The Writings of Herman Melville

The Northwestern–Newberry Edition

VOLUME THREE

Mardi

This volume edited by
Harrison Hayford
Hershel Parker
G. Thomas Tanselle

Historical Note by
Elizabeth S. Foster

Mardi

and

A Voyage Thither

HERMAN MELVILLE

NORTHWESTERN UNIVERSITY PRESS

and

THE NEWBERRY LIBRARY

Evanston and Chicago

1970

THE RESEARCH *reported herein was prepared pursuant to a contract with the United States Department of Health, Education, and Welfare, Office of Education, under the provisions of the Coöperative Research Program, and is in the public domain.*

Publication of the Northwestern–Newberry Edition of THE WRITINGS OF HERMAN MELVILLE *has been made possible through the financial support of Northwestern University and its Research Committee, and of The Newberry Library. This edition originated with Northwestern University Press, Inc., which reserves all rights against commercial reproduction by offset-lithographic or equivalent copying processes.*

LIBRARY OF CONGRESS CATALOG CARD NUMBER 67–21602

PRINTED IN THE UNITED STATES OF AMERICA

Cloth Edition, SBN 8101–0015–0
Paper Edition, SBN 8101–0014–2

CENTER FOR EDITIONS OF
AMERICAN AUTHORS

AN APPROVED TEXT

MODERN LANGUAGE
ASSOCIATION OF AMERICA

®

DEDICATED
TO MY BROTHER,
Allan Melville

Contents

VOLUME ONE

Preface	xvii
Chapter 1 · *Foot in Stirrup*	3
Chapter 2 · *A Calm*	9
Chapter 3 · *A King for a Comrade*	11
Chapter 4 · *A Chat in the Clouds*	16
Chapter 5 · *Seats secured and Portmanteaus packed*	19
Chapter 6 · *Eight Bells*	22
Chapter 7 · *A Pause*	24
Chapter 8 · *They push off, Velis et Remis*	26
Chapter 9 · *The Watery World is all before Them*	29
Chapter 10 · *They arrange their Canopies and Lounges, and try to make Things comfortable*	32
Chapter 11 · *Jarl afflicted with the Lockjaw*	35
Chapter 12 · *More about being in an open Boat*	37
Chapter 13 · *Of the Chondropterygii, and other uncouth Hordes infesting the South Seas*	39
Chapter 14 · *Jarl's Misgivings*	43

Chapter 15 · *A Stitch in Time saves Nine*   46

Chapter 16 · *They are Becalmed*   48

Chapter 17 · *In high Spirits they push on for the Terra Incognita*   51

Chapter 18 · *My Lord Shark and his Pages*   53

Chapter 19 · *Who goes there?*   56

Chapter 20 · *Noises and Portents*   62

Chapter 21 · *Man ho!*   65

Chapter 22 · *What befel the Brigantine at the Pearl Shell Islands*   68

Chapter 23 · *Sailing from the Island they pillage the Cabin*   74

Chapter 24 · *Dedicated to the College of Physicians and Surgeons*   77

Chapter 25 · *Peril a Peace-maker*   80

Chapter 26 · *Containing a Pennyweight of Philosophy*   83

Chapter 27 · *In which the past History of the Parki is concluded*   85

Chapter 28 · *Suspicions laid, and something about the Calmuc*   89

Chapter 29 · *What they lighted upon in further searching the Craft, and the*   93
Resolution they came to

Chapter 30 · *Hints for a full length of Samoa*   98

Chapter 31 · *Rovings Alow and Aloft*   100

Chapter 32 · *Xiphius Platypterus*   103

Chapter 33 · *Otard*   106

Chapter 34 · *How they steered on their Way*   108

Chapter 35 · *Ah, Annatoo!*   113

Chapter 36 · *The Parki gives up the Ghost*   116

Chapter 37 · *Once more they take to the Chamois*   119

Chapter 38 · *The Sea on Fire*   121

Chapter 39 · *They fall in with Strangers*   125

Chapter 40 · *Sire and Sons*   129

Chapter 41 · *A Fray*   131

Chapter 42 · *Remorse*   134

Chapter 43 · *The Tent entered*   136

Chapter 44 · *Away!*   139

Chapter 45 · *Reminiscences*   142

Chapter 46 · *The Chamois with a roving Commission*   144

Chapter 47 · *Yillah, Jarl, and Samoa*   146

Chapter 48 · *Something under the Surface* 148

Chapter 49 · *Yillah* 152

Chapter 50 · *Yillah in Ardair* 154

Chapter 51 · *The Dream begins to fade* 158

Chapter 52 · *World ho!* 160

Chapter 53 · *The Chamois Ashore* 163

Chapter 54 · *A Gentleman from the Sun* 165

Chapter 55 · *Tiffin in a Temple* 168

Chapter 56 · *King Media a Host* 171

Chapter 57 · *Taji takes Counsel with himself* 174

Chapter 58 · *Mardi by Night and Yillah by Day* 178

Chapter 59 · *Their Morning Meal* 180

Chapter 60 · *Belshazzar on the Bench* 182

Chapter 61 · *An Incognito* 186

Chapter 62 · *Taji retires from the World* 188

Chapter 63 · *Odo and its Lord* 190

Chapter 64 · *Yillah a Phantom* 193

Chapter 65 · *Taji makes three Acquaintances* 196

Chapter 66 · *With a fair Wind at Sunrise they sail* 199

Chapter 67 · *Little King Peepi* 201

Chapter 68 · *How Teeth were regarded in Valapee* 205

Chapter 69 · *The Company discourse, and Braid-Beard rehearses a Legend* 208

Chapter 70 · *The Minstrel leads off with a Paddle-Song; and a Message is received from Abroad* 213

Chapter 71 · *They land upon the Island of Juam* 216

Chapter 72 · *A Book from the Chronicles of Mohi* 219

Chapter 73 · *Something more of the Prince* 223

Chapter 74 · *Advancing deeper into the Vale, they encounter Donjalolo* 225

Chapter 75 · *Time and Temples* 228

Chapter 76 · *A pleasant Place for a Lounge* 231

Chapter 77 · *The House of the Afternoon* 233

Chapter 78 · *Babbalanja solus* 236

Chapter 79 · *The Center of many Circumferences* 239

Chapter 80 · *Donjalolo in the Bosom of his Family* 241

Chapter 81 · *Wherein Babbalanja relates the Adventure of one Karkeke in the*   245
Land of Shades

Chapter 82 · *How Donjalolo sent Agents to the surrounding Isles; with the*   248
Result

Chapter 83 · *They visit the Tributary Islets*   251

Chapter 84 · *Taji sits down to Dinner with five-and-twenty Kings, and a royal*   253
Time they have

Chapter 85 · *After Dinner*   260

Chapter 86 · *Of those Scamps the Plujii*   262

Chapter 87 · *Nora-Bamma*   265

Chapter 88 · *In a Calm, Hautia's Heralds approach*   267

Chapter 89 · *Braid-Beard rehearses the Origin of the Isle of Rogues*   269

Chapter 90 · *Rare Sport at Ohonoo*   272

Chapter 91 · *Of King Uhia and his Subjects*   275

Chapter 92 · *The God Keevi and the Precipice of Mondo*   277

Chapter 93 · *Babbalanja steps in between Mohi and Yoomy; and Yoomy relates*   280
a Legend

Chapter 94 · *Of that jolly old Lord, Borabolla; and that jolly Island of his,*   285
Mondoldo; and of the Fish-ponds, and the Hereafters of Fish

Chapter 95 · *That jolly old Lord Borabolla laughs on both Sides of his Face*   290

Chapter 96 · *Samoa a Surgeon*   294

Chapter 97 · *Faith and Knowledge*   296

Chapter 98 · *The Tale of a Traveler*   298

Chapter 99 · *"Marnee Ora, Ora Marnee."*   300

Chapter 100 · *The Pursuer himself is pursued*   305

Chapter 101 · *The Iris*   309

Chapter 102 · *They depart from Mondoldo*   311

Chapter 103 · *As they sail*   313

Chapter 104 · *Wherein Babbalanja broaches a diabolical Theory, and in his*   316
own Person proves it

VOLUME TWO

Chapter 105 · *Maramma*   323

Chapter 106 · *They land*   326

Chapter 107 · *They pass through the Woods*   330

Chapter 108 · *Hivohitee MDCCCXLVIII* 332

Chapter 109 · *They visit the great Morai* 335

Chapter 110 · *They discourse of the Gods of Mardi, and Braid-Beard tells of* 340
one Foni

Chapter 111 · *They visit the Lake of Yammo* 343

Chapter 112 · *They meet the Pilgrims at the Temple of Oro* 346

Chapter 113 · *They discourse of Alma* 348

Chapter 114 · *Mohi tells of one Ravoo, and they land to visit Hevaneva, a* 351
flourishing Artisan

Chapter 115 · *A Nursery-tale of Babbalanja's* 355

Chapter 116 · *Landing to visit Hivohitee the Pontiff, they encounter an* 358
extraordinary old Hermit; with whom Yoomy has a confidential Interview, but
learns little

Chapter 117 · *Babbalanja endeavors to explain the Mystery* 362

Chapter 118 · *Taji receives Tidings and Omens* 364

Chapter 119 · *Dreams* 366

Chapter 120 · *Media and Babbalanja discourse* 369

Chapter 121 · *They regale themselves with their Pipes* 371

Chapter 122 · *They visit an extraordinary old Antiquary* 378

Chapter 123 · *They go down into the Catacombs* 382

Chapter 124 · *Babbalanja quotes from an antique Pagan; and earnestly presses* 387
it upon the Company, that what he recites is not his but another's

Chapter 125 · *They visit a wealthy old Pauper* 391

Chapter 126 · *Yoomy sings some odd Verses, and Babbalanja quotes from the* 393
old Authors right and left

Chapter 127 · *What manner of Men the Tapparians were* 398

Chapter 128 · *Their adventures upon landing at Pimminee* 401

Chapter 129 · *A, I, and O* 405

Chapter 130 · *A Reception-day at Pimminee* 408

Chapter 131 · *Babbalanja falleth upon Pimminee Tooth and Nail* 411

Chapter 132 · *Babbalanja regales the Company with some Sandwiches* 414

Chapter 133 · *They still remain upon the Rock* 419

Chapter 134 · *Behind and Before* 422

Chapter 135 · *Babbalanja discourses in the Dark* 424

Chapter 136 · *My Lord Media summons Mohi to the Stand*   431

Chapter 137 · *Wherein Babbalanja and Yoomy embrace*   435

Chapter 138 · *Of the Isle of Diranda*   439

Chapter 139 · *They visit the Lords Piko and Hello*   443

Chapter 140 · *They attend the Games*   446

Chapter 141 · *Taji still hunted and beckoned*   450

Chapter 142 · *They embark from Diranda*   452

Chapter 143 · *Wherein Babbalanja discourses of himself*   455

Chapter 144 · *Of the Sorcerers in the Isle of Minda*   461

Chapter 145 · *Chiefly of King Bello*   465

Chapter 146 · *Dominora and Vivenza*   471

Chapter 147 · *They land at Dominora*   475

Chapter 148 · *Through Dominora, they wander after Yillah*   478

Chapter 149 · *They behold King Bello's State Canoe*   481

Chapter 150 · *Wherein Babbalanja bows thrice*   484

Chapter 151 · *Babbalanja philosophizes, and my Lord Media passes round the*   486
Calabashes

Chapter 152 · *They sail round an Island without landing; and talk round*   491
a Subject without getting at it

Chapter 153 · *They draw nigh to Porpheero; where they behold a terrific Eruption*   497

Chapter 154 · *Wherein King Media celebrates the Glories of Autumn;*   501
the Minstrel, the Promise of Spring

Chapter 155 · *In which Azzageddi seems to use Babbalanja for a Mouth-piece*   503

Chapter 156 · *The charming Yoomy sings*   509

Chapter 157 · *They draw nigh unto Land*   511

Chapter 158 · *They visit the great central Temple of Vivenza*   514

Chapter 159 · *Wherein Babbalanja comments upon the Speech of Alanno*   519

Chapter 160 · *A Scene in the Land of Warwicks, or King-makers*   521

Chapter 161 · *They hearken unto a Voice from the Gods*   523

Chapter 162 · *They visit the extreme South of Vivenza*   531

Chapter 163 · *They converse of the Mollusca, Kings, Toad-stools, and other*   536
Matters

Chapter 164 · *Wherein, that gallant Gentleman and Demi-god, King Media,*   539
Scepter in Hand, throws himself into the Breach

CONTENTS

Chapter 165 · *They round the stormy Cape of Capes*   543

Chapter 166 · *They encounter Gold-hunters*   545

Chapter 167 · *They seek through the Isles of Palms; and pass the Isles of Myrrh*   549

Chapter 168 · *Concentric, inward, with Mardi's Reef, they leave their Wake*   551
around the World

Chapter 169 · *Sailing on*   556

Chapter 170 · *A flight of Nightingales from Yoomy's Mouth*   558

Chapter 171 · *They visit one Doxodox*   562

Chapter 172 · *King Media dreams*   565

Chapter 173 · *After a long Interval, by Night they are becalmed*   567

Chapter 174 · *They land at Hooloomooloo*   569

Chapter 175 · *A Book from the "Ponderings of old Bardianna"*   574

Chapter 176 · *Babbalanja starts to his Feet*   579

Chapter 177 · *At last, the last Mention is made of old Bardianna; and His last*   582
Will and Testament is recited at Length

Chapter 178 · *A Death-cloud sweeps by them as they sail*   586

Chapter 179 · *They visit the palmy King Abrazza*   588

Chapter 180 · *Some pleasant, shady Talk in the Groves, between my Lords*   591
Abrazza and Media, Babbalanja, Mohi, and Yoomy

Chapter 181 · *They sup*   603

Chapter 182 · *They embark*   610

Chapter 183 · *Babbalanja at the Full of the Moon*   612

Chapter 184 · *Morning*   615

Chapter 185 · *L'Ultima sera*   617

Chapter 186 · *They sail from Night to Day*   622

Chapter 187 · *They land*   625

Chapter 188 · *Babbalanja relates to them a Vision*   632

Chapter 189 · *They depart from Serenia*   637

Chapter 190 · *They meet the Phantoms*   640

Chapter 191 · *They draw nigh to Flozella*   642

Chapter 192 · *They land*   644

Chapter 193 · *They enter the Bower of Hautia*   647

Chapter 194 · *Taji with Hautia*   650

Chapter 195 · *Mardi behind: an Ocean before*   652

EDITORIAL APPENDIX

HISTORICAL NOTE · *By Elizabeth S. Foster*   657

TEXTUAL RECORD · *By the Editors*
   Note on the Text   683
   Discussions of Adopted Readings   697
   List of Emendations   703
   Report of Line-End Hyphenation   711
   List of Substantive Variants   717

RELATED DOCUMENTS
   Manuscript Fragments   723

Preface

NOT LONG AGO, having published two narratives of voyages in the Pacific, which, in many quarters, were received with incredulity, the thought occurred to me, of indeed writing a romance of Polynesian adventure, and publishing it as such; to see whether, the fiction might not, possibly, be received for a verity: in some degree the reverse of my previous experience.

This thought was the germ of others, which have resulted in Mardi.

New York, *January*, 1849.

Mardi

Chapter 1

Foot in Stirrup

W E ARE OFF! The courses and topsails are set: the coral-hung anchor swings from the bow: and together, the three royals are given to the breeze, that follows us out to sea like the baying of a hound. Out spreads the canvas—alow, aloft—boom-stretched, on both sides, with many a stun' sail; till like a hawk, with pinions poised, we shadow the sea with our sails, and reelingly cleave the brine.

But whence, and whither wend ye, mariners?

We sail from Ravavai, an isle in the sea, not very far northward from the tropic of Capricorn, nor very far westward from Pitcairn's island, where the mutineers of the Bounty settled. At Ravavai I had stepped ashore some few months previous; and now was embarked on a cruise for the whale, whose brain enlightens the world.

And from Ravavai we sail for the Gallipagos, otherwise called the Enchanted Islands, by reason of the many wild currents and eddies there met.

Now, round about those isles, which Dampier once trod, where the Spanish bucaniers once hived their gold moidores, the Cachalot, or sperm whale, at certain seasons abounds.

But thither, from Ravavai, your craft may not fly, as flies the sea-gull, straight to her nest. For, owing to the prevalence of the trade winds, ships bound to the northeast from the vicinity of Ravavai are fain to take something of a circuit; a few thousand miles or so. First, in pursuit of the variable

3

winds, they make all haste to the south; and there, at length picking up a stray breeze, they stand for the main: then, making their easting, up helm, and away down the coast, toward the Line.

This round-about way did the Arcturion take; and in all conscience a weary one it was. Never before had the ocean appeared so monotonous; thank fate, never since.

But bravo! in two weeks' time, an event. Out of the gray of the morning, and right ahead, as we sailed along, a dark object rose out of the sea; standing dimly before us, mists wreathing and curling aloft, and creamy breakers frothing round its base.—We turned aside, and, at length, when day dawned, passed Massafuero. With a glass, we spied two or three hermit goats winding down to the sea, in a ravine; and presently, a signal: a tattered flag upon a summit beyond. Well knowing, however, that there was nobody on the island but two or three noose-fulls of runaway convicts from Chili, our captain had no mind to comply with their invitation to land. Though, haply, he may have erred in not sending a boat off with his card.

A few days more and we "took the trades." Like favors snappishly conferred, they came to us, as is often the case, in a very sharp squall; the shock of which carried away one of our spars; also our fat old cook off his legs; depositing him plump in the scuppers to leeward.

In good time making the desired longitude upon the equator, a few leagues west of the Gallipagos, we spent several weeks chassezing across the Line, to and fro, in unavailing search for our prey. For some of their hunters believe, that whales, like the silver ore in Peru, run in veins through the ocean. So, day after day, daily; and week after week, weekly, we traversed the self-same longitudinal intersection of the self-same Line; till we were almost ready to swear that we felt the ship strike every time her keel crossed that imaginary locality.

At length, dead before the equatorial breeze, we threaded our way straight along the very Line itself. Westward sailing; peering right, and peering left, but seeing naught.

It was during this weary time, that I experienced the first symptoms of that bitter impatience of our monotonous craft, which ultimately led to the adventures herein recounted.

But hold you! Not a word against that rare old ship, nor its crew. The sailors were good fellows all, the half-score of pagans we had shipped at the islands included. Nevertheless, they were not precisely to my mind. There was no soul a magnet to mine; none with whom to mingle sympathies; save in deploring the calms with which we were now and then overtaken;

or in hailing the breeze when it came. Under other and livelier auspices the
tarry knaves might have developed qualities more attractive. Had we sprung
a leak, been "stove" by a whale, or been blessed with some despot of a
captain against whom to stir up some spirited revolt, these shipmates of
mine might have proved limber lads, and men of mettle. But as it was,
there was naught to strike fire from their steel.

There were other things, also, tending to make my lot on ship-board
very hard to be borne. True, the skipper himself was a trump; stood upon
no quarter-deck dignity; and had a tongue for a sailor. Let me do him justice, furthermore: he took a sort of fancy for me in particular; was sociable,
nay, loquacious, when I happened to stand at the helm. But what of that?
Could he talk sentiment or philosophy? Not a bit. His library was eight
inches by four: Bowditch, and Hamilton Moore.

And what to me, thus pining for some one who could page me a quotation from Burton on Blue Devils; what to me, indeed, were flat repetitions
of long-drawn yarns, and the everlasting stanzas of Black-eyed Susan sung
by our full forecastle choir? Staler than stale ale.

Ay, ay, Arcturion! I say it in no malice, but thou wast exceedingly dull.
Not only at sailing: hard though it was, that I could have borne; but in every
other respect. The days went slowly round and round, endless and unevent-
ful as cycles in space. Time, and time-pieces! How many centuries did my
hammock tell, as pendulum-like it swung to the ship's dull roll, and ticked
the hours and ages. Sacred forever be the Arcturion's fore-hatch—alas! sea-
moss is over it now—and rusty forever the bolts that held together that old
sea hearth-stone, about which we so often lounged. Nevertheless, ye lost
and leaden hours, I will rail at ye while life lasts.

Well: weeks, chronologically speaking, went by. Bill Marvel's stories
were told over and over again, till the beginning and end dovetailed into
each other, and were united for aye. Ned Ballad's songs were sung till the
echoes lurked in the very tops, and nested in the bunts of the sails. My poor
patience was clean gone.

But, at last after some time sailing due westward we quitted the Line
in high disgust; having seen there, no sign of a whale.

But whither now? To the broiling coast of Papua? That region of sun-
strokes, typhoons, and bitter pulls after whales unattainable. Far worse. We
were going, it seemed, to illustrate the Whistonian theory concerning the
damned and the comets;—hurried from equinoctial heats to arctic frosts.
To be short, with the true fickleness of his tribe, our skipper had abandoned
all thought of the Cachalot. In desperation, he was bent upon bobbing for

the Right whale on the Nor'-West Coast and in the Bay of Kamschatka.

To the uninitiated in the business of whaling, my feelings at this juncture may perhaps be hard to understand. But this much let me say: that Right whaling on the Nor'-West Coast, in chill and dismal fogs, the sullen inert monsters rafting the sea all round like Hartz forest logs on the Rhine, and submitting to the harpoon like half-stunned bullocks to the knife; this horrid and indecent Right whaling, I say, compared to a spirited hunt for the gentlemanly Cachalot in southern and more genial seas, is as the butchery of white bears upon blank Greenland icebergs to zebra hunting in Caffraria, where the lively quarry bounds before you through leafy glades.

Now, this most unforeseen determination on the part of my captain to measure the arctic circle was nothing more nor less than a tacit contravention of the agreement between us. That agreement needs not to be detailed. And having shipped but for a single cruise, I had embarked aboard his craft as one might put foot in stirrup for a day's following of the hounds. And here, Heaven help me, he was going to carry me off to the Pole! And on such a vile errand too! For there was something degrading in it. Your true whaleman glories in keeping his harpoon unspotted by blood of aught but Cachalot. By my halidome, it touched the knighthood of a tar. Sperm and spermaceti! It was unendurable.

"Captain," said I, touching my sombrero to him as I stood at the wheel one day, "It's very hard to carry me off this way to purgatory. I shipped to go elsewhere."

"Yes, and so did I," was his reply. "But it can't be helped. Sperm whales are not to be had. We've been out now three years, and something or other must be got; for the ship is hungry for oil, and her hold a gulf to look into. But cheer up my boy! once in the Bay of Kamschatka, and we'll be all afloat with what we want, though it be none of the best."

Worse and worse! The oleaginous prospect extended into an immensity of Macassar. "Sir," said I, "I did not ship for it; put me ashore somewhere, I beseech." He stared, but no answer vouchsafed; and for a moment I thought I had roused the domineering spirit of the sea-captain, to the prejudice of the more kindly nature of the man.

But not so. Taking three turns on the deck, he placed his hand on the wheel, and said, "Right or wrong, my lad, go with us you must. Putting you ashore is now out of the question. I make no port till this ship is full to the combings of her hatchways. However, you may leave her if you can." And so saying he entered his cabin, like Julius Cæsar into his tent.

He may have meant little by it, but that last sentence rung in my ear like

a bravado. It savored of the turnkey's compliments to the prisoner in New-
gate, when he shoots to the bolt on him.

"Leave the ship if I can!" Leave the ship when neither sail nor shore was
in sight! Ay, my fine captain, stranger things have been done. For on board
that very craft, the old Arcturion, were four tall fellows, whom two years
previous our skipper himself had picked up in an open boat, far from the
farthest shoal. To be sure, they spun a long yarn about being the only survivors of an Indiaman burnt down to the water's edge. But who credited
their tale? Like many others, they were keepers of a secret: had doubtless
contracted a disgust for some ugly craft still afloat and hearty, and stolen
away from her, off soundings. Among seamen in the Pacific such adventures
not seldom occur. Nor are they accounted great wonders. They are but incidents, not events, in the career of the brethren of the order of South Sea
rovers. For what matters it, though hundreds of miles from land, if a good
whale-boat be under foot, the Trades behind, and mild, warm seas before?
And herein lies the difference between the Atlantic and Pacific:—that once
within the Tropics, the bold sailor who has a mind to quit his ship round
Cape Horn, waits not for port. He regards that ocean as one mighty harbor.

Nevertheless, the enterprise hinted at was no light one; and I resolved
to weigh well the chances. It's worth noticing, this way we all have of pondering for ourselves the enterprise, which, for others, we hold a bagatelle.

My first thoughts were of the boat to be obtained, and the right or wrong
of abstracting it, under the circumstances. But to split no hairs on this point,
let me say, that were I placed in the same situation again, I would repeat the
thing I did then. The captain well knew that he was going to detain me unlawfully: against our agreement; and it was he himself who threw out the
very hint, which I merely adopted, with many thanks to him.

In some such willful mood as this, I went aloft one day, to stand my
allotted two hours at the mast-head. It was toward the close of a day, serene
and beautiful. There I stood, high upon the mast, and away, away, illim-
itably rolled the ocean beneath. Where we then were was perhaps the most
unfrequented and least known portion of these seas. Westward, however,
lay numerous groups of islands, loosely laid down upon the charts, and invested with all the charms of dream-land. But soon these regions would be
past; the mild equatorial breeze exchanged for cold, fierce squalls, and all
the horrors of northern voyaging.

I cast my eyes downward to the brown planks of the dull, plodding ship,
silent from stem to stern; then abroad.

In the distance what visions were spread! The entire western horizon high piled with gold and crimson clouds; airy arches, domes, and minarets; as if the yellow, Moorish sun were setting behind some vast Alhambra. Vistas seemed leading to worlds beyond. To and fro, and all over the towers of this Nineveh in the sky, flew troops of birds. Watching them long, one crossed my sight, flew through a low arch, and was lost to view. My spirit must have sailed in with it; for directly, as in a trance, came upon me the cadence of mild billows laving a beach of shells, the waving of boughs, and the voices of maidens, and the lulled beatings of my own dissolved heart, all blended together.

Now, all this, to be plain, was but one of the many visions one has up aloft. But coming upon me at this time, it wrought upon me so, that thenceforth my desire to quit the Arcturion became little short of a frenzy.

Chapter 2

A Calm

NEXT DAY there was a calm, which added not a little to my impatience of the ship. And, furthermore, by certain nameless associations revived in me my old impressions upon first witnessing as a landsman this phenomenon of the sea. Those impressions may merit a page.

To a landsman a calm is no joke. It not only revolutionizes his abdomen, but unsettles his mind; tempts him to recant his belief in the eternal fitness of things; in short, almost makes an infidel of him.

At first he is taken by surprise, never having dreamt of a state of existence where existence itself seems suspended. He shakes himself in his coat, to see whether it be empty or no. He closes his eyes, to test the reality of the glassy expanse. He fetches a deep breath, by way of experiment, and for the sake of witnessing the effect. If a reader of books, Priestley on Necessity occurs to him; and he believes in that old Sir Anthony Absolute to the very last chapter. His faith in Malte Brun, however, begins to fail; for the geography, which from boyhood he had implicitly confided in, always assured him, that though expatiating all over the globe, the sea was at least margined by land. That over against America, for example, was Asia. But it is a calm, and he grows madly skeptical.

To his alarmed fancy, parallels and meridians become emphatically what

9

they are merely designated as being: imaginary lines drawn round the earth's surface.

The log assures him that he is in such a place; but the log is a liar; for no place, nor any thing possessed of a local angularity, is to be lighted upon in the watery waste.

At length horrible doubts overtake him as to the captain's competency to navigate his ship. The ignoramus must have lost his way, and drifted into the outer confines of creation, the region of the everlasting lull, introductory to a positive vacuity.

Thoughts of eternity thicken. He begins to feel anxious concerning his soul.

The stillness of the calm is awful. His voice begins to grow strange and portentous. He feels it in him like something swallowed too big for the esophagus. It keeps up a sort of involuntary interior humming in him, like a live beetle. His cranium is a dome full of reverberations. The hollows of his very bones are as whispering galleries. He is afraid to speak loud, lest he be stunned; like the man in the bass drum.

But more than all else is the consciousness of his utter helplessness. Succor or sympathy there is none. Penitence for embarking avails not. The final satisfaction of despairing may not be his with a relish. Vain the idea of idling out the calm. He may sleep if he can, or purposely delude himself into a crazy fancy, that he is merely at leisure. All this he may compass; but he may not lounge; for to lounge is to be idle; to be idle implies an absence of any thing to do; whereas there is a calm to be endured: enough to attend to, Heaven knows.

His physical organization, obviously intended for locomotion, becomes a fixture; for where the calm leaves him, there he remains. Even his un-doubted vested rights, comprised in his glorious liberty of volition, become as naught. For of what use? He wills to go: to get away from the calm: as ashore he would avoid the plague. But he can not; and how foolish to revolve expedients. It is more hopeless than a bad marriage in a land where there is no Doctors' Commons. He has taken the ship to wife, for better or for worse, for calm or for gale; and she is not to be shuffled off. With yards akimbo, she says unto him scornfully, as the old beldam said to the little dwarf:—"Help yourself."

And all this, and more than this, is a calm.

Chapter 3

A King for a Comrade

AT THE TIME I now write of, we must have been something more
than sixty degrees to the west of the Gallipagos. And having attained
a desirable longitude, we were standing northward for our arctic
destination: around us one wide sea.

But due west, though distant a thousand miles, stretched north and
south an almost endless Archipelago, here and there inhabited, but little
known; and most unfrequented, even by whalemen, who go almost every
where. Beginning at the southerly termination of this great chain, it com-
prises the islands loosely known as Ellice's group; then, the Kingsmill isles;
then, the Radack and Mulgrave clusters. These islands had been represented
to me as mostly of coral formation, low and fertile, and abounding in a
variety of fruits. The language of the people was said to be very similar to
that of the Navigator's islands, from which, their ancestors are supposed to
have emigrated.

And thus much being said, all has been related that I then knew of the
islands in question. Enough, however, that they existed at all; and that our
path thereto lay over a pleasant sea, and before a reliable Trade-wind. The
distance, though great, was merely an extension of water; so much blank-
ness to be sailed over; and in a craft, too, that properly managed has been
known to outlive great ships in a gale. For this much is true of a whale-boat,
the cunningest thing in its way ever fabricated by man.

Upon one of the Kingsmill islands, then, I determined to plant my foot, come what come would. And I was equally determined that one of the ship's boats should float me thither. But I had no idea of being without a companion. It would be a weary watch to keep all by myself, with naught but the horizon in sight.

Now, among the crew was a fine old seaman, one Jarl; how old, no one could tell, not even himself. Forecastle chronology is ever vague and defective. "Man and boy," said honest Jarl, "I have lived ever since I can remember." And truly, who may call to mind when he was not? To ourselves, we all seem coeval with creation. Whence it comes, that it is so hard to die, ere the world itself is departed.

Jarl hailed from the isle of Skye, one of the constellated Hebrides. Hence, they often called him the Skyeman. And though he was far from being piratical of soul, he was yet an old Norseman to behold. His hands were brawny as the paws of a bear; his voice hoarse as a storm roaring round the old peak of Mull; and his long yellow hair waved round his head like a sunset. My life for it, Jarl, thy ancestors were Vikings, who many a time sailed over the salt German sea and the Baltic; who wedded their Brynhildas in Jutland; and are now quaffing mead in the halls of Valhalla, and beating time with their cans to the hymns of the Scalds. Ah! how the old Sagas run through me!

Yet Jarl, the descendant of heroes and kings, was a lone, friendless mariner on the main, only true to his origin in the sea-life that he led. But so it has been, and forever will be. What yeoman shall swear that he is not descended from Alfred? what dunce, that he is not sprung of old Homer? King Noah, God bless him! fathered us all. Then hold up your heads, oh ye Helots, blood potential flows through your veins. All of us have monarchs and sages for kinsmen; nay, angels and archangels for cousins; since in antediluvian days, the sons of God did verily wed with our mothers, the irresistible daughters of Eve. Thus all generations are blended: and heaven and earth of one kin: the hierarchies of seraphs in the uttermost skies; the thrones and principalities in the zodiac; the shades that roam throughout space; the nations and families, flocks and folds of the earth; one and all, brothers in essence—oh, be we then brothers indeed! All things form but one whole; the universe a Judea, and God Jehovah its head. Then no more let us start with affright. In a theocracy, what is to fear? Let us compose ourselves to death as fagged horsemen sleep in the saddle. Let us welcome even ghosts when they rise. Away with our stares and grimaces. The New Zealander's tattooing is not a prodigy; nor the Chinaman's ways an enigma.

No custom is strange; no creed is absurd; no foe, but who will in the end prove a friend. In heaven, at last, our good, old, white-haired father Adam will greet all alike, and sociality forever prevail. Christian shall join hands between Gentile and Jew; grim Dante forget his Infernos, and shake sides with fat Rabelais; and monk Luther, over a flagon of old nectar, talk over old times with Pope Leo. Then, shall we sit by the sages, who of yore gave laws to the Medes and Persians in the sun; by the cavalry captains in Perseus, who cried, "To horse!" when waked by their Last Trump sounding to the charge; by the old hunters, who eternities ago, hunted the moose in Orion; by the minstrels, who sang in the Milky Way when Jesus our Saviour was born. Then shall we list to no shallow gossip of Magellans and Drakes; but give ear to the voyagers who have circumnavigated the Ecliptic; who rounded the Polar Star as Cape Horn. Then shall the Stagirite and Kant be forgotten, and another folio than theirs be turned over for wisdom; even the folio now spread with horoscopes as yet undeciphered, the heaven of heavens on high.

Now, in old Jarl's lingo there was never an idiom. Your aboriginal tar is too much of a cosmopolitan for that. Long companionship with seamen of all tribes: Manilla-men, Anglo-Saxons, Cholos, Lascars, and Danes, wear away in good time all mother-tongue stammerings. You sink your clan; down goes your nation; you speak a world's language, jovially jabbering in the Lingua-Franca of the forecastle.

True to his calling, the Skyeman was very illiterate; witless of Salamanca, Heidelberg, or Brazen-Nose; in Delhi, had never turned over the books of the Brahmins. For geography, in which sailors should be adepts, since they are forever turning over and over the great globe of globes, poor Jarl was deplorably lacking. According to his view of the matter, this terraqueous world had been formed in the manner of a tart; the land being a mere marginal crust, within which rolled the watery world proper. Such seemed my good Viking's theory of cosmography. As for other worlds, he weened not of them; yet full as much as Chrysostom.

Ah, Jarl! an honest, earnest wight; so true and simple, that the secret operations of thy soul were more inscrutable than the subtle workings of Spinoza's.

Thus much be said of the Skyeman; for he was exceedingly taciturn, and but seldom will speak for himself.

Now, higher sympathies apart, for Jarl I had a wonderful liking; for he loved me; from the first had cleaved to me.

It is sometimes the case, that an old mariner like him will conceive a

very strong attachment for some young sailor, his shipmate; an attachment
so devoted, as to be wholly inexplicable, unless originating in that heart-
loneliness which overtakes most seamen as they grow aged; impelling them
to fasten upon some chance object of regard. But however it was, my Viking,
thy unbidden affection was the noblest homage ever paid me. And frankly,
I am more inclined to think well of myself, as in some way deserving thy
devotion, than from the rounded compliments of more cultivated minds.

Now, at sea, and in the fellowship of sailors, all men appear as they are.
No school like a ship for studying human nature. The contact of one man
with another is too near and constant to favor deceit. You wear your
character as loosely as your flowing trowsers. Vain all endeavors to assume
qualities not yours; or to conceal those you possess. Incognitos, however
desirable, are out of the question. And thus aboard of all ships in which I
have sailed, I have invariably been known by a sort of drawing-room title.
Not,—let me hurry to say,—that I put hand in tar bucket with a squeamish
air, or ascended the rigging with a Chesterfieldian mince. No, no, I was
never better than my vocation; and mine have been many. I showed as
brown a chest, and as hard a hand, as the tarriest tar of them all. And never
did shipmate of mine upbraid me with a genteel disinclination to duty,
though it carried me to truck of main-mast, or jib-boom-end, in the most
wolfish blast that ever howled.

Whence then, this annoying appellation? for annoying it most assuredly
was. It was because of something in me that could not be hidden; stealing
out in an occasional polysyllable; an otherwise incomprehensible deliberation in dining; remote, unguarded allusions to Belles-Lettres affairs; and
other trifles superfluous to mention.

But suffice it to say, that it had gone abroad among the Arcturion's
crew, that at some indefinite period of my career, I had been a "nob." But
Jarl seemed to go further. He must have taken me for one of the House of
Hanover in disguise; or, haply, for bonneted Charles Edward the Pretender,
who, like the Wandering Jew, may yet be a vagrant. At any rate, his loyalty
was extreme. Unsolicited, he was my laundress and tailor; a most expert
one, too; and when at meal-times my turn came round to look out at the
mast-head, or stand at the wheel, he catered for me among the "kids" in
the forecastle with unwearied assiduity. Many's the good lump of "duff"
for which I was indebted to my good Viking's good care of me. And like
Sesostris I was served by a monarch. Yet in some degree the obligation was
mutual. For be it known that, in sea-parlance, we were *chummies*.

Now this *chummying* among sailors is like the brotherhood subsisting between a brace of collegians (chums) rooming together. It is a Fidus-Achates-ship, a league of offense and defense, a copartnership of chests and toilets, a bond of love and good feeling, and a mutual championship of the absent one. True, my nautical reminiscences remind me of sundry lazy, ne'er-do-well, unprofitable, and abominable chummies; chummies, who at meal times were last at the "kids," when their unfortunate partners were high upon the spars; chummies, who affected awkwardness at the needle, and conscientious scruples about dabbling in the suds; so that chummy the simple was made to do all the work of the firm, while chummy the cunning played the sleeping partner in his hammock. Out upon such chummies!

But I appeal to thee, honest Jarl, if I was ever chummy the cunning. Never mind if thou didst fabricate my tarpaulins; and with Samaritan charity bind up the rents, and pour needle and thread into the frightful gashes that agonized my hapless nether integuments, which thou calledst "ducks;"—Didst thou not expressly declare, that all these things, and more, thou wouldst do for me, despite my own quaint thimble, fashioned from the ivory tusk of a whale? Nay; could I even wrest from thy willful hands my very shirt, when once thou hadst it steaming in an unsavory pickle in thy capacious vat, a decapitated cask? Full well thou knowest, Jarl, that these things are true; and I am bound to say it, to disclaim any lurking desire to reap advantage from thy great good nature.

Now my Viking for me, thought I, when I cast about for a comrade; and my Viking alone.

Chapter 4

A Chat in the Clouds

THE SKYEMAN seemed so earnest and upright a seaman, that to tell the plain truth, in spite of his love for me, I had many misgivings as to his readiness to unite in an undertaking which apparently savored of a moral dereliction. But all things considered, I deemed my own resolution quite venial; and as for inducing another to join me, it seemed a precaution so indispensable, as to outweigh all other considerations.

Therefore I resolved freely to open my heart to him; for that special purpose paying him a visit, when, like some old albatross in the air, he happened to be perched at the fore-mast-head, all by himself, on the lookout for whales never seen.

Now this standing upon a bit of stick 100 feet aloft for hours at a time, swiftly sailing over the sea, is very much like crossing the Channel in a balloon. Manfred-like, you talk to the clouds: you have a fellow feeling for the sun. And when Jarl and I got conversing up there, smoking our dwarfish "dudeens," any sea-gull passing by might have taken us for Messrs. Blanchard and Jeffries, socially puffing their after-dinner Bagdads, bound to Calais, via Heaven, from Dover. Honest Jarl, I acquainted with all: my conversation with the captain, the hint implied in his last words, my firm resolve to quit the ship in one of her boats, and the facility with which I thought the thing could be done. Then I threw out many inducements, in the shape of pleasant anticipations of bearing right down before the wind upon the sunny isles under our lee.

He listened attentively; but so long remained silent that I almost fancied there was something in Jarl which would prove too much for me and my eloquence.

At last he very bluntly declared that the scheme was a crazy one; he had never known of such a thing but thrice before; and in every case the runaways had never afterwards been heard of. He entreated me to renounce my determination, not be a boy, pause and reflect, stick to the ship, and go home in her like a man. Verily, my Viking talked to me like my uncle.

But to all this I turned a deaf ear; affirming that my mind was made up; and that as he refused to accompany me, and I fancied no one else for a comrade, I would go stark alone rather than not at all. Upon this, seeing my resolution immovable, he bluntly swore that he would follow me through thick and thin.

Thanks, Jarl! thou wert one of those devoted fellows who will wrestle hard to convince one loved of error; but failing, forthwith change their wrestling to a sympathetic hug.

But now his elderly prudence came into play. Casting his eye over the boundless expanse below, he inquired how far off were the islands in question.

"A thousand miles and no less."

"With a fair trade breeze, then, and a boat sail, that is a good twelve days' passage, but calms and currents may make it a month, perhaps more." So saying, he shook his old head, and his yellow hair streamed.

But trying my best to chase away these misgivings, he at last gave them over. He assured me I might count upon him to his uttermost keel.

My Viking secured, I felt more at ease; and thoughtfully considered how the enterprise might best be accomplished.

There was no time to be lost. Every hour was carrying us farther and farther from the parallel most desirable for us to follow in our route to the westward. So, with all possible dispatch, I matured my plans, and communicated them to Jarl, who gave several old hints—having ulterior probabilities in view—which were not neglected.

Strange to relate, it was not till my Viking, with a rueful face, reminded me of the fact, that I bethought me of a circumstance somewhat alarming at the first blush. We must push off without chart or quadrant; though, as will shortly be seen, a compass was by no means out of the question. The chart, to be sure, I did not so much lay to heart; but a quadrant was more

than desirable. Still, it was by no means indispensable. For this reason.
When we started, our latitude would be exactly known; and whether, on
our voyage westward, we drifted north or south therefrom, we could not,
by any possibility, get so far out of our reckoning, as to fail in striking some
one of a long chain of islands, which, for many degrees, on both sides of
the equator, stretched right across our track.

For much the same reason, it mattered little, whether on our passage
we daily knew our longitude; for no known land lay between us and the
place we desired to reach. So what could be plainer than this: that if westward we patiently held on our way, we must eventually achieve our destination?

As for intervening shoals or reefs, if any there were, they intimidated
us not. In a boat that drew but a few inches of water, but an indifferent
look-out would preclude all danger on that score. At all events, the thing
seemed feasible enough, notwithstanding old Jarl's superstitious reverence
for nautical instruments, and the philosophical objections which might have
been urged by a pedantic disciple of Mercator.

Very often, as the old maxim goes, the simplest things are the most
startling, and that, too, from their very simplicity. So cherish no alarms,
if thus we addressed the setting sun—"Be thou, old pilot, our guide!"

Chapter 5

Seats secured and Portmanteaus packed

B UT THOUGHTS OF SEXTANTS and quadrants were the least
of our cares.

Right from under the very arches of the eyebrows of thirty men
—captain, mates, and crew—a boat was to be abstracted; they knowing
nothing of the event, until all knowledge would prove unavailing.

Hark ye:

At sea, the boats of a South Sea-man (generally four in number, spare
ones omitted,) are suspended by tackles, hooked above, to curved timbers
called "davits," vertically fixed to the ship's sides.

Now, no fair one with golden locks is more assiduously waited upon,
or more delicately handled by her tire-women, than the slender whale-boat
by her crew. And out of its element, it seems fragile enough to justify the
utmost solicitude. For truly, like a fine lady, the fine whale-boat is most
delicate when idle, though little coy at a pinch.

Besides the "davits," the following supports are provided. Two small
cranes are swung under the keel, on which the latter rests, preventing the
settling of the boat's middle, while hanging suspended by the bow and stern.
A broad, braided, hempen band, usually worked in a tasteful pattern, is also
passed round both gunwales; and secured to the ship's bulwarks, firmly
lashes the craft to its place. Being elevated above the ship's rail, the boats
are in plain sight from all parts of the deck.

Now, one of these boats was to be made way with. No facile matter, truly. Harder than for any dashing young Janizary to run off with a sultana from the Grand Turk's seraglio. Still, the thing could be done, for, by Jove, it had been.

What say you to slyly loosing every thing by day; and when night comes, cast off the band and swing in the cranes? But how lower the tackles, even in the darkest night, without a creaking more fearful than the death rattle? Easily avoided. Anoint the ropes, and they will travel deftly through the subtle windings of the blocks.

But though I had heard of this plan being pursued, there was a degree of risk in it, after all, which I was far from fancying. Another plan was hit upon; still bolder; and hence more safe. What it was, in the right place will be seen.

In selecting my craft for this good voyage, I would fain have traversed the deck, and eyed the boats like a cornet choosing his steed from out a goodly stud. But this was denied me. And the "bow boat" was, perforce, singled out, as the most remote from the quarter-deck, that region of sharp eyes and relentless purposes.

Then, our larder was to be thought of; also, an abundant supply of water; concerning which last I determined to take good heed. There were but two to be taken care of; but I resolved to lay in sufficient store of both meat and drink for four; at the same time that the supplemental twain thus provided for were but imaginary. And if it came to the last dead pinch, of which we had no fear, however, I was food for no man but Jarl.

Little time was lost in catering for our mess. Biscuit and salt beef were our sole resource; and, thanks to the generosity of the Arcturion's owners, our ship's company had a plentiful supply. Casks of both, with heads knocked out, were at the service of all. In bags which we made for the purpose, a sufficiency of the biscuit was readily stored away, and secreted in a corner of easy access. The salt beef was more difficult to obtain; but, little by little, we managed to smuggle out of the cask enough to answer our purpose.

As for water, most luckily a day or two previous several "breakers" of it had been hoisted from below for the present use of the ship's company.

These "breakers" are casks, long and slender, but very strong. Of various diameters, they are made on purpose to stow into spaces intervening between the immense butts in a ship's hold.

The largest we could find was selected, first carefully examining it to detect any leak. On some pretense or other, we then rolled them all over to that side of the vessel where our boat was suspended, the selected breaker being placed in their middle.

Our compendious wardrobes were snugly packed into bundles and laid aside for the present. And at last, by due caution, we had every thing arranged preliminary to the final start. Let me say, though, perhaps to the credit of Jarl, that whenever the most strategy was necessary, he seemed ill at ease, and for the most part left the matter to me. It was well that he did; for as it was, by his untimely straight-forwardness, he once or twice came near spoiling every thing. Indeed, on one occasion he was so unseasonably blunt, that curiously enough, I had almost suspected him of taking that odd sort of interest in one's welfare, which leads a philanthropist, all other methods failing, to frustrate a project deemed bad, by pretending clumsily to favor it. But no inuendoes; Jarl was a Viking, frank as his fathers; though not so much of a bucanier.

Chapter 6

Eight Bells

THE MOON must be monstrous coy, or some things fall out opportunely, or else almanacs are consulted by nocturnal adventurers; but so it is, that when Cynthia shows a round and chubby disk, few daring deeds are done. Though true it may be, that of moonlight nights, jewelers' caskets and maidens' hearts have been burglariously broken into—and rifled, for aught Copernicus can tell.

The gentle planet was in her final quarter, and upon her slender horn I hung my hopes of withdrawing from the ship undetected.

Now, making a tranquil passage across the ocean, we kept at this time what are called among whalemen "boats-crew-watches." That is, instead of the sailors being divided at night into two bands, alternately on deck every four hours, there were four watches, each composed of a boat's crew, the "headsman" (always one of the mates) excepted. To the officers, this plan gives uninterrupted repose—"all-night-in," as they call it, and of course greatly lightens the duties of the crew.

The harpooneers head the boats' crews, and are responsible for the ship during the continuance of their watches.

Now, my Viking being a stalwart seaman, pulled the midship oar of the boat of which I was bowsman. Hence, we were in the same watch; to which, also, three others belonged, including Mark, the harpooneer. One of these seamen, however, being an invalid, there were only two left for us to manage.

Voyaging in these seas, you may glide along for weeks without starting tack or sheet, hardly moving the helm a spoke, so mild and constant are the Trades. At night, the watch seldom trouble themselves with keeping much of a look-out; especially, as a strange sail is almost a prodigy in these lonely waters. In some ships, for weeks in and weeks out, you are puzzled to tell when your nightly turn on deck really comes round; so little heed is given to the standing of watches, where in the license of presumed safety, nearly every one nods without fear.

But remiss as you may be in the boats-crew-watch of a heedless whale-man, the man who heads it is bound to maintain his post on the quarter-deck until regularly relieved. Yet drowsiness being incidental to all natures, even to Napoleon, beside his own sentry napping in the snowy bivouac; so, often, in snowy moonlight, or ebon eclipse, dozed Mark, our harpooneer. Lethe be his portion this blessed night, thought I, as during the morning which preceded our enterprise, I eyed the man who might possibly cross my plans.

But let me come closer to this part of my story. During what are called at sea the "dog-watches" (between four o'clock and eight in the evening), sailors are quite lively and frolicsome; their spirits even flow far into the first of the long "night-watches;" but upon its expiration at "eight bells" (midnight), silence begins to reign; if you hear a voice it is no cherub's: all exclamations are oaths.

At eight bells, the mariners on deck, now relieved from their cares, crawl out from their sleepy retreats in old monkey jackets, or coils of rigging, and hie to their hammocks, almost without interrupting their dreams: while the sluggards below lazily drag themselves up the ladder to resume their slumbers in the open air.

For these reasons then, the moonless sea midnight was just the time to escape. Hence, we suffered a whole day to pass unemployed; waiting for the night, when the starboard-quarter-boats'-watch, to which we belonged, would be summoned on deck at the eventful eight of the bell.

But twenty-four hours soon glide away; and "Starboleens ahoy! eight bells there below!" at last started me from a troubled doze.

I sprang from my hammock, and would have lighted my pipe. But the forecastle lamp had gone out. An old sea-dog was talking about sharks in his sleep. Jarl and our solitary watch-mate were groping their way into their trowsers. And little was heard but the humming of the still sails aloft; the dash of the waves against the bow; and the deep breathing of the dreaming sailors around.

Chapter 7

A Pause

GOOD OLD ARCTURION! Maternal craft, that rocked me so often in thy heart of oak, I grieve to tell how I deserted thee on the broad deep. So far from home, with such a motley crew, so many islanders, whose heathen babble echoing through thy Christian hull, must have grated harshly on every carline.

Old ship! where sails thy lone ghost now? For of the stout Arcturion no word was ever heard, from the dark hour we pushed from her fated planks. In what time of tempest, to what seagull's scream, the drowning eddies did their work, knows no mortal man. Sunk she silently, helplessly, into the calm depths of that summer sea, assassinated by the ruthless blade of the swordfish? Such things have been. Or was hers a better fate? Stricken down while gallantly battling with the blast; her storm-sails set; helm manned; and every sailor at his post; as sunk the Hornet, her men at quarters, in some distant gale.

But surmises are idle. A very old craft, she may have foundered; or laid her bones upon some treacherous reef; but as with many a far rover, her fate is a mystery.

Pray Heaven, the spirit of that lost vessel roaming abroad through the troubled mists of midnight gales—as old mariners believe of missing ships—may never haunt my future path upon the waves. Peacefully may she rest

24

at the bottom of the sea; and sweetly sleep my shipmates in the lowest watery zone, where prowling sharks come not, nor billows roll.

By quitting the Arcturion when we did, Jarl and I unconsciously eluded a sailor's grave. We hear of providential deliverances. Was this one? But life is sweet to all, death comes as hard. And for myself I am almost tempted to hang my head, that I escaped the fate of my shipmates; something like him who blushed to have escaped the fell carnage at Thermopylæ.

Though I can not repress a shudder when I think of that old ship's end, it is impossible for me so much as to imagine, that our deserting her could have been in any way instrumental in her loss. Nevertheless, I would to Heaven the Arcturion still floated; that it was given me once more to tread her familiar decks.

Chapter 8

They push off, Velis et Remis

AND NOW TO TELL HOW, tempted by devil or good angel, and a thousand miles from land, we embarked upon this western voyage.

It was midnight, mark you, when our watch began; and my turn at the helm now coming on was of course to be avoided. On some plausible pretense, I induced our solitary watchmate to assume it; thus leaving myself untrammeled, and at the same time satisfactorily disposing of him. For being a rather fat fellow, an enormous consumer of "duff," and with good reason supposed to be the son of a farmer, I made no doubt, he would pursue his old course and fall to nodding over the wheel. As for the leader of the watch—our harpooneer—he fell heir to the nest of old jackets, under the lee of the mizzen-mast, left nice and warm by his predecessor.

The night was even blacker than we had anticipated; there was no trace of a moon; and the dark purple haze, sometimes encountered at night near the Line, half shrouded the stars from view.

Waiting about twenty minutes after the last man of the previous watch had gone below, I motioned to Jarl, and we slipped our shoes from our feet. He then descended into the forecastle, and I sauntered aft toward the quarter-deck. All was still. Thrice did I pass my hand full before the face of the slumbering lubber at the helm, and right between him and the light of the binnacle.

Mark, the harpooneer, was not so easily sounded. I feared to approach him. He lay quietly, though; but asleep or awake, no more delay. Risks must be run, when time presses. And our ears were a pointer's to catch a sound.

To work we went, without hurry, but swiftly and silently. Our various stores were dragged from their lurking-places, and placed in the boat, which hung from the ship's lee side, the side depressed in the water, an indispensable requisite to an attempt at escape. And though at sundown the boat was to windward, yet, as we had foreseen, the vessel having been tacked during the first watch, brought it to leeward.

Endeavoring to manhandle our clumsy breaker, and lift it into the boat, we found, that by reason of the intervention of the shrouds, it could not be done without risking a jar; besides straining the craft in lowering. An expedient, however, though at the eleventh hour, was hit upon. Fastening a long rope to the breaker, which was perfectly tight, we cautiously dropped it overboard; paying out enough line, to insure its towing astern of the ship, so as not to strike against the copper. The other end of the line we then secured to the boat's stern.

Fortunately, this was the last thing to be done; for the breaker, acting as a clog to the vessel's way in the water, so affected her steering as to fling her perceptibly into the wind. And by causing the helm to work, this must soon rouse the lubber there stationed, if not already awake. But our dropping overboard the breaker greatly aided us in this respect: it diminished the ship's headway; which owing to the light breeze had not been very great at any time during the night. Had it been so, all hope of escaping without first arresting the vessel's progress, would have been little short of madness. As it was, the sole daring of the deed that night achieved, consisted in our lowering away while the ship yet clove the brine, though but moderately.

All was now ready: the cranes swung in, the lashings adrift, and the boat fairly suspended; when, seizing the ends of the tackle ropes, we silently stepped into it, one at each end. The dead weight of the breaker astern now dragged the craft horizontally through the air, so that her tackle ropes strained hard. She quivered like a dolphin. Nevertheless, had we not feared her loud splash upon striking the wave, we might have quitted the ship almost as silently as the breath the body. But this was out of the question, and our plans were laid accordingly.

"All ready, Jarl?"

"Ready."

"A man overboard!" I shouted at the top of my compass; and like lightning the cords slid through our blistering hands, and with a tremendous shock the boat bounded on the sea's back. One mad sheer and plunge, one terrible strain on the tackles as we sunk in the trough of the waves, tugged upon by the towing breaker, and our knives severed the tackle ropes—we hazarded not unhooking the blocks—our oars were out, and the good boat headed round, with prow to leeward.

"Man overboard!" was now shouted from stem to stern. And directly we heard the confused tramping and shouting of the sailors, as they rushed from their dreams into the almost inscrutable darkness.

"Man overboard! Man overboard!" My heart smote me as the human cry of horror came out of the black vaulted night.

"Down helm!" was soon heard from the chief mate. "Back the main-yard! Quick to the boats! How's this? One down already? Well done! Hold on, then, those other boats!"

Meanwhile several seamen were shouting as they strained at the braces.

"Cut! cut all! Lower away! lower away!" impatiently cried the sailors, who already had leaped into the boats.

"Heave the ship to, and hold fast every thing," cried the captain, apparently just springing to the deck. "One boat's enough. Steward! show a light there from the mizzen-top. Boat ahoy!—Have you got that man?"

No reply. The voice came out of a cloud; the ship dimly showing like a ghost. We had desisted from rowing, and hand over hand were now hauling in upon the rope attached to the breaker, which we soon lifted into the boat, instantly resuming our oars.

"Pull! pull, men! and save him!" again shouted the captain.

"Ay, ay, sir," answered Jarl instinctively, "pulling as hard as ever we can, sir."

And pull we did, till nothing could be heard from the ship but a confused tumult; and, ever and anon, the hoarse shout of the captain, too distant to be understood.

We now set our sail to a light air; and right into the darkness, and dead to leeward, we rowed and sailed till morning dawned.

Chapter 9

The Watery World is all before Them

AT SEA IN AN OPEN BOAT, and a thousand miles from land! Shortly after the break of day, in the gray transparent light, a speck to windward broke the even line of the horizon. It was the ship wending her way north-eastward.

Had I not known the final indifference of sailors to such disasters as that which the Arcturion's crew must have imputed to the night past (did not the skipper suspect the truth) I would have regarded that little speck with many compunctions of conscience. Nor, as it was, did I feel in any very serene humor. For the consciousness of being deemed dead, is next to the presumable unpleasantness of being so in reality. One feels like his own ghost unlawfully tenanting a defunct carcass. Even Jarl's glance seemed so queer, that I begged him to look another way.

Secure now from all efforts of the captain to recover those whom he most probably supposed lost; and equally cut off from all hope of returning to the ship even had we felt so inclined; the resolution that had thus far nerved me, began to succumb in a measure to the awful loneliness of the scene. Ere this, I had regarded the ocean as a slave, the steed that bore me whither I listed, and whose vicious propensities, mighty though they were, often proved harmless, when opposed to the genius of man. But now, how changed! In our frail boat, I would fain have built an altar to Neptune.

What a mere toy we were to the billows, that jeeringly shouldered us from crest to crest, as from hand to hand lost souls may be tossed along by the chain of shades which enfilade the route to Tartarus.

But drown or swim, here's overboard with care! Cheer up, Jarl! Ha! ha! how merrily, yet terribly, we sail! Up, up—slowly up—toiling up the long, calm wave; then balanced on its summit a while, like a plank on a rail; and down, we plunge headlong into the seething abyss, till arrested, we glide upward again. And thus did we go. Now buried in watery hollows —our sail idly flapping; then lifted aloft—canvas bellying; and beholding the furthest horizon.

Had not our familiarity with the business of whaling divested our craft's wild motions of its first novel horrors, we had been but a rueful pair. But day-long pulls after whales, the ship left miles astern; and entire dark nights passed moored to the monsters, killed too late to be towed to the ship far to leeward:—all this, and much more, accustoms one to strange things. Death, to be sure, has a mouth as black as a wolf's, and to be thrust into his jaws is a serious thing. But true it most certainly is—and I speak from no hearsay—that to sailors, as a class, the grisly king seems not half so hideous as he appears to those who have only regarded him on shore, and at a deferential distance. Like many ugly mortals, his features grow less frightful upon acquaintance; and met over often and sociably, the old adage holds true, about familiarity breeding contempt. Thus too with soldiers. Of the quaking recruit, three pitched battles make a grim grenadier; and he who shrank from the muzzle of a cannon, is now ready to yield his mustache for a sponge.

And truly, since death is the last enemy of all, valiant souls will taunt him while they may. Yet rather, should the wise regard him as the inflexible friend, who, even against our own wills, from life's evils triumphantly re-lieves us.

And there is but little difference in the manner of dying. To die, is all. And death has been gallantly encountered by those who never beheld blood that was red, only its light azure seen through the veins. And to yield the ghost proudly, and march out of your fortress with all the honors of war, is not a thing of sinew and bone. Though in prison, Geoffry Hudson, the dwarf, died more bravely than Goliah, the giant; and the last end of a butterfly shames us all. Some women have lived nobler lives, and died nobler deaths, than men. Threatened with the stake, mitred Cranmer re-canted; but through her fortitude, the lorn widow of Edessa stayed the tide of Valens' persecutions. 'Tis no great valor to perish sword in hand, and bravado on lip; cased all in panoply complete. For even the alligator dies in his mail, and the swordfish never surrenders. To expire, mild-eyed, in one's bed, transcends the death of Epaminondas.

Chapter 10

They arrange their Canopies and Lounges,
and try to make Things comfortable

O UR LITTLE CRAFT was soon in good order. From the spare rigging brought along, we made shrouds to the mast, and converted the boat-hook into a handy boom for the jib. Going large before the wind, we set this sail wing-and-wing with the main-sail. The latter, in accordance with the customary rig of whale-boats, was worked with a sprit and sheet. It could be furled or set in an instant. The bags of bread we stowed away in the covered space about the loggerhead, a useless appurtenance now, and therefore removed. At night, Jarl used it for a pillow; saying, that when the boat rolled it gave easy play to his head. The precious breaker we lashed firmly amidships; thereby much improving our sailing.

Now, previous to leaving the ship, we had seen to it well, that our craft was supplied with all those equipments, with which, by the regulations of the fishery, a whale-boat is constantly provided: night and day, afloat or suspended. Hanging along our gunwales inside, were six harpoons, three lances, and a blubber-spade; all keen as razors, and sheathed with leather. Besides these, we had three waifs, a couple of two-gallon water-kegs, several bailers, the boat-hatchet for cutting the whale-line, two auxiliary knives for the like purpose, and several minor articles, also employed in hunting the leviathan. The line and line-tub, however, were on ship-board.

And here it may be mentioned, that to prevent the strain upon the boat when suspended to the ship's side, the heavy whale-line, over two hundred fathoms in length, and something more than an inch in diameter, when not in use is kept on ship-board, coiled away like an endless snake in its tub. But this tub is always in readiness to be launched into the boat. Now, having no use for the line belonging to our craft, we had purposely left it behind.

But well had we marked that by far the most important item of a whale-boat's furniture was snugly secured in its place. This was the water-tight keg, at both ends firmly headed, containing a small compass, tinder-box and flint, candles, and a score or two of biscuit. This keg is an invariable precaution against what so frequently occurs in pursuing the sperm whale —prolonged absence from the ship, losing sight of her, or never seeing her more, till years after you reach home again. In this same keg of ours seemed coopered up life and death, at least so seemed it to honest Jarl. No sooner had we got clear from the Arcturion, than dropping his oar for an instant, he clutched at it in the dark.

And when day at last came, we knocked out the head of the keg with the little hammer and chisel, always attached to it for that purpose, and removed the compass, that glistened to us like a human eye. Then filling up the vacancy with biscuit, we again made all tight, driving down the hoops till they would budge no more.

At first we were puzzled to fix our compass. But at last the Skyeman out knife, and cutting a round hole in the aftermost thwart, or seat of the boat, there inserted the little brass case containing the needle.

Over the stern of the boat, with some old canvas which my Viking's forethought had provided, we spread a rude sort of awning, or rather counterpane. This, however, proved but little or no protection from the glare of the sun; for the management of the main-sail forbade any considerable elevation of the shelter. And when the breeze was fresh, we were fain to strike it altogether; for the wind being from aft, and getting underneath the canvas, almost lifted the light boat's stern into the air, vexing the counterpane as if it were a petticoat turning a gusty corner. But when a mere breath rippled the sea, and the sun was fiery hot, it was most pleasant to lounge in this shady asylum. It was like being transferred from the roast to cool in the cupboard. And Jarl, much the toughest fowl of the two, out of an abundant kindness for his comrade, during the day voluntarily remained exposed at the helm, almost two hours to my one. No lady-like scruples had he, the old Viking, about marring his complexion, which already was more than bronzed. Over the ordinary tanning of the sailor, he seemed masked by a visor of japanning, dotted all over with freckles, so intensely yellow, and symmetrically circular, that they seemed scorched there by a burning glass.

In the tragico-comico moods which at times overtook me, I used to look upon the brown Skyeman with humorous complacency. If we fall in with cannibals, thought I, then, ready-roasted Norseman that thou art, shall I survive to mourn thee; at least, during the period I revolve upon the spit.

But of such a fate, it needs hardly be said, we had no apprehension.

Chapter 11

Jarl afflicted with the Lockjaw

IF EVER AGAIN I launch whale-boat from sheer-plank of ship at sea, I shall take good heed, that my comrade be a sprightly fellow, with a rattle-box head. Be he never so silly, his very silliness, so long as he be lively at it, shall be its own excuse.

Upon occasion, who likes not a lively loon, one of your giggling, gamesome oafs, whose mouth is a grin? Are not such, well-ordered dispensations of Providence? filling up vacuums, in intervals of social stagnation relieving the tedium of existing? besides keeping up, here and there, in very many quarters indeed, sundry people's good opinion of themselves? What, if at times their speech is insipid as water after wine? What, if to ungenial and irascible souls, their very "mug" is an exasperation to behold, their clack an inducement to suicide? Let us not be hard upon them for this; but let them live on for the good they may do.

But Jarl, dear, dumb Jarl, thou wert none of these. Thou didst carry a phiz like an excommunicated deacon's. And no matter what happened, it was ever the same. Quietly, in thyself, thou didst revolve upon thine own sober axis, like a wheel in a machine which forever goes round, whether you look at it or no. Ay, Jarl! wast thou not forever intent upon minding that which so many neglect—thine own especial business? Wast thou not forever at it, too, with no likelihood of ever winding up thy moody affairs, and striking a balance sheet?

35

But at times how wearisome to me these everlasting reveries in my one solitary companion. I longed for something enlivening; a burst of words; human vivacity of one kind or other. After in vain essaying to get something of this sort out of Jarl, I tried it all by myself; playing upon my body as upon an instrument; singing, halloing, and making empty gestures, till my Viking stared hard; and I myself paused to consider whether I had run crazy or no.

But how account for the Skyeman's gravity? Surely, it was based upon no philosophic taciturnity; he was nothing of an idealist; an aerial architect; a constructor of flying buttresses. It was inconceivable, that his reveries were Manfred-like and exalted, reminiscent of unutterable deeds, too mysterious even to be indicated by the remotest of hints. Suppositions all out of the question.

His ruminations were a riddle. I asked him anxiously, whether, in any part of the world, Savannah, Surat, or Archangel, he had ever a wife to think of; or children, that he carried so lengthy a phiz. Nowhere neither. Therefore, as by his own confession he had nothing to think of but himself, and there was little but honesty in him (having which, by the way, he may be thought full to the brim), what could I fall back upon but my original theory: namely, that in repose, his intellects stepped out, and left his body to itself.

Chapter 12

More about being in an open Boat

O N THE THIRD MORNING, at break of day, I sat at the steering oar, an hour or two previous having relieved Jarl, now fast
asleep. Somehow, and suddenly, a sense of peril so intense, came
over me, that it could hardly have been aggravated by the completest
solitude.

On a ship's deck, the mere feeling of elevation above the water, and the
reach of prospect you command, impart a degree of confidence which dis-
poses you to exult in your fancied security. But in an open boat, brought
down to the very plane of the sea, this feeling almost wholly deserts you.
Unless the waves, in their gambols, toss you and your chip upon one of their
lordly crests, your sphere of vision is little larger than it would be at the
bottom of a well. At best, your most extended view in any one direction,
at least, is in a high, slow-rolling sea; when you descend into the dark, misty
spaces, between long and uniform swells. Then, for the moment, it is like
looking up and down in a twilight glade, interminable; where two dawns,
one on each hand, seem struggling through the semi-transparent tops of the
fluid mountains.

But, lingering not long in those silent vales, from watery cliff to cliff,
a sea-chamois, sprang our solitary craft,—a goat among the Alps!

How undulated the horizon; like a vast serpent with ten thousand folds coiled all round the globe; yet so nigh, apparently, that it seemed as if one's hand might touch it.

What loneliness; when the sun rose, and spurred up the heavens, we hailed him as a wayfarer in Sahara the sight of a distant horseman. Save ourselves, the sun and the Chamois seemed all that was left of life in the universe. We yearned toward its jocund disk, as in strange lands the traveler joyfully greets a face from home, which there had passed unheeded. And was not the sun a fellow-voyager? were we not both wending westward? But how soon he daily overtook and passed us; hurrying to his journey's end.

When a week had gone by, sailing steadily on, by day and by night, and nothing in sight but this self-same sea, what wonder if disquieting thoughts at last entered our hearts? If unknowingly we should pass the spot where, according to our reckoning, our islands lay, upon what shoreless sea would we launch? At times, these forebodings bewildered my idea of the positions of the groups beyond. All became vague and confused; so that westward of the Kingsmill isles and the Radack chain, I fancied there could be naught but an endless sea.

Chapter 13

Of the Chondropterygii, and other uncouth Hordes
infesting the South Seas

A T INTERVALS in our lonely voyage, there were sights which
diversified the scene; especially when the constellation Pisces was
in the ascendant.

It's famous botanizing, they say, in Arkansas' boundless prairies; I
commend the student of Ichthyology to an open boat, and the ocean moors
of the Pacific. As your craft glides along, what strange monsters float by.
Elsewhere, was never seen their like. And nowhere are they found in the
books of the naturalists.

Though America be discovered, the Cathays of the deep are unknown.
And whoso crosses the Pacific might have read lessons to Buffon. The sea-
serpent is not a fable; and in the sea, that snake is but a garden worm. There
are more wonders than the wonders rejected, and more sights unrevealed
than you or I ever ever dreamt of. Moles and bats alone should be skeptics;
and the only true infidelity is for a live man to vote himself dead. Be Sir
Thomas Brown our ensample; who, while exploding "Vulgar Errors,"
heartily hugged all the mysteries in the Pentateuch.

But look! fathoms down in the sea; where ever saw you a phantom like
that? An enormous crescent with antlers like a reindeer, and a Delta of
mouths. Slowly it sinks, and is seen no more.

Doctor Faust saw the devil; but you have seen the "Devil Fish."

Look again! Here comes another. Jarl calls it a Bone Shark. Full as large as a whale, it is spotted like a leopard; and tusk-like teeth overlap its jaws like those of the walrus. To seamen, nothing strikes more terror than the near vicinity of a creature like this. Great ships steer out of its path. And well they may; since the good craft Essex, and others, have been sunk by sea-monsters, as the alligator thrusts his horny snout through a Caribbean canoe.

Ever present to us, was the apprehension of some sudden disaster from the extraordinary zoological specimens we almost hourly passed.

For the sharks, we saw them, not by units, nor by tens, nor by hundreds; but by thousands and by myriads. Trust me, there are more sharks in the sea than mortals on land.

And of these prolific fish there are full as many species as of dogs. But by the German naturalists Müller and Henle, who, in christening the sharks, have bestowed upon them the most heathenish names, they are classed under one family; which family, according to Müller, king-at-arms, is an undoubted branch of the ancient and famous tribe of the Chondropterygii.

To begin. There is the ordinary Brown Shark, or sea-attorney, so called by sailors; a grasping, rapacious varlet, that in spite of the hard knocks received from it, often snapped viciously at our steering oar. At times, these gentry swim in herds; especially about the remains of a slaughtered whale. They are the vultures of the deep.

Then we often encountered the dandy Blue Shark, a long, taper and mighty genteel looking fellow, with a slender waist, like a Bond-street beau, and the whitest tiers of teeth imaginable. This dainty spark invariably lounged by with a careless fin and an indolent tail. But he looked infernally heartless.

How his cold-blooded, gentlemanly air, contrasted with the rude, savage swagger of the Tiger Shark; a round, portly gourmand; with distended mouth and collapsed conscience, swimming about seeking whom he might devour. These gluttons are the scavengers of navies, following ships in the South Seas, picking up odds and ends of garbage, and sometimes a tit-bit, a stray sailor. No wonder, then, that sailors denounce them. In substance, Jarl once assured me, that under any temporary misfortune, it was one of his sweetest consolations to remember, that in his day, he had murdered, not killed, shoals of Tiger Sharks.

Yet this is all wrong. As well hate a seraph, as a shark. Both were made by the same hand. And that sharks are lovable, witness their domestic endearments. No Fury so ferocious, as not to have some amiable side. In the wild wilderness, a leopard-mother caresses her cub, as Hagar did Ishmael;

or a queen of France the dauphin. We know not what we do when we hate. And I have the word of my gentlemanly friend Stanhope, for it; that he who declared he loved a good hater was but a respectable sort of Hottentot, at best. No very genteel epithet this, though coming from the genteelest of men. But when the digger of dictionaries said that saying of his, he was assuredly not much of a Christian. However, it is hard for one given up to constitutional hypos like him, to be filled with the milk and meekness of the gospels. Yet, with deference, I deny that my old uncle Johnson really believed in the sentiment ascribed to him. Love a hater, indeed! Who smacks his lips over gall? Now hate is a thankless thing. So, let us only hate hatred; and once give love play, we will fall in love with a unicorn. Ah! the easiest way is the best; and to hate, a man must work hard. Love is a delight; but hate a torment. And haters are thumbscrews, Scotch boots, and Spanish inquisitions to themselves. In five words—would they were a Siamese diphthong—he who hates is a fool.

For several days our Chamois was followed by two of these aforesaid Tiger Sharks. A brace of confidential inseparables, jogging along in our wake, side by side, like a couple of highwaymen, biding their time till you come to the cross-roads. But giving it up at last, for a bootless errand, they dropped farther and farther astern, until completely out of sight. Much to the Skyeman's chagrin; who long stood in the stern, lance poised for a dart.

But of all sharks, save me from the ghastly White Shark. For though we should hate naught, yet some dislikes are spontaneous; and disliking is not hating. And never yet could I bring myself to be loving, or even sociable, with a White Shark. He is not the sort of creature to enlist young affections.

This ghost of a fish is not often encountered, and shows plainer by night than by day. Timon-like, he always swims by himself; gliding along just under the surface, revealing a long, vague shape, of a milky hue; with glimpses now and then of his bottomless white pit of teeth. No need of a dentist hath he. Seen at night, stealing along like a spirit in the water, with horrific serenity of aspect, the White Shark sent many a thrill to us twain in the Chamois.

By day, and in the profoundest calms, oft were we startled by the ponderous sigh of the grampus, as lazily rising to the surface, he fetched a long breath after napping below.

And time and again we watched the darting albicore, the fish with the chain-plate armor and golden scales; the Nimrod of the seas, to whom so many flying fish fall a prey. Flying from their pursuers, many of them flew into our boat. But invariably they died from the shock. No nursing could restore them. One of their wings I removed, spreading it out to dry under a weight. In two days' time the thin membrane, all over tracings like those of a leaf, was transparent as isinglass, and tinted with brilliant hues, like those of a changing silk.

Almost every day, we spied Black Fish; coal-black and glossy. They seemed to swim by revolving round and round in the water, like a wheel; their dorsal fins, every now and then shooting into view, like spokes.

Of a somewhat similar species, but smaller, and clipper-built about the nose, were the Algerines; so called, probably, from their corsair propensities; waylaying peaceful fish on the high seas, and plundering them of body and soul at a gulp. Atrocious Turks! a crusade should be preached against them.

Besides all these, we encountered Killers and Thrashers, by far the most spirited and "spunky" of the finny tribes. Though little larger than a porpoise, a band of them think nothing of assailing leviathan himself. They bait the monster, as dogs a bull. The Killers seizing the Right whale by his immense, sulky lower lip, and the Thrashers fastening on to his back, and beating him with their sinewy tails. Often they come off conquerors, worrying the enemy to death. Though, sooth to say, if leviathan gets but one sweep at them with his terrible tail, they go flying into the air, as if tossed from Taurus' horn.

This sight we beheld. Had old Wouvermans, who once painted a bull bait, been along with us, a rare chance, that, for his pencil. And Gudin or Isabey might have thrown the blue rolling sea into the picture. Lastly, one of Claude's setting summer suns would have glorified the whole. Oh, believe me, God's creatures fighting, fin for fin, a thousand miles from land, and with the round horizon for an arena, is no ignoble subject for a masterpiece.

Such are a few of the sights of the great South Sea. But there is no telling all. The Pacific is populous as China.

Chapter 14

Jarl's Misgivings

ABOUT THIS TIME an event took place. My good Viking opened his mouth, and spoke. The prodigy occurred, as, jackknife in hand, he was bending over the midship oar; on the loom, or handle, of which he kept our almanac; making a notch for every set sun. For some forty-eight hours past, the wind had been light and variable. It was more than suspected that a current was sweeping us northward.

Now, marking these things, Jarl threw out the thought, that the more wind, and the less current, the better; and if a long calm came on, of which there was some prospect, we had better take to our oars.

Take to our oars! as if we were crossing a ferry, and no ocean leagues to traverse. The idea indirectly suggested all possible horrors. To be rid of them forthwith, I proceeded to dole out our morning meal. For to make away with such things, there is nothing better than bolting something down on top of them; albeit, oft repeated, the plan is very apt to beget dyspepsia; and the dyspepsia the blues.

But what of our store of provisions? So far as enough to eat was concerned, we felt not the slightest apprehension; our supplies proving more abundant than we had anticipated. But, curious to tell, we felt but little inclination for food. It was water, bright water, cool, sparkling water, alone, that we craved. And of this, also, our store at first seemed ample.

43

But as our voyage lengthened, and breezes blew faint, and calms fell fast, the idea of being deprived of the precious fluid grew into something little short of a monomania; especially with Jarl.

Every hour or two with the hammer and chisel belonging to the tinder box keg, he tinkered away at the invaluable breaker; driving down the hoops, till in his over solicitude, I thought he would burst them outright.

Now the breaker lay on its bilge, in the middle of the boat, where more or less sea-water always collected. And ever and anon, dipping his finger therein, my Viking was troubled with the thought, that this sea-water tasted less brackish than that alongside. Of course the breaker must be leaking. So, he would turn it over, till its wet side came uppermost; when it would quickly become dry as a bone. But now, with his knife, he would gently probe the joints of the staves; shake his head; look up; look down; taste of the water in the bottom of the boat; then that of the sea; then lift one end of the breaker; going through with every test of leakage he could dream of. Nor was he ever fully satisfied, that the breaker was in all respects sound. But in reality it was tight as the drum-heads that beat at Cerro-Gordo. Oh! Jarl, Jarl: to me in the boat's quiet stern, steering and philosophizing at one time and the same, thou and thy breaker were a study.

Besides the breaker, we had, full of water, the two boat-kegs, previously alluded to. These were first used. We drank from them by their leaden spouts; so many swallows three times in the day; having no other means of measuring an allowance. But when we came to the breaker, which had only a bung-hole, though a very large one, dog-like, it was so many laps apiece; jealously counted by the observer. This plan, however, was only good for a single day; the water then getting beyond the reach of the tongue. We therefore daily poured from the breaker into one of the kegs; and drank from its spout. But to obviate the absorption inseparable from decanting, we at last hit upon something better,—my comrade's shoe, which, deprived of its quarters, narrowed at the heel, and diligently rinsed out in the sea, was converted into a handy but rather limber ladle. This we kept suspended in the bung-hole of the breaker, that it might never twice absorb the water.

Now pewter imparts flavor to ale; a Meerschaum bowl, the same to the tobacco of Smyrna; and goggle green glasses are deemed indispensable to the bibbing of Hock. What then shall be said of a leathern goblet for water? Try it, ye mariners who list.

One morning, taking his wonted draught, Jarl fished up in his ladle a deceased insect; something like a Daddy-long-legs, only more corpulent. Its fate? A sea-toss? Believe it not; with all those precious drops clinging to its lengthy legs. It was held over the ladle till the last globule dribbled; and even then, being moist, honest Jarl was but loth to drop it overboard.

For our larder, we could not endure the salt beef; it was raw as a live Abyssinian steak, and salt as Cracow. Besides, the Feegee simile would not have held good with respect to it. It was far from being "tender as a dead man." The biscuit only could we eat; not to be wondered at; for even on shipboard, seamen in the tropics are but sparing feeders.

And here let not a suggestion be omitted, most valuable to any future castaway or sailaway as the case may be. Eat not your biscuit dry; but dip it in the sea: which makes it more bulky and palatable. During meal times it was soak and sip with Jarl and me: one on each side of the Chamois dipping our biscuit in the brine. This plan obviated finger-glasses at the conclusion of our repast. Upon the whole, dwelling upon the water is not so bad after all. The Chinese are no fools. In the operation of making your toilet, how handy to float in your ewer!

Chapter 15

A Stitch in Time saves Nine

L IKE MOST silent earnest sort of people, my good Viking was a pattern of industry. When in the boats after whales, I have known him carry along a roll of sinnate to stitch into a hat. And the boats lying motionless for half an hour or so, waiting the rising of the chase, his fingers would be plying at their task, like an old lady knitting. Like an experienced old-wife too, his digits had become so expert and conscientious, that his eyes left them alone; deeming optic supervision unnecessary. And on this trip of ours, when not otherwise engaged, he was quite as busy with his fingers as ever:—unraveling old Cape Horn hose, for yarn wherewith to darn our woolen frocks; with great patches from the skirts of a condemned reefing-jacket, panneling the seats of our "ducks;" in short, veneering our broken garments with all manner of choice old broadcloths.

With the true forethought of an old tar, he had brought along with him nearly the whole contents of his chest. His precious "Ditty Bag," containing his sewing utensils, had been carefully packed away in the bottom of one of his bundles; of which he had as many as an old maid on her travels. In truth, an old salt is very much of an old maid, though, strictly speaking, far from deserving that misdeemed appellative. Better be an old maid, a woman with herself for a husband, than the wife of a fool; and Solomon more than hints that all men are fools; and every wise man knows himself to be one.

When playing the sempstress, Jarl's favorite perch was the triangular little platform in the bow; which being the driest and most elevated part of the boat, was best adapted to his purpose. Here for hours and hours together the honest old tailor would sit darning and sewing away, heedless of the wide ocean around; while forever, his slouched Guayaquil hat kept bobbing up and down against the horizon before us.

It was a most solemn avocation with him. Silently he nodded like the still statue in the opera of Don Juan. Indeed he never spoke, unless to give pithy utterance to the wisdom of keeping one's wardrobe in repair. But herein my Viking at times waxed oracular. And many's the hour we glided along, myself deeply pondering in the stern, hand upon helm; while crosslegged at the other end of the boat Jarl laid down patch upon patch, and at long intervals precept upon precept; here several saws, and there innumerable stitches.

Chapter 16

They are Becalmed

O N THE EIGHTH DAY there was a calm.
   It came on by night: so that waking at daybreak, and folding my arms over the gunwale, I looked out upon a scene very hard to describe. The sun was still beneath the horizon; perhaps not yet out of sight from the plains of Paraguay. But the dawn was too strong for the stars; which, one by one, had gone out, like waning lamps after a ball.

Now, as the face of a mirror is a blank, only borrowing character from what it reflects; so in a calm in the Tropics, a colorless sky overhead, the ocean, upon its surface, hardly presents a sign of existence. The deep blue is gone; and the glassy element lies tranced; almost viewless as the air.

But that morning, the two gray firmaments of sky and water seemed collapsed into a vague ellipsis. And alike, the Chamois seemed drifting in the atmosphere as in the sea. Every thing was fused into the calm: sky, air, water, and all. Not a fish was to be seen. The silence was that of a vacuum. No vitality lurked in the air. And this inert blending and brooding of all things seemed gray chaos in conception.

This calm lasted four days and four nights; during which, but a few cat's-paws of wind varied the scene. They were faint as the breath of one dying.

At times the heat was intense. The heavens, at mid-day, glowing like an

48

ignited coal mine. Our skin curled up like lint; our vision became dim; the brain dizzy.

To our consternation, the water in the breaker became lukewarm, brackish, and slightly putrescent; notwithstanding we kept our spare clothing piled upon the breaker, to shield it from the sun. At last, Jarl enlarged the vent, carefully keeping it exposed. To this precaution, doubtless, we owed more than we then thought. It was now deemed wise to reduce our allowance of water to the smallest modicum consistent with the present preservation of life; strangling all desire for more.

Nor was this all. The upper planking of the boat began to warp; here and there, cracking and splintering. But though we kept it moistened with brine, one of the plank-ends started from its place; and the sharp, sudden sound, breaking the scorching silence, caused us both to spring to our feet. Instantly the sea burst in; but we made shift to secure the rebellious plank with a cord, not having a nail; we then bailed out the boat, nearly half full of water.

On the second day of the calm, we unshipped the mast, to prevent its being pitched out by the occasional rolling of the vast smooth swells now overtaking us. Leagues and leagues away, after its fierce raging, some tempest must have been sending to us its last dying waves. For as a pebble dropped into a pond ruffles it to its marge; so, on all sides, a sea-gale operates as if an asteroid had fallen into the brine; making ringed mountain billows, interminably expanding, instead of ripples.

The great September waves breaking at the base of the Neversink Highlands, far in advance of the swiftest pilot-boat, carry tidings. And full often, they know the last secret of many a stout ship, never heard of from the day she left port. Every wave in my eyes seems a soul.

As there was no steering to be done, Jarl and I sheltered ourselves as well as we could under the awning. And for the first two days, one at a time, and every three or four hours, we dropped overboard for a bath, clinging to the gunwale; a sharp look-out being kept for prowling sharks. A foot or two below the surface, the water felt cool and refreshing.

On the third day a change came over us. We relinquished bathing, the exertion taxing us too much. Sullenly we laid ourselves down; turned our backs to each other; and were impatient of the slightest casual touch of our persons. What sort of expression my own countenance wore, I know not; but I hated to look at Jarl's. When I did it was a glare, not a glance. I became more taciturn than he. I can not tell what it was that came over me, but I wished I was alone. I felt that so long as the calm lasted, we were without help; that neither could assist the other; and above all, that for one, the water would hold out longer than for two. I felt no remorse, not the slightest, for these thoughts. It was instinct. Like a desperado giving up the ghost, I desired to gasp by myself.

From being cast away with a brother, good God deliver me!

The four days passed. And on the morning of the fifth, thanks be to Heaven, there came a breeze. Dancingly, mincingly it came, just rippling the sea, until it struck our sails, previously set at the very first token of its advance. At length it slightly freshened; and our poor Chamois seemed raised from the dead.

Beyond expression delightful! Once more we heard the low humming of the sea under our bow, as our boat, like a bird, went singing on its way.

How changed the scene! Overhead, a sweet blue haze, distilling sunlight in drops. And flung abroad over the visible creation was the sun-spangled, azure, rustling robe of the ocean, ermined with wave crests; all else, infinitely blue. Such a cadence of musical sounds! Waves chasing each other, and sporting and frothing in frolicsome foam: painted fish rippling past; and anon the noise of wings as sea-fowls flew by.

Oh, Ocean, when thou choosest to smile, more beautiful thou art than flowery mead or plain!

Chapter 17

In high Spirits, they push on for the Terra Incognita

T HERE WERE NOW fourteen notches on the loom of the Skyeman's oar:—So many days since we had pushed from the fore-
chains of the Arcturion. But as yet, no floating bough, no tern,
noddy, nor reef-bird, to denote our proximity to land. In that long calm,
whither might not the currents have swept us?

Where we were precisely, we knew not; but according to our reckoning, the loose estimation of the knots run every hour, we must have sailed
due west but little more than one hundred and fifty leagues; for the most
part having encountered but light winds, and frequent intermitting calms,
besides that prolonged one described. But spite of past calms and currents,
land there must be to the westward. Sun, compass, stout hearts, and steady
breezes, pointed our prow thereto. So courage! my Viking, and never say
drown!

At this time, our hearts were much lightened by discovering that our
water was improving in taste. It seemed to have been undergoing anew
that sort of fermentation, or working, occasionally incident to ship water
shortly after being taken on board. Sometimes, for a period, it is more or
less offensive to taste and smell; again, however, becoming comparatively
limpid.

But as our water improved, we grew more and more miserly of so price-
less a treasure.

51

And here it may be well to make mention of another little circumstance, however unsentimental. Thorough-paced tar that he was, my Viking was an inordinate consumer of the Indian weed. From the Arcturion, he had brought along with him a small half-keg, at bottom impacted with a solitary layer of sable Negrohead, fossil-marked, like the primary stratum of the geologists. It was the last tier of his abundant supply for the long whaling voyage upon which he had embarked upwards of three years previous. Now during the calm, and for some days after, poor Jarl's accustomed quid was no longer agreeable company. To pun: he eschewed his chew. I asked him wherefore. He replied that it puckered up his mouth, above all provoked thirst, and had somehow grown every way distasteful. I was sorry; for the absence of his before ever present wad impaired what little fullness there was left in his cheek; though, sooth to say, I no longer called upon him as of yore to shift over the enormous morsel to starboard or larboard, and so trim our craft.

The calm gone by, once again my sea-tailor plied needle and thread; or turning laundress, hung our raiment to dry on oars peaked obliquely in the thole-pins. All of which tattered pennons, the wind being astern, helped us gayly on our way; as jolly poor devils, with rags flying in the breeze, sail blithely through life; and are merry although they are poor!

Chapter 18

My Lord Shark and his Pages

THERE IS A FISH in the sea that evermore, like a surly lord, only goes abroad attended by his suite. It is the Shovel-nosed Shark. A clumsy lethargic monster, unshapely as his name, and the last species of his kind, one would think, to be so bravely waited upon, as he is. His suite is composed of those dainty little creatures called Pilot fish by sailors. But by night his retinue is frequently increased by the presence of several small luminous fish, running in advance, and flourishing their flambeaux like link-boys lighting the monster's way. Pity there were no ray-fish in rear, page-like, to carry his caudal train.

Now the relation subsisting between the Pilot fish above mentioned and their huge ungainly lord, seems one of the most inscrutable things in nature. At any rate, it poses poor me to comprehend. That a monster so ferocious, should suffer five or six little sparks, hardly fourteen inches long, to gambol about his grim hull with the utmost impunity, is of itself something strange. But when it is considered, that by a reciprocal understanding, the Pilot fish seem to act as scouts to the shark, warning him of danger, and apprising him of the vicinity of prey; and moreover, in case of his being killed, evincing their anguish by certain agitations, otherwise inexplicable; the whole thing becomes a mystery unfathomable. Truly marvels abound. It needs no dead man to be raised, to convince us of some things. Even my Viking

53

marveled full as much at those Pilot fish as he would have marveled at the Pentecost.

But perhaps a little incident, occurring about this period, will best illustrate the matter in hand.

We were gliding along, hardly three knots an hour, when my comrade, who had been dozing over the gunwale, suddenly started to his feet, and pointed out an immense Shovel-nosed Shark, less than a boat's length distant, and about half a fathom beneath the surface. A lance was at once snatched from its place; and true to his calling, Jarl was about to dart it at the fish, when, interested by the sight of its radiant little scouts, I begged him to desist.

One of them was right under the shark, nibbling at his ventral fin; another above, hovering about his dorsal appurtenance; one on each flank; and a frisking fifth pranking about his nose, seemingly having something to say of a confidential nature. They were of a bright, steel-blue color, alternated with jet black stripes; with glistening bellies of a silver-white. Clinging to the back of the shark, were four or five Remoras, or sucking-fish; snaky parasites, impossible to remove from whatever they adhere to, without destroying their lives. The Remora has little power in swimming; hence its sole locomotion is on the backs of larger fish. Leech-like, it sticketh closer than a false brother in prosperity; closer than a beggar to the benevolent; closer than Webster to the Constitution. But it feeds upon what it clings to; its feelers having a direct communication with the esophagus.

The shark swam sluggishly; creating no sign of a ripple; but ever and anon shaking his Medusa locks, writhing and curling with horrible life. Now and then, the nimble Pilot fish darted from his side—this way and that—mostly toward our boat; but previous to taking a fresh start ever returning to their liege lord to report progress.

A thought struck me. Baiting a rope's end with a morsel of our almost useless salt beef, I suffered it to trail in the sea. Instantly the foremost scout swam toward it; hesitated; paused; but at last advancing, briskly snuffed at the line, and taking one finical little nibble, retreated toward the shark. Another moment, and the great Tamerlane himself turned heavily about; pointing his black, cannon-like nose directly toward our broadside. Meanwhile, the little Pilot fish darted hither and thither; keeping up a mighty fidgeting, like men of small minds in a state of nervous agitation.

Presently, Tamerlane swam nearer and nearer, all the while lazily eyeing the Chamois, as a wild boar a kid. Suddenly making a rush for it, in the foam he made away with the bait. But the next instant, the uplifted lance sped at his skull; and thrashing his requiem with his sinewy tail, he sunk slowly, through his own blood, out of sight. Down with him swam the terrified Pilot fish; but soon after, three of them were observed close to the boat, gliding along at a uniform pace; one on each side, and one in advance; even as they had attended their lord. Doubtless, one was under our keel.

"A good omen," said Jarl; "no harm will befall us so long as they stay."

But however that might be, follow us they did, for many days after: until an event occurred, which necessitated their withdrawal.

Chapter 19

Who goes there?

JARL'S OAR showed sixteen notches on the loom, when one evening, as the expanded sun touched the horizon's rim, a ship's uppermost spars were observed, traced like a spider's web against its crimson disk. It looked like a far-off craft on fire.

In bright weather at sea, a sail, invisible in the full flood of noon, becomes perceptible toward sunset. It is the reverse in the morning. In sight at gray dawn, the distant vessel, though in reality approaching, recedes from view, as the sun rises higher and higher. This holds true, till its vicinity makes it readily fall within the ordinary scope of vision. And thus, too, here and there, with other distant things: the more light you throw on them, the more you obscure. Some revelations show best in a twilight.

The sight of the stranger not a little surprised us. But brightening up, as if the encounter were welcome, Jarl looked happy and expectant. He quickly changed his demeanor, however, upon perceiving that I was bent upon shunning a meeting.

Instantly our sails were struck; and calling upon Jarl, who was somewhat backward to obey, I shipped the oars; and, both rowing, we stood away obliquely from our former course.

I divined that the vessel was a whaler; and hence, that by help of the glass, with which her look-outs must be momentarily sweeping the horizon, they might possibly have descried us; especially, as we were due east from the ship; a direction, which at sunset is the one most favorable for perceiving a far-off object at sea. Furthermore, our canvas was snow-white and conspicuous. To be sure, we could not be certain what kind of a vessel it was; but whatever it might be, I, for one, had no mind to risk an encounter; for it was quite plain, that if the stranger came within hailing distance, there would be no resource but to link our fortunes with hers; whereas I desired to pursue none but the Chamois'. As for the Skyeman, he kept looking wistfully over his shoulder; doubtless, praying Heaven, that we might not escape what I sought to avoid.

Now, upon a closer scrutiny, being pretty well convinced that the stranger, after all, was steering a nearly westerly course—right away from us— we reset our sail; and as night fell, my Viking's entreaties, seconded by my own curiosity, induced me to resume our original course; and so follow after the vessel, with a view of obtaining a nearer glimpse, without danger of detection. So, boldly we steered for the sail.

But not gaining much upon her, spite of the lightness of the breeze (a circumstance in our favor: the chase being a ship, and we but a boat), at my comrade's instigation, we added oars to sails, readily guiding our way by the former, though the helm was left to itself.

As we came nearer, it was plain that the vessel was no whaler; but a small, two-masted craft; in short, a brigantine. Her sails were in a state of unaccountable disarray; only the foresail, mainsail, and jib being set. The first was much tattered; and the jib was hoisted but half way up the stay, where it idly flapped, the breeze coming from over the taffrail. She continually yawed in her course; now almost presenting her broadside, then showing her stern.

Striking our sails once more, we lay on our oars, and watched her in the starlight. Still she swung from side to side, and still sailed on.

Not a little terrified at the sight, superstitious Jarl more than insinuated that the craft must be a gold-huntress, haunted. But I told him, that if such were the case, we must board her, come gold or goblins. In reality, however, I began to think that she must have been abandoned by her crew; or else, that from sickness, those on board were incapable of managing her.

After a long and anxious reconnoiter, we came still nearer, using our oars, but very reluctantly on Jarl's part; who, while rowing, kept his eyes over his shoulder, as if about to beach the little Chamois on the back of a whale as of yore. Indeed, he seemed full as impatient to quit the vicinity of the vessel, as before he had been anxiously courting it.

Now, as the silent brigantine again swung round her broadside, I hailed her loudly. No return. Again. But all was silent. With a few vigorous strokes, we closed with her, giving yet another unanswered hail; when, laying the Chamois right alongside, I clutched at the main-chains. Instantly we felt her dragging us along. Securing our craft by its painter, I sprang over the rail, followed by Jarl, who had snatched his harpoon, his favorite arms. Long used with that weapon to overcome the monsters of the deep, he doubted not it would prove equally serviceable in any other encounter.

The deck was a complete litter. Tossed about were pearl oyster shells, husks of cocoa-nuts, empty casks, and cases. The deserted tiller was lashed; which accounted for the vessel's yawing. But we could not conceive, how going large before the wind, the craft could, for any considerable time, at least, have guided herself without the help of a hand. Still, the breeze was light and steady.

Now, seeing the helm thus lashed, I could not but distrust the silence that prevailed. It conjured up the idea of miscreants concealed below, and meditating treachery; unscrupulous mutineers—Lascars, or Manilla-men; who, having murdered the Europeans of the crew, might not be willing to let strangers depart unmolested. Or yet worse, the entire ship's company might have been swept away by a fever, its infection still lurking in the poisoned hull. And though the first conceit, as the last, was a mere surmise, it was nevertheless deemed prudent to secure the hatches, which for the present we accordingly barred down with the oars of our boat. This done, we went about the deck in search of water. And finding some in a clumsy cask, drank long and freely, and to our thirsty souls' content.

The wind now freshening, and the rent sails like to blow from the yards, we brought the brigantine to the wind, and brailed up the canvas. This left us at liberty to examine the craft, though, unfortunately, the night was growing hazy.

All this while our boat was still towing alongside; and I was about to drop it astern, when Jarl, ever cautious, declared it safer where it was; since, if there were people on board, they would most likely be down in the cabin, from the dead-lights of which, mischief might be done to the Chamois.

It was then, that my comrade observed, that the brigantine had no boats, a circumstance most unusual in any sort of a vessel at sea. But marking this, I was exceedingly gratified. It seemed to indicate, as I had opined, that from some cause or other, she must have been abandoned of her crew. And in a good measure this dispelled my fears of foul play, and the apprehension of contagion. Encouraged by these reflections, I now resolved to descend, and explore the cabin, though sorely against Jarl's counsel. To be sure, as he earnestly said, this step might have been deferred till daylight; but it seemed too wearisome to wait. So bethinking me of our tinder-box and candles, I sent him into the boat for them. Presently, two candles were lit; one of which the Skyeman tied up and down the barbed end of his harpoon; so that upon going below, the keen steel might not be far off, should the light be blown out by a dastard.

Unfastening the cabin scuttle, we stepped downward into the smallest and murkiest den in the world. The altar-like transom, surmounted by the closed dead-lights in the stern, together with the dim little sky-light over-head, and the somber aspect of every thing around, gave the place the air of some subterranean oratory, say a Prayer Room of Peter the Hermit. But coils of rigging, bolts of canvas, articles of clothing, and disorderly heaps of rubbish, harmonized not with this impression. Two doors, one on each side, led into wee little state-rooms, the berths of which also were littered. Among other things, was a large box, sheathed with iron and stoutly clamped, containing a keg partly filled with powder, the half of an old cutlass, a pouch of bullets, and a case for a sextant—a brass plate on the lid, with the maker's name, London. The broken blade of the cutlass was very rusty and stained; and the iron hilt bent in. It looked so tragical that I thrust it out of sight.

Removing a small trap-door, opening into the space beneath, called the "run," we lighted upon sundry cutlasses and muskets, lying together at sixes and sevens, as if pitched down in a hurry.

Casting round a hasty glance, and satisfying ourselves, that through the bulkhead of the cabin, there was no passage to the forward part of the hold, we caught up the muskets and cutlasses, the powder keg and the pouch of bullets, and bundling them on deck, prepared to visit the other end of the vessel. Previous to so doing, however, I loaded a musket, and belted a cut-lass to my side. But my Viking preferred his harpoon.

In the forecastle reigned similar confusion. But there was a snug little lair, cleared away in one corner, and furnished with a grass mat and bolster, like those used among the Islanders of these seas. This little lair looked to us as if some leopard had crouched there. And as it turned out, we were not far from right. Forming one side of this retreat, was a sailor's chest, stoutly secured by a lock, and monstrous heavy withal. Regardless of Jarl's entreaties, I managed to burst the lid; thereby revealing a motley assemblage of millinery, and outlandish knick-knacks of all sorts; together with sundry rude calico contrivances, which though of unaccountable cut, nevertheless possessed a certain petticoatish air, and latitude of skirt, betokening them the habiliments of some feminine creature; most probably of the human species.

In this strong box, also, was a canvas bag, jingling with rusty old bell-buttons, gangrened copper bolts, and sheathing nails; damp, greenish Carolus dollars (true coin all), besides divers iron screws, and battered chisels, and belaying-pins. Sounded on the chest lid, the dollars rang clear as convent bells. These were put aside by Jarl; the sight of substantial dollars doing away, for the nonce, with his superstitious misgivings. True to his kingship, he loved true coin; though abroad on the sea, and no land but dollarless dominions around, all this silver was worthless as charcoal or diamonds. Nearly one and the same thing, say the chemists; but tell that to the marines, say the illiterate Jews and the jewelers. Go, buy a house, or a ship, if you can, with your charcoal! Yea, all the woods in Canada charred down to cinders would not be worth the one famed Brazilian diamond, though no bigger than the egg of a carrier pigeon. Ah! but these chemists are liars, and Sir Humphrey Davy a cheat. Many's the poor devil they've deluded into the charcoal business, who otherwise might have made his fortune with a mattock.

Groping again into the chest, we brought to light a queer little hair trunk, very bald and rickety. At every corner was a mighty clamp, the weight of which had no doubt debilitated the box. It was jealously secured with a padlock, almost as big as itself; so that it was almost a question, which was meant to be security to the other. Prying at it hard, we at length effected an entrance; but saw no golden moidores, no ruddy doubloons; nothing under heaven but three pewter mugs, such as are used in a ship's cabin, several brass screws, and brass plates, which must have belonged to a quadrant; together with a famous lot of glass beads, and brass rings; while, pasted on the inside of the cover, was a little colored print, representing the harlots, the shameless hussies, having a fine time with the Prodigal Son.

It should have been mentioned ere now, that while we were busy in the forecastle, we were several times startled by strange sounds aloft. And just after, crashing into the little hair trunk, down came a great top-block, right through the scuttle, narrowly missing my Viking's crown; a much stronger article, by the way, than your goldsmiths turn out in these days. This startled us much; particularly Jarl, as one might suppose; but accustomed to the strange creakings and wheezings of the masts and yards of old vessels at sea, and having many a time dodged stray blocks accidentally falling from aloft, I thought little more of the matter; though my comrade seemed to think the noises somewhat different from any thing of that kind he had ever heard before.

After a little more turning over of the rubbish in the forecastle, and much marveling thereat, we ascended to the deck; where we found every thing so silent, that, as we moved toward the taffrail, the Skyeman unconsciously addressed me in a whisper.

Chapter 20

Noises and Portents

I LONGED FOR DAY. For however now inclined to believe that the brigantine was untenanted, I desired the light of the sun to place that fact beyond a misgiving.

Now, having observed, previous to boarding the vessel, that she lay rather low in the water, I thought proper to sound the well. But there being no line-and-sinker at hand, I sent Jarl to hunt them up in the arm-chest on the quarter-deck, where doubtless they must be kept. Meanwhile I searched for the "brakes," or pump-handles, which, as it turned out, could not have been very recently used; for they were found lashed up and down to the mainmast.

Suddenly Jarl came running toward me, whispering that all doubt was dispelled;—there were spirits on board, to a dead certainty. He had overheard a supernatural sneeze. But by this time I was all but convinced, that we were alone in the brigantine. Since, if otherwise, I could assign no earthly reason for the crew's hiding away from a couple of sailors, whom, were they so minded, they might easily have mastered. And furthermore, this alleged disturbance of the atmosphere aloft by a sneeze, Jarl averred to have taken place in the main-top; directly underneath which I was all this time standing, and had heard nothing. So complimenting my good Viking upon the exceeding delicacy of his auriculars, I bade him trouble himself no more

with his piratical ghosts and goblins, which existed nowhere but in his own
imagination.

Not finding the line-and-sinker, with the spare end of a bowline we
rigged a substitute; and sounding the well, found nothing to excite our
alarm. Under certain circumstances, however, this sounding a ship's well
is a nervous sort of business enough. 'Tis like feeling your own pulse in the
last stage of a fever.

At the Skyeman's suggestion, we now proceeded to throw round the
brigantine's head on the other tack. For until daylight we desired to alter
the vessel's position as little as possible, fearful of coming unawares upon
reefs.

And here be it said, that for all his superstitious misgivings about the
brigantine; his imputing to her something equivalent to a purely phantom-
like nature, honest Jarl was nevertheless exceedingly downright and prac-
tical in all hints and proceedings concerning her. Wherein, he resembled
my Right Reverend friend, Bishop Berkeley—truly, one of your lords
spiritual—who, metaphysically speaking, holding all objects to be mere
optical delusions, was, notwithstanding, extremely matter-of-fact in all
matters touching matter itself. Besides being pervious to the points of pins,
and possessing a palate capable of appreciating plum-puddings:—which
sentence reads off like a pattering of hailstones.

Now, while we were employed bracing round the yards, whispering
Jarl must needs pester me again with his confounded suspicions of goblins
on board. He swore by the main-mast, that when the fore-yard swung
round, he had heard a half-stifled groan from that quarter; as if one of his
bugbears had been getting its aerial legs jammed. I laughed:—hinting that
goblins were incorporeal. Whereupon he besought me to ascend the fore-
rigging and test the matter for myself. But here my mature judgment got
the better of my first crude opinion. I civilly declined. For assuredly, there
was still a possibility, that the fore-top might be tenanted, and that too by
living miscreants; and a pretty hap would be mine, if, with hands full of
rigging, and legs dangling in air, while surmounting the oblique futtock-
shrouds, some unseen arm should all at once tumble me overboard. Therefore I held my peace; while Jarl went on to declare, that with regard to the
character of the brigantine, his mind was now pretty fully made up;—she
was an arrant impostor, a shade of a ship, full of sailors' ghosts, and before
we knew where we were, would dissolve in a supernatural squall, and leave
us twain in the water. In short, Jarl, the descendant of the superstitious old
Norsemen, was full of old Norse conceits, and all manner of Valhalla

marvels concerning the land of goblins and goblets. No wonder then, that with this catastrophe in prospect, he again entreated me to quit the ill-starred craft, carrying off nothing from her ghostly hull. But I refused.

One can not relate every thing at once. While in the cabin, we came across a "barge" of biscuit, and finding its contents of a quality much superior to our own, we had filled our pockets and occasionally regaled ourselves in the intervals of rummaging. Now this sea cake-basket we had brought on deck. And for the first time since bidding adieu to the Arcturion having fully quenched our thirst, our appetite returned with a rush; and having nothing better to do till day dawned, we planted the bread-barge in the middle of the quarter-deck; and crossing our legs before it, laid close seige thereto, like the Grand Turk and his Vizier Mustapha sitting down before Vienna.

Our castle, the Bread-Barge was of the common sort; an oblong oaken box, much battered and bruised, and like the Elgin Marbles, all over inscriptions and carving:—foul anchors, skewered hearts, almanacs, Burton-blocks, love verses, links of cable, Kings of Clubs; and divers mystic diagrams in chalk, drawn by old Finnish mariners, in casting horoscopes and prophecies. Your old tars are all Daniels. There was a round hole in one side, through which, in getting at the bread, invited guests thrust their hands.

And mighty was the thrusting of hands that night; also, many and earnest the glances of Mustapha at every sudden creaking of the spars or rigging. Like Belshazzar, my royal Viking ate with great fear and trembling; ever and anon pausing to watch the wild shadows flitting along the bulwarks.

Chapter 21

Man ho!

SLOWLY, FITFULLY, broke the morning in the East, showing the desolate brig forging heavily through the water, which sluggishly thumped under her bows. While leaping from sea to sea, our faithful Chamois, like a faithful dog, still gamboled alongside, confined to the main-chains by its painter. At times, it would long lag behind; then, pushed by a wave like lightning dash forward; till bridled by its leash, it again fell in rear.

As the gray light came on, anxiously we scrutinized the features of the craft, as one by one they became more plainly revealed. Every thing seemed stranger now, than when partially visible in the dingy night. The stanchions, or posts of the bulwarks, were of rough stakes, still incased in the bark. The unpainted sides were of a dark-colored, heathenish looking wood. The tiller was a wry-necked, elbowed bough, thrusting itself through the deck, as if the tree itself was fast rooted in the hold. The binnacle, containing the compass, was defended at the sides by yellow matting. The rigging—shrouds, halyards and all—was of "Kaiar," or cocoa-nut fibres; and here and there the sails were patched with plaited rushes.

But this was not all. Whoso will pry, must needs light upon matters for suspicion. Glancing over the side, in the wake of every scupper-hole, we beheld a faded, crimson stain, which Jarl averred to be blood. Though now he betrayed not the slightest trepidation; for what he saw pertained not to ghosts; and all his fears hitherto had been of the supernatural.

Indeed, plucking up a heart, with the dawn of the day my Viking looked bold as a lion; and soon, with the instinct of an old seaman cast his eyes up aloft.

Directly, he touched my arm,—"Look: what stirs in the main-top?"

Sure enough, something alive was there.

Fingering our arms, we watched it; till as the day came on, a crouching stranger was beheld.

Presenting my piece, I hailed him to descend or be shot. There was silence for a space, when the black barrel of a musket was thrust forth, leveled at my head. Instantly, Jarl's harpoon was presented at a dart;—two to one;—and my hail was repeated. But no reply.

"Who are you?"

"Samoa," at length said a clear, firm voice.

"Come down from the rigging. We are friends."

Another pause; when, rising to his feet, the stranger slowly descended, holding on by one hand to the rigging, for but one did he have; his musket partly slung from his back, and partly griped under the stump of his muti-lated arm.

He alighted about six paces from where we stood; and balancing his weapon, eyed us bravely as the Cid.

He was a tall, dark Islander, a very devil to behold, theatrically arrayed in kilt and turban; the kilt of a gay calico print, the turban of a red China silk. His neck was jingling with strings of beads.

"Who else is on board?" I asked; while Jarl, thus far covering the stranger with his weapon, now dropped it to the deck.

"Look there:—Annatoo!" was his reply in broken English, pointing aloft to the fore-top. And lo! a woman, also an Islander; and barring her skirts, dressed very much like Samoa, was beheld descending.

"Any more?"

"No more."

"Who are *you* then; and what craft is this?"

"Ah, ah—you are no ghost;—but are you my friend?" he cried, advancing nearer as he spoke; while the woman, having gained the deck, also approached, eagerly glancing.

We said we were friends; that we meant no harm; but desired to know what craft this was; and what disaster had befallen her; for that something untoward had occurred, we were certain.

Whereto, Samoa made answer, that it was true that something dreadful had happened; and that he would gladly tell us all, and tell us the truth. And about it he went.

Now, this story of his was related in the mixed phraseology of a Polynesian sailor. With a few random reflections, in substance, it will be found in the six following chapters.

Chapter 22

What befel the Brigantine at the Pearl Shell Islands

THE VESSEL was the Parki, of Lahina, a village and harbor on the coast of Mowee, one of the Hawaian isles, where she had been miserably cobbled together with planks of native wood, and fragments of a wreck, there drifted ashore.

Her appellative had been bestowed in honor of a high chief, the tallest and goodliest looking gentleman in all the Sandwich Islands. With a mixed European and native crew, about thirty in number (but only four whites in all, captain included), the Parki, some four months previous, had sailed from her port on a voyage southward, in quest of pearls, and pearl oyster shells, sea-slugs, and other matters of that sort.

Samoa, a native of the Navigator Islands, had long followed the sea, and was well versed in the business of oyster diving and its submarine mysteries. The native Lahineese on board were immediately subordinate to him; the captain having bargained with Samoa for their services as divers.

The woman, Annatoo, was a native of a far-off, anonymous island to the westward: whence, when quite young, she had been carried by the commander of a ship, touching there on a passage from Macao to Valparaiso. At Valparaiso her protector put her ashore; most probably, as I afterward had reason to think, for a nuisance.

By chance it came to pass that when Annatoo's first virgin bloom had

departed, leaving nothing but a lusty frame and a lustier soul, Samoa, the
Navigator, had fallen desperately in love with her. And thinking the lady
to his mind, being brave like himself, and doubtless well adapted to the
vicissitudes of matrimony at sea, he meditated suicide—I would have said,
wedlock—and the twain became one. And some time after, in capacity of
wife, Annatoo the dame, accompanied in the brigantine, Samoa her lord.
Now, as Antony flew to the refuse embraces of Cæsar, so Samoa solaced
himself in the arms of this discarded fair one. And the sequel was the same.
For not harder the life Cleopatra led my fine frank friend, poor Mark, than
Queen Annatoo did lead this captive of her bow and her spear. But all in
good time.

They left their port; and crossing the Tropic and the Line, fell in with
a cluster of islands, where the shells they sought were found in round numbers. And here—not at all strange to tell—besides the natives, they encountered a couple of Cholos, or half-breed Spaniards, from the Main; one half
Spanish, the other half quartered between the wild Indian and the devil;
a race, that from Baldivia to Panama are notorious for their unscrupulous
villainy.

Now, the half-breeds having long since deserted a ship at these islands,
had risen to high authority among the natives. This hearing, the Parki's
captain was much gratified; he, poor ignorant, never before having fallen
in with any of their treacherous race. And, no doubt, he imagined that their
influence over the Islanders would tend to his advantage. At all events, he
made presents to the Cholos; who, in turn, provided him with additional
divers from among the natives. Very kindly, also, they pointed out the best
places for seeking the oysters. In a word, they were exceedingly friendly;
often coming off to the brigantine, and sociably dining with the captain in
the cabin; placing the salt between them and him.

All things went on very pleasantly until, one morning, the half-breeds
prevailed upon the captain to go with them, in his whale-boat, to a shoal
on the thither side of the island, some distance from the spot where lay the
brigantine. They so managed it, moreover, that none but the Lahineese
under Samoa, in whom the captain much confided, were left in custody of
the Parki; the three white men going along to row; for there happened to
be little or no wind for a sail.

Now, the fated brig lay anchored within a deep, smooth, circular lagoon,
margined on all sides but one by the most beautiful groves. On that side, was
the outlet to the sea; perhaps a cable's length or more from where the brigantine had been moored. An hour or two after the party were gone, and

when the boat was completely out of sight, the natives in shoals were perceived coming off from the shore; some in canoes, and some swimming. The former brought bread fruit and bananas, ostentatiously piled up in their proas; the latter dragged after them long strings of cocoanuts; for all of which, on nearing the vessel, they clamorously demanded knives and hatchets in barter.

From their actions, suspecting some treachery, Samoa stood in the gangway, and warned them off; saying that no barter could take place until the captain's return. But presently one of the savages stealthily climbed up from the water, and nimbly springing from the bob-stays to the bow-sprit, darted a javelin full at the foremast, where it vibrated. The signal of blood! With terrible outcries, the rest, pulling forth their weapons, hitherto concealed in the canoes, or under the floating cocoanuts, leaped into the low chains of the brigantine; sprang over the bulwarks; and, with clubs and spears, attacked the aghast crew with the utmost ferocity.

After one faint rally, the Lahineese scrambled for the rigging; but to a man were overtaken and slain.

At the first alarm, Annatoo, however, had escaped to the fore-top-gallant-yard, higher than which she could not climb, and whither the savages durst not venture. For though after their nuts these Polynesians will climb palm trees like squirrels; yet, at the first blush, they decline a ship's mast like Kennebec farmers.

Upon the first token of an onslaught, Samoa, having rushed toward the cabin scuttle for arms, was there fallen upon by two young savages. But after a desperate momentary fray, in which his arm was mangled, he made shift to spring below, instantly securing overhead the slide of the scuttle. In the cabin, while yet the uproar of butchery prevailed, he quietly bound up his arm; then laying on the transom the captain's three loaded muskets, undauntedly awaited an assault.

The object of the natives, it seems, was to wreck the brigantine upon the sharp coral beach of the lagoon. And with this intent, one of their number had plunged into the water, and cut the cable, which was of hemp. But the tide ebbing, cast the Parki's head seaward—toward the outlet; and the savages, perceiving this, clumsily boarded the fore-tack, and hauled aft the sheet; thus setting, after a fashion, the fore-sail, previously loosed to dry.

Meanwhile, a gray-headed old chief stood calmly at the tiller, endeavoring to steer the vessel shoreward. But not managing the helm aright, the brigantine, now gliding apace through the water, only made more way toward the outlet. Seeing which, the ringleaders, six or eight in number, ran to help the old graybeard at the helm. But it was a black hour for them. Of a sudden, while they were handling the tiller, three muskets were rapidly discharged upon them from the cabin skylight. Two of the savages dropped dead. The old steersman, clutching wildly at the helm, fell over it, mortally wounded; and in a wild panic at seeing their leaders thus unaccountably slain, the rest of the natives leaped overboard and made for the shore.

Hearing the splashing, Samoa flew on deck; and beholding the foresail set, and the brigantine heading right out to sea, he cried out to Annatoo, still aloft, to descend to the topsail-yard, and loose the canvas there. His command was obeyed. Annatoo deserved a gold medal for what she did that day. Hastening down the rigging, after loosing the topsail, she strained away at the sheets; in which operation she was assisted by Samoa, who snatched an instant from the helm.

The foresail and fore-topsail were now tolerably well set; and as the craft drew seaward, the breeze freshened. And well that it did; for, recovered from their alarm, the savages were now in hot pursuit; some in canoes, and some swimming as before. But soon the main-topsail was given to the breeze, which still freshening, came from over the quarter. And with this brave show of canvas, the Parki made gallantly for the outlet; and loud shouted Samoa as she shot by the reef, and parted the long swells without. Against these, the savages could not swim. And at that turn of the tide, paddling a canoe therein was almost equally difficult. But the fugitives were not yet safe. In full chase now came in sight the whale-boat manned by the Cholos, and four or five Islanders. Whereat, making no doubt, that all the whites who left the vessel that morning had been massacred through the treachery of the half-breeds; and that the capture of the brigantine had been premeditated; Samoa now saw no other resource than to point his craft dead away from the land.

Now on came the devils buckling to their oars. Meantime Annatoo was still busy aloft, loosing the smaller sails—t'gallants and royals, which she managed partially to set.

The strong breeze from astern now filling the ill-set sails, they bellied, and rocked in the air, like balloons, while, from the novel strain upon it, every spar quivered and sprung. And thus, like a frightened gull fleeing from sea-hawks, the little Parki swooped along, and bravely breasted the brine.

His shattered arm in a hempen sling, Samoa stood at the helm, the muskets reloaded, and planted full before him on the binnacle. For a time, so badly did the brigantine steer, by reason of her ill-adjusted sails, made still more unmanageable by the strength of the breeze,—that it was doubtful, after all, notwithstanding her start, whether the fugitives would not yet fall a prey to their hunters. The craft wildly yawed, and the boat drew nearer and nearer. Maddened by the sight, and perhaps thinking more of revenge for the past, than of security for the future, Samoa, yielding the helm to Annatoo, rested his muskets on the bulwarks, and taking long, sure aim, discharged them, one by one at the advancing foe.

The three reports were answered by loud jeers from the savages, who brandished their spears, and made gestures of derision; while with might and main the Cholos tugged at their oars.

The boat still gaining on the brigantine, the muskets were again reloaded. And as the next shot sped, there was a pause; when, like lightning, the headmost Cholo bounded upwards from his seat, and oar in hand, fell into the sea. A fierce yell; and one of the natives springing into the water, caught the sinking body by its long hair; and the dead and the living were dragged into the boat. Taking heart from this fatal shot, Samoa fired yet again; but not with the like sure result; merely grazing the remaining half-breed, who, crouching behind his comrades, besought them to turn the boat round, and make for the shore. Alarmed at the fate of his brother, and seemingly distrustful of the impartiality of Samoa's fire, the pusillanimous villain refused to expose a limb above the gunwale.

Fain now would the pursuers have made good their escape; but an accident forbade. In the careening of the boat, when the stricken Cholo sprung overboard, two of their oars had slid into the water; and together with that death-griped by the half-breed, were now floating off; occasionally lost to view, as they sunk in the trough of the sea. Two of the Islanders swam to recover them; but frightened by the whirring of a shot over their heads, as they unavoidably struck out towards the Parki, they turned quickly about; just in time to see one of their comrades smite his body with his hand, as he received a bullet from Samoa.

Enough: darting past the ill-fated boat, they swam rapidly for land, followed by the rest; who plunged overboard, leaving in the boat the surviving Cholo—who it seems could not swim—the wounded savage, and the dead man.

"Load away now, and take thy revenge, my fine fellow," said Samoa to himself. But not yet. Seeing all at his mercy, and having none, he quickly laid his fore-topsail to the mast; "hove to" the brigantine; and opened fire anew upon the boat; every swell of the sea heaving it nearer and nearer. Vain all efforts to escape. The wounded man paddled wildly with his hands;

the dead one rolled from side to side; and the Cholo, seizing the solitary oar, in his frenzied heedlessness, spun the boat round and round; while all the while shot followed shot, Samoa firing as fast as Annatoo could load. At length both Cholo and savage fell dead upon their comrades, canting the boat over sideways, till well nigh awash; in which manner she drifted off.

Chapter 23

Sailing from the Island they pillage the Cabin

T HERE WAS A SMALL CARRONADE on the forecastle, un-shipped from its carriage, and lashed down to ringbolts on the deck. This Samoa now loaded; and with an ax knocking off the round knob upon the breech, rammed it home in the tube. When, running the cannon out at one of the ports, and studying well his aim, he let fly, sunk the boat, and buried his dead.

It was now late in the afternoon; and for the present bent upon avoiding land, and gaining the shoreless sea, never mind where, Samoa again forced round his craft before the wind, leaving the island astern. The decks were still cumbered with the bodies of the Lahineese, which heel to point and crosswise, had, log-like, been piled up on the main-hatch. These, one by one, were committed to the sea; after which, the decks were washed down.

At sunrise next morning, finding themselves out of sight of land, with little or no wind, they stopped their headway, and lashed the tiller alee, the better to enable them to overhaul the brigantine; especially the recesses of the cabin. For there, were stores of goods adapted for barter among the Islanders; also several bags of dollars.

Now, nothing can exceed the cupidity of the Polynesian, when, through partial commerce with the whites, his eyes are opened to his nakedness, and he perceives that in some things they are richer than himself.

74

The poor skipper's wardrobe was first explored; his chests of clothes being capsized, and their contents strown about the cabin floor.

Then took place the costuming. Samoa and Annatoo trying on coats and pantaloons, shirts and drawers, and admiring themselves in the little mirror panneled in the bulkhead. Then, were broken open boxes and bales; rolls of printed cotton were inspected, and vastly admired; insomuch, that the trumpery found in the captain's chests was disdainfully doffed: and donned were loose folds of calico, more congenial to their tastes.

As case after case was opened and overturned, slippery grew the cabin deck with torrents of glass beads; and heavy the necks of Samoa and Annatoo with goodly bunches thereof.

Among other things, came to light brass jewelry,—Rag Fair gewgaws and baubles a plenty, more admired than all; Annatoo, bedecking herself like a tragedy queen: one blaze of brass. Much mourned the married dame, that thus arrayed, there was none to admire but Samoa her husband; but he was all the while admiring himself, and not her.

And here must needs be related, what has hitherto remained unsaid. Very often this husband and wife were no Darby and Joan. Their married life was one long campaign, whereof the truces were only by night. They billed and they cooed on their arms, rising fresh in the morning to battle, and often Samoa got more than a hen-pecking. To be short, Annatoo was a Tartar, a regular Calmuc, and Samoa—Heaven help him—her husband.

Yet awhile, joined together by a sense of common danger, and long engrossed in turning over their tinsel acquisitions without present thought of proprietorship, the pair refrained from all squabbles. But soon burst the storm. Having given every bale and every case a good shaking, Annatoo, making an estimate of the whole, very coolly proceeded to set apart for herself whatever she fancied. To this, Samoa objected; to which objection Annatoo objected; and then they went at it.

The lady vowed that the things were no more Samoa's than hers; nay, not so much; and that whatever she wanted, that same would she have. And furthermore, by way of codicil, she declared that she was slave to nobody.

Now, Samoa, sad to tell, stood in no little awe of his bellicose spouse. What, though a hero in other respects; what, though he had slain his savages, and gallantly carried his craft from their clutches:—Like the valiant captains Marlborough and Belisarius, he was a poltroon to his wife. And Annatoo was worse than either Sarah or Antonina.

However, like every thing partaking of the nature of a scratch, most conjugal squabbles are quickly healed; for if they healed not, they would never anew break out: which is the beauty of the thing. So at length they made up; but the treaty stipulations of Annatoo told much against the interests of Samoa. Nevertheless, ostensibly, it was agreed upon, that they should strictly go halves; the lady, however, laying special claim to certain valuables, more particularly fancied. But as a set-off to this, she generously renounced all claims upon the spare rigging; all claims upon the foremast and mainmast; and all claims upon the captain's arms and ammunition. Of the latter, by the way, Dame Antonina stood in no need. Her voice was a park of artillery; her talons a charge of bayonets.

Chapter 24

Dedicated to the College of Physicians and Surgeons

B Y THIS TIME Samoa's wounded arm was in such a state, that amputation became necessary. Among savages, severe personal injuries are, for the most part, accounted but trifles. When a European would be taking to his couch in despair, the savage would disdain to recline.

More yet. In Polynesia, every man is his own barber and surgeon, cutting off his beard or arm, as occasion demands. No unusual thing, for the warriors of Varvoo to saw off their own limbs, desperately wounded in battle. But owing to the clumsiness of the instrument employed—a flinty, serrated shell—the operation has been known to last several days. Nor will they suffer any friend to help them; maintaining, that a matter so nearly concerning a warrior is far better attended to by himself. Hence it may be said, that they amputate themselves at their leisure, and hang up their tools when tired. But, though thus beholden to no one for aught connected with the practice of surgery, they never cut off their own heads, that ever I heard; a species of amputation to which, metaphorically speaking, many would-be independent sort of people in civilized lands are addicted.

Samoa's operation was very summary. A fire was kindled in the little caboose, or cook-house, and so made as to produce much smoke. He then placed his arm upon one of the windlass bitts (a short upright timber, breast-high), and seizing the blunt cook's ax would have struck the blow; but for some reason distrusting the precision of his aim, Annatoo was assigned to the task. Three strokes, and the limb, from just above the elbow, was no longer Samoa's; and he saw his own bones; which many a centenarian can not say. The very clumsiness of the operation was safety to the subject. The weight and bluntness of the instrument both deadened the pain and lessened the hemorrhage. The wound was then scorched, and held over the smoke of the fire, till all signs of blood vanished. From that day forward it healed, and troubled Samoa but little.

But shall the sequel be told? How that, superstitiously averse to burying in the sea the dead limb of a body yet living; since in that case Samoa held, that he must very soon drown and follow it; and how, that equally dreading to keep the thing near him, he at last hung it aloft from the topmast-stay; where yet it was suspended, bandaged over and over in cerements. The hand that must have locked many others in friendly clasp, or smote a foe, was no food, thought Samoa, for fowls of the air nor fishes of the sea.

Now, which was Samoa? The dead arm swinging high as Haman? Or the living trunk below? Was the arm severed from the body, or the body from the arm? The residual part of Samoa was alive, and therefore we say it was he. But which of the writhing sections of a ten times severed worm, is the worm proper?

For myself, I ever regarded Samoa as but a large fragment of a man, not a man complete. For was he not an entire limb out of pocket? And the action at Teneriffe over, great Nelson himself—physiologically speaking— was but three-quarters of a man. And the smoke of Waterloo blown by, what was Anglesea but the like? After Saratoga, what Arnold? To say no-thing of Mutius Scævola minus a hand, General Knox a thumb, and Hanni-bal an eye; and that old Roman grenadier, Dentatus, nothing more than a bruised and battered trunk, a knotty sort of hemlock of a warrior, hard to hack and hew into chips, though much marred in symmetry by battle-ax blows. Ah! but these warriors, like anvils, will stand a deal of hard ham-mering. Especially in the old knight-errant times. For at the battle of Bre-vieux in Flanders, my glorious old gossiping ancestor, Froissart, informs me, that ten good knights, being suddenly unhorsed, fell stiff and powerless to the plain, fatally encumbered by their armor. Whereupon, the rascally burglarious peasants, their foes, fell to picking their visors; as burglars, locks; or oystermen, oysters; to get at their lives. But all to no purpose. And at last they were fain to ask aid of a blacksmith; and not till then, were the inmates of the armor dispatched. Now it was deemed very hard, that the mysterious state-prisoner of France should be riveted in an iron mask; but these knight-errants did voluntarily prison themselves in their own iron Bastiles; and thus

helpless were murdered therein. Days of chivalry these, when gallant cheva-
liers died chivalric deaths!

And this was the epic age, over whose departure my late eloquent and
prophetic friend and correspondent, Edmund Burke, so movingly mourned.
Yes, they were glorious times. But no sensible man, given to quiet domestic
delights, would exchange his warm fireside and muffins, for a heroic bivouac, in a wild beechen wood, of a raw gusty morning in Normandy; every
knight blowing his steel-gloved fingers, and vainly striving to cook his cold
coffee in his helmet.

Chapter 25

Peril a Peace-maker

A FEW DAYS PASSED: the brigantine drifting hither and thither, and nothing in sight but the sea, when forth again on its stillness rung Annatoo's domestic alarum. The truce was up. Most egregiously had the lady infringed it; appropriating to herself various objects previously disclaimed in favor of Samoa. Besides, forever on the prowl, she was perpetually going up and down; with untiring energy, exploring every nook and cranny; carrying off her spoils and diligently secreting them. Having little idea of feminine adaptations, she pilfered whatever came handy:—iron hooks, dollars, bolts, hatchets, and stopping not at balls of marline and sheets of copper. All this, poor Samoa would have borne with what patience he might, rather than again renew the war, were it not, that the audacious dame charged him with peculations upon her own private stores; though of any such thing he was innocent as the bowsprit.

This insulting impeachment got the better of the poor islander's philosophy. He keenly resented it. And the consequence was, that seeing all domineering useless, Annatoo flew off at a tangent; declaring that, for the future, Samoa might stay by himself; she would have nothing more to do with him. Save when unavoidable in managing the brigantine, she would not even speak to him, that she wouldn't, the monster! She then boldly demanded the forecastle—in the brig's case, by far the pleasantest end of the ship—for her own independent suite of apartments. As for hapless Belisarius, he might do what he pleased in his dark little den of a cabin.

Concerning the division of the spoils, the termagant succeeded in carrying the day; also, to her quarters, bale after bale of goods, together with numerous odds and ends, sundry and divers. Moreover, she laid in a fine stock of edibles, so as, in all respects possible, to live independent of her spouse.

Unlovely Annatoo! Unfortunate Samoa! Thus did the pair make a divorce of it; the lady going upon a separate maintenance,—and Belisarius resuming his bachelor loneliness. In the captain's state room, all cold and comfortless, he slept; his lady whilome retiring to her forecastle boudoir; beguiling the hours in saying her pater-nosters, and tossing over and assorting her ill-gotten trinkets and finery; like Madame De Maintenon dedicating her last days and nights to continence and calicoes.

But think you this was the quiet end of their conjugal quarrels? Ah, no! No end to those feuds, till one or t'other gives up the ghost.

Now, exiled from the nuptial couch, Belisarius bore the hardship without a murmur. And hero that he was, who knows that he felt not like a soldier on a furlough? But as for Antonina, she could neither get along with Belisarius, nor without him. She made advances. But of what sort? Why, breaking into the cabin and purloining sundry goods therefrom; in artful hopes of breeding a final reconciliation out of the temporary outburst that might ensue.

Then followed a sad scene of altercation; interrupted at last by a sudden loud roaring of the sea. Rushing to the deck, they beheld themselves sweeping head-foremost toward a shoal making out from a cluster of low islands, hitherto, by banks of clouds, shrouded from view.

The helm was instantly shifted; and the yards braced about. But for several hours, owing to the freshness of the breeze, the set of the currents, and the irregularity and extent of the shoal, it seemed doubtful whether they would escape a catastrophe. But Samoa's seamanship, united to Annatoo's industry, at last prevailed; and the brigantine was saved.

Of the land where they came so near being wrecked, they knew nothing; and for that reason, they at once steered away. For after the fatal events which had overtaken the Parki at the Pearl Shell islands, so fearful were they of encountering any Islanders, that from the first they had resolved to keep open sea, shunning every appearance of land; relying upon being eventually picked up by some passing sail.

Doubtless this resolution proved their salvation. For to the navigator in these seas, no risk so great, as in approaching the isles; which mostly are so guarded by outpost reefs, and far out from their margins environed by perils, that the green flowery field within, lies like a rose among thorns; and hard to be reached as the heart of proud maiden. Though once attained, all three—red rose, bright shore, and soft heart—are full of love, bloom, and all manner of delights. The Pearl Shell islands excepted.

Besides, in those generally tranquil waters, Samoa's little craft, though hundreds of miles from land, was very readily managed by himself and Annatoo. So small was the Parki, that one hand could brace the main-yard; and a very easy thing it was, even to hoist the small top-sails; for after their first clumsy attempt to perform that operation by hand, they invariably led the halyards to the windlass, and so managed it, with the utmost facility.

Chapter 26

Containing a Pennyweight of Philosophy

STILL MANY DAYS PASSED and the Parki yet floated. The little flying-fish got used to her familiar, loitering hull; and like swallows building their nests in quiet old trees, they spawned in the great green barnacles that clung to her sides.

The calmer the sea, the more the barnacles grow. In the tropical Pacific, but a few weeks suffice thus to encase your craft in shell armor. Vast bunches adhere to the very cutwater, and if not stricken off, much impede the ship's sailing. And, at intervals, this clearing away of barnacles was one of Anna-too's occupations. For be it known, that, like most termagants, the dame was tidy at times, though capriciously; loving cleanliness by fits and starts. Wherefore, these barnacles oftentimes troubled her; and with a long pole she would go about, brushing them aside. It beguiled the weary hours, if nothing more; and then she would return to her beads and her trinkets; telling them all over again; murmuring forth her devotions, and marking whether Samoa had been pilfering from her store.

Now, the escape from the shoal did much once again to heal the differences of the good lady and her spouse. And keeping house, as they did, all alone by themselves, in that lonely craft, a marvel it is, that they should ever have quarreled. And then to divorce, and yet dwell in the same tenement, was only aggravating the evil. So Belisarius and Antonina again came together. But now, grown wise by experience, they neither loved over-keenly, nor hated; but took things as they were; found themselves joined, without hope of a sundering, and did what they could to make a match of the mate. Annatoo concluded that Samoa was not wholly to be enslaved; and Samoa thought best to wink at Annatoo's foibles, and let her purloin when she pleased.

But as in many cases, all this philosophy about wedlock is not proof against the perpetual contact of the parties concerned; and as it is far better to revive the old days of courtship, when men's mouths are honey-combs: and, to make them still sweeter, the ladies the bees which there store their sweets; when fathomless raptures glimmer far down in the lover's fond eye; and best of all, when visits are alternated by absence: so, like my dig-nified lord duke and his duchess, Samoa and Annatoo, man and wife, dwelling in the same house, still kept up their separate quarters. Marl-borough visiting Sarah; and Sarah, Marlborough, whenever the humor suggested.

Chapter 27

In which the past History of the Parki is concluded

STILL DAYS, days, days sped by; and steering now this way, now that, to avoid the green treacherous shores, which frequently rose into view, the Parki went to and fro in the sea; till at last, it seemed hard to tell, in what watery world she floated. Well knowing the risks they ran, Samoa desponded. But blessed be ignorance. For in the day of his despondency, the lively old lass his wife bade him be of stout heart, cheer up, and steer away manfully for the setting sun; following which, they must inevitably arrive at her own dear native island, where all their cares would be over. So squaring their yards, away they glided; far sloping down the liquid sphere.

Upon the afternoon of the day we caught sight of them in our boat, they had sighted a cluster of low islands, which put them in no small panic, because of their resemblance to those where the massacre had taken place. Whereas, they must have been full five hundred leagues from that fearful vicinity. However, they altered their course to avoid it; and a little before sunset, dropping the islands astern, resumed their previous track. But very soon after, they espied our little sea-goat, bounding over the billows from afar.

This they took for a canoe giving chase to them. It renewed and augmented their alarm.

And when at last they perceived that the strange object was a boat, their fears, instead of being allayed, only so much the more increased. For their wild superstitions led them to conclude, that a white man's craft coming upon them so suddenly, upon the open sea, and by night, could be naught but a phantom. Furthermore, marking two of us in the Chamois, they fancied us the ghosts of the Cholos. A conceit which effectually damped Samoa's courage, like my Viking's, only proof against things tangible. So seeing us bent upon boarding the brigantine; after a hurried overturning of their chattels, with a view of carrying the most valuable aloft for safe keeping, they secreted what they could; and together made for the fore-top; the man with a musket, the woman with a bag of beads. Their endeavoring to secure these treasures against ghostly appropriation originated in no real fear, that otherwise they would be stolen: it was simply incidental to the vacant panic into which they were thrown. No reproach this, to Belisarius' heart of game; for the most intrepid Feegee warrior, he who has slain his hecatombs, will not go ten yards in the dark alone, for fear of ghosts.

Their purpose was to remain in the top until daylight; by which time, they counted upon the withdrawal of their visitants; who, sure enough, at last sprang on board, thus verifying their worst apprehensions.

They watched us long and earnestly. But curious to tell, in that very strait of theirs, perched together in that airy top, their domestic differences again broke forth; most probably, from their being suddenly forced into such very close contact.

However that might be, taking advantage of our descent into the cabin, Samoa, in desperation fled from his wife, and one-armed as he was, sailor-like, shifted himself over by the fore and aft-stays to the main-top, his musket being slung to his back. And thus divided, though but a few yards intervened, the pair were as much asunder as if at the opposite Poles.

During the live-long night they were both in great perplexity as to the extraordinary goblins on board. Such inquisitive, meddlesome spirits, had never before been encountered. So cool and systematic; sagaciously stopping the vessel's headway the better to rummage;—the very plan they themselves had adopted. But what most surprised them, was our striking a light, a thing of which no true ghost would be guilty. Then, our eating and drinking on the quarter-deck including the deliberate investment of Vienna; and many other actions equally strange, almost led Samoa to fancy that we were no shades, after all, but a couple of men from the moon.

Yet they had dimly caught sight of the frocks and trowsers we wore, similar to those which the captain of the Parki had bestowed upon the two Cholos, and in which those villains had been killed. This, with the presence of the whale-boat, united to chase away the conceit of our lunar origin. But these considerations renewed their first superstitious impressions of our being the ghosts of the murderous half-breeds.

Nevertheless, while during the latter part of the night we were reclining beneath him, munching our biscuit, Samoa eyeing us intently, was half a mind to open fire upon us by way of testing our corporeality. But most luckily, he concluded to defer so doing till sunlight; if by that time we should not have evaporated.

For dame Annatoo, almost from our first boarding the brigantine, something in our manner had bred in her a lurking doubt as to the genuineness of our atmospheric organization; and abandoned to her speculations when Samoa fled from her side, her incredulity waxed stronger and stronger. Whence we came she knew not; enough, that we seemed bent upon pillaging her own precious purloinings. Alas! thought she, my buttons, my nails, my tappa, my dollars, my beads, and my boxes!

Wrought up to desperation by these dismal forebodings, she at length shook the ropes leading from her own perch to Samoa's; adopting this method of arousing his attention to the heinousness of what was in all probability going on in the cabin, a prelude most probably to the invasion of her own end of the vessel. Had she dared raise her voice, no doubt she would have suggested the expediency of shooting us so soon as we emerged from the cabin. But failing to shake Samoa into an understanding of her views on the subject, her malice proved futile.

When her worst fears were confirmed, however, and we actually descended into the forecastle; there ensued such a reckless shaking of the ropes, that Samoa was fain to hold on hard, for fear of being tossed out of the rigging. And it was this violent rocking that caused the loud creaking of the yards, so often heard by us while below in Annatoo's apartment.

And the fore-top being just over the open forecastle scuttle, the dame could look right down upon us; hence our proceedings were plainly revealed by the lights that we carried. Upon our breaking open her strong-box, her indignation almost completely overmastered her fears. Unhooking a top-block, down it came into the forecastle, charitably commissioned with the demolition of Jarl's cocoa-nut, then more exposed to the view of an aerial observer than my own. But as it turned out, no harm was done to our porcelain.

At last, morning dawned; when ensued Jarl's discovery of the occupant of the main-top; which event, with what followed, has been duly recounted.

And such, in substance, was the first, second, third and fourth acts of the Parki drama. The fifth and last, including several scenes, now follows.

Chapter 28

Suspicions laid, and something about the Calmuc

THOUGH ABOUNDING IN DETAILS full of the savor of reality, Samoa's narrative did not at first appear altogether satisfactory. Not that it was so strange; for stranger recitals I had heard.

But one reason, perhaps, was that I had anticipated a narrative quite different; something agreeing with my previous surmises.

Not a little puzzling, also, was his account of having seen islands the day preceding; though, upon reflection, that might have been the case, and yet, from his immediately altering the Parki's course, the Chamois, unknowingly might have sailed by their vicinity. Still, those islands could form no part of the chain we were seeking. They must have been some region hitherto undiscovered.

But seems it likely, thought I, that one, who, according to his own account, has conducted himself so heroically in rescuing the brigantine, should be the victim of such childish terror at the mere glimpse of a couple of sailors in an open boat, so well supplied, too, with arms, as he was, to resist their capturing his craft, if such proved their intention? On the contrary, would it not have been more natural, in his dreary situation, to have hailed our approach with the utmost delight? But then again, we were taken for phantoms, not flesh and blood. Upon the whole, I regarded the narrator of these things somewhat distrustfully. But he met my gaze like a man.

While Annatoo, standing by, looked so expressively the Amazonian character imputed to her, that my doubts began to waver. And recalling all the little incidents of their story, so hard to be conjured up on the spur of a presumed necessity to lie; nay, so hard to be conjured up at all; my suspicions at last gave way. And I could no longer harbor any misgivings.

For, to be downright, what object could Samoa have, in fabricating such a narrative of horrors—those of the massacre, I mean—unless to conceal some tragedy, still more atrocious, in which he himself had been criminally concerned? A supposition, which, for obvious reasons, seemed out of the question. True, instances were known to me of half-civilized beings, like Samoa, forming part of the crews of ships in these seas, rising suddenly upon their white shipmates, and murdering them, for the sake of wrecking the ship on the shore of some island near by, and plundering her hull, when stranded.

But had this been purposed with regard to the Parki, where the rest of the mutineers? There was no end to my conjectures; the more I indulged in them, the more they multiplied. So, unwilling to torment myself, when nothing could be learned, but what Samoa related, and stuck to like a hero; I gave over conjecturing at all; striving hard to repose full faith in the Islander.

Jarl, however, was skeptical to the last; and never could be brought completely to credit the tale. He stoutly maintained that the hobgoblins must have had something or other to do with the Parki.

My own curiosity satisfied with respect to the brigantine, Samoa himself turned inquisitor. He desired to know who we were; and whence we came in our marvelous boat. But on these heads I thought best to withhold from him the truth; among other things, fancying that if disclosed, it would lessen his deference for us, as men superior to himself. I therefore spoke vaguely of our adventures, and assumed the decided air of a master; which I perceived was not lost upon the rude Islander. As for Jarl, and what he might reveal, I embraced the first opportunity to impress upon him the importance of never divulging our flight from the Arcturion; nor in any way to commit himself on that head: injunctions which he faithfully promised to observe.

If not wholly displeased with the fine form of Samoa, despite his savage lineaments, and mutilated member, I was much less conciliated by the person of Annatoo; who, being sinewy of limb, and neither young, comely, nor amiable, was exceedingly distasteful in my eyes. Besides, she was a tigress. Yet how avoid admiring those Penthesilian qualities which so signally had aided Samoa, in wresting the Parki from its treacherous captors. Nevertheless, it was indispensable that she should at once be brought under prudent subjection; and made to know, once for all, that though conjugally a rebel, she must be nautically submissive. For to keep the sea with a Calmuc on board, seemed next to impossible. In most military marines, they are prohibited by law; no officer may take his Pandora and her bandbox off soundings.

By the way, this self-same appellative, Pandora, has been bestowed upon vessels. There was a British ship by that name, dispatched in quest of the mutineers of the Bounty. But any old tar might have prophesied her fate. Bound home she was wrecked on a reef off New South Wales. Pandora, indeed! A pretty name for a ship: fairly smiting Fate in the face. But in this matter of christening ships of war, Christian nations are but too apt to be dare-devils. Witness the following: British names all.—The Conqueror, the Defiance, the Revenge, the Spitfire, the Dreadnaught, the Thunderer, and the Tremendous; not omitting the Etna, which, in the Roads of Corfu, was struck by lightning, coming nigh being consumed by fire from above. But almost potent as Moses' rod, Franklin's proved her salvation.

With the above catalogue, compare we the Frenchman's; quite characteristic of the aspirations of Monsieur:—The Destiny, the Glorious, the Magnanimous, the Magnificent, the Conqueror, the Triumphant, the Indomitable, the Intrepid, the Mont-Blanc. Lastly, the Dons; who have ransacked the theology of the religion of peace for fine names for their fighting ships; stopping not at designating one of their three-deckers, The Most Holy Trinity. But though, at Trafalgar, the Santissima Trinidada thundered like Sinai, her thunders were silenced by the victorious cannonade of the Victory.

And without being blown into splinters by artillery, how many of these Redoubtables and Invincibles have succumbed to the waves, and like braggarts gone down before hurricanes, with their bravadoes broad on their bows.

Much better the American names (barring Scorpions, Hornets, and Wasps;) Ohio, Virginia, Carolina, Vermont. And if ever these Yankees fight great sea engagements—which Heaven forefend!—how glorious, poetically speaking, to range up the whole federated fleet, and pour forth a broadside from Florida to Maine. Ay, ay, very glorious indeed! yet in that proud crowing of cannon, how shall the shade of peace-loving Penn be astounded, to see the mightiest murderer of them all, the great Pennsylvania, a very namesake of his. Truly, the Pennsylvania's guns should be the wooden ones, called by men-of-war's-men, Quakers.

But all this is an episode, made up of digressions. Time to tack ship, and return.

Now, in its proper place, I omitted to mention, that shortly after descending from the rigging, and while Samoa was rehearsing his adventures, dame Annatoo had stolen below into the forecastle, intent upon her chattels. And finding them all in mighty disarray, she returned to the deck prodigiously excited, and glancing angrily toward Jarl and me, showered a whole torrent of objurgations into both ears of Samoa.

This contempt of my presence surprised me at first; but perhaps women are less apt to be impressed by a pretentious demeanor, than men.

Now, to use a fighting phrase, there is nothing like boarding an enemy in the smoke. And therefore, upon this first token of Annatoo's termagant qualities, I gave her to understand—craving her pardon—that neither the vessel nor aught therein was hers; but that every thing belonged to the owners in Lahina. I added, that at all hazards, a stop must be put to her pilferings. Rude language for feminine ears; but how to be avoided? Here was an infatuated woman, who, according to Samoa's account, had been repeatedly detected in the act of essaying to draw out the screw-bolts which held together the planks. Tell me; was she not worse than the Load-Stone Rock, sailing by which a stout ship fell to pieces?

During this scene, Samoa said little. Perhaps he was secretly pleased that his matrimonial authority was reinforced by myself and my Viking, whose views of the proper position of wives at sea, so fully corresponded with his own; however difficult to practice, those purely theoretical ideas of his had hitherto proved.

Once more turning to Annatoo, now looking any thing but amiable, I observed, that all her clamors would be useless; and that if it came to the worst, the Parki had a hull that would hold her.

In the end she went off in a fit of the sulks; sitting down on the windlass and glaring; her arms akimbo, and swaying from side to side; while ever and anon she gave utterance to a dismal chant. It sounded like an invocation to the Cholos to rise and dispatch us.

Chapter 29

What they lighted upon in further searching the Craft,
and the Resolution they came to

DESCENDING INTO THE CABIN with Samoa, I bade him hunt up the brigantine's log, the captain's writing-desk, and nautical instruments; in a word, aught that could throw light on the previous history of the craft, or aid in navigating her homeward.

But nearly every thing of the kind had disappeared: log, quadrant, and ship's papers. Nothing was left but the sextant-case, which Jarl and I had lighted upon in the state-room.

Upon this, vague though they were, my suspicions returned; and I closely questioned the Islander concerning the disappearance of these important articles. In reply, he gave me to understand, that the nautical instruments had been clandestinely carried down into the forecastle by Annatoo; and by that indefatigable and inquisitive dame they had been summarily taken apart for scientific inspection. It was impossible to restore them; for many of the fixtures were lost, including the colored glasses, sights, and little mirrors; and many parts still recoverable, were so battered and broken as to be entirely useless. For several days afterward, we now and then came across bits of the quadrant or sextant; but it was only to mourn over their fate.

However, though sextant and quadrant were both unattainable, I did not so quickly renounce all hope of discovering a chronometer, which, if in good order, though at present not ticking, might still be made in some degree serviceable. But no such instrument was to be seen. No: nor to be heard of; Samoa himself professing utter ignorance.

Annatoo, I threatened and coaxed; describing the chronometer—a live, round creature like a toad, that made a strange noise, which I imitated; but she knew nothing about it. Whether she had lighted upon it unbeknown to Samoa, and dissected it as usual, there was now no way to determine. Indeed, upon this one point, she maintained an air of such inflexible stupidity, that if she were really fibbing, her dead-wall countenance superseded the necessity for verbal deceit.

It may be, however, that in this particular she was wronged; for, as with many small vessels, the Parki might never have possessed the instrument in question. All thought, therefore, of feeling our way, as we should penetrate farther and farther into the watery wilderness, was necessarily abandoned.

The log book had also formed a portion of Annatoo's pilferings. It seems she had taken it into her studio to ponder over. But after amusing herself by again and again counting over the leaves, and wondering how so many distinct surfaces could be compacted together in so small a compass, she had very suddenly conceived an aversion to literature, and dropped the book overboard as worthless. Doubtless, it met the fate of many other ponderous tomes; sinking quickly and profoundly. What Camden or Stowe hereafter will dive for it?

One evening Samoa brought me a quarto half-sheet of yellowish, ribbed paper, much soiled and tarry, which he had discovered in a dark hole of the forecastle. It had plainly formed part of the lost log; but all the writing thereon, at present decipherable, conveyed no information upon the subject then nearest my heart.

But one could not but be struck by a tragical occurrence, which the page very briefly recounted; as well, as by a noteworthy pictorial illustration of the event in the margin of the text. Save the cut, there was no further allusion to the matter than the following:—"This day, being calm, Tooboi, one of the Lahina men, went overboard for a bath, and was eaten up by a shark. Immediately sent forward for his bag."

Now, this last sentence was susceptible of two meanings. It is truth, that immediately upon the decease of a friendless sailor at sea, his shipmates oftentimes seize upon his effects, and divide them; though the dead man's clothes are seldom worn till a subsequent voyage. This proceeding seems heartless. But sailors reason thus: Better we, than the captain. For by law, either scribbled or unscribbled, the effects of a mariner, dying on shipboard, should be held in trust by that officer. But as sailors are mostly foundlings and castaways, and carry all their kith and kin in their arms and their legs, there hardly ever appears any heir-at-law to claim their estate; seldom worth inheriting, like Esterhazy's. Wherefore, the withdrawal of a dead man's "kit" from the forecastle to the cabin, is often held tantamount to its virtual appropriation by the captain. At any rate, in small ships on long voyages, such things have been done.

Thus much being said, then, the sentence above quoted from the Parki's log, may be deemed somewhat ambiguous. At the time it struck me as singular; for the poor diver's grass bag could not have contained much of any thing valuable; unless, peradventure, he had concealed therein some Cleopatra pearls, feloniously abstracted from the shells brought up from the sea.

Aside of the paragraph, copied above, was a pen-and-ink sketch of the casualty, most cruelly executed; the poor fellow's legs being represented half way in the process of deglutition; his arms firmly grasping the monster's teeth, as if heroically bent upon making as tough a morsel of himself as possible.

But no doubt the honest captain sketched this cenotaph to the departed in all sincerity of heart; perhaps, during the melancholy leisure which followed the catastrophe. Half obliterated were several stains upon the page; seemingly, lingering traces of a salt tear or two.

From this unwonted embellishment of the text, I was led to infer, that the designer, at one time or other, must have been engaged in the vocation of whaling. For, in India ink, the logs of certain whalemen are decorated by somewhat similar illustrations.

When whales are seen, but not captured, the fact is denoted by an outline figure representing the creature's flukes, the broad, curving lobes of his tail. But in those cases where the monster is both chased and killed, this outline is filled up jet black; one for every whale slain; presenting striking objects in turning over the log; and so facilitating reference. Hence, it is quite imposing to behold, all in a row, three or four, sometime five or six, of these drawings; showing that so many monsters that day jetted their last spout. And the chief mate, whose duty it is to keep the ship's record, generally prides himself upon the beauty, and flushy likeness to life, of his flukes; though, sooth to say, many of these artists are no Landseers.

After vainly searching the cabin for those articles we most needed, we proceeded to explore the hold, into which as yet we had not penetrated.

Here, we found a considerable quantity of pearl shells; cocoanuts; an abundance of fresh water in casks; spare sails and rigging; and some fifty barrels or more of salt beef and biscuit. Unromantic as these last mentioned objects were, I lingered over them long, and in a revery. Branded upon each barrel head was the name of a place in America, with which I was very familiar. It is from America chiefly, that ship's stores are originally procured for the few vessels sailing out of the Hawaiian Islands.

Having now acquainted myself with all things respecting the Parki, which could in any way be learned, I repaired to the quarter-deck, and summoning round me Samoa, Annatoo, and Jarl, gravely addressed them.

I said, that nothing would give me greater satisfaction than forthwith to return to the scene of the massacre, and chastise its surviving authors. But as there were only four of us in all; and the place of those islands was wholly unknown to me; and even if known, would be altogether out of our reach, since we possessed no instruments of navigation; it was quite plain that all thought of returning thither was entirely useless. The last mentioned reason, also, prevented our voyaging to the Hawaiian group, where the vessel belonged; though that would have been the most advisable step, resulting, as it would, if successful, in restoring the ill-fated craft to her owners.

But all things considered, it seemed best, I added, cautiously to hold on our way to the westward. It was our easiest course; for we would ever have the wind from astern; and though we could not so much as hope to arrive at any one spot previously designated, there was still a positive certainty, if we floated long enough, of falling in with islands whereat to refresh ourselves; and whence, if we thought fit, we might afterward embark for more agreeable climes. I then reminded them of the fact, that so long as we kept the sea, there was always some prospect of encountering a friendly sail; in which event, our solicitude would be over.

All this I said in the mild, firm tone of a superior; being anxious, at once to assume the unquestioned supremacy. For, otherwise, Jarl and I might better quit the vessel forthwith, than remain on board subject to the outlandish caprices of Annatoo, who through Samoa would then have the sway. But I was sure of my Viking; and if Samoa proved docile, had no fear of his dame.

And therefore during my address, I steadfastly eyed him; thereby learning enough to persuade me, that though he deferred to me at present, he was, notwithstanding, a man who, without precisely meditating mischief, could upon occasion act an ugly part. But of his courage, and savage honor, such as it was, I had little doubt. Then, wild buffalo that he was, tamed down in the yoke matrimonial, I could not but fancy, that if upon no other account, our society must please him, as rendering less afflictive the tyranny of his spouse.

For a hen-pecked husband, by the way, Samoa was a most terrible fellow to behold. And though, after all, I liked him; it was as you fancy a fiery steed with mane disheveled, as young Alexander fancied Bucephalus; which wild horse, when he patted, he preferred holding by the bridle. But more of Samoa anon.

Our course determined, and the command of the vessel tacitly yielded up to myself, the next thing done was to put every thing in order. The tattered sails were replaced by others, dragged up from the sail-room below; in several places, new running-rigging was rove; blocks restrapped; and the slackened stays and shrouds set taught. For all of which, we were mostly indebted to my Viking's unwearied and skillful marling-spike, which he swayed like a scepter.

The little Parki's toilet being thus thoroughly made for the first time since the massacre, we gave her new raiment to the breeze, and daintily squaring her yards, she gracefully glided away; honest old Jarl at the helm, watchfully guiding her path, like some devoted old foster-father.

As I stood by his side like a captain, or walked up and down on the quarter-deck, I felt no little importance upon thus assuming for the first time in my life, the command of a vessel at sea. The novel circumstances of the case only augmented this feeling; the wild and remote seas where we were; the character of my crew, and the consideration, that to all purposes, I was owner, as well as commander of the craft I sailed.

Chapter 30

Hints for a full length of Samoa

M Y ORIGINAL INTENTION to touch at the Kingsmill Chain, or the countries adjacent, was greatly strengthened by thus encountering Samoa; and the more I had to do with my Belisarius, the more I was pleased with him. Nor could I avoid congratulating myself, upon having fallen in with a hero, who in various ways, could not fail of proving exceedingly useful.

Like any man of mark, Samoa best speaks for himself; but we may as well convey some idea of his person. Though manly enough, nay, an obelisk in stature, the savage was far from being sentimentally prepossessing. Be not alarmed; but he wore his knife in the lobe of his dexter ear, which, by constant elongation almost drooped upon his shoulder. A mode of sheathing it exceedingly handy, and far less brigandish than the Highlander's dagger concealed in his leggins.

But it was the mother of Samoa, who at a still earlier day had punctured him through and through in still another direction. The middle cartilage of his nose was slightly pendent, peaked, and Gothic, and perforated with a hole; in which, like a Newfoundland dog carrying a cane, Samoa sported a trinket: a well polished nail.

In other respects he was equally a coxcomb. In his style of tattooing, for instance, which seemed rather incomplete; his marks embracing but a vertical half of his person, from crown to sole; the other side being free from the slightest stain. Thus clapped together, as it were, he looked like a union of the unmatched moieties of two distinct beings; and your fancy was lost in conjecturing, where roamed the absent ones. When he turned round upon you suddenly, you thought you saw some one else, not him whom you had been regarding before.

But there was one feature in Samoa beyond the reach of the innovations of art:—his eye; which in civilized man or savage, ever shines in the head, just as it shone at birth. Truly, our eyes are miraculous things. But alas, that in so many instances, these divine organs should be mere lenses inserted into the socket, as glasses in spectacle rims.

But my Islander had a soul in his eye; looking out upon you there, like somebody in him. What an eye, to be sure! At times, brilliantly changeful as opal; in anger, glowing like steel at white heat.

Belisarius, be it remembered, had but very recently lost an arm. But you would have thought he had been born without it; so Lord Nelson-like and cavalierly did he sport the honorable stump.

But no more of Samoa; only this: that his name had been given him by a sea-captain; to whom it had been suggested by the native designation of the islands to which he belonged; the Saviian or Samoan group, otherwise known as the Navigator Islands. The island of Upolua, one of that cluster, claiming the special honor of his birth, as Corsica does Napoleon's, we shall occasionally hereafter speak of Samoa as the Upoluan; by which title he most loved to be called.

It is ever ungallant to pass over a lady. But what shall be said of Annatoo? As I live, I can make no pleasing portrait of the dame; for as in most ugly subjects, flattering would but make the matter worse. Furthermore, unalleviated ugliness should ever go unpainted, as something unnecessary to duplicate. But the only ugliness is that of the heart, seen through the face. And though beauty be obvious, the only loveliness is invisible.

Chapter 31

Rovings Alow and Aloft

EVERY ONE KNOWS what a fascination there is in wandering up
and down in a deserted old tenement in some warm, dreamy country; where the vacant halls seem echoing of silence, and the doors
creak open like the footsteps of strangers; and into every window the old
garden trees thrust their dark boughs, like the arms of night-burglars; and
ever and anon the nails start from the wainscot; while behind it the mice
rattle like dice. Up and down in such old specter houses one loves to wander;
and so much the more, if the place be haunted by some marvelous story.

And during the drowsy stillness of the tropical sea-day, very much such
a fancy had I, for prying about our little brigantine, whose tragic hull was
haunted by the memory of the massacre, of which it still bore innumerable
traces.

And so far as the indulgence of quiet strolling and reverie was concerned,
it was well nigh the same as if I were all by myself. For Samoa, for a time,
was rather reserved, being occupied with thoughts of his own. And Annatoo seldom troubled me with her presence. She was taken up with her
calicoes and jewelry; which I had permitted her to retain, to keep her in
good humor if possible. And as for my royal old Viking, he was one of
those individuals who seldom speak, unless personally addressed.

Besides, all that by day was necessary to navigating the Parki was, that somebody should stand at the helm; the craft being so small, and the grating, whereon the steersman stood, so elevated, that he commanded a view far beyond the bowsprit; thus keeping Argus eyes on the sea, as he steered us along. In all other respects we left the brigantine to the guardianship of the gentle winds.

My own turn at the helm—for though commander, I felt constrained to do duty with the rest—came but once in the twenty-four hours. And not only did Jarl and Samoa, officiate as helmsmen, but also Dame Annatoo, who had become quite expert at the business. Though Jarl always maintained that there was a slight drawback upon her usefulness in this vocation. Too much taken up by her lovely image partially reflected in the glass of the binnacle before her, Annatoo now and then neglected her duty, and led us some devious dances. Nor was she, I ween, the first woman that ever led men into zigzags.

For the reasons above stated, I had many spare hours to myself. At times, I mounted aloft, and lounging in the slings of the topsail yard—one of the many snug nooks in a ship's rigging—I gazed broad off upon the blue boundless sea, and wondered what they were doing in that unknown land, toward which we were fated to be borne. Or feeling less meditative, I roved about hither and thither; slipping over, by the stays, from one mast to the other; climbing up to the truck; or lounging out to the ends of the yards; exploring wherever there was a foothold. It was like climbing about in some mighty old oak, and resting in the crotches.

To a sailor, a ship's ropes are a study. And to me, every rope-yarn of the Parki's was invested with interest. The outlandish fashion of her shrouds, the collars of her stays, the stirrups, seizings, Flemish-horses, gaskets,—all the wilderness of her rigging, bore unequivocal traces of her origin.

But, perhaps, my pleasantest hours were those which I spent, stretched out on a pile of old sails, in the fore-top; lazily dozing to the craft's light roll.

Frequently, I descended to the cabin: for the fiftieth time, exploring the lockers and state-rooms for some new object of curiosity. And often, with a glimmering light, I went into the midnight hold, as into old vaults and catacombs; and creeping between damp ranges of casks, penetrated into its farthest recesses.

Sometimes, in these under-ground burrowings, I lighted upon sundry out-of-the-way hiding places of Annatoo's; where were snugly secreted divers articles, with which she had been smitten. In truth, no small portion of the hull seemed a mine of stolen goods, stolen out of its own bowels. I found a jaunty shore-cap of the captain's, hidden away in the hollow heart of a coil of rigging; covered over in a manner most touchingly natural, with a heap of old ropes; and near by, in a breaker, discovered several entire pieces of calico, heroically tied together with cords almost strong enough to sustain the mainmast.

Near the stray light, which, when the hatch was removed, gleamed down into this part of the hold, was a huge ground-tier butt, headless as Charles the First. And herein was a mat nicely spread for repose; a discovery which accounted for what had often proved an enigma. Not seldom Annatoo had been among the missing; and though, from stem to stern, loudly invoked to come forth and relieve the poignant distress of her anxious friends, the dame remained perdu; silent and invisible as a spirit. But in her own good time, she would mysteriously emerge; or be suddenly espied lounging quietly in the forecastle, as if she had been there from all eternity.

Useless to inquire, "Where hast thou been, sweet Annatoo?" For no sweet rejoinder would she give.

But now the problem was solved. Here, in this silent cask in the hold, Annatoo was wont to coil herself away, like a garter-snake under a stone.

Whether she thus stood sentry over her goods secreted round about: whether she here performed penance like a nun in her cell; or was moved to this unaccountable freak by the powers of the air; no one could tell. Can you?

Verily, her ways were as the ways of the inscrutable penguins in building their inscrutable nests, which baffle all science, and make a fool of a sage.

Marvelous Annatoo! who shall expound thee?

Chapter 32

Xiphius Platypterus

ABOUT THIS TIME, the loneliness of our voyage was relieved by an event worth relating.

Ever since leaving the Pearl Shell Islands, the Parki had been followed by shoals of small fish, pleasantly enlivening the sea, and socially swimming by her side. But in vain did Jarl and I search among their ranks for the little, steel-blue Pilot fish, so long outriders of the Chamois. But perhaps since the Chamois was now high and dry on the Parki's deck, our bright little avant-couriers were lurking out of sight, far down in the brine; racing along close to the keel.

But it is not with the Pilot fish that we now have to do.

One morning our attention was attracted to a mighty commotion in the water. The shoals of fish were darting hither and thither, and leaping into the air in the utmost affright. Samoa declared, that their deadly foe the Sword fish must be after them.

And here let me say, that, since of all the bullies, and braggarts, and bravoes, and free-booters, and Hectors, and fish-at-arms, and knight-errants, and moss-troopers, and assassins, and foot-pads, and gallant soldiers, and immortal heroes that swim the seas, the Indian Sword fish is by far the most remarkable, I propose to dedicate this chapter to a special description of the warrior. In doing which, I but follow the example of all chroniclers

103

and historians, my Peloponnesian friend Thucydides and others, who are ever mindful of devoting much space to accounts of eminent destroyers; for the purpose, no doubt, of holding them up as ensamples to the world.

Now, the fish here treated of is a very different creature from the Sword fish frequenting the Northern Atlantic; being much larger every way, and a more dashing varlet to boot. Furthermore, he is denominated the Indian Sword fish, in contradistinction from his namesake above mentioned. But by seamen in the Pacific, he is more commonly known as the Bill fish; while for those who love science and hard names, be it known, that among the erudite naturalists he goeth by the outlandish appellation of "*Xiphius Platypterus.*"

But I waive for my hero all these his cognomens, and substitute a much better one of my own: namely, the Chevalier. And a Chevalier he is, by good right and title. A true gentleman of Black Prince Edward's bright day, when all gentlemen were known by their swords; whereas, in times present, the Sword fish excepted, they are mostly known by their high polished boots and rattans.

A right valiant and jaunty Chevalier is our hero; going about with his long Toledo perpetually drawn. Rely upon it, he will fight you to the hilt, for his bony blade has never a scabbard. He himself sprang from it at birth; yea, at the very moment he leaped into the Battle of Life; as we mortals ourselves spring all naked and scabbardless into the world. Yet, rather, are we scabbards to our souls. And the drawn soul of genius is more glittering than the drawn cimeter of Saladin. But how many let their steel sleep, till it eat up the scabbard itself, and both corrode to rust-chips. Saw you ever the hillocks of old Spanish anchors, and anchor-stocks of ancient galleons, at the bottom of Callao Bay? The world is full of old Tower armories, and dilapidated Venetian arsenals, and rusty old rapiers. But true warriors polish their good blades by the bright beams of the morning; and gird them on to their brave sirloins; and watch for rust spots as for foes; and by many stout thrusts and stoccadoes keep their metal lustrous and keen, as the spears of the Northern Lights charging over Greenland.

Fire from the flint is our Chevalier enraged. He takes umbrage at the cut of some ship's keel crossing his road; and straightway runs a tilt at it; with one mad lunge thrusting his Andrea Ferrara clean through and through; not seldom breaking it short off at the haft, like a bravo leaving his poignard in the vitals of his foe.

In the case of the English ship Foxhound, the blade penetrated through the most solid part of her hull, the bow; going completely through the copper plates and timbers, and showing for several inches in the hold. On the return of the ship to London, it was carefully sawn out; and, imbedded in the original wood, like a fossil, is still preserved. But this was a comparatively harmless onslaught of the valiant Chevalier. With the Rousseau, of Nantucket, it fared worse. She was almost mortally stabbed; her assailant withdrawing his blade. And it was only by keeping the pumps clanging, that she managed to swim into a Tahitian harbor, "heave down," and have her wound dressed by a ship-surgeon with tar and oakum. This ship I met with at sea, shortly after the disaster.

At what armory our Chevalier equips himself after one of his spiteful tilting-matches, it would not be easy to say. But very hard for him, if ever after he goes about in the lists, swordless and disarmed, at the mercy of any caitiff shark he may meet.

Now, seeing that our fellow-voyagers, the little fish alongside, were sorely tormented and thinned out by the incursions of a pertinacious Chevalier, bent upon making a hearty breakfast out of them, I determined to interfere in their behalf, and capture the enemy.

With shark-hook and line I succeeded, and brought my brave gentleman to the deck. He made an emphatic landing; lashing the planks with his sinewy tail; while a yard and a half in advance of his eyes, reached forth his terrible blade.

As victor, I was entitled to the arms of the vanquished; so, quickly dispatching him, and sawing off his Toledo, I bore it away for a trophy. It was three-sided, slightly concave on each, like a bayonet; and some three inches through at the base, it tapered from thence to a point.

And though tempered not in Tagus or Guadalquiver, it yet revealed upon its surface that wavy grain and watery fleckiness peculiar to tried blades of Spain. It was an aromatic sword; like the ancient caliph's, giving out a peculiar musky odor by friction. But far different from steel of Tagus or Damascus, it was inflexible as Crockett's rifle tube; no doubt, as deadly.

Long hung that rapier over the head of my hammock. Was it not storied as the good trenchant blade of brave Bayard, that other chevalier? The knight's may have slain its scores, or fifties; but the weapon I preserved had, doubtless, run through and riddled its thousands.

Chapter 33

Otard

A ND HERE is another little incident.

One afternoon while all by myself curiously penetrating into the hold, I most unexpectedly obtained proof, that the ill-fated captain of the Parki had been a man of sound judgment and most excellent taste. In brief, I lighted upon an aromatic cask of prime old Otard.

Now, I mean not to speak lightly of any thing immediately connected with the unfortunate captain. Nor, on the other hand, would I resemble the inconsolable mourner, who among other tokens of affliction, bound in funereal crape his deceased friend's copy of Joe Miller. Is there not a fitness in things?

But let that pass. I found the Otard, and drank thereof; finding it, moreover, most pleasant to the palate, and right cheering to the soul. My next impulse was to share my prize with my shipmates. But here a judicious reflection obtruded. From the sea-monarchs, his ancestors, my Viking had inherited one of their cardinal virtues, a detestation and abhorrence of all vinous and spirituous beverages; insomuch, that he never could see any, but he instantly quaffed it out of sight. To be short, like Alexander the Great and other royalties, Jarl was prone to overmuch bibbing. And though at sea more sober than a Fifth Monarchy Elder, it was only because he was then removed from temptation. But having thus divulged my Viking's weak side, I earnestly entreat, that it may not disparage him in any charitable man's estimation. Only think, how many more there are like him—to say nothing further of Alexander the Great—especially among his own class; and consider, I beseech, that the most capacious-souled fellows, for that very reason, are the most apt to be too liberal in their libations; since, being so large-hearted, they hold so much more good cheer than others.

For Samoa, from his utter silence hitherto as to aught inebriating on board, I concluded, that, along with his other secrets, the departed captain had very wisely kept his Otard to himself.

Nor did I doubt, but that the Upoluan, like all Polynesians, much loved getting high of head; and in that state, would be more intractable than a Black Forest boar. And concerning Annatoo, I shuddered to think, how that Otard might inflame her into a Fury more fierce than the foremost of those that pursued Orestes.

In good time, then, bethinking me of the peril of publishing my dis-covery;—bethinking me of the quiet, lazy, everpresent perils of the voyage, of all circumstances, the very worst under which to introduce an intox-icating beverage to my companions, I resolved to withhold it from them altogether.

So impressed was I with all this, that for a moment, I was almost tempted to roll over the cask on its bilge, remove the stopper, and suffer its contents to mix with the foul water at the bottom of the hold.

But no, no: What: dilute the brine with the double distilled soul of the precious grape? Hafiz himself would have haunted me!

Then again, it might come into play medicinally; and Paracelsus him-self stands sponsor for every cup drunk for the good of the abdomen. So at last, I determined to let it remain where it was: visiting it occasionally, by myself, for inspection.

But by way of advice to all ship-masters, let me say, that if your Otard magazine be exposed to view—then, in the evil hour of wreck, stave in your spirit-casks, ere rigging the life-boat.

Chapter 34

How they steered on their Way

WHEN WE QUITTED the Chamois for the brigantine, we must have been at least two hundred leagues to the westward of the spot, where we had abandoned the Arcturion. Though how far we might then have been, North or South of the Equator, I could not with any certainty divine.

But that we were not removed any considerable distance from the Line, seemed obvious. For in the starriest night no sign of the extreme Polar constellations was visible; though often we scanned the northern and southern horizon in search of them. So far as regards the aspect of the skies near the ocean's rim, the difference of several degrees in one's latitude at sea, is readily perceived by a person long accustomed to surveying the heavens.

If correct in my supposition, concerning our longitude at the time here alluded to, and allowing for what little progress we had been making in the Parki, there now remained some one hundred leagues to sail, ere the country we sought would be found. But for obvious reasons, how long precisely we might continue to float out of sight of land, it was impossible to say. Calms, light breezes, and currents made every thing uncertain. Nor had we any method of estimating our due westward progress, except by what is called Dead Reckoning,—the computation of the knots run hourly;

allowances being made for the supposed deviations from our course, by reason of the ocean streams; which at times in this quarter of the Pacific run with very great velocity.

Now, in many respects we could not but feel safer aboard the Parki than in the Chamois. The sense of danger is less vivid, the greater the number of lives involved. He who is ready to despair in solitary peril, plucks up a heart in the presence of another. In a plurality of comrades is much countenance and consolation.

Still, in the brigantine there were many sources of uneasiness and anxiety unknown to me in the whale-boat. True, we had now between us and the deep, five hundred good planks to one lath in our buoyant little chip. But the Parki required more care and attention; especially by night, when a vigilant look-out was indispensable. With impunity, in our whale-boat, we might have run close to shoal or reef; whereas, similar carelessness or temerity now, might prove fatal to all concerned.

Though in the joyous sunlight, sailing through the sparkling sea, I was little troubled with serious misgivings; in the hours of darkness it was quite another thing. And the apprehensions, nay terrors I felt, were much augmented by the remissness of both Jarl and Samoa, in keeping their night-watches. Several times I was seized with a deadly panic, and earnestly scanned the murky horizon, when rising from slumber I found the steersman, in whose hands for the time being were life and death, sleeping upright against the tiller, as much of a fixture there, as the open-mouthed dragon rudely carved on our prow.

Were it not, that on board of other vessels, I myself had many a time dozed at the helm, spite of all struggles, I would have been almost at a loss to account for this heedlessness in my comrades. But it seemed as if the mere sense of our situation, should have been sufficient to prevent the like conduct in all on board our craft.

Samoa's aspect, sleeping at the tiller, was almost appalling. His large opal eyes were half open; and turned toward the light of the binnacle, gleamed between the lids like bars of flame. And added to all, was his giant stature and savage lineaments.

It was in vain, that I remonstrated, begged, or threatened: the occasional drowsiness of my fellow-voyagers proved incurable. To no purpose, I reminded my Viking that sleeping in the night-watch in a craft like ours, was far different from similar heedlessness on board the Arcturion. For there, our place upon the ocean was always known, and our distance from land; so that when by night the seamen were permitted to be drowsy, it was mostly, because the captain well knew that strict watchfulness could be dispensed with.

Though in all else, the Skyeman proved a most faithful ally, in this one thing he was either perversely obtuse, or infatuated. Or, perhaps, finding himself once more in a double-decked craft, which rocked him as of yore, he was lulled into a deceitful security.

For Samoa, his drowsiness was the drowsiness of one bent on sleep, come dreams or death. He seemed insensible to the peril we ran. Often I sent the sleepy savage below, and steered myself till morning. At last I made a point of slumbering much by day, the better to stand watch by night; though I made Samoa and Jarl regularly go through with their allotted four hours each.

It has been mentioned, that Annatoo took her turn at the helm; but it was only by day. And in justice to the lady, I must affirm, that upon the whole she acquitted herself well. For notwithstanding the syren face in the binnacle, which dimly allured her glances, Annatoo after all was tolerably heedful of her steering. Indeed she took much pride therein; always ready for her turn; with marvelous exactitude calculating the approaching hour, as it came on in regular rotation. Her time-piece was ours, the sun. By night it must have been her guardian star; for frequently she gazed up at a particular section of the heavens, like one regarding the dial in a tower.

By some odd reasoning or other, she had cajoled herself into the notion, that whoever steered the brigantine, for that period was captain. Wherefore, she gave herself mighty airs at the tiller; with extravagant gestures issuing unintelligible orders about trimming the sails, or pitching overboard something to see how fast we were going. All this much diverted my Viking, who several times was delivered of a laugh; a loud and healthy one to boot: a phenomenon worthy the chronicling.

And thus much for Annatoo, preliminary to what is further to be said. Seeing the drowsiness of Jarl and Samoa, which so often kept me from my hammock at night, forcing me to repose by day, when I far preferred being broad awake, I decided to let Annatoo take her turn at the night watches; which several times she had solicited me to do; railing at the sleepiness of her spouse; though abstaining from all reflections upon Jarl, toward whom she had of late grown exceedingly friendly.

Now the Calmuc stood her first night watch to admiration; if anything, was altogether too wakeful. The mere steering of the craft employed not sufficiently her active mind. Ever and anon she must needs rush from the tiller to take a parenthetical pull at the fore-brace, the end of which led down to the bulwarks near by; then refreshing herself with a draught or two of water and a biscuit, she would continue to steer away, full of the importance of her office. At any unusual flapping of the sails, a violent stamping on deck announced the fact to the startled crew. Finding her thus indefatigable, I readily induced her to stand two watches to Jarl's and Samoa's one; and when she was at the helm, I permitted myself to doze on a pile of old sails, spread every evening on the quarter-deck.

It was the Skyeman, who often admonished me to "heave the ship to" every night, thus stopping her headway till morning; a plan which, under other circumstances, might have perhaps warranted the slumbers of all. But as it was, such a course would have been highly imprudent. For while making no onward progress through the water, the rapid currents we en-countered would continually be drifting us eastward; since, contrary to our previous experience, they seemed latterly to have reversed their flow, a phenomenon by no means unusual in the vicinity of the Line in the Pacific. And this it was that so prolonged our passage to the westward. Even in a moderate breeze, I sometimes fancied, that the impulse of the wind little more than counteracted the glide of the currents; so that with much show of sailing, we were in reality almost a fixture on the sea.

The equatorial currents of the South Seas may be regarded as among the most mysterious of the mysteries of the deep. Whence they come, whither go, who knows? Tell us, what hidden law regulates their flow. Regardless of the theory which ascribes to them a nearly uniform course from east to west, induced by the eastwardly winds of the Line, and the collateral action of the Polar streams; these currents are forever shifting. Nor can the period of their revolutions be at all relied upon or predicted.

But however difficult it may be to assign a specific cause for the ocean streams, in any part of the world, one of the wholesome effects thereby produced would seem obvious enough. And though the circumstance here alluded to is perhaps known to every body, it may be questioned, whether it is generally invested with the importance it deserves. Reference is here made to the constant commingling and purification of the sea-water by reason of the currents.

For, that the ocean, according to the popular theory, possesses a special purifying agent in its salts, is somewhat to be doubted. Nor can it be ex-plicitly denied, that those very salts might corrupt it, were it not for the brisk circulation of its particles consequent upon the flow of the streams. It is well known to seamen, that a bucket of sea-water, left standing in a tropical climate, very soon becomes highly offensive; which is not the case with rain-water.

But I build no theories. And by way of obstructing the one, which might possibly be evolved from the statement above, let me add, that the offensiveness of sea-water left standing, may arise in no small degree from the presence of decomposed animal matter.

Chapter 35

Ah, Annatoo!

IN ORDER to a complete revelation, I must needs once again discourse of Annatoo and her pilferings; and to what those pilferings led. In the simplicity of my soul, I fancied that the dame, so much flattered as she needs must have been, by the confidence I began to repose in her, would now mend her ways, and abstain from her larcenies. But not so. She was possessed by some scores of devils, perpetually inciting her to mischief on their own separate behoof, and not hers; for many of her pranks were of no earthly advantage to her, present or prospective.

One day the log-reel was missing. Summon Annatoo. She came; but knew nothing about it. Jarl spent a whole morning in contriving a substitute; and a few days after, pop, we came upon the lost article hidden away in the main-top.

Another time, discovering the little vessel to "gripe" hard in steering, as if some one under water were jerking her backward, we instituted a diligent examination, to see what was the matter. When lo; what should we find but a rope, cunningly attached to one of the chain-plates under the starboard main-channel. It towed heavily in the water. Upon dragging it up—much as you would the cord of a ponderous bucket far down in a well—a stout wooden box was discovered at the end; which opened, disclosed sundry knives, hatchets, and ax-heads.

Called to the stand, the Upoluan deposed, that thrice he had rescued that identical box from Annatoo's all-appropriating clutches.

Now, here were four human beings shut up in this little oaken craft, and, for the time being, their interests the same. What sane mortal, then, would forever be committing thefts, without rhyme or reason. It was like stealing silver from one pocket and decanting it into the other. And what might it not lead to in the end?

Why, ere long, in good sooth, it led to the abstraction of the compass from the binnacle; so that we were fain to substitute for it, the one brought along in the Chamois.

It was Jarl that first published this last and alarming theft. Annatoo being at the helm at dawn, he had gone to relieve her; and looking to see how we headed, was horror-struck at the emptiness of the binnacle.

I started to my feet; sought out the woman, and ferociously demanded the compass. But her face was a blank; every word a denial.

Further lenity was madness. I summoned Samoa, told him what had happened, and affirmed that there was no safety for us except in the nightly incarceration of his spouse. To this he privily assented; and that very evening, when Annatoo descended into the forecastle, we barred over her the scuttle-slide. Long she clamored, but unavailingly. And every night this was repeated; the dame saying her vespers most energetically.

It has somewhere been hinted, that Annatoo occasionally cast sheep's eyes at Jarl. So I was not a little surprised when her manner toward him decidedly changed. Pulling at the ropes with us, she would give him sly pinches, and then look another way, innocent as a lamb. Then again, she would refuse to handle the same piece of rigging with him; with wry faces, rinsed out the wooden can at the water cask, if it so chanced that my Viking had previously been drinking therefrom. At other times, when the honest Skyeman came up from below, she would set up a shout of derision, and loll out her tongue; accompanying all this by certain indecorous and exceedingly unladylike gestures, significant of the profound contempt in which she held him.

Yet, never did Jarl heed her ill-breeding; but patiently overlooked and forgave it. Inquiring the reason of the dame's singular conduct, I learned, that with eye averted, she had very lately crept close to my Viking, and met with no tender reception.

Doubtless, Jarl, who was much of a philosopher, innocently imagined that ere long the lady would forgive and forget him. But what knows a philosopher about women?

Ere long, so outrageous became Annatoo's detestation of him, that the honest old tar could stand it no longer, and like most good-natured men when once fairly roused, he was swept through and through with a terrible typhoon of passion. He proposed, that forthwith the woman should be sacked and committed to the deep; he could stand it no longer.

Murder is catching. At first I almost jumped at the proposition; but as quickly rejected it. Ah! Annatoo: Woman unendurable: deliver me, ye gods, from being shut up in a ship with such a hornet again.

But are we yet through with her? Not yet. Hitherto she had continued to perform the duties of the office assigned her since the commencement of the voyage: namely, those of the culinary department. From this she was now deposed. Her skewer was broken. My Viking solemnly averring, that he would eat nothing more of her concocting, for fear of being poisoned. For myself, I almost believed, that there was malice enough in the minx to give us our henbane broth.

But what said Samoa to all this? Passing over the matter of the cookery, will it be credited, that living right among us as he did, he was yet blind to the premeditated though unachieved peccadilloes of his spouse? Yet so it was. And thus blind was Belisarius himself, concerning the intrigues of Antonina.

Witness that noble dame's affair with the youth Theodosius; when her deluded lord charged upon the scandalmongers with the very horns she had bestowed upon him.

Upon one occasion, seized with a sudden desire to palliate Annatoo's thievings, Samoa proudly intimated, that the lady was the most virtuous of her sex.

But alas, poor Annatoo, why say more? And bethinking me of the hard fate that so soon overtook thee, I almost repent what has already and too faithfully been portrayed.

Chapter 36

The Parki gives up the Ghost

A LONG CALM in the boat, and now, God help us, another in the brigantine. It was airless and profound.

In that hot calm, we lay fixed and frozen in like Parry at the Pole. The sun played upon the glassy sea like the sun upon the glaciers.

At the end of two days we lifted up our eyes and beheld a low, creeping, hungry cloud expanding like an army, wing and wing, along the eastern horizon. Instantly Jarl bade me take heed.

Here be it said, that though for weeks and weeks reign over the equatorial latitudes of the Pacific, the mildest and sunniest of days; that nevertheless, when storms do come, they come in their strength: spending in a few, brief blasts their concentrated rage. They come like the Mamelukes: they charge, and away.

It wanted full an hour to sunset; but the sun was well nigh obscured. It seemed toiling among bleak Scythian steeps in the hazy background. Above the storm-cloud flitted ominous patches of scud, rapidly advancing and receding: Attila's skirmishers, thrown forward in the van of his Huns. Beneath, a fitful shadow slid along the surface. As we gazed, the cloud came nearer; accelerating its approach.

With all haste we proceeded to furl the sails, which, owing to the calm, had been hanging loose in the brails. And by help of a spare boom, used on the forecastle-deck as a sweep or great oar, we endeavored to cast the brig-antine's head toward the foe.

The storm seemed about to overtake us; but we felt no breeze. The noiseless cloud stole on; its advancing shadow lowering over a distinct and prominent milk-white crest upon the surface of the ocean. But now this line of surging foam came rolling down upon us like a white charge of cavalry: mad Hotspur and plumed Murat at its head; pouring right forward in a continuous frothy cascade, which curled over, and fell upon the glassy sea before it.

Still, no breath of air. But of a sudden, like a blow from a man's hand, and before our canvas could be secured, the stunned craft, giving one lurch to port, was stricken down on her beam-ends; the roaring tide dashed high up against her windward side, and drops of brine fell upon the deck, heavy as drops of gore.

It was all a din and a mist; a crashing of spars and of ropes; a horrible blending of sights and of sounds; as for an instant we seemed in the hot heart of the gale; our cordage, like harp-strings, shrieking above the fury of the blast. The masts rose, and swayed, and dipped their trucks in the sea. And like unto some stricken buffalo brought low to the plain, the brigantine's black hull, shaggy with sea-weed, lay panting on its flank in the foam.

Frantically we clung to the uppermost bulwarks. And now, loud above the roar of the sea, was suddenly heard a sharp, splintering sound, as of a Norway woodman felling a pine in the forest. It was brave Jarl, who fore-most of all had snatched from its rack against the mainmast, the ax, always there kept.

"Cut the lanyards to windward!" he cried; and again buried his ax into the mast. He was quickly obeyed. And upon cutting the third lanyard of the five, he shouted for us to pause. Dropping his ax, he climbed up to windward. As he clutched the rail, the wounded mast snapped in twain with a report like a cannon. A slight smoke was perceptible where it broke. The remaining lanyards parted. From the violent strain upon them, the two shrouds flew madly into the air, and one of the great blocks at their ends, striking Annatoo upon the forehead, she let go her hold upon a stan-chion, and sliding across the aslant deck, was swallowed up in the whirlpool under our lea. Samoa shrieked. But there was no time to mourn; no hand could reach to save.

By the connecting stays, the mainmast carried over with it the foremast; when we instantly righted, and for the time were saved; my own royal Viking our saviour.

The first fury of the gale was gone. But far to leeward was seen the even, white line of its onset, pawing the ocean into foam. All round us, the sea boiled like ten thousand caldrons; and through eddy, wave, and surge, our almost water-logged craft waded heavily; every dead dash ringing hollow against her hull, like blows upon a coffin.

We floated a wreck. With every pitch we lifted our dangling jib-boom into the air; and beating against the side, were the shattered fragments of the masts. From these we made all haste to be free, by cutting the rigging that held them.

Soon, the worst of the gale was blown over. But the sea ran high. Yet the rack and scud of the tempest, its mad, tearing foam, was subdued into immense, long-extended, and long-rolling billows; the white cream on their crests like snow on the Andes. Ever and anon we hung poised on their brows; when the furrowed ocean all round looked like a panorama from Chimborazo.

A few hours more, and the surges went down. There was a moderate sea, a steady breeze, and a clear, starry sky.

Such was the storm that came after our calm.

Chapter 37

Once more they take to the Chamois

T RY THE PUMPS. We dropped the sinker, and found the Parki bleeding at every pore. Up from her well, the water, spring-like, came bubbling, pure and limpid as the water of Saratoga. Her time had come. But by keeping two hands at the pumps, we had no doubt she would float till daylight; previous to which we liked not to abandon her.

The interval was employed in clanging at the pump-brakes, and preparing the Chamois for our reception. So soon as the sea permitted, we lowered it over the side; and letting it float under the stern, stowed it with water and provisions, together with various other things, including muskets and cutlasses.

Shortly after daylight, a violent jostling and thumping under foot showed that the water, gaining rapidly in the hold, spite of all pumping, had floated the lighter casks upward to the deck, against which they were striking.

Now, owing to the number of empty butts in the hold, there would have been, perhaps, but small danger of the vessel's sinking outright—all awash as her decks would soon be—were it not, that many of her timbers were of a native wood, which, like the Teak of India, is specifically heavier than water. This, with the pearl shells on board, counteracted the buoyancy of the casks.

At last, the sun—long waited for—arose; the Parki meantime sinking lower and lower.

All things being in readiness, we proceeded to embark from the wreck, as from a wharf.

But not without some show of love for our poor brigantine.

To a seaman, a ship is no piece of mechanism merely; but a creature of thoughts and fancies, instinct with life. Standing at her vibrating helm, you feel her beating pulse. I have loved ships, as I have loved men.

To abandon the poor Parki was like leaving to its fate something that could feel. It was meet that she should die decently and bravely.

All this thought the Skyeman. Samoa and I were in the boat, calling upon him to enter quickly, lest the vessel should sink, and carry us down in the eddies; for already she had gone round twice. But cutting adrift the last fragments of her broken shrouds, and putting her decks in order, Jarl buried his ax in the splintered stump of the mainmast, and not till then did he join us.

We slowly cheered, and sailed away.

Not ten minutes after, the hull rolled convulsively in the sea; went round once more; lifted its sharp prow as a man with arms pointed for a dive; gave a long seething plunge; and went down.

Many of her old planks were twice wrecked; once strown upon ocean's beach; now dropped into its lowermost vaults, with the bones of drowned ships and drowned men.

Once more afloat in our shell! But not with the intrepid spirit that shoved off with us from the deck of the Arcturion. A bold deed done from impulse, for the time carries few or no misgivings along with it. But forced upon you, its terrors stare you in the face. So now. I had pushed from the Arcturion with a stout heart; but quitting the sinking Parki, my heart sunk with her.

With a fair wind, we held on our way westward, hoping to see land before many days.

Chapter 38

The Sea on Fire

THE NIGHT following our abandonment of the Parki, was made memorable by a remarkable spectacle.

Slumbering in the bottom of the boat, Jarl and I were suddenly awakened by Samoa. Starting, we beheld the ocean of a pallid white color, corruscating all over with tiny golden sparkles. But the pervading hue of the water cast a cadaverous gleam upon the boat, so that we looked to each other like ghosts. For many rods astern our wake was revealed in a line of rushing illuminated foam; while here and there beneath the surface, the tracks of sharks were denoted by vivid, greenish trails, crossing and re-crossing each other in every direction. Farther away, and distributed in clusters, floated on the sea, like constellations in the heavens, innumerable Medusæ, a species of small, round, refulgent fish, only to be met with in the South Seas and the Indian Ocean.

Suddenly, as we gazed, there shot high into the air a bushy jet of flashes, accompanied by the unmistakable deep breathing sound of a sperm whale. Soon, the sea all round us spouted in fountains of fire; and vast forms, emitting a glare from their flanks, and ever and anon raising their heads above water, and shaking off the sparkles, showed where an immense shoal of Cachalots had risen from below to sport in these phosphorescent billows.

The vapor jetted forth was far more radiant than any portion of the sea; ascribable perhaps to the originally luminous fluid contracting still more brilliancy from its passage through the spouting canal of the whales.

We were in great fear, lest without any vicious intention the Leviathans might destroy us, by coming into close contact with our boat. We would have shunned them; but they were all round and round us. Nevertheless we were safe; for as we parted the pallid brine, the peculiar irradiation which shot from about our keel seemed to deter them. Apparently discovering us of a sudden, many of them plunged headlong down into the water, tossing their fiery tails high into the air, and leaving the sea still more sparkling from the violent surging of their descent.

Their general course seemed the same as our own; to the westward. To remove from them, we at last out oars, and pulled toward the north. So doing, we were steadily pursued by a solitary whale, that must have taken our Chamois for a kindred fish. Spite of all our efforts, he drew nearer and nearer; at length rubbing his fiery flank against the Chamois' gunwale, here and there leaving long strips of the glossy transparent substance which thin as gossamer invests the body of the Cachalot.

In terror at a sight so new, Samoa shrank. But Jarl and I, more used to the intimate companionship of the whales, pushed the boat away from it with our oars: a thing often done in the fishery.

The close vicinity of the whale revived in the so long astute Skyeman all the enthusiasm of his daring vocation. However quiet by nature, a thorough-bred whaleman betrays no little excitement in sight of his game. And it required some persuasion to prevent Jarl from darting his harpoon: insanity under present circumstances; and of course without object. But "Oh! for a dart," cried my Viking. And "Where's now our old ship?" he added reminiscently.

But to my great joy the monster at last departed; rejoining the shoal, whose lofty spoutings of flame were still visible upon the distant line of the horizon; showing there, like the fitful starts of the Aurora Borealis.

The sea retained its luminosity for about three hours; at the expiration of half that period beginning to fade; and excepting occasional faint illuminations consequent upon the rapid darting of fish under water, the phenomenon at last wholly disappeared.

Heretofore, I had beheld several exhibitions of marine phosphorescence, both in the Atlantic and Pacific. But nothing in comparison with what was seen that night. In the Atlantic, there is very seldom any portion of the ocean luminous, except the crests of the waves; and these mostly appear so during wet, murky weather. Whereas, in the Pacific, all instances of the sort, previously coming under my notice, had been marked by patches of greenish light, unattended with any pallidness of sea. Save twice on the coast of Peru, where I was summoned from my hammock to the alarming midnight cry of "All hands ahoy! tack ship!" And rushing on deck, beheld the sea white as a shroud; for which reason it was feared we were on soundings.

Now, sailors love marvels, and love to repeat them. And from many an old shipmate I have heard various sage opinings, concerning the phenomenon in question. Dismissing, as destitute of sound philosophic probability, the extravagant notion of one of my nautical friends—no less a philosopher than my Viking himself—namely: that the phosphorescence of the sea is caused by a commotion among the mermaids, whose golden locks, all torn and disheveled, do irradiate the waters at such times; I proceed to record more reliable theories.

Faraday might, perhaps, impute the phenomenon to a peculiarly electrical condition of the atmosphere; and to that solely. But herein, my scientific friend would be stoutly contradicted by many intelligent seamen, who, in part, impute it to the presence of large quantities of putrescent animal matter, with which the sea is well known to abound.

And it would seem not unreasonable to suppose, that it is by this means that the fluid itself becomes charged with the luminous principle. Draw a bucket of water from the phosphorescent ocean, and it still retains traces of fire; but, standing awhile, this soon subsides. Now pour it along the deck, and it is a stream of flame; caused by its renewed agitation. Empty the bucket, and for a space sparkles cling to it tenaciously; and every stave seems ignited.

But after all, this seeming ignition of the sea can not be wholly produced by dead matter therein. There are many living fish, phosphorescent; and, under certain conditions, by a rapid throwing off of luminous particles must largely contribute to the result. Not to particularize this circumstance as true of divers species of sharks, cuttle-fish, and many others of the larger varieties of the finny tribes; the myriads of microscopic mollusca, well known to swarm off soundings, might alone be deemed almost sufficient to kindle a fire in the brine.

But these are only surmises; likely, but uncertain.

After science comes sentiment.

A French naturalist maintains, that the nocturnal radiance of the fire-fly is purposely intended as an attraction to the opposite sex; that the artful insect illuminates its body for a beacon to love. Thus: perched upon the

edge of a leaf, and waiting the approach of her Leander, who comes buffet-
ing with his wings the aroma of the flowers, some insect Hero may show
a torch to her gossamer gallant.

But alas, thrice alas, for the poor little fire-fish of the sea, whose radiance
but reveals them to their foes, and lights the way to their destruction.

Chapter 39

They fall in with Strangers

AFTER QUITTING the Parki, we had much calm weather, varied by light breezes. And sailing smoothly over a sea, so recently one sheet of foam, I could not avoid bethinking me, how fortunate it was, that the gale had overtaken us in the brigantine, and not in the Chamois. For deservedly high as the whale-shallop ranks as a sea boat; still, in a severe storm, the larger your craft the greater your sense of security. Wherefore, the thousand reckless souls tenanting a line-of-battle ship scoff at the most awful hurricanes; though, in reality, they may be less safe in their wooden-walled Troy, than those who contend with the gale in a clipper.

But not only did I congratulate myself upon salvation from the past, but upon the prospect for the future. For storms happening so seldom in these seas, one just blown over is almost a sure guarantee of very many weeks' calm weather to come.

Now sun followed sun; and no land. And at length it almost seemed as if we must have sailed past the remotest presumable westerly limit of the chain of islands we sought; a lurking suspicion which I sedulously kept to myself. However, I could not but nourish a latent faith that all would yet be well.

On the ninth day my forebodings were over. In the gray of the dawn, perched upon the peak of our sail, a noddy was seen fast asleep. This freak was true to the nature of that curious fowl, whose name is significant of its drowsiness. Its plumage was snow-white, its bill and legs blood-red; the latter looking like little pantalettes. In a sly attempt at catching the bird, Samoa captured three tail-feathers; the alarmed creature flying away with a scream, and leaving its quills in his hand.

Sailing on, we gradually broke in upon immense low-sailing flights of other aquatic fowls, mostly of those species which are seldom found far from land: terns, frigate-birds, mollymeaux, reef-pigeons, boobies, gulls, and the like. They darkened the air; their wings making overhead an incessant rustling like the simultaneous turning over of ten thousand leaves. The smaller sort skimmed the sea like pebbles sent skipping from the shore. Over these, flew myriads of birds of broader wing. While high above all, soared in air the daring "Diver," or sea-kite, the power of whose vision is truly wonderful. It perceives the little flying-fish in the water, at a height which can not be less than four hundred feet. Spirally wheeling and screaming as it goes, the sea-kite, bill foremost, darts downward, swoops into the water, and for a moment altogether disappearing, emerges at last; its prey firmly trussed in its claws. But bearing it aloft, the bold bandit is quickly assailed by other birds of prey, that strive to wrest from him his booty. And snatched from his talons, you see the fish falling through the air, till again caught up in the very act of descent, by the fleetest of its pursuers.

Leaving these sights astern, we presently picked up the slimy husk of a cocoanut, all over green barnacles. And shortly after, passed two or three limbs of trees, and the solitary trunk of a palm; which, upon sailing nearer, seemed but very recently started on its endless voyage. As noon came on, the dark purple land-haze, which had been dimly descried resting upon the western horizon, was very nearly obscured. Nevertheless, behind that dim drapery we doubted not bright boughs were waving.

We were now in high spirits. Samoa between times humming to himself some heathenish ditty, and Jarl ten times more intent on his silence than ever; yet his eye full of expectation and gazing broad off from our bow. Of a sudden, shading his face with his hand, he gazed fixedly for an instant, and then springing to his feet, uttered the long-drawn sound—"Sail ho!"

Just tipping the furthest edge of the sky was a little speck, dancing into view every time we rose upon the swells. It looked like one of many birds; for half intercepting our view, fell showers of plumage: a flight of milk-white noddies flying downward to the sea.

But soon the birds are seen no more. Yet there remains the speck; plainly a sail; but too small for a ship. Was it a boat after a whale? The vessel to which it belonged far astern, and shrouded by the haze? So it seemed.

Quietly, however, we waited the stranger's nearer approach; confident, that for some time he would not be able to perceive us, owing to our being in what mariners denominate the "sun-glade," or that part of the ocean upon which the sun's rays flash with peculiar intensity.

As the sail drew nigh, its failing to glisten white led us to doubt whether it was indeed a whale-boat. Presently, it showed yellow; and Samoa declared, that it must be the sail of some island craft. True. The stranger proving a large double-canoe, like those used by the Polynesians in making passages between distant islands.

The Upoluan was now clamorous for a meeting, to which Jarl was averse. Deliberating a moment, I directed the muskets to be loaded; then setting the sail—the wind on our quarter—we headed away for the canoe, now sailing at right angles with our previous course.

Here it must be mentioned, that from the various gay cloths and other things provided for barter by the captain of the Parki, I had very strikingly improved my costume; making it free, flowing, and eastern. I looked like an Emir. Nor had my Viking neglected to follow my example; though with some few modifications of his own. With his long tangled hair and harpoon, he looked like the sea-god, that boards ships, for the first time crossing the Equator. For tatooed Samoa, he yet sported both kilt and turban, reminding one of a tawny leopard, though his spots were all in one place. Besides this raiment of ours, against emergencies we had provided our boat with divers nankeens and silks.

But now into full view comes a yoke of huge clumsy prows, shaggy with carving, and driving through the water with considerable velocity; the immense sprawling sail holding the wind like a bag. She seemed full of men; and from the dissonant cries borne over to us, and the canoe's widely yawing, it was plain that we had occasioned no small sensation. They seemed undetermined what course to pursue: whether to court a meeting, or avoid it; whether to regard us as friends or foes.

As we came still nearer, distinctly beholding their faces, we loudly hailed them, inviting them to furl their sails, and allow us to board them. But no answer was returned; their confusion increasing. And now, within less than two ships'-lengths, they swept right across our bow, gazing at us with blended curiosity and fear.

Their craft was about thirty feet long, consisting of a pair of parallel canoes, very narrow, and at the distance of a yard or so, lengthwise, united by stout cross-timbers, lashed across the four gunwales. Upon these timbers was a raised platform or dais, quite dry; and astern an arched cabin or tent;

behind which, were two broad-bladed paddles terminating in rude shark-tails, by which the craft was steered.

The yard, spreading a yellow sail, was a crooked bough, supported obliquely in the crotch of a mast, to which the green bark was still clinging. Here and there were little tufts of moss. The high, beaked prow of that canoe in which the mast was placed, resembled a rude altar; and all round it was suspended a great variety of fruits, including scores of cocoanuts, unhusked. This prow was railed off, forming a sort of chancel within.

The foremost beam, crossing the gunwales, extended some twelve feet beyond the side of the dais; and at regular intervals hereupon, stout cords were fastened, which, leading up to the head of the mast, answered the purpose of shrouds. The breeze was now streaming fresh; and, as if to force down into the water the windward side of the craft, five men stood upon this long beam, grasping five shrouds. Yet they failed to counterbalance the pressure of the sail; and owing to the opposite inclination of the twin canoes, these living statues were elevated high above the water; their appearance rendered still more striking by their eager attitudes, and the apparent peril of their position, as the mad spray from the bow dashed over them. Suddenly, the Islanders threw their craft into the wind; while, for ourselves, we lay on our oars, fearful of alarming them by now coming nearer. But hailing them again, we said we were friends, and had friendly gifts for them, if they would peaceably permit us to approach. This understood, there ensued a mighty clamor; insomuch, that I bade Jarl and Samoa out oars, and row very gently toward the strangers. Whereupon, amid a storm of vociferations, some of them hurried to the furthest side of their dais; standing with arms arched over their heads, as if for a dive; others menacing us with clubs and spears; and one, an old man with a bamboo trellis on his head forming a sort of arbor for his hair, planted himself full before the tent, stretching behind him a wide plaited sling.

Upon this hostile display, Samoa dropped his oar, and brought his piece to bear upon the old man, who, by his attitude, seemed to menace us with the fate of the great braggart of Gath. But I quickly knocked down the muzzle of his musket, and forbade the slightest token of hostility; enjoining it upon my companions, nevertheless, to keep well on their guard.

We now ceased rowing, and after a few minutes' uproar in the canoe, they ran to the steering-paddles, and forcing round their craft before the wind, rapidly ran away from us. With all haste we set our sail, and pulling also at our oars, soon overtook them, determined upon coming into closer communion.

Chapter 40

Sire and Sons

SEEING FLIGHT WAS USELESS, the Islanders again stopped their canoe, and once more we cautiously drew nearer; myself crying out to them not to be fearful; and Samoa, with the odd humor of his race, averring that he had known every soul of them from his infancy.

We approached within two or three yards; when we paused, which somewhat allayed their alarm. Fastening a red China handkerchief to the blade of our long mid-ship oar, I waved it in the air. A lively clapping of hands, and many wild exclamations.

While yet waving the flag, I whispered to Jarl to give the boat a sheer toward the canoe, which being adroitly done, brought the bow, where I stood, still nearer to the Islanders. I then dropped the silk among them; and the Islander, who caught it, at once handed it to the warlike old man with the sling; who, on seating himself, spread it before him; while the rest crowding round, glanced rapidly from the wonderful gift, to the more wonderful donors.

This old man was the superior of the party. And Samoa asserted, that he must be a priest of the country to which the Islanders belonged; that the craft could be no other than one of their sacred canoes, bound on some priestly voyage. All this he inferred from the altar-like prow, and there being no women on board.

Bent upon conciliating the old priest, I dropped into the canoe another silk handkerchief; while Samoa loudly exclaimed, that we were only three men, and were peaceably inclined. Meantime, old Aaron, fastening the two silks crosswise over his shoulders, like a brace of Highland plaids, cross-legged sat, and eyed us.

It was a curious sight. The old priest, like a scroll of old parchment, covered all over with hieroglyphical devices, harder to interpret, I'll warrant, than any old Sanscrit manuscript. And upon his broad brow, deep-graven in wrinkles, were characters still more mysterious, which no Champollion nor gipsy could have deciphered. He looked old as the elderly hills; eyes sunken, though bright; and head white as the summit of Mont Blanc.

The rest were a youthful and comely set: their complexion that of Gold Sherry, and all tattooed after this pattern: two broad cross-stripes on the chest and back, reaching down to the waist, like a foot-soldier's harness. Their faces were full of expression; and their mouths were full of fine teeth; so that the parting of their lips, was as the opening of pearl oysters. Marked, here and there, after the style of Tahiti, with little round figures in blue, dotted in the middle with a spot of vermilion, their brawny brown thighs looked not unlike the gallant hams of Westphalia, spotted with the red dust of Cayenne.

But what a marvelous resemblance in the features of all. Were they born at one birth? This resemblance was heightened by their uniform marks. But it was subsequently ascertained, that they were the children of one sire; and that sire, old Aaron; who, no doubt, reposed upon his sons, as an old general upon the trophies of his youth.

They were the children of as many mothers; and he was training them up for the priesthood.

Chapter 41

A Fray

SO BENT were the strangers upon concealing who they were, and the object of their voyage, that it was some time ere we could obtain the information we desired.

They pointed toward the tent, as if it contained their Eleusinian mysteries. And the old priest gave us to know, that it would be profanation to enter it.

But all this only roused my curiosity to unravel the wonder.

At last I succeeded.

In that mysterious tent was concealed a beautiful maiden. And, in pursuance of a barbarous custom, by Aleema, the priest, she was being borne an offering from the island of Amma to the gods of Tedaidee.

Now, hearing of the maiden, I waited for no more. Need I add, how stirred was my soul toward this invisible victim; and how hotly I swore, that precious blood of hers should never smoke upon an altar. If we drowned for it, I was bent upon rescuing the captive. But as yet, no gentle signal of distress had been waved to us from the tent. Thence, no sound could be heard, but an occasional rustle of the matting. Was it possible, that one about to be immolated could proceed thus tranquilly to her fate?

But desperately as I resolved to accomplish the deliverance of the maiden, it was best to set heedfully about it. I desired no shedding of blood; though the odds were against us.

The old priest seemed determined to prevent us from boarding his craft. But being equally determined the other way, I cautiously laid the bow of the Chamois against the canoe's quarter, so as to present the smallest possible chance for a hostile entrance into our boat. Then, Samoa, knife in ear, and myself with a cutlass, stepped upon the dais, leaving Jarl in the boat's head, equipped with his harpoon; three loaded muskets lying by his side. He was strictly enjoined to resist the slightest demonstration toward our craft.

As we boarded the canoe, the Islanders slowly retreated; meantime earnestly conferring in whispers; all but the old priest, who, still seated, presented an undaunted though troubled front. To our surprise, he motioned us to sit down by him; which we did; taking care, however, not to cut off our communication with Jarl.

With the hope of inspiring good will, I now unfolded a roll of printed cotton, and spreading it before the priest, directed his attention to the pictorial embellishments thereon, representing some hundreds of sailor boys simultaneously ascending some hundreds of uniform sections of a ship's rigging. Glancing at them a moment, by a significant sign, he gave me to know, that long previous he himself had ascended the shrouds of a ship. Making this allusion, his countenance was overcast with a ferocious expression, as if something terrific was connected with the reminiscence. But it soon passed away, and somewhat abruptly he assumed an air of much merriment.

While we were thus sitting together, and my whole soul full of the thoughts of the captive, and how best to accomplish my purpose, and often gazing toward the tent; I all at once noticed a movement among the strangers. Almost in the same instant, Samoa, right across the face of Aleema, and in his ordinary tones, bade me take heed to myself, for mischief was brewing. Hardly was this warning uttered, when, with carved clubs in their hands, the Islanders completely surrounded us. Then up rose the old priest, and gave us to know, that we were wholly in his power, and if we did not swear to depart in our boat forthwith, and molest him no more, the peril be ours.

"Depart and you live; stay and you die."

Fifteen to three. Madness to gainsay his mandate. Yet a beautiful maiden was at stake.

The knife before dangling in Samoa's ear was now in his hand. Jarl cried out for us to regain the boat, several of the Islanders making a rush for it. No time to think. All passed quicker than it can be said. They closed in

upon us, to push us from the canoe. Rudely the old priest flung me from
his side, menacing me with his dagger, the sharp spine of a fish. A thrust
and a threat! Ere I knew it, my cutlass made a quick lunge. A curse from
the priest's mouth; red blood from his side; he tottered, stared about him,
and fell over like a brown hemlock into the sea. A yell of maledictions rose
on the air. A wild cry was heard from the tent. Making a dead breach
among the crowd, we now dashed side by side for the boat. Springing into
it, we found Jarl battling with two Islanders; while the rest were still howling upon the dais. Rage and grief had almost disabled them.

With one stroke of my cutlass, I now parted the line that held us to the
canoe, and with Samoa falling upon the two Islanders, by Jarl's help, we
quickly mastered them; forcing them down into the bottom of the boat.

The Skyeman and Samoa holding passive the captives, I quickly set our
sail, and snatching the sheet at the cavil, we rapidly shot from the canoe.
The strangers defying us with their spears; several couching them as if to
dart; while others held back their hands, as if to prevent them from jeop-
ardizing the lives of their countrymen in the Chamois.

Seemingly untoward events oftentimes lead to successful results. Far
from destroying all chance of rescuing the captive, our temporary flight,
indispensable for the safety of Jarl, only made the success of our enterprise
more probable. For having made prisoners two of the strangers, I determined to retain them as hostages, through whom to effect my plans without further bloodshed.

And here it must needs be related, that some of the natives were wounded
in the fray: while all three of their assailants had received several bruises.

Chapter 42

Remorse

DURING THE SKIRMISH not a single musket had been discharged. The first snatched by Jarl had missed fire, and ere he could seize another, it was close quarters with him, and no gestures to spare. His harpoon was his all. And truly, there is nothing like steel in a fray. It comes and it goes with a will, and is never a-weary. Your sword is your life, and that of your foe; to keep or to take as it happens. Closer home does it go than a rammer; and fighting with steel is a play without ever an interlude. There are points more deadly than bullets; and stocks packed full of subtle tubes, whence comes an impulse more reliable than powder.

Binding our prisoners lengthwise across the boat's seats, we rowed for the canoe, making signs of amity.

Now, if there be any thing fitted to make a high tide ebb in the veins, it is the sight of a vanquished foe, inferior to yourself in powers of destruction; but whom some necessity has forced you to subdue. All victories are not triumphs, nor all who conquer, heroes.

As we drew near the canoe, it was plain, that the loss of their sire had again for the instant overcome the survivors. Raising hands, they cursed us; and at intervals sent forth a low, piercing wail, peculiar to their race. As before, faint cries were heard from the tent. And all the while rose and fell on the sea, the ill-fated canoe.

As I gazed at this sight, what iron mace fell on my soul; what curse rang sharp in my ear! It was I, who was the author of the deed that caused the shrill wails that I heard. By this hand, the dead man had died. Remorse smote me hard; and like lightning I asked myself, whether the death-deed I had done was sprung of a virtuous motive, the rescuing a captive from thrall; or whether beneath that pretense, I had engaged in this fatal affray for some other, and selfish purpose; the companionship of a beautiful maid. But throttling the thought, I swore to be gay. Am I not rescuing the maiden? Let them go down who withstand me.

At the dismal spectacle before him, Jarl, hitherto menacing our prisoners with his weapon, in order to intimidate their countrymen, honest Jarl dropped his harpoon. But shaking his knife in the air, Samoa yet defied the strangers; nor could we prevent him. His heathenish blood was up.

Standing foremost in the boat, I now assured the strangers, that all we sought at their hands was the maiden in the tent. That captive surrendered, our own, unharmed, should be restored. If not, they must die. With a cry, they started to their feet, and brandished their clubs; but, seeing Jarl's harpoon quivering over the hearts of our prisoners, they quickly retreated; at last signifying their acquiescence in my demand. Upon this, I sprang to the dais, and across it indicating a line near the bow, signed the Islanders to retire beyond it. Then, calling upon them one by one to deliver their weapons, they were passed into the boat.

The Chamois was now brought round to the canoe's stern; and leaving Jarl to defend it as before, the Upoluan rejoined me on the dais. By these precautions—the hostages still remaining bound hand and foot in the boat—we deemed ourselves entirely secure.

Attended by Samoa, I stood before the tent, now still as the grave.

Chapter 43

The Tent entered

B Y MEANS OF THIN SPACES between the braids of matting, the place was open to the air, but not to view. There was also a round opening on one side, only large enough, however, to admit the arm; but this aperture was partially closed from within. In front, a deep-dyed rug of osiers, covering the entrance way, was intricately laced to the standing part of the tent. As I divided this lacing with my cutlass, there arose an outburst of voices from the Islanders. And they covered their faces, as the interior was revealed to my gaze.

Before me crouched a beautiful girl. Her hands were drooping. And, like a saint from a shrine, she looked sadly out from her long, fair hair. A low wail issued from her lips, and she trembled like a sound. There were tears on her cheek, and a rose-colored pearl on her bosom.

Did I dream?—A snow-white skin: blue, firmament eyes: Golconda locks. For an instant spell-bound I stood; while with a slow, apprehensive movement, and still gazing fixedly, the captive gathered more closely about her a gauze-like robe. Taking one step within, and partially dropping the curtain of the tent, I so stood, as to have both sight and speech of Samoa, who tarried without; while the maiden, crouching in the farther corner of the retreat, was wholly screened from all eyes but mine.

Crossing my hands before me, I now stood without speaking. For the soul of me, I could not link this mysterious creature with the tawny strangers. She seemed of another race. So powerful was this impression, that unconsciously, I addressed her in my own tongue. She started, and bending over, listened intently, as if to the first faint echo of something dimly remembered. Again I spoke, when throwing back her hair, the maiden looked up with a piercing, bewildered gaze. But her eyes soon fell, and bending over once more, she resumed her former attitude. At length she slowly chanted to herself several musical words, unlike those of the Islanders; but though I knew not what they meant, they vaguely seemed familiar.

Impatient to learn her story, I now questioned her in Polynesian. But with much earnestness, she signed me to address her as before. Soon perceiving, however, that without comprehending the meaning of the words I employed, she seemed merely touched by something pleasing in their sound, I once more addressed her in Polynesian; saying that I was all eagerness to hear her history.

After much hesitation she complied; starting with alarm at every sound from without; yet all the while deeply regarding me.

Broken as these disclosures were at the time, they are here presented in the form in which they were afterward more fully narrated.

So unearthly was the story, that at first I little comprehended it; and was almost persuaded that the luckless maiden was some beautiful maniac.

She declared herself more than mortal, a maiden from Oroolia, the Island of Delights, somewhere in the paradisiacal archipelago of the Polynesians. To this isle, while yet an infant, by some mystical power, she had been spirited from Amma, the place of her nativity. Her name was Yillah. And hardly had the waters of Oroolia washed white her olive skin, and tinged her hair with gold, when one day strolling in the woodlands, she was snared in the tendrils of a vine. Drawing her into its bowers, it gently transformed her into one of its blossoms, leaving her conscious soul folded up in the transparent petals.

Here hung Yillah in a trance, the world without all tinged with the rosy hue of her prison. At length when her spirit was about to burst forth in the opening flower, the blossom was snapped from its stem; and borne by a soft wind to the sea; where it fell into the opening valve of a shell; which in good time was cast upon the beach of the Island of Amma.

In a dream, these events were revealed to Aleema the priest; who by a spell unlocking its pearly casket, took forth the bud, which now showed signs of opening in the reviving air, and bore faint shadowy revealings, as of the dawn behind crimson clouds. Suddenly expanding, the blossom exhaled away in perfumes; floating a rosy mist in the air. Condensing at last, there emerged from this mist the same radiant young Yillah as before; her locks all moist, and a rose-colored pearl on her bosom. Enshrined as a goddess, the wonderful child now tarried in the sacred temple of Apo, buried in a dell; never beheld of mortal eyes save Aleema's.

Moon after moon passed away, and at last, only four days gone by, Aleema came to her with a dream; that the spirits in Oroolia had recalled her home by the way of Tedaidee, on whose coast gurgled up in the sea an enchanted spring; which streaming over upon the brine, flowed on between blue watery banks; and, plunging into a vortex, went round and round, descending into depths unknown. Into this whirlpool Yillah was to descend in a canoe, at last to well up in an inland fountain of Oroolia.

Chapter 44

Away!

THOUGH CLOTHED in language of my own, the maiden's story is in substance the same as she related. Yet were not these things narrated as past events; she merely recounted them as impressions of her childhood, and of her destiny yet unaccomplished. And mystical as the tale most assuredly was, my knowledge of the strange arts of the island priesthood, and the rapt fancies indulged in by many of their victims, deprived it in good part of the effect it otherwise would have produced.

For ulterior purposes connected with their sacerdotal supremacy, the priests of these climes oftentimes secrete mere infants in their temples; and jealously secluding them from all intercourse with the world, craftily delude them, as they grow up, into the wildest conceits.

Thus wrought upon, their pupils almost lose their humanity in the constant indulgence of seraphic imaginings. In many cases becoming inspired as oracles; and as such, they are sometimes resorted to by devotees; always screened from view, however, in the recesses of the temples. But in every instance, their end is certain. Beguiled with some fairy tale about revisiting the islands of Paradise, they are led to the secret sacrifice, and perish unknown to their kindred.

But, would that all this had been hidden from me at the time. For Yillah was lovely enough to be really divine; and so I might have been tranced into a belief of her mystical legends.

But with what passionate exultation did I find myself the deliverer of this beautiful maiden; who, thinking no harm, and rapt in a dream, was being borne to her fate on the coast of Tedaidee. Nor now, for a moment, did the death of Aleema her guardian seem to hang heavy upon my heart. I rejoiced that I had sent him to his gods; that in place of the sea moss growing over sweet Yillah drowned in the sea, the vile priest himself had sunk to the bottom.

But though he had sunk in the deep, his ghost sunk not in the deep waters of my soul. However in exultations its surface foamed up, at bottom guilt brooded. Sifted out, my motives to this enterprise justified not the mad deed, which, in a moment of rage, I had done: though, those motives had been covered with a gracious pretense; concealing myself from myself. But I beat down the thought.

In relating her story, the maiden frequently interrupted it with questions concerning myself:—Whence I came: being white, from Oroolia? Whither I was going: to Amma? And what had happened to Aleema? For she had been dismayed at the fray, though knowing not what it could mean; and she had heard the priest's name called upon in lamentations. These questions for the time I endeavored to evade; only inducing her to fancy me some gentle demi-god, that had come over the sea from her own fabulous Oroolia. And all this she must verily have believed. For whom, like me, ere this could she have beheld? Still fixed she her eyes upon me strangely, and hung upon the accents of my voice.

While this scene was passing, the strangers began to show signs of impatience, and a voice from the Chamois repeatedly hailed us to accelerate our movements.

My course was quickly decided. The only obstacle to be encountered was the possibility of Yillah's alarm at being suddenly borne into my prow. For this event I now sought to prepare her. I informed the damsel that Aleema had been dispatched on a long errand to Oroolia; leaving to my care, for the present, the guardianship of the lovely Yillah; and that therefore, it was necessary to carry her tent into my own canoe, then waiting to receive it.

This intelligence she received with the utmost concern; and not knowing to what her perplexity might lead, I thought fit to transport her into the Chamois, while yet overwhelmed by the announcement of my intention.

Quitting her retreat, I apprised Jarl of my design; and then, no more delay!

At bottom, the tent was attached to a light framework of bamboos;

and from its upper corners, four cords, like those of a marquee, confined it to the dais. These, Samoa's knife soon parted; when lifting the light tent, we speedily transferred it to the Chamois; a wild yell going up from the Islanders, which drowned the faint cries of the maiden. But we heeded not the din. Toss in the fruit, hanging from the altar-prow! It was done; and then running up our sail, we glided away;—Chamois, tent, hostages, and all. Rushing to the now vacant stern of their canoe, the Islanders once more lifted up their hands and their voices in curses.

A suitable distance gained, we paused to fling overboard the arms we had taken; and Jarl proceeded to liberate the hostages.

Meanwhile, I entered the tent, and by many tokens, sought to allay the maiden's alarm. Thus engaged, violent plunges were heard: our prisoners taking to the sea to regain their canoe. All dripping, they were received by their brethren with wild caresses.

From something now said by the captives, the rest seemed suddenly inspirited with hopes of revenge; again wildly shaking their spears, just before picked up from the sea. With great clamor and confusion they soon set their mat-sail; and instead of sailing southward for Tedaidee, or northward for Amma their home, they steered straight after us, in our wake.

Foremost in the prow stood three; javelins poised for a dart; at intervals, raising a yell.

Did they mean to pursue me? Full in my rear they came on, baying like hounds on their game. Yillah trembled at their cries. My own heart beat hard with undefinable dread. The corpse of Aleema seemed floating before: its avengers were raging behind.

But soon these phantoms departed. For very soon it appeared that in vain the pagans pursued. Their craft, our fleet Chamois outleaped. And farther and farther astern dropped the evil-boding canoe, till at last but a speck; when a great swell of the sea surged up before it, and it was seen no more. Samoa swore that it must have swamped, and gone down. But however it was, my heart lightened apace. I saw none but ourselves on the sea: I remembered that our keel left no track as it sailed.

Let the Oregon Indian through brush, bramble, and brier, hunt his enemy's trail, far over the mountains and down in the vales; comes he to the water, he snuffs idly in air.

Chapter 45

Reminiscences

IN RESCUING the gentle Yillah from the hands of the Islanders, a
design seemed accomplished. But what was now to be done? Here,
in our adventurous Chamois, was a damsel more lovely than the flushes
of morning; and for companions, whom had she but me and my comrades?
Besides, her bosom still throbbed with alarms, her fancies all roving through
mazes.

How subdue these dangerous imaginings? How gently dispel them?

But one way there was: to lead her thoughts toward me, as her friend
and preserver; and a better and wiser than Aleema the priest. Yet could not
this be effected but by still maintaining my assumption of a divine origin
in the blessed isle of Oroolia; and thus fostering in her heart the mysterious
interest, with which from the first she had regarded me. But if punctilious
reserve on the part of her deliverer should teach her to regard him as some
frigid stranger from the Arctic Zone, what sympathy could she have for
him? and hence, what peace of mind, having no one else to cling to?

Now re-entering the tent, she again inquired where tarried Aleema.

"Think not of him, sweet Yillah," I cried. "Look on me. Am I not white
like yourself? Behold, though since quitting Oroolia the sun has dyed my
cheek, am I not even as you? Am I brown like the dusky Aleema? They
snatched you away from your isle in the sea, too early for you to remember

me there. But you have not been forgotten by me, sweetest Yillah. Ha! ha! shook we not the palm-trees together, and chased we not the rolling nuts down the glen? Did we not dive into the grotto on the sea-shore, and come up together in the cool cavern in the hill? In my home in Oroolia, dear Yillah, I have a lock of your hair, ere yet it was golden: a little dark tress like a ring. How your cheeks were then changing from olive to white. And when shall I forget the hour, that I came upon you sleeping among the flowers, with roses and lilies for cheeks. Still forgetful? Know you not my voice? Those little spirits in your eyes have seen me before. They mimic me now as they sport in their lakes. All the past a dim blank? Think of the time when we ran up and down in our arbor, where the green vines grew over the great ribs of the stranded whale. Oh Yillah, little Yillah, has it all come to this? am I forever forgotten? Yet over the wide watery world have I sought thee: from isle to isle, from sea to sea. And now we part not. Aleema is gone. My prow shall keep kissing the waves, till it kisses the beach at Oroolia. Yillah, look up."

Sunk the ghost of Aleema: Sweet Yillah was mine!

Chapter 46

The Chamois with a roving Commission

THROUGH THE ASSIDUITY of my Viking, ere nightfall our Chamois was again in good order. And with many subtle and sea-manlike splices the light tent was lashed in its place; the sail taken up by a reef.

My comrades now questioned me, as to my purposes; whether they had been modified by the events of the day. I replied that our destination was still the islands to the westward.

But from these we had steadily been drifting all the morning long; so that now no loom of the land was visible. But our prow was kept pointing as before.

As evening came on, my comrades fell fast asleep, leaving me at the helm.

How soft and how dreamy the light of the hour. The rays of the sun, setting behind golden-barred clouds, came to me like the gleaming of a shaded light behind a lattice. And the low breeze, pervaded with the pecul-iar balm of the mid-Pacific near land, was fragrant as the breath of a bride.

Such was the scene; so still and witching that the hand of Yillah in mine seemed no hand, but a touch. Visions flitted before me and in me; something hummed in my ear; all the air was a lay.

And now entered a thought into my heart. I reflected how serenely we might thus glide along, far removed from all care and anxiety. And then, what different scenes might await us upon any of the shores roundabout. But there seemed no danger in the balmy sea; the assured vicinity of land imparting a sense of security. We had ample supplies for several days more, and thanks to the Pagan canoe, an abundance of fruit.

Besides, what cared I now for the green groves and bright shore? Was not Yillah my shore and my grove? my meadow, my mead, my soft shady vine, and my arbor? Of all things desirable and delightful, the full-plumed sheaf, and my own right arm the band? Enough: no shore for me yet. One sweep of the helm, and our light prow headed round toward the vague land of song, sun, and vine: the fabled South.

As we glided along, strange Yillah gazed down in the sea, and would fain have had me plunge into it with her, to rove through its depths. But I started dismayed; in fancy, I saw the stark body of the priest drifting by. Again that phantom obtruded; again guilt laid his red hand on my soul. But I laughed. Was not Yillah my own? by my arm rescued from ill? To do her a good, I had periled myself. So down, down, Aleema.

When next morning, starting from slumber, my comrades beheld the sun on our beam, instead of astern as before at that hour, they eagerly inquired, "Whither now?" But very briefly I gave them to know, that after devoting the night to the due consideration of a matter so important, I had determined upon voyaging for the island Tedaidee, in place of the land to the westward.

At this, they were not displeased. But to tell the plain truth, I harbored some shadowy purpose of merely hovering about for a while, till I felt more landwardly inclined.

But had I not declared to Yillah, that our destination was the fairy isle she spoke of, even Oroolia? Yet that shore was so exceedingly remote, and the folly of endeavoring to reach it in a craft built with hands, so very apparent, that what wonder I really nourished no thought of it?

So away floated the Chamois, like a vagrant cloud in the heavens: bound, no one knew whither.

Chapter 47

Yillah, Jarl, and Samoa

BUT TIME TO TELL, how Samoa and Jarl regarded this mystical Yillah; and how Yillah regarded them.

As Beauty from the Beast, so at first shrank the damsel from my one-armed companion. But seeing my confidence in the savage, a reaction soon followed. And in accordance with that curious law, by which, under certain conditions, the ugliest mortals become only amiably hideous, Yillah at length came to look upon Samoa as a sort of harmless and good-natured goblin. Whence came he, she cared not; or what was his history; or in what manner his fortunes were united to mine.

May be, she held him a being of spontaneous origin.

Now, as every where women are the tamers of the menageries of men; so Yillah in good time tamed down Samoa to the relinquishment of that horrible thing in his ear, and persuaded him to substitute a vacancy for the bauble in his nose. On his part, however, all this was conditional. He stipulated for the privilege of restoring both trinkets upon suitable occasions.

But if thus gayly the damsel sported with Samoa; how different his emotions toward her? The fate to which she had been destined, and every nameless thing about her, appealed to all his native superstitions, which ascribed to beings of her complexion a more than terrestrial origin. When permitted to approach her, he looked timid and awkwardly strange; sug-

146

gesting the likeness of some clumsy satyr, drawing in his horns; slowly wagging his tail; crouching abashed before some radiant spirit.

And this reverence of his was most pleasing to me. Bravo! thought I; be a pagan forever. No more than myself; for, after a different fashion, Yillah was an idol to both.

But what of my Viking? Why, of good Jarl I grieve to say, that the old-fashioned interest he took in my affairs led him to look upon Yillah as a sort of intruder, an Ammonite syren, who might lead me astray. This would now and then provoke a philippic; but he would only turn toward my resentment his devotion; and then I was silent.

Unsophisticated as a wild flower in the germ, Yillah seemed incapable of perceiving the contrasted lights in which she was regarded by our companions. And like a true beauty seemed to cherish the presumption, that it was quite impossible for such a person as hers to prove otherwise than irresistible to all.

She betrayed much surprise at my Viking's appearance. But most of all was she struck by a characteristic device upon the arm of the wonderful mariner—our Saviour on the cross, in blue; with the crown of thorns, and three drops of blood in vermilion, falling one by one from each hand and foot.

Now, honest Jarl did vastly pride himself upon this ornament. It was the only piece of vanity about him. And like a lady keeping gloveless her hand to show off a fine Turquoise ring, he invariably wore that sleeve of his frock rolled up, the better to display the embellishment.

And round and round would Yillah turn Jarl's arm, till Jarl was fain to stand firm, for fear of revolving all over. How such untutored homage would have thrilled the heart of the ingenious artist!

Eventually, through the Upoluan, she made overtures to the Skyeman, concerning the possession of his picture in her own proper right. In her very simplicity, little heeding, that like a landscape in fresco, it could not be removed.

Chapter 48

Something under the Surface

NOT TO OMIT an occurrence of considerable interest, we must needs here present some account of a curious retinue of fish which overtook our Chamois, a day or two after parting with the canoe.

A violent creaming and frothing in our rear announced their approach. Soon we found ourselves the nucleus of an incredible multitude of finny creatures, mostly anonymous.

First, far in advance of our prow, swam the helmeted Silver-heads; side by side, in uniform ranks, like an army. Then came the Boneetas, with their flashing blue flanks. Then, like a third distinct regiment, wormed and twisted through the water like Archimedean screws, the quivering Wriggle-tails; followed in turn by the rank and file of the Trigger-fish—so called from their quaint dorsal fins being set in their backs with a comical curve, as if at half-cock. Far astern the rear was brought up by endless battalions of Yellow-backs, right martially vested in buff.

And slow sailing overhead were flights of birds; a wing in the air for every fin in the sea.

But let the sea-fowls fly on: turn we to the fish.

Their numbers were amazing; countless as the tears shed for perfidious lovers. Far abroad on both flanks, they swam in long lines, tier above tier; the water alive with their hosts. Locusts of the sea, peradventure, going to fall with a blight upon some green, mossy province of Neptune. And tame and fearless they were, as the first fish that swam in Euphrates; hardly evading the hand; insomuch that Samoa caught many without lure or line.

They formed a decorous escort; paddling along by our barnacled sides, as if they had been with us from the very beginning; neither scared by our craft's surging in the water; nor in the least sympathetic at losing a comrade by the hand of Samoa. They closed in their ranks and swam on.

How innocent, yet heartless they looked! Had a plank dropped out of our boat, we had sunk to the bottom; and belike, our cheerful retinue would have paid the last rites to our remains.

But still we kept company; as sociably as you please; Samoa helping himself when he listed, and Yillah clapping her hands as the radiant creatures, by a simultaneous turning round on their silvery bellies, caused the whole sea to glow like a burnished shield.

But what has befallen this poor little Boneeta astern, that he swims so toilingly on, with gills showing purple? What has he there, towing behind? It is tangled sea-kelp clinging to its fins. But the clogged thing strains to keep up with its fellows. Yet little they heed. Away they go; every fish for itself, and any fish for Samoa.

At last the poor Boneeta is seen no more. The myriad fins swim on; a lonely waste, where the lost one drops behind.

Strange fish! All the live-long day, they were there by our side; and at night still tarried and shone; more crystal and scaly in the pale moonbeams, than in the golden glare of the sun.

How prettily they swim; all silver life; darting hither and thither between their long ranks, and touching their noses, and scraping acquaintance. No mourning they wear for the Boneeta left far astern; nor for those so cruelly killed by Samoa. No, no; all is glee, fishy glee, and frolicking fun; light hearts and light fins; gay backs and gay spirits.—Swim away, swim away! my merry fins all. Let us roam the flood; let us follow this monster fish with the barnacled sides; this strange-looking fish, so high out of water; that goes without fins. What fish can it be? What rippling is that? Dost hear the great monster breathe? Why, 'tis sharp at both ends; a tail either way; nor eyes has it any, nor mouth. What a curious fish! what a comical fish! But more comical far, those creatures above, on its hollow back, clinging thereto like the snaky eels, that cling and slide on the back of the Sword fish, our terrible foe. But what curious eels these are! Do they deem themselves pretty as we? No, no; for sure, they behold our limber fins, our speckled and beautiful scales. Poor, powerless things! How they must wish they were

we, that roam the flood, and scour the seas with a wish. Swim away; merry
fins, swim away! Let him drop, that fellow that halts; make a lane; close
in, and fill up. Let him drown, if he can not keep pace. No laggards for us:—

> We fish, we fish, we merrily swim,
> We care not for friend nor for foe:
>   Our fins are stout,
>   Our tails are out,
> As through the seas we go.
>
> Fish, fish, we are fish with red gills;
>   Naught disturbs us, our blood is at zero:
> We are buoyant because of our bags,
>   Being many, each fish is a hero.
> We care not what is it, this life
>   That we follow, this phantom unknown:
> To swim, it's exceedingly pleasant,—
>   So swim away, making a foam.
> This strange looking thing by our side,
>   Not for safety, around it we flee:—
> Its shadow's so shady, that's all,—
>   We only swim under its lee.
> And as for the eels there above,
>   And as for the fowls in the air,
> We care not for them nor their ways,
>   As we cheerily glide afar!
>
> We fish, we fish, we merrily swim,
> We care not for friend nor for foe:
>   Our fins are stout,
>   Our tails are out,
> As through the seas we go.

But how now, my fine fish! what alarms your long ranks, and tosses
them all into a hubbub of scales and of foam? Never mind that long knave
with the spear there, astern. Pipe away, merry fish, and give us a stave or two
more, keeping time with your doggerel tails. But no, no! their singing was
over. Grim death, in the shape of a Chevalier, was after them.

How they changed their boastful tune! How they hugged the vilified
boat! How they wished they were in it, the braggarts! And how they all
tingled with fear!

For, now here, now there, is heard a terrific rushing sound under water, betokening the onslaught of the dread fish of prey, that with spear ever in rest, charges in upon the outskirts of the shoal, transfixing the fish on his weapon. Retreating and shaking them off, the Chevalier devours them; then returns to the charge.

Hugging the boat to desperation, the poor fish fairly crowded themselves up to the surface, and floundered upon each other, as men are lifted off their feet in a mob. They clung to us thus, out of a fancied security in our presence. Knowing this, we felt no little alarm for ourselves, dreading lest the Chevalier might despise our boat, full as much as his prey; and in pursuing the fish, run through the poor Chamois with a lunge. A jacket, rolled up, was kept in readiness to be thrust into the first opening made; while as the thousand fins audibly patted against our slender planks, we felt nervously enough; as if treading upon thin, crackling ice.

At length, to our no small delight, the enemy swam away; and again by our side merrily paddled our escort; ten times merrier than ever.

Chapter 49

Yillah

WHILE FOR A FEW DAYS, now this way, now that, as our craft glides along, surrounded by these locusts of the deep, let the story of Yillah flow on.

Of her beauty say I nothing. It was that of a crystal lake in a fathomless wood: all light and shade; full of fleeting revealings; now shadowed in depths; now sunny in dimples; but all sparkling and shifting, and blending together.

But her wild beauty was a vail to things still more strange. As often she gazed so earnestly into my eyes, like some pure spirit looking far down into my soul, and seeing therein some upturned faces, I started in amaze, and asked what spell was on me, that thus she gazed.

Often she entreated me to repeat over and over again certain syllables of my language. These she would chant to herself, pausing now and then, as if striving to discover wherein lay their charm.

In her accent, there was something very different from that of the people of the canoe. Wherein lay the difference, I knew not; but it enabled her to pronounce with readiness all the words which I taught her; even as if recalling sounds long forgotten.

If all this filled me with wonder, how much was that wonder increased, and yet baffled again, by considering her complexion, and the cast of her features.

After endeavoring in various ways to account for these things, I was led to imagine, that the damsel must be an Albino (Tulla) occasionally to be met with among the people of the Pacific. These persons are of an exceedingly delicate white skin, tinted with a faint rose hue, like the lips of a shell. Their hair is golden. But, unlike the Albinos of other climes, their eyes are invariably blue, and no way intolerant of light.

As a race, the Tullas die early. And hence the belief, that they pertain to some distant sphere, and only through irregularities in the providence of the gods, come to make their appearance upon earth: whence, the oversight discovered, they are hastily snatched. And it is chiefly on this account, that in those islands where human sacrifices are offered, the Tullas are deemed the most suitable oblations for the altar, to which from their birth many are prospectively devoted. It was these considerations, united to others, which at times induced me to fancy, that by the priest, Yillah was regarded as one of these beings. So mystical, however, her revelations concerning her past history, that often I knew not what to divine. But plainly they showed that she had not the remotest conception of her real origin.

But these conceits of a state of being anterior to an earthly existence may have originated in one of those celestial visions seen transparently stealing over the face of a slumbering child. And craftily drawn forth and re-echoed by another, and at times repeated over to her with many additions, these imaginings must at length have assumed in her mind a hue of reality, heightened into conviction by the dreamy seclusion of her life.

But now, let her subsequent and more credible history be related, as from time to time she rehearsed it.

Chapter 50

Yillah in Ardair

IN THE VERDANT GLEN of Ardair, far in the silent interior of Amma, shut in by hoar old cliffs, Yillah the maiden abode.

So small and so deep was this glen, so surrounded on all sides by steep acclivities, and so vividly green its verdure, and deceptive the shadows that played there; that, from above, it seemed more like a lake of cool, balmy air, than a glen: its woodlands and grasses gleaming shadowy all, like sea groves and mosses beneath the calm sea.

Here, none came but Aleema the priest, who at times was absent for days together. But at certain seasons, an unseen multitude with loud chants stood upon the verge of the neighboring precipices, and traversing those shaded wilds, slowly retreated; their voices lessening and lessening, as they wended their way through the more distant groves.

At other times, Yillah being immured in the temple of Apo, a band of men entering the vale, surrounded her retreat, dancing there till evening came. Meanwhile, heaps of fruit, garlands of flowers, and baskets of fish, were laid upon an altar without, where stood Aleema, arrayed in white tappa, and muttering to himself, as the offerings were laid at his feet.

When Aleema was gone, Yillah went forth into the glen, and wandered among the trees, and reposed by the banks of the stream. And ever as she strolled, looked down upon her the grim old cliffs, bearded with trailing moss.

Toward the lower end of the vale, its lofty walls advancing and over-hanging their base, almost met in mid air. And a great rock, hurled from an adjacent height, and falling into the space intercepted, there remained fixed. Aerial trees shot up from its surface; birds nested in its clefts; and strange vines roved abroad, overrunning the tops of the trees, lying thereon in coils and undulations, like anacondas basking in the light. Beneath this rock, was a lofty wall of ponderous stones. Between its crevices, peeps were had of a long and leafy arcade, quivering far away to where the sea rolled in the sun. Lower down, these crevices gave an outlet to the waters of the brook, which, in a long cascade, poured over sloping green ledges near the foot of the wall, into a deep shady pool; whose rocky sides, by the perpetual eddying of the water, had been worn into a grotesque resemblance to a group of giants, with heads submerged, indolently reclining about the basin.

In this pool, Yillah would bathe. And once, emerging, she heard the echoes of a voice, and called aloud. But the only reply, was the rustling of branches, as some one, invisible, fled down the valley beyond. Soon after, a stone rolled inward, and Aleema the priest stood before her; saying that the voice she had heard was his. But it was not.

At last the weary days grew longer and longer, and the maiden pined for companionship. When the breeze blew not, but slept in the caves of the mountains, and all the leaves of the trees stood motionless as tears in the eye, Yillah would sadden, and call upon the spirits in her soul to awaken. She sang low airs, she thought she had heard in Oroolia; but started affrighted, as from dingles and dells, came back to her strains more wild than hers. And ever, when sad, Aleema would seek to cheer her soul, by calling to mind the bright scenes of Oroolia the Blest, to which place, he averred, she was shortly to return, never more to depart.

Now, at the head of the vale of Ardair, rose a tall, dark peak, presenting at the top the grim profile of a human face; whose shadow, every afternoon, crept down the verdant side of the mountain: a silent phantom, stealing all over the bosom of the glen.

At times, when the phantom drew near, Aleema would take Yillah forth, and waiting its approach, lay her down by the shadow, disposing her arms in a caress; saying, "Oh, Apo! dost accept thy bride?" And at last, when it crept beyond the place where he stood, and buried the whole valley in gloom; Aleema would say, "Arise Yillah; Apo hath stretched himself to sleep in Ardair. Go, slumber where thou wilt; for thou wilt slumber in his arms."

And so, every night, slept the maiden in the arms of grim Apo.

One day when Yillah had come to love the wild shadow, as something that every day moved before her eyes, where all was so deathfully still; she went forth alone to watch it, as softly it slid down from the peak. Of a sudden, when its face was just edging a chasm, that made it to look as if parting its lips, she heard a loud voice, and thought it was Apo calling "Yillah! Yillah!" But now it seemed like the voice she had heard while bathing in the pool. Glancing upward, she beheld a beautiful open-armed youth, gazing down upon her from an inaccessible crag. But presently, there was a rustling in the groves behind, and swift as thought, something darted through the air. The youth bounded forward. Yillah opened her arms to receive him; but he fell upon the cliff, and was seen no more. As alarmed, and in tears, she fled from the scene, some one out of sight ran before her through the wood.

Upon recounting this adventure to Aleema, he said, that the being she had seen, must have been a bad spirit come to molest her; and that Apo had slain him.

The sight of this youth, filled Yillah with wild yearnings to escape from her lonely retreat; for a glimpse of some one beside the priest and the phantom, suggested vague thoughts of worlds of fair beings, in regions beyond Ardair. But Aleema sought to put away these conceits; saying, that ere long she would be journeying to Oroolia, there to rejoin the spirits she dimly remembered.

Soon after, he came to her with a shell—one of those ever moaning of ocean—and placing it to her ear, bade her list to the being within, which in that little shell had voyaged from Oroolia to bear her company in Amma.

Now, the maiden oft held it to her ear, and closing her eyes, listened and listened to its soft inner breathings, till visions were born of the sound, and her soul lay for hours in a trance of delight.

And again the priest came, and brought her a milk-white bird, with a bill jet-black, and eyes like stars. "In this, lurks the soul of a maiden; it hath flown from Oroolia to greet you." The soft stranger willingly nestled in her bosom; turning its bright eyes upon hers, and softly warbling.

Many days passed; and Yillah, the bird, and the shell were inseparable. The bird grew familiar; pecked seeds from her mouth; perched upon her shoulder, and sang in her ear; and at night, folded its wings in her bosom, and, like a sea-fowl, went softly to sleep: rising and falling upon the maiden's heart. And every morning it flew from its nest, and fluttered and chirped; and sailed to and fro; and blithely sang; and brushed Yillah's cheek till she woke. Then came to her hand: and Yillah, looking earnestly in its eyes, saw strange faces there; and said to herself as she gazed—"These are two souls, not one."

But at last, going forth into the groves with the bird, it suddenly flew from her side, and perched in a bough; and throwing back its white downy throat, there gushed from its bill a clear warbling jet, like a little fountain in air. Now the song ceased; when up and away toward the head of the vale, flew the bird. "Lil! Lil! come back, leave me not, blest souls of the maidens." But on flew the bird, far up a defile, winging its way till a speck.

It was shortly after this, and upon the evening of a day which had been tumultuous with sounds of warfare beyond the lower wall of the glen; that Aleema came to Yillah in alarm; saying—"Yillah, the time has come to follow thy bird; come, return to thy home in Oroolia." And he told her the way she would voyage there: by the vortex on the coast of Tedaidee. That night, being veiled and placed in the tent, the maiden was borne to the sea-side, where the canoe was in waiting. And setting sail quickly, by next morning the island of Amma was no longer in sight.

And this was the voyage, whose sequel has already been recounted.

Chapter 51

The Dream begins to fade

STRIPPED OF THE STRANGE ASSOCIATIONS, with which a mind like Yillah's must have invested every incident of her life, the story of her abode in Ardair seemed not incredible.

But so etherealized had she become from the wild conceits she nourished, that she verily believed herself a being of the lands of dreams. Her fabulous past was her present.

Yet as our intimacy grew closer and closer, these fancies seemed to be losing their hold. And often she questioned me concerning my own reminiscences of her shadowy isle. And cautiously I sought to produce the impression, that whatever I had said of that clime, had been revealed to me in dreams; but that in these dreams, her own lineaments had smiled upon me; and hence the impulse which had sent me roving after the substance of this spiritual image.

And true it was to say so; and right it was to swear it, upon her white arms crossed. For oh, Yillah; were you not the earthly semblance of that sweet vision, that haunted my earliest thoughts?

At first she had wildly believed, that the nameless affinities between us, were owing to our having in times gone by dwelt together in the same ethereal region. But thoughts like these were fast dying out. Yet not without many strange scrutinies. More intently than ever she gazed into my eyes; rested her ear against my heart, and listened to its beatings. And love, which in the eye of its object ever seeks to invest itself with some rare superiority, love, sometimes induced me to prop my failing divinity; though it was I myself who had undermined it.

But if it was with many regrets, that in the sight of Yillah, I perceived myself thus dwarfing down to a mortal; it was with quite contrary emotions, that I contemplated the extinguishment in her heart of the notion of her own spirituality. For as such thoughts were chased away, she clung the more closely to me, as unto one without whom she would be desolate indeed.

And now, at intervals, she was sad, and often gazed long and fixedly into the sea. Nor would she say why it was, that she did so; until at length she yielded; and replied, that whatever false things Aleema might have instilled into her mind; of this much she was certain: that the whirlpool on the coast of Tedaidee prefigured her fate; that in the waters she saw lustrous eyes, and beckoning phantoms, and strange shapes smoothing her a couch among the mosses.

Her dreams seemed mine. Many visions I had of the green corse of the priest, outstretching its arms in the water, to receive pale Yillah, as she sunk in the sea.

But these forebodings departed, no happiness in the universe like ours. We lived and we loved; life and love were united; in gladness glided our days.

Chapter 52

World ho!

F IVE SUNS ROSE AND SET. And Yillah pining for the shore, we
turned our prow due west, and next morning came in sight of land.
It was innumerable islands; lifting themselves bluely through the
azure air, and looking upon the distant sea, like haycocks in a hazy field.
Towering above all, and midmost, rose a mighty peak; one fleecy cloud
sloping against its summit; a column wreathed. Beyond, like purple steeps
in heaven at set of sun, stretched far away, what seemed lands on lands, in
infinite perspective.

Gliding on, the islands grew more distinct; rising up from the billows
to greet us; revealing hills, vales, and peaks, grouped within a milk-white
zone of reef, so vast, that in the distance all was dim. The jeweled vapors, erewhile hovering over these violet shores, now seemed to be shedding their
gems; and as the almost level rays of the sun, shooting through the air like
a variegated prism, touched the verdant land, it trembled all over with
dewy sparkles.

Still nearer we came: our sail faintly distended as the breeze died away
from our vicinity to the isles. The billows rolled listlessly by, as if conscious
that their long task was nigh done; while gleamed the white reef, like the
trail of a great fish in a calm. But as yet, no sign of paddle or canoe; no
distant smoke; no shining thatch. Bravo! good comrades, we've discovered
some new constellation in the sea.

Sweet Yillah, no more of Oroolia; see you not this flowery land? Nevermore shall we desire to roam.

Voyaging along the zone, we came to an opening; and quitting the firmament blue of the open sea, we glided in upon the still, green waters of the wide lagoon. Mapped out in the broad shadows of the isles, and tinted here and there with the reflected hues of the sun clouds, the mild waters stretched all around us like another sky. Near by the break in the reef, was a little island, with palm trees harping in the breeze; an aviary of alluring sounds, that seemed calling upon us to land. And here, Yillah, whom the sight of the verdure had made glad, threw out a merry suggestion. Nothing less, than to plant our mast, sail-set, upon the highest hill; and fly away, island and all; trees rocking, birds caroling, flowers springing; away, away, across the wide waters, to Oroolia! But alas! how weigh the isle's coral anchor, leagues down in the fathomless sea?

We glanced around; but all the islands seemed slumbering in the flooding light.

"A canoe! a canoe!" cried Samoa, as three proas showed themselves rounding a neighboring shore. Instantly we sailed for them; but after shooting to and fro for a time, and standing up and gazing at us, the Islanders retreated behind the headland. Hardly were they out of sight, when from many a shore roundabout, other proas pushed off. Soon the water all round us was enlivened by fleets of canoes, darting hither and thither like frighted water-fowls. Presently they all made for one island.

From their actions we argued that these people could have had but little or no intercourse with whites; and most probably knew not how to account for our appearance among them. Desirous, therefore, of a friendly meeting, ere any hostile suspicions might arise, we pointed our craft for the island, whither all the canoes were now hastening. Whereupon, those which had not yet reached their destination, turned and fled; while the occupants of the proas that had landed, ran into the groves, and were lost to view.

Crossing the distinct outer line of the isle's shadow on the water, we gained the shore; and gliding along its margin, passing canoe after canoe, hauled up on the silent beach, which otherwise seemed entirely innocent of man.

A dilemma. But I decided at last upon disembarking Jarl and Samoa, to seek out and conciliate the natives. So, landing them upon a jutting buttress of coral, whence they waded to the shore; I pushed off with Yillah into the water beyond, to await the event.

Full an hour must have elapsed; when, to our great joy, loud shouts were heard; and there burst into view a tumultuous crowd, in the midst of which my Viking was descried, mounted upon the shoulders of two brawny natives; while the Upoluan, striding on in advance, seemed resisting a similar attempt to elevate him in the world.

Good omens both.

"Come ashore!" cried Jarl. "Aramai!" cried Samoa; while storms of interjections went up from the Islanders, who with extravagant gestures danced about the beach.

Further caution seemed needless: I pointed our prow for the shore. No sooner was this perceived, than, raising an applauding shout, the Islanders ran up to their waists in the sea. And skimming like a gull over the smooth lagoon, the light shallop darted in among them. Quick as thought, fifty hands were on the gunwale: and, with all its contents, lifted bodily into the air, the little Chamois, upon many a dripping shoulder, was borne deep into the groves. Yillah shrieked at the rocking motion, and when the boughs of the trees brushed against the tent.

With his staff, an old man now pointed to a couple of twin-like trees, some four paces apart; and a little way from the ground conveniently crotched.

And here, eftsoons, they deposited their burden; lowering the Chamois gently between the forks of the trees, whose willow-like foliage fringed the tent and its inmate.

Chapter 53

The Chamois Ashore

UNTIL NOW, enveloped in her robe, and crouching like a fawn, Yillah had been well nigh hidden from view. But presently she withdrew her hood.

What saw the Islanders, that they so gazed and adored in silence: some retreating, some creeping nearer, and the women all in a flutter? Long they gazed; and following Samoa's example, stretched forth their arms in reverence.

The adoration of the maiden was extended to myself. Indeed, from the singular gestures employed, I had all along suspected, that we were being received with unwonted honors.

I now sought to get speech of my comrades. But so obstreperous was the crowd, that it was next to impossible. Jarl was still in his perch in the air; his enthusiastic bearers not yet suffering him to alight. Samoa, however, who had managed to keep out of the saddle, by-and-by contrived to draw nearer to the Chamois.

He advised me, by no means to descend for the present; since in any event we were sure of remaining unmolested therein; the Islanders regarding it as sacred.

The Upoluan attracted a great deal of attention; chiefly from his style of tattooing, which, together with other peculiarities, so interested the natives,

163

that they were perpetually hanging about him, putting eager questions, and all the time keeping up a violent clamor.

But despite the large demand upon his lungs, Samoa made out to inform me, that notwithstanding the multitude assembled, there was no high chief, or person of consequence present; the king of the place, also those of the islands adjacent, being absent at a festival in another quarter of the Archipelago. But upon the first distant glimpse of the Chamois, fleet canoes had been dispatched to announce the surprising event that had happened.

In good time, the crowd becoming less tumultuous, and abandoning the siege of Samoa, I availed myself of this welcome lull, and called upon him and my Viking to enter the Chamois; desirous of condensing our forces against all emergencies.

Samoa now gave me to understand, that from all he could learn, the Islanders regarded me as a superior being. They had inquired of him, whether I was not white Taji, a sort of half-and-half deity, now and then an Avatar among them, and ranking among their inferior ex-officio demi-gods. To this, Samoa had said ay; adding, moreover, all he could to encourage the idea.

He now entreated me, at the first opportunity, to announce myself as Taji: declaring that if once received under that title, the unbounded hospitality of our final reception would be certain; and our persons fenced about from all harm.

Encouraging this. But it was best to be wary. For although among some barbarians the first strangers landing upon their shores, are frequently hailed as divine; and in more than one wild land have been actually styled gods, as a familiar designation; yet this has not exempted the celestial visitants from peril, when too much presuming upon the reception extended to them. In sudden tumults they have been slain outright, and while full faith in their divinity had in no wise abated. The sad fate of an eminent navigator is a well-known illustration of this unaccountable waywardness.

With no small anxiety, therefore, we awaited the approach of some of the dignitaries of Mardi; for by this collective appellation, the people informed us, their islands were known.

We waited not long. Of a sudden, from the sea-side, a single shrill cry was heard. A moment more, and the blast of numerous conch shells startled the air; a confused clamor drew nearer and nearer; and fixing our eyes in the direction of these sounds, we impatiently awaited what was to follow.

Chapter 54

A Gentleman from the Sun

NEVER BEFORE had I seen the deep foliage of woodlands navigated by canoes. But on they came sailing through the leaves; two abreast; borne on men's shoulders; in each a chief, carried along to the measured march of his bearers; paddle-blades reversed under arms. As they emerged, the multitude made gestures of homage. At the distance of some eight or ten paces the procession halted; when the kings alighted to the ground.

They were fine-looking men, arrayed in various garbs. Rare the show of stained feathers, and jewels, and other adornments. Brave the floating of dyed mantles.

The regal bearing of these personages, the deference paid them, and their entire self-possession, not a little surprised me. And it seemed preposterous, to assume a divine dignity in the presence of these undoubted potentates of *terra firma*. Taji seemed oozing from my fingers' ends. But courage! and erecting my crest, I strove to look every inch the character I had determined to assume.

For a time, it was almost impossible to tell with what emotions precisely the chiefs were regarding me. They said not a word.

But plucking up heart of grace, I crossed my cutlass on my chest, and reposing my hand on the hilt, addressed their High Mightinesses thus. "Men of Mardi, I come from the sun. When this morning it rose and touched the wave, I pushed my shallop from its golden beach, and hither sailed before its level rays. I am Taji."

More would have been added, but I paused for the effect of my exordium.

Stepping back a pace or two, the chiefs eagerly conversed.

Emboldened, I returned to the charge, and labored hard to impress them with just such impressions of me and mine, as I deemed desirable. The gentle Yillah was a seraph from the sun; Samoa I had picked off a reef in my route from that orb; and as for the Skyeman, why, as his name imported, he came from above. In a word, we were all strolling divinities.

Advancing toward the Chamois, one of the kings, a calm old man, now addressed me as follows:—"Is this indeed Taji? he, who according to a tradition, was to return to us after five thousand moons? But that period is yet unexpired. What bring'st thou hither then, Taji, before thy time? Thou wast but a quarrelsome demi-god, say the legends, when thou dwelt among our sires. But wherefore comest thou, Taji? Truly, thou wilt interfere with the worship of thy images, and we have plenty of gods besides thee. But comest thou to fight?—We have plenty of spears, and desire not thine. Comest thou to dwell?—Small are the houses of Mardi. Or comest thou to fish in the sea? Tell us, Taji."

Now, all this was a series of posers hard to be answered; furnishing a curious example, moreover, of the reception given to strange demi-gods when they travel without their portmanteaus; and also of the familiar manner in which these kings address the immortals. Much I mourned that I had not previously studied better my part, and learned the precise nature of my previous existence in the land.

But nothing like carrying it bravely.

"Attend. Taji comes, old man, because it pleases him to come. And Taji will depart when it suits him. Ask the shades of your sires whether Taji thus scurvily greeted them, when they came stalking into his presence in the land of spirits. No. Taji spread the banquet. He removed their mantles. He kindled a fire to drive away the damp. He said not, 'Come you to fight, you fogs and vapors? come you to dwell? or come you to fish in the sea?' Go to, then, kings of Mardi!"

Upon this, the old king fell back; and his place was supplied by a noble chief, of a free, frank bearing. Advancing quickly toward the boat, he exclaimed—"I am Media, the son of Media. Thrice welcome, Taji. On my island of Odo hast thou an altar. I claim thee for my guest." He then reminded the rest, that the strangers had voyaged far, and needed repose. And, furthermore, that he proposed escorting them forthwith to his own dominions; where, next day, he would be happy to welcome all visitants.

And good as his word, he commanded his followers to range themselves under the Chamois. Springing out of our prow, the Upoluan was followed by Jarl; leaving Yillah and Taji to be borne therein toward the sea.

Soon, we were once more afloat; by our side, Media sociably seated; six of his paddlers, perched upon the gunwale, swiftly urging us over the lagoon.

The transition from the grove to the sea was instantaneous. All seemed a dream.

The place to which we were hastening, being some distance away, as we rounded isle after isle, the extent of the Archipelago grew upon us greatly.

Chapter 55

Tiffin in a Temple

UPON AT LAST drawing nigh to Odo, its appearance somewhat disappointed me. A small island, of moderate elevation.

But plumb not the height of the house that feasts you.

The beach was lined with expectant natives, who, lifting the Chamois, carried us up the beach.

Alighting, as they were bearing us along, King Media, designating a canoe-house hard by, ordered our craft to be deposited therein. This being done, we stepped upon the soil. It was the first we had pressed in very many days. It sent a sympathetic thrill through our frames.

Turning his steps inland, Media signed us to follow.

Soon we came to a rude sort of inclosure, fenced in by an imposing wall. Here a halt was sounded, and in great haste the natives proceeded to throw down a portion of the stones. This accomplished, we were signed to enter the fortress thus carried by storm. Upon an artificial mound, opposite the breach, stood a small structure of bamboo, open in front. Within, was a long pedestal, like a settee, supporting three images, also of wood, and about the size of men; bearing, likewise, a remote resemblance to that species of animated nature. Before these idols was an altar, and at its base many fine mats.

Entering the temple, as if he felt very much at home, Media disposed these mats so as to form a very pleasant lounge; where he deferentially entreated Yillah to recline. Then deliberately removing the first idol, he motioned me to seat myself in its place. Setting aside the middle one, he quietly established himself in its stead. The displaced ciphers, meanwhile, standing upright before us, and their blank faces looking upon this occasion unusually expressive. As yet, not a syllable as to the meaning of this cavalier treatment of their wooden godships.

We now tranquilly awaited what next might happen, and I earnestly prayed, that if sacrilege was being committed, the vengeance of the gods might be averted from an ignoramus like me; notwithstanding the petitioner himself hailed from the other world. Perfect silence was preserved: Jarl and Samoa standing a little without the temple; the first looking quite composed, but his comrade casting wondering glances at my sociable apotheosis with Media.

Now happening to glance upon the image last removed, I was not long in detecting a certain resemblance between it and our host. Both were decorated in the same manner; the carving on the idol exactly corresponding with the tattooing of the king.

Presently, the silence was relieved by a commotion without: and a butler approached, staggering under an immense wooden trencher; which, with profound genuflexions, he deposited upon the altar before us. The tray was loaded like any harvest wain; heaped up with good things sundry and divers: Bread-fruit, and cocoanuts, and plantains, and guavas; all pleasant to the eye, and furnishing good earnest of something equally pleasant to the palate.

Transported at the sight of these viands, after so long an estrangement from full indulgence in things green, I was forthwith proceeding to help Yillah and myself, when, like lightning, a most unwelcome query obtruded. Did deities dine? Then also recurred what Media had declared about my shrine in Odo. Was this it? Self-sacrilegious demigod that I was, was I going to gluttonize on the very offerings, laid before me in my own sacred fane? Give heed to thy ways, oh Taji, lest thou stumble and be lost.

But hereupon, what saw we, but his cool majesty of Odo tranquilly proceeding to lunch in the temple?

How now? Was Media too a god? Egad, it must be so. Else, why his image here in the fane, and the original so entirely at his ease, with legs full cosily tucked away under the very altar itself. This put to flight all appalling apprehensions of the necessity of starving to keep up the assumption of my divinity. So without more ado I helped myself right and left;

taking the best care of Yillah; who ever fed her flushed beauty with juicy fruits, thereby transferring to her cheek the sweet glow of the guava.

Our hunger appeased, and Media in token thereof celestially laying his hand upon the appropriate region, we proceeded to quit the inclosure. But coming to the wall where the breach had been made, lo, and behold, no breach was to be seen. But down it came tumbling again, and forth we issued.

This overthrowing of walls, be it known, is an incidental compliment paid distinguished personages in this part of Mardi. It would seem to signify, that such gentry can go nowhere without creating an impression; even upon the most obdurate substances.

But to return to our ambrosial lunch.

Sublimate, as you will, the idea of our ethereality as intellectual beings; no sensible man can harbor a doubt, but that there is a vast deal of satisfaction in dining. More: there is a savor of life and immortality in substantial fare. Like balloons, we are nothing till filled.

And well knowing this, nature has provided this jolly round board, our globe, which in an endless sequence of courses and crops, spreads a perpetual feast. Though, as with most public banquets, there is no small crowding, and many go away famished from plenty.

Chapter 56

King Media a Host

STRIKING INTO A GROVE, about sunset we emerged upon a
fine, clear space, and spied a city in the woods.

In the middle of all, like a generalissimo's marquee among tents, was
a structure more imposing than the rest. Here, abode King Media.

Disposed round a space some fifty yards square, were many palm posts
staked firmly in the earth. A man's height from the ground, these supported
numerous horizontal trunks, upon which lay a flooring of habiscus. High
over this dais, but resting upon independent supports beyond, a gable-ended
roof sloped away to within a short distance of the ground.

Such was the palace.

We entered it by an arched, arbored entrance, at one of its palmetto-
thatched ends. But not through this exclusive portal entered the Islanders.
Humbly stooping, they found ingress under the drooping eaves. A custom
immemorial, and well calculated to remind all contumacious subjects of
the dignity of the habitation thus entered.

Three steps led to the summit of the dais, where piles of soft mats, and
light pillows of woven grass, stuffed with the golden down of a wild thistle,
invited all loiterers to lounge.

How pleasant the twilight that welled up from under the low eaves,
above which we were seated. And how obvious now the design of the roof.

No shade more grateful and complete; the garish sun lingering without like some lackey in waiting.

But who is this in the corner, gaping at us like a butler in a quandary? Media's household deity, in the guise of a plethoric monster, his enormous head lolling back, and wide, gaping mouth stuffed full of fresh fruits and green leaves. Truly, had the idol possessed a soul under his knotty ribs, how tantalizing to hold so glorious a mouthful without the power of deglutition. Far worse than the inexorable lock-jaw, which will not admit of the step preliminary to a swallow.

This jolly Josh image was that of an inferior deity, the god of Good Cheer, and often after, we met with his merry round mouth in many other abodes in Mardi. Daily, his jaws are replenished, as a flower vase in summer.

But did the demi-divine Media thus brook the perpetual presence of a subaltern divinity? Still more; did he render it homage? But ere long the Mardian mythology will be discussed, thereby making plain what may now seem anomalous.

Politely escorting us into his palace, Media did the honors by inviting his guests to recline. He then seemed very anxious to impress us with the fact, that, by bringing us to his home, and thereby charging the royal larder with our maintenance, he had taken no hasty or imprudent step. His merry butlers kept piling round us viands, till we were well nigh walled in. At every fresh deposit, Media directing our attention to the same, as yet additional evidence of his ample resources as a host. The evidence was finally closed by dragging under the eaves a felled plantain tree, the spike of red ripe fruit, sprouting therefrom, blushing all over, at so rude an introduction to the notice of strangers.

During this scene, Jarl was privily nudging Samoa, in wonderment, to know what upon earth it all meant. But Samoa, scarcely deigning to notice interrogatories propounded through the elbow, only let drop a vague hint or two.

It was quite amusing, what airs Samoa now gave himself, at least toward my Viking. Among the Mardians he was at home. And who, when there, stretches not out his legs, and says unto himself, "Who is greater than I?"

To be plain: concerning himself and the Skyeman, the tables were turned. At sea, Jarl had been the oracle: an old sea-sage, learned in hemp and helm. But our craft high and dry, the Upoluan lifted his crest as the erudite pagan; master of Gog and Magog, expounder of all things heathenish and obscure.

An hour or two was now laughed away in very charming conversation with Media; when I hinted, that a couch and solitude would be acceptable. Whereupon, seizing a taper, our host escorted us without the palace. And ushering us into a handsome unoccupied mansion, gave me to understand that the same was mine. Mounting to the dais, he then instituted a vigorous investigation, to discern whether every thing was in order. Not fancying something about the mats, he rolled them up into bundles, and one by one sent them flying at the heads of his servitors; who, upon that gentle hint made off with them, soon after returning with fresh ones. These, with mathematical precision, Media in person now spread on the dais; looking carefully to the fringes or ruffles with which they were bordered, as if striving to impart to them a sentimental expression.

This done, he withdrew.

Chapter 57

Taji takes Counsel with himself

M Y BRIEF INTERCOURSE with our host, had by this time enabled me to form a pretty good notion of the light, in which I was held by him and his more intelligent subjects.

His free and easy carriage evinced, that though acknowledging my assumptions, he was no way overawed by them; treating me as familiarly, indeed, as if I were a mere mortal, one of the abject generation of mushrooms.

The scene in the temple, however, had done much toward explaining this demeanor of his. A demi-god in his own proper person, my claims to a similar dignity neither struck him with wonder, nor lessened his good opinion of himself.

As for any thing foreign in my aspect, and my ignorance of Mardian customs:—all this, instead of begetting a doubt unfavorable to my pretensions, but strengthened the conviction of them as verities. Thus has it been in similar instances; but to a much greater extent. The celebrated navigator referred to in a preceding chapter, was hailed by the Hawaiians as one of their demi-gods, returned to earth, after a wide tour of the universe. And they worshiped him as such, though incessantly he was interrogating them, as to who under the sun his worshipers were; how their ancestors came on the island; and whether they would have the kindness to provide his followers with plenty of pork during his stay.

But a word or two concerning the idols in the shrine at Odo. Superadded to the homage rendered him as a temporal prince, Media was there worshiped as a spiritual being. In his corporeal absence, his effigy receiving all oblations intended for him. And in the days of his boyhood, listening to the old legends of the Mardian mythology, Media had conceived a strong liking for the fabulous Taji; a deity whom he had often declared was worthy a niche in any temple extant. Hence he had honored my image with a place in his own special shrine; placing it side by side with his worshipful likeness.

I appreciated the compliment. But of the close companionship of the other image there, I was heartily ashamed. And with reason. The nuisance in question being the image of a deified maker of plantain-pudding, lately deceased; who had been famed far and wide as the most notable fellow of his profession in the whole Archipelago. During his sublunary career, having been attached to the household of Media, his grateful master had afterward seen fit to crown his celebrity by this posthumous distinction: a circumstance sadly subtracting from the dignity of an apotheosis. Nor must it here be omitted, that in this part of Mardi culinary artists are accounted worthy of high consideration. For among these people of Odo, the matter of eating and drinking is held a matter of life and of death. "Drag away my queen from my arms," said old Tyty when overcome of Adommo, "but leave me my cook."

Now, among the Mardians there were plenty of incarnated deities to keep me in countenance. Most of the kings of the Archipelago, besides Media, claiming homage as demi-gods; and that, too, by virtue of hereditary descent, the divine spark being transmissible from father to son. In illustration of this, was the fact, that in several instances the people of the land addressed the supreme god Oro, in the very same terms employed in the political adoration of their sublunary rulers.

Ay: there were deities in Mardi far greater and taller than I: right royal monarchs to boot, living in jolly round tabernacles of jolly brown clay; and feasting, and roystering, and lording it in yellow tabernacles of bamboo. These demi-gods had wherewithal to sustain their lofty pretensions. If need were, could crush out of him the infidelity of a non-conformist. And by this immaculate union of church and state, god and king, in their own proper persons reigned supreme Cæsars over the souls and bodies of their subjects.

Beside these mighty magnates, I and my divinity shrank into nothing. In their woodland ante-chambers plebeian deities were kept lingering. For be it known, that in due time we met with several decayed, broken down demi-gods: magnificos of no mark in Mardi; having no temples wherein to feast personal admirers, or spiritual devotees. They wandered about forlorn and friendless. And oftentimes in their dinnerless despair hugely gluttonized, and would fain have grown fat, by reflecting upon the magnificence of their genealogies. But poor fellows! like shabby Scotch lords in London in King James's time, the very multitude of them confounded distinction. And since they could show no rent-roll, they were permitted to fume unheeded.

Upon the whole, so numerous were living and breathing gods in Mardi, that I held my divinity but cheaply. And seeing such a host of immortals, and hearing of multitudes more, purely spiritual in their nature, haunting woodlands and streams; my views of theology grew strangely confused; I began to bethink me of the Jew that rejected the Talmud, and his all-permeating principle, to which Goethe and others have subscribed.

Instead, then, of being struck with the audacity of endeavoring to palm myself off as a god—the way in which the thing first impressed me—I now perceived that I might be a god as much as I pleased, and yet not whisk a lion's tail after all; at least on that special account.

As for Media's reception, its graciousness was not wholly owing to the divine character imputed to me. His, he believed to be the same. But to a whim, a freakishness in his soul, which led him to fancy me as one among many, not as one with no peer.

But the apparent unconcern of King Media with respect to my godship, by no means so much surprised me, as his unaffected indifference to my amazing voyage from the sun; his indifference to the sun itself; and all the wonderful circumstances that must have attended my departure. Whether he had ever been there himself, that he regarded a solar trip with so much unconcern, almost became a question in my mind. Certain it is, that as a mere traveler he must have deemed me no very great prodigy.

My surprise at these things was enhanced by reflecting, that to the people of the Archipelago the map of Mardi was the map of the world. With the exception of certain islands out of sight and at an indefinite distance, they had no certain knowledge of any isles but their own.

And, no long time elapsed ere I had still additional reasons to cease wondering at the easy faith accorded to the story which I had given of myself. For these Mardians were familiar with still greater marvels than mine; verily believing in prodigies of all sorts. Any one of them put my exploits to the blush.

Look to thy ways then, Taji, thought I, and carry not thy crest too high. Of a surety, thou hast more peers than inferiors. Thou art overtopped all round. Bear thyself discreetly and not haughtily, Taji. It will not answer to give thyself airs. Abstain from all consequential allusions to the other world, and the genteel deities among whom thou hast circled. Sport not too jauntily thy raiment, because it is novel in Mardi; nor boast of the fleetness of thy Chamois, because it is unlike a canoe. Vaunt not of thy pedigree, Taji; for Media himself will measure it with thee there by the furlong. Be not a "snob," Taji.

So then, weighing all things well, and myself severely, I resolved to follow my Mentor's wise counsel; neither arrogating aught, nor abating of just dues; but circulating freely, sociably, and frankly, among the gods, heroes, high-priests, kings, and gentlemen, that made up the principalities of Mardi.

Chapter 58

Mardi by Night and Yillah by Day

D URING THE NIGHT following our arrival, many dreams were no doubt dreamt in Odo. But my thoughts were wakeful. And while all others slept, obeying a restless impulse, I stole without into the magical starlight. There are those who in a strange land ever love to view it by night.

It has been said, that the opening in the groves where was situated Media's city, was elevated above the surrounding plains. Hence was commanded a broad reach of prospect.

Far and wide was deep low-sobbing repose of man and nature. The groves were motionless; and in the meadows, like goblins, the shadows advanced and retreated. Full before me, lay the Mardian fleet of isles, profoundly at anchor within their coral harbor. Near by was one belted round by a frothy luminous reef, wherein it lay, like Saturn in its ring.

From all their summits, went up a milk-white smoke, as from Indian wigwams in the hazy harvest-moon. And floating away, these vapors blended with the faint mist, as of a cataract, hovering over the circumvallating reef. Far beyond all, and far into the infinite night, surged the jet-black ocean.

But how tranquil the wide lagoon, which mirrored the burning spots in heaven! Deep down into its innermost heart penetrated the slanting rays of Hesperus like a shaft of light, sunk far into mysterious Golcondas, where myriad gnomes seemed toiling. Soon a light breeze rippled the water, and the shaft was seen no more. But the moon's bright wake was still revealed: a silver track, tipping every wave-crest in its course, till each seemed a pearly, scroll-prowed nautilus, buoyant with some elfin crew.

From earth to heaven! High above me was Night's shadowy bower, traversed, vine-like, by the Milky Way, and heavy with golden clusterings. Oh stars! oh eyes, that see me, wheresoe'er I roam: serene, intent, inscrutable for aye, tell me Sybils, what I am.—Wondrous worlds on worlds! Lo, round and round me, shining, awful spells: all glorious, vivid constellations, God's diadem ye are! To you, ye stars, man owes his subtlest raptures, thoughts unspeakable, yet full of faith.

But how your mild effulgence stings the boding heart. Am I a murderer, stars?

Hours pass. The starry trance is departed. Long waited for, the dawn now comes.

First, breaking along the waking face; peeping from out the languid lids; then shining forth in longer glances; till, like the sun, up comes the soul, and sheds its rays abroad.

When thus my Yillah did daily dawn, how she lit up my world; tinging more rosily the roseate clouds, that in her summer cheek played to and fro, like clouds in Italian air.

Chapter 59

Their Morning Meal

NOT WHOLLY is our world made up of bright stars and bright eyes: so now to our story.

A conscientious host should ever be up betimes, to look after the welfare of his guests, and see to it that their day begin auspiciously. King Media announced the advent of the sun, by rustling at my bower's eaves in person.

A repast was spread in an adjoining arbor, which Media's pages had smoothed for our reception, and where his subordinate chiefs were in attendance. Here we reclined upon mats. Balmy and fresh blew the breath of the morning; golden vapors were upon the mountains, silver sheen upon the grass; and the birds were at matins in the groves; their bright plumage flashing into view, here and there, as if some rainbow were crouching in the foliage.

Spread before us were viands, served in quaint-shaped, curiously-dyed gourds, not Sèvres, but almost as tasteful; and like true porcelain, fire had tempered them. Green and yielding, they are plucked from the tree; and emptied of their pulp, are scratched over with minute marks, like those of a line engraving. The ground prepared, the various figures are carefully etched. And the outlines filled up with delicate punctures, certain vegetable oils are poured over them, for coloring. Filled with a peculiar species of earth, the gourd is now placed in an oven in the ground. And in due time exhumed, emptied of its contents, and washed in the stream, it presents a deep-dyed exterior; every figure distinctly traced and opaque, but the ground semi-transparent. In some cases, owing to the variety of dyes employed, each figure is of a different hue.

More glorious goblets than these for the drinking of wine, went never from hand to mouth. Capacious as pitchers, they almost superseded decanters.

Now, in a tropical climate, fruit, with light wines, forms the only fit meal of a morning. And with orchards and vineyards forever in sight, who but the Hetman of the Cossacs would desire more? We had plenty of the juice of the grape. But of this hereafter; there are some fine old cellars, and plenty of good cheer in store.

During the repast, Media, for a time, was much taken up with our raiment. He begged me to examine for a moment the texture of his right royal robe, and observe how much superior it was to my own. It put my mantle to the blush; being tastefully stained with rare devices in red and black; and bordered with dyed fringes of feathers, and tassels of red birds' claws.

Next came under observation the Skyeman's Guayaquil hat; at whose preposterous shape, our host laughed in derision; clapping a great conical calabash upon the head of an attendant, and saying that now he was Jarl. At this, and all similar sallies, Samoa was sure to roar louder than any; though mirth was no constitutional thing with him. But he seemed rejoiced at the opportunity of turning upon us the ridicule, which as a barbarian among whites, he himself had so often experienced.

These pleasantries over, King Media very slightly drew himself up, as if to make amends for his previous unbending. He discoursed imperially with his chiefs; nodded his sovereign will to his pages; called for another gourd of wine; in all respects carrying his royalty bravely.

The repast concluded, we journeyed to the canoe-house, where we found the little Chamois stabled like a steed. One solitary depredation had been committed. Its sides and bottom had been completely denuded of the minute green barnacles, and short sea-grass, which, like so many leeches, had fastened to our planks during our long, lazy voyage.

By the people they had been devoured as dainties.

Chapter 60

Belshazzar on the Bench

N OW, MEDIA WAS KING OF ODO. And from the simplicity of his manners hitherto, and his easy, frank demeanor toward ourselves, had we foolishly doubted that fact, no skepticism could have survived an illustration of it, which this very day we witnessed at noon.

For at high noon, Media was wont to don his dignity with his symbols of state; and sit on his judgment divan or throne, to hear and try all causes brought before him, and fulminate his royal decrees.

This divan was elevated at one end of a spacious arbor, formed by an avenue of regal palms, which in brave state, held aloft their majestical canopy.

The crown of the island prince was of the primitive old Eastern style; in shape, similar, perhaps, to that jauntily sported as a foraging cap by his sacred majesty King Nimrod, who so lustily followed the hounds. It was a plaited turban of red tappa, radiated by the pointed and polished white bones of the Ray-fish. These diverged from a bandeau or fillet of the most precious pearls; brought up from the sea by the deepest diving mermen of Mardi. From the middle of the crown rose a tri-foiled spear-head. And a spear-headed scepter graced the right hand of the king.

Now, for all the rant of your democrats, a fine king on a throne is a very fine sight to behold. He looks very much like a god. No wonder that

his more dutiful subjects so swore, that their good lord and master King
Media was demi-divine.

A king on his throne! Ah, believe me, ye Gracchi, ye Acephali, ye
Levelers, it is something worth seeing, be sure; whether beheld at Babylon
the Tremendous, when Nebuchadnezzar was crowned; at old Scone in the
days of Macbeth; at Rheims, among Oriflammes, at the coronation of
Louis le Grand; at Westminster Abbey, when the gentlemanly George
doffed his beaver for a diadem; or under the soft shade of palm trees on an
isle in the sea.

Man lording it over man, man kneeling to man, is a spectacle that
Gabriel might well travel hitherward to behold; for never did he behold
it in heaven. But Darius giving laws to the Medes and the Persians, or the
conqueror of Bactria with king-cattle yoked to his car, was not a whit more
sublime, than Beau Brummel magnificently ringing for his valet.

A king on his throne! It is Jupiter nodding in the councils of Olympus;
Satan, seen among the coronets in Hell.

A king on his throne! It is the sun over a mountain; the sun over law-
giving Sinai; the sun in our system: planets, duke-like, dancing attendance,
and baronial satellites in waiting.

A king on his throne! After all, but a gentleman seated.

And thus sat the good lord, King Media.

Time passed. And after trying and dismissing several minor affairs,
Media called for certain witnesses to testify concerning one Jiromo, a fool-
hardy wight, who had been silly enough to plot against the majesty now
sitting judge and jury upon him.

His guilt was clear. And the witnesses being heard, from a bunch of
palm plumes Media taking a leaf, placed it in the hand of a runner or pur-
suivant, saying, "This to Jiromo, where he is prisoned; with his king's
compliments; say we here wait for his head."

It was doffed like a turban before a Dey, and brought back on the
instant.

Now came certain lean-visaged, poverty-stricken, and hence suspicious-
looking varlets, grumbling and growling, and amiable as Bruin. They came
muttering some wild jargon about "bulwarks," "bulkheads," "coffer-
dams," "safeguards," "noble charters," "shields," and "paladiums," "great
and glorious birthrights," and other unintelligible gibberish.

Of the pursuivants, these worthies asked audience of Media.

"Go, kneel at the throne," was the answer.

"Our knee-pans are stiff with sciatics," was the rheumatic reply.

"An artifice to keep on your legs," said the pursuivants.

And advancing they salamed, and told Media the excuse of those sour-looking varlets. Whereupon my lord commanded them to down on their marrow-bones instanter, either before him or the headsman, whichsoever they pleased.

They preferred the former. And as they there kneeled, in vain did men with sharp ears (who abound in all courts) prick their auriculars, to list to that strange crackling and firing off of bone balls and sockets, ever incident to the genuflections of rheumatic courtiers.

In a row, then, these selfsame knee-pans did kneel before the king; who eyed them as eagles in air do goslings on dunghills; or hunters, hounds crouching round their calves.

"Your prayer?" said Media.

It was a petition, that thereafter all differences between man and man in Odo, together with all alleged offenses against the state, might be tried by twelve good men and true. These twelve to be unobnoxious to the party or parties concerned; their peers; and previously unbiased touching the matter at issue. Furthermore, that unanimity in these twelve should be indispensable to a verdict; and no dinner be vouchsafed till unanimity came.

Loud and long laughed King Media in scorn.

"This be your judge," he cried, swaying his scepter. "What! are twelve wise men more wise than one? or will twelve fools, put together, make one sage? Are twelve honest men more honest than one? or twelve knaves less knavish than one? And if, of twelve men, three be fools, and three wise, three knaves, and three upright, how obtain real unanimity from such?

"But if twelve judges be better than one, then are twelve hundred better than twelve. But take the whole populace for a judge, and you will long wait for a unanimous verdict.

"If upon a thing dubious, there be little unanimity in the conflicting opinions of one man's mind, how expect it in the uproar of twelve puzzled brains? though much unanimity be found in twelve hungry stomachs.

"Judges unobnoxious to the accused! Apply it to a criminal case. Ha! ha! if peradventure a Cadi be rejected, because he had seen the accused commit the crime for which he is arraigned. Then, his mind would be biased: no impartiality from him! Or your testy accused might object to another, because of his tomahawk nose, or a cruel squint of the eye.

"Of all follies the most foolish! Know ye from me, that true peers render not true verdicts. Jiromo was a rebel. Had I tried him by his peers, I had tried him by rebels; and the rebel had rebelled to some purpose.

"Away! As unerring justice dwells in a unity, and as one judge will at last judge the world beyond all appeal; so—though often here below justice be hard to attain—does man come nearest the mark, when he imitates that model divine. Hence, one judge is better than twelve.

"And as Justice, in ideal, is ever painted high lifted above the crowd; so, from the exaltation of his rank, an honest king is the best of those unical judges, which individually are better than twelve. And therefore am I, King Media, the best judge in this land.

"Subjects! so long as I live, I will rule you and judge you alone. And though you here kneeled before me till you grew into the ground, and there took root, no yea to your petition will you get from this throne. I am king: ye are slaves. Mine to command: yours to obey. And this hour I decree, that henceforth no gibberish of bulwarks and bulkheads be heard in this land. For a dead bulwark and a bulkhead, to dam off sedition, will I make of that man, who again but breathes those bulky words. Ho! spears! see that these knee-pans here kneel till set of sun."

High noon was now passed; and removing his crown, and placing it on the dais for the kneelers to look at during their devotions, King Media departed from that place, and once more played the agreeable host.

Chapter 61

An Incognito

FOR THE REST of that day, and several that followed, we were continually receiving visits from the neighboring islands; whose inhabitants in fleets and flotillas flocked round Odo to behold the guests of its lord. Among them came many messengers from the neighboring kings with soft speeches and gifts.

But it were needless to detail our various interviews, or relate in what manifold ways, the royal strangers gave token of their interest concerning us.

Upon the third day, however, there was noticed a mysterious figure, like the inscrutable incognitos sometimes encountered, crossing the tower-shadowed Plaza of Assignations at Lima. It was enveloped in a dark robe of tappa, so drawn and plaited about the limbs; and with one hand, so wimpled about the face, as only to expose a solitary eye. But that eye was a world. Now it was fixed upon Yillah with a sinister glance, and now upon me, but with a different expression. However great the crowd, however tumultuous, that fathomless eye gazed on; till at last it seemed no eye, but a spirit, forever prying into my soul. Often I strove to approach it, but it would evade me, soon reappearing.

Pointing out the apparition to Media, I intreated him to take means to fix it, that my suspicions might be dispelled, as to its being incorporeal.

He replied that, by courtesy, incognitos were sacred. Insomuch that the close-plaited robe and the wimple were secure as a castle. At last, to my relief, the phantom disappeared, and was seen no more.

Numerous and fervent the invitations received to return the calls wherewith we were honored. But for the present we declined them; preferring to establish ourselves firmly in the heart of Media, ere encountering the vicissitudes of roaming. In a multitude of acquaintances is less security, than in one faithful friend.

Now, while these civilities were being received, and on the fourth morning after our arrival, there landed on the beach three black-eyed damsels, deep brunettes, habited in long variegated robes, and with gay blossoms on their heads.

With many salams, the strangers were ushered into my presence by an old white-haired servitor of Media's, who with a parting congé murmured, "From Queen Hautia," then departed. Surprised, I stood mute, and welcomed them.

The first, with many smiles and blandishments, waved before me a many-tinted Iris: the flag-flower streaming with pennons. Advancing, the second then presented three rose-hued purple-veined Circea flowers, the dew still clinging to them. The third placed in my hand a moss-rose bud; then, a Venus-car.

"Thanks for your favors! now your message."

Starting at this reception, graciously intended, they conferred a moment; when the Iris-bearer said in winning phrase, "We come from Hautia, whose moss-rose you hold."

"All thanks to Hautia then; the bud is very fragrant."

Then she pointed to the Venus-car.

"This too is sweet; thanks to Hautia for her flowers. Pray, bring me more."

"He mocks our mistress," and gliding from me, they waved witch-hazels, leaving me alone and wondering.

Informing Media of this scene, he smiled; threw out queer hints of Hautia; but knew not what her message meant.

At first this affair occasioned me no little uneasiness, with much matter for marveling; but in the novel pleasure of our sojourn in Odo, it soon slipped from my mind; nor for some time, did I again hear aught of Queen Hautia.

Chapter 62

Taji retires from the World

AFTER A WHILE, when the strangers came not in shoals as before, I proposed to our host, a stroll over his dominions; desirous of beholding the same, and secretly induced by the hope of selecting an abode, more agreeable to my fastidious taste, than the one already assigned me.

The ramble over—a pleasant one it was—it resulted in a determination on my part to quit Odo. Yet not to go very far; only ten or twelve yards, to a little green tuft of an islet; one of many, which here and there, all round the island, nestled like birds' nests in the branching boughs of the coral grove, whose roots laid hold of the foundations of the deep. Between these islets and the shore, extended shelving ledges, with shallows above, just sufficient to float a canoe. One of these islets was wooded and vined; an arbor in the sea. And here, Media permitting, I decided to dwell.

Not long was Media in complying; nor long, ere my retreat was in readiness. Laced together, the twisting boughs were closely thatched. And thatched were the sides also, with deep crimson pandannus leaves; whose long, forked spears, lifted by the breeze, caused the whole place to blaze, as with flames. Canes, laid on palm trunks, formed the floor. How elastic! In vogue all over Odo, among the chiefs, it imparted such a buoyancy to the person, that to this special cause may be imputed in good part the famous fine spirits of the nobles.

Hypochondriac! essay the elastic flooring! It shall so pleasantly and gently jolt thee, as to shake up, and pack off the stagnant humors mantling thy pool-like soul.

Such was my dwelling. But I make no mention of sundry little appurtenances of tropical housekeeping: calabashes, cocoanut shells, and rolls of fine tappa; till with Yillah seated at last in my arbor, I looked round, and wanted for naught.

But what of Jarl and Samoa? Why Jarl must needs be fanciful, as well as myself. Like a bachelor in chambers, he settled down right opposite to me, on the main land, in a little wigwam in the grove.

But Samoa, following not his comrade's example, still tarried in the camp of the Hittites and Jebusites of Odo. Beguiling men of their leisure by his marvelous stories: and maidens of their hearts by his marvelous wiles.

When I chose, I was completely undisturbed in my arbor; an ukase of Media's forbidding indiscriminate intrusion. But thrice in the day came a garrulous old man with my viands.

Thus sequestered, however, I could not entirely elude the pryings of the people of the neighboring islands; who often passed by, slowly paddling, and earnestly regarding my retreat. But gliding along at a distance, and never essaying a landing, their occasional vicinity troubled me but little. But now and then of an evening, when thick and fleet the shadows were falling, dim glimpses of a canoe would be spied; hovering about the place like a ghost. And once, in the stillness of the night, hearing the near ripple of a prow, I sallied forth, but the phantom quickly departed.

That night, Yillah shuddered as she slept. "The whirlpool," she murmured, "sweet mosses." Next day she was lost in reveries, plucking pensive hyacinths, or gazing intently into the lagoon.

Chapter 63

Odo and its Lord

TIME NOW TO ENTER upon some further description of the island and its lord.

And first for Media: a gallant gentleman and king. From a goodly stock he came. In his endless pedigree, reckoning deities by decimals, innumerable kings, and scores of great heroes, chiefs, and priests. Nor in person, did he belie his origin. No far-descended dwarf was he, the least of a receding race. He stood like a palm tree; about whose acanthus capital droops not more gracefully the silken fringes, than Media's locks upon his noble brow. Strong was his arm to wield the club, or hurl the javelin; and potent, I ween, round a maiden's waist.

Thus much here for Media. Now comes his isle.

Our pleasant ramble found it a little round world by itself; full of beauties as a garden; chequered by charming groves; watered by roving brooks; and fringed all round by a border of palm trees, whose roots drew nourishment from the water. But though abounding in other quarters of the Archipelago, not a solitary bread-fruit grew in Odo. A noteworthy circumstance, observable in these regions, where islands close adjoining, so differ in their soil, that certain fruits growing genially in one, are foreign to another. But Odo was famed for its guavas, whose flavor was likened to the flavor of new-blown lips; and for its grapes, whose juices prompted many a laugh and many a groan.

Beside the city where Media dwelt, there were few other clusters of habitations in Odo. The higher classes living, here and there, in separate households; but not as eremites. Some buried themselves in the cool, quivering bosoms of the groves. Others, fancying a marine vicinity, dwelt hard by the beach in little cages of bamboo; whence of mornings they sallied out with jocund cries, and went plunging into the refreshing bath, whose frothy margin was the threshold of their dwellings. Others still, like birds, built their nests among the sylvan nooks of the elevated interior; whence all below, and hazy green, lay steeped in languor the island's throbbing heart.

Thus dwelt the chiefs and merry men of mark. The common sort, including serfs, and Helots, war-captives held in bondage, lived in secret places, hard to find. Whence it came, that, to a stranger, the whole isle looked care-free and beautiful. Deep among the ravines and the rocks, these beings lived in noisome caves, lairs for beasts, not human homes; or built them coops of rotten boughs—living trees were banned them—whose mouldy hearts hatched vermin. Fearing infection of some plague, born of this filth, the chiefs of Odo seldom passed that way; and looking round within their green retreats, and pouring out their wine, and plucking from orchards of the best, marveled how these swine could grovel in the mire, and wear such sallow cheeks. But they offered no sweet homes; from that mire they never sought to drag them out; they open threw no orchard; and intermitted not the mandates that condemned their drudges to a life of deaths. Sad sight! to see those round-shouldered Helots, stooping in their trenches: artificial, three in number, and concentric: the isle well nigh surrounding. And herein, fed by oozy loam, and kindly dew from heaven, and bitter sweat from men, grew as in hot-beds the nutritious Taro.

Toil is man's allotment; toil of brain, or toil of hands, or a grief that's more than either, the grief and sin of idleness. But when man toils and slays himself for masters who withhold the life he gives to them—then, then, the soul screams out, and every sinew cracks. So with these poor serfs. And few of them could choose but be the brutes they seemed.

Now needs it to be said, that Odo was no land of pleasure unalloyed, and plenty without a pause?—Odo, in whose lurking-places infants turned from breasts, whence flowed no nourishment.—Odo, in whose inmost haunts, dark groves were brooding, passing which you heard most dismal cries, and voices cursing Media. There, men were scourged; their crime, a heresy; the heresy, that Media was no demi-god. For this they shrieked. Their fathers shrieked before; their fathers, who, tormented, said, "Happy we to groan, that our children's children may be glad." But their children's children howled. Yet these, too, echoed previous generations, and loudly swore, "The pit that's dug for us may prove another's grave."

But let all pass. To look at, and to roam about of holidays, Odo seemed a happy land. The palm-trees waved—though here and there you marked one sear and palsy-smitten; the flowers bloomed—though dead ones moldered in decay; the waves ran up the strand in glee—though, receding, they sometimes left behind bones mixed with shells.

But else than these, no sign of death was seen throughout the isle. Did men in Odo live for aye? Was Ponce de Leon's fountain there? For near and far, you saw no ranks and files of graves, no generations harvested in windrows. In Odo, no hard-hearted nabob slept beneath a gentle epitaph; no *requiescat-in-pace* mocked a sinner damned; no *memento-mori* admonished men to live while yet they might. Here Death hid his skull; and hid it in the sea, the common sepulcher of Odo. Not dust to dust, but dust to brine; not hearses but canoes. For all who died upon that isle were carried out beyond the outer reef, and there were buried with their sires' sires. Hence came the thought, that of gusty nights, when round the isles, and high toward heaven, flew the white reef's rack and foam, that then and there, kept chattering watch and ward, the myriads that were ocean-tombed.

But why these watery obsequies?

Odo was but a little isle, and must the living make way for the dead, and Life's small colony be dislodged by Death's grim hosts; as the gaunt tribes of Tamerlane o'erspread the tented pastures of the Khan?

And now, what follows, said these Islanders: "Why sow corruption in the soil which yields us life? We would not pluck our grapes from over graves. This earth's an urn for flowers, not for ashes."

They said that Oro, the supreme, had made a cemetery of the sea.

And what more glorious grave? Was Mausolus more sublimely urned? Or do the minster-lamps that burn before the tomb of Charlemagne, show more of pomp, than all the stars, that blaze above the shipwrecked mariner?

But no more of the dead; men shrug their shoulders, and love not their company; though full soon we shall all have them for fellows.

Chapter 64

Yillah a Phantom

FOR A TIME we were happy in Odo: Yillah and I in our islet. Nor did the pearl on her bosom glow more rosily than the roses in her cheeks; though at intervals they waned and departed; and deadly pale was her glance, when she murmured of the whirlpool and mosses. As pale my soul, bethinking me of Aleema the priest.

But day by day, did her spell weave round me its magic, and all the hidden things of her being grew more lovely and strange. Did I commune with a spirit? Often I thought that Paradise had overtaken me on earth, and that Yillah was verily an angel, and hence the mysteries that hallowed her.

But how fleeting our joys. Storms follow bright dawnings.—Long memories of short-lived scenes, sad thoughts of joyous hours—how common are ye to all mankind. When happy, do we pause and say—"Lo, thy felicity, my soul?" No: happiness seldom seems happiness, except when looked back upon from woes. A flowery landscape, you must come out of, to behold.

Sped the hours, the days, the one brief moment of our joys. Fairy bower in the fair lagoon, scene of sylvan ease and heart's repose,—Oh, Yillah, Yillah! All the woods repeat the sound, the wild, wild woods of my wild

193

soul. Yillah! Yillah! cry the small strange voices in me, and evermore, and far and deep, they echo on.

Days passed. When one morning I found the arbor vacant. Gone! A dream. I closed my eyes, and would have dreamed her back. In vain. Starting, I called upon her name; but none replied. Fleeing from the islet, I gained the neighboring shore, and searched among the woods; and my comrades meeting, besought their aid. But idle all. No glimpse of aught, save trees and flowers. Then Media was sought out; the event made known; and quickly, bands were summoned to range the isle.

Noon came; but no Yillah. When Media averred she was no longer in Odo. Whither she was gone, or how, he knew not; nor could any imagine.

At this juncture, there chanced to arrive certain messengers from abroad; who, presuming that all was well with Taji, came with renewed invitations to visit various pleasant places round about. Among these, came Queen Hautia's heralds, with their Iris flag, once more bringing flowers. But they came and went unheeded.

Setting out to return, these envoys were accompanied by numerous followers of Media, dispatched to the neighboring islands, to seek out the missing Yillah. But three days passed; and, one by one, they all returned; and stood before me silently.

For a time I raved. Then, falling into outer repose, lived for a space in moods and reveries, with eyes that knew no closing, one glance forever fixed.

They strove to rouse me. Girls danced and sang; and tales of fairy times were told; of monstrous imps, and youths enchanted; of groves and gardens in the sea. Yet still I moved not, hearing all, yet noting naught. Media cried, "For shame, oh Taji; thou, a god?" and placed a spear in my nerveless hand. And Jarl loud called upon me to awake. Samoa marveled.

Still sped the days. And at length, my memory was restored. The thoughts of things broke over me like returning billows on a beach long bared. A rush, a foam of recollections!—Sweet Yillah gone, and I bereaved.

Another interval, and that mood was past. Misery became a memory. The keen pang a deep vibration. The remembrance seemed the thing remembered; though bowed with sadness. There are thoughts that lie and glitter deep: tearful pearls beneath life's sea, that surges still, and rolls sunlit, whatever it may hide. Common woes, like fluids, mix all round. Not so with that other grief. Some mourners load the air with lamentations; but the loudest notes are struck from hollows. Their tears flow fast: but the deep spring only wells.

At last I turned to Media, saying I must hie from Odo, and rove throughout all Mardi; for Yillah might yet be found.

But hereafter, in words, little more of the maiden, till perchance her fate be learned.

Chapter 65

Taji makes three Acquaintances

DOWN TO THIS PERIOD, I had restrained Samoa from wandering to the neighboring islands, though he had much desired it, in compliance with the invitations continually received. But now I informed both him, and his comrade, of the tour I purposed; desiring their company.

Upon the announcement of my intention to depart, to my no small surprise Media also proposed to accompany me: a proposition gladly embraced. It seems, that for some reason, he had not as yet extended his travels to the more distant islands. Hence the voyage in prospect was particularly agreeable to him. Nor did he forbear any pains to insure its prosperity; assuring me, furthermore, that its object must eventually be crowned with success. "I myself am interested in this pursuit," said he; "and trust me, Yillah will be found."

For the tour of the lagoon, the docile Chamois was proposed; but Media dissented; saying, that it befitted not the lord of Odo to voyage in the equipage of his guest. Therefore, three canoes were selected from his own royal fleet.

One for ourselves, and a trio of companions whom he purposed introducing to my notice; the rest were reserved for attendants.

Thanks to Media's taste and heedfulness, the strangers above mentioned proved truly acceptable.

The first was Mohi, or Braid-Beard, so called from the manner in which he wore that appendage, exceedingly long and gray. He was a venerable teller of stories and legends, one of the Keepers of the Chronicles of the Kings of Mardi.

The second was Babbalanja, a man of a mystical aspect, habited in a voluminous robe. He was learned in Mardian lore; much given to quotations from ancient and obsolete authorities: the Ponderings of Old Bardi-anna: the Pandects of Alla-Malolla.

Third and last, was Yoomy, or the Warbler. A youthful, long-haired, blue-eyed minstrel; all fits and starts; at times, absent of mind, and wan of cheek; but always very neat and pretty in his apparel; wearing the most becoming of turbans, a Bird of Paradise feather its plume, and sporting the gayest of sashes. Most given was Yoomy to amorous melodies, and rondos, and roundelays, very witching to hear. But at times disdaining the oaten reed, like a clarion he burst forth with lusty lays of arms and battle; or, in mournful strains, sounded elegies for departed bards and heroes.

Thus much for Yoomy as a minstrel. In other respects, it would be hard to depict him. He was so capricious a mortal; so swayed by contrary moods; so lofty, so humble, so sad, so merry; so made up of a thousand contra-dictions, that we must e'en let him depict himself as our story progresses. And herein it is hoped he will succeed; since no one in Mardi comprehended him.

Now the trio, thus destined for companions on our voyage, had for some time been anxious to take the tour of the Archipelago. In particular, Babbalanja had often expressed the most ardent desire to visit every one of the isles, in quest of some object, mysteriously hinted. He murmured deep concern for my loss, the sincerest sympathy; and pressing my hand more than once, said lowly, "Your pursuit is mine, noble Taji. Where'er you search, I follow."

So, too, Yoomy addressed me; but with still more feeling. And some-thing like this, also, Braid-Beard repeated.

But to my sorrow, I marked that both Mohi and Babbalanja, especially the last, seemed not so buoyant of hope, concerning lost Yillah, as the youth-ful Yoomy, and his high-spirited lord, King Media.

As our voyage would embrace no small period of time, it behoved King Media to appoint some trustworthy regent, to rule during his absence. This regent was found in Almanni, a stern-eyed, resolute warrior, a kinsman of the king.

All things at last in readiness, and the ensuing morning appointed for a start, Media, on the beach, at eventide, when both light and water waned, drew a rude map of the lagoon, to compensate for the obstructions in the way of a comprehensive glance at it from Odo.

And thus was sketched the plan of our voyage; which islands first to visit; and which to touch at, when we should be homeward bound.

Chapter 66

With a fair Wind, at Sunrise they sail

TRUE EACH TO HIS WORD, up came the sun, and round to my isle came Media.

How glorious a morning! The new-born clouds all dappled with gold, and streaked with violet; the sun in high spirits; and the pleasant air cooled overnight by the blending circumambient fountains, forever playing all round the reef; the lagoon within, the coral-rimmed basin, into which they poured, subsiding, hereabouts, into green tranquillity.

But what monsters of canoes! Would they devour an innocent voyager? their great black prows curling aloft, and thrown back like trunks of elephants; a dark, snaky length behind, like the sea-serpent's train.

The prow of the foremost terminated in a large, open, shark's mouth, garnished with ten rows of pearly human teeth, curiously inserted into the sculptured wood. The gunwale was ornamented with rows of rich spotted Leopard and Tiger-shells; here and there, varied by others, flat and round, and spirally traced; gay serpents petrified in coils. These were imbedded in a grooved margin, by means of a resinous compound, exhaling such spices, that the canoes were odoriferous as the Indian chests of the Maldives.

The likeness of the foremost canoe to an elephant, was helped by a sort of canopied Howdah in its stern, of heavy, russet-dyed tappa, tasselled at the corners with long bunches of cocoanut fibres, stained red. These swayed to and fro, like the fox-tails on a Tuscarora robe.

But what is this, in the head of the canoe, just under the shark's mouth?

A grinning little imp of an image; a ring in its nose; cowrie shells jingling at its ears; with an abominable leer, like that of Silenus reeling on his ass. It was taking its ease; cosily smoking a pipe; its bowl, a duodecimo edition of the face of the smoker. This image looked sternward; everlastingly mocking us.

Of these canoes, it may be well to state, that although during our stay in Odo, so many barges and shallops had touched there, nothing similar to Media's had been seen. But inquiring whence his sea-equipage came, we were thereupon taught to reverence the same as antiquities and heir-looms; claw-keeled, dragon-prowed crafts of a bygone generation; at present, superseded in general use by the more swan-like canoes, significant of the advanced stage of marine architecture in Mardi. No sooner was this known, than what had seemed almost hideous in my eyes, became merely grotesque. Nor could I help being greatly delighted with the good old family pride of our host.

The upper corners of our sails displayed the family crest of Media; three upright boars' tusks, in an heraldic field argent. A fierce device: Whom rends he?

All things in readiness, we glided away: the multitude waving adieu; and our flotilla disposed in the following order.

First went the royal Elephant, carrying Media, myself, Jarl, and Samoa; Mohi the Teller of Legends, Babbalanja, and Yoomy, and six vivacious paddlers; their broad paddle-blades carved with the royal boars' tusks, the same tattooed on their chests for a livery.

And thus, as Media had promised, we voyaged in state. To crown all, seated sideways in the high, open shark's-mouth of our prow was a little dwarf of a boy, one of Media's pages, a red conch-shell, bugle-wise sus-pended at his side. Among various other offices, it was the duty of little Vee-Vee to announce the advent of his master, upon drawing near to the islands in our route. Two short bars, projecting from one side of the prow, furnished him the means of ascent to his perch.

As we gained the open lagoon with bellied sails, and paddles playing, a sheaf of foam borne upright at our prow; Yoomy, standing where the spicy spray flew over him, stretched forth his hand and cried—"The dawn of day is passed, and Mardi lies all before us: all her isles, and all her lakes; all her stores of good and evil. Storms may come, our barks may drown. But blow before us, all ye winds; give us a lively blast, good clarion; rally round us all our wits; and be this voyage full gayly sailed, for Yillah will yet be found."

Chapter 67

Little King Peepi

VALAPEE, or the Isle of Yams, being within plain sight of Media's dominions, we were not very long in drawing nigh to its shores.

Two long parallel elevations, rising some three arrow-flights into the air, double-ridge the island's entire length, lapping between, a widening vale, so level withal, that at either extremity, the green of its groves blends with the green of the lagoon; and the isle seems divided by a strait.

Within several paces of the beach, our canoes keeled the bottom, and camel-like mutely hinted that we voyagers must dismount.

Hereupon, the assembled islanders ran into the water, and with bent shoulders obsequiously desired the honor of transporting us to land. The beach gained, all present wearing robes instantly stripped them to the waist; a naked chest being their salute to kings. Very convenient for the common people, this; their half-clad forms presenting a perpetual and profound salutation.

Presently, Peepi, the ruler of Valapee drew near: a boy, hardly ten years old, striding the neck of a burly mute, bearing a long spear erect before him, to which was attached a canopy of five broad banana leaves, new plucked. Thus shaded, little Peepi advanced, steadying himself by the forelock of his bearer.

Besides his bright red robe, the young prince wore nothing but the symbol of Valapeean royalty; a string of small, close-fitting, concave shells, coiled and ambushed in his profuse, curly hair; one end falling over his ear, revealing a serpent's head, curiously carved from a nutmeg.

Quite proverbial, the unembarrassed air of young slips of royalty. But there was something so surprisingly precocious in this young Peepi, that at first one hardly knew what to conclude.

The first compliments over, the company were invited inland to a shady retreat.

As we pursued the path, walking between old Mohi the keeper of chronicles and Samoa the Upoluan, Babbalanja besought the former to enlighten a stranger concerning the history of this curious Peepi. Whereupon the chronicler gave us the following account; for all of which he alone is responsible.

Peepi, it seems, had been proclaimed king before he was born; his sire dying some few weeks previous to that event; and vacating his divan, declared that he left a monarch behind.

Marvels were told of Peepi. Along with the royal dignity, and superadded to the soul possessed in his own proper person, the infant monarch was supposed to have inherited the valiant spirits of some twenty heroes, sages, simpletons, and demi-gods, previously lodged in his sire.

Most opulent in spiritual gifts was this lord of Valapee; the legatee, moreover, of numerous anonymous souls, bequeathed to him by their late loyal proprietors. By a slavish act of his convocation of chiefs, he also possessed the reversion of all and singular the immortal spirits, whose first grantees might die intestate in Valapee. Servile, yet audacious senators! thus prospectively to administrate away the inalienable rights of posterity. But while yet unborn, the people of Valapee had been deprived of more than they now sought to wrest from their descendants. And former Peepies, infant and adult, had received homage more profound, than Peepi the Present. Witness the demeanor of the chieftains of old, upon every new investiture of the royal serpent. In a fever of loyalty, they were wont to present themselves before the heir to the isle, to go through with the court ceremony of the Pupera; a curious proceeding, so called: inverted endeavors to assume an erect posture: the nasal organ the base.

It was to the frequent practice of this ceremony, that most intelligent observers imputed the flattened noses of the elderly chiefs of the island; who, nevertheless, much gloried therein.

It was these chiefs, also, who still observed the old-fashioned custom of retiring from the presence of royalty with their heads between their thighs;

so that while advancing in the contrary direction, their faces might be still deferentially turned toward their lord and master. A fine view of him did they obtain. All objects look well through an arch.

But to return to Peepi, the inheritor of souls and subjects. It was an article of faith with the people of Valapee, that Peepi not only actually possessed the souls bequeathed to him; but that his own was enriched by their peculiar qualities: The headlong valor of the late Tongatona; the pusillanimous discretion of Blandoo; the cunning of Voyo; the simplicity of Raymonda; the prodigality of Zonoree; the thrift of Titonti.

But had all these, and similar opposite qualities, simultaneously acted as motives upon Peepi, certes, he would have been a most pitiable mortal, in a ceaseless eddy of resolves, incapable of a solitary act.

But blessed be the gods, it was otherwise. Though it fared little better for his subjects as it was. His assorted souls were uppermost and active in him, one by one. To-day, valiant Tongatona ruled the isle, meditating wars and invasions; to-morrow, thrice discreet Blandoo, who, disbanding the levies, turned his attention to the terraces of yams. And so on in rotation to the end.

Whence, though capable of action, Peepi, by reason of these revolving souls in him, was one of the most unreliable of beings. What the open-handed Zonoree promised freely to-day, the parsimonious Titonti withheld to-morrow; and forever Raymonda was annulling the doings of Voyo; and Voyo the doings of Raymonda.

What marvel then, that in Valapee all was legislative uproar and confusion; advance and retreat; abrogations and revivals; foundations without superstructures; nothing permanent but the island itself.

Nor were there those in the neighboring countries, who failed to reap profit from this everlasting transition state of the affairs of the kingdom. All boons from Peepi were entreated when the prodigal Zonoree was lord of the ascendant. And audacious claims were urged upon the state when the pusillanimous Blandoo shrank from the thought of resisting them.

Thus subject to contrary impulses, over which he had not the faintest control, Peepi was plainly denuded of all moral obligation to virtue. He was no more a free agent, than the heart which beat in his bosom. Wherefore, his complaisant parliament had passed a law, recognizing that curious, but alarming fact; solemnly proclaiming, that King Peepi was minus a conscience. Agreeable to truth. But when they went further, and vowed by statute, that Peepi could do no wrong, they assuredly did violence to the truth; besides, making a sad blunder in their logic. For far from possessing an absolute aversion to evil, by his very nature it was the hardest thing in the world for Peepi to do right.

Taking all these things into consideration, then, no wonder that this wholly irresponsible young prince should be a lad of considerable assurance, and the easiest manners imaginable.

Chapter 68

How Teeth were regarded in Valapee

COILING THROUGH THE THICKETS, like the track of a serpent, wound along the path we pursued. And ere long we came to a spacious grove, embowering an oval arbor. Here, we reclined at our ease, and refreshments were served.

Little worthy of mention occurred, save this. Happening to catch a glimpse of the white even teeth of Hohora one of our attendants, King Peepi coolly begged of Media the favor, to have those same dentals drawn on the spot, and presented to him.

Now human teeth, extracted, are reckoned among the most valuable ornaments in Mardi. So open wide thy strong box, Hohora, and show thy treasures. What a gallant array! standing shoulder to shoulder, without a hiatus between. A complete set of jewelry, indeed, thought Peepi. But, it seems, not destined for him; Media leaving it to the present proprietor, whether his dentals should change owners or not.

And here, to prepare the way for certain things hereafter to be narrated, something farther needs be said concerning the light in which men's molars are regarded in Mardi.

Strung together, they are sported for necklaces, or hung in drops from the ear; they are wrought into dice; in lieu of silken locks, are exchanged for love tokens.

205

As in all lands, men smite their breasts, and tear their hair, when transported with grief; so, in some countries, teeth are stricken out under the sway of similar emotions. To a very great extent, this was once practiced in the Hawaiian Islands, ere idol and altar went down. Still living in Oahu, are many old chiefs, who were present at the famous obsequies of their royal old generalissimo, Tammahammaha, when there is no telling how many pounds of ivory were cast upon his grave.

Ah! had the regal white elephants of Siam been there, doubtless they had offered up their long, hooked tusks, whereon they impale the leopards, their foes; and the unicorn had surrendered that fixed bayonet in his forehead; and the imperial Cachalot-whale, the long chain of white towers in his jaw; yea, over that grim warrior's grave, the mooses, and elks, and stags, and fallow-deer had stacked their antlers, as soldiers their arms on the field.

Terrific shade of tattooed Tammahammaha! if, from a vile dragon's molars, rose mailed men, what heroes shall spring from the cannibal canines once pertaining to warriors themselves!—Am I the witch of Endor, that I conjure up this ghost? Or, King Saul, that I so quake at the sight? For, lo! roundabout me Tammahammaha's tattooing expands, till all the sky seems a tiger's skin. But now, the spotted phantom sweeps by; as a man-of-war's main-sail, cloud-like, blown far to leeward in a gale.

Banquo down, we return.

In Valapee, prevails not the barbarous Hindoo custom of offering up widows to the shades of their lords; for, bereaved, the widows there marry again. Nor yet prevails the savage Hawaiian custom of offering up teeth to the manes of the dead; for, at the decease of a friend, the people rob not their own mouths to testify their woe. On the contrary, they extract the teeth from the departed, distributing them among the mourners for memorial legacies; as elsewhere, silver spoons are bestowed.

From the high value ascribed to dentals throughout the archipelago of Mardi, and also from their convenient size, they are circulated as money; strings of teeth being regarded by these people very much as belts of wampum among the Winnebagoes of the North; or cowries, among the Bengalese. So, that in Valapee the very beggars are born with a snug investment in their mouths; too soon, however, to be appropriated by their lords; leaving them toothless for the rest of their days, and forcing them to diet on poee-pudding and banana blanc-mange.

As a currency, teeth are far less clumsy than cocoanuts; which, among certain remote barbarians, circulate for coin; one nut being equivalent, perhaps, to a penny. The voyager who records the fact, chuckles over it hugely; as evincing the simplicity of those heathens; not knowing that he himself was the simpleton; since that currency of theirs was purposely devised by the men, to check the extravagance of their women; cocoanuts, for spending money, being such a burden to carry.

It only remains to be added, that the most solemn oath of a native of Valapee is that sworn by his tooth. "By this tooth," said Bondo to Noojoomo, "by this tooth I swear to be avenged upon thee, oh Noojoomo!"

Chapter 69

The Company discourse, and Braid-Beard rehearses a Legend

FINDING IN VALAPEE no trace of her whom we sought, and but little pleased with the cringing demeanor of the people, and the wayward follies of Peepi their lord, we early withdrew from the isle.

As we glided away, King Media issued a sociable decree. He declared it his royal pleasure, that throughout the voyage, all stiffness and state etiquette should be suspended: nothing must occur to mar the freedom of the party. To further this charming plan, he doffed his symbols of royalty, put off his crown, laid aside his scepter, and assured us that he would not wear them again, except when we landed; and not invariably, then.

"Are we not all now friends and companions?" he said. "So companions and friends let us be. I unbend my bow; do ye likewise."

"But are we not to be dignified?" asked Babbalanja.

"If dignity be free and natural, be as dignified as you please; but away with rigidities."

"Away they go," said Babbalanja; "and, my lord, now that you mind me of it, I have often thought, that it is all folly and vanity for any man to attempt a dignified carriage. Why, my lord,"—frankly crossing his legs where he lay—"the king, who receives his embassadors with a majestic toss of the head, may have just recovered from the tooth-ache. That thought should cant over the spine he bears so bravely."

"Have a care, sir! there is a king within hearing."

"Pardon, my lord; I was merely availing myself of the immunity bestowed upon the company. Hereafter, permit a subject to rebel against your sociable decrees. I will not be so frank any more."

"Well put, Babbalanja; come nearer; here, cross your legs by mine; you have risen a cubit in my regard. Vee-Vee, bring us that gourd of wine; so, pass it round with the cups. Now, Yoomy, a song!"

And a song was sung.

And thus did we sail; pleasantly reclining on the mats stretched out beneath the canopied howdah.

At length, we drew nigh to a rock, called Pella, or The Theft. A high, green crag, toppling over its base, and flinging a cavernous shadow upon the lagoon beneath, bubbling with the moisture that dropped.

Passing under this cliff was like finding yourself, as some sea-hunters unexpectedly have, beneath the open, upper jaw of a whale; which, descending, infallibly entombs you. But familiar with the rock, our paddlers only threw back their heads, to catch the cool, pleasant tricklings from the mosses above.

Wiping away several glittering beads from his beard, old Mohi turning round where he sat, just outside the canopy, solemnly affirmed, that the drinking of that water had cured many a man of ambition.

"How so, old man?" demanded Media.

"Because of its passing through the ashes of ten kings, of yore buried in a sepulcher, hewn in the heart of the rock."

"Mighty kings, and famous, doubtless," said Babbalanja, "whose bones were thought worthy of so noble and enduring an urn. Pray, Mohi, their names and terrible deeds."

"Alas! their sepulcher only remains."

"And, no doubt, like many others, they made that sepulcher for themselves. They sleep sound, my word for it, old man. But I very much question, if, were the rock rent, any ashes would be found. Mohi, I deny that those kings ever had any bones to bury."

"Why, Babbalanja," said Media, "since you intimate that they never had ghosts to give up, you ignore them in toto; denying the very fact of their being even defunct."

"Ten thousand pardons, my lord, no such discourtesy would I do the anonymous memory of the illustrious dead. But whether they ever lived or not, it is all the same with them now. Yet, grant that they lived; then, if death be a deaf-and-dumb death, a triumphal procession over their graves would concern them not. If a birth into brightness, then Mardi must seem to them the most trivial of reminiscences. Or, perhaps, theirs may be an utter lapse of memory concerning sublunary things; and they themselves be not themselves, as the butterfly is not the larva."

Said Yoomy, "Then, Babbalanja, you account that a fit illustration of the miraculous change to be wrought in man after death?"

"No; for the analogy has an unsatisfactory end. From its chrysalis state, the silkworm but becomes a moth, that very quickly expires. Its longest existence is as a worm. All vanity, vanity, Yoomy, to seek in nature for positive warranty to these aspirations of ours. Through all her provinces, nature seems to promise immortality to life, but destruction to beings. Or, as old Bardianna has it, if not against us, nature is not for us."

Said Media, rising, "Babbalanja, you have indeed put aside the courtier; talking of worms and caterpillars to me, a king and a demi-god! To renown, for your theme: a more agreeable topic."

"Pardon, once again, my lord. And since you will, let us discourse of that subject. First, I lay it down for an indubitable maxim, that in itself all posthumous renown, which is the only renown, is valueless. Be not offended, my lord. To the nobly ambitious, renown hereafter may be something to anticipate. But analyzed, that feverish typhoid feeling of theirs may be nothing more than a flickering fancy, that now, while living, they are recognized as those who will be as famous in their shrouds, as in their girdles."

Said Yoomy, "But those great and good deeds, Babbalanja, of which the philosophers so often discourse: must it not be sweet to believe that their memory will long survive us; and we ourselves in them?"

"I speak now," said Babbalanja, "of the ravening for fame; which even appeased, like thirst slaked in the desert, yields no felicity, but only relief; and which discriminates not in aught that will satisfy its cravings. But let me resume. Not an hour ago, Braid-Beard was telling us that story of prince Ottimo, who inodorous while living, expressed much delight at the prospect of being perfumed and embalmed, when dead. But was not Ottimo the most eccentric of mortals? For few men issue orders for their shrouds, to inspect their quality beforehand. Far more anxious are they about the texture of the sheets in which their living limbs lie. And, my lord, with some rare exceptions, does not all Mardi, by its actions, declare, that it is far better to be notorious now, than famous hereafter?"

"A base sentiment, my lord," said Yoomy. "Did not poor Bonja, the unappreciated poet, console himself for the neglect of his contemporaries, by inspiriting thoughts of the future?"

"In plain words by bethinking him of the glorious harvest of bravos his ghost would reap for him," said Babbalanja; "but Banjo,—Bonjo,—Binjo,—I never heard of him."

"Nor I," said Mohi.

"Nor I," said Media.

"Poor fellow!" cried Babbalanja; "I fear me his harvest is not yet ripe."

"Alas!" cried Yoomy; "he died more than a century ago."

"But now that you speak of unappreciated poets, Yoomy," said Babbalanja, "shall I give you a piece of my mind?"

"Do," said Mohi, stroking his beard.

"He, who on all hands passes for a cypher to-day, if at all remembered hereafter, will be sure to pass for the same. For there is more likelihood of being overrated while living, than of being underrated when dead. And to insure your fame, you must die."

"A rather discouraging thought for your race. But answer: I assume that King Media is but a mortal like you; now, how may I best perpetuate my name?"

Long pondered Babbalanja; then said, "Carve it, my lord, deep into a ponderous stone, and sink it, face downward, into the sea; for the unseen foundations of the deep are more enduring than the palpable tops of the mountains."

Sailing past Pella, we gained a view of its farther side; and seated in a lofty cleft, beheld a lonely fisherman; solitary as a seal on an iceberg; his motionless line in the water.

"What recks he of the ten kings," said Babbalanja.

"Mohi," said Media, "methinks there is another tradition concerning that rock: let us have it."

"In old times of genii and giants, there dwelt in barren lands, not very remote from our outer reef, but since submerged, a band of evil-minded, envious goblins, furlongs in stature, and with immeasurable arms; who from time to time cast covetous glances upon our blooming isles. Long they lusted; till at last, they waded through the sea, strode over the reef, and seizing the nearest islet, rolled it over and over, toward an adjoining outlet.

"But the task was hard; and day-break surprised them in the midst of their audacious thieving; while in the very act of giving the devoted land another doughty surge and somerset. Leaving it bottom upward and midway poised, gardens under water, its foundations in air, they precipitately fled; in their great haste, deserting a comrade, vainly struggling to liberate his foot caught beneath the overturned land.

"This poor fellow now raised such an outcry, as to awaken the god Upi, or the Archer, stretched out on a long cloud in the East; who forthwith resolved to make an example of the unwilling lingerer. Snatching his bow, he let fly an arrow. But overshooting its mark, it pierced through and through, the lofty promontory of a neighboring island; making an arch in it, which remaineth even unto this day. A second arrow, however, accomplished its errand: the slain giant sinking prone to the bottom."

"And now," added Mohi, "glance over the gunwale, and you will see his remains petrified into white ribs of coral."

"Ay, there they are," said Yoomy, looking down into the water where they gleamed. "A fanciful legend, Braid-Beard."

"Very entertaining," said Media.

"Even so," said Babbalanja. "But perhaps we lost time in listening to it; for though we know it, we are none the wiser."

"Be not a cynic," said Media. "No pastime is lost time."

Musing a moment, Babbalanja replied, "My lord, that maxim may be good as it stands; but had you made six words of it, instead of six syllables, you had uttered a better and a deeper."

Chapter 70

The Minstrel leads off with a Paddle-Song;
and a Message is received from Abroad

FROM SEAWARD now came a breeze so blithesome and fresh, that it made us impatient of Babbalanja's philosophy, and Mohi's incredible legends. One and all, we called upon the minstrel Yoomy to give us something in unison with the spirited waves wide-foaming around us.

"If my lord will permit, we will give Taji the Paddle-Chant of the warriors of King Bello."

"By all means," said Media.

So the three canoes were brought side to side; their sails rolled up; and paddles in hand, our paddlers seated themselves sideways on the gunwales; Yoomy, as leader, occupying the place of the foremast, or Bow-Paddler of the royal barge.

Whereupon the six rows of paddle-blades being uplifted, and every eye on the minstrel, this song was sung, with actions corresponding; the canoes at last shooting through the water, with a violent roll.

(*All.*)
Thrice waved on high,
Our paddles fly:
Thrice round the head, thrice dropt to feet:
And then well timed,
Of one stout mind,
All fall, and back the waters heap!

(*Bow-Paddler.*)
Who lifts this chant?
Who sounds this vaunt?

(*All.*)
The wild sea song, to the billows' throng,
Rising, falling,
Hoarsely calling,
Now high, now low, as fast we go,
Fast on our flying foe!

(*Bow-Paddler.*)
Who lifts this chant?
Who sounds this vaunt?

(*All.*)
Dip, dip, in the brine our paddles dip,
Dip, dip, the fins of our swimming ship!
How the waters part,
As on we dart;
Our sharp prows fly,
And curl on high,
As the upright fin of the rushing shark,
Rushing fast and far on his flying mark!
Like him we prey;
Like him we slay;
Swim on the foe,
Our prow a blow!

(*Bow-Paddler.*)
Who lifts this chant?
Who sounds this vaunt?

(*All.*)
Heap back; heap back; the waters back!
Pile them high astern, in billows black;
Till we leave our wake,
In the slope we make;
And rush and ride,
On the torrent's tide!

Here we were overtaken by a swift gliding canoe, which, bearing down upon us before the wind, lowered its sail when close by: its occupants signing our paddlers to desist.

I started.

The strangers were three hooded damsels: the enigmatical Queen Hautia's heralds.

Their pursuit surprised and perplexed me. Nor was there wanting a vague feeling of alarm to heighten these emotions. But perhaps I was mistaken, and this time they meant not me.

Seated in the prow, the foremost waved her Iris flag.

Cried Yoomy, "Some message! Taji, that Iris points to you."

It was then, I first divined, that some meaning must have lurked in those flowers they had twice brought me before.

The second damsel now flung over to me Circe flowers; then, a faded jonquil, buried in a tuft of wormwood leaves.

The third sat in the shallop's stern, and as it glided from us, thrice waved oleanders.

"What dumb show is this?" cried Media. "But it looks like poetry: minstrel, you should know."

"Interpret then," said I.

"Shall I, then, be your Flora's flute, and Hautia's dragoman? Held aloft, the Iris signified a message. These purple-woven Circe flowers mean that some spell is weaving. That golden, pining jonquil, which you hold, buried in those wormwood leaves, says plainly to you—Bitter love in absence."

Said Media, "Well done, Taji, you have killed a queen."

"Yet no Queen Hautia have these eyes beheld."

Said Babbalanja, "The thrice waved oleanders, Yoomy; what meant they?"

"Beware—beware—beware."

"Then that, at least, seems kindly meant," said Babbalanja; "Taji, beware of Hautia."

Chapter 71

They land upon the Island of Juam

CROSSING THE LAGOON, our course now lay along the reef to Juam; a name bestowed upon one of the largest islands hereabout; and also, collectively, upon several wooded isles engirdling it, which together were known as the dominions of one monarch. That monarch was Donjalolo. Just turned of twenty-five, he was accounted not only the handsomest man in his dominions, but throughout the lagoon. His comeliness, however, was so feminine, that he was sometimes called "Fonoo," or the Girl.

Our first view of Juam was imposing. A dark green pile of cliffs, towering some one hundred toises; at top, presenting a range of steep, gable-pointed projections; as if some Titanic hammer and chisel had shaped the mass.

Sailing nearer, we perceived an extraordinary rolling of the sea, which bursting into the lagoon through an adjoining breach in the reef, surged toward Juam in enormous billows. At last, dashing against the wall of the cliff, they played there in unceasing fountains. But under the brow of a beetling crag, the spray came and went unequally. There, the blue billows seemed swallowed up, and lost.

Right regally was Juam guarded. For, at this point, the rock was pierced by a cave, into which the great waves chased each other like lions; after a hollow, subterraneous roaring issuing forth with manes disheveled.

Cautiously evading the dangerous currents here ruffling the lagoon, we rounded the wall of cliff, and shot upon a smooth expanse; on one side, hemmed in by the long, verdent, northern shore of Juam; and across the water, sentineled by its tributary islets.

With sonorous Vee-Vee in the shark's mouth, we swept toward the beach, tumultuous with a throng.

Our canoes were secured. And surrounded by eager glances, we passed the lower ends of several populous valleys; and crossing a wide, open meadow, gradually ascending, came to a range of light-green bluffs. Here, we wended our way down a narrow defile, almost cleaving this quarter of the island to its base. Black crags frowned overhead: among them the shouts of the Islanders reverberated. Yet steeper grew the defile, and more overhanging the crags; till at last, the keystone of the arch seemed dropped into its place. We found ourselves in a subterranean tunnel, dimly lighted by a span of white day at the end.

Emerging, what a scene was revealed! All round, embracing a circuit of some three leagues, stood heights inaccessible, here and there, forming buttresses, sheltering deep recesses between. The bosom of the place was vivid with verdure.

Shining aslant into this wild hollow, the afternoon sun lighted up its eastern side with tints of gold. But opposite, brooded a somber shadow, double-shading the secret places between the salient spurs of the mountains. Thus cut in twain by masses of day and night, it seemed as if some Last Judgment had been enacted in the glen.

No sooner did we emerge from the defile, than we became sensible of a dull, jarring sound; and Yoomy was almost tempted to turn and flee, when informed that the sea-cavern, whose mouth we had passed, was believed to penetrate deep into the opposite hills; and that the surface of the amphitheater was depressed beneath that of the lagoon. But all over the lowermost hill-sides, and sloping into the glen, stood grand old groves; still and stately, as if no insolent waves were throbbing in the mountain's heart.

Such was Willamilla, the hereditary abode of the young monarch of Juam.

Was Yillah immured in this strange retreat? But from those around us naught could we learn.

Our attention was now directed to the habitations of the glen; comprised in two handsome villages; one to the west, the other to the east; both stretching along the base of the cliffs.

Said Media, "Had we arrived at Willamilla in the morning, we had found Donjalolo and his court in the eastern village; but being afternoon, we must travel farther, and seek him in his western retreat; for that is now in the shade."

Wending our way, Media added, that aside from his elevated station as a monarch, Donjalolo was famed for many uncommon traits; but more especially for certain peculiar deprivations, under which he labored.

Whereupon Braid-Beard unrolled his old chronicles; and regaled us with the history, which will be found in the following chapter.

Chapter 72

A Book from the Chronicles of Mohi

MANY AGES AGO, there reigned in Juam a king called Teei. This Teei's succession to the sovereignty was long disputed by his brother Marjora; who at last rallying round him an army, after many vicissitudes, defeated the unfortunate monarch in a stout fight of clubs on the beach.

In those days, Willamilla during a certain period of the year was a place set apart for royal games and diversions; and was furnished with suitable accommodations for king and court. From its peculiar position, moreover, it was regarded as the last stronghold of the Juam monarchy: in remote times having twice withstood the most desperate assaults from without. And when Roonoonoo, a famous upstart, sought to subdue all the isles in this part of the Archipelago, it was to Willamilla that the banded kings had repaired to take counsel together; and while there conferring, were surprised at the sudden onslaught of Roonoonoo in person. But in the end, the rebel was captured, he and all his army, and impaled on the tops of the hills.

Now, defeated and fleeing for his life, Teei with his surviving followers was driven across the plain toward the mountains. But to cut him off from all escape to inland Willamilla, Marjora dispatched a fleet band of warriors to occupy the entrance of the defile. Nevertheless, Teei the pursued ran faster than his pursuers; first gained the spot; and with his chiefs, fled swiftly down the gorge, closely hunted by Marjora's men. But arriving at the further end, they in vain sought to defend it. And after much desperate fighting, the main body of the foe coming up, with great slaughter the fugitives were driven into the glen.

They ran to the opposite wall of cliff; where turning, they fought at bay, blood for blood, and life for life, till at last, overwhelmed by numbers, they were all put to the point of the spear.

With fratricidal hate, singled out by the ferocious Marjora, Teei fell by that brother's hand. When stripping from the body the regal girdle, the victor wound it round his own loins; thus proclaiming himself king over Juam.

Long torn by this intestine war, the island acquiesced in the new sovereignty. But at length a sacred oracle declared, that since the conqueror had slain his brother in deep Willamilla, so that Teei never more issued from that refuge of death; therefore, the same fate should be Marjora's; for never, thenceforth, from that glen, should he go forth; neither Marjora; nor any son of his girdled loins; nor his son's sons; nor the uttermost scion of his race.

But except this denunciation, naught was denounced against the usurper; who, mindful of the tenure by which he reigned, ruled over the island for many moons; at his death bequeathing the girdle to his son.

In those days, the wildest superstitions concerning the interference of the gods in things temporal, prevailed to a much greater extent than at present. Hence Marjora himself, called sometimes in the traditions of the island, The-Heart-of-Black-Coral, even unscrupulous Marjora had quailed before the oracle. "He bowed his head," say the legends. Nor was it then questioned, by his most devoted adherents, that had he dared to act counter to that edict, he had dropped dead, the very instant he went under the shadow of the defile. This persuasion also guided the conduct of the son of Marjora, and that of his grandson.

But there at last came to pass a change in the popular fancies concerning this ancient anathema. The penalty denounced against the posterity of the usurper should they issue from the glen, came to be regarded as only applicable to an invested monarch, not to his relatives, or heirs.

A most favorable construction of the ban; for all those related to the king, freely passed in and out of Willamilla.

From the time of the usurpation, there had always been observed a certain ceremony upon investing the heir to the sovereignty with the girdle of Teei. Upon these occasions, the chief priests of the island were present, acting an important part. For the space of as many days, as there had reigned kings of Marjora's dynasty, the inner mouth of the defile remained sealed; the new monarch placing the last stone in the gap. This symbolized his relinquishment forever of all purpose of passing out of the glen. And without this observance, was no king girdled in Juam.

It was likewise an invariable custom, for the heir to receive the regal investiture immediately upon the decease of his sire. No delay was permitted. And instantly upon being girdled, he proceeded to take part in the ceremony of closing the cave; his predecessor yet remaining uninterred on the purple mat where he died.

In the history of the island, three instances were recorded; wherein, upon the vacation of the sovereignty, the immediate heir had voluntarily renounced all claim to the succession, rather than surrender the privilege of roving, to which he had been entitled, as a prince of the blood.

Said Rani, one of these young princes, in reply to the remonstrances of his friends, "What! shall I be a king, only to be a slave? Teei's girdle would clasp my waist less tightly, than my soul would be banded by the mountains of Willamilla. A subject, I am free. No slave in Juam but its king; for all the tassels round his loins."

To guard against a similar resolution in the mind of his only son, the wise sire of Donjalolo, ardently desirous of perpetuating his dignities in a child so well beloved, had from his earliest infancy, restrained the boy from passing out of the glen, to contract in the free air of the Archipelago, tastes and predilections fatal to the inheritance of the girdle.

But as he grew in years, so impatient became young Donjalolo of the king his father's watchfulness over him, though hitherto a most dutiful son, that at last he was prevailed upon by his youthful companions to appoint a day, on which to go abroad, and visit Mardi. Hearing this determination, the old king sought to vanquish it. But in vain. And early on the morning of the day, that Donjalolo was to set out, he swallowed poison, and died; in order to force his son into the instant assumption of the honors thus suddenly inherited.

The event, but not its dreadful circumstances, was communicated to the prince; as with a gay party of young chiefs, he was about to enter the mouth of the defile.

"My sire dead!" cried Donjalolo. "So sudden, it seems a bolt from Heaven." And bursting into exclamations of grief, he wept upon the bosom of Talara his friend.

But starting from his side:—"My fate converges to a point. If I but cross that shadow, my kingdom is lost. One lifting of my foot, and the girdle goes to my proud uncle Darfi, who would so joy to be my master. Haughty Darfi! Oh Oro! would that I had ere this passed thee, fatal cavern; and seen for myself, what outer Mardi is. Say ye true, comrades, that Willamilla is less lovely than the valleys without? that there is bright light in the eyes of the maidens of Mina? and wisdom in the hearts of the old priests of Maramma; that it is pleasant to tread the green earth where you will; and breathe the free ocean air? Would, oh would, that I were but the least of yonder sun-clouds, that look down alike on Willamilla and all places besides, that I might determine aright. Yet why do I pause? did not Rani, and Atama, and Mardonna, my ancestors, each see for himself, free Mardi; and did they not fly the proffered girdle; choosing rather to be free to come and go, than bury themselves forever in this fatal glen? Oh Mardi! Mardi! art thou then so fair to see? Is liberty a thing so glorious? Yet can I be no king, and behold thee! Too late, too late, to view thy charms and then return. My sire! my sire! thou hast wrung my heart with this agony of doubt. Tell me, comrades,—for ye have seen it,—is Mardi sweeter to behold, than it is royal to reign over Juam? Silent, are ye? Knowing what ye do, were ye me, would ye be kings? Tell me, Talara.—No king: no king:— that were to obey, and not command. And none hath Donjalolo ere obeyed but the king his father. A king, and my voice may be heard in farthest Mardi, though I abide in narrow Willamilla. My sire! my sire! Ye flying clouds, what look ye down upon? Tell me, what ye see abroad? Methinks sweet spices breathe from out the cave."

"Hail, Donjalolo, King of Juam," now sounded with acclamations from the groves.

Starting, the young prince beheld a multitude approaching: warriors with spears, and maidens with flowers; and Kubla, a priest, lifting on high the tasseled girdle of Teei, and waving it toward him.

The young chiefs fell back. Kubla, advancing, came close to the prince, and unclasping the badge of royalty, exclaimed, "Donjalolo, this instant it is king or subject with thee: wilt thou be girdled monarch?"

Gazing one moment up the dark defile, then staring vacantly, Donjalolo turned and met the eager gaze of Darfi. Stripping off his mantle, the next instant he was a king.

Loud shouted the multitude, and exulted; but after mutely assisting at the closing of the cavern, the new-girdled monarch retired sadly to his dwelling, and was not seen again for many days.

Chapter 73

Something more of the Prince

PREVIOUS TO RECORDING our stay in his dominions, it only remains to be related of Donjalolo, that after assuming the girdle, a change came over him.

During the lifetime of his father, he had been famed for his temperance and discretion. But when Mardi was forever shut out; and he remembered the law of his isle, interdicting abdication to its kings; he gradually fell into desperate courses, to drown the emotions at times distracting him.

His generous spirit thirsting after some energetic career, found itself narrowed down within the little glen of Willamilla, where ardent impulses seemed idle. But these are hard to die; and repulsed all round, recoil upon themselves.

So with Donjalolo; who, in many a riotous scene, wasted the powers which might have compassed the noblest designs.

Not many years had elapsed since the death of the king, his father. But the still youthful prince was no longer the bright-eyed and elastic boy who at the dawn of day had sallied out to behold the landscapes of the neighboring isles.

Not more effeminate Sardanapalus, than he. And, at intervals, he was the victim of unaccountable vagaries; haunted by specters, and beckoned to by the ghosts of his sires.

At times, loathing his vicious pursuits, which brought him no solid satisfaction, but ever filled him with final disgust, he would resolve to amend his ways; solacing himself for his bitter captivity, by the society of the wise and discreet. But brief the interval of repentance. Anew, he burst into excesses, a hundred fold more insane than ever.

Thus vacillating between virtue and vice; to neither constant, and upbraided by both; his mind, like his person in the glen, was continually passing and repassing between opposite extremes.

Chapter 74

Advancing deeper into the Vale, they encounter Donjalolo

FROM THE MOUTH of the cavern, a broad shaded way over-arched by fraternal trees embracing in mid-air, conducted us to a cross-path, on either hand leading to the opposite cliffs, shading the twin villages before mentioned.

Level as a meadow, was the bosom of the glen. Here, nodding with green orchards of the Bread-fruit and the Palm; there, flashing with golden plantations of the Banana. Emerging from these, we came out upon a grassy mead, skirting a projection of the mountain. And soon we crossed a bridge of boughs, spanning a trench, thickly planted with roots of the Tara, like alligators, or Hollanders, reveling in the soft alluvial. Strolling on, the wild beauty of the mountains excited our attention. The topmost crags poured over with vines; which, undulating in the air, seemed leafy cascades; their sources the upland groves.

Midway up the precipice, along a shelf of rock, sprouted the multi-tudinous roots of an apparently trunkless tree. Shooting from under the shallow soil, they spread all over the rocks below, covering them with an intricate net-work. While far aloft, great boughs—each a copse—clambered to the very summit of the mountain; then bending over, struck anew into the soil; forming along the verge an interminable colonnade; all manner of antic architecture standing against the sky.

According to Mohi, this tree was truly wonderful; its seed having been dropped from the moon; where were plenty more similar forests, causing the dark spots on its surface.

Here and there, the cool fluid in the veins of the mountains gushed forth in living springs; their waters received in green mossy tanks, half buried in grasses.

In one place, a considerable stream, bounding far out from a wooded height, ere reaching the ground was dispersed in a wide misty shower, falling so far from the base of the cliff, that walking close underneath, you felt little moisture. Passing this fall of vapors, we spied many Islanders taking a bath.

But what is yonder swaying of the foliage? And what now issues forth, like a habitation astir? Donjalolo drawing nigh to his guests.

He came in a fair sedan; a bower, resting upon three long, parallel poles, borne by thirty men, gayly attired; five at each pole-end. Decked with dyed tappas, and looped with garlands of newly-plucked flowers, from which, at every step, the fragrant petals were blown; with a sumptuous, elastic motion the gay sedan came on; leaving behind it a long, rosy wake of fluttering leaves and odors.

Drawing near, it revealed a slender, enervate youth, of pallid beauty, reclining upon a crimson mat, near the festooned arch of the bower. His anointed head was resting against the bosom of a girl; another stirred the air, with a fan of Pintado plumes. The pupils of his eyes were as floating isles in the sea. In a soft low tone he murmured "Media!"

The bearers paused; and Media advancing, the Island Kings bowed their foreheads together.

Through tubes ignited at the end, Donjalolo's reclining attendants now blew an aromatic incense around him. These were composed of the stimulating leaves of the "Aina," mixed with the long yellow blades of a sweet-scented upland grass; forming a hollow stem. In general, the agreeable fumes of the "Aina" were created by one's own inhalations; but Donjalolo deeming the solace too dearly purchased by any exertion of the royal lungs, regaled himself through those of his attendants, whose lips were as moss-rose buds after a shower.

In silence the young prince now eyed us attentively; meanwhile gently waving his hand, to obtain a better view through the wreaths of vapor. He was about to address us, when chancing to catch a glimpse of Samoa, he suddenly started; averted his glance; and wildly commanded the warrior out of sight. Upon this, his attendants would have soothed him; and Media desired the Upoluan to withdraw.

While we were yet lost in wonder at this scene, Donjalolo, with eyes closed, fell back into the arms of his damsels. Recovering, he fetched a deep sigh, and gazed vacantly around.

It seems, that he had fancied Samoa the noon-day specter of his ancestor Marjora; the usurper having been deprived of an arm in the battle which gained him the girdle. Poor prince: this was one of those crazy conceits, so puzzling to his subjects.

Media now hastened to assure Donjalolo, that Samoa, though no cherub to behold, was good flesh and blood, nevertheless. And soon the king unconcernedly gazed; his monomania having departed as a dream.

But still suffering from the effects of an overnight feast, he presently murmured forth a desire to be left to his women; adding that his people would not fail to provide for the entertainment of his guests.

The curtains of the sedan were now drawn; and soon it disappeared in the groves. Journeying on, ere long we arrived at the western side of the glen; where one of the many little arbors scattered among the trees, was assigned for our abode. Here, we reclined to an agreeable repast. After which, we strolled forth to view the valley at large; more especially the far-famed palaces of the prince.

Chapter 75

Time and Temples

IN THE ORIENTAL Pilgrimage of the pious old Purchas, and in the fine old folio Voyages of Hakluyt, Thevenot, Ramusio, and De Bry, we read of many glorious old Asiatic temples, very long in erecting. And veracious Gaudentio di Lucca hath a wondrous narration of the time consumed in rearing that mighty three-hundred-and-sixty-five-pillared Temple of the Year, somewhere beyond Libya; whereof, the columns did signify days, and all round fronted upon concentric zones of palaces, cross-cut by twelve grand avenues symbolizing the signs of the zodiac, all radiating from the sun-dome in their midst. And in that wild eastern tale of his, Marco Polo tells us, how the Great Mogul began him a pleasure-palace on so imperial a scale, that his grandson had much ado to complete it.

But no matter for marveling all this: great towers take time to construct. And so of all else.

And that which long endures full-fledged, must have long lain in the germ. And duration is not of the future, but of the past; and eternity is eternal, because it has been; and though a strong new monument be builded to-day, it only is lasting because its blocks are old as the sun. It is not the Pyramids that are ancient, but the eternal granite whereof they are made; which had been equally ancient though yet in the quarry. For to make an eternity, we must build with eternities; whence, the vanity of the cry for any thing alike durable and new; and the folly of the reproach—Your granite hath come from the old-fashioned hills. For we are not gods and creators; and the controversialists have debated, whether indeed the All-Plastic Power itself can do more than mold. In all the universe is but one original; and the very suns must to their source for their fire; and we Prometheuses must to them for ours; which, when had, only perpetual Vestal tending will keep alive.

But let us back from fire to stone. No fine firm fabric ever yet grew like a gourd. Nero's House of Gold was not raised in a day; nor the Mexican House of the Sun; nor the Alhambra; nor the Escurial; nor Titus's Amphitheater; nor the Illinois Mounds; nor Diana's great columns at Ephesus; nor Pompey's proud Pillar; nor the Parthenon; nor the Altar of Belus; nor Stonehenge; nor Solomon's Temple; nor Tadmor's towers; nor Susa's bastions; nor Persepolis' pediments. Round and round, the Moorish turret at Seville was not wound heavenward in the revolution of a day; and from its first founding, five hundred years did circle, ere Strasbourg's great spire lifted its five hundred feet into the air. No: nor were the great grottos of Elephanta hewn out in an hour; nor did the Troglodytes dig Kentucky's Mammoth Cave in a sun; nor that of Trophonius, nor Antiparos; nor the Giant's Causeway. Nor were the subterranean arched sewers of Etruria channeled in a trice; nor the airy arched aqueducts of Nerva thrown over their vallies in the ides of a month. Nor was Virginia's Natural Bridge worn under in a year; nor, in geology, were the eternal Grampians upheaved in an age. And who shall count the cycles that revolved ere earth's interior sedimentary strata were crystalized into stone. Nor Peak of Piko, nor Teneriffe, were chiseled into obelisks in a decade; nor had Mount Athos been turned into Alexander's statue so soon. And the bower of Artaxerxes took a whole Persian summer to grow; and the Czar's Ice Palace a long Muscovite winter to congeal. No, no: nor was the Pyramid of Cheops masoned in a month; though, once built, the sands left by the deluge might not have submerged such a pile. Nor were the broad boughs of Charles' Oak grown in a spring; though they outlived the royal dynasties of Tudor and Stuart. Nor were the parts of the great Iliad put together in haste; though old Homer's temple shall lift up its dome, when St. Peter's is a legend. Even man himself lives months ere his Maker deems him fit to be born; and ere his proud shaft gains its full stature, twenty-one long Julian years must elapse. And his whole mortal life brings not his immortal soul to maturity; nor will all eternity perfect him. Yea, with uttermost reverence, as to human understanding, increase of dominion seems increase of power; and day by day new planets are being added to elder-born Saturns, even as six thousand years ago our own Earth made one more in this system; so, in incident, not in essence, may the Infinite himself be not less than more infinite now, than when old Aldebaran rolled forth from his hand. And if time was, when this round Earth, which to innumerable mortals has seemed an empire never to be wholly explored; which, in its seas, concealed all the Indies over four thousand five hundred years; if time was, when this great quarry of Assyrias and Romes was not extant; then, time may have been, when the whole material universe lived its Dark Ages; yea, when the Ineffable Silence, proceeding from its unimaginable remoteness, espied it as an isle in the sea. And herein is no derogation. For the Immeasurable's altitude is not heightened by the arches of Mahomet's heavens; and were all space a vacuum, yet would it be a fullness; for to Himself His own universe is He.

Thus deeper and deeper into Time's endless tunnel, does the winged soul, like a night-hawk, wend her wild way; and finds eternities before and behind; and her last limit is her everlasting beginning.

But sent over the broad flooded sphere, even Noah's dove came back, and perched on his hand. So comes back my spirit to me, and folds up her wings.

Thus, then, though Time be the mightiest of Alarics, yet is he the mightiest mason of all. And a tutor, and a counselor, and a physician, and a scribe, and a poet, and a sage, and a king.

Yea, and a gardener, as ere long will be shown.

But first must we return to the glen.

Chapter 76

A pleasant Place for a Lounge

WHETHER THE HARD CONDITION of their kingly state, very naturally demanding some luxurious requital, prevailed upon the monarchs of Juam to house themselves so delightfully as they did; whether buried alive in their glen, they sought to center therein a secret world of enjoyment; however it may have been, throughout the Archipelago this saying was a proverb—"You are lodged like the king in Willamilla." Hereby was expressed the utmost sumptuousness of a palace.

A well warranted saying; for of all the bright places, where my soul loves to linger, the haunts of Donjalolo are most delicious.

In the eastern quarter of the glen was the House of the Morning. This fanciful palace was raised upon a natural mound, many rods square, almost completely filling up a deep recess between deep-green and projecting cliffs, overlooking many abodes distributed in the shadows of the groves beyond.

Now, if it indeed be, that from the time employed in its construction, any just notion may be formed of the stateliness of an edifice, it must needs be determined, that this retreat of Donjalolo could not be otherwise than imposing.

Full five hundred moons was the palace in completing; for by some architectural arborist, its quadrangular foundations had been laid in seed-cocoanuts, requiring that period to sprout up into pillars. In front, these were horizontally connected, by elaborately carved beams, of a scarlet hue, inserted into the vital wood; which, swelling out, and overlapping, firmly secured them. The beams supported the rafters, inclining from the rear; while over the aromatic grasses covering the roof, waved the tufted tops of the Palms, green capitals to their dusky shafts.

Through and through this vibrating verdure, bright birds flitted and sang; the scented and variegated thatch seemed a hanging-garden; and between it and the Palm tops, was leaf-hung an arbor in the air.

Without these columns, stood a second and third colonnade, forming the most beautiful bowers; advancing through which, you fancied that the palace beyond must be chambered in a fountain, or frozen in a crystal. Three sparkling rivulets flowing from the heights were led across its summit, through great trunks half buried in the thatch; and emptying into a sculptured channel, running along the eaves, poured over in one wide sheet, plaited and transparent. Received into a basin beneath, they were thence conducted down the vale.

The sides of the palace were hedged by Diomi bushes bearing a flower, from its perfume, called Lenora, or Sweet Breath; and within these odorous hedges, were heavy piles of mats, richly dyed and embroidered.

Here lounging of a glowing noon, the plaited cascade playing, the verdure waving, and the birds melodious, it was hard to say, whether you were an inmate of a garden in the glen, or a grotto in the sea.

But enough for the nonce, of the House of the Morning. Cross we the hollow, to the House of the Afternoon.

Chapter 77

The House of the Afternoon

FOR THE MOST PART, the House of the Afternoon was but a wing built against a mansion wrought by the hand of Nature herself; a grotto running into the side of the mountain.

From high over the mouth of this grotto, sloped a long arbor, supported by great blocks of stone, rudely chiseled into the likeness of idols, each bearing a carved lizard on its chest: a sergeant's guard of the gods condescendingly doing duty as posts.

From the grotto thus vestibuled, issued hilariously forth the most considerable stream of the glen; which, seemingly overjoyed to find daylight in Willamilla, sprang into the arbor with a cheery, white bound. But its youthful enthusiasm was soon repressed; its waters being caught in a large stone basin, scooped out of the natural rock; whence, staid and decorous, they traversed sundry moats; at last meandering away, to join floods with the streams trained to do service at the other end of the vale.

Truant streams: the livelong day wending their loitering path to the subterraneous outlet, flowing into which, they disappeared. But no wonder they loitered; passing such ravishing landscapes. Thus with life: man bounds out of night; runs and babbles in the sun; then returns to his darkness again; though, peradventure, once more to emerge.

But the grotto was not a mere outlet to the stream. Flowing through a dark flume in the rock, on both sides it left a dry, elevated shelf, to which you ascend from the arbor by three artificially-wrought steps, sideways disposed, to avoid the spray of the rejoicing cataract. Mounting these, and pursuing the edge of the flume, the grotto gradually expands and heightens; your way lighted by rays in the inner distance. At last you come to a lofty subterraneous dome, lit from above by a cleft in the mountain; while full before you, in the opposite wall, from a low, black arch, midway up, and inaccessible, the stream, with a hollow ring and a dash, falls in a long, snowy column into a bottomless pool, whence, after many an eddy and whirl, it entered the flume, and away with a rush. Half hidden from view by an overhanging brow of the rock, the white fall looked like the sheeted ghost of the grotto.

Yet gallantly bedecked was the cave, as any old armorial hall hung round with banners and arras. Streaming from the cleft, vines swung in the air; or crawled along the rocks, wherever a tendril could be fixed. High up, their leaves were green; but lower down, they were shriveled; and dyed of many colors; and tattered and torn with much rustling; as old banners again; sore raveled with much triumphing.

In the middle of this hall in the hill was incarcerated the stone image of one Demi, the tutelar deity of Willamilla. All green and oozy like a stone under water, poor Demi looked as if sore harassed with sciatics and lumbagos.

But he was cheered from aloft, by the promise of receiving a garland all blooming on his crown; the Dryads sporting in the woodlands above, forever peeping down the cleft, and essaying to drop him a coronal.

Now, the still, panting glen of Willamilla, nested so close by the mountains, and a goodly green mark for the archer in the sun, would have been almost untenable were it not for the grotto. Hereby, it breathed the blessed breezes of Omi; a mountain promontory buttressing the island to the east, receiving the cool stream of the upland Trades; much pleasanter than the currents beneath.

At all times, even in the brooding noon-day, a gush of cool air came hand-in-hand with the cool waters, that burst with a shout into the palace of Donjalolo. And as, after first refreshing the king, as in loyalty bound, the stream flowed at large through the glen, and bathed its verdure; so, the blessed breezes of Omi, not only made pleasant the House of the Afternoon; but finding ample outlet in its wide, open front, blew forth upon the bosom of all Willamilla.

"Come let us take the air of Omi," was a very common saying in the glen. And the speaker would hie with his comrade toward the grotto; and flinging himself on the turf, pass his hand through his locks, and recline; making a joy and a business of breathing; for truly the breezes of Omi were as air-wine to the lungs.

Yet was not this breeze over-cool; though at times the zephyrs grew boisterous. Especially at the season of high sea, when the strong Trades drawn down the cleft in the mountain, rushed forth from the grotto with wonderful force. Crossing it then, you had much ado to keep your robe on your back.

Thus much for the House of the Afternoon. Whither—after spending the shady morning under the eastern cliffs of the glen—daily, at a certain hour, Donjalolo in his palanquin was borne; there, finding new shades; and there tarrying till evening; when again he was transported whence he came: thereby anticipating the revolution of the sun. Thus dodging day's luminary through life, the prince hied to and fro in his dominions; on his smooth, spotless brow Sol's rays never shining.

Chapter 78

Babbalanja solus

O F THE HOUSE OF THE AFTERNOON something yet remains to be said.

It was chiefly distinguished by its pavement, where, according to the strange customs of the isle, were inlaid the reputed skeletons of Donjalolo's sires; each surrounded by a mosaic of corals,—red, white, and black, intermixed with vitreous stones fallen from the skies in a meteoric shower. These delineated the tattooing of the departed. Near by, were imbedded their arms: mace, bow, and spear, in similar marquetry; and over each skull was the likeness of a scepter.

First and conspicuous lay the half-decayed remains of Marjora, the father of these Coral Kings; by his side, the storied, sickle-shaped weapon, wherewith he slew his brother Teei.

"Line of kings and row of scepters," said Babbalanja as he gazed. "Donjalolo, come forth and ponder on thy sires. Here they lie, from dread Marjora down to him who fathered thee. Here are their bones, their spears, and their javelins; their scepters, and the very fashion of their tattooing: all that can be got together of what they were. Tell me, oh king, what are thy thoughts? Dotest thou on these thy sires? Art thou more truly royal, that they were kings? Or more a man, that they were men? Is it a fable, or a verity about Marjora and the murdered Teei? But here is the mighty conqueror,—ask him. Speak to him: son to sire: king to king. Prick him; beg; buffet; entreat; spurn; split the globe, he will not budge. Walk over and over thy whole ancestral line, and they will not start. They are not here. Ay, the dead are not to be found, even in their graves. Nor have they simply departed; for they willed not to go; they died not by choice; whithersoever they have gone, thither have they been dragged; and if so be, they are extinct, their nihilities went not more against their grain, than their forced quitting of Mardi. Either way, something has become of them that they sought not. Truly, had stout-hearted Marjora sworn to live here in Willamilla for ay, and kept the vow, *that* would have been royalty indeed; but here he lies. Marjora! rise! Juam revolteth! Lo, I stamp upon thy scepter; base menials tread upon thee where thou liest! Up, king, up! What? no reply? Are not these bones thine? Oh, how the living triumph over the dead! Marjora! answer. Art thou? or art thou not? I see thee not; I hear thee not; I feel thee not; eyes, ears, hands, are worthless to test thy being; and if thou art, thou art something beyond all human thought to compass. We must have other faculties to know thee by. Why, thou art not even a sightless sound; not the echo of an echo; here are thy bones. Donjalolo, methinks I see thee fallen upon by assassins:—which of thy fathers riseth to the rescue? I see thee dying:—which of them telleth thee what cheer beyond the grave? But they have gone to the land unknown. Meet phrase. Where is it? Not one of Oro's priests telleth a straight story concerning it; 'twill be hard finding their paradises. Touching the life of Alma, in Mohi's chronicles, 'tis related, that a man was once raised from the tomb. But rubbed he not his eyes, and stared he not most vacantly? Not one revelation did he make. Ye gods! to have been a bystander there!

"At best, 'tis but a hope. But will a longing bring the thing desired? Doth dread avert its object? An instinct is no preservative. The fire I shrink from, may consume me.—But dead, and yet alive; alive, yet dead;—thus say the sages of Maramma. But die we then living? Yet if our dead fathers somewhere and somehow live, why not our unborn sons? For backward or forward, eternity is the same; already have we been the nothing we dread to be. Icy thought! But bring it home,—it will not stay. What ho, hot heart of mine: to beat thus lustily awhile, to feel in the red rushing blood, and then be ashes,—can this be so? But peace, peace, thou liar in me, telling me I am immortal—shall I not be as these bones? To come to this! But the balsam-dropping palms, whose boles run milk, whose plumes wave boastful in the air, they perish in their prime, and bow their blasted trunks. Nothing abideth; the river of yesterday floweth not to-day; the sun's rising is a setting; living is dying; the very mountains melt; and all revolve:—systems and asteroids; the sun wheels through the zodiac, and the zodiac is a revolution. Ah gods! in all this universal stir, am *I* to prove one stable thing?

"Grim chiefs in skeletons, avaunt! Ye are but dust; belike the dust of beggars; for on this bed, paupers may lie down with kings, and filch their skulls. *This*, great Marjora's arm? No, some old paralytic's. *Ye*, kings? *ye*, men? Where are your vouchers? I do reject your brotherhood, ye libelous remains. But no, no; despise them not, oh Babbalanja! Thy own skeleton, thou thyself dost carry with thee, through this mortal life; and aye would view it, but for kind nature's screen; thou art death alive; and e'en to what's before thee wilt thou come. Ay, thy children's children will walk over thee: thou, voiceless as a calm."

And over the Coral Kings, Babbalanja paced in profound meditation.

Chapter 79

The Center of many Circumferences

LIKE DONJALOLO HIMSELF, we hie to and fro; for back now
must we pace to the House of the Morning.

In its rear, there diverged three separate arbors, leading to less public
apartments.

Traversing the central arbor, and fancying it will soon lead you to open
ground, you suddenly come upon the most private retreat of the prince:
a square structure; plain as a pyramid; and without, as inscrutable. Down
to the very ground, its walls are thatched; but on the farther side a passage-
way opens, which you enter. But not yet are you within. Scarce a yard
distant, stands an inner thatched wall, blank as the first. Passing along the
intervening corridor, lighted by narrow apertures, you reach the opposite
side, and a second opening is revealed. This entering, another corridor;
lighted as the first, but more dim, and a third blank wall. And thus, three
times three, you worm round and round, the twilight lessening as you proceed; until at last, you enter the citadel itself: the innermost arbor of a nest;
whereof, each has its roof, distinct from the rest.

The heart of the place is but small; illuminated by a range of open sky-
lights, downward contracting.

Innumerable as the leaves of an endless folio, multitudinous mats cover
the floor; whereon reclining by night, like Pharaoh on the top of his

patrimonial pile, the inmate looks heavenward, and heavenward only; gazing at the torch-light processions in the skies, when, in state, the suns march to be crowned.

And here, in this impenetrable retreat, centrally slumbered the universe-rounded, zodiac-belted, horizon-zoned, sea-girt, reef-sashed, mountain-locked, arbor-nested, royalty-girdled, arm-clasped, self-hugged, indivisible Donjalolo, absolute monarch of Juam:—the husk-inhusked meat in a nut; the innermost spark in a ruby; the juice-nested seed in a golden-rinded orange; the red royal stone in an effeminate peach; the insphered sphere of spheres.

Chapter 80

Donjalolo in the Bosom of his Family

TO PRETEND TO RELATE the manner in which Juam's ruler passed his captive days, without making suitable mention of his harem, would be to paint one's full-length likeness and omit the face. For it was his harem that did much to stamp the character of Donjalolo.

And had he possessed but a single spouse, most discourteous, surely, to have overlooked the princess; much more, then, as it is; and by how much the more, a plurality exceeds a unit.

Exclusive of the female attendants, by day waiting upon the person of the king, he had wives thirty in number, corresponding in name to the nights of the moon. For, in Juam, time is not reckoned by days, but by nights; each night of the lunar month having its own designation; which, relatively only, is extended to the day.

In uniform succession, the thirty wives ruled queen of the king's heart. An arrangement most wise and judicious; precluding much of that jealousy and confusion prevalent in ill-regulated seraglios. For as thirty spouses must be either more desirable, or less desirable than one; so is a harem thirty times more difficult to manage than an establishment with one solitary mistress. But Donjalolo's wives were so nicely drilled, that for the most part, things went on very smoothly. Nor were his brows much furrowed with wrinkles referable to domestic cares and tribulations. Although, as in due time will be seen, from these he was not altogether exempt.

Now, according to Braid-Beard, who, among other abstruse political researches, had accurately informed himself concerning the internal administration of Donjalolo's harem, the following was the method pursued therein.

On the Aquella, or First Night of the month, the queen of that name assumes her diadem, and reigns. So too with Azzolino the Second, and Velluvi the Third Night of the Moon; and so on, even unto the utter eclipse thereof; through Calends, Nones, and Ides.

For convenience, the king is furnished with a card, whereon are copied the various ciphers upon the arms of his queens; and parallel thereto, the hieroglyphics significant of the corresponding Nights of the month. Glancing over this, Donjalolo predicts the true time of the rising and setting of all his stars.

This Moon of wives was lodged in two spacious seraglios, which few mortals beheld. For, so deeply were they buried in a grove; so overpowered with verdure; so overrun with vines; and so hazy with the incense of flowers; that they were almost invisible, unless closely approached. Certain it was, that it demanded no small enterprise, diligence, and sagacity, to explore the mysterious wood in search of them. Though a strange, sweet, humming sound, as of the clustering and swarming of warm bees among roses, at last hinted the royal honey at hand. High in air, toward the summit of the cliff, overlooking this side of the glen, a narrow ledge of rocks might have been seen, from which, rumor whispered, was to be caught an angular peep at the tip of the apex of the roof of the nearest seraglio. But this wild report had never been established. Nor, indeed, was it susceptible of a test. For was not that rock inaccessible as the eyrie of young eagles? But to guard against the possibility of any visual profanation, Donjalolo had authorized an edict, forever tabooing that rock to foot of man or pinion of fowl. Birds and bipeds both trembled and obeyed; taking a wide circuit to avoid the spot.

Access to the seraglios was had by corresponding arbors leading from the palace. The seraglio to the right was denominated "Ravi" (Before), that to the left "Zono" (After). The meaning of which was, that upon the termination of her reign the queen wended her way to the Zono; there tarrying with her predecessors till the Ravi was emptied; when the entire Moon of wives, swallow-like, migrated back whence they came; and the procession was gone over again.

In due order, the queens reposed upon mats inwoven with their respective ciphers. In the Ravi, the mat of the queen-apparent, or next in succession, was spread by the portal. In the Zono, the newly-widowed queen reposed furthest from it.

But alas for all method where thirty wives are concerned. Notwithstanding these excellent arrangements, the mature result of ages of progressive improvement in the economy of the royal seraglios in Willamilla, it must needs be related, that at times the order of precedence became confused, and was very hard to restore.

At intervals, some one of the wives was weeded out, to the no small delight of the remainder; but to their equal vexation her place would soon after be supplied by some beautiful stranger; who assuming the denomination of the vacated Night of the Moon, thenceforth commenced her monthly revolutions in the king's infallible calendar.

In constant attendance, was a band of old men; woe-begone, thin of leg, and puny of frame; whose grateful task it was, to tarry in the garden of Donjalolo's delights, without ever touching the roses. Along with innumerable other duties, they were perpetually kept coming and going upon ten thousand errands; for they had it in strict charge to obey the slightest behests of the damsels; and with all imaginable expedition to run, fly, swim, or dissolve into impalpable air, at the shortest possible notice.

So laborious their avocations, that none could discharge them for more than a twelvemonth, at the end of that period giving up the ghost out of pure exhaustion of the locomotive apparatus. It was this constant drain upon the stock of masculine old age in the glen, that so bethinned its small population of gray-beards and hoary-heads. And any old man hitherto exempted, who happened to receive a summons to repair to the palace, and there wait the pleasure of the king: this unfortunate, at once suspecting his doom, put his arbor in order; oiled and suppled his joints; took a long farewell of his friends; selected his burial-place; and going resigned to his fate, in due time expired like the rest.

Had any one of them cast about for some alleviating circumstance, he might possibly have derived some little consolation from the thought, that though a slave to the whims of thirty princesses, he was nevertheless one of their guardians, and as such, he might ingeniously have concluded, their superior. But small consolation this. For the damsels were as blithe as larks, more playful than kittens; never looking sad and sentimental, projecting clandestine escapes. But supplied with the thirtieth part of all that Aspasia could desire; glorying in being the spouses of a king; nor in the remotest degree anxious about eventual dowers; they were care-free, content, and rejoicing, as the rays of the morning.

Poor old men, then; it would be hard to distill out of your fate, one drop of the balm of consolation. For, commissioned to watch over those who forever kept you on the trot, affording you no time to hunt up peccadilloes; was not this circumstance an aggravation of hard times? a sharpening and edge-giving to the steel in your souls?

But much yet remains unsaid.

To dwell no more upon the eternal wear-and-tear incident to these attenuated old warders, they were intensely hated by the damsels. Inasmuch, as it was archly opined, for what ulterior purposes they were retained.

Nightly couching, on guard, round the seraglio, like fangless old bronze dragons round a fountain enchanted, the old men ever and anon cried out mightily, by reason of sore pinches and scratches received in the dark. And tri-trebly-tri-triply girt about as he was, Donjalolo himself started from his slumbers, raced round and round through his ten thousand corridors; at last bursting all dizzy among his twenty-nine queens, to see what under the seventh-heavens was the matter. When, lo and behold! there lay the innocents all sound asleep; the dragons moaning over their mysterious bruises.

Ah me! his harem, like all large families, was the delight and the torment of the days and nights of Donjalolo.

And in one special matter was he either eminently miserable, or otherwise: for all his multiplicity of wives, he had never an heir. Not his, the proud paternal glance of the Grand Turk Solyman, looking round upon a hundred sons, all bone of his bone, and squinting with his squint.

Chapter 81

Wherein Babbalanja relates the Adventure of one Karkeke in the Land of Shades

AT OUR MORNING REPAST on the second day of our stay in the hollow, our party indulged in much lively discourse.

"Samoa," said I, "those isles of yours, of whose beauty you so often make vauntful mention, can those isles, good Samoa, furnish a valley in all respects equal to Willamilla?"

Disdainful answer was made, that Willamilla might be endurable enough for a sojourn, but as a permanent abode, any glen of his own natal isle was unspeakably superior.

"In the great valley of Savaii," cried Samoa, "for every leaf grown here in Willamilla, grows a stately tree; and for every tree here waving, in Savaii flourishes a goodly warrior."

Immeasurable was the disgust of the Upoluan for the enervated subjects of Donjalolo; and for Donjalolo himself; though it was shrewdly divined, that his annoying reception at the hands of the royalty of Juam, had something to do with his disdain.

To Jarl, no similar question was put; for he was sadly deficient in a taste for the picturesque. But he cursorily observed, that in his blue-water opinion, Willamilla was next to uninhabitable, all view of the sea being intercepted.

And here it may be well to relate a comical blunder on the part of honest Jarl; concerning which, Samoa, the savage, often afterward twitted him;

245

as indicating a rusticity, and want of polish in his breeding. It rather originated, however, in his not heeding the conventionalities of the strange
people among whom he was thrown.

The anecdote is not an epic; but here it is.

Reclining in our arbor, we breakfasted upon a marble slab; so frost-
white, and flowingly traced with blue veins, that it seemed a little lake
sheeted over with ice: Diana's virgin bosom congealed.

Before each guest was a richly carved bowl and gourd, fruit and wine
freighted; also the empy hemisphere of a small nut, the purpose of which
was a problem. Now, King Jarl scorned to admit the slightest degree of
under-breeding in the matter of polite feeding. So nothing was a problem
to him. At once reminded of the morsel of Arva-root in his mouth, a
substitute for another sort of sedative then unattainable, he was instantly illuminated concerning the purpose of the nut; and very complacently introduced each to the other; in the innocence of his ignorance making no doubt
that he had acquitted himself with discretion; the little hemisphere plainly
being intended as a place of temporary deposit for the Arva of the guests.

The company were astounded: Samoa more than all. King Jarl, meanwhile, looking at all present with the utmost serenity. At length, one of the
horrified attendants, using two sticks for a forceps, disappeared with the
obnoxious nut. Upon which, the meal proceeded.

This attendant was not seen again for many days; which gave rise to
the supposition, that journeying to the sea-side, he had embarked for some
distant strand; there, to bury out of sight the abomination with which he
was freighted.

Upon this, his egregious misadventure, calculated to do discredit to our
party, and bring Media himself into contempt, Babbalanja had no scruples
in taking Jarl roundly to task. He assured him, that it argued but little brains
to evince a desire to be thought familiar with all things; that however
desirable as incidental attainments, conventionalities, in themselves, were
the very least of arbitrary trifles; the knowledge of them, innate with no
man. "Moreover, Jarl," he added, "in essence, conventionalities are but
mimickings, at which monkeys succeed best. Hence, when you find yourself at a loss in these matters, wait patiently, and mark what the other
monkeys do: and then follow suit. And by so doing, you will gain a vast
reputation as an accomplished ape. Above all things, follow not the silly
example of the young spark Karkeke, of whom Mohi was telling me. Dying, and entering the other world with a mincing gait, and there finding
certain customs quite strange and new; such as friendly shades passing

through each other by way of a salutation;—Karkeke, nevertheless, resolved to show no sign of embarrassment. Accosted by a phantom, with
wings folded pensively, plumes interlocked across its chest, he off head;
and stood obsequiously before it. Staring at him for an instant, the spirit
cut him dead; murmuring to itself, 'Ah, some terrestrial bumpkin, I fancy,'
and passed on with its celestial nose in the highly rarified air. But silly
Karkeke undertaking to replace his head, found that it would no more stay
on; but forever tumbled off; even in the act of nodding a salute; which
calamity kept putting him out of countenance. And thus through all eternity
is he punished for his folly, in having pretended to be wise, wherein he
was ignorant. Head under arm, he wanders about, the scorn and ridicule
of the other world."

Our repast concluded, messengers arrived from the prince, courteously
inviting our presence at the House of the Morning. Thither we went;
journeying in sedans, sent across the hollow, for that purpose, by Donjalolo.

Chapter 82

How Donjalolo sent Agents to the surrounding Isles;
with the Result

RE RECOUNTING what was beheld on entering the House of the
Morning, some previous information is needful. Though so many
of Donjalolo's days were consumed by sloth and luxury, there came
to him certain intervals of thoughtfulness, when all his curiosity concerning
the things of outer Mardi revived with augmented intensity. In these moods,
he would send abroad deputations, inviting to Willamilla the kings of the
neighboring islands; together with the most celebrated priests, bards, story-
tellers, magicians, and wise men; that he might hear them converse of those
things, which he could not behold for himself.

But at last, he bethought him, that the various narrations he had heard,
could not have been otherwise than unavoidably faulty; by reason that they
had been principally obtained from the inhabitants of the countries described; who, very naturally, must have been inclined to partiality or un-
candidness in their statements. Wherefore he had very lately dispatched to
the isles special agents of his own; honest of heart, keen of eye, and shrewd
of understanding; to seek out every thing that promised to illuminate him
concerning the places they visited, and also to collect various specimens
of interesting objects; so that at last he might avail himself of the researches
of others, and see with their eyes.

But though two observers were sent to every one of the neighboring lands; yet each was to act independently; make his own inquiries; form his own conclusions; and return with his own specimens; wholly regardless of the proceedings of the other.

It so came to pass, that on the very day of our arrival in the glen, these pilgrims returned from their travels. And Donjalolo had set apart the following morning to giving them a grand public reception. And it was to this, that our party had been invited, as related in the chapter preceding.

In the great Palm-hall of the House of the Morning, we were assigned distinguished mats, to the right of the prince; his chiefs, attendants, and subjects assembled in the open colonnades without.

When all was in readiness, in marched the company of savans and travelers; and humbly standing in a semi-circle before the king, their numerous hampers were deposited at their feet.

Donjalolo was now in high spirits, thinking of the rich store of reliable information about to be furnished.

"Zuma," said he, addressing the foremost of the company, "you and Varnopi were directed to explore the island of Rafona. Proceed now, and relate all you know of that place. Your narration heard, we will list to Varnopi."

With a profound inclination the traveler obeyed.

But soon Donjalolo interrupted him. "What say you, Zuma, about the secret cavern, and the treasures therein? A very different account, this, from all I have heard hitherto; but perhaps yours is the true version. Go on."

But very soon, poor Zuma was again interrupted by exclamations of surprise. Nay, even to the very end of his recountings.

But when he had done, Donjalolo observed, that if from any cause Zuma was in error or obscure, Varnopi would not fail to set him right.

So Varnopi was called upon.

But not long had Varnopi proceeded, when Donjalolo changed color.

"What!" he exclaimed, "will ye contradict each other before our very face? Oh Oro! how hard is truth to be come at by proxy! Fifty accounts have I had of Rafona; none of which wholly agreed; and here, these two varlets, sent expressly to behold and report, these two lying knaves, speak crookedly both. How is it? Are the lenses in their eyes diverse-hued, that objects seem different to both; for undeniable is it, that the things they thus clashingly speak of are to be known for the same; though represented with unlike colors and qualities. But dumb things can not lie nor err. Unpack thy hampers, Zuma. Here, bring them close: now: what is this?"

"That," tremblingly replied Zuma, "is a specimen of the famous reef-bar on the west side of the island of Rafona; your highness perceives its deep red dyes."

Said Donjalolo, "Varnopi, hast thou a piece of this coral, also?"

"I have, your highness," said Varnopi; "here it is."

Taking it from his hand, Donjalolo gazed at its bleached, white hue; then dashing it to the pavement, "Oh mighty Oro! Truth dwells in her fountains; where every one must drink for himself. For me, vain all hope of ever knowing Mardi! Away! Better know nothing, than be deceived. Break up!"

And Donjalolo rose, and retired.

All present now broke out in a storm of vociferations; some siding with Zuma; others with Varnopi; each of whom, in turn, was declared the man to be relied upon.

Marking all this, Babbalanja, who had been silently looking on, leaning against one of the palm pillars, quietly observed to Media:—"My lord, I have seen this same reef at Rafona. In various places, it is of various hues. As for Zuma and Varnopi, both are wrong, and both are right."

Chapter 83

They visit the Tributary Islets

IN WILLAMILLA, no Yillah being found, on the third day we took
leave of Donjalolo; who lavished upon us many caresses; and, somewhat reluctantly on Media's part, we quitted the vale.

One by one, we now visited the outer villages of Juam; and crossing
the waters, wandered several days among its tributary isles. There we saw
the viceroys of him who reigned in the hollow: chieftains of whom Donjalolo was proud; so honest, humble, and faithful; so bent upon amelio-
rating the condition of those under their rule. For, be it said, Donjalolo was
a charitable prince; in his serious intervals, ever seeking the welfare of his
subjects, though after an imperial view of his own. But alas, in that sunny
donjon among the mountains, where he dwelt, how could Donjalolo be
sure, that the things he decreed were executed in regions forever remote
from his view. Ah! very bland, very innocent, very pious, the faces his
viceroys presented during their monthly visits to Willamilla. But as cruel
their visage, when, returned to their islets, they abandoned themselves to
all the license of tyrants; like Verres reveling down the rights of the Sicilians.

Like Carmelites, they came to Donjalolo, barefooted; but in their
homes, their proud latchets were tied by their slaves. Before their king-
belted prince, they stood rope-girdled like self-abased monks of St. Francis;
but with those ropes, before their palaces, they hung Innocence and Truth.

As still seeking Yillah, and still disappointed, we roved through the lands which these chieftains ruled, Babbalanja exclaimed—"Let us depart; idle our search, in isles that have viceroys for kings."

At early dawn, about embarking for a distant land, there came to us certain messengers of Donjalolo, saying that their lord the king, repenting of so soon parting company with Media and Taji, besought them to return with all haste; for that very morning, in Willamilla, a regal banquet was preparing; to which many neighboring kings had been invited, most of whom had already arrived.

Declaring that there was no alternative but compliance, Media acceded; and with the king's messengers we returned to the glen.

Chapter 84

Taji sits down to Dinner with five-and-twenty Kings,
and a royal Time they have

IT WAS AFTERNOON when we emerged from the defile. And informed that our host was receiving his guests in the House of the Afternoon, thither we directed our steps.

Soft in our face, blew the blessed breezes of Omi, stirring the leaves overhead; while, here and there, through the trees, showed the idol-bearers of the royal retreat, hand in hand, linked with festoons of flowers. Still beyond, on a level, sparkled the nodding crowns of the kings, like the constellation Corona-Borealis, the horizon just gained.

Close by his noon-tide friend, the cascade at the mouth of the grotto, reposed on his crimson mat, Donjalolo:—arrayed in a vestment of the finest white tappa of Mardi, figured all over with bright yellow lizards, so curiously stained in the gauze, that he seemed overrun, as with golden mice.

Marjora's girdle girdled his loins, tasseled with the congregated teeth of his sires. A jeweled turban-tiara, milk-white, surmounted his brow, over which waved a copse of Pintado plumes.

But what sways in his hand? A scepter, similar to those likenesses of scepters, imbedded among the corals at his feet. A polished thigh-bone; by Braid-Beard declared once Teei's the Murdered. For to emphasize his intention utterly to rule, Marjora himself had selected this emblem of dominion over mankind.

But even this last despite done to dead Teei had once been transcended.

In the usurper's time, prevailed the belief, that the saliva of kings must never touch ground; and Mohi's Chronicles made mention, that during the life time of Marjora, Teei's skull had been devoted to the basest of purposes: Marjora's, the hate no turf could bury.

Yet, traditions like these ever seem dubious. There be many who deny the hump, moral and physical, of Gloster Richard.

Still advancing unperceived, in social hilarity we descried their High-nesses, chatting together like the most plebeian of mortals; full as merry as the monks of old. But marking our approach, all changed. A pair of potentates, who had been playfully trifling, hurriedly adjusted their dia-dems, threw themselves into attitudes, looking stately as statues. Phidias turned not out his Jupiter so soon.

In various-dyed robes the five-and-twenty kings were arrayed; and various their features, as the rows of lips, eyes and ears in John Caspar Lavater's physiognomical charts. Nevertheless, to a king, all their noses were aquiline.

There were long fox-tail beards of silver gray, and enameled chins, like those of girls; bald pates and Merovingian locks; smooth brows and wrinkles: forms erect and stooping; an eye that squinted; one king was deaf; by his side, another that was halt; and not far off, a dotard. They were old and young, tall and short, handsome and ugly, fat and lean, cun-ning and simple.

With animated courtesy our host received us; assigning a neighboring bower for Babbalanja and the rest; and among so many right-royal, demi-divine guests, how could the demi-gods Media and Taji be otherwise than at home?

The unwonted sprightliness of Donjalolo surprised us. But he was in one of those relapses of desperate gayety invariably following his failures in efforts to amend his life. And the bootless issue of his late mission to outer Mardi had thrown him into a mood for revelry. Nor had he lately shunned a wild wine, called Morando.

A slave now appearing with a bowl of this beverage, it circulated freely.

Not to gainsay the truth, we fancied the Morando much. A nutty, pungent flavor it had; like some kinds of arrack distilled in the Philippine isles. And a marvelous effect did it have, in dissolving the crystalization of the brain; leaving nothing but precious little drops of good humor, beading round the bowl of the cranium.

Meanwhile, garlanded boys, climbing the limbs of the idol-pillars, and stirruping their feet in their most holy mouths, suspended hangings of crimson tappa all round the hall; so that sweeping the pavement they rustled in the breeze from the grot.

Presently, stalwart slaves advanced; bearing a mighty basin of a porphyry hue, deep-hollowed out of a tree. Outside, were innumerable grotesque conceits; conspicuous among which, for a border, was an endless string of the royal lizards circumnavigating the basin in inverted chase of their tails.

Peculiar to the groves of Willamilla, the yellow lizard formed part of the arms of Juam. And when Donjalolo's messengers went abroad, they carried its effigy, as the emblem of their royal master; themselves being known, as the Gentlemen of the Golden Lizard.

The porphyry-hued basin planted full in our midst, the attendants forthwith filled the same with the living waters from the cascade; a proceeding, for which some of the company were at a loss to account, unless his highness, our host, with all the coolness of royalty, purposed cooling himself still further, by taking a bath in presence of his guests. A conjecture, most premature; for directly, the basin being filled to within a few inches of the lizards, the attendants fell to launching therein divers goodly sized trenchers, all laden with choice viands:—wild boar meat; humps of grampuses; embrowned bread-fruit, roasted in odoriferous fires of sandal wood, but suffered to cool; gold fish, dressed with the fragrant juices of berries; citron sauce; rolls of the baked paste of yams; juicy bananas, steeped in a saccharine oil; marmalade of plantains; jellies of guava; confections of the treacle of palm sap; and many other dainties; besides numerous stained calabashes of Morando, and other beverages, fixed in carved floats to make them buoyant.

The guests assigned seats, by the woven handles attached to his purple mat, the prince, our host, was now gently moved by his servitors to the head of the porphyry-hued basin. Where, flanked by lofty crowned-heads, white-tiaraed, and radiant with royalty, he sat; like snow-turbaned Mont Blanc, at sunrise presiding over the head waters of the Rhone; to right and left, looming the gilded summits of the Simplon, the Gothard, the Jungfrau, the Great St. Bernard, and the Grand Glockner.

Yet turbid from the launching of its freight, Lake Como tossed to and fro its navies of good cheer, the shadows of the king-peaks wildly flitting thereupon.

But no frigid wine and fruit cooler, Lake Como; as at first it did seem; but a tropical dining table, its surface a slab of light blue St. Pons marble in a state of fluidity.

Now, many a crown was doffed; scepters laid aside; girdles slackened; and among those verdant viands the bearded kings like goats did browse; or tusking their wild boar's meat, like mastiffs ate.

And like unto some well-fought fight, beginning calmly, but pressing forward to a fiery rush, this well-fought feast did now wax warm.

A few royal epicures, however, there were: epicures intent upon concoctions, admixtures, and masterly compoundings; who comported themselves with all due deliberation and dignity; hurrying themselves into no reckless deglutition of the dainties. Ah! admirable conceit, Lake Como: superseding attendants. For, from hand to hand the trenchers sailed; no sooner gaining one port, than dispatched over sea to another.

Well suited they were for the occasion; sailing high out of water, to resist the convivial swell at times ruffling the sociable sea; and sharp at both ends, still better adapting them to easy navigation.

But soon, the Morando, in triumphant decanters, went round, reeling like barks before a breeze. But their voyages were brief; and ere long, in certain havens, the accumulation of empty vessels threatened to bridge the lake with pontoons. In those directions, Trade winds were setting. But full soon, cut out were all unladen and unprofitable gourds; and replaced by jolly-bellied calabashes, for a time sailing deep, yawing heavily to the push.

At last, the whole flotilla of trenchers—wrecks and all—were sent swimming to the further end of Lake Como; and thence removed, gave place to ruddy hillocks of fruit, and floating islands of flowers. Chief among the former, a quince-like, golden sphere, that filled the air with such fragrance, you thought you were tasting its flavor.

Nor did the wine cease flowing. That day the Juam grape did bleed; that day the tendril ringlets of the vines, did all uncurl; and grape by grape, in sheer dismay, the sun-ripe clusters dropped. Grape-glad were five-and-twenty kings: five-and-twenty kings were merry.

Morando's vintage had no end; nor other liquids, in the royal cellar stored, somewhere secret in the grot. Oh! where's the endless Niger's source? Search ye here, or search ye there; on, on, through ravine, vega, vale—no head waters will ye find. But why need gain the hidden spring, when its lavish stream flows by? At three-fold mouths that Delta-grot discharged; rivers golden, white, and red.

But who may sing for aye? Down I come, and light upon the old and prosy plain.

Among other decanters set afloat, was a pompous, lordly-looking demi-john, but old and reverend withal, that sailed about, consequential as an autocrat going to be crowned, or a treasure-freighted argosie bound home before the wind. It looked solemn, however, though it reeled; peradventure, far gone with its own potent contents.

Oh! russet shores of Rhine and Rhone! oh, mellow memories of ripe old vintages! oh, cobwebs in the Pyramids! oh, dust on Pharaoh's tomb!—all, all recur, as I bethink me of that glorious gourd, its contents cogent as Tokay, itself as old as Mohi's legends; more venerable to look at than his beard. Whence came it? Buried in vases, so saith the label, with the heart of old Marjora, now dead one hundred thousand moons. Exhumed at last, it looked no wine, but was shrunk into a subtle syrup.

This special calabash was distinguished by numerous trappings, caparisoned like the sacred bay steed led before the Great Khan of Tartary. A most curious and betasseled net-work encased it; and the royal lizard was jealously twisted about its neck, like a hand on a throat containing some invaluable secret.

All Hail, Marzilla! King's Own Royal Particular! A vinous Percy! Dating back to the Conquest! Distilled of yore from purple berries growing in the purple valley of Ardair! Thrice hail.

But the imperial Marzilla was not for all; gods only could partake; the Kings and demigods of the isles; excluding left-handed descendants of sad rakes of immortals, in old times breaking heads and hearts in Mardi, bequeathing bars-sinister to many mortals, who now in vain might urge a claim to a cup-full of right regal Marzilla.

The Royal Particular was pressed upon me, by the now jovial Donjalolo. With his own sceptered hand charging my flagon to the brim, he declared his despotic pleasure, that I should quaff it off to the last lingering globule. No hard calamity, truly; for the drinking of this wine was as the singing of a mighty ode, or frenzied lyric to the soul.

"Drink, Taji," cried Donjalolo, "drink deep. In this wine a king's heart is dissolved. Drink long; in this wine lurk the seeds of the life everlasting. Drink deep; drink long: thou drinkest wisdom and valor at every draught. Drink forever, oh Taji, for thou drinkest that which will enable thee to stand up and speak out before mighty Oro himself."

"Borabolla," he added, turning round upon a domed old king at his left, "Was it not the god Xipho, who begged of my great-great-grandsire a draught of this same wine, saying he was about to beget a hero?"

"Even so. And thy glorious Marzilla produced thrice valiant Ononna, who slew the giants of the reef."

"Ha, ha, hear'st that, oh Taji?" And Donjalolo drained another cup.

Amazing! the flexibility of the royal elbow, and the rigidity of the royal spine! More especially as we had been impressed with a notion of their debility. But, sometimes these seemingly enervated young blades approve themselves steadier of limb, than veteran revelers of very long standing.

"Discharge the basin, and refill it with wine," cried Donjalolo. "Break all empty gourds! Drink, kings, and dash your cups at every draught."

So saying, he started from his purple mat; and with one foot planted unknowingly upon the skull of Marjora; while all the skeletons grinned at him from the pavement; Donjalolo, holding on high his blood-red goblet, burst forth with the following invocation:—

> Ha, ha, gods and kings; fill high, one and all;
> Drink, drink! shout and drink! mad respond to the call!
> Fill fast, and fill full; 'gainst the goblet ne'er sin;
> Quaff there, at high tide, to the uttermost rim:—
>   Flood-tide, and soul-tide to the brim!
>
> Who with wine in him fears? who thinks of his cares?
> Who sighs to be wise, when wine in him flares?
> Water sinks down below, in currents full slow;
> But wine mounts on high with its genial glow:—
>   Welling up, till the brain overflow!
>
> As the spheres, with a roll, some fiery of soul,
> Others golden, with music, revolve round the pole;
> So let our cups, radiant with many hued wines,
> Round and round in groups circle, our Zodiac's Signs:—
>   Round reeling, and ringing their chimes!
>
> Then drink, gods and kings; wine merriment brings;
> It bounds through the veins; there, jubilant sings.
> Let it ebb, then, and flow; wine never grows dim;
> Drain down that bright tide at the foam beaded rim:—
>   Fill up, every cup, to the brim!

Caught by all present, the chorus resounded again and again. The beaded wine danced on many a beard; the cataract lifted higher its voice; the grotto sent back a shout; the ghosts of the Coral Monarchs seemed starting from their insulted bones. But ha, ha, ha, roared forth the five-and-twenty kings —alive, not dead—holding both hands to their girdles, and baying out their laughter from abysses; like Nimrod's hounds over some fallen elk.

Mad and crazy revelers, how ye drank and roared! but kings no more: vestures loosed; and scepters rolling on the ground.

Glorious agrarian, thou wine! bringing all hearts on a level, and at last all legs to the earth; even those of kings, who, to do them justice, have been much maligned for imputed qualities not theirs. For whoso has touched flagons with monarchs, bear they their back bones never so stiffly on the throne, well know the rascals, to be at bottom royal good fellows; capable of a vinous frankness exceeding that of base-born men. Was not Alexander a boon companion? And daft Cambyses? and what of old Rowley, as good a judge of wine and other matters, as ever sipped claret or kisses.

If ever Taji joins a club, be it a Beef-Steak Club of Kings!

Donjalolo emptied yet another cup.

The mirth now blew a gale; like a ship's shrouds in a Typhoon, every tendon vibrated; the breezes of Omi came forth with a rush; the hangings shook; the goblets danced fandangos; and Donjalolo, clapping his hands, called before him his dancing women.

Forth came from the grotto a reed-like burst of song, making all start, and look that way to behold such enchanting strains. Sounds heralding sights! Swimming in the air, emerged the nymphs, lustrous arms interlocked like Indian jugglers' glittering snakes. Round the cascade they thronged; then paused in its spray. Of a sudden, seemed to spring from its midst, a young form of foam, that danced into the soul like a thought. At last, sideways floating off, it subsided into the grotto, a wave. Evening drawing on apace, the crimson draperies were lifted, and festooned to the arms of the idol-pillars, admitting the rosy light of the even.

Yielding to the re-action of the banquet, the kings now reclined; and two mute damsels entered: one with a gourd of scented waters; the other with napkins. Bending over Donjalolo's steaming head, the first let fall a shower of aromatic drops, slowly absorbed by her companion. Thus, in turn, all were served; nothing heard but deep breathing.

In a marble vase they now kindled some incense: a handful of spices.

Shortly after, came three of the king's beautiful smokers; who, lighting their tubes at this odorous fire, blew over the company the sedative fumes of the Aina.

Steeped in languor, I strove against it long; essayed to struggle out of the enchanted mist. But a syren hand seemed ever upon me, pressing me back.

Half-revealed, as in a dream, and the last sight that I saw, was Donjalolo:—eyes closed, face pale, locks moist, borne slowly to his sedan, to cross the hollow, and wake in the seclusion of his harem.

Chapter 85

After Dinner

A S IN DREAMS I behold thee again, Willamilla! as in dreams, once again I stroll through thy cool shady groves, oh fairest of the vallies of Mardi! the thought of that mad merry feasting steals over my soul till I faint.

Prostrate here and there over the bones of Donjalolo's sires, the royal bacchanals lay slumbering till noon.

"Which are the deadest?" said Babbalanja, peeping in, "the live kings, or the dead ones?"

But the former were drooping flowers sought to be revived by watering. At intervals the sedulous attendants went to and fro, besprinkling their heads with the scented contents of their vases.

At length, one by one, the five-and-twenty kings lifted their ambrosial curls; and shaking the dew therefrom, like eagles opened their right royal eyes, and dilated their aquiline nostrils, full upon the golden rays of the sun.

But why absented himself, Donjalolo? Had he cavalierly left them to survive the banquet by themselves? But this apparent incivility was soon explained by heralds, announcing to their prone majesties, that through the over solicitude of his slaves, their lord the king had been borne to his harem, without being a party to the act. But to make amends, in his sedan, Donjalolo was even now drawing nigh. Not, however, again to make merry; but socially to sleep in company with his guests; for, together they had all got high, and together they must all lie low.

So at it they went: each king to his bones, and slumbered like heroes till evening; when, availing themselves of the cool moonlight approaching, the royal guests bade adieu to their host; and summoning their followers, quitted the glen.

Early next day, having determined to depart for our canoes, we proceeded to the House of the Morning, to take leave of Donjalolo.

An amazing change, one night of solitude had wrought! Pale and languid, we found him reclining: one hand on his throbbing temples.

Near an overturned vessel of wine, the royal girdle lay tossed at his feet. He had waved off his frightened attendants, who crouched out of sight.

We advanced.

"Do ye too leave me? Ready enough are ye to partake of my banquetings, which, to such as ye, are but mad incidents in one round of more tranquil diversions. But heed me not, Media;—I am mad. Oh, ye gods! am I forever a captive?—Ay, free king of Odo, when you list, condescend to visit the poor slave in Willamilla. I account them but charity, your visits; would fain allure ye by sumptuous fare. Go, leave me; go, and be rovers again throughout blooming Mardi. For me, I am here for aye.—Bring me wine, slaves! quick! that I may pledge my guests fitly. Alas, Media, at the bottom of this cup are no sparkles as at top. Oh, treacherous, treacherous friend! full of smiles and daggers. Yet for such as me, oh wine, thou art e'en a prop, though it pierce the side; for man must lean. Thou wine art the friend of the friendless, though a foe to all. King Media, let us drink. More cups!—And now, farewell."

Falling back, he averted his face; and silently we quitted the palace.

Chapter 86

Of those Scamps the Plujii

THE BEACH GAINED, we embarked.

In good time our party recovered from the seriousness into which we had been thrown; and a rather long passage being now before us, we whiled away the hours as best we might.

Among many entertaining narrations, old Braid-Beard, crossing his calves, and peaking his beard, regaled us with some account of certain invisible spirits, ycleped the Plujii, arrant little knaves as ever gulped moonshine.

They were spoken of as inhabiting the island of Quelquo, in a remote corner of the lagoon; the innocent people of which island were sadly fretted and put out by their diabolical proceedings. Not to be wondered at; since, dwelling as they did in the air, and completely inaccessible, these spirits were peculiarly provocative of ire.

Detestable Plujii! With malice aforethought, they brought about high winds that destroyed the banana plantations, and tumbled over the heads of its occupants many a bamboo dwelling. They cracked the calabashes; soured the "poee;" induced the colic; begat the spleen; and almost rent people in twain with stitches in the side. In short, of whatever evil, the cause of which the Islanders could not directly impute to their gods, or in their own opinion was not referable to themselves,—of that very thing must the invisible Plujii be guilty. With horrible dreams, and blood-thirsty gnats, they invaded the most innocent slumbers.

All things they bedeviled. A man with a wry neck ascribed it to the Plujii; he with a bad memory railed against the Plujii; and the boy, bruising his finger, also cursed those abominable spirits.

Nor, to some minds, at least, was there wanting strong presumptive evidence, that at times, with invisible fingers, the above mentioned Plujii did leave direct and tangible traces of their presence; pinching and pounding the unfortunate Islanders; pulling their hair; plucking their ears, and tweaking their beards and their noses. And thus perpetually vexing, incensing, tormenting, and exasperating their helpless victims, the atrocious Plujii reveled in their malicious dominion over the souls and bodies of the people of Quelquo.

What it was, that induced them to enact such a part, Oro only knew; and never but once, it seems, did old Mohi endeavor to find out.

Once upon a time, visiting Quelquo, he chanced to encounter an old woman almost doubled together, both hands upon her abdomen; in that manner running about distracted.

"My good woman," said he, "what under the firmament is the matter?"

"The Plujii! the Plujii!" affectionately caressing the field of their operations.

"But why do they torment you?" he soothingly inquired.

"How should I know? and what good would it do me if I did?"

And on she ran.

At this part of his narration, Mohi was interrupted by Media; who, much to the surprise of all present, observed, that, unbeknown to him (Braid-Beard), he happened to have been on that very island, at that very time, and saw that identical old lady in the very midst of those abdominal tribulations.

"That she was really in great distress," he went on to say, "was plainly to be seen; but that in that particular instance, your Plujii had any hand in tormenting her, I had some boisterous doubts. For, hearing that an hour or two previous she had been partaking of some twenty unripe bananas, I rather fancied that that circumstance might have had something to do with her sufferings. But however it was, all the herb-leeches on the island would not have altered her own opinions on the subject."

"No," said Braid-Beard; "a post-mortem examination would not have satisfied her ghost."

"Curious to relate," he continued, "the people of that island never abuse the Plujii, notwithstanding all they suffer at their hands, unless under direct provocation; and a settled matter of faith is it, that at such times all bitter words and hasty objurgations are entirely overlooked, nay, pardoned on the spot, by the unseen genii against whom they are directed."

"Magnanimous Plujii!" cried Media. "But, Babbalanja, do you, who run a tilt at all things, suffer this silly conceit to be uttered with impunity in your presence? Why so silent?"

"I have been thinking, my lord," said Babbalanja, "that though the people of that island may at times err, in imputing their calamities to the Plujii; that, nevertheless, upon the whole, they indulge in a reasonable belief. For, Plujii or no Plujii, it is undeniable, that in ten thousand ways, as if by a malicious agency, we mortals are woefully put out and tormented; and that, too, by things in themselves so exceedingly trivial, that it would seem almost impiety to ascribe them to the august gods. No; there must exist some greatly inferior spirits; so insignificant, comparatively, as to be overlooked by the supernal powers; and through them it must be, that we are thus grievously annoyed. At any rate, such a theory would supply a hiatus in my system of metaphysics."

"Well, peace to the Plujii," said Media; "they trouble not me."

Chapter 87

Nora-Bamma

STILL ONWARD GLIDING, the lagoon a calm.
Hours pass; and full before us, round and green, a Moslem turban by us floats—Nora-Bamma, Isle of Nods.

Noon-tide rolls its flood. Vibrates the air, and trembles. And by illusion optical, thin-draped in azure haze, drift here and there the brilliant lands: swans, peacock-plumaged, sailing through the sky. Down to earth hath heaven come; hard telling sun-clouds from the isles.

And high in air nods Nora-Bamma. Nid-nods its tufted summit like three ostrich plumes; its beetling crags, bent poppies, shadows, willowy shores, all nod; its streams are murmuring down the hills; its wavelets hush the shore.

Who dwells in Nora-Bamma? Dreamers, hypochondriacs, somnambulists; who, from the cark and care of outer Mardi fleeing, in the poppy's jaded odors, seek oblivion for the past, and ecstasies to come.

Open-eyed, they sleep and dream; on their roof-trees, grapes unheeded drop. In Nora-Bamma, whispers are as shouts; and at a zephyr's breath, from the woodlands shake the leaves, as of humming-birds, a flight.

All this spake Braid-Beard, of the isle. How that none ere touched its strand, without rendering instant tribute of a nap; how that those who thither voyaged, in golden quest of golden gourds, fast dropped asleep, ere one was plucked; waking not till night; how that you must needs rub hard your eyes, would you wander through the isle; and how that silent specters would be met, haunting twilight groves, and dreamy meads; hither gliding, thither fading, end or purpose none.

True or false, so much for Mohi's Nora-Bamma.

But as we floated on, it looked the place described. We yawned, and yawned, as crews of vessels may; as in warm Indian seas, their winnowing sails all swoon, when by them glides some opium argosie.

Chapter 88

In a Calm, Hautia's Heralds approach

H OW STILL!" cried Babbalanja. "This calm is like unto Oro's
everlasting serenity, and like unto man's last despair."
But now the silence was broken by a strange, distant, intermitted
melody in the water.

Gazing over the side, we saw naught but a far-darting ray in its depths.

Then Yoomy, before buried in a reverie, burst forth with a verse, sudden as a jet from a Geyser.

> Like the fish of the bright and twittering fin,
>   Bright fish! diving deep as high soars the lark,
> So, far, far, far, doth the maiden swim,
>   Wild song, wild light, in still ocean's dark.

"What maiden, minstrel?" cried Media.

"None of these," answered Yoomy, pointing out a shallop gliding near.

"The damsels three:—Taji, they pursue you yet."

That still canoe drew nigh, the Iris in its prow.

Gliding slowly by, one damsel flung a Venus-car, the leaves yet fresh.

Said Yoomy—"Fly to love."

The second maiden flung a pallid blossom, buried in hemlock leaves.

Said Yoomy, starting—"I have wrought a death."

267

Then came showering Venus-cars, and glorious moss-roses numberless, and odorous handfuls of Verbena.

Said Yoomy—"Yet fly, oh fly to me: all rosy joys and sweets are mine." Then the damsels floated on.

"Was ever queen more enigmatical?" cried Media—"Love,—death,—joy,—fly to me? But what says Taji?"

"That I turn not back for Hautia; whoe'er she be, that wild witch I contemn."

"Then spread our pinions wide! a breeze! up sails! ply paddles all! Come, Flora's flute, float forth a song."

To pieces picking the thorny roses culled from Hautia's gifts, and holding up their blighted cores, thus plumed and turbaned Yoomy sang, leaning against the mast:—

> Oh! royal is the rose,
>   But barbed with many a dart;
> Beware, beware the rose,
>   'Tis cankered at the heart.
>
> Sweet, sweet the sunny down,
> Oh! lily, lily, lily down!
>   Sweet, sweet, Verbena's bloom!
> Oh! pleasant, gentle, musky bloom!
>
> Dread, dread the sunny down;
>   Lo! lily-hooded asp;
> Blooms, blooms no more Verbena;
>   White-withered in your clasp.

Chapter 89

Braid-Beard rehearses the Origin of the Isle of Rogues

JUDGE NOT things by their names. This, the maxim illustrated respecting the isle toward which we were sailing.

Ohonoo was its designation, in other words the Land of Rogues. So what but a nest of villains and pirates could one fancy it to be: a downright Tortuga, swarming with "Brethren of the coast,"—such as Montbars, L'Ollonais, Bartolomeo, Peter of Dieppe, and desperadoes of that kidney. But not so. The men of Ohonoo were as honest as any in Mardi. They had a suspicious appellative for their island, true; but not thus seemed it to them. For, upon nothing did they so much plume themselves as upon this very name. Why? Its origin went back to old times; and being venerable they gloried therein; though they disclaimed its present applicability to any of their race; showing, that words are but algebraic signs, conveying no meaning except what you please. And to be called one thing, is oftentimes to be another.

But how came the Ohonoose by their name?

Listen, and Braid-Beard, our Herodotus, will tell.

Long and long ago, there were banished to Ohonoo all the bucaniers, flibustiers, thieves, and malefactors of the neighboring islands; who, becoming at last quite a numerous community, resolved to make a stand for their dignity, and number one among the nations of Mardi. And even as before they had been weeded out of the surrounding countries; so now, they went to weeding out themselves; banishing all objectionable persons to still another island. These events happened at a period so remote, that at present it was uncertain whether those twice banished, were thrust into their second exile by reason of their superlative knavery, or because of their comparative honesty. If the latter, then must the residue have been a precious enough set of scoundrels.

However it was, the commonwealth of knaves now mustered together their gray-beards, and wise-pates, and knowing-ones, of which last there was a plenty, chose a king to rule over them, and went to political house-keeping for themselves.

And in the fullness of time, this people became numerous and mighty. And the more numerous and mighty they waxed, by so much the more did they take pride and glory in their origin, frequently reverting to it with manifold boastings. The proud device of their monarch was a hand with the forefinger crooked, emblematic of the peculatory propensities of his ancestors.

And all this, at greater length, said Mohi.

"It would seem, then, my lord," said Babbalanja, reclining, "as if these men of Ohonoo had canonized the derelictions of their progenitors, though the same traits are deemed scandalous among themselves. But it is time that makes the difference. The knave of a thousand years ago seems a fine old fellow full of spirit and fun, little malice in his soul; whereas, the knave of to-day seems a sour-visaged wight, with nothing to redeem him. Many great scoundrels of our Chronicler's chronicles are heroes to us:—witness, Marjora the usurper. Ay, time truly works wonders. It sublimates wine; it sublimates fame; nay, is the creator thereof; it enriches and darkens our spears of the Palm; enriches and enlightens the mind; it ripens cherries and young lips; festoons old ruins, and ivies old heads; imparts a relish to old yams, and a pungency to the Ponderings of old Bardianna; of fables distills truths; and finally, smooths, levels, glosses, softens, melts, and meliorates all things. Why, my lord, round Mardi itself is all the better for its antiquity, and the more to be revered; to the cozy-minded, more comfortable to dwell in. Ah! if ever it lay in embryo like a green seed in the pod, what a damp, shapeless thing it must have been, and how unpleasant from the traces of its recent creation. The first man, quoth old Bardianna, must have felt like one going into a new habitation, where the bamboos are green. Is there not a legend in Maramma, that his family were long troubled with influenzas and catarrhs?"

"Oh Time, Time, Time!" cried Yoomy—"it is Time, old midsummer Time, that has made the old world what it is. Time hoared the old mountains, and balded their old summits, and spread the old prairies, and built the old forests, and molded the old vales. It is Time that has worn glorious old channels for the glorious old rivers, and rounded the old lakes, and deepened the old sea! It is Time—"

"Ay, full time to cease," cried Media. "What have you to do with cogitations not in verse, minstrel? Leave prose to Babbalanja, who is prosy enough."

"Even so," said Babbalanja, "Yoomy, you have overstepped your province. My lord Media well knows, that your business is to make the metal in you jingle in tags, not ring in the ingot."

Chapter 90

Rare Sport at Ohonoo

APPROACHED FROM THE NORTHWARD, Ohonoo, midway cloven down to the sea, one half a level plain; the other, three mountain terraces—Ohonoo looks like the first steps of a gigantic way to the sun. And such, if Braid-Beard spoke truth, it had formerly been.

"Ere Mardi was made," said that true old chronicler, "Vivo, one of the genii, built a ladder of mountains whereby to go up and go down. And of this ladder, the island of Ohonoo was the base. But wandering here and there, incognito in a vapor, so much wickedness did Vivo spy out, that in high dudgeon he hurried up his ladder, knocking the mountains from under him as he went. These here and there fell into the lagoon, forming many isles, now green and luxuriant; which, with those sprouting from seeds dropped by a bird from the moon, comprise all the groups in the reef."

Surely, oh, surely, if I live till Mardi be forgotten by Mardi, I shall not forget the sight that greeted us, as we drew nigh the shores of this same island of Ohonoo; for was not all Ohonoo bathing in the surf of the sea?

But let the picture be painted.

Where eastward the ocean rolls surging against the outer reef of Mardi, there, facing a flood-gate in the barrier, stands cloven Ohonoo; her plains sloping outward to the sea, her mountains a bulwark behind. As at Juam, where the wild billows from seaward roll in upon its cliffs; much more at Ohonoo, in billowy battalions charge they hotly into the lagoon, and fall on the isle like an army from the deep. But charge they never so boldly, and charge they forever, old Ohonoo gallantly throws them back till all before her is one scud and rack. So charged the bright billows of cuirassiers at Waterloo: so hurled them off the long line of living walls, whose base was as the sea-beach, wreck-strown, in a gale.

Without the break in the reef, wide banks of coral shelve off, creating the bar, where the waves muster for the onset, thundering in water-bolts, that shake the whole reef, till its very spray trembles. And then is it, that the swimmers of Ohonoo most delight to gambol in the surf.

For this sport, a surf-board is indispensable: some five feet in length; the width of a man's body; convex on both sides; highly polished; and rounded at the ends. It is held in high estimation; invariably oiled after use; and hung up conspicuously in the dwelling of the owner.

Ranged on the beach, the bathers, by hundreds dash in; and diving under the swells, make straight for the outer sea, pausing not till the comparatively smooth expanse beyond has been gained. Here, throwing themselves upon their boards, tranquilly they wait for a billow that suits. Snatching them up, it hurries them landward, volume and speed both increasing, till it races along a watery wall, like the smooth, awful verge of Niagara. Hanging over this scroll, looking down from it as from a precipice, the bathers halloo; every limb in motion to preserve their place on the very crest of the wave. Should they fall behind, the squadrons that follow would whelm them; dismounted, and thrown forward, as certainly would they be run over by the steed they ride. 'Tis like charging at the head of cavalry: you must on.

An expert swimmer shifts his position on his plank; now half striding it; and anon, like a rider in the ring, poising himself upright in the scud, coming on like a man in the air.

At last all is lost in scud and vapor, as the overgrown billow bursts like a bomb. Adroitly emerging, the swimmers thread their way out; and like seals at the Orkneys, stand dripping upon the shore.

Landing in smooth water, some distance from the scene, we strolled forward; and meeting a group resting, inquired for Uhia, their king. He was pointed out in the foam. But presently drawing nigh, he embraced Media, bidding all welcome.

The bathing over, and evening at hand, Uhia and his subjects repaired to their canoes; and we to ours.

Landing at another quarter of the island, we journeyed up a valley called Monlova, and were soon housed in a very pleasant retreat of our host.

Soon supper was spread. But though the viands were rare, and the red wine went round and round like a foaming bay horse in the ring; yet we marked, that despite the stimulus of his day's good sport, and the stimulus of his brave good cheer, Uhia our host was moody and still.

Said Babbalanja, "My lord, he fills wine cups for others to quaff."

But whispered King Media, "Though Uhia be sad, be we merry, merry men."

And merry some were, and merrily went to their mats.

Chapter 91

Of King Uhia and his Subjects

AS BESEEMED HIM, Uhia was royally lodged. Ample his roof. Beneath it a hundred attendants nightly laying their heads. But long since, he had disbanded his damsels.

Springing from syren embrace—"They shall sap and mine me no more," he cried; "my destiny commands me. I will don my manhood. By Keevi! no more will I clasp a waist."

"From that time forth," said Braid-Beard, "young Uhia spread like the tufted top of the Palm; his thigh grew brawny as the limb of the Banian; his arm waxed strong as the back bone of the shark; yea, his voice grew sonorous as a conch.

"And now he bent his whole soul to the accomplishment of the destiny believed to be his. Nothing less than bodily to remove Ohonoo to the center of the lagoon, in fulfillment of an old prophecy running thus— 'When a certain island shall stir from its foundations and stand in the middle of the still water, then shall the ruler of that island be ruler of all Mardi.'

"The task was hard, but how glorious the reward! So at it he went, and all Ohonoo helped him. Not by hands, but by calling in the magicians. Thus far, nevertheless, in vain. But Uhia had hopes."

Now, informed of all this, said Babbalanja to Media, "My lord, if the continual looking-forward to something greater, be better than an

275

acquiescence in things present; then, wild as it is, this belief of Uhia's he should hug to his heart, as erewhile his wives. But my lord, this faith it is, that robs his days of peace; his nights of sweet unconsciousness. For holding himself foreordained to the dominion of the entire Archipelago, he upbraids the gods for laggards, and curses himself as deprived of his rights; nay, as having had wrested from him, what he never possessed. Discontent dwarfs his horizon till he spans it with his hand. 'Most miserable of demigods,' he cries, 'here am I cooped up in this insignificant islet, only one hundred leagues by fifty, when scores of broad empires own me not for their lord.' Yet Uhia himself is envied. 'Ah!' cries Karrolono, one of his chieftains, master of a snug little glen, 'Here am I cabined in this paltry cell among the mountains, when that great King Uhia is lord of the whole island, and every cubic mile of matter therein.' But this same Karrolono is envied. 'Hard, oh beggarly lot is mine,' cries Donno, one of his retainers. 'Here am I fixed and screwed down to this paltry plantation, when my lord Karrolono owns the whole glen, ten long parasangs from cliff to sea.' But Donno too is envied. 'Alas, cursed fate!' cries his servitor Flavona. 'Here am I made to trudge, sweat, and labor all day, when Donno my master does nothing but command.' But others envy Flavona; and those who envy him are envied in turn; even down to poor bed-ridden Manta, who dying of want, groans forth, 'Abandoned wretch that I am! here I miserably perish, while so many beggars gad about and live!' But surely, none envy Manta! Yes; great Uhia himself. 'Ah!' cries the king. 'Here am I vexed and tormented by ambition; no peace night nor day; my temples chafed sore by this cursed crown that I wear; while that ignoble wight Manta, gives up the ghost with none to molest him.'"

In vain we wandered up and down in this isle, and peered into its innermost recesses: no Yillah was there.

Chapter 92

The God Keevi and the Precipice of Mondo

ONE OBJECT OF INTEREST in Ohonoo was the original image
of Keevi the god of Thieves; hence, from time immemorial, the
tutelar deity of the isle.

His shrine was a natural niche in a cliff, walling in the valley of Monlova.
And here stood Keevi, with his five eyes, ten hands, and three pair of legs,
equipped at all points for the vocation over which he presided. Of mighty
girth, his arms terminated in hands, every finger a limb, spreading in multiplied digits: palms twice five, and fifty fingers.

According to the legend, Keevi fell from a golden cloud, burying himself to the thighs in the earth, tearing up the soil all round. Three meditative
mortals, strolling by at the time, had a narrow escape.

A wonderful recital; but none of us voyagers durst flout it. Did they
not show us the identical spot where the idol fell? We descended into the
hollow, now verdant. Questionless, Keevi himself would have vouched
for the truth of the miracle, had he not been unfortunately dumb. But by
far the most cogent, and pointed argument advanced in support of this
story, is a spear which the priests of Keevi brought forth, for Babbalanja
to view.

"Let me look at it closer," said Babbalanja.

277

And turning it over and over and curiously inspecting it, "Wonderful spear," he cried. "Doubtless, my reverends, this self-same spear must have persuaded many recusants!"

"Nay, the most stubborn," they answered.

"And all afterward quoted as additional authority for the truth of the legend?"

"Assuredly."

From the sea to the shrine of this god, the fine valley of Monlova ascends with a gentle gradation, hardly perceptible; but upon turning round toward the water, one is surprised to find himself high elevated above its surface. Pass on, and the same silent ascent deceives you; and the valley contracts; and on both sides the cliffs advance; till at last you come to a narrow space, shouldered by buttresses of rock. Beyond, through this cleft, all is blue sky. If the Trades blow high, and you came unawares upon the spot, you would think Keevi himself pushing you forward with all his hands; so powerful is the current of air rushing through this elevated defile. But expostulate not with the tornado that blows you along; sail on; but soft; look down; the land breaks off in one sheer descent of a thousand feet, right down to the wide plain below. So sudden and profound this precipice, that you seem to look off from one world to another. In a dreamy, sunny day, the spangled plain beneath assumes an uncertain fleeting aspect. Had you a deep-sea-lead you would almost be tempted to sound the ocean-haze at your feet.

This, mortal! is the precipice of Mondo.

From this brink, spear in hand, sprang fifty rebel warriors, driven back into the vale by a superior force. Finding no spot to stand at bay, with a fierce shout they took the fatal leap.

Said Mohi, "Their souls ascended, ere their bodies touched."

This tragical event took place many generations gone by, and now a dizzy, devious way conducts one, firm of foot, from the verge to the plain. But none ever ascended. So perilous, indeed, is the descent itself, that the islanders venture not the feat, without invoking supernatural aid. Flanking the precipice, beneath beetling rocks, stand the guardian deities of Mondo; and on altars before them, are placed the propitiatory offerings of the traveler.

To the right of the brink of the precipice, and far over it, projects a narrow ledge. The test of legitimacy in the Ohonoo monarchs is to stand hereon, arms folded, and javelins darting by.

And there in his youth Uhia stood.

"How felt you, cousin?" asked Media.

"Like the King of Ohonoo," he replied. "As I *shall* again feel, when King of all Mardi."

Chapter 93

*Babbalanja steps in between Mohi and Yoomy; and Yoomy
relates a Legend*

EMBARKING FROM OHONOO, we at length found ourselves
gliding by the pleasant shores of Tupia, an islet which according
to Braid-Beard had for ages remained uninhabited by man. Much
curiosity being expressed to know more of the isle, Mohi was about to
turn over his chronicles, when, with modesty, the minstrel Yoomy interposed; saying, that if my Lord Media permitted, he himself would relate
the legend. From its nature, deeming the same pertaining to his province
as poet; though, as yet, it had not been versified. But he added, that true
pearl shells rang musically, though not strung upon a cord.

Upon this presumptuous interference, Mohi looked highly offended;
and nervously twitching his beard, uttered something invidious about frip-
pery young poetasters being too full of silly imaginings to tell a plain tale.

Said Yoomy, in reply, adjusting his turban, "Old Mohi, let us not clash.
I honor your calling; but, with submission, your chronicles are more wild
than my cantos. I deal in pure conceits of my own; which have a shapeliness
and a unity, however unsubstantial; but you, Braid-Beard, deal in mangled
realities. In all your chapters, you yourself grope in the dark. Much truth
is not in thee, historian. Besides, Mohi: my songs perpetuate many things
which you sage scribes entirely overlook. Have you not oftentimes come
to me, and my ever dewy ballads for information, in which you and your

280

musty old chronicles were deficient? In much that is precious, Mohi, we poets are the true historians; we embalm; you corrode."

To this Mohi, with some ire, was about to make answer, when, flinging over his shoulder a new fold of his mantle, Babbalanja spoke thus: "Peace, rivals. As Bardianna has it, like all who dispute upon pretensions of their own, you are each nearest the right, when you speak of the other; and furthest therefrom, when you speak of yourselves."

Said Mohi and Yoomy in a breath, "Who sought your opinion, philosopher? you filcher from old Bardianna, and monger of maxims!"

"You, who have so long marked the vices of Mardi, that you flatter yourself you have none of your own," added Braid-Beard.

"You, who only seem wise, because of the contrasting follies of others, and not of any great wisdom in yourself," continued the minstrel, with unwonted asperity.

"Now here," said Babbalanja, "am I charged upon by a bearded old ram, and a lamb. One butting with his carious and brittle old frontlet; the other pushing with its silly head before its horns are sprouted. But this comes of being impartial. Had I espoused the cause of Yoomy versus Mohi, or that of Mohi versus Yoomy, I had been sure to have had at least one voice in my favor. The impartialist insulteth all sides, saith old Bardianna; but smite with but one hand, and the other shall be kissed.—Oh incomparable Bardianna!"

"Will no one lay that troubled old ghost," exclaimed Media, devoutly. "Proceed with thy legend, Yoomy; and see to it, that it be brief; for I mistrust me, these legends do but test the patience of the hearers. But draw a long breath, and begin."

"A long bow," muttered Mohi.

And Yoomy began.

"It is now about ten hundred thousand moons—"

"Great Oro! How long since, say you?" cried Mohi, making Gothic arches of his brows.

Looking at him disdainfully, but vouchsafing no reply, Yoomy began over again.

"It is now above ten hundred thousand moons, since there died the last of a marvelous race, once inhabiting the very shores by which we are sailing. They were a very diminutive people, only a few inches high—"

"Stop, minstrel," cried Mohi; "how many pennyweights did they weigh?"

Continued Yoomy, unheedingly, "They were covered all over with a soft, silky down, like that on the rind of the Avee; and there grew upon their heads a green, lance-leaved vine, of a most delicate texture. For convenience, the manikins reduced their tendrils, sporting nothing but coronals. Whereas, priding themselves upon the redundancy of their tresses, the little maidens assiduously watered them with the early dew of the morning; so that all wreathed and festooned with verdure, they moved about in arbors, trailing after them trains."

"I can hear no more," exclaimed Mohi, stopping his ears.

Continued Yoomy, "The damsels lured to their bowers, certain red-plumaged insect-birds, and taught them to nestle therein, and warble; which, with the pleasant vibrating of the leaves, when the little maidens moved, produced a strange blending of sweet, singing sounds. The little maidens embraced not with their arms, but with their viny locks; whose tendrils instinctively twined about their lovers, till both were lost in the bower."

"And what then?" asked Mohi, who, notwithstanding the fingers in his ears, somehow contrived to listen; "What then?"

Vouchsafing no reply, Yoomy went on.

"At a certain age, but while yet the maidens were very young, their vines bore blossoms. Ah! fatal symptoms. For soon as they burst, the maidens died in their arbors; and were buried in the valleys; and their vines spread forth; and the flowers bloomed; but the maidens themselves were no more. And now disdaining the earth, the vines shot upward: climbing to the topmost boughs of the trees; and flowering in the sunshine forever and aye."

Yoomy here paused for a space; but presently continued:

"The little eyes of the people of Tupia were very strange to behold: full of stars, that shone from within, like the Pleiades, deep-bosomed in blue. And like the stars, they were intolerant of sunlight; and slumbering through the day, the people of Tupia only went abroad by night. But it was chiefly when the moon was at full, that they were mostly in spirits.

"Then the little manikins would dive down into the sea, and rove about in the coral groves, making love to the mermaids. Or, racing round, make a mad merry night of it with the sea-urchins:—plucking the reverend mullets by the beard; serenading the turtles in their cells; worrying the sea-nettles; or tormenting with their antics the touchy torpedos. Sometimes they went prying about with the star-fish, that have an eye at the end of each ray; and often with coral files in their hands stole upon slumbering swordfish, slyly blunting their weapons. In short, these stout little manikins

were passionately fond of the sea, and swore by wave and billow, that
sooner or later they would embark thereon in nautilus shells, and spend
the rest of their roving days thousands of inches from Tupia. Too true, they
were shameless little rakes. Oft would they return to their sweethearts,
sporting musky girdles of sea-kelp, tasseled with green little pouches of grass,
brimful of seed-pearls; and jingling their coin in the ears of the damsels,
throw out inuendoes about the beautiful and bountiful mermaids: how
wealthy and amorous they were, and how they delighted in the company of
the brave gallants of Tupia. Ah! at such heartless bravadoes, how mourned
the poor little nymphs. Deep into their arbors they went; and their little
hearts burst like rose-buds, and filled the whole air with an odorous grief.
But when their lovers were gentle and true, no happier maidens haunted
the lilies than they. By some mystical process they wrought minute balls
of light: touchy, mercurial globules, very hard to handle; and with these, at
pitch and toss, they played in the groves. Or mischievously inclined, they
toiled all night long at braiding the moonbeams together, and entangling
the plaited end to a bough; so that at night, the poor planet had much ado
to set."

Here Yoomy once more was mute.

"Pause you to invent as you go on?" said old Mohi, elevating his chin,
till his beard was horizontal.

Yoomy resumed.

"Little or nothing more, my masters, is extant of the legend; only it
must be mentioned, that these little people were very tasteful in their personal adornings; the manikins wearing girdles of fragrant leaves, and necklaces of aromatic seeds; and the little damsels, not content with their vines,
and their verdure, sporting pearls in their ears; bracelets of wee little porpoise teeth; and oftentimes dancing with their mates in the moonlit glades,
coquettishly fanned themselves with the transparent wings of the flying
fish."

"Now, I appeal to you, royal Media; to you, noble Taji; to you,
Babbalanja;" said the chronicler, with an impressive gesture, "whether
this seems a credible history: Yoomy has invented."

"But perhaps he has entertained, old Mohi," said Babbalanja.

"He has not spoken the truth," persisted the chronicler.

"Mohi," said Babbalanja, "truth is in things, and not in words: truth
is voiceless; so at least saith old Bardianna. And I, Babbalanja, assert, that
what are vulgarly called fictions are as much realities as the gross mattock
of Dididi, the digger of trenches; for things visible are but conceits of the

eye: things imaginative, conceits of the fancy. If duped by one, we are equally duped by the other."

"Clear as this water," said Yoomy.

"Opaque as this paddle," said Mohi. "But, come now, thou oracle, if all things are deceptive, tell us what is truth?"

"The old interrogatory; did they not ask it when the world began? But ask it no more. As old Bardianna hath it, that question is more final than any answer."

Chapter 94

Of that jolly old Lord, Borabolla; and that jolly Island of his,
Mondoldo; and of the Fish-ponds, and the Hereafters of Fish

D RAWING NEAR MONDOLDO, our next place of destination,
we were greeted by six fine canoes, gayly tricked out with
streamers, and all alive with the gestures of their occupants.
King Borabolla and court were hastening to welcome our approach;
Media, unbeknown to all, having notified him at the Banquet of the
Five-and-Twenty Kings, of our intention to visit his dominions.

Soon, side by side, these canoes floated with ours; each barge of Odo
courteously flanked by those of Mondoldo.

Not long were we in identifying Borabolla: the portly, pleasant old
monarch, seated cross-legged upon a dais, projecting over the bow of the
largest canoe of the six, close-grappling to the side of the Sea Elephant.

Was he not a goodly round sight to behold? Round all over; round of
eye and of head; and like the jolly round Earth, roundest and biggest about
the Equator. A girdle of red was his Equinoctial Line, giving a compact-
ness to his plumpness.

This old Borabolla permitted naught to come between his head and
the sun; not even gray hairs. Bald as a gourd, right down on his brazen
skull, the rays of the luminary converged.

He was all hilarity; full of allusions to the feast at Willamilla, where he
had done royal execution. Rare old Borabolla! thou wert made for dining

out; thy ample mouth an inlet for good cheer, and a sally-port for good humor.

Bustling about on his dais, he now gave orders for the occupants of our canoes to be summarily emptied into his own; saying, that in that manner only did he allow guests to touch the beach of Mondoldo.

So, with no little trouble—for the waves were grown somewhat riotous—we proceeded to comply; bethinking ourselves all the while, how annoying is sometimes an overstrained act of hospitality.

We were now but little less than a mile from the shore. But what of that? There was plenty of time, thought Borabolla, for a hasty lunch, and the getting of a subsequent appetite ere we effected a landing. So viands were produced; to which the guests were invited to pay heedful attention; or take the consequences, and famish till the long voyage in prospect was ended.

Soon the water shoaled (approaching land is like nearing truth in metaphysics), and ere we yet touched the beach, Borabolla declared, that we were already landed. Which paradoxical assertion implied, that the hospitality of Mondoldo was such, that in all directions it radiated far out upon the lagoon, embracing a great circle; so that no canoe could sail by the island, without its occupants being so long its guests.

In most hospitable vicinity to the water, was a fine large structure, inclosed by a stockade; both rather dilapidated; as if the cost of entertaining its guests, prevented outlays for repairing the place. But it was one of Borabolla's maxims, that generally your tumble-down old homesteads yield the most entertainment; their very dilapidation betokening their having seen good service in hospitality; whereas, spruce-looking, finical portals, have a phiz full of meaning; for niggards are oftentimes neat.

Now, after what has been said, who so silly as to fancy, that because Borabolla's mansion was inclosed by a stockade, that the same was intended as a defense against guests? By no means. In the palisade was a mighty breach, not an entrance-way, wide enough to admit six Daniel Lamberts abreast.

"Look," cried Borabolla, as landing we stepped toward the place. "Look Media! look all. These gates, you here see, lashed back with osiers, have been so lashed during my life-time; and just where they stand, shall they rot; ay, they shall perish wide open."

"But why have them at all?" inquired Media.

"Ah! there you have old Borabolla," cried the other.

"No," said Babbalanja, "a fence whose gate is ever kept open, seems unnecessary, I grant; nevertheless, it gives a notable hint, otherwise not so aptly conveyed; for is not the open gate the sign of the open heart?"

"Right, right," cried Borabolla; "so enter both, cousin Media;" and with one hand smiting his chest, with the other he waved us on.

But if the stockade seemed all open gate, the structure within seemed only a roof; for nothing but a slender pillar here and there, supported it.

"This is my mode of building," said Borabolla; "I will have no outside to my palaces. Walls are superfluous. And to a high-minded guest, the entering a narrow doorway is like passing under a yoke; every time he goes in, or comes out, it reminds him, that he is being entertained at the cost of another. So storm in all round."

Within, was one wide field-bed; where reclining, we looked up to endless rows of brown calabashes, and trenchers suspended along the rafters; promissory of ample cheer as regiments of old hams in a baronial refectory.

They were replenished with both meat and drink; the trenchers readily accessible by means of cords; but the gourds containing arrack, suspended neck downward, were within easy reach where they swung.

Seeing all these indications of hard roystering; like a cautious young bridegroom at his own marriage merry-making, Taji stood on his guard. And when Borabolla urged him to empty a gourd or two, by way of making room in him for the incidental repast about to be served, Taji civilly declined; not wishing to cumber the floor, before the cloth was laid.

Jarl, however, yielding to importunity, and unmindful of the unities of time and place, went freely about, from gourd to gourd, concocting in him a punch. At which, Samoa expressed much surprise, that he should be so unobservant as not to know, that in Mardi, guests might be pressed to demean themselves, without its being expected that so they would do. A true toss-pot himself, he bode his time.

The second lunch over, Borabolla placed both hands to the ground, and giving the sigh of the fat man, after three vigorous efforts, succeeded in gaining his pins; which pins of his, were but small for his body; insomuch that they hugely staggered about, under the fine old load they carried.

The specific object of his thus striving after an erect posture, was to put himself in motion, and conduct us to his fish-ponds, famous throughout the Archipelago as the hobby of the king of Mondoldo. Furthermore, as the great repast of the day, yet to take place, was to be a grand piscatory one, our host was all anxiety, that we should have a glimpse of our fish, while yet alive and hearty.

We were alarmed at perceiving, that certain servitors were preparing to accompany us with trenchers of edibles. It begat the notion, that our trip to the fish-ponds was to prove a long journey. But they were not three hundred yards distant; though Borabolla being a veteran traveler, never stirred from his abode without his battalion of butlers.

The ponds were four in number, close bordering the water, embracing about an acre each, and situated in a low fen, draining several valleys. The excavated soil was thrown up in dykes, made tight by being beaten all over, while in a soft state, with the heavy, flat ends of Palm stalks. Lying side by side, by three connecting trenches, these ponds could be made to communicate at pleasure; while two additional canals afforded means of letting in upon them the salt waters of the lagoon on one hand, or those of an inland stream on the other. And by a third canal with four branches, together or separately, they could be partially drained. Thus, the waters could be mixed to suit any gills; and the young fish taken from the sea, passed through a stated process of freshening; so that by the time they graduated, the salt was well out of them, like the brains out of some diplomaed collegians.

Fresh-water fish are only to be obtained in Mondoldo by the artificial process above mentioned; as the streams and brooks abound not in trout or other Waltonian prey.

Taken all floundering from the sea, Borabolla's fish, passing through their regular training for the table, and daily tended by their keepers, in course of time became quite tame and communicative. To prove which, calling his Head Ranger, the king bade him administer the customary supply of edibles.

Accordingly, mouthfuls were thrown into the ponds. Whereupon, the fish darted in a shoal toward the margin; some leaping out of the water in their eagerness. Crouching on the bank, the Ranger now called several by name, patted their scales, carrying on some heathenish nursery-talk, like St. Anthony, in ancient Coptic, instilling virtuous principles into his finny flock on the sea shore.

But alas, for the hair-shirted old dominie's backsliding disciples. For, of all nature's animated kingdoms, fish are the most unchristian, inhospitable, heartless, and cold-blooded of creatures. At least, so seem they to strangers; though at bottom, somehow, they must be all right. And truly it is not to be wondered at, that the very reverend Anthony strove after the conversion of fish. For, whoso shall Christianize, and by so doing, humanize the sharks, will do a greater good, by the saving of human life in all time to come, than though he made catechumens of the head-hunting Dyaks of Borneo, or the blood-bibbing Battas of Sumatra. And are these

Dyaks and Battas one whit better than tiger-sharks? Nay, are they so good? Were a Batta your intimate friend, you would often mistake an orang-outang for him; and have orang-outangs immortal souls? True, the Battas believe in a hereafter; but of what sort? Full of Blue-Beards and bloody bones. So, also, the sharks; who hold that Paradise is one vast Pacific, ploughed by navies of mortals, whom an endless gale forever drops into their maws.

Not wholly a surmise. For, does it not appear a little unreasonable to imagine, that there is any creature, fish, flesh, or fowl, so little in love with life, as not to cherish hopes of a future state? Why does man believe in it? One reason, reckoned cogent, is, that he desires it. Who shall say, then, that the leviathan this day harpooned on the coast of Japan, goes not straight to his ancestor, who rolled all Jonah, as a sweet morsel, under his tongue?

Though herein, some sailors are slow believers, or at best hold themselves in a state of philosophical suspense. Say they—"That catastrophe took place in the Mediterranean; and the only whales frequenting the Mediterranean, are of a sort having not a swallow large enough to pass a man entire; for those Mediterranean whales feed upon small things, as horses upon oats." But hence, the sailors draw a rash inference. Are not the Straits of Gibraltar wide enough to admit a sperm-whale, even though none have sailed through, since Nineveh and the gourd in its suburbs dried up?

As for the possible hereafter of the whales; a creature eighty feet long without stockings, and thirty feet round the waist before dinner, is not inconsiderately to be consigned to annihilation.

Chapter 95

That jolly old Lord Borabolla laughs on both Sides of his Face

A VERY GOOD PALACE, this, coz, for you and me," said waddling old Borabolla to Media, as, returned from our excursion, he slowly lowered himself down to his mat, sighing like a grampus.

By this, he again made known the vastness of his hospitality, which led him for the nonce to parcel out his kingdom with his guests.

But apart from these extravagant expressions of good feeling, Borabolla was the prince of good fellows. His great tun of a person was indispensable to the housing of his bullock-heart; under which, any lean wight would have sunk. But alas! unlike Media and Taji, Borabolla, though a crowned king, was accounted no demi-god; his obesity excluding him from that honor. Indeed, in some quarters of Mardi, certain pagans maintain, that no fat man can be even immortal. A dogma! truly, which should be thrown to the dogs. For fat men are the salt and savor of the earth; full of good humor, high spirits, fun, and all manner of jollity. Their breath clears the atmosphere: their exhalations air the world. Of men, they are the good measures; brimmed, heaped, pressed down, piled up, and running over. They are as ships from Teneriffe; swimming deep, full of old wine, and twenty steps down into their holds. Soft and susceptible, all round they are easy of entreaty. Wherefore, for all their rotundity, they are too often circumnavigated by hatchet-faced knaves. Ah! a fat uncle, with a fat paunch, and a fat purse, is a joy and a delight to all nephews; to philosophers, a subject of endless speculation, as to how many droves of oxen and Lake Eries of wine might have run through his great mill during the full term of his mortal career. Fat men not immortal! This very instant, old Lambert is rubbing his jolly abdomen in Paradise.

Now, to the fact of his not being rated a demi-god, was perhaps ascribable the circumstance, that Borabolla comported himself with less dignity, than was the wont of their Mardian majesties. And truth to say, to have seen him regaling himself with one of his favorite cuttle-fish, its long snaky arms and feelers instinctively twining round his head as he ate; few intelligent observers would have opined that the individual before them was the sovereign lord of Mondoldo.

But what of the banquet of fish? Shall we tell how the old king ungirdled himself thereto; how as the feast waxed toward its close, with one sad exception, he still remained sunny-sided all round; his disc of a face joyous as the South Side of Madeira in the hilarious season of grapes? Shall we tell how we all grew glad and frank; and how the din of the dinner was heard far into night?

We will.

When Media ate slowly, Borabolla took him to task, bidding him dispatch his viands more speedily.

Whereupon said Media, "But Borabolla, my round fellow, that would abridge the pleasure."

"Not at all, my dear demi-god; do like me: eat fast and eat long."

In the middle of the feast, a huge skin of wine was brought in. The portly peltry of a goat; its horns embattling its effigy head; its mouth the nozzle; and its long beard flowed to its jet-black hoofs. With many ceremonial salams, the attendants bore it along, placing it at one end of the convivial mats, full in front of Borabolla; where seated upon its haunches it made one of the party.

Brimming a ram's horn, the mellowest of bugles, Borabolla bowed to his silent guest, and thus spoke—"In this wine, which yet smells of the grape, I pledge you, my reverend old toper, my lord Capricornus; you alone have enough; and here's full skins to the rest!"

"How jolly he is," whispered Media to Babbalanja.

"Ay, his lungs laugh loud; but is laughing, rejoicing?"

"Help! help!" cried Borabolla, "lay me down! lay me down! good gods, what a twinge!"

The goblet fell from his hand; the purple flew from his wine to his face;

and Borabolla fell back into the arms of his servitors. "That gout! that gout!" he groaned. "Lord! lord! no more cursed wine will I drink!"

Then at ten paces distant, a clumsy attendant let fall a trencher—"Take it off my foot, you knave!"

Afar off another entered gallanting a calabash—"Look out for my toe, you hound!"

During all this, the attendants tenderly nursed him. And in good time, with its thousand fangs, the gout-fiend departed for a while.

Reprieved, the old king brightened up; by degrees becoming jolly as ever.

"Come! let us be merry again," he cried, "what shall we eat? and what shall we drink? that infernal gout is gone; come, what will your worships have?"

So at it once more we went.

But of our feast, little more remains to be related than this;—that out of it, grew a wondrous kindness between Borabolla and Jarl. Strange to tell, from the first our fat host had regarded my Viking with a most friendly eye. Still stranger to add, this feeling was returned. But though they thus fancied each other, they were very unlike; Borabolla and Jarl. Nevertheless, thus is it ever. And as the convex fits not into the convex, but into the concave; so do men fit into their opposites; and so fitted Borabolla's arched paunch into Jarl's, hollowed out to receive it.

But how now? Borabolla was jolly and loud: Jarl demure and silent; Borabolla a king: Jarl only a Viking;—how came they together? Very plain, to repeat:—because they were heterogeneous; and hence the affinity. But as the affinity between those chemical opposites chlorine and hydrogen, is promoted by caloric; so the affinity between Borabolla and Jarl was promoted by the warmth of the wine that they drank at this feast. For of all blessed fluids, the juice of the grape is the greatest foe to cohesion. True, it tightens the girdle; but then it loosens the tongue, and opens the heart.

In sum, Borabolla loved Jarl; and Jarl, pleased with this sociable monarch, for all his garrulity, esteemed him the most sensible old gentleman and king he had as yet seen in Mardi. For this reason, perhaps; that his talkativeness favored that silence in listeners, which was my Viking's delight in himself.

Repeatedly during the banquet, our host besought Taji to allow his henchman to remain on the island, after the rest of our party should depart; and he faithfully promised to surrender Jarl, whenever we should return to claim him.

But though I harbored no distrust of Borabolla's friendly intentions, I could not so readily consent to his request; for with Jarl for my one only companion, had I not both famished and feasted? was he not my only link to things past?—

Things past!—Ah Yillah! for all its mirth, and though we hunted wide, we found thee not in Mondoldo.

Chapter 96

Samoa a Surgeon

THE SECOND DAY of our stay in Mondoldo was signalized by a noteworthy exhibition of the surgical skill of Samoa; who had often boasted, that though well versed in the science of breaking men's heads, he was equally an adept in mending their crockery.

Overnight, Borabolla had directed his corps of sea-divers to repair early on the morrow, to a noted section of the great Mardian reef, for the purpose of procuring for our regalement some of the fine Hawk's-bill turtle, whose secret retreats were among the cells and galleries of that submerged wall of coral, from whose foamy coping no plummet dropped ever yet touched bottom.

These turtles were only to be obtained by diving far down under the surface; and then swimming along horizontally, and peering into the coral honeycomb; snatching at a flipper when seen, as at a pinion in a range of billing dove-cotes.

As the king's divers were thus employed, one of them, Karhownoo by name, perceived a Devil-shark, so called, swimming wistfully toward him from out his summer grotto in the reef. No way petrified by the sight, and pursuing the usual method adopted by these divers in such emergencies, Karhownoo, splashing the water, instantly swam toward the stranger. But the shark, undaunted, advanced: a thing so unusual, and fearful, that, in an agony of fright, the diver shot up for the surface. Heedless, he looked

294

not up as he went; and when within a few inches of the open air, dashed his head against a projection of the reef. He would have sunk into the live tomb beneath, were it not that three of his companions, standing on the brink, perceived his peril, and dragged him into safety.

Seeing the poor fellow was insensible, they endeavored, ineffectually, to revive him; and at last, placing him in their canoe, made all haste for the shore. Here a crowd soon gathered, and the diver was borne to a habitation, close adjoining Borabolla's; whence, hearing of the disaster, we sallied out to render assistance.

Upon entering the hut, the benevolent old king commanded it to be cleared; and then proceeded to examine the sufferer.

The skull proved to be very badly fractured; in one place, splintered.

"Let me mend it," said Samoa, with ardor.

And being told of his experience in such matters, Borabolla surrendered the patient.

With a gourd of water, and a tappa cloth, the one-armed Upoluan carefully washed the wound; and then calling for a sharp splinter of bamboo, and a thin, semi-transparent cup of cocoa-nut shell, he went about the operation: nothing less than the "Tomoti" (head-mending), in other words the trepan.

The patient still continuing insensible, the fragments were disengaged by help of a bamboo scalpel; when a piece of the drinking cup—previously dipped in the milk of a cocoa-nut—was nicely fitted into the vacancy, the skin as nicely adjusted over it, and the operation was complete.

And now, while all present were crying out in admiration of Samoa's artistic skill, and Samoa himself stood complacently regarding his workmanship, Babbalanja suggested, that it might be well to ascertain whether the patient survived. When, upon sounding his heart, the diver was found to be dead.

The bystanders loudly lamented; but declared the surgeon a man of marvelous science.

Returning to Borabolla's, much conversation ensued, concerning the sad scene we had witnessed, which presently branched into a learned discussion upon matters of surgery at large.

At length, Samoa regaled the company with a story; for the truth of which no one but him can vouch, for no one but him was by, at the time; though there is testimony to show that it involves nothing at variance with the customs of certain barbarous tribes.

Read on.

Chapter 97

Faith and Knowledge

A THING INCREDIBLE is about to be related; but a thing may be incredible and still be true; sometimes it is incredible because it is true. And many infidels but disbelieve the least incredible things; and many bigots reject the most obvious. But let us hold fast to all we have; and stop all leaks in our faith; lest an opening, but of a hand's breadth, should sink our seventy-fours. The wide Atlantic can rush in at one port-hole; and if we surrender a plank, we surrender the fleet. Panoplied in all the armor of St. Paul, morion, hauberk, and greaves, let us fight the Turks inch by inch, and yield them naught but our corpse.

But let us not turn round upon friends, confounding them with foes. For dissenters only assent to more than we. Though Milton was a heretic to the creed of Athanasius, his faith exceeded that of Athanasius himself; and the faith of Athanasius that of Thomas, the disciple, who with his own eyes beheld the mark of the nails. Whence it comes that though we be all Christians now, the best of us had perhaps been otherwise in the days of Thomas.

The higher the intelligence, the more faith, and the less credulity: Gabriel rejects more than we, but out-believes us all. The greatest marvels are first truths; and first truths the last unto which we attain. Things nearest are furthest off. Though your ear be next-door to your brain, it is forever removed from your sight. Man has a more comprehensive view of the moon, than the man in the moon himself. We know the moon is round; he only infers it. It is because we ourselves are in ourselves, that we know ourselves not. And it is only of our easy faith, that we are not infidels throughout; and only of our lack of faith, that we believe what we do.

In some universe-old truths, all mankind are disbelievers. Do you believe that you lived three thousand years ago? That you were at the taking of Tyre, were overwhelmed in Gomorrah? No. But for me, I was at the subsiding of the Deluge, and helped swab the ground, and build the first house. With the Israelites, I fainted in the wilderness; was in court, when Solomon outdid all the judges before him. I, it was, who suppressed the lost work of Manetho, on the Egyptian theology, as containing mysteries not to be revealed to posterity, and things at war with the canonical scriptures; I, who originated the conspiracy against that purple murderer, Domitian; I, who in the senate moved, that great and good Aurelian be emperor. I instigated the abdication of Diocletian, and Charles the Fifth; I touched Isabella's heart, that she hearkened to Columbus. I am he, that from the king's minions hid the Charter in the old oak at Hartford; I harbored Goffe and Whalley: I am the leader of the Mohawk masks, who in the Old Commonwealth's harbor, overboard threw the East India Company's Souchong; I am the Vailed Persian Prophet; I, the man in the iron mask; I, Junius.

Chapter 98

The Tale of a Traveler

IT WAS SAMOA, who told the incredible tale; and he told it as a traveler. But stay-at-homes say travelers lie. Yet a voyage to Ethiopia would cure them of that; for few skeptics are travelers; fewer travelers liars, though the proverb respecting them lies. It is false, as some say, that Bruce was cousin-german to Baron Munchausen; but true, as Bruce said, that the Abyssinians cut live steaks from their cattle. It was, in good part, his villainous transcribers, who made monstrosities of Mandeville's travels. And though all liars go to Gehenna; yet, assuming that Mandeville died before Dante; still, though Dante took the census of Hell, we find not Sir John, under the likeness of a roasted neat's tongue, in that infernalest of infernos, The Inferno.

But let not the truth be postponed. To the stand, Samoa, and through your interpreter, speak.

Once upon a time, during his endless sea-rovings, the Upoluan was called upon to cobble the head of a friend, grievously hurt in a desperate fight of slings.

Upon examination, that part of the brain proving as much injured as the cranium itself, a young pig was obtained; and preliminaries being over, part of its live brain was placed in the cavity, the trepan accomplished with cocoanut shell, and the scalp drawn over and secured.

This man died not, but lived. But from being a warrior of great sense and spirit, he became a perverse-minded and piggish fellow, showing many of the characteristics of his swinish grafting. He survived the operation more than a year; at the end of that period, however, going mad, and dying in his delirium.

Stoutly backed by the narrator, this anecdote was credited by some present. But Babbalanja held out to the last.

"Yet, if this story be true," said he, "and since it is well settled, that our brains are somehow the organs of sense; then, I see not why human reason could not be put into a pig, by letting into its cranium the contents of a man's. I have long thought, that men, pigs, and plants, are but curious physiological experiments; and that science would at last enable philosophers to produce new species of beings, by somehow mixing, and concocting the essential ingredients of various creatures; and so forming new combinations. My friend Atahalpa, the astrologer and alchymist, has long had a jar, in which he has been endeavoring to hatch a fairy, the ingredients being compounded according to a receipt of his own."

But little they heeded Babbalanja. It was the traveler's tale that most arrested attention.

Tough the thews, and tough the tales of Samoa.

Chapter 99

"Marnee Ora, Ora Marnee"

DURING THE AFTERNOON of the day of the diver's decease, preparations were making for paying the last rites to his remains, and carrying them by torch-light to their sepulcher, the sea; for, as in Odo, so was the custom here.

Meanwhile, all over the isle, to and fro went heralds, dismally arrayed, beating shark-skin drums; and, at intervals, crying—"A man is dead; let no fires be kindled; have mercy, oh Oro!—Let no canoes put to sea till the burial. This night, oh Oro!—Let no food be cooked."

And ever and anon, passed and repassed these, others in brave attire; with castanets of pearl shells, making gay music; and these sang—

> Be merry, oh men of Mondoldo,
> A maiden this night is to wed:
> Be merry, oh damsels of Mardi,—
> Flowers, flowers for the bridal bed.

Informed that the preliminary rites were about being rendered, we repaired to the arbor, whither the body had been removed.

Arrayed in white, it was laid out on a mat; its arms mutely crossed, between its lips an asphodel; at the feet, a withered hawthorn bough.

The relatives were wailing, and cutting themselves with shells, so that blood flowed, and spotted their vesture.

Upon remonstrating with the most abandoned of these mourners, the wife of the diver, she exclaimed, "Yes; great is the pain, but greater my affliction."

Another, the deaf sire of the dead, went staggering about, and groping; saying, that he was now quite blind; for some months previous he had lost one eye in the death of his eldest son; and now the other was gone.

"I am childless," he cried; "henceforth call me Roi Mori," that is, Twice-Blind.

While the relatives were thus violently lamenting, the rest of the company occasionally scratched themselves with their shells; but very slightly, and mostly on the soles of their feet; from long exposure, quite callous. This was interrupted, however, when the real mourners averted their eyes; though at no time was there any deviation in the length of their faces.

But on all sides, lamentations afresh broke forth, upon the appearance of a person who had been called in to assist in solemnizing the obsequies, and also to console the afflicted.

In rotundity, he was another Borabolla. He puffed and panted.

As he approached the corpse, a sobbing silence ensued; when holding the hand of the dead, between his, the stranger thus spoke:—

"Mourn not, oh friends of Karhownoo, that this your brother lives not. His wounded head pains him no more; he would not feel it, did a javelin pierce him. Yea; Karhownoo is exempt from all the ills and evils of this miserable Mardi!"

Hereupon, the Twice-Blind, who being deaf, heard not what was said, tore his gray hair, and cried, "Alas! alas! my boy; thou wert the merriest man in Mardi, and now thy pranks are over!"

But the other proceeded—"Mourn not, I say, oh friends of Karhownoo; the dead whom ye deplore is happier than the living; is not his spirit in the aerial isles?"

"True! true!" responded the raving wife, mingling her blood with her tears, "my own poor hapless Karhownoo is thrice happy in Paradise!" And anew she wailed, and lacerated her cheeks.

"Rave not, I say."

But she only raved the more.

And now the good stranger departed; saying, he must hie to a wedding, waiting his presence in an arbor adjoining.

Understanding that the removal of the body would not take place till midnight, we thought to behold the mode of marrying in Mondoldo.

Drawing near the place, we were greeted by merry voices, and much singing, which greatly increased when the good stranger was perceived.

Gayly arrayed in fine robes, with plumes on their heads, the bride and groom stood in the middle of a joyous throng, in readiness for the nuptial bond to be tied.

Standing before them, the stranger was given a cord, so bedecked with flowers, as to disguise its stout fibers; and taking the bride's hands, he bound them together to a ritual chant; about her neck, in festoons, disposing the flowery ends of the cord. Then turning to the groom, he was given another, also beflowered; but attached thereto was a great stone, very much carved, and stained; indeed, so every way disguised, that a person not knowing what it was, and lifting it, would be greatly amazed at its weight. This cord being attached to the waist of the groom, he leaned over toward the bride, by reason of the burden of the drop.

All present now united in a chant, and danced about the happy pair, who meanwhile looked ill at ease; the one being so bound by the hands, and the other sorely weighed down by his stone.

A pause ensuing, the good stranger, turning them back to back, thus spoke:—

"By thy flowery gyves, oh bride, I make thee a wife; and by thy burdensome stone, oh groom, I make thee a husband. Live and be happy, both; for the wise and good Oro hath placed us in Mardi to be glad. Doth not all nature rejoice in her green groves and her flowers? and woo and wed not the fowls of the air, trilling their bliss in their bowers? Live then, and be happy, oh bride and groom; for Oro is offended with the unhappy, since he meant them to be gay."

And the ceremony ended with a joyful feast.

But not all nuptials in Mardi were like these. Others were wedded with different rites; without the stone and flowery gyves. These were they who plighted their troth with tears not smiles, and made responses in the heart.

Returning from the house of the merry to the house of the mournful, we lingered till midnight to witness the issuing forth of the body.

By torch light, numerous canoes, with paddlers standing by, were drawn up on the beach, to accommodate those who purposed following the poor diver to his home.

The remains embarked, some confusion ensued concerning the occupancy of the rest of the shallops. At last the procession glided off, our party included. Two by two, forming a long line of torches trailing round the isle, the canoes all headed toward the opening in the reef.

For a time, a decorous silence was preserved; but presently, some whispering was heard; perhaps melancholy discoursing touching the close of the diver's career. But we were shocked to discover, that poor Karhownoo was not much in their thoughts; they were conversing about the next bread-fruit harvest, and the recent arrival of King Media and party at Mondoldo. From far in advance, however, were heard the lamentations of the true mourners, the relatives of the diver.

Passing the reef, and sailing a little distance therefrom, the canoes were disposed in a circle; the one bearing the corpse in the center. Certain ceremonies over, the body was committed to the waves; the white foam lighting up the last, long plunge of the diver, to see sights more strange, than ever he saw in the brooding cells of the Turtle Reef.

And now, while in the still midnight, all present were gazing down into the ocean, watching the white wake of the corpse, ever and anon illuminated by sparkles, an unknown voice was heard, and all started and vacantly stared, as this wild song was sung:—

> We drop our dead in the sea,
>   The bottomless, bottomless sea;
> Each bubble a hollow sigh,
>   As it sinks forever and aye.
>
> We drop our dead in the sea,—
>   The dead reck not of aught;
> We drop our dead in the sea,—
>   The sea ne'er gives it a thought.
>
> Sink, sink, oh corpse, still sink,
>   Far down in the bottomless sea,
> Where the unknown forms do prowl,
>   Down, down in the bottomless sea.
>
> 'Tis night above, and night all round,
>   And night will it be with thee;
> As thou sinkest, and sinkest for aye,
>   Deeper down in the bottomless sea.

The mysterious voice died away; no sign of the corpse was now seen; and mute with amaze, the company long listed to the low moan of the billows and the sad sough of the breeze.

At last, without speaking, the obsequies were concluded by sliding into the ocean a carved tablet of Palmetto, to mark the place of the burial. But a wave-crest received it, and fast it floated away.

Returning to the isle, long silence prevailed. But at length, as if the scene in which they had just taken part, afresh reminded them of the mournful event which had called them together, the company again recurred to it; some present, sadly and incidentally alluding to Borabolla's banquet of turtle, thereby postponed.

Chapter 100

The Pursuer himself is pursued

N
EXT MORNING, when much to the chagrin of Borabolla we
were preparing to quit his isle, came tidings to the palace, of a
wonderful event, occurring in one of the "Motoos," or little
islets of the great reef; which "Motoo" was included in the dominions of
the king.

The men who brought these tidings were highly excited; and no sooner
did they make known what they knew, than all Mondoldo was in a tumult
of marveling.

Their story was this.

Going at day break to the Motoo to fish, they perceived a strange proa
beached on its seaward shore; and presently were hailed by voices; and
saw among the palm trees, three specter-like men, who were not of Mardi.

The first amazement of the fishermen over, in reply to their eager
questions, the strangers related, that they were the survivors of a company
of men, natives of some unknown island to the northeast; whence they had
embarked for another country, distant three days' sail to the southward
of theirs. But falling in with a terrible adventure, in which their sire had
been slain, they altered their course to pursue the fugitive who murdered
him; one and all vowing, never more to see home, until their father's fate
was avenged. The murderer's proa outsailing theirs, soon ran out of sight;

305

yet after him they blindly steered by day and by night: steering by the blood-red star in Boötes. Soon, a violent gale overtook them; driving them to and fro; leaving them they knew not where. But still struggling against strange currents, at times counteracting their sailing, they drifted on their way; nigh to famishing for water; and no shore in sight. In long calms, in vain they held up their dry gourds to heaven, and cried "send us a breeze, sweet gods!" The calm still brooded; and ere it was gone, all but three gasped; and dead from thirst, were plunged into the sea. The breeze which followed the calm, soon brought them in sight of a low, uninhabited isle; where tarrying many days, they laid in good store of cocoanuts and water, and again embarked.

The next land they saw was Mardi; and they landed on the Motoo, still intent on revenge.

This recital filled Taji with horror.

Who could these avengers be, but the sons of him I had slain. I had thought them far hence, and myself forgotten; and now, like adders, they started up in my path, as I hunted for Yillah.

But I dissembled my thoughts.

Without waiting to hear more, Borabolla, all curiosity to behold the strangers, instantly dispatched to the Motoo one of his fleetest canoes, with orders to return with the voyagers.

Ere long they came in sight; and perceiving that strange proa in tow of the king's, Samoa cried out: "Lo! Taji, the canoe that was going to Tedaidee!"

Too true; the same double-keeled craft, now sorely broken, the fatal dais in wild disarray: the canoe, the canoe of Aleema! And with it came the spearmen three, who, when the Chamois was fleeing from their bow, had poised their javelins. But so wan their aspect now, their faces looked like skulls.

Then came over me the wild dream of Yillah; and, for a space, like a madman, I raved. It seemed as if the mysterious damsel must still be there; the rescue yet to be achieved. In my delirium I rushed upon the skeletons, as they landed—"Hide not the maiden!" But interposing, Media led me aside; when my transports abated.

Now, instantly, the strangers knew who I was; and, brandishing their javelins, they rushed upon me, as I had on them, with a yell. But deeming us all mad, the crowd held us apart; when, writhing in the arms that restrained them, the pale specters foamed out their curses again and again:—"Oh murderer! white curses upon thee! Bleached be thy soul with our hate! Living, our brethren cursed thee; and dying, dry-lipped, they cursed thee again. They died not through famishing for water, but for revenge upon thee! Thy blood, their thirst would have slaked!"

I lay fainting against the hard-throbbing heart of Samoa, while they showered their yells through the air. Once more, in my thoughts, the green corpse of the priest drifted by.

Among the people of Mondoldo, a violent commotion now raged. They were amazed at Taji's recognition by the strangers, and at the deadly ferocity they betrayed.

Rallying upon this, and perceiving that by divulging all they knew, these sons of Aleema might stir up the Islanders against me, I resolved to anticipate their story; and, turning to Borabolla, said—"In these strangers, oh, king! you behold the survivors of a band we encountered on our voyage. From them I rescued a maiden, called Yillah, whom they were carrying captive. Little more of their history do I know."

"Their maledictions?" exclaimed Borabolla.

"Are they not delirious with suffering?" I cried. "They know not what they say."

So, moved by all this, he commanded them to be guarded, and conducted within his palisade; and having supplied them with cheer, entered into earnest discourse. Yet all the while, the pale strangers on me fixed their eyes; deep, dry, crater-like hollows, lurid with flames, reflected from the fear-frozen glacier, my soul.

But though their hatred appalled, spite of that spell, again the sweet dream of Yillah stole over me, with all the mysterious things by her narrated, but left unexplained. And now, before me were those who might reveal the lost maiden's whole history, previous to the fatal affray.

Thus impelled, I besought them to disclose what they knew.

But, "Where now is your Yillah?" they cried. "Is the murderer wedded and merry? Bring forth the maiden!"

Yet, though they tore out my heart's core, I told them not of my loss.

Then, anxious, to learn the history of Yillah, all present commanded them to divulge it; and breathlessly I heard what follows.

"Of Yillah, we know only this:—that many moons ago, a mighty canoe, full of beings, white, like this murderer Taji, touched at our island of Amma. Received with wonder, they were worshiped as gods; were feasted all over the land. Their chief was a tower to behold; and with him, was a being, whose cheeks were of the color of the red coral; her eye, tender as the blue of the sky. Every day our people brought her offerings of fruit and flowers;

which last she would not retain for herself, but hung them round the neck of her child, Yillah; then only an infant in her mother's arms; a bud, nestling close to a flower, full-blown. All went well between our people and the gods, till at last they slew three of our countrymen, charged with stealing from their great canoe. Our warriors retired to the hills, brooding over revenge. Three days went by; when by night, descending to the plain, in silence they embarked; gained the great vessel, and slaughtered every soul but Yillah. The bud was torn from the flower; and, by our father Aleema, was carried to the Valley of Ardair; there set apart as a sacred offering for Apo, our deity. Many moons passed; and there arose a tumult, hostile to our sire's longer holding custody of Yillah; when, foreseeing that the holy glen would ere long be burst open, he embarked the maiden in yonder canoe, to accelerate her sacrifice at the great shrine of Apo, in Tedaidee.— The rest thou knowest, murderer!"

"Yillah! Yillah!" now hunted again that sound through my soul. "Oh, Yillah! too late, too late have I learned what thou art!"

Apprised of the disappearance of their former captive, the meager strangers exulted; declaring that Apo had taken her to himself. For me, ere long, my blood they would quaff from my skull.

But though I shrunk from their horrible threats, I dissembled anew; and turning, again swore that they raved.

"Ay!" they retorted, "we rave and raven for you; and your white heart will we have!"

Perceiving the violence of their rage, and persuaded from what I said, that much suffering at sea must have maddened them; Borabolla thought fit to confine them for the present; so that they could not molest me.

Chapter 101

The Iris

THAT EVENING, in the groves, came to me three gliding forms:—
Hautia's heralds: the Iris mixed with nettles.
Said Yoomy, "A cruel message!"

With the right hand, the second syren presented glossy, green wax-myrtle berries, those that burn like tapers; the third, a lily of the valley, crushed in its own broad leaf.

This done, they earnestly eyed Yoomy; who, after much pondering, said—"I speak for Hautia; who by these berries says, I will enlighten you."

"Oh, give me then that light! say, where is Yillah?" and I rushed upon the heralds.

But eluding me, they looked reproachfully at Yoomy; and seemed offended.

"Then, I am wrong," said Yoomy. "It is thus:—Taji, you have been enlightened, but the lily you seek is crushed."

Then fell my heart, and the phantoms nodded; flinging upon me bilberries, like rose pearls, which bruised against my skin, left stains.

Waving oleanders, they retreated.

"Harm! treachery! beware!" cried Yoomy.

Then they glided through the wood: one showering dead leaves along the path I trod, the others gayly waving bunches of spring-crocuses, yellow, white, and purple; and thus they vanished.

Said Yoomy, "Sad your path, but merry Hautia's."

"Then merry may she be, whoe'er she is; and though woe be mine, I turn not from that to Hautia; nor ever will I woo her, though she woo me till I die;—though Yillah never bless my eyes."

Chapter 102

They depart from Mondoldo

NIGHT PASSED; and next morning we made preparations for leaving Mondoldo that day.

But fearing anew, lest after our departure, the men of Amma might stir up against me the people of the isle, I determined to yield to the earnest solicitations of Borabolla, and leave Jarl behind, for a remembrance of Taji; if necessary, to vindicate his name. Apprised hereof, my follower was loth to acquiesce. His guiltless spirit feared not the strangers: less selfish considerations prevailed. He was willing to remain on the island for a time, but not without me. Yet, setting forth my reasons; and assuring him, that our tour would not be long in completing, when we would not fail to return, previous to sailing for Odo, he at last, but reluctantly, assented.

At Mondoldo, we also parted with Samoa. Whether it was, that he feared the avengers, whom he may have thought would follow on my track; or whether the islands of Mardi answered not in attractiveness to the picture his fancy had painted; or whether the restraint put upon him by the domineering presence of King Media, was too irksome withal; or whether, indeed, he relished not those disquisitions with which Babbalanja regaled us: however it may have been, certain it was, that Samoa was impatient of the voyage. He besought permission to return to Odo, there to await my return; and a canoe of Mondoldo being about to proceed in that direction, permission was granted; and departing for the other side of the island, from thence he embarked.

Long after, dark tidings came, that at early dawn he had been found dead in the canoe: three arrows in his side.

Yoomy was at a loss to account for the departure of Samoa; who, while ashore, had expressed much desire to roam.

Media, however, declared that he must be returning to some inamorata.

But Babbalanja averred, that the Upoluan was not the first man, who had turned back, after beginning a voyage like our own.

To this, after musing, Yoomy assented. Indeed, I had noticed, that already the Warbler had abated those sanguine assurances of success, with which he had departed from Odo. The futility of our search thus far, seemed ominous to him, of the end.

On the eve of embarking, we were accompanied to the beach by Borabolla; who, with his own hand, suspended from the shark's mouth of Media's canoe, three red-ripe bunches of plantains, a farewell gift to his guests.

Though he spoke not a word, Jarl was long in taking leave. His eyes seemed to say, I will see you no more.

At length we pushed from the strand; Borabolla waving his adieus with a green leaf of banana; our comrade ruefully eyeing the receding canoes; and the multitude loudly invoking for us a prosperous voyage.

But to my horror, there suddenly dashed through the crowd, the three specter sons of Aleema, escaped from their prison. With clenched hands, they stood in the water, and cursed me anew. And with that curse in our sails, we swept off.

Chapter 103

As they sail

A S THE CANOES now glided across the lagoon, I gave myself up
to reverie; and revolving over all that the men of Amma had rehearsed of the history of Yillah, I one by one unriddled the mysteries,
before so baffling. Now, all was made plain: no secret remaining, but the
subsequent event of her disappearance. Yes, Hautia! enlightened I had been
—but where was Yillah?

Then I recalled that last interview with Hautia's messengers, so full of
enigmas; and wondered, whether Yoomy had interpreted aright. Unseen,
and unsolicited; still pursuing me with omens, with taunts, and with woo-
ings, mysterious Hautia appalled me. Vaguely I began to fear her. And the
thought, that perhaps again and again, her heralds would haunt me, filled
me with a nameless dread, which I almost shrank from acknowledging.
Inwardly I prayed, that never more they might appear.

While full of these thoughts, Media interrupted them by saying, that
the minstrel was about to begin one of his chants, a thing of his own composing; and therefore, as he himself said, all critics must be lenient; for
Yoomy, at times, not always, was a timid youth, distrustful of his own
sweet genius for poesy.

The words were about a curious hereafter, believed in by some people

in Mardi: a sort of nocturnal Paradise, where the sun and its heat are ex-
cluded: one long, lunar day, with twinkling stars to keep company.

THE SONG.

Far off in the sea is Marlena,
A land of shades and streams,
A land of many delights.
Dark and bold, thy shores, Marlena;
But green, and timorous, thy soft knolls,
Crouching behind the woodlands.
All shady thy hills; all gleaming thy springs,
Like eyes in the earth looking at you.
How charming thy haunts, Marlena!—
Oh, the waters that flow through Onimoo:
Oh, the leaves that rustle through Ponoo:
Oh, the roses that blossom in Tarma.
Come, and see the valley of Vina:
How sweet, how sweet, the Isles from Hina:
'Tis aye afternoon of the full, full moon,
And ever the season of fruit,
And ever the hour of flowers,
And never the time of rains and gales,
All in and about Marlena.
Soft sigh the boughs in the stilly air,
Soft lap the beach the billows there;
And in the woods or by the streams,
You needs must nod in the Land of Dreams.

"Yoomy," said old Mohi with a yawn, "you composed that song, then,
did you?"

"I did," said Yoomy, placing his turban a little to one side.

"Then, minstrel, you shall sing me to sleep every night, especially with
that song of Marlena; it is soporific as the airs of Nora-Bamma."

"Mean you, old man, that my lines, setting forth the luxurious repose
to be enjoyed hereafter, are composed with such skill, that the description
begets the reality; or would you ironically suggest, that the song is a sleepy
thing itself?"

"An important discrimination," said Media; "which mean you, Mohi?"

"Now, are you not a silly boy," said Babbalanja, "when from the ambiguity of his speech, you could so easily have derived something flattering,

thus to seek to extract unpleasantness from it? Be wise, Yoomy; and here-after, whenever a remark like that seems equivocal, be sure to wrest com-mendation from it, though you torture it to the quick."

"And most sure am I, that I would ever do so; but often I so incline to a distrust of my powers, that I am far more keenly alive to censure, than to praise; and always deem it the more sincere of the two; and no praise so much elates me, as censure depresses."

Chapter 104

*Wherein Babbalanja broaches a diabolical Theory,
and, in his own Person, proves it*

A TRUCE!" cried Media, "here comes a gallant before the wind.
—Look, Taji!"
Turning, we descried a sharp-prowed canoe, dashing on, under
the pressure of an immense triangular sail, whose outer edges were streaming with long, crimson pennons. Flying before it, were several small craft,
belonging to the poorer sort of Islanders.

"Out of his way there, ye laggards," cried Media, "or that mad prince,
Tribonnora, will ride over ye with a rush!"

"And who is Tribonnora," said Babbalanja, "that he thus bravely
diverts himself, running down innocent paddlers?"

"A harum-scarum young chief," replied Media, "heir to three islands;
he likes nothing better than the sport you now see him at."

"He must be possessed by a devil," said Mohi.

Said Babbalanja, "Then he is only like all of us."

"What say you?" cried Media.

"I say, as old Bardianna in the Nine hundred and ninety ninth book of
his immortal Ponderings saith, that all men—"

"As I live, my lord, he has swamped three canoes," cried Mohi, pointing
off the beam.

But just then a fiery fin-back whale, having broken into the paddock of the lagoon, threw up a high fountain of foam, almost under Tribonnora's nose; who, quickly turning about his canoe, cur-like slunk off; his steering-paddle between his legs.

Comments over; "Babbalanja, you were going to quote," said Media. "Proceed."

"Thank you, my lord. Says old Bardianna, 'All men are possessed by devils; but as these devils are sent into men, and kept in them, for an additional punishment; not garrisoning a fortress, but limboed in a bride-well; so, it may be more just to say, that the devils themselves are possessed by men, not men by them.'"

"Faith!" cried Media, "though sometimes a bore, your old Bardianna is a trump."

"I have long been of that mind, my lord. But let me go on. Says Bardianna, 'Devils are divers;—strong devils, and weak devils; knowing devils, and silly devils; mad devils, and mild devils; devils, merely devils; devils, themselves bedeviled; devils, doubly bedeviled.'"

"And in the devil's name, what sort of a devil is yours?" cried Mohi.

"Of him anon; interrupt me not, old man. Thus, then, my lord, as devils are divers, divers are the devils in men. Whence, the wide difference we see. But after all, the main difference is this:—that one man's devil is only more of a devil than another's; and be bedeviled as much as you will; yet, may you perform the most bedeviled of actions with impunity, so long as you only bedevil yourself. For it is only when your deviltry injures another, that the other devils conspire to confine yours for a mad one. That is to say, if you be easily handled. For there are many bedeviled Bedlamites in Mardi, doing an infinity of mischief, who are too brawny in the arms to be tied."

"A very devilish doctrine that," cried Mohi. "I don't believe it."

"My lord," said Babbalanja, "here's collateral proof;—the sage law-giver Yamjamma, who flourished long before Bardianna, roundly asserts, that all men who knowingly do evil are bedeviled; for good is happiness; happiness the object of living; and evil is not good."

"If the sage Yamjamma said that," said old Mohi, "the sage Yamjamma might have bettered the saying; it's not quite so plain as it might be."

"Yamjamma disdained to be plain; he scorned to be fully comprehended by mortals. Like all oracles, he dealt in dark sayings. But old Bardianna was of another sort; he spoke right out, going straight to the point like a javelin; especially when he laid it down for a universal maxim, that minus exceptions, all men are bedeviled."

"Of course, then," said Media, "you include yourself among the number."

"Most assuredly; and so did old Bardianna; who somewhere says, that being thoroughly bedeviled himself, he was so much the better qualified to discourse upon the deviltries of his neighbors. But in another place he seems to contradict himself, by asserting, that he is not so sensible of his own deviltry as of other people's."

"Hold!" cried Media, "who have we here?" and he pointed ahead of our prow to three men in the water, urging themselves along, each with a paddle.

We made haste to overtake them.

"Who are you?" said Media, "where from, and where bound?"

"From Variora," they answered, "and bound to Mondoldo."

"And did that devil Tribonnora swamp your canoe?" asked Media, offering to help them into ours.

"We had no such useless incumbrance to lose," they replied, resting on their backs, and panting with their exertions. "If we had had a canoe, we would have had to paddle it along with us; whereas we have only our bodies to paddle."

"You are a parcel of loons," exclaimed Media. "But go your ways, if you are satisfied with your locomotion, well and good."

"Now, it is an extreme case, I grant," said Babbalanja, "but those poor devils there, help to establish old Bardianna's position. They belong to that species of our bedeviled race, called simpletons; but their devils harming none but themselves, are permitted to be at large with the fish. Whereas, Tribonnora's devil, who daily runs down canoes, drowning their occupants, belongs to the species of out and out devils; but being high in station, and strongly backed by kith and kin, Tribonnora can not be mastered, and put in a strait-jacket. For myself, I think my devil is somewhere between these two extremes; at any rate, he belongs to that class of devils who harm not other devils."

"I am not so sure of that," retorted Media. "Methinks this doctrine of yours, about all mankind being bedeviled, will work a deal of mischief; seeing that by implication it absolves you mortals from moral accountability. Furthermore; as your doctrine is exceedingly evil, by Yamjamma's theory it follows, that you must be proportionably bedeviled; and since it harms others, your devil is of the number of those whom it is best to limbo; and since he is one of those that *can* be limboed, limboed he shall be in you."

And so saying, he humorously commanded his attendants to lay hands upon the bedeviled philosopher, and place a bandage upon his mouth, that he might no more disseminate his devilish doctrine.

Against this, Babbalanja demurred, protesting that he was no orang-outang, to be so rudely handled.

"Better and better," said Media, "you but illustrate Bardianna's theory; that men are not sensible of their being bedeviled."

Thus tantalized, Babbalanja displayed few signs of philosophy.

Whereupon, said Media, "Assuredly his devil is foaming; behold his mouth!" And he commanded him to be bound hand and foot.

At length, seeing all resistance ineffectual, Babbalanja submitted; but not without many objurgations.

Presently, however, they released him; when Media inquired, how he relished the application of his theory; and whether he was still of old Bardianna's mind?

To which, haughtily adjusting his robe, Babbalanja replied, "The strong arm, my lord, is no argument, though it overcomes all logic."

END OF VOLUME ONE

Volume Two

Chapter 105

Maramma

W E WERE NOW voyaging straight for Maramma; where lived and reigned, in mystery, the High Pontiff of the adjoining isles: prince, priest, and god, in his own proper person: great lord paramount over many kings in Mardi; his hands full of scepters and crosiers.

Soon, rounding a lofty and insulated shore, the great central peak of the island came in sight; domineering over the neighboring hills; the same aspiring pinnacle, descried in drawing near the archipelago in the Chamois.

"Tall Peak of Ofo!" cried Babbalanja, "how comes it that thy shadow so broods over Mardi; flinging new shades upon spots already shaded by the hill-sides; shade upon shade!"

"Yet so it is," said Yoomy, sadly, "that where that shadow falls, gay flowers refuse to spring; and men long dwelling therein become shady of face and of soul. 'Hast thou come from out the shadows of Ofo?' inquires the stranger, of one with a clouded brow."

"It was by this same peak," said Mohi, "that the nimble god Roo, a great sinner above, came down from the skies, a very long time ago. Three skips and a jump, and he landed on the plain. But alas, poor Roo! though easy the descent, there was no climbing back."

323

"No wonder, then," said Babbalanja, "that the peak is inaccessible to man. Though, with a strange infatuation, many still make pilgrimages thereto; and wearily climb and climb, till slipping from the rocks, they fall headlong backward, and oftentimes perish at its base."

"Ay," said Mohi, "in vain, on all sides of the Peak, various paths are tried; in vain new ones are cut through the cliffs and the brambles:—Ofo yet remains inaccessible."

"Nevertheless," said Babbalanja, "by some it is believed, that those, who by dint of hard struggling climb so high as to become invisible from the plain; that these have attained the summit; though others much doubt, whether their becoming invisible is not because of their having fallen, and perished by the way."

"And wherefore," said Media, "do you mortals undertake the ascent at all? why not be content on the plain? and even if attainable, what would you do upon that lofty, clouded summit? Or how can you hope to breathe that rarefied air, unfitted for your human lungs?"

"True, my lord," said Babbalanja; "and Bardianna asserts that the plain alone was intended for man; who should be content to dwell under the shade of its groves, though the roots thereof descend into the darkness of the earth. But, my lord, you well know, that there are those in Mardi, who secretly regard all stories connected with this peak, as inventions of the people of Maramma. They deny that any thing is to be gained by making a pilgrimage thereto. And for warranty, they appeal to the sayings of the great prophet Alma."

Cried Mohi, "But Alma is also quoted by others, in vindication of the pilgrimages to Ofo. They declare that the prophet himself was the first pilgrim that thitherward journeyed: that from thence he departed to the skies."

Now, excepting this same peak, Maramma is all rolling hill and dale, like the sea after a storm; which then seems not to roll, but to stand still, poising its mountains. Yet the landscape of Maramma has not the merriness of meadows; partly because of the shadow of Ofo, and partly because of the solemn groves in which the Morais and temples are buried.

According to Mohi, not one solitary tree bearing fruit, not one esculent root, grows in all the isle; the population wholly depending upon the large tribute remitted from the neighboring shores.

"It is not that the soil is unproductive," said Mohi, "that these things are so. It is extremely fertile; but the inhabitants say that it would be wrong to make a Bread-fruit orchard of the holy island."

"And hence, my lord," said Babbalanja, "while others are charged with the business of their temporal welfare, these Islanders take no thought of the morrow; and broad Maramma lies one fertile waste in the lagoon."

Chapter 106

They land

COMING CLOSE TO THE ISLAND, the pennons and trappings of our canoes were removed; and Vee-Vee was commanded to descend from the shark's mouth; and for a time to lay aside his conch. In token of reverence, our paddlers also stripped to the waist; an example which even Media followed; though, as a king, the same homage he rendered, was at times rendered himself.

At every place, hitherto visited, joyous crowds stood ready to hail our arrival; but the shores of Maramma were silent, and forlorn.

Said Babbalanja, "It looks not as if the lost one were here."

At length we landed in a little cove nigh a valley, which Mohi called Uma; and here in silence we beached our canoes.

But presently, there came to us an old man, with a beard white as the mane of the pale horse. He was clad in a midnight robe. He fanned himself with a fan of faded leaves. A child led him by the hand, for he was blind, wearing a green plantain leaf over his plaited brow.

Him, Media accosted, making mention who we were, and on what errand we came: to seek out Yillah, and behold the isle.

Whereupon Pani, for such was his name, gave us a courteous reception; and lavishly promised to discover sweet Yillah; declaring that in Maramma, if any where, the long-lost maiden must be found. He assured us, that

326

throughout the whole land he would lead us; leaving no place, desirable to be searched, unexplored.

And so saying, he conducted us to his dwelling, for refreshment and repose.

It was large and lofty. Near by, however, were many miserable hovels, with squalid inmates. But the old man's retreat was exceedingly comfortable; especially abounding in mats for lounging; his rafters were bowed down by calabashes of good cheer.

During the repast which ensued, blind Pani, freely partaking, enlarged upon the merit of abstinence; declaring that a thatch overhead, and a cocoanut tree, comprised all that was necessary for the temporal welfare of a Mardian. More than this, he assured us was sinful.

He now made known, that he officiated as guide in this quarter of the country; and that as he had renounced all other pursuits to devote himself to showing strangers the island; and more particularly the best way to ascend lofty Ofo; he was necessitated to seek remuneration for his toil.

"My lord," then whispered Mohi to Media, "the great prophet Alma always declared, that, without charge, this island was free to all."

"What recompense do you desire, old man?" said Media to Pani.

"What I seek is but little:—twenty rolls of fine tappa; two score mats of best upland grass; one canoe-load of bread-fruit and yams; ten gourds of wine; and forty strings of teeth;—you are a large company, but my requisitions are small."

"Very small," said Mohi.

"You are extortionate, good Pani," said Media. "And what wants an aged mortal like you with all these things?"

"I thought superfluities were worthless; nay, sinful," said Babbalanja.

"Is not this your habitation already more than abundantly supplied with all desirable furnishings?" asked Yoomy.

"I am but a lowly laborer," said the old man, meekly crossing his arms, "but does not the lowliest laborer ask and receive his reward? and shall I miss mine?—But I beg charity of none. What I ask, I demand; and in the dread name of great Alma, who appointed me a guide." And to and fro he strode, groping as he went.

Marking his blindness, whispered Babbalanja to Media, "My lord, methinks this Pani must be a poor guide. In his journeys inland, his little child leads him; why not, then, take the guide's guide?"

But Pani would not part with the child.

Then said Mohi in a low voice, "My lord Media, though I am no appointed guide; yet, will I undertake to lead you aright over all this island; for I am an old man, and have been here oft by myself; though I can not undertake to conduct you up the peak of Ofo, and to the more secret temples."

Then Pani said: "And what mortal may this be, who pretends to thread the labyrinthine wilds of Maramma? Beware!"

"He is one with eyes that see," made answer Babbalanja.

"Follow him not," said Pani, "for he will lead thee astray; no Yillah will he find; and having no warrant as a guide, the curses of Alma will accompany him."

Now, this was not altogether without effect; for Pani and his fathers before him had always filled the office of guide.

Nevertheless, Media at last decided, that, this time, Mohi should conduct us; which being communicated to Pani, he desired us to remove from his roof. So withdrawing to the skirt of a neighboring grove, we lingered awhile, to refresh ourselves for the journey in prospect.

As we here reclined, there came up from the sea-side a party of pilgrims, but newly arrived.

Apprized of their coming, Pani and his child went out to meet them; and standing in the path he cried, "I am the appointed guide; in the name of Alma I conduct all pilgrims to the temples."

"This must be the worthy Pani," said one of the strangers, turning upon the rest.

"Let us take him, then, for our guide," cried they; and all drew near.

But upon accosting him; they were told, that he guided none without recompense.

And now, being informed, that the foremost of the pilgrims was one Divino, a wealthy chief of a distant island, Pani demanded of him his requital.

But the other demurred; and by many soft speeches at length abated the recompense to three promissory cocoanuts, which he covenanted to send Pani at some future day.

The next pilgrim accosted, was a sad-eyed maiden, in decent but scanty raiment; who without seeking to diminish Pani's demands promptly placed in his hands a small hoard of the money of Mardi.

"Take it, holy guide," she said, "it is all I have."

But the third pilgrim, one Fanna, a hale matron, in handsome apparel, needed no asking to bestow her goods. Calling upon her attendants to advance with their burdens, she quickly unrolled them; and wound round and

round Pani, fold after fold of the costliest tappas; and filled both his hands
with teeth; and his mouth with some savory marmalade; and poured oil
upon his head; and knelt and besought of him a blessing.

"From the bottom of my heart I bless thee," said Pani; and still holding
her hands exclaimed, "Take example from this woman, oh Divino; and
do ye likewise, ye pilgrims all."

"Not to-day," said Divino.

"We are not rich, like unto Fanna," said the rest.

Now, the next pilgrim was a very old and miserable man; stone-blind,
covered with rags; and supporting his steps with a staff.

"My recompense," said Pani.

"Alas! I have naught to give. Behold my poverty."

"I can not see," replied Pani; but feeling of his garments, he said, "Thou
wouldst deceive me; hast thou not this robe, and this staff?"

"Oh! Merciful Pani, take not my all!" wailed the pilgrim. But his
worthless gaberdine was thrust into the dwelling of the guide.

Meanwhile, the matron was still enveloping Pani in her interminable
tappas.

But the sad-eyed maiden, removing her upper mantle, threw it over
the naked form of the beggar.

The fifth pilgrim was a youth of an open, ingenuous aspect; and with
an eye, full of eyes; his step was light.

"Who art thou?" cried Pani, as the stripling touched him in passing.

"I go to ascend the Peak," said the boy.

"Then take me for guide."

"No, I am strong and lithesome. Alone must I go."

"But how knowest thou the way?"

"There are many ways: the right one I must seek for myself."

"Ah, poor deluded one," sighed Pani; "but thus is it ever with youth;
and rejecting the monitions of wisdom, suffer they must. Go on, and
perish!"

Turning, the boy exclaimed—"Though I act counter to thy counsels,
oh Pani, I but follow the divine instinct in me."

"Poor youth!" murmured Babbalanja. "How earnestly he struggles in
his bonds. But though rejecting a guide, still he clings to that legend of the
Peak."

The rest of the pilgrims now tarried with the guide, preparing for their
journey inland.

Chapter 107

They pass through the Woods

REFRESHED BY OUR STAY in the grove, we rose, and placed ourselves under the guidance of Mohi; who went on in advance.

Winding our way among jungles, we came to a deep hollow, planted with one gigantic palm-shaft, belted round by saplings, springing from its roots. But, Laocoon-like, sire and sons stood locked in the serpent folds of gnarled, distorted banians; and the banian-bark, eating into their vital wood, corrupted their veins of sap, till all those palm-nuts were poisoned chalices.

Near by stood clean-limbed, comely manchineels, with lustrous leaves and golden fruit. You would have deemed them Trees of Life; but underneath their branches grew no blade of grass, no herb, nor moss; the bare earth was scorched by heaven's own dews, filtrated through that fatal foliage.

Farther on, there frowned a grove of blended banian boughs, thick-ranked manchineels, and many a upas; their summits gilded by the sun; but below, deep shadows, darkening night-shade ferns, and mandrakes. Buried in their midst, and dimly seen among large leaves, all halberd-shaped, were piles of stone, supporting falling temples of bamboo. Thereon frogs leaped in dampness, trailing round their slime. Thick hung the rafters with lines of pendant sloths; the upas trees dropped darkness round; so

330

dense the shade, nocturnal birds found there perpetual night; and, throve on poisoned air. Owls hooted from dead boughs; or, one by one, sailed by on silent pinions; cranes stalked abroad, or brooded in the marshes; adders hissed; bats smote the darkness; ravens croaked; and vampires, fixed on slumbering lizards, fanned the sultry air.

Chapter 108

Hivohitee MDCCCXLVIII

N OW, THOSE DOLEFUL WOODLANDS PASSED, straightway converse was renewed, and much discourse took place, concerning Hivohitee, Pontiff of the isle.

For, during our first friendly conversation with Pani, Media had inquired for Hivohitee, and sought to know in what part of the island he abode.

Whereto Pani had replied, that the Pontiff would be invisible for several days to come; being engaged with particular company.

And upon further inquiry, as to who were the personages monopolizing his hospitalities, Media was dumb when informed, that they were no other than certain incorporeal deities from above, passing the Capricorn Solstice at Maramma.

As on we journeyed, much curiosity being expressed to know more of the Pontiff and his guests, old Mohi, familiar with these things, was commanded to enlighten the company. He complied; and his recital was not a little significant, of the occasional credulity of chroniclers.

According to his statement, the deities entertained by Hivohitee belonged to the third class of immortals. These, however, were far elevated above the corporeal demi-gods of Mardi. Indeed, in Hivohitee's eyes, the greatest demi-gods were as gourds. Little wonder, then, that their superiors were accounted the most genteel characters on his visiting list.

These immortals were wonderfully fastidious and dainty as to the atmosphere they breathed; inhaling no sublunary air, but that of the elevated interior; where the Pontiff had a rural lodge for the special accommodation of impalpable guests; who were entertained at very small cost; dinners being unnecessary, and dormitories superfluous.

But Hivohitee permitted not the presence of these celestial grandees, to interfere with his own solid comfort. Passing his mornings in highly intensified chat, he thrice reclined at his ease; partaking of a fine plantain-pudding, and pouring out from a calabash of celestial old wine; meanwhile, carrying on the flow of soul with his guests. And truly, the sight of their entertainer thus enjoying himself in the flesh, while they themselves starved on the ether, must have been exceedingly provoking to these aristocratic and aerial strangers.

It was reported, furthermore, that Hivohitee, one of the haughtiest of Pontiffs, purposely treated his angelical guests thus cavalierly; in order to convince them, that though a denizen of earth; a sublunarian; and in respect of heaven, a mere provincial; he (Hivohitee) accounted himself full as good as seraphim from the capital; and that too at the Capricorn Solstice, or any other time of the year. Strongly bent was Hivohitee upon humbling their supercilious pretensions.

Besides, was he not accounted a great god in the land? supreme? having power of life and death? essaying the deposition of kings? and dwelling in moody state, all by himself, in the goodliest island of Mardi? Though here, be it said, that his assumptions of temporal supremacy were but seldom made good by express interference with the secular concerns of the neighboring monarchs; who, by force of arms, were too apt to argue against his claims to authority; however, in theory, they bowed to it. And now, for the genealogy of Hivohitee; for eighteen hundred and forty-seven Hivohitees were alleged to have gone before him. He came in a right line from the divine Hivohitee I.: the original grantee of the empire of men's souls and the first swayer of a crosier. The present Pontiff's descent was unquestionable; his dignity having been transmitted through none but heirs male; the whole procession of High Priests being the fruit of successive marriages between uterine brother and sister. A conjunction deemed incestuous in some lands; but, here, held the only fit channel for the pure transmission of elevated rank.

Added to the hereditary appellation, Hivohitee, which simply denoted the sacerdotal station of the Pontiffs, and was but seldom employed in current discourse, they were individualized by a distinctive name, bestowed upon them at birth. And the degree of consideration in which they were held, may be inferred from the fact, that during the lifetime of a Pontiff, the leading sound in his name was banned to ordinary uses. Whence, at every new accession to the archiepiscopal throne, it came to pass, that multitudes of words and phrases were either essentially modified, or wholly dropped. Wherefore, the language of Maramma was incessantly fluctuating; and had become so full of jargonings, that the birds in the groves were greatly puzzled; not knowing where lay the virtue of sounds, so incoherent.

And, in a good measure, this held true of all tongues spoken throughout the Archipelago; the birds marveling at mankind, and mankind at the birds; wondering how they could continually sing; when, for all man knew to the contrary, it was impossible they could be holding intelligent discourse. And thus, though for thousands of years, men and birds had been dwelling together in Mardi, they remained wholly ignorant of each other's secrets; the Islander regarding the fowl as a senseless songster, forever in the clouds; and the fowl him, as a screeching crane, destitute of pinions and lofty aspirations.

Over and above numerous other miraculous powers imputed to the Pontiffs as spiritual potentates, there was ascribed to them one special privilege of a secular nature: that of healing with a touch the bites of the ravenous sharks, swarming throughout the lagoon. With these they were supposed to be upon the most friendly terms; according to popular accounts, sociably bathing with them in the sea; permitting them to rub their noses against their priestly thighs; playfully mouthing their hands, with all their tiers of teeth.

At the ordination of a Pontiff, the ceremony was not deemed complete, until embarking in his barge, he was saluted High Priest by three sharks drawing near; with teeth turned up, swimming beside his canoe.

These monsters were deified in Maramma; had altars there; it was deemed worse than homicide to kill one. "And what if they destroy human life?" say the Islanders, "are they not sacred?"

Now many more wonderful things were related touching Hivohitee; and though one could not but doubt the validity of many prerogatives ascribed to him, it was nevertheless hard to do otherwise, than entertain for the Pontiff that sort of profound consideration, which all render to those who indisputably possess the power of quenching human life with a wish.

Chapter 109

They visit the great Morai

AS GARRULOUS GUIDE to the party, Braid-Beard soon brought us nigh the great Morai of Maramma, the burial-place of the Pontiffs, and a rural promenade, for certain idols there inhabiting.

Our way now led through the bed of a shallow water-course; Mohi observing, as we went, that our feet were being washed at every step; whereas, to tread the dusty earth would be to desecrate the holy Morai, by transferring thereto, the base soil of less sacred ground.

Here and there, thatched arbors were thrown over the stream, for the accommodation of devotees; who, in these consecrated waters, issuing from a spring in the Morai, bathed their garments, that long life might ensue. Yet, as Braid-Beard assured us, sometimes it happened, that divers feeble old men zealously donning their raiment immediately after immersion became afflicted with rheumatics; and instances were related of their falling down dead, in this their pursuit of longevity.

Coming to the Morai, we found it inclosed by a wall; and while the rest were surmounting it, Mohi was busily engaged in the apparently childish occupation of collecting pebbles. Of these, however, to our no small surprise, he presently made use, by irreverently throwing them at all objects to which he was desirous of directing attention. In this manner, was pointed out a black boar's head, suspended from a bough. Full twenty of these sentries were on post in the neighboring trees.

Proceeding, we came to a hillock of bone-dry sand, resting upon the otherwise loamy soil. Possessing a secret, preservative virtue, this sand had, ages ago, been brought from a distant land, to furnish a sepulcher for the Pontiffs; who here, side by side, and sire by son, slumbered all peacefully in the fellowship of the grave. Mohi declared, that were the sepulcher to be opened, it would be the resurrection of the whole line of High Priests. "But a resurrection of bones, after all," said Babbalanja, ever osseous in his allusions to the departed.

Passing on, we came to a number of Runic-looking stones, all over hieroglyphical inscriptions, and placed round an elliptical aperture; where welled up the sacred spring of the Morai, clear as crystal, and showing through its waters, two tiers of sharp, tusk-like stones; the mouth of Oro, so called; and it was held, that if any secular hand should be immersed in the spring, straight upon it those stony jaws would close.

We next came to a large image of a dark-hued stone, representing a burly man, with an overgrown head, and abdomen hollowed out, and open for inspection; therein, were relics of bones. Before this image we paused. And whether or no it was Mohi's purpose to make us tourists quake with his recitals, his revelations were far from agreeable. At certain seasons, human beings were offered to the idol, which being an epicure in the matter of sacrifices, would accept of no ordinary fare. To insure his digestion, all indirect routes to the interior were avoided; the sacrifices being packed in the ventricle itself.

Near to this image of Doleema, so called, a solitary forest-tree was pointed out; leafless and dead to the core. But from its boughs hung numerous baskets, brimming over with melons, grapes, and guavas. And daily these baskets were replenished.

As we here stood, there passed a hungry figure, in ragged raiment: hollow cheeks, and hollow eyes. Wistfully he eyed the offerings; but retreated; knowing it was sacrilege to touch them. There, they must decay, in honor of the god Ananna; for so this dead tree was denominated by Mohi.

Now, as we were thus strolling about the Morai, the old chronicler elucidating its mysteries, we suddenly spied Pani and the pilgrims approaching the image of Doleema; his child leading the guide.

"This," began Pani, pointing to the idol of stone, "is the holy god Ananna who lives in the sap of this green and flourishing tree."

"Thou meanest not, surely, this stone image we behold?" said Divino.

"I mean the tree," said the guide. "It is no stone image."

"Strange," muttered the chief; "were it not a guide that spoke, I would deny it. As it is, I hold my peace."

"Mystery of mysteries!" cried the blind old pilgrim; "is it, then, a stone image that Pani calls a tree? Oh, Oro, that I had eyes to see, that I might verily behold it, and then believe it to be what it is not; that so I might prove the largeness of my faith; and so merit the blessing of Alma."

"Thrice sacred Ananna," murmured the sad-eyed maiden, falling upon her knees before Doleema, "receive my adoration. Of thee, I know nothing, but what the guide has spoken. I am but a poor, weak-minded maiden, judging not for myself, but leaning upon others that are wiser. These things are above me. I am afraid to think. In Alma's name, receive my homage."

And she flung flowers before the god.

But Fanna, the hale matron, turning upon Pani, exclaimed, "Receive more gifts, oh guide." And again she showered them upon him.

Upon this, the willful boy who would not have Pani for his guide, entered the Morai; and perceiving the group before the image, walked rapidly to where they were. And beholding the idol, he regarded it attentively, and said:—"This must be the image of Doleema; but I am not sure."

"Nay," cried the blind pilgrim, "it is the holy tree Ananna, thou wayward boy."

"A tree? whatever it may be, it is not that; thou art blind, old man."

"But though blind, I have that which thou lackest."

Then said Pani, turning upon the boy, "Depart from the holy Morai, and corrupt not the hearts of these pilgrims. Depart, I say; and, in the sacred name of Alma, perish in thy endeavors to climb the Peak."

"I may perish there in truth," said the boy, with sadness; "but it shall be in the path revealed to me in my dream. And think not, oh guide, that I perfectly rely upon gaining that lofty summit. I will climb high Ofo with hope, not faith; Oh, mighty Oro, help me!"

"Be not impious," said Pani; "pronounce not Oro's sacred name too lightly."

"Oro is but a sound," said the boy. "They call the supreme god, Ati, in my native isle; it is the soundless thought of him, oh guide, that is in me."

"Hark to his rhapsodies! Hark, how he prates of mysteries, that not even Hivohitee can fathom."

"Nor he, nor thou, nor I, nor any; Oro, to all, is Oro the unknown."

"Why claim to know Oro, then, better than others?"

"I am not so vain; and I have little to substitute for what I can not receive. I but feel Oro in me, yet can not declare the thought."

"Proud boy! thy humility is a pretense; at heart, thou deemest thyself wiser than Mardi."

"Not near so wise. To believe is a haughty thing; my very doubts humiliate me. I weep and doubt; all Mardi may be right; and I too simple to discern."

"He is mad," said the chief Divino; "never before heard I such words."

"They are thoughts," muttered the guide.

"Poor fool!" cried Fanna.

"Lost youth!" sighed the maiden.

"He is but a child," said the beggar. "These whims will soon depart; once I was like him; but, praise be to Alma, in the hour of sickness I repented, feeble old man that I am!"

"It is because I am young and in health," said the boy, "that I more nourish the thoughts, that are born of my youth and my health. I am fresh from my Maker, soul and body unwrinkled. On thy sick couch, old man, they took thee at advantage."

"Turn from the blasphemer," cried Pani. "Hence! thou evil one, to the perdition in store."

"I will go my ways," said the boy, "but Oro will shape the end."

And he quitted the Morai.

After conducting the party round the sacred inclosure, assisting his way with his staff, for his child had left him, Pani seated himself on a low, mossy stone, grimly surrounded by idols; and directed the pilgrims to return to his habitation; where, ere long he would rejoin them.

The pilgrims departed, he remained in profound meditation; while, backward and forward, an invisible ploughshare turned up the long furrows on his brow.

Long he was silent; then muttered to himself, "That boy, that wild, wise boy, has stabbed me to the heart. His thoughts are my suspicions. But he is honest. Yet I harm none. Multitudes must have unspoken meditations as well as I. Do we then mutually deceive? Off masks, mankind, that I may know what warranty of fellowship with others, my own thoughts possess. Why, upon this one theme, oh Oro! must all dissemble? Our thoughts are not our own. Whate'er it be, an honest thought must have some germ of truth. But we must set, as flows the general stream; I blindly follow, where I seem to lead; the crowd of pilgrims is so great, they see not there is none to guide.—It hinges upon this: Have we angelic spirits? But in vain, in vain, oh Oro! I essay to live out of this poor, blind body, fit dwelling for my sightless soul. Death, death:—blind, am I dead? for blindness seems a consciousness of death. Will my grave be more dark, than all is now?— From dark to dark!—What is this subtle something that is in me, and eludes me? Will it have no end? When, then, did it begin? All, all is chaos! What is this shining light in heaven, this sun they tell me of? Or, do they lie? Methinks, it might blaze convictions; but I brood and grope in blackness; I am dumb with doubt; yet, 'tis not doubt, but worse: I doubt my doubt. Oh, ye all-wise spirits in the air, how can ye witness all this woe, and give no sign? Would, would that mine were a settled doubt, like that wild boy's, who without faith, seems full of it. The undoubting doubter believes the most. Oh! that I were he. Methinks that daring boy hath Alma in him, struggling to be free. But those pilgrims: that trusting girl.—What, if they saw me as I am? Peace, peace, my soul; on, mask, again."

And he staggered from the Morai.

Chapter 110

*They discourse of the Gods of Mardi, and Braid-Beard
tells of one Foni*

WALKING FROM THE SACRED INCLOSURE, Mohi dis-
coursed of the plurality of gods in the land, a subject suggested
by the multitudinous idols we had just been beholding.

Said Mohi, "These gods of wood and of stone are nothing in number
to the gods in the air. You breathe not a breath without inhaling, you
touch not a leaf without ruffling a spirit. There are gods of heaven, and gods
of earth; gods of sea and of land; gods of peace and of war; gods of rock and
of fell; gods of ghosts and of thieves; of singers and dancers; of lean men
and of house-thatchers. Gods glance in the eyes of birds, and sparkle in the
crests of the waves; gods merrily swing in the boughs of the trees, and
merrily sing in the brook. Gods are here, and there, and every where; you
are never alone for them."

"If this be so, Braid-Beard," said Babbalanja, "our inmost thoughts are
overheard; but not by eaves-droppers. However, my lord, these gods to
whom he alludes, merely belong to the semi-intelligibles, the divided
unities in unity, this side of the First Adyta."

"Indeed?" said Media.

"Semi-intelligible, say you, philosopher?" cried Mohi. "Then, prithee,
make it appear so; for what you say, seems gibberish to me."

"Babbalanja," said Media, "no more of your abstrusities; what know you mortals of us gods and demi-gods? But tell me, Mohi, how many of your deities of rock and fell think you there are? Have you no statistical table?"

"My lord, at the lowest computation, there must be at least three billion trillion of quintillions."

"A mere unit!" said Babbalanja. "Old man, would you express an infinite number? Then take the sum of the follies of Mardi for your multiplicand; and for your multiplier, the totality of sublunarians, that never have been heard of since they became no more; and the product shall exceed your quintillions, even though all their units were nonillions."

"Have done, Babbalanja!" cried Media; "you are showing the sinister vein in your marble. Have done. Take a warm bath, and make tepid your cold blood. But come, Mohi, tell us of the ways of this Maramma; something of the Morai and its idols, if you please."

And straightway Braid-Beard proceeded with a narration, in substance as follows:—

It seems, there was a particular family upon the island, whose members, for many generations, had been set apart as sacrifices for the deity called Doleema. They were marked by a sad and melancholy aspect, and a certain involuntary shrinking, when passing the Morai. And though, when it came to the last, some of these unfortunates went joyfully to their doom, declaring that they gloried to die in the service of holy Doleema; still, were there others, who audaciously endeavored to shun their fate; upon the approach of a festival, fleeing to the innermost wilderness of the island. But little availed their flight. For swift on their track sped the hereditary butler of the insulted god, one Xiki, whose duty it was to provide the sacrifices. And when crouching in some covert, the fugitive spied Xiki's approach, so fearful did he become of the vengeance of the deity he sought to evade, that renouncing all hope of escape, he would burst from his lair, exclaiming, "Come on, and kill!" baring his breast for the javelin that slew him.

The chronicles of Maramma were full of horrors.

In the wild heart of the island, was said still to lurk the remnant of a band of warriors, who, in the days of the sire of the present pontiff, had risen in arms to dethrone him, headed by Foni, an upstart prophet, a personage distinguished for the uncommon beauty of his person. With terrible carnage, these warriors had been defeated; and the survivors, fleeing into the interior, for thirty days were pursued by the victors. But though many were overtaken and speared, a number survived; who, at last, wandering forlorn and in despair, like demoniacs, ran wild in the woods. And the islanders, who at times penetrated into the wilderness, for the purpose of procuring rare herbs, often scared from their path some specter, glaring through the foliage. Thrice had these demoniacs been discovered prowling about the inhabited portions of the isle; and at day-break, an attendant of the holy Morai once came upon a frightful figure, doubled with age, helping itself to the offerings in the image of Doleema. The demoniac was slain; and from his ineffaceable tatooing, it was proved that this was no other than Foni, the false prophet; the splendid form he had carried into the rebel fight, now squalid with age and misery.

Chapter 111

They visit the Lake of Yammo

FROM THE MORAI, we bent our steps toward an unoccupied arbor; and here, refreshing ourselves with the viands presented by Borabolla, we passed the night. And next morning proceeded to voyage round to the opposite quarter of the island; where, in the sacred lake of Yammo, stood the famous temple of Oro, also the great gallery of the inferior deities.

The lake was but a portion of the smooth lagoon, made separate by an arm of wooded reef, extending from the high western shore of the island, and curving round toward a promontory, leaving a narrow channel to the sea, almost invisible, however, from the land-locked interior.

In this lake were many islets, all green with groves. Its main-shore was a steep acclivity, with jutting points, each crowned with mossy old altars of stone, or ruinous temples, darkly reflected in the green, glassy water; while, from its long line of stately trees, the low reef-side of the lake looked one verdant bluff.

Gliding in upon Yammo, its many islets greeted us like a little Mardi; but ever and anon we started at long lines of phantoms in the water, reflections of the long line of images on the shore.

Toward the islet of Dolzono we first directed our way; and there we beheld the great gallery of the gods; a mighty temple, resting on one hundred tall pillars of palm, each based, below the surface, on the buried body

343

of a man; its nave one vista of idols; names carved on their foreheads: Ogro, Tripoo, Indrimarvoki, Parzillo, Vivivi, Jojijojorora, Jorkraki, and innumerable others.

Crowds of attendants were new-grouping the images.

"My lord, you behold one of their principal occupations," said Mohi.

Said Media: "I have heard much of the famed image of Mujo, the Nursing Mother;—can you point it out, Braid-Beard?"

"My lord, when last here, I saw Mujo at the head of this file; but they must have removed it; I see it not now."

"Do these attendants, then," said Babbalanja, "so continually new-marshal the idols, that visiting the gallery to-day, you are at a loss to-morrow?"

"Even so," said Braid-Beard. "But behold, my lord, this image is Mujo."

We stood before an obelisk-idol, so towering, that gazing at it, we were fain to throw back our heads. According to Mohi, winding stairs led up through its legs; its abdomen a cellar, thick-stored with gourds of old wine; its head, a hollow dome; in rude alto-relievo, its scores of hillock-breasts were carved over with legions of baby deities, frog-like sprawling; while, within, were secreted whole litters of infant idols, there placed, to imbibe divinity from the knots of the wood.

As we stood, a strange subterranean sound was heard, mingled with a gurgling as of wine being poured. Looking up, we beheld, through arrow-slits and port-holes, three masks, cross-legged seated in the abdomen, and holding stout wassail. But instantly upon descrying us, they vanished deeper into the interior; and presently was heard a sepulchral chant, and many groans and grievous tribulations.

Passing on, we came to an image, with a long anaconda-like posterior development, wound round and round its own neck.

"This must be Oloo, the god of Suicides," said Babbalanja.

"Yes," said Mohi, "you perceive, my lord, how he lays violent tail upon himself."

At length, the attendants having, in due order, new-disposed the long lines of sphinxes and griffins, and many-limbed images, a band of them, in long flowing robes, began their morning chant.

"Awake Rarni! awake Foloona!
Awake unnumbered deities!"

With many similar invocations, to which the images made not the slightest rejoinder. Not discouraged, however, the attendants now separately proceeded to offer up petitions on behalf of various tribes, retaining them for that purpose.

One prayed for abundance of rain, that the yams of Valapee might not wilt in the ground; another for dry sunshine, as most favorable for the present state of the Bread-fruit crop in Mondoldo.

Hearing all this, Babbalanja thus spoke:—"Doubtless, my lord Media, besides these petitions we hear, there are ten thousand contradictory prayers ascending to these idols. But methinks the gods will not jar the eternal progression of things, by any hints from below; even were it possible to satisfy conflicting desires."

Said Yoomy, "But I would pray, nevertheless, Babbalanja; for prayer draws us near to our own souls, and purifies our thoughts. Nor will I grant that our supplications are altogether in vain."

Still wandering among the images, Mohi had much to say, concerning their respective claims to the reverence of the devout.

For though, in one way or other, all Mardians bowed to the supremacy of Oro, they were not so unanimous concerning the inferior deities; those supposed to be intermediately concerned in sublunary things. Some nations sacrificed to one god; some to another; each maintaining, that their own god was the most potential.

Observing that all the images were more or less defaced, Babbalanja sought the reason.

To which, Braid-Beard made answer, that they had been thus defaced by hostile devotees; who quarreling in the great gallery of the gods, and getting beside themselves with rage, often sought to pull down, and demolish each other's favorite idols.

"But behold," cried Babbalanja, "there seems not a single image unmutilated. How is this, old man?"

"It is thus. While one faction defaces the images of its adversaries, its own images are in like manner assailed; whence it comes that no idol escapes."

"No more, no more, Braid-Beard," said Media. "Let us depart, and visit the islet, where the god of all these gods is enshrined."

Chapter 112

They meet the Pilgrims at the Temple of Oro

D EEP, DEEP, in deep groves, we found the great temple of Oro, Spreader-of-the-Sky, and deity supreme.

While here we silently stood eyeing this Mardi-renowned image, there entered the fane a great multitude of its attendants, holding pearl-shells on their heads, filled with a burning incense. And ranging themselves in a crowd round Oro, they began a long-rolling chant, a sea of sounds; and the thick smoke of their incense went up to the roof.

And now approached Pani and the pilgrims; followed, at a distance, by the willful boy.

"Behold great Oro," said the guide.

"We see naught but a cloud," said the chief Divino.

"My ears are stunned by the chanting," said the blind pilgrim.

"Receive more gifts, oh guide!" cried Fanna the matron.

"Oh Oro! invisible Oro! I kneel," slow murmured the sad-eyed maid.

But now, a current of air swept aside the eddying incense; and the willful boy, all eagerness to behold the image, went hither and thither; but the gathering of attendants was great; and at last he exclaimed, "Oh Oro! I can not see thee, for the crowd that stands between thee and me."

"Who is this babbler?" cried they with the censers, one and all turning upon the pilgrims; "let him speak no more; but bow down, and grind the

346

dust where he stands; and declare himself the vilest creature that crawls. So Oro and Alma command."

"I feel nothing in me so utterly vile," said the boy, "and I cringe to none. But I would as lief *adore* your image, as that in my heart, for both mean the same; but more, how can I? I love great Oro, though I comprehend him not. I marvel at his works, and feel as nothing in his sight; but because he is thus omnipotent, and I a mortal, it follows not that I am vile. Nor so doth he regard me. We do ourselves degrade ourselves, not Oro us. Hath not Oro made me? And therefore am I not worthy to stand erect before him? Oro is almighty, but no despot. I wonder; I hope; I love; I weep; I have in me a feeling nigh to fear, that is not fear; but wholly vile I am not; nor can we love and cringe. But Oro knows my heart, which I can not speak."

"Impious boy," cried they with the censers, "we will offer thee up, before the very image thou contemnest. In the name of Alma, seize him."

And they bore him away unresisting.

"Thus perish the ungodly," said Pani to the shuddering pilgrims.

And they quitted the temple, to journey toward the Peak of Ofo.

"My soul bursts!" cried Yoomy. "My lord, my lord, let us save the boy."

"Speak not," said Media. "His fate is fixed. Let Mardi stand."

"Then let us away from hence, my lord; and join the pilgrims; for, in these inland vales, the lost one may be found, perhaps at the very base of Ofo."

"Not there; not there;" cried Babbalanja, "Yillah may have touched these shores; but long since she must have fled."

Chapter 113

They discourse of Alma

SAILING TO AND FRO in the lake, to view its scenery, much discourse took place concerning the things we had seen; and far removed from the censer-bearers, the sad fate that awaited the boy was now the theme of all.

A good deal was then said of Alma, to whom the guide, the pilgrims, and the censer-bearers had frequently alluded, as to some paramount authority.

Called upon to reveal what his chronicles said on this theme, Braid-Beard complied; at great length narrating, what now follows condensed.

Alma, it seems, was an illustrious prophet, and teacher divine; who, ages ago, at long intervals, and in various islands, had appeared to the Mardians under the different titles of Brami, Manko, and Alma. Many thousands of moons had elapsed since his last and most memorable avatar, as Alma on the isle of Maramma. Each of his advents had taken place in a comparatively dark and benighted age. Hence, it was devoutly believed, that he came to redeem the Mardians from their heathenish thrall; to instruct them in the ways of truth, virtue, and happiness; to allure them to good by promises of beatitude hereafter; and to restrain them from evil by denunciations of woe. Separated from the impurities and corruptions, which in a long series of centuries had become attached to every thing originally

348

uttered by the prophet, the maxims, which as Brami he had taught, seemed similar to those inculcated by Manko. But as Alma, adapting his lessons to the improved condition of humanity, the divine prophet had more completely unfolded his scheme; as Alma, he had made his last revelation.

This narration concluded, Babbalanja mildly observed, "Mohi: without seeking to accuse you of uttering falsehoods; since what you relate rests not upon testimony of your own; permit me, to question the fidelity of your account of Alma. The prophet came to dissipate errors, you say; but superadded to many that have survived the past, ten thousand others have originated in various constructions of the principles of Alma himself. The prophet came to do away all gods but one; but since the days of Alma, the idols of Maramma have more than quadrupled. The prophet came to make us Mardians more virtuous and happy; but along with all previous good, the same wars, crimes, and miseries, which existed in Alma's day, under various modifications are yet extant. Nay: take from your chronicles, Mohi, the history of those horrors, one way or other, resulting from the doings of Alma's nominal followers, and your chronicles would not so frequently make mention of blood. The prophet came to guarantee our eternal felicity; but according to what is held in Maramma, that felicity rests on so hard a proviso, that to a thinking mind, but very few of our sinful race may secure it. For one, then, I wholly reject your Alma; not so much, because of all that is hard to be understood in his histories; as because of obvious and undeniable things all round us; which, to me, seem at war with an unreserved faith in his doctrines as promulgated here in Maramma. Besides; every thing in this isle strengthens my incredulity; I never was so thorough a disbeliever as now."

"Let the winds be laid," cried Mohi, "while your rash confession is being made in this sacred lake."

Said Media, "Philosopher; remember the boy, and they that seized him."

"Ah! I do indeed remember him. Poor youth! in his agony, how my heart yearned toward his. But that very prudence which you deny me, my lord, prevented me from saying aught in his behalf. Have you not observed, that until now, when we are completely by ourselves, I have refrained from freely discoursing of what we have seen in this island? Trust me, my lord, there is no man, that bears more in mind the necessity of being either a believer or a hypocrite in Maramma, and the imminent peril of being honest here, than I, Babbalanja. And have I not reason to be wary, when in my boyhood, my own sire was burnt for his temerity; and in this very isle?

Just Oro! it was done in the name of Alma,—what wonder then, that, at times, I almost hate that sound. And from those flames, they devoutly swore he went to others,—horrible fable!"

Said Mohi: "Do you deny, then, the everlasting torments?"

" 'Tis not worth a denial. Nor by formally denying it, will I run the risk of shaking the faith of thousands, who in that pious belief find infinite consolation for all they suffer in Mardi."

"How?" said Media; "are there those who soothe themselves with the thought of everlasting flames?"

"One would think so, my lord, since they defend that dogma more resolutely than any other. Sooner will they yield you the isles of Paradise, than it. And in truth, as liege followers of Alma, they would seem but right in clinging to it as they do; for, according to all one hears in Maramma, the great end of the prophet's mission seems to have been the revealing to us Mardians the existence of horrors, most hard to escape. But better we were all annihilated, than that one man should be damned."

Rejoined Media: "But think you not, that possibly, Alma may have been misconceived? Are you certain that doctrine is his?"

"I know nothing more than that such is the belief in this land. And in these matters, I know not where else to go for information. But, my lord, had I been living in those days when certain men are said to have been actually possessed by spirits from hell, I had not let slip the opportunity— as our forefathers did—to cross-question them concerning the place they came from."

"Well, well," said Media, "your Alma's faith concerns not me: I am a king, and a demi-god; and leave vulgar torments to the commonality."

"But it concerns me," muttered Mohi; "yet I know not what to think."

"For me," said Yoomy, "I reject it. Could I, I would not believe it. It is at variance with the dictates of my heart; instinctively my heart turns from it, as a thirsty man from gall."

"Hush; say no more," said Mohi; "again we approach the shore."

Chapter 114

Mohi tells of one Ravoo, and they land to visit Hevaneva,
a flourishing Artisan

HAVING SEEN all worth viewing in Yammo, we departed, to
complete the circumnavigation of the island, by returning to
Uma without reversing our prows. As we glided along, we passed
many objects of interest, concerning which, Mohi, as usual, was very
diffuse.

Among other things pointed out, were certain little altars, like mile-
stones, planted here and there upon bright bluffs, running out into the
lagoon. Dedicated respectively to the guardian spirits of Maramma, these
altars formed a chain of spiritual defenses; and here were presumed to stand
post the most vigilant of warders; dread Hivohitee, all by himself, garrisoning the impregnable interior.

But these sentries were only subalterns, subject to the beck of the Pontiff;
who frequently sent word to them, concerning the duties of their watch.
His mandates were intrusted to one Ravoo, the hereditary pontifical messenger; a long-limbed varlet, so swift of foot, that he was said to travel
like a javelin. "Art thou Ravoo, that thou so pliest thy legs?" say these
islanders, to one encountered in a hurry.

Hivohitee's postman held no oral communication with the sentries.
Dispatched round the island with divers bits of tappa, hieroglyphically

351

stamped, he merely deposited one upon each altar; superadding a stone, to keep the missive in its place; and so went his rounds.

Now, his route lay over hill and over dale, and over many a coral rock; and to preserve his feet from bruises, he was fain to wear a sort of buskin, or boot, fabricated of a durable tappa, made from the thickest and toughest of fibers. As he never wore his buskins except when he carried the mail, Ravoo sorely fretted with his Hessians; though it would have been highly imprudent to travel without them. To make the thing more endurable, therefore, and, at intervals, to cool his heated pedals, he established a series of stopping-places, or stages; at each of which a fresh pair of buskins, hanging from a tree, were taken down and vaulted into by the ingenious traveler. Those relays of boots were exceedingly convenient; next, indeed, to being lifted upon a fresh pair of legs.

"Now, to what purpose that anecdote?" demanded Babbalanja of Mohi, who in substance related it.

"Marry! 'tis but the simple recital of a fact; and I tell it to entertain the company."

"But has it any meaning you know of?"

"Thou art wise, find out," retorted Braid-Beard.

"But what comes of it?" persisted Babbalanja.

"Beshrew me, this senseless catechising of thine," replied Mohi; "naught else, it seems, save a grin or two."

"And pray, what may you be driving at, philosopher?" interrupted Media.

"I am intent upon the essence of things; the mystery that lieth beyond; the elements of the tear which much laughter provoketh; that which is beneath the seeming; the precious pearl within the shaggy oyster. I probe the circle's center; I seek to evolve the inscrutable."

"Seek on; and when aught is found, cry out, that we may run to see."

"My lord the king is merry upon me. To him my more subtle cogitations seem foolishness. But believe me, my lord, there is more to be thought of than to be seen. There is a world of wonders insphered within the spontaneous consciousness; or, as old Bardianna hath it, a mystery within the obvious, yet an obviousness within the mystery."

"And did I ever deny that?" said Media.

"As plain as my hand in the dark," said Mohi.

"I dreamed a dream," said Yoomy.

"They banter me; but enough; I am to blame for discoursing upon the deep world wherein I live. I am wrong in seeking to invest sublunary sounds with celestial sense. Much that is in me is incommunicable by this ether we breathe. But I blame ye not." And wrapping round him his mantle, Babbalanja retired into its most private folds.

Ere coming in sight of Uma, we put into a little bay, to pay our respects to Hevaneva, a famous character there dwelling; who, assisted by many journeymen, carried on the lucrative business of making idols for the surrounding isles.

Know ye, that all idols not made in Maramma, and consecrated by Hivohitee; and, what is more, in strings of teeth paid down for to Hevaneva; are of no more account, than logs, stocks, or stones. Yet does not the cunning artificer monopolize the profits of his vocation; for Hevaneva being but the vassal of the Pontiff, the latter lays claim to King Leo's share of the spoils, and secures it.

The place was very prettily lapped in a pleasant dell, nigh to the margin of the water; and here, were several spacious arbors; wherein, prostrate upon their sacred faces, were all manner of idols, in every imaginable stage of statuary development.

With wonderful industry the journeymen were plying their tools;— some chiseling noses; some trenching for mouths; and others, with heated flints, boring for ears: a hole drilled straight through the occiput, representing the auricular organs.

"How easily they are seen through," said Babbalanja, taking a sight through one of the heads.

The last finish is given to their godships, by rubbing them all over with dried slips of consecrated shark-skin, rough as sand paper, tacked over bits of wood.

In one of the farther arbors, Hevaneva pointed out a goodly array of idols, all complete and ready for the market. They were of every variety of pattern; and of every size; from that of a giant, to the little images worn in the ears of the ultra devout.

"Of late," said the artist, "there has been a lively demand for the image of Arbino the god of fishing; the present being the principal season for that business. For Nadams (Nadam presides over love and wine), there has also been urgent call; it being the time of the grape; and the maidens growing frolicsome withal, and devotional."

Seeing that Hevaneva handled his wares with much familiarity, not to say irreverence, Babbalanja was minded to learn from him, what he thought of his trade; whether the images he made were genuine or spurious; in a word, whether he believed in his gods.

His reply was curious. But still more so, the marginal gestures where-with he helped out the text.

"When I cut down the trees for my idols," said he, "they are nothing but logs; when upon those logs, I chalk out the figures of my images, they yet remain logs; when the chisel is applied, logs they are still; and when all complete, I at last stand them up in my studio, even then they are logs. Nevertheless, when I handle the pay, they are as prime gods, as ever were turned out in Maramma."

"You must make a very great variety," said Babbalanja.

"All sorts, all sorts."

"And from the same material, I presume."

"Ay, ay, one grove supplies them all. And, on an average, each tree stands us in full fifty idols. Then, we often take second-hand images in part pay for new ones. These we work over again into new patterns; touching up their eyes and ears; resetting their noses; and more especially new-foot-ing their legs, where they always decay first."

Under sanction of the Pontiff, Hevaneva, in addition to his large com-merce in idols, also carried on the highly lucrative business of canoe-build-ing; the profits whereof, undivided, he dropped into his private exchequer. But Mohi averred, that the Pontiff often charged him with neglecting his images, for his canoes. Be that as it may, Hevaneva drove a thriving trade at both avocations. And in demonstration of the fact, he directed our atten-tion to three long rows of canoes, upheld by wooden supports. They were in perfect order; at a moment's notice, ready for launching; being furnished with paddles, out-riggers, masts, sails, and a human skull, with a short handle thrust through one of its eyes, the ordinary bailer of Maramma; besides other appurtenances, including on the prow a duodecimo idol to match.

Owing to a superstitious preference bestowed upon the wood and work of the sacred island, Hevaneva's canoes were in as high repute as his idols; and sold equally well.

In truth, in several ways one trade helped the other. The larger images being dug out of the hollow part of the canoes; and all knotty odds and ends reserved for the idol ear-rings.

"But after all," said the artificer, "I find a readier sale for my images, than for my canoes."

"And so it will ever be," said Babbalanja.—"Stick to thy idols, man! a trade, more reliable than the baker's."

Chapter 115

A Nursery-tale of Babbalanja's

H AVING TAKEN to our canoes once again, we were silently
sailing along, when Media observed, "Babbalanja; though I
seldom trouble myself with such thoughts, I have just been thinking, how difficult it must be, for the more ignorant sort of people, to decide
upon what particular image to worship as a guardian deity, when in Maramma, it seems, there exists such a multitude of idols, and a thousand more are
to be heard of."

"Not at all, your highness. The more ignorant the better. The multitude
of images distracts them not. But I am in no mood for serious discourse; let
me tell you a story."

"A story! hear him: the solemn philosopher is desirous of regaling us
with a tale! But pray, begin."

"Once upon a time, then," said Babbalanja, indifferently adjusting his
girdle, "nine blind men, with uncommonly long noses, set out on their
travels to see the great island on which they were born."

"A precious beginning," muttered Mohi. "Nine blind men setting out
to see sights."

Continued Babbalanja, "Staff in hand, they traveled; one in advance of
the other; each man with his palm upon the shoulder next him; and he
with the longest nose took the lead of the file. Journeying on in this manner,

they came to a valley, in which reigned a king called Tammaro. Now, in a
certain inclosure toward the head of the valley, there stood an immense
wild banian tree; all over moss, and many centuries old, and forming quite
a wood in itself; its thousand boughs striking into the earth, and fixing there
as many gigantic trunks. With Tammaro, it had long been a question, which
of those many trunks was the original and true one; a matter that had
puzzled the wisest heads among his subjects; and in vain had a reward been
offered for the solution of the perplexity. But the tree was so vast, and its
fabric so complex; and its rooted branches so similar in appearance; and so
numerous, from the circumstance that every year had added to them, that
it was quite impossible to determine the point. Nevertheless, no sooner did
the nine blind men hear that there was a reward offered for discovering the
trunk of a tree, standing all by itself, than, one and all, they assured Tammaro, that they would quickly settle that little difficulty of his; and loudly
inveighed against the stupidity of his sages, who had been so easily posed.
So, being conducted into the inclosure, and assured that the tree was somewhere within, they separated their forces, so as at wide intervals to surround
it at a distance; when feeling their way, with their staves and their noses,
they advanced to the search, crying out—'Pshaw! make room there; let us
wise men feel of the mystery.' Presently, striking with his nose one of the
rooted branches, the foremost blind man quickly knelt down; and feeling
that it struck into the earth, gleefully shouted:—'Here it is! here it is!' But
almost in the same breath, his companions, also, each striking a branch with
his staff or his nose, cried out in like manner, 'Here it is! here it is!' Whereupon they were all confounded: but directly, the man who first cried out,
thus addressed the rest:—'Good friends, surely you're mistaken. There is
but one tree in the place, and here it is.' 'Very true,' said the others, all together; 'there is only *one* tree; but *here* it is.' 'Nay,' said the others, 'it is
here!' and so saying, each blind man triumphantly felt of the branch, where
it penetrated into the earth. Then again said the first speaker:—'Good
friends, if you will not believe what I say, come hither, and feel for yourselves.' 'Nay, nay,' replied they, 'why seek further? *here* it is; and nowhere
else can it be.' 'You blind fools, you, you contradict yourselves,' continued
the first speaker, waxing wroth; 'how can you each have hold of a separate
trunk, when there is but one in the place?' Whereupon, they redoubled
their cries, calling each other all manner of opprobrious names, and presently they fell to beating each other with their staves, and charging upon each
other with their noses. But soon after, being loudly called upon by Tammaro and his people; who all this while had been looking on; being loudly

called upon, I say, to clap their hands on the trunk, they again rushed for their respective branches; and it so happened, that, one and all, they changed places; but still cried out, '*Here* it is; *here* it is!' 'Peace! peace! ye silly blind men,' said Tammaro. 'Will ye without eyes presume to see more sharply than those who have them? The tree is too much for us all. Hence! depart from the valley.' "

"An admirable story," cried Media. "I had no idea that a mere mortal, least of all a philosopher, could acquit himself so well. By my scepter, but it is well done! Ha, ha! blind men round a banian! Why, Babbalanja, no demi-god could surpass it. Taji, could you?"

"But, Babbalanja, what under the sun, mean you by your blind story!" cried Mohi. "Obverse, or reverse, I can make nothing out of it."

"Others may," said Babbalanja. "It is a polysensuum, old man."

"A pollywog!" said Mohi.

Chapter 116

Landing to visit Hivohitee the Pontiff, they encounter an extraordinary old Hermit; with whom Yoomy has a confidential Interview, but learns little

GLIDING ON, suddenly we spied a solitary Islander putting out in his canoe from a neighboring cove.

Drawing near, the stranger informed us, that he was just from the face of the great Pontiff, Hivohitee, who, having dismissed his celestial guests, had retired to his private sanctuary. Upon this, Media resolved to land forthwith, and under the guidance of Mohi, proceed inland, and pay a visit to his Holiness.

Quitting the beach, our path penetrated into the solitudes of the groves. Skirting the way were tall Casuarinas, a species of cypress, standing motionless in the shadows, as files of mutes at a funeral. But here and there, they were overrun with the adventurous vines of the Convolvulus, the Morning-glory of the Tropics, whose tendrils, bruised by the twigs, dropped milk upon the dragon-like scales of the trees.

This vine is of many varieties. Lying perdu, and shunning the garish sun through the day, one species rises at night with the stars; bursting forth in dazzling constellations of blossoms, which close at dawn. Others, slumbering through the darkness, are up and abroad with their petals, by peep of morn; and after inhaling its breath, again drop their lids in repose. While a third species, more capricious, refuse to expand at all, unless in the most brilliant sunshine, and upon the very tops of the loftiest trees. Ambitious flowers! that will not blow, unless in high places, with the bright day looking on and admiring.

Here and there, we passed open glades in the woods, delicious with the incense of violets. Balsamic ferns, stirred by the breeze, fanned all the air with aromas. These glades were delightful.

Journeying on, we at length came to a dark glen so deftly hidden by the surrounding copses, that were it not for the miasma thence wafted, an ignorant wayfarer might pass and repass it, time and again, never dreaming of its vicinity.

Down into the gloom of this glen we descended. Its sides were mantled with noxious shrubs, whose exhalations, half way down, unpleasantly blended with the piny breeze from the uplands. Through its bed ran a brook, whose incrusted margin had a strange metallic luster, from the polluted waters here flowing; their source a sulphur spring, of vile flavor and odor, where many invalid pilgrims resorted.

The woods all round were haunted by the dismal cawings of crows; tap, tap, the black hawk whetted his bill on the boughs; each trunk stalked a ghost; and from those trunks, Hevaneva procured the wood for his idols.

Rapidly crossing this place, Yoomy's hands to his ears, old Mohi's to his nostrils, and Babbalanja vainly trying to walk with closed eyes, we toiled among steep, flinty rocks, along a wild, zigzag pathway; like a mule-track in the Andes, not so much onward as upward; Yoomy above Babbalanja, my lord Media above him, and Braid-Beard, our guide, in the air, above all.

Strown over with cinders, the vitreous marl seemed tumbled together, as if belched from a volcano's throat.

Presently, we came to a tall, slender structure, hidden among the scenic projections of the cliffs, like a monument in the dark, vaulted ways of an abbey. Surrounding it, were five extinct craters. The air was sultry and still, as if full of spent thunderbolts.

Like a Hindoo pagoda, this bamboo edifice rose story above story; its many angles and points decorated with pearl-shells suspended by cords. But the uppermost story, some ten toises in the air, was closely thatched from apex to floor; which summit was gained by a series of ascents.

What eremite dwelleth here, like St. Stylites at the top of his column?—a question which Mohi seemed all eagerness to have answered.

Dropping upon his knees, he gave a peculiar low call: no response. Another: all was silent. Marching up to the pagoda, and again dropping upon his knees, he shook the bamboos till the edifice rocked, and its pearl-shells jingled, as if a troop of Andalusian mules, with bells round their necks, were galloping along the defile.

At length the thatch aloft was thrown open, and a head was thrust forth. It was that of an old, old man; with steel-gray eyes, hair and beard, and a horrible necklace of jaw-bones.

Now, issuing from the pagoda, Mohi turned about to gain a view of the ghost he had raised; and no sooner did he behold it, than with King Media and the rest, he made a marked salutation.

Presently, the eremite pointed to where Yoomy was standing; and waved his hand upward; when Mohi informed the minstrel, that it was St. Stylites' pleasure, that he should pay him a visit.

Wondering what was to come, Yoomy proceeded to mount; and at last arriving toward the top of the pagoda, was met by an opening, from which an encouraging arm assisted him to gain the ultimate landing.

Here, all was murky enough; for the aperture from which the head of the apparition had been thrust, was now closed; and what little twilight there was, came up through the opening in the floor.

In this dismal seclusion, silently the hermit confronted the minstrel; his gray hair, eyes, and beard all gleaming, as if streaked with phosphorus; while his ghastly gorget grinned hideously, with all its jaws.

Mutely Yoomy waited to be addressed; but hearing no sound, and becoming alive to the strangeness of his situation, he meditated whether it would not be well to subside out of sight, even as he had come—through the floor. An intention which the eremite must have anticipated; for of a sudden, something was slid over the opening; and the apparition seating itself thereupon, the twain were in darkness complete.

Shut up thus, with an inscrutable stranger posted at the only aperture of escape, poor Yoomy fell into something like a panic; hardly knowing what step to take next. As for endeavoring to force his way out, it was alarming to think of; for aught he knew, the eremite, availing himself of the gloom, might be bristling all over with javelin points.

At last, the silence was broken.

"What see you, mortal?"

"Chiefly darkness," said Yoomy, wondering at the audacity of the question.

"I dwell in it. But what else see you, mortal?"

"The dim gleaming of thy gorget."

"But that is not me. What else dost thou see?"

"Nothing."

"Then thou hast found me out, and seen all! Descend."

And with that, the passage-way opened, and groping through the twi-light, Yoomy obeyed the mandate, and retreated; full of vexation at his enigmatical reception.

On his alighting, Mohi inquired whether the hermit was not a wonder-ful personage.

But thinking some sage waggery lurked in the question; and at present too indignant to enter into details, the minstrel made some impatient reply; and winding through a defile, the party resumed its journey.

Straggling behind, to survey the strange plants and flowers in his path, Yoomy became so absorbed, as almost to forget the scene in the pagoda; yet every moment expected to be nearing the stately abode of the Pontiff.

But suddenly, the scene around grew familiar; the path seemed that which had been followed just after leaving the canoes; and at length, the place of debarkation was in sight.

Surprised that the object of our visit should have been thus abandoned, the minstrel ran forward, and sought an explanation.

Whereupon, Mohi lifted his hands in amazement; exclaiming at the blindness of the eyes, which had beheld the supreme Pontiff of Maramma, without knowing it.

The old hermit was no other than the dread Hivohitee; the pagoda, the inmost oracle of the isle.

Chapter 117

Babbalanja endeavors to explain the Mystery

T HIS GREAT MOGUL of a personage, then; this woundy Ahasuerus; this man of men; this same Hivohitee, whose name rumbled
among the mountains like a peal of thunder, had been seen face to
face, and taken for naught, but a bearded old hermit, or at best, some
equivocal conjuror.

So great was his wonderment at the time, that Yoomy could not avoid
expressing it in words.

Whereupon thus discoursed Babbalanja:

"Gentle Yoomy, be not astounded, that Hivohitee is so far behind your
previous conceptions. The shadows of things are greater than themselves;
and the more exaggerated the shadow, the more unlike to the substance."

"But knowing now, what manner of person Hivohitee is," said Yoomy,
"much do I long to behold him again."

But Mohi assured him it was out of the question; that the Pontiff always
acted toward strangers as toward him (Yoomy); and that but one dim
blink at the eremite was all that mortal could obtain.

Debarred thus from a second and more satisfactory interview with one,
concerning whom his curiosity had been violently aroused, the minstrel
again turned to Mohi for enlightenment; especially touching that magnate's
Egyptian reception of him in his aerial den.

Whereto, the chronicler made answer, that the Pontiff affected darkness because he liked it: that he was a ruler of few words, but many deeds; and that, had Yoomy been permitted to tarry longer with him in the pagoda, he would have been privy to many strange attestations of the divinity imputed to him. Voices would have been heard in the air, gossiping with Hivohitee; noises inexplicable proceeding from him; in brief, light would have flashed out of his darkness.

"But who has seen these things, Mohi?" said Babbalanja, "have you?"

"Nay."

"Who then?—Media?—Any one you know?"

"Nay: but the whole Archipelago has."

"Thus," exclaimed Babbalanja, "does Mardi, blind though it be in many things, collectively behold the marvels, which one pair of eyes sees not."

Chapter 118

Taji receives Tidings and Omens

SLOWLY SAILING ON, we were overtaken by a shallop; whose inmates grappling to the side of Media's, said they came from Borabolla.

Dismal tidings!—My faithful follower's death.

Absent over night, that morning early, he had been discovered lifeless in the woods, three arrows in his heart. And the three pale strangers were nowhere to be found. But a fleet canoe was missing from the beach.

Slain for me! my soul sobbed out. Nor yet appeased Aleema's manes; nor yet seemed sated the avengers' malice; who, doubtless, were on my track.

But I turned; and instantly the three canoes had been reversed; and full soon, Jarl's dead hand in mine, had not Media interposed.

"To death, your presence will not bring life back."

"And we must on," said Babbalanja. "We seek the living, not the dead."

Thus they overruled me; and Borabolla's messengers departed.

Soon evening came, and in its shades, three shadows,—Hautia's heralds. Their shallop glided near.

A leaf tri-foiled was first presented; then another, arrow-shaped.

Said Yoomy, "Still I swiftly follow, behind revenge."

Then were showered faded, pallid daffodils.

Said Yoomy, "Thy hopes are blighted all."

"Not dead, but living with the life of life. Sirens! I heed ye not."

They would have showered more flowers; but crowding sail we left them.

Much converse followed. Then, beneath the canopy all sought repose. And ere long slouched sleep drew nigh, tending dreams innumerable; silent dotting all the downs; a shepherd with his flock.

Chapter 119

Dreams

DREAMS! DREAMS! golden dreams: endless, and golden, as the flowery prairies, that stretch away from the Rio Sacramento, in whose waters Danae's shower was woven;—prairies like rounded eternities: jonquil leaves beaten out; and my dreams herd like buffaloes, browsing on to the horizon, and browsing on round the world; and among them, I dash with my lance, to spear one, ere they all flee.

Dreams! dreams! passing and repassing, like Oriental empires in history; and scepters wave thick, as Bruce's pikes at Bannockburn; and crowns are plenty as marigolds in June. And far in the background, hazy and blue, their steeps let down from the sky, loom Andes on Andes, rooted on Alps; and all round me, long rushing oceans, roll Amazons and Oronocos; waves, mounted Parthians; and, to and fro, toss the wide woodlands: all the world an elk, and the forests its antlers.

But far to the South, past my Sicily suns and my vineyards, stretches the Antarctic barrier of ice: a China wall, built up from the sea, and nodding its frosted towers in the dun, clouded sky. Do Tartary and Siberia lie beyond? Deathful, desolate dominions those; bleak and wild the ocean, beating at that barrier's base, hovering 'twixt freezing and foaming; and freighted with navies of ice-bergs,—warring worlds crossing orbits; their long icicles, projecting like spears to the charge. Wide away stream the floes of drift ice,

366

frozen cemeteries of skeletons and bones. White bears howl as they drift from their cubs; and the grinding islands crush the skulls of the peering seals.

But beneath me, at the Equator, the earth pulses and beats like a warrior's heart; till I know not, whether it be not myself. And my soul sinks down to the depths, and soars to the skies; and comet-like reels on through such boundless expanses, that methinks all the worlds are my kin, and I invoke them to stay in their course. Yet, like a mighty three-decker, towing argosies by scores, I tremble, gasp, and strain in my flight, and fain would cast off the cables that hamper.

And like a frigate, I am full with a thousand souls; and as on, on, on, I scud before the wind, many mariners rush up from the orlop below, like miners from caves; running shouting across my decks; opposite braces are pulled; and this way and that, the great yards swing round on their axes; and boisterous speaking-trumpets are heard; and contending orders, to save the good ship from the shoals. Shoals, like nebulous vapors, shoreing the white reef of the Milky Way, against which the wrecked worlds are dashed; strowing all the strand, with their Himmaleh keels and ribs.

Ay: many, many souls are in me. In my tropical calms, when my ship lies tranced on Eternity's main, speaking one at a time, then all with one voice: an orchestra of many French bugles and horns, rising, and falling, and swaying, in golden calls and responses.

Sometimes, when these Atlantics and Pacifics thus undulate round me, I lie stretched out in their midst: a land-locked Mediterranean, knowing no ebb, nor flow. Then again, I am dashed in the spray of these sounds: an eagle at the world's end, tossed skyward, on the horns of the tempest.

Yet, again, I descend, and list to the concert.

Like a grand, ground swell, Homer's old organ rolls its vast volumes under the light frothy wave-crests of Anacreon and Hafiz; and high over my ocean, sweet Shakespeare soars, like all the larks of the spring. Throned on my sea-side, like Canute, bearded Ossian smites his hoar harp, wreathed with wild-flowers, in which warble my Wallers; blind Milton sings bass to my Petrarchs and Priors, and laureats crown me with bays.

In me, many worthies recline, and converse. I list to St. Paul who argues the doubts of Montaigne; Julian the Apostate cross-questions Augustine; and Thomas-a-Kempis unrolls his old black letters for all to decipher. Zeno murmurs maxims beneath the hoarse shout of Democritus; and though Democritus laugh loud and long, and the sneer of Pyrrho be seen; yet, divine Plato, and Proclus, and Verulam are of my counsel; and Zoroaster whispered me before I was born. I walk a world that is mine; and enter many nations, as Mungo Park rested in African cots; I am served like Bajazet: Bacchus my butler, Virgil my minstrel, Philip Sidney my page. My memory is a life beyond birth; my memory, my library of the Vatican, its alcoves all endless perspectives, eve-tinted by cross-lights from Middle-Age oriels.

And as the great Mississippi musters his watery nations: Ohio, with all his leagued streams; Missouri, bringing down in torrents the clans from the highlands; Arkansas, his Tartar rivers from the plain;—so, with all the past and present pouring in me, I roll down my billow from afar.

Yet not I, but another: God is my Lord; and though many satellites revolve around me, I and all mine revolve round the great central Truth, sun-like, fixed and luminous forever in the foundationless firmament.

Fire flames on my tongue; and though of old the Bactrian prophets were stoned, yet the stoners in oblivion sleep. But whoso stones me, shall be as Erostratus, who put torch to the temple; though Genghis Khan with Cambyses combine to obliterate him, his name shall be extant in the mouth of the last man that lives. And if so be, down unto death, whence I came, will I go, like Xenophon retreating on Greece, all Persia brandishing her spears in his rear.

My cheek blanches white while I write; I start at the scratch of my pen; my own mad brood of eagles devours me; fain would I unsay this audacity; but an iron-mailed hand clenches mine in a vice, and prints down every letter in my spite. Fain would I hurl off this Dionysius that rides me; my thoughts crush me down till I groan; in far fields I hear the song of the reaper, while I slave and faint in this cell. The fever runs through me like lava; my hot brain burns like a coal; and like many a monarch, I am less to be envied, than the veriest hind in the land.

Chapter 120

Media and Babbalanja discourse

O

UR VISITING the Pontiff at a time previously unforeseen, somewhat altered our plans. All search in Maramma for the lost one
proving fruitless, and nothing of note remaining to be seen, we
returned not to Uma; but proceeded with the tour of the lagoon.

When day came, reclining beneath the canopy, Babbalanja would fain
have seriously discussed those things we had lately been seeing, which, for
all the occasional levity he had recently evinced, seemed very near his heart.

But my lord Media forbade; saying that they necessarily included a
topic which all gay, sensible Mardians, who desired to live and be merry,
invariably banished from social discourse.

"Meditate as much as you will, Babbalanja, but say little aloud, unless
in a merry and mythical way. Lay down the great maxims of things, but
let inferences take care of themselves. Never be special; never, a partisan.
In safety, afar off, you may batter down a fortress; but at your peril you
essay to carry a single turret by escalade. And if doubts distract you, in vain
will you seek sympathy from your fellow men. For upon this one theme,
not a few of you free-minded mortals, even the otherwise honest and
intelligent, are the least frank and friendly. Discourse with them, and it is
mostly formulas, or prevarications, or hollow assumption of philosophical

indifference, or urbane hypocrisies, or a cool, civil deference to the dominant belief; or still worse, but less common, a brutality of indiscriminate
skepticism. Furthermore, Babbalanja, on this head, final, last thoughts you
mortals have none; nor can have; and, at bottom, your own fleeting fancies
are too often secrets to yourselves; and sooner may you get another's
secret, than your own. Thus with the wisest of you all; you are ever un-
fixed. Do you show a tropical calm without? then, be sure a thousand contrary currents whirl and eddy within. The free, airy robe of your philosophy
is but a dream, which seems true while it lasts; but waking again into the
orthodox world, straightway you resume the old habit. And though in
your dreams you may hie to the uttermost Orient, yet all the while you
abide where you are. Babbalanja, you mortals dwell in Mardi, and it is
impossible to get elsewhere."

Said Babbalanja, "My lord, you school me. But though I dissent from
some of your positions, I am willing to confess, that this is not the first
time a philosopher has been instructed by a man."

"A demi-god, sir; and therefore I the more readily discharge my mind
of all seriousness, touching the subject, with which you mortals so vex and
torment yourselves."

Silence ensued. And seated apart, on both sides of the barge, solemnly
swaying, in fixed meditation, to the roll of the waves, Babbalanja, Mohi,
and Yoomy, drooped lower and lower, like funeral plumes; and our
gloomy canoe seemed a hearse.

Chapter 121

They regale themselves with their Pipes

H O! MORTALS! mortals!" cried Media. "Go we to bury our
dead? Awake, sons of men! Cheer up, heirs of immortality! Ho,
Vee-Vee! bring forth our pipes: we'll smoke off this cloud."

Nothing so beguiling as the fumes of tobacco, whether inhaled through
hookah, narghil, chibouque, Dutch porcelain, pure Principe, or Regalia.
And a great oversight had it been in King Media, to have omitted pipes
among the appliances of this voyage that we went. Tobacco in rouleaus
we had none; cigar nor cigarret; which little the company esteemed. Pipes
were preferred; and pipes we often smoked; testify, oh! Vee-Vee, to that.
But not of the vile clay, of which mankind and Etruscan vases were made,
were these jolly fine pipes of ours. But all in good time.

Now, the leaf called tobacco is of divers species and sorts. Not to dwell
upon vile Shag, Pig-tail, Plug, Nail-rod, Negro-head, Cavendish, and mis-
named Lady's-twist, there are the following varieties:—Gold-leaf,
Oronoco, Cimaroza, Smyrna, Bird's-eye, James-river, Sweet-scented,
Honey-dew, Kentucky, Cnaster, Scarfalati, and famed Shiraz, or Persian.
Of all of which, perhaps the last is the best.

But smoked by itself, to a fastidious wight, even Shiraz is not gentle
enough. It needs mitigation. And the cunning craft of so mitigating even

371

the mildest tobacco was well understood in the dominions of Media. There, in plantations ever covered with a brooding, blue haze, they raised its fine leaf in the utmost luxuriance; almost as broad as the broad fans of the broad-bladed banana. The stalks of the leaf withdrawn, the remainder they cut up, and mixed with soft willow-bark, and the aromatic leaves of the Betel.

"Ho! Vee-Vee, bring forth the pipes," cried Media. And forth they came, followed by a quaint, carved cocoa-nut, agate-lidded, containing ammunition sufficient for many stout charges and primings.

Soon we were all smoking so hard, that the canopied howdah, under which we reclined, sent up purple wreaths like a Michigan wigwam. There we sat in a ring, all smoking in council—every pipe a halcyon pipe of peace.

And among those calumets, my lord Media's showed like the turbaned Grand Turk among his Bashaws. It was an extraordinary pipe, be sure; of right royal dimensions. Its mouth-piece an eagle's beak; its long stem, a bright, red-barked cherry-tree branch, partly covered with a close net-work of purple dyed porcupine quills; and toward the upper end, stream-ing with pennons, like a Versailles flag-staff of a coronation day. These pennons were managed by halyards; and after lighting his prince's pipe, it was little Vee-Vee's part to run them up toward the mast-head, or mouth-piece, in token that his lord was fairly under weigh.

But Babbalanja's was of a different sort; an immense, black, serpentine stem of ebony, coiling this way and that, in endless convolutions, like an anaconda round a traveler in Brazil. Smoking this hydra, Babbalanja looked as if playing upon the trombone.

Next, gentle Yoomy's. Its stem, a slender golden reed, like musical Pan's; its bowl very merry with tassels.

Lastly, old Mohi the chronicler's. Its Death's-head bowl forming its latter end, continually reminding him of his own. Its shank was an ostrich's leg, some feathers still waving nigh the mouth-piece.

"Here, Vee-Vee! fill me up again," cried Media, through the blue vapors sweeping round his great gonfalon, like plumed Marshal Ney, waving his baton in the smoke of Waterloo; or thrice gallant Anglesea, crossing his wooden leg mid the reek and rack of the Apsley House banquet.

Vee-Vee obeyed; and quickly, like a howitzer, the pipe-bowl was re-loaded to the muzzle, and King Media smoked on.

"Ah! this is pleasant indeed," he cried. "Look, it's a calm on the waters, and a calm in our hearts, as we inhale these sedative odors."

"So calm," said Babbalanja; "the very gods must be smoking now."

"And thus," said Media, "we demi-gods hereafter shall cross-legged sit, and smoke out our eternities. Ah, what a glorious puff! Mortals, methinks these pipe-bowls of ours must be petrifactions of roses, so scented they seem. But, old Mohi, you have smoked this many a long year; doubtless, you know something about their material—the Froth-of-the-Sea they call it, I think—ere my handicraft subjects obtain it, to work into bowls. Tell us the tale."

"Delighted to do so, my lord," replied Mohi, slowly disentangling his mouth-piece from the braids of his beard. "I have devoted much time and attention to the study of pipe-bowls, and groped among many learned authorities, to reconcile the clashing opinions concerning the origin of the so-called Farnoo, or Froth-of-the-Sea."

"Well, then, my old centenarian, give us the result of your investigations. But smoke away: a word and a puff: go on."

"May it please you, then, my right worshipful lord, this Farnoo is an unctuous, argillaceous substance; in its natural state, soft, malleable, and easily worked as the cornelian-red clay from the famous pipe-quarries of the wild tribes to the North. But though mostly found buried in terra-firma, especially in the isles toward the East, this Farnoo, my lord, is sometimes thrown up by the ocean; in seasons of high sea, being plentifully found on the reefs. But, my lord, like amber, the precise nature and origin of this Farnoo are points widely mooted."

"Stop there!" cried Media; "our mouth-pieces are of amber; so, not a word more of the Froth-of-the-Sea, until something be said to clear up the mystery of amber. What is amber, old man?"

"A still more obscure thing to trace than the other, my worshipful lord. Ancient Plinnee maintained, that originally it must be a juice, exuding from balsam firs and pines; Borhavo, that, like camphor, it is the crystalized oil of aromatic ferns; Berzilli, that it is the concreted scum of the lake Cephioris; and Vondendo, against scores of antagonists, stoutly held it a sort of bituminous gold, trickling from antediluvian smugglers' caves, nigh the sea."

"Why, old Braid-Beard," cried Media, placing his pipe in rest, "you are almost as erudite as our philosopher here."

"Much more so, my lord," said Babbalanja; "for Mohi has somehow picked up all my worthless forgettings, which are more than my valuable rememberings."

"What say you, wise one?" cried Mohi, shaking his braids, like an enraged elephant with many trunks.

Said Yoomy: "My lord, I have heard that amber is nothing less than the congealed tears of broken-hearted mermaids."

"Absurd, minstrel," cried Mohi. "Hark ye; I know what it is. All other authorities to the contrary, amber is nothing more than gold-fishes' brains, made waxy, then firm, by the action of the sea."

"Nonsense!" cried Yoomy.

"My lord," said Braid-Beard, waving his pipe, "this thing is just as I say. Imbedded in amber, do we not find little fishes' fins, porpoise-teeth, sea-gulls' beaks and claws; nay, butterflies' wings, and sometimes a topaz? And how could that be, unless the substance was first soft? Amber is gold-fishes' brains, I say."

"For one," said Babbalanja, "I'll not believe that, till you prove to me, Braid-Beard, that ideas themselves are found imbedded therein."

"Another of your crazy conceits, philosopher," replied Mohi, disdainfully; "yet, sometimes plenty of strange black-letter characters have been discovered in amber." And throwing back his hoary old head, he jetted forth his vapors like a whale.

"Indeed?" cried Babbalanja. "Then, my lord Media, it may be earnestly inquired, whether the gentle laws of the tribes before the flood, were not sought to be embalmed and perpetuated between transparent and sweet scented tablets of amber."

"That, now, is not so unlikely," said Mohi; "for old King Rondo the Round once set about getting him a coffin-lid of amber; much desiring a famous mass of it owned by the ancestors of Donjalolo of Juam. But no navies could buy it. So Rondo had himself urned in a crystal."

"And that immortalized Rondo, no doubt," said Babbalanja. "Ha! ha! pity he fared not like the fat porpoise frozen and tombed in an iceberg; its icy shroud drifting south, soon melted away, and down, out of sight, sunk the dead."

"Well, so much for amber," cried Media. "Now, Mohi, go on about Farnoo."

"Know, then, my lord, that Farnoo is more like ambergris than amber."

"Is it? then, pray, tell us something on that head. You know all about ambergris, too, I suppose."

"Every thing about all things, my lord. Ambergris is found both on land and at sea. But especially, are lumps of it picked up on the spicy coasts of Jovanna; indeed, all over the atolls and reefs in the eastern quarter of Mardi."

"But *what* is this ambergris? Braid-Beard," said Babbalanja.

"Aquovi, the chymist, pronounced it the fragments of mushrooms growing at the bottom of the sea; Voluto held, that like naptha, it springs from fountains down there. But it is neither."

"I have heard," said Yoomy, "that it is the honey-comb of bees, fallen from flowery cliffs into the brine."

"Nothing of the kind," said Mohi. "Do I not know all about it, minstrel? Ambergris is the petrified gall-stones of crocodiles."

"What!" cried Babbalanja, "comes sweet scented ambergris from those musky and chain-plated river cavalry? No wonder, then, their flesh is so fragrant; their upper jaws as the visors of vinaigrettes."

"Nay, you are all wrong," cried King Media.

Then, laughing to himself:—"It's pleasant to sit by, a demi-god, and hear the surmisings of mortals, upon things they know nothing about; theology, or amber, or ambergris, it's all the same. But then, did I always out with every thing I know, there would be no conversing with these comical creatures.

"Listen, old Mohi; ambergris is a morbid secretion of the Spermaceti whale; for like you mortals, the whale is at times a sort of hypochondriac and dyspeptic. You must know, subjects, that in antediluvian times, the Spermaceti whale was much hunted by sportsmen, that being accounted better pastime, than pursuing the Behemoths on shore. Besides, it was a lucrative diversion. Now, sometimes upon striking the monster, it would start off in a dastardly fright, leaving certain fragments in its wake. These fragments the hunters picked up, giving over the chase for a while. For in those days, as now, a quarter-quintal of ambergris was more valuable than a whole ton of spermaceti."

"Nor, my lord," said Babbalanja, "would it have been wise to kill the fish that dropped such treasures: no more than to murder the noddy that laid the golden eggs."

"Beshrew me! a noddy it must have been," gurgled Mohi through his pipe-stem, "to lay golden eggs for others to hatch."

"Come, no more of that now," cried Media. "Mohi, how long think you, may one of these pipe-bowls last?"

"My lord, like one's cranium, it will endure till broken. I have smoked this one of mine more than half a century."

"But unlike our craniums, stocked full of concretions," said Babbalanja, "our pipe-bowls never need clearing out."

"True," said Mohi, "they absorb the oil of the smoke, instead of allowing it offensively to incrust."

"Ay, the older the better," said Media, "and the more delicious the flavor imparted to the fumes inhaled."

"Farnoos forever! my lord," cried Yoomy. "By much smoking, the bowl waxes russet and mellow, like the berry-brown cheek of a sunburnt brunette."

"And as like smoked hams," cried Braid-Beard, "we veteran old smokers grow browner and browner; hugely do we admire to see our jolly noses and pipe-bowls mellowing together."

"Well said, old man," cried Babbalanja; "for, like a good wife, a pipe is a friend and companion for life. And whoso weds with a pipe, is no longer a bachelor. After many vexations, he may go home to that faithful counselor, and ever find it full of kind consolations and suggestions. But not thus with cigars or cigarrets: the acquaintances of a moment, chatted with in by-places, whenever they come handy; their existence so fugitive, uncertain, unsatisfactory. Once ignited, nothing like longevity pertains to them. They never grow old. Why, my lord, the stump of a cigarret is an abomination; and two of them crossed are more of a *memento-mori*, than a brace of thigh-bones at right angles."

"So they are, so they are," cried King Media. "Then, mortals, puff we away at our pipes. Puff, puff, I say. Ah! how we puff! But thus we demigods ever puff at our ease."

"Puff, puff, how we puff," cried Babbalanja. "But life itself is a puff and a wheeze. Our lungs are two pipes which we constantly smoke."

"Puff, puff! how we puff," cried old Mohi. "All thought is a puff."

"Ay," said Babbalanja, "not more smoke in that skull-bowl of yours than in the skull on your shoulders: both ends alike."

"Puff! puff! how we puff," cried Yoomy. "But in every puff, there hangs a wreath. In every puff, off flies a care."

"Ay, there they go," cried Mohi, "there goes another—and there, and there;—this is the way to get rid of them my worshipful lord; puff them aside."

"Yoomy," said Media, "give us that pipe song of thine. Sing it, my sweet and pleasant poet. We'll keep time with the flageolets of ours."

So with pipes and puffs for a chorus, thus Yoomy sang:—

> Care is all stuff:—
> Puff! Puff!
> To puff is enough:—
> Puff! Puff!

> More musky than snuff,
> And warm is a puff:—
>   Puff! Puff!
> Here we sit mid our puffs,
> Like old lords in their ruffs,
> Snug as bears in their muffs:—
>   Puff! Puff!
> Then puff, puff, puff,
> For care is all stuff,
> Puffed off in a puff:—
>   Puff! Puff!

"Ay, puff away," cried Babbalanja, "puff, puff, so we are born, and so die. Puff, puff, my volcanos: the great sun itself will yet go out in a snuff, and all Mardi smoke out its last wick."

"Puffs enough," said King Media. "Vee-Vee! haul down my flag. There, lie down before me, oh Gonfalon! and, subjects, hear,—when I die, lay this spear on my right, and this pipe on my left, its colors at half mast; so shall I be ambidexter, and sleep between eloquent symbols."

Chapter 122

They visit an extraordinary old Antiquary

ABOUT PROWS THERE, ye paddlers," cried Media. "In this fog
we've been raising, we have sailed by Padulla, our destination."
Now Padulla, was but a little island, tributary to a neighboring king;
its population embracing some hundreds of thousands of leaves, and flowers,
and butterflies, yet only two solitary mortals; one, famous as a venerable
antiquarian: a collector of objects of Mardian vertu; a cognoscenti, and
dilettante in things old and marvelous; and for that reason, very choice of
himself.

He went by the exclamatory cognomen of "Oh-Oh;" a name bestowed upon him, by reason of the delighted interjections, with which he
welcomed all accessions to his museum.

Now, it was to obtain a glimpse of this very museum, that Media was
anxious to touch at Padulla.

Landing, and passing through a grove, we were accosted by Oh-Oh
himself; who, having heard the shouts of our paddlers, had sallied forth,
staff in hand.

The old man was a sight to see; especially his nose; a remarkable one.
And all Mardi over, a remarkable nose is a prominent feature: an ever
obvious passport to distinction. For, after all, this gaining a name, is but the
individualizing of a man; as well achieved by an extraordinary nose, as by

an extraordinary epic. Far better, indeed; for you may pass poets without knowing them. Even a hero, is no hero without his sword; nor Beelzebub himself a lion, minus that lasso-tail of his, wherewith he catches his prey. Whereas, he who is famous through his nose, it is impossible to overlook. He is a celebrity without toiling for a name. Snugly ensconced behind his proboscis, he revels in its shadow, receiving tributes of attention wherever he goes.

Not to enter at large upon the topography of Oh-Oh's nasal organ, all must be content with this; that it was of a singular magnitude, and boldly aspiring at the end; an exclamation point in the face of the wearer, forever wondering at the visible universe. The eyes of Oh-Oh were like the creature's that the Jew abhors: placed slanting in his head, and converging their rays toward the mouth; which was no mouth, but a gash.

I mean not to be harsh, or unpleasant upon thee, Oh-Oh; but I must paint thee as thou wert.

The rest of his person was crooked, and dwarfed, and surmounted by a hump, that sat on his back like a burden. And a weary load is a hump, Heaven knows, only to be cast off in the grave.

Thus old, and antiquated, and gable-ended, was the tabernacle of Oh-Oh's soul. But his person was housed in as curious a structure. Built of old boughs of trees blown down in the groves, and covered over with unruly thatching, it seemed, without, some ostrich nest. But within, so intricate, and grotesque, its brown alleys and cells, that the interior of no walnut was more labyrinthine.

And here, strewn about, all dusty and disordered, were the precious antiques, and *curios*, and obsoletes, which to Oh-Oh were dear as the apple of his eye, or the memory of departed days.

The old man was exceedingly importunate, in directing attention to his relics; concerning each of which, he had an endless story to tell. Time would fail; nay, patience, to repeat his legends. So, in order, here follow the most prominent of his rarities:—

The identical Canoe, in which, ages back, the god Unja came from the bottom of the sea.
(Very ponderous; of lignum-vitæ wood).
A stone Flower-pot, containing in the original soil, Unja's last footprints, when he embarked from Mardi for parts unknown.
(One foot-print unaccountably reversed).
The Jaw-bones of Tooroorooloo, a great orator in the days of Unja.
(Somewhat twisted).

A quaint little Fish-hook.

>(Made from the finger-bones of Kravi the Cunning).

The mystic Gourd; carved all over with cabalistic triangles, and hypogriffs; by study of which a reputed prophet, was said to have obtained his inspiration.

>(Slightly redolent of vineyards).

The complete Skeleton of an immense Tiger-shark; the bones of a Pearl-shell-diver's leg inside.

>(Picked off the reef at low tide).

An inscrutable, shapeless block of a mottled-hued, smoke-dried wood.

>(Three unaccountable holes drilled through the middle).

A sort of ecclesiastical Fasces, being the bony blades of nine sword-fish, basket-hilted with shark's jaws, braided round and tasseled with cords of human hair.

>(Now obsolete).

The mystic Fan with which Unja fanned himself when in trouble.

>(Woven from the leaves of the Water-Lily).

A Tripod of a Stork's Leg, supporting a nautilus shell, containing the fragments of a bird's egg; into which, was said to have been magically decanted the soul of a deceased chief.

>(Unfortunately crushed in by atmospheric pressure).

Two clasped Right Hands, embalmed; being those of twin warriors, who thus died on a battle-field.

>(Impossible to sunder).

A curious Pouch, or Purse, formed from the skin of an Albatross' foot, and decorated with three sharp claws, naturally pertaining to it.

>(Originally the property of a notorious old Tooth-per-Tooth).

A long tangled lock of Mermaid's Hair, much resembling the curling silky fibres of the finer sea-weed.

>(Preserved between fins of the dolphin).

A Mermaid's Comb for the toilet. The stiff serrated crest of a Cock Storm-petrel.

>(Oh-Oh was particularly curious concerning Mermaids).

Files, Rasps, and Pincers, all bone, the implements of an eminent Chiropodist, who flourished his tools before the flood.

>(Owing to the excessive unevenness of the surface in those times, the diluvians were peculiarly liable to pedal afflictions).

The back Tooth, that Zozo the Enthusiast, in token of grief, recklessly knocked out at the decease of a friend.

(Worn to a stump and quite useless).

These wonders inspected, Oh-Oh conducted us to an arbor, to show
us the famous telescope, by help of which, he said he had discovered an ant-
hill in the moon. It rested in the crotch of a Bread-fruit tree; and was a
prodigiously long and hollow trunk of a Palm; a scale from a sea-kraken
its lens.

Then returning to his cabinet, he pointed to a bamboo microscope,
which had wonderfully assisted him in his entomological pursuits.

"By this instrument, my masters," said he, "I have satisfied myself,
that in the eye of a dragon-fly there are precisely twelve thousand five
hundred and forty-one triangular lenses; and in the leg of a flea, scores on
scores of distinct muscles. Now, my masters, how far think you a flea may
leap at one spring? Why, two hundred times its own length; I have often
measured their leaps, with a small measure I use for scientific purposes."

"Truly, Oh-Oh," said Babbalanja, "your discoveries must ere long
result in something grand; since you furnish such invaluable data for
theorists. Pray, attend, my lord Media. If, at one spring, a flea leaps two
hundred times its own length, then, with the like proportion of muscles in
his calves, a bandit might pounce upon the unwary traveler from a quarter
of a mile off. Is it not so, Oh-Oh?"

"Indeed, but it is, my masters. And one of the greatest consolations I
draw from these studies, is the ever-strengthening conviction of the bene-
ficent wisdom that framed our Mardi. For did men possess thighs in proportion to fleas, verily, the wicked would grievously leap about, and curvet in
the isles."

"But Oh-Oh," said Babbalanja, "what other discoveries have you
made? Hast yet put a usurer under your lens, to find his conscience? or a
libertine, to find his heart? Hast yet brought your microscope to bear
upon a downy peach, or a rosy cheek?"

"I have," said Oh-Oh, mournfully; "and from the moment I so did, I
have had no heart to eat a peach, or salute a cheek."

"Then dash your lens!" cried Media.

"Well said, my lord. For all the eyes we get beyond our own, but
minister to infelicity. The microscope disgusts us with our Mardi; and the
telescope sets us longing for some other world."

Chapter 123

They go down into the Catacombs

WITH A DULL FLAMBEAU, we now descended some narrow stone steps, to view Oh-Oh's collection of ancient and curious manuscripts, preserved in a vault.

"This way, this way, my masters," cried Oh-Oh, aloft, swinging his dim torch. "Keep your hands before you; it's a dark road to travel."

"So it seems," said Babbalanja, wide-groping, as he descended lower and lower. "My lord, this is like going down to posterity."

Upon gaining the vault, forth flew a score or two of bats, extinguishing the flambeau, and leaving us in darkness, like Belzoni deserted by his Arabs in the heart of a pyramid. The torch at last relumed, we entered a tomb-like excavation, at every step raising clouds of dust; and at last stood before long rows of musty, mummyish parcels, so dingy-red, and so rolled upon sticks, that they looked like stiff sausages of Bologna; but smelt like some fine old Stilton or Cheshire.

Most ancient of all, was a hieroglyphical Elegy on the Dumps, consisting of one thousand and one lines; the characters,—herons, weeping-willows, and ravens, supposed to have been traced by a quill from the sea-noddy.

Then there were plenty of rare old ballads:—

> "King Kroko, and the Fisher Girl."
> "The Fight at the Ford of Spears."
> "The Song of the Skulls."

And brave old chronicles, that made Mohi's mouth water:—

> "The Rise and Setting of the Dynasty of Foofoo."
> "The Heroic History of the Noble Prince Dragoni; showing how he killed ten Pinioned Prisoners with his Own Hand."
> "The whole Pedigree of the King of Kandidee, with that of his famous horse, Znorto."

And Tarantula books:—

> "Sour Milk for the Young, by a Dairyman."
> "The Devil adrift, by a Corsair."
> "Grunts and Groans, by a Mad Boar."
> "Stings, by a Scorpion."

And poetical productions:—

> "Suffusions of a Lily in a Shower."
> "Sonnet on the last Breath of an Ephemera."
> "The Gad-fly, and Other Poems."

And metaphysical treatises:—

> "Necessitarians not Predestinarians."
> "Philosophical Necessity and Predestination One Thing and The Same."
> "Whatever is not, is."
> "Whatever is, is not."

And scarce old memoirs:—

> "The One Hundred Books of the Biography of the Great and Good King Grandissimo."
> "The Life of old Philo, the Philanthropist, in one Chapter."

And popular literature:—

> "A most Sweet, Pleasant, and Unctuous Account of the Manner in which Five-and-Forty Robbers were torn asunder by Swiftly-Going Canoes."

And books by chiefs and nobles:—

> "The Art of Making a Noise in Mardi."

"On the Proper Manner of Saluting a Bosom Friend."
"Letters from a Father to a Son, inculcating the Virtue of Vice."
"Pastorals by a Younger Son."
"A Catalogue of Chieftains who have been Authors, by a Chieftain, who disdains to be deemed an Author."
"A Canto on a Cough caught by my Consort."
"The Philosophy of Honesty, by a late Lord, who died in disgrace."

And theological works:—

"Pepper for the Perverse."
"Pudding for the Pious."
"Pleas for Pardon."
"Pickles for the Persecuted."

And long and tedious romances with short and easy titles:—

"The Buck."
"The Belle."
"The King and the Cook, or the Cook and the King."

And books of voyages:—

"A Sojourn among the Anthropophagi, by One whose Hand was eaten off at Tiffin among the Savages."
"Franko: its King, Court, and Tadpoles."
"Three Hours in Vivenza, containing a Full and Impartial Account of that Whole Country: by a Subject of King Bello."

And works of nautical poets:—

"Sky-Sail-Pole Lyrics."

And divers brief books, with panic-striking titles:—

"Are you safe?"
"A Voice from Below."
"Hope for none."
"Fire for all."

And pamphlets by retired warriors:—

"On the Best Gravy for Wild Boar's Meat."
"Three Receipts for Bottling New Arrack."
"To Brown Bread Fruit without Burning."
"Advice to the Dyspeptic."
"On Starch for Tappa."

All these MSS. were highly prized by Oh-Oh. He averred, that they spoke of the mighty past, which he reverenced more than the paltry present, the dross and sediment of what had been.

Peering into a dark crypt, Babbalanja drew forth a few crumbling, illegible, black-letter sheets of his favorite old essayist, brave Bardianna. They seemed to have formed parts of a work, whose title only remained— "Thoughts, by a Thinker."

Silently Babbalanja pressed them to his heart. Then at arm's length held them, and said, "And is all this wisdom lost? Can not the divine cunning in thee, Bardianna, transmute to brightness these sullied pages? Here, perhaps, thou didst dive into the deeps of things, treating of the normal forms of matter and of mind; how the particles of solids were first molded in the interstices of fluids; how the thoughts of men are each a soul, as the lung-cells are each a lung; how that death is but a mode of life; while midmost is the Pharzi.—But all is faded. Yea, here the Thinker's thoughts lie cheek by jowl with phrasemen's words. Oh Bardianna! these pages were off-spring of thee, thought of thy thought, soul of thy soul. Instinct with mind, they once spoke out like living voices; now, they're dust; and would not prick a fool to action. Whence then is this? If the fogs of some few years can make soul linked to matter naught; how can the unhoused spirit hope to live when mildewed with the damps of death."

Piously he folded the shreds of manuscript together, kissed them, and laid them down.

Then approaching Oh-Oh, he besought him for one leaf, one shred of those most precious pages, in memory of Bardianna, and for the love of him.

But learning who he was, one of that old Ponderer's commentators, Oh-Oh tottered toward the manuscripts; with trembling fingers told them over, one by one, and said—"Thank Oro! all are here.—Philosopher, ask me for my limbs, my life, my heart, but ask me not for these. Steeped in wax, these shall be my cerements."

All in vain; Oh-Oh was an antiquary.

Turning in despair, Babbalanja spied a heap of worm-eaten parchment covers, and many clippings and parings. And whereas the rolls of manuscripts did smell like unto old cheese; so these relics did marvelously resemble the rinds of the same.

Turning over this pile, Babbalanja lighted upon something that restored his good humor. Long he looked it over delighted; but bethinking him, that he must have dragged to day some lost work of the collection, and much desirous of possessing it, he made bold again to ply Oh-Oh; offering a tempting price for his discovery.

Glancing at the title—"A Happy Life"—the old man cried—"Oh, rubbish! rubbish! take it for nothing."

And Babbalanja placed it in his vestment.

The catacombs surveyed, and day-light gained, we inquired the way to Ji-Ji's, also a collector, but of another sort; one miserly in the matter of teeth, the money of Mardi.

At the mention of his name, Oh-Oh flew out into scornful philippics upon the insanity of that old dotard, who hoarded up teeth, as if teeth were of any use, but to purchase rarities. Nevertheless, he pointed out our path; following which, we crossed a meadow.

Chapter 124

Babbalanja quotes from an antique Pagan; and earnestly presses it upon the Company, that what he recites is not his, but another's

JOURNEYING ON, we stopped by a gurgling spring, in a beautiful grove; and here, we stretched out on the grass, and our attendants unpacked their hampers, to provide us a lunch.

But as for that Babbalanja of ours, he must needs go and lunch by himself, and, like a cannibal, feed upon an author; though in other respects he was not so partial to bones.

Bringing forth the treasure he had buried in his bosom, he was soon buried in it; and motionless on his back, looked as if laid out, to keep an appointment with his undertaker.

"What, ho! Babbalanja!" cried Media from under a tree, "don't be a duck, there, with your bill in the air; drop your metaphysics, man, and fall to on the solids. Do you hear?"

"Come, philosopher," said Mohi, handling a banana, "you will weigh more after you have eaten."

"Come, list, Babbalanja," cried Yoomy, "I am going to sing."

"Up! up! I say," shouted Media again. "But go, old man, and wake him: rap on his head, and see whether he be in."

Mohi, obeying, found him at home; and Babbalanja started up.

"In Oro's name, what ails you, philosopher? See you Paradise, that you look so wildly?"

"A Happy Life! a Happy Life!" cried Babbalanja, in an ecstasy. "My lord, I am lost in the dream of it, as here recorded. Marvelous book! its goodness transports me. Let me read:—'I would bear the same mind, whether I be rich or poor, whether I get or lose in the world. I will reckon benefits well placed as the fairest part of my possession, not valuing them by number or weight, but by the profit and esteem of the receiver; accounting myself never the poorer for any thing I give. What I do shall be done for conscience, not ostentation. I will eat and drink, not to gratify my palate, but to satisfy nature. I will be cheerful to my friends, mild and placable to my enemies. I will prevent an honest request, if I can foresee it; and I will grant it, without asking. I will look upon the whole world as my country; and upon Oro, both as the witness and the judge of my words and my deeds. I will live and die with this testimony: that I loved a good conscience; that I never invaded another man's liberty; and that I preserved my own. I will govern my life and my thoughts, as if the whole world were to see the one, and to read the other; for what does it signify, to make any thing a secret to my neighbor, when to Oro all our privacies are open.' "

"Very fine," said Media.

"The very spirit of the first followers of Alma, as recorded in the legends," said Mohi.

"Inimitable," said Yoomy.

Said Babbalanja, "Listen again:—'Righteousness is sociable and gentle; free, steady, and fearless; full of inexhaustible delights.' And here again, and here, and here:—'The true felicity of life is to understand our duty to Oro.'—'True joy is a serene and sober motion.' And here, and here,—my lord, 'tis hard quoting from this book;—but listen—'A peaceful conscience, honest thoughts, and righteous actions are blessings without end, satiety, or measure. The poor man wants many things; the covetous man, all. It is not enough to know Oro, unless we obey him.' "

"Alma all over," cried Mohi; "sure, you read from his sayings?"

"I read but odd sentences from one, who though he lived ages ago, never saw, scarcely heard of Alma. And mark me, my lord, this time I improvise nothing. What I have recited, is here. Mohi, this book is more marvelous than the prophecies. My lord, that a mere man, and a heathen, in that most heathenish time, should give utterance to such heavenly wisdom, seems more wonderful than that an inspired prophet should reveal it. And is it not more divine in this philosopher, to love righteousness for its own sake, and in view of annihilation, than for pious sages to extol it as the means of everlasting felicity?"

"Alas," sighed Yoomy, "and does he not promise us any good thing, when we are dead?"

"He speaks not by authority. He but woos us to goodness and happiness here."

"Then, Babbalanja," said Media, "keep your treasure to yourself. Without authority, and a full right hand, Righteousness better be silent. Mardi's religion must seem to come direct from Oro, and the mass of you mortals endeavor it not, except for a consideration, present or to come."

"And call you that righteousness, my lord, which is but the price paid down for something else?"

"I called it not righteousness; it is religion so called. But let us prate no more of these things; with which I, a demi-god, have but little in common. It ever impairs my digestion. No more, Babbalanja."

"My lord! my lord! out of itself, Religion has nothing to bestow. Nor will she save us from aught, but from the evil in ourselves. Her one grand end is to make us wise; her only manifestations are reverence to Oro and love to man; her only, but ample reward, herself. He who has this, has all. He who has this, whether he kneel to an image of wood, calling it Oro; or to an image of air, calling it the same; whether he fasts or feasts; laughs or weeps;—that man can be no richer. And this religion, faith, virtue, right-eousness, good, whate'er you will, I find in this book I hold. No written page can teach me more."

"Have you that, then, of which you speak, Babbalanja? Are you content, there where you stand?"

"My lord, you drive me home. I am not content. The mystery of mysteries is still a mystery. How this author came to be so wise, perplexes me. How he led the life he did, confounds me. Oh, my lord, I am in dark-ness, and no broad blaze comes down to flood me. The rays that come to me are but faint cross lights, mazing the obscurity wherein I live. And after all, excellent as it is, I can be no gainer by this book. For the more we learn, the more we unlearn; we accumulate not, but substitute; and take away, more than we add. We dwindle while we grow; we sally out for wisdom, and retreat beyond the point whence we started; we essay the Fondiza, and get but the Phe. Of all simpletons, the simplest! Oh! that I were another sort of fool than I am, that I might restore my good opinion of myself. Con-tinually I stand in the pillory, am broken on the wheel, and dragged asunder by wild horses. Yes, yes, Bardianna, all is in a nut, as thou sayest; but all my back teeth can not crack it; I but crack my own jaws. All round me, my fellow men are new-grafting their vines, and dwelling in flourishing arbors; while I am forever pruning mine, till it is become but a stump. Yet in this pruning will I persist; I will not add, I will diminish; I will train myself down to the standard of what is unchangeably true. Day by day I drop off my redundancies; ere long I shall have stripped my ribs; when I die, they will but bury my spine. Ah! where, where, where, my lord, is the everlasting Tekana? Tell me, Mohi, where the Ephina? I may have come to the Penultimate, but where, sweet Yoomy, is the Ultimate? Ah, companions! I faint, I am wordless:—something,—nothing,—riddles,—does Mardi hold her?"

"He swoons!" cried Yoomy.

"Water! water!" cried Media.

"Away:" said Babbalanja serenely, "I revive."

Chapter 125

They visit a wealthy old Pauper

CONTINUING OUR ROUTE to Jiji's, we presently came to a miserable hovel. Half projecting from the low, open entrance, was a bald overgrown head, intent upon an upright row of dark-colored bags:—pelican pouches—prepared by dropping a stone within, and suspending them, when moist.

Ever and anon, the great head shook with a tremulous motion, as one by one, to a clicking sound from the old man's mouth, the strings of teeth were slowly drawn forth, and let fall, again and again, with a rattle.

But perceiving our approach, the old miser suddenly swooped his pouches out of sight; and, like a turtle into its shell, retreated into his den. But soon he decrepitly emerged upon his knees, asking what brought us thither?—to steal the teeth, which lying rumor averred he possessed in abundance? And opening his mouth, he averred he had none; not even a sentry in his head.

But Babbalanja declared, that long since he must have drawn his own dentals, and bagged them with the rest.

Now this miserable old miser must have been idiotic; for soon forgetting what he had but just told us of his utter toothlessness, he was so smitten with the pearly mouth of Hohora, one of our attendants (the same for whose pearls, little King Peepi had taken such a fancy), that he made the

391

following overture to purchase its contents: namely: one tooth of the buyer's, for every three of the seller's. A proposition promptly rejected, as involving a mercantile absurdity.

"Why?" said Babbalanja. "Doubtless, because that proposed to be given, is less than that proposed to be received. Yet, says a philosopher, this is the very principle which regulates all barterings. For where the sense of a simple exchange of quantities, alike in value?"

"Where, indeed?" said Hohora with open eyes, "though I never heard it before, that's a staggering question. I beseech you, who was the sage that asked it?"

"Vivo, the Sophist," said Babbalanja, turning aside.

In the hearing of Jiji, allusion was made to Oh-Oh, as a neighbor of his. Whereupon he vented much slavering opprobrium upon that miserable old hump-back; who accumulated useless monstrosities; throwing away the precious teeth, which otherwise might have sensibly rattled in his own pelican pouches.

When we quitted the hovel, Jiji, marking little Vee-Vee, from whose shoulder hung a calabash of edibles, seized the hem of his garment and besought him for one mouthful of food; for nothing had he tasted that day.

The boy tossed him a yam.

Chapter 126

*Yoomy sings some odd Verses, and Babbalanja quotes from
the old Authors right and left*

SAILING FROM PADULLA, after many pleasant things had been
said concerning the sights there beheld; Babbalanja thus addressed
Yoomy—"Warbler, the last song you sung was about moonlight,
and paradise, and fabulous pleasures evermore: now, have you any hymns
about earthly felicity?"

"If so, minstrel," said Media, "jet it forth, my fountain, forthwith."

"Just now, my lord," replied Yoomy, "I was singing to myself, as I
often do, and by your leave, I will continue aloud."

"Better begin at the beginning, I should think," said the chronicler,
both hands to his chin, beginning at the top to new braid his beard.

"No: like the roots of your beard, old Mohi, all beginnings are stiff,"
cried Babbalanja. "We are lucky in living midway in eternity. So sing
away, Yoomy, where you left off," and thus saying he unloosed his girdle
for the song, as Apicius would for a banquet.

"Shall I continue aloud, then, my lord?"

My lord nodded, and Yoomy sang:—

> Full round, full soft, her dewy arms,—
> Sweet shelter from all Mardi's harms!

"Whose arms?" cried Mohi.

Sang Yoomy:—
          Diving deep in the sea,
            She takes sunshine along:
          Down flames in the sea,
            As of dolphins a throng.

"What mermaid is this?" cried Mohi.

Sang Yoomy:—
          Her foot, a falling sound,
          That all day long might bound,
            Over the beach,
            The soft sand beach,
          And none would find
          A trace behind.

"And why not?" demanded Media, "why could no trace be found?"

Said Braid-Beard, "Perhaps owing, my lord, to the flatness of the mermaid's foot. But no; that can not be; for mermaids are all vertebræ below the waist."

"Your fragment is pretty good, I dare say, Yoomy," observed Media, "but as Braid-Beard hints, rather flat."

"Flat as the foot of a man with his mind made up," cried Braid-Beard. "Yoomy, did you sup on flounders last night?"

But Yoomy vouchsafed no reply, he was ten thousand leagues off in a reverie: somewhere in the Hyades perhaps.

Conversation proceeding, Braid-Beard happened to make allusion to one Rotato, a portly personage, who, though a sagacious philosopher, and very ambitious to be celebrated as such, was only famous in Mardi as the fattest man of his tribe.

Said Media, "Then, Mohi, Rotato could not pick a quarrel with Fame, since she did not belie him. Fat he was, and fat she published him."

"Right, my lord," said Babbalanja, "for Fame is not always so honest. Not seldom to be famous, is to be widely known for what you are not, says Alla-Malolla. Whence it comes, as old Bardianna has it, that for years a man may move unnoticed among his fellows; but all at once, by some chance attitude, foreign to his habit, become a trumpet-full for fools; though, in himself, the same as ever. Nor has he shown himself yet; for the entire merit of a man can never be made known; nor the sum of his demerits, if he have them. We are only known by our names; as letters sealed up, we but read each other's superscriptions.

"So with the commonalty of us Mardians. How then with those beings who every way are but too apt to be riddles. In many points the works of our great poet Vavona, now dead a thousand moons, still remain a mystery. Some call him a mystic; but wherein he seems obscure, it is, perhaps, we that are in fault; not by premeditation spoke he those archangel thoughts, which made many declare, that Vavona, after all, was but a crack-pated god, not a mortal of sound mind. But had he been less, my lord, he had seemed more. Saith Fulvi, 'Of the highest order of genius, it may be truly asserted, that to gain the reputation of superior power, it must partially disguise itself; it must come down, and then it will be applauded for soaring.' And furthermore, 'that there are those who falter in the common tongue, because they think in another; and these are accounted stutterers and stammerers.' "

"Ah! how true!" cried the Warbler.

"And what says the archangel Vavona, Yoomy, in that wonderful drama of his, 'The Souls of the Sages?'—'Beyond most barren hills, there are landscapes ravishing; with but one eye to behold; which no pencil can portray.' What wonder then, my lord, that Mardi itself is so blind. 'Mardi is a monster,' says old Bardianna, 'whose eyes are fixed in its head, like a whale's; it can see but two ways, and those comprising but a small arc of a perfect vision. Poets, heroes, and men of might, are all around this monster Mardi. But stand before me on stilts, or I will behold you not, says the monster; brush back your hair; inhale the wind largely; lucky are all men with dome-like foreheads; luckless those with pippin-heads; loud lungs are a blessing; a lion is no lion that can not roar.' Says Aldina, 'There are those looking on, who know themselves to be swifter of foot than the racers, but are confounded with the simpletons that stare.' "

"The mere carping of a disappointed cripple," cried Mohi. "His biographer states, that Aldina had only one leg."

"Braid-Beard, you are witty," said Babbalanja, adjusting his robe. "My lord, there are heroes without armies, who hear martial music in their souls."

"Why not blow their trumpets louder, then," cried Media, "that all Mardi may hear?"

"My lord Media, too, is witty, Babbalanja," said Mohi.

Breathed Yoomy, "There are birds of divinest plumage, and most glorious song, yet singing their lyrics to themselves."

Said Media, "The lark soars high, cares for no auditor, yet its sweet notes are heard here below. It sings, too, in company with myriads of mates. Your soliloquists, Yoomy, are mostly herons and owls."

Said Babbalanja, "Very clever, my lord; but think you not, there are men eloquent, who never babble in the market-place?"

"Ay, and arrant babblers at home. In few words, Babbalanja, you espouse a bad cause. Most of you mortals are peacocks; some having tails, and some not; those who have them will be sure to thrust their plumes in your face; for the rest, they will display their bald cruppers, and still screech for admiration. But when a great genius is born into Mardi, he nods, and is known."

"More wit, but, with deference, perhaps less truth, my lord. Say what you will, Fame is an accident; merit a thing absolute. But what matter? Of what available value reputation, unless wedded to power, dentals, or place? To those who render him applause, a poet's may seem a thing tangible; but to the recipient, 'tis a fantasy; the poet never so stretches his imagination, as when striving to comprehend what it is; often, he is famous without knowing it."

"At the sacred games of Lazella," said Yoomy, "slyly crowned from behind with a laurel fillet, for many hours, the minstrel Jarmi wandered about ignorant of the honors he bore. But enlightened at last, he doffed the wreath; then, holding it at arm's length, sighed forth—'Oh, ye laurels! to be visible to me, ye must be removed from my brow!' "

"And what said Botargo," cried Babbalanja, "hearing that his poems had been translated into the language of the remote island of Bertranda? —'It stirs me little; already, in merry fancies, have I dreamed of their being trilled by the blessed houris in paradise; I can only imagine the same of the damsels of Bertranda.' Says Boldo, the Materialist,—'Substances alone are satisfactory.'"

"And so thought the mercenary poet, Zenzi," said Yoomy. "Upon receiving fourteen ripe yams for a sonnet, one for every line, he said to me, —'Yoomy, I shall make a better meal upon these, than upon so many compliments.' "

"Ay," cried Babbalanja, " 'Bravos,' saith old Bardianna, 'but induce flatulency.' "

Said Media, "And do you famous mortals, then, take no pleasure in hearing your bravos?"

"Much, my good lord; at least such famous mortals, so enamored of a clamorous notoriety, as to bravo for themselves, when none else will huzza; whose whole existence is an unintermitting consciousness of self; whose very persons stand erect and self-sufficient as their infallible index, the capital letter I; who relish and comprehend no reputation but what attaches to the carcass; who would as lief be renowned for a splendid mustache, as for a splendid drama: who know not how it was that a personage, to posterity so universally celebrated as the poet Vavona, ever passed through the crowd unobserved; who deride the very thunder for making such a noise in Mardi, and yet disdain to manifest itself to the eye."

"Wax not so warm, Babbalanja; but tell us, if to his contemporaries Vavona's person was almost unknown, what satisfaction did he derive from his genius?"

"Had he not its consciousness?—an empire boundless as the West. What to him were huzzas? Why, my lord, from his privacy, the great and good Logodora sent liniment to the hoarse throats without. But what said Bardianna, when they dunned him for autographs?—'Who keeps the register of great men? who decides upon noble actions? and how long may ink last? Alas! Fame has dropped more rolls than she displays; and there are more lost chronicles, than the perished books of the historian Livella.' But what is lost forever, my lord, is nothing to what is now unseen. There are more treasures in the bowels of the earth, than on its surface."

"Ah! no gold," cried Yoomy, "but that comes from dark mines."

Said Babbalanja, " 'Bear witness, ye gods!' cries fervent old Bardianna, 'that besides disclosures of good and evil undreamed of now, there will be other, and more astounding revelations hereafter, of what has passed in Mardi unbeheld.' "

"A truce to your everlasting pratings of old Bardianna," said King Media; "why not speak your own thoughts, Babbalanja? then would your discourse possess more completeness; whereas, its warp and woof are of all sorts,—Bardianna, Alla-Malolla, Vavona, and all the writers that ever have written. Speak for yourself, mortal!"

"May you not possibly mistake, my lord? for I do not so much quote Bardianna, as Bardianna quoted me, though he flourished before me; and no vanity, but honesty to say so. The catalogue of true thoughts is but small; they are ubiquitous; no man's property; and unspoken, or bruited, are the same. When we hear them, why seem they so natural, receiving our spontaneous approval? why do we think we have heard them before? Because they but reiterate ourselves; they were in us, before we were born. The truest poets are but mouth-pieces; and some men are duplicates of each other; I see myself in Bardianna."

"And there, for Oro's sake, let it rest, Babbalanja; Bardianna in you, and you in Bardianna forever!"

Chapter 127

What manner of Men the Tapparians were

THE CANOES SAILED ON. But we leave them awhile. For our visit to Jiji, the last visit we made, suggests some further revelations concerning the dental money of Mardi.

Ere this, it should have been mentioned, that throughout the Archipelago, there was a restriction concerning incisors and molars, as ornaments for the person; none but great chiefs, brave warriors, and men distinguished by rare intellectual endowments, orators, romancers, philosophers, and poets, being permitted to sport them as jewels. Though, as it happened, among the poets there were many who had never a tooth, save those employed at their repasts; which, coming but seldom, their teeth almost corroded in their mouths. Hence, in commerce, poets' teeth were at a discount.

For these reasons, then, many mortals blent with the promiscuous mob of Mardians, who, by any means, accumulated teeth, were fain to assert their dental claims to distinction, by clumsily carrying their treasures in pelican pouches slung over their shoulders; which pouches were a huge burden to carry about, and defend. Though, in good truth, from any of these porters, it was harder to wrench his pouches, than his limbs. It was also a curious circumstance that at the slightest casual touch, these bags seemed to convey a simultaneous thrill to the owners.

Besides these porters, there were others, who exchanged their teeth for richly stained calabashes, elaborately carved canoes, and more especially, for costly robes, and turbans; in which last, many outshone the noblest-born nobles. Nevertheless, this answered not the end they had in view; some of the crowd only admiring what they wore, and not them; breaking out into laudation of the inimitable handiwork of the artisans of Mardi.

And strange to relate, these artisans themselves often came to be men of teeth and turbans, sporting their bravery with the best. A circumstance, which accounted for the fact, that many of the class above alluded to, were considered capital judges of tappa and tailoring.

Hence, as a general designation, the whole tribe went by the name of Tapparians; otherwise, Men of Tappa.

Now, many moons ago, according to Braid-Beard, the Tapparians of a certain cluster of islands, seeing themselves hopelessly confounded with the plebeian race of mortals; such as artificers, honest men, bread-fruit bakers, and the like; seeing, in short, that nature had denied them every inborn mark of distinction; and furthermore, that their external assumptions were derided by so many in Mardi, these selfsame Tapparians, poor devils, resolved to secede from the rabble; form themselves into a community of their own; and conventionally pay that homage to each other, which universal Mardi could not be prevailed upon to render to them.

Jointly, they purchased an island, called Pimminee, toward the extreme west of the lagoon; and thither they went; and framing a code of laws— amazingly arbitrary, considering they themselves were the framers— solemnly took the oath of allegiance to the commonwealth thus established. Regarded section by section, this code of laws seemed exceedingly trivial; but taken together, made a somewhat imposing aggregation of particles.

By this code, the minutest things in life were all ordered after a specific fashion. More especially one's dress was legislated upon, to the last warp and woof. All girdles must be so many inches in length, and with such a number of tassels in front. For a violation of this ordinance, before the face of all Mardi, the most dutiful of sons would cut the most affectionate of fathers.

Now, though like all Mardi, kings and slaves included, the people of Pimminee had dead dust for grandsires, they seldom reverted to that fact; for, like all founders of families, they had no family vaults. Nor were they much encumbered by living connections; connections, some of them appeared to have none. Like poor Logan the last of his tribe, they seemed to have monopolized the blood of their race, having never a cousin to own.

Wherefore it was, that many ignorant Mardians, who had not pushed

their investigations into the science of physiology, sagely divined, that the
Tapparians must have podded into life like peas, instead of being otherwise
indebted for their existence. Certain it is, they had a comical way of backing
up their social pretensions. When the respectability of his clan was mooted,
Paivai, one of their bucks, disdained all reference to the Dooms-day Book,
and the ancients. More reliable evidence was had. He referred the anxious
world to a witness, still alive and hearty,—his contemporary tailor; the
varlet who cut out his tappa doublets, and rejoiced his soul with good fits.

"Ah!" sighed Babbalanja, "how it quenches in one the thought of
immortality, to think that these Tapparians too, will hereafter claim each
a niche!"

But we rove. Our visit to Pimminee itself, will best make known the
ways of its denizens.

Chapter 128

Their adventures upon landing at Pimminee

A LONG SAIL OVER, the island of Pimminee came in sight; one
dead flat, wreathed in a thin, insipid vapor.

"My lord, why land?" said Babbalanja; "no Yillah is here."

"'Tis my humor, Babbalanja."

Said Yoomy, "Taji would leave no isle unexplored."

As we neared the beach, the atmosphere became still closer and more
languid. Much did we miss the refreshing balm which breathed in the fine
breezy air of the open lagoon. Of a slender and sickly growth seemed the
trees; in the meadows, the grass grew small and mincing.

Said Media, "Taji, from the accounts which Braid-Beard gives, there
must be much to amuse, in the ways of these Tapparians."

"Yes," said Babbalanja, "their lives are a continual farce, gratuitously
performed for the diversion of Mardi. My lord, perhaps we had best doff
our dignity, and land among them as persons of lowly condition; for then,
we shall receive more diversion, though less hospitality."

"A good proposition," said Media.

And so saying, he put off his robe for one less pretentious.

All followed suit; Yoomy doffing turban and sash; and, at last, completely metamorphosed, we looked like Hungarian gipsies.

401

Voyaging on, we entered a bay, where numbers of menials were standing in the water, engaged in washing the carved work of certain fantastic
canoes, belonging to the Tapparians, their masters.

Landing at some distance, we followed a path that soon conducted us
to a betwisted dwelling of bamboos, where, gently, we knocked for admittance. So doing, we were accosted by a servitor, his portliness all in his
calves. Marking our appearance, he monopolized the threshold, and gruffly
demanded what was wanted.

"Strangers, kind sir, fatigued with travel, and in need of refreshment
and repose."

"Then hence with ye, vagabonds!" and with an emphasis, he closed
the portal in our face.

Said Babbalanja, turning, "You perceive, my lord Media, that these
varlets take after their masters; who feed none but the well-fed, and house
none but the well-housed."

"Faith! but they furnish most rare entertainment, nevertheless," cried
Media. "Ha! ha! Taji, we had missed much, had we missed Pimminee."

As this was said, we observed, at a distance, three menials running from
seaward, as if conveying important intelligence.

Halting here and there, vainly seeking admittance at other habitations,
and receiving nothing but taunts for our pains, we still wandered on; and at
last came upon a village, toward which, those from the sea-side had been
running.

And now, to our surprise, we were accosted by an eager and servile
throng.

"Obsequious varlets," said Media, "where tarry your masters?"

"Right royal, and thrice worshipful Lord of Odo, do you take us for
our domestics? We are Tapparians, may it please your illustrious Highness;
your most humble and obedient servants. We beseech you, supereminent
Sir, condescend to visit our habitations, and partake of our cheer."

Then turning upon their attendants, "Away with ye, hounds! and set
our dwellings in order."

"How know ye me to be king?" asked Media.

"Is it not in your serene Highness's regal port, and eye?"

"'Twas their menials," muttered Mohi, "who from the paddlers in
charge of our canoes must have learned who my lord was, and published
the tidings."

After some further speech, Media made a social surrender of himself to the foremost of the Tapparians, one Nimni; who, conducting us to his abode, with much deference introduced us to a portly old Begum, and three slender damsels; his wife and daughters.

Soon, refreshments appeared:—green and yellow compounds, and divers enigmatical dainties; besides vegetable liqueurs of a strange and alarming flavor served in fragile little leaves, folded into cups, and very troublesome to handle.

Excessively thirsty, Babbalanja made bold to inquire for water; which called forth a burst of horror from the old Begum, and minor shrieks from her daughters; who declared, that the beverage to which remote reference had been made, was far too widely diffused in Mardi, to be at all esteemed in Pimminee.

"But though we seldom imbibe it," said the old Begum, ceremoniously adjusting her necklace of cowrie-shells, "we occasionally employ it for medicinal purposes."

"Ah, indeed?" said Babbalanja.

"But oh! believe me; even then, we imbibe not the ordinary fluid of the springs and streams; but that which in afternoon showers softly drains from our palm-trees into the little hollow or miniature reservoir beneath its compacted roots."

A goblet of this beverage was now handed Babbalanja; but having a curious, gummy flavor, it proved any thing but palatable.

Presently, in came a company of young men, relatives of Nimni. They were slender as sky-sail-poles; standing in a row, resembled a picket-fence; and were surmounted by enormous heads of hair, combed out all round, variously dyed, and evened by being singed with a lighted wisp of straw. Like milliners' parcels, they were very neatly done up; wearing redolent robes.

"How like the woodlands they smell," whispered Yoomy.

"Ay, marvelously like sap," said Mohi.

One part of their garniture consisted of numerous tasseled cords, like those of an aigulette, depending from the neck, and attached here and there about the person. A separate one, at a distance, united their ankles. These served to measure and graduate their movements; keeping their gestures, paces, and attitudes, within the prescribed standard of Tapparian gentility. When they went abroad, they were preceded by certain footmen; who placed before them small, carved boards, whereon their masters stepped; thus avoiding contact with the earth. The simple device of a shoe, as a fixture for the foot, was unknown in Pimminee.

Being told, that Taji was lately from the sun, they manifested not the slightest surprise; one of them incidentally observing, however, that the eclipses there, must be a sad bore to endure.

Chapter 129

A, I, and O

THE OLD BEGUM went by the euphonious appellation of Ohiro-Moldona-Fivona; a name, from its length, deemed highly genteel; though scandal averred, that it was nothing more than her real name transposed; the appellation by which she had been formerly known, signifying a "Getter-up-of-Fine-Tappa." But as this would have let out an ancient secret, it was thought wise to disguise it.

Her daughters respectively reveled in the pretty diminutives of A, I, and O; which, from their brevity, comical to tell, were considered equally genteel with the dame's.

The habiliments of the three Vowels must not be omitted. Each damsel garrisoned an ample, circular farthingale of canes, serving as the framework, whereon to display a gayly dyed robe. Perhaps their charms intrenched themselves in these impregnable petticoats, as feeble armies fly to fortresses, to hide their weakness, and better resist an onset.

But polite and politic it is, to propitiate your hostess. So seating himself by the Begum, Taji led off with earnest inquiries after her welfare. But the Begum was one of those, who relieve the diffident from the embarrassment of talking; all by themselves carrying on conversation for two. Hence, no wonder that my Lady was esteemed invaluable at all assemblies in the groves

of Pimminee; contributing so largely to that incessant din, which is held
the best test of the enjoyment of the company, as making them deaf to the
general nonsense, otherwise audible.

Learning that Taji had been making the tour of certain islands in Mardi,
the Begum was surprised that he could have thus hazarded his life among
the barbarians of the East. She desired to know whether his constitution
was not impaired by inhaling the unrefined atmosphere of those remote
and barbarous regions. For her part, the mere thought of it made her faint
in her innermost citadel; nor went she ever abroad with the wind at East,
dreading the contagion which might lurk in the air.

Upon accosting the three damsels, Taji very soon discovered that the
tongue which had languished in the presence of the Begum, was now
called into active requisition, to entertain the Polysyllables, her daughters.
So assiduously were they occupied in silent endeavors to look sentimental
and pretty, that it proved no easy task to sustain with them an ordinary
chat. In this dilemma, Taji diffused not his remarks among all three; but
discreetly centered them upon O. Thinking she might be curious concerning the sun, he made some remote allusion to that luminary as the place of
his nativity. Upon which, O inquired where that country was, of which
mention was made.

"Some distance from here; in the air above; the sun that gives light to
Pimminee, and Mardi at large."

She replied, that if that were the case, she had never beheld it; for such
was the construction of her farthingale, that her head could not be thrown
back, without impairing its set. Wherefore, she had always abstained from
astronomical investigations.

Hereupon, rude Mohi laughed out. And that lucky laugh happily relieved Taji from all further necessity of entertaining the Vowels. For at so
vulgar, and in Pimminee, so unwonted a sound, as a genuine laugh, the
three startled nymphs fainted away in a row, their round farthingales falling
over upon each other, like a file of empty tierces. But they presently revived.

Meanwhile, without stirring from their mats, the polite young bucks
in the aigulettes did nothing but hold semi-transparent leaves to their eyes,
by the stems; which leaves they directed downward, toward the disordered
hems of the farthingales; in wait, perhaps, for the revelation of an ankle,
and its accompaniments. What the precise use of these leaves could have
been, it would be hard to say, especially as the observers invariably peeped
over and under them.

The calamity of the Vowels was soon followed by the breaking up of the party; when, evening coming on, and feeling much wearied with the labor of seeing company in Pimminee, we retired to our mats; there finding that repose which ever awaits the fatigued.

Chapter 130

A Reception day at Pimminee

NEXT MORNING, Nimni apprized us, that throughout the day he proposed keeping open house, for the purpose of enabling us to behold whatever of beauty, rank, and fashion, Pimminee could boast; including certain strangers of note from various quarters of the lagoon, who doubtless would honor themselves with a call.

As inmates of the mansion, we unexpectedly had a rare opportunity of witnessing the final toilets of the Begum and her daughters, preparatory to receiving their guests.

Their four farthingales were placed standing in the middle of the dwelling; when their future inmates, arrayed in rudimental vestments, went round and round them, attaching various articles of finery, dyed scarfs, ivory trinkets, and other decorations. Upon the propriety of this or that adornment, the three Vowels now and then pondered apart, or together consulted. They talked and they laughed; they were silent and sad; now merry at their bravery; now pensive at the thought of the charms to be hidden.

It was O who presently suggested the expediency of an artful fold in their draperies, by the merest accident in Mardi, to reveal a tantalizing glimpse of their ankles, which were thought to be pretty.

But the old Begum was more active than any; by far the most disinterested in the matter of advice. Her great object seemed to be to pile on the finery at all hazards; and she pointed out many as yet vacant and unappropriated spaces, highly susceptible of adornment.

At last, all was in readiness; when, taking a valedictory glance, at their intrenchments, the Begum and damsels simultaneously dipped their heads, directly after emerging from the summit, all ready for execution.

And now to describe the general reception that followed. In came the Roes, the Fees, the Lol-Lols, the Hummee-Hums, the Bidi-Bidies, and the Dedidums; the Peenees, the Yamoyamees, the Karkies, the Fanfums, the Diddledees, and the Fiddlefies; in a word, all the aristocracy of Pimminee; people with exceedingly short names; and some all name, and nothing else. It was an imposing array of sounds; a circulation of ciphers; a marshaling of tappas; a getting together of grimaces and furbelows; a masquerade of vapidities.

Among the crowd was a bustling somebody, one Gaddi, arrayed in much apparel to little purpose; who, singling out Babbalanja, for some time adhered to his side, and with excessive complaisance, enlightened him as to the people assembled.

"*That* is rich Marmonora, accounted a mighty man in Pimminee; his bags of teeth included, he is said to weigh upwards of fourteen stone; and is much sought after by tailors for his measure, being but slender in the region of the heart. His riches are great. And that old vrow is the widow Roo; very rich; plenty of teeth; but has none in her head. And *this* is Finfi; said to be not very rich, and a maid. Who would suppose she had ever beat tappa for a living?"

And so saying, Gaddi sauntered off; his place by Babbalanja's side being immediately supplied by the damsel Finfi. That vivacious and amiable nymph at once proceeded to point out the company, where Gaddi had left off; beginning with Gaddi himself, who, she insinuated, was a mere parvenu, a terrible infliction upon society, and not near so rich as he was imagined to be.

Soon we were accosted by one Nonno, a sour, saturnine personage. "I know nobody here; not a soul have I seen before; I wonder who they all are." And just then he was familiarly nodded to by nine worthies abreast. Whereupon Nonno vanished. But after going the rounds of the company, and paying court to many, he again sauntered by Babbalanja, saying, "Nobody, nobody; nobody but nobodies; I see nobody I know."

Advancing, Nimni now introduced many strangers of distinction, parading their titles after a fashion, plainly signifying that he was bent upon convincing us, that there were people present at this little affair of his, who were men of vast reputation; and that we erred, if we deemed him unaccustomed to the society of the illustrious.

But not a few of his magnates seemed shy of Media and their laurels. Especially a tall robustious fellow, with a terrible javelin in his hand, much notched and splintered, as if it had dealt many a thrust. His left arm was gallanted in a sling, and there was a patch upon his sinister eye. Him Nimni made known as a famous captain, from King Piko's island (of which anon) who had been all but mortally wounded somewhere, in a late desperate though nameless encounter.

"Ah," said Media as this redoubtable withdrew, "Fofi is a cunning knave; a braggart, driven forth, by King Piko for his cowardice. He has blent his tattooing into one mass of blue, and thus disguised, must have palmed himself off here in Pimminee, for the man he is not. But I see many more like him."

"Oh ye Tapparians," said Babbalanja, "none so easily humbugged as humbugs. Taji: to behold this folly makes one wise. Look, look; it is all round us. Oh Pimminee, Pimminee!"

Chapter 131

Babbalanja falleth upon Pimminee Tooth and Nail

THE LEVEE OVER, waiving further civilities, we took courteous leave of the Begum and Nimni, and proceeding to the beach, very soon were embarked.

When all were pleasantly seated beneath the canopy, pipes in full blast, calabashes revolving, and the paddlers quietly urging us along, Media proposed that, for the benefit of the company, some one present, in a pithy, whiffy sentence or two, should sum up the character of the Tapparians; and ended by nominating Babbalanja to that office.

"Come, philosopher: let us see in how few syllables you can put the brand on those Tapparians."

"Pardon me, my lord, but you must permit me to ponder awhile; nothing requires more time, than to be brief. An example: they say that in conversation old Bardianna dealt in nothing but trisyllabic sentences. His talk was thunder peals: sounding reports, but long intervals."

"The devil take old Bardianna. And would that the grave-digger had buried his Ponderings, along with his other remains. Can none be in your company, Babbalanja, but you must perforce make them hob-a-nob with that old prater? A brand for the Tapparians! that is what we seek."

"You shall have it, my lord. Full to the brim of themselves, for that reason, the Tapparians are the emptiest of mortals."

"A good blow and well planted, Babbalanja."

"In sooth, a most excellent saying; it should be carved upon his tombstone," said Mohi, slowly withdrawing his pipe.

"What! would you have my epitaph read thus:—'Here lies the emptiest of mortals, who was full of himself?' At best, your words are exceedingly ambiguous, Mohi."

"Now have I the philosopher," cried Yoomy, with glee. "What did some one say to me, not long since, Babbalanja, when in the matter of that sleepy song of mine, Braid-Beard bestowed upon me an equivocal compliment? Was I not told to wrest commendation from it, though I tortured it to the quick?"

"Take thy own pills, philosopher," said Mohi.

"Then would he be a great original," said Media.

"Tell me, Yoomy," said Babbalanja, "are you not in fault? Because I sometimes speak wisely, you must not imagine that I should always act so."

"I never imagined that," said Yoomy, "and, if I did, the truth would belie me. It is you who are in fault, Babbalanja; not I, craving your pardon."

"The minstrel's sides are all edges to-day," said Media.

"This, then, thrice gentle Yoomy, is what I would say;" resumed Babbalanja, "that since we philosophers bestow so much wisdom upon others, it is not to be wondered at, if now and then we find what is left in us too small for our necessities. It is from our very abundance that we want."

"And from the fool's poverty," said Media, "that he is opulent; for his very simplicity, is sometimes of more account than the wisdom of the sage. But we were discoursing of the Tapparians. Babbalanja: sententiously you have acquitted yourself to admiration; now amplify, and tell us more of the people of Pimminee."

"My lord, I might amplify forever."

"Then, my worshipful lord, let him not begin," interposed Braid-Beard.

"I mean," said Babbalanja, "that all subjects are inexhaustible, however trivial; as the mathematical point, put in motion, is capable of being produced into an infinite line."

"But forever extending into nothing," said Media. "A very bad example to follow. Do you, Babbalanja, come to the point, and not travel off with it, which is too much your wont."

"Since my lord insists upon it then, thus much for the Tapparians, though but a thought or two of many in reserve. They ignore the rest of

Mardi, while they themselves are but a rumor in the isles of the East; where the business of living and dying goes on with the same uniformity, as if there were no Tapparians in existence. They think themselves Mardi in full; whereas, by the mass, they are stared at as prodigies; exceptions to the law, ordaining that no Mardian shall undertake to live, unless he set out with at least the average quantity of brains. For these Tapparians have no brains. In lieu, they carry in one corner of their craniums, a drop or two of attar of roses; charily used, the supply being small. They are the victims of two incurable maladies: stone in the heart, and ossification of the head. They are full of fripperies, fopperies, and finesses; knowing not, that nature should be the model of art. Yet, they might appear less silly than they do, were they content to be the plain idiots which at bottom they are. For there be grains of sense in a simpleton, so long as he be natural. But what can be expected from them? They are irreclaimable Tapparians; not so much fools by contrivance of their own, as by an express, though inscrutable decree of Oro's. For one, my lord, I can not abide them."

Nor could Taji.

In Pimminee were no hilarious running and shouting: none of the royal good cheer of old Borabolla; none of the mysteries of Maramma; none of the sentiment and romance of Donjalolo; no rehearsing of old legends: no singing of old songs; no life; no jolly commotion: in short, no men and women; nothing but their integuments; stiff trains and farthingales.

Chapter 132

Babbalanja regales the Company with some Sandwiches

I T WAS NIGHT. But the moon was brilliant, far and near illuminating
the lagoon.
    Over silvery billows we glided.
    "Come Yoomy," said Media, "moonlight and music for aye—a song!
a song! my bird of paradise."
    And folding his arms, and watching the sparkling waters, thus Yoomy
sang:—

> A ray of the moon on the dancing waves
>   Is the step, light step of that beautiful maid:
> Mardi, with music, her footfall paves,
>   And her voice, no voice, but a song in the glade.

    "Hold!" cried Media, "yonder is a curious rock. It looks black as a
whale's hump in blue water, when the sun shines."
    "That must be the Isle of Fossils," said Mohi. "Ay, my lord, it is."
    "Let us land, then," said Babbalanja.
    And none dissenting, the canoes were put about, and presently we de-
barked.
    It was a dome-like surface, here and there fringed with ferns, sprouting

from clefts. But at every tide the thin soil seemed gradually washing into the lagoon.

Like antique tablets, the smoother parts were molded in strange devices:—Luxor marks, Tadmor ciphers, Palenque inscriptions. In long lines, as on Denderah's architraves, were bas-reliefs of beetles, turtles, ant-eaters, armadilloes, guanos, serpents, tongueless crocodiles:—a long procession, frosted and crystalized in stone, and silvered by the moon.

"Strange sight!" cried Media. "Speak, antiquarian Mohi."

But the chronicler was twitching his antiquarian beard, nonplussed by these wondrous records. The cowled old father, Piaggio, bending over his calcined Herculanean manuscripts, looked not more at fault than he.

Said Media, "Expound *you*, then, sage Babbalanja."

Muffling his face in his mantle, and his voice in sepulchral tones, Babbalanja thus:—

"These are the leaves of the book of Oro. Here we read how worlds are made; here read the rise and fall of Nature's kingdoms. From where this old man's furthest histories start, these unbeginning records end. These are the secret memoirs of times past; whose evidence, at last divulged, gives the grim lie to Mohi's gossipings, and makes a rattling among the dry-bone relics of old Maramma."

Braid-Beard's old eyes flashed fire. With bristling beard, he cried, "Take back the lie you send!"

"Peace! everlasting foes," cried Media, interposing, with both arms outstretched. "Philosopher, probe not too deep. All you say is very fine, but very dark. I would know something more precise. But, prithee, ghost, unmuffle! chatter no more! wait till you're buried for that."

"Ay, death's cold ague will set us all shivering, my lord. We'll swear our teeth are icicles."

"Will you quit driving your sleet upon us? have done: expound these rocks."

"My lord, if you desire, I'll turn over these stone tablets till they're dog-eared."

"Heaven and Mardi!—Go on, Babbalanja."

"'Twas thus. These were tombs burst open by volcanic throes; and hither hurled from the lowermost vaults of the lagoon. All Mardi's rocks are one wide resurrection. But look. Here, now, a pretty story's told. Ah, little thought these grand old lords, that lived and roared before the flood, that they would come to this. Here, King Media, look and learn."

He looked; and saw a picture petrified, and plain as any on the pediments of Petra.

It seemed a stately banquet of the dead, where lords in skeletons were ranged around a board heaped up with fossil fruits, and flanked with vit-reous vases, grinning like empty skulls. There they sat, exchanging rigid courtesies. One's hand was on his stony heart; his other pledged a lord who held a hollow beaker. Another sat, with earnest face beneath a mitred brow. He seemed to whisper in the ear of one who listened trustingly. But on the chest of him who wore the miter, an adder lay, close-coiled in flint.

At the further end, was raised a throne, its canopy surmounted by a crown, in which now rested the likeness of a raven on an egg.

The throne was void. But half-concealed by drapery, behind the good-liest lord, sideway leaned a figure diademed, a lifted poniard in its hand:— a monarch fossilized in very act of murdering his guest.

"Most high and sacred majesty!" cried Babbalanja, bowing to his feet.

While all stood gazing on this sight, there came two servitors of Media's, who besought of Babbalanja to settle a dispute, concerning certain tracings upon the islet's other side.

Thither we followed them.

Upon a long layer of the slaty stone were marks of ripplings of some now waveless sea; mid which were tri-toed foot-prints of some huge heron, or wading fowl.

Pointing to one of which, the foremost disputant thus spoke:—"I main-tain that these are three toes."

"And I, that it is one foot," said the other.

"And now decide between us," joined the twain.

Said Babbalanja, starting, "Is not this the very question concerning which they made such dire contention in Maramma, whose tertiary rocks are chiseled all over with these marks? Yes; this it is, concerning which they once shed blood. This it is, concerning which they still divide."

"Which of us is right?" again demanded the impatient twain.

"Unite, and both are right; divide, and both are wrong. Every unit is made up of parts, as well as every plurality. Nine is three threes; a unit is as many thirds; or, if you please, a thousand thousandths; no special need to stop at thirds."

"Away, ye foolish disputants!" cried Media. "Full before you is the thing disputed."

Strolling on, many marvels did we mark; and Media said:—"Babba-lanja, you love all mysteries; here's a fitting theme. You have given us the history of the rock; can your sapience tell the origin of all the isles? how Mardi came to be?"

"Ah, that once mooted point is settled. Though hard at first, it proved a bagatelle. Start not my lord; there are those who have measured Mardi by perch and pole, and with their wonted lead sounded its utmost depths. Listen: it is a pleasant story. The coral wall which circumscribes the isles but continues upward the deep buried crater of the primal chaos. In the first times this crucible was charged with vapors nebulous, boiling over fires volcanic. Age by age, the fluid thickened; dropping, at long intervals, heavy sediment to the bottom; which layer on layer concreted, and at length, in crusts, rose toward the surface. Then, the vast volcano burst; rent the whole mass; upthrew the ancient rocks; which now in divers mountain tops tell tales of what existed ere Mardi was completely fashioned. Hence many fossils on the hills, whose kith and kin still lurk beneath the vales. Thus Nature works, at random warring, chaos a crater, and this world a shell."

Mohi stroked his beard.

Yoomy yawned.

Media cried, "Preposterous!"

"My lord, then take another theory—which you will—the celebrated sandwich System. Nature's first condition was a soup, wherein the agglomerating solids formed granitic dumplings, which, wearing down, deposited the primal stratum made up of series, sandwiching strange shapes of mollusks, and zoophytes; then snails, and periwinkles:—marmalade to sip, and nuts to crack, ere the substantials came.

"And next, my lord, we have the fine old time of the Old Red Sandstone sandwich, clapped on the underlying layer, and among other dainties, imbedding the first course of fish,—all quite in rule,—sturgeon-forms, cephalaspis, glyptolepis, pterichthys; and other finny things, of flavor rare, but hard to mouth for bones. Served up with these, were sundry greens,—lichens, mosses, ferns, and fungi.

"Now comes the New Red Sandstone sandwich: marly and magnesious, spread over with old patriarchs of crocodiles and alligators,—hard carving these,—and prodigious lizards, spine-skewered, tails tied in bows, and swimming in saffron sauces."

"What next?" cried Media.

"The Ool, or Oily sandwich:—rare gormandizing then; for oily it was called, because of fat old joints, and hams, and rounds, and barons of sea-beeves and walrusses, which then crowned the stratum-board. All piled together, glorious profusion!—fillets and briskets, rumps, and saddles, and haunches; shoulder to shoulder, loin 'gainst sirloin, ribs rapping knuckles, and quarter to none. And all these sandwiched right over all that went before. Course after course, and course on course, my lord; no time to clear the wreck; no stop nor let; lay on and slash; cut, thrust, and come.

"Next the Chalk, or Coral sandwich; but no dry fare for that; made up of rich side-courses,—eocene, miocene, and pliocene. The first was wild game for the delicate,—bantam larks, curlews, quails, and flying weazels; with a slight sprinkling of pilaus,—capons, pullets, plovers, and garnished with petrels' eggs. Very savory, that, my lord. The second side-course— miocene—was out of course, flesh after fowl:—marine mammalia,—seals, grampuses, and whales, served up with sea-weed on their flanks, hearts and kidneys deviled, and fins and flippers fricasseed. All very nice, my lord. The third side-course, the pliocene, was goodliest of all:—whole-roasted elephants, rhinoceroses, and hippopotamuses, stuffed with boiled ostriches, condors, cassowaries, turkeys. Also barbacued mastodons and megathe- riums, gallantly served up with fir-trees in their mouths, and tails cock- billed.

"Thus fared the old diluvians: arrant gormandizers and beef-bolters. We Mardians famish on the superficial strata of deposits; cracking our jaws on walnuts, filberts, cocoa-nuts, and clams. My lord, I've done."

"And bravely done it is. Mohi tells us, that Mardi was made in six days; but you, Babbalanja, have built it up from the bottom in less than six minutes."

"Nothing for us geologists, my lord. At a word we turn you out whole systems, suns, satellites, and asteroids included. Why, my good lord, my friend Annonimo is laying out a new Milky Way, to intersect with the old one, and facilitate cross-cuts among the comets."

And so saying, Babbalanja turned aside.

Chapter 133

They still remain upon the Rock

"GOGLE-GOGGLE, fugle-fi, fugle-fogle-orum," so hummed to himself Babbalanja, slowly pacing over the fossils.

"Is he crazy again?" whispered Yoomy.

"Are you crazy, Babbalanja?" asked Media.

"From my very birth have I been so, my lord; am I not possessed by a devil?"

"Then I'll e'en interrogate him," cried Media.—"Hark ye, sirrah;—why rave you thus in this poor mortal?"

" 'Tis he, not I. I am the mildest devil that ever entered man; in propria persona, no antlers do I wear; my tail has lost its barb, as at last your Mardian lions lose their caudal horns."

"A very sing-song devil this. But, prithee, who are you, sirrah?"

"The mildest devil that ever entered man; in propria persona, no antlers do I wear; my tail has lost its barb, as at last your Mardian lions lose their caudal horns."

"A very iterating devil this. Sirrah! mock me not. Know you aught yet unrevealed by Babbalanja?"

"Many things I know, not good to tell; whence they call me Azzageddi."

"A very confidential devil, this; that tells no secrets. Azzageddi, can I drive thee out?"

419

"Only with this mortal's ghost:—together we came in, together we depart."

"A very terse, and ready devil, this. Whence come you, Azzageddi?"

"Whither my catechist must go—a torrid clime, cut by a hot equator."

"A very keen, and witty devil, this. Azzageddi, whom have you there?"

"A right down merry, jolly set, that at a roaring furnace sit and toast their hoofs for aye; so used to flames, they poke the fire with their horns, and light their tails for torches."

"A very funny devil, this. Azzageddi, is not Mardi a place far pleasanter, than that from whence you came?"

"Ah, home! sweet, sweet, home! would, would that I were home again!"

"A very sentimental devil, this. Azzageddi, would you had a hand,—I'd shake it."

"Not so with us; who, rear to rear, shake each other's tails, and courteously inquire, 'Pray, worthy sir, how now stands the great thermometer?'"

"The very prince of devils, this."

"How mad our Babbalanja is," cried Mohi. "My lord, take heed; he'll bite."

"Alas! alas!" sighed Yoomy.

"Hark ye, Babbalanja," cried Media, "enough of this: doff your devil, and be a man."

"My lord, I can not doff him; but I'll down him for a time: Azzageddi! down, imp; down, down, down! so: now, my lord, I'm only Babbalanja."

"Shall I test his sanity, my lord?" cried Mohi.

"Do, old man."

"Philosopher, our great reef is surrounded by an ocean; what think you lies beyond?"

"Alas!" sighed Yoomy, "the very subject to renew his madness."

"Peace, minstrel!" said Media. "Answer, Babbalanja."

"I will, my lord. Fear not, sweet Yoomy; you see how calm I am. Braid-Beard, those strangers, that came to Mondoldo prove isles afar, as a philosopher of old surmised, but was hooted at for his surmisings. Nor is it at all impossible, Braid-Beard, that beyond their land may exist other regions, of which those strangers know not; peopled with races something like us Mardians; but perhaps with more exalted faculties, and organs that we lack. They may have some better seeing sense than ours; perhaps, have fins or wings for arms."

"This seems not like sanity," muttered Mohi.

"A most crazy hypothesis, truly," said Media.

"And are all inductions vain?" cried Babbalanja. "Have we mortals naught to rest on, but what we see with eyes? Is no faith to be reposed in that inner microcosm, wherein we see the charted universe in little, as the whole horizon is mirrored in the iris of a gnat? Alas! alas! my lord, is there no blest Odonphi? no Astrazzi?"

"His devil's uppermost again, my lord," cried Braid-Beard.

"He's stark, stark mad!" sighed Yoomy.

"Ay, the moon's at full," said Media. "Ho, paddlers! we depart."

Chapter 134

Behind and Before

I T WAS YET MOONLIGHT when we pushed from the islet. But
soon, the sky grew dun; the moon went into a cavern among the
clouds; and by that secret sympathy between our hearts and the elements, the thoughts of all but Media became overcast.

Again discourse was had of that dark intelligence from Mondoldo,—
the fell murder of Taji's follower.

Said Mohi, "Those specter sons of Aleema must have been the assassins."

"They harbored deadly malice," said Babbalanja.

"Which poor Jarl's death must now have sated," sighed Yoomy.

"Then all the happier for Taji," said Media. "But away with gloom!
because the sky is clouded, why cloud your brows? Babbalanja, I grieve
the moon is gone. Yet start some paradox, that we may laugh. Say a woman
is a man, or you yourself a stork."

At this they smiled. When hurtling came an arrow, which struck our
stern, and quivered. Another! and another! Grazing the canopy, they darted
by, and hissing, dived like red-hot bars beneath the waves.

Starting, we beheld a corruscating wake, tracking the course of a low
canoe, far flying for a neighboring mountain. The next moment it was lost
within the mountain's shadow and pursuit was useless.

"Let us fly!" cried Yoomy.

"Peace! What murderers these?" said Media, calmly; "whom can they seek?—you, Taji?"

"The three avengers fly three bolts," said Babbalanja.

"See if the arrow yet remain astern," cried Media.

They brought it to him.

"By Oro! Taji on the barb!"

"Then it missed its aim. But I will not mine. And whatever arrows follow, still will I hunt on. Nor does the ghost, that these pale specters would avenge, at all disquiet me. The priest I slew, but to gain her, now lost; and I would slay again, to bring her back. Ah, Yillah! Yillah."

All started.

Then said Babbalanja, "Aleema's sons raved not; 'tis true, then, Taji, that an evil deed gained you your Yillah: no wonder she is lost."

Said Media, unconcernedly, "Perhaps better, Taji, to have kept your secret; but tell no more; I care not to be your foe."

"Ah, Taji! I had shrank from you," cried Yoomy, "but for the mark upon your brow. That undoes the tenor of your words. But look, the stars come forth, and who are these? A waving Iris! ay, again they come:— Hautia's heralds!"

They brought a black thorn, buried in withered rose-balm blossoms, red and blue.

Said Yoomy, "For that which stings, there is no cure."

"Who, who is Hautia, that she stabs me thus?"

"And this wild sardony mocks your misery."

"Away! ye fiends."

"Again a Venus car; and lo! a wreath of strawberries!—Yet fly to me, and be garlanded with joys."

"Let the wild witch laugh. She moves me not. Neither hurtling arrows nor Circe flowers appall."

Said Yoomy, "They wait reply."

"Tell your Hautia, that I know her not; nor care to know. I defy her incantations; she lures in vain. Yillah! Yillah! still I hope!"

Slowly they departed; heeding not my cries no more to follow.

Silence, and darkness fell.

Chapter 135

Babbalanja discourses in the Dark

NEXT DAY CAME AND WENT; and still we onward sailed. At last, by night, there fell a calm, becalming the water of the wide lagoon, and becalming all the clouds in heaven, vailing the constellations. But though our sails were useless, our paddlers plied their broad stout blades. Thus sweeping by a rent and hoar old rock, Vee-Vee, impatient of the calm, sprang to his crow's nest in the shark's mouth, and seizing his conch, sounded a blast which ran in and out among the hollows, reverberating with the echoes.

Be sure, it was startling. But more so with respect to one of our paddlers, upon whose shoulders, elevated Vee-Vee, his balance lost, all at once came down by the run. But the heedless little bugler himself was most injured by the fall; his arm nearly being broken.

Some remedies applied, and the company grown composed, Babbalanja thus:—"My lord Media, was there any human necessity for that accident?"

"None that I know, or care to tell, Babbalanja."

"Vee-Vee," said Babbalanja, "did you fall on purpose?"

"Not I," sobbed little Vee-Vee, slinging his ailing arm in its mate.

"Woe! woe to us all, then," cried Babbalanja; "for what direful events may be in store for us which we can not avoid."

"How now, mortal?" cried Media; "what now?"

"My lord, think of it. Minus human inducement from without, and minus volition from within, Vee-Vee has met with an accident, which has almost maimed him for life. Is it not terrifying to think of? Are not all mortals exposed to similar, nay, worse calamities, ineffably unavoidable? Woe, woe, I say, to us Mardians! Here, take my last breath; let me give up this beggarly ghost!"

"Nay," said Media; "pause, Babbalanja. Turn it not adrift prematurely. Let it house till midnight; the proper time for you mortals to dissolve. But, philosopher, if you harp upon Vee-Vee's mishap, know that it was owing to nothing but his carelessness."

"And what was that owing to, my lord?"

"To Vee-Vee himself."

"Then, my lord, what brought such a careless being into Mardi?"

"A long course of generations. He's some one's great-great-grandson, doubtless; who was great-great-grandson to some one else; who also had grandsires."

"Many thanks then to your highness; for you establish the doctrine of Philosophical Necessity."

"No. I establish nothing; I but answer your questions."

"All one, my lord: you are a Necessitarian; in other words, you hold that every thing takes place through absolute necessity."

"Do you take me, then, for a fool, and a Fatalist? Pardie! a bad creed for a monarch, the distributor of rewards and punishments."

"Right there, my lord. But, for all that, your highness is a Necessitarian, yet no Fatalist. Confound not the distinct. Fatalism presumes express and irrevocable edicts of heaven concerning particular events. Whereas, Necessity holds that all events are naturally linked, and inevitably follow each other, without providential interposition, though by the eternal letting of Providence."

"Well, well, Babbalanja, I grant it all. Go on."

"On high authority, we are told that in times past the fall of certain nations in Mardi was prophesied of seers."

"Most true, my lord," said Mohi; "it is all down in the chronicles."

"Ha! ha!" cried Media. "Go on, philosopher."

Continued Babbalanja, "Previous to the time assigned to their fulfillment, those prophecies were bruited through Mardi; hence, previous to the time assigned to their fulfillment, full knowledge of them may have come to the nations concerned. Now, my lord, was it possible for those nations, thus forwarned, so to conduct their affairs, as at the prophesied time, to prove false the events revealed to be in store for them?"

"However that may be," said Mohi, "certain it is, those events did assuredly come to pass:—Compare the ruins of Babbelona with book ninth, chapter tenth, of the chronicles. Yea, yea, the owl inhabits where the seers predicted; the jackals yell in the tombs of the kings."

"Go on, Babbalanja," said Media. "Of course those nations could not have resisted their doom. Go on, then: vault over your premises."

"If it be, then, my lord, that—"

"My very worshipful lord," interposed Mohi, "is not our philosopher getting off soundings; and may it not be impious to meddle with these things?"

"Were it so, old man, he should have known it. The king of Odo is something more than you mortals."

"But are we the great gods themselves," cried Yoomy, "that we discourse of these things?"

"No, minstrel," said Babbalanja; "and no need have the great gods to discourse of things perfectly comprehended by them, and by themselves ordained. But you and I, Yoomy, are men, and not gods; hence is it for us, and not for them, to take these things for our themes. Nor is there any impiety in the right use of our reason, whatever the issue. Smote with superstition, shall we let it wither and die out, a dead limb to a live trunk, as the mad devotee's arm held up motionless for years? Or shall we employ it but for a paw, to help us to our bodily needs, as the brutes use their instinct? Is not reason subtle as quicksilver—live as lightning—a neighing charger to advance, but a snail to recede? Can we starve that noble instinct in us, and hope that it will survive? Better slay the body than the soul; and if it be the direst of sins to be the murderers of our own bodies, how much more to be a soul-suicide. Yoomy, we are men, we are angels. And in his faculties, high Oro is but what a man would be, infinitely magnified. Let us aspire to all things. Are we babes in the woods, to be scared by the shadows of the trees? What shall appall us? If eagles gaze at the sun, may not men at the gods?"

"For one," said Media, "you may gaze at me freely. Gaze on. But talk not of my kinsmen so fluently, Babbalanja. Return to your argument."

"I go back then, my lord. By implication, you have granted, that in times past the future was foreknown of Oro; hence, in times past, the future must have been foreordained. But in all things Oro is immutable. Wherefore our own future is foreknown and foreordained. Now, if things fore-

ordained concerning nations have in times past been revealed to them previous to their taking place, then something similar may be presumable
concerning individual men now living. That is to say, out of all the events
destined to befall any one man, it is not impossible that previous knowledge
of some one of these events might supernaturally come to him. Say, then,
it is revealed to me, that ten days hence I shall, of my own choice, fall upon
my javelin; when the time comes round, could I refrain from suicide?
Grant the strongest presumable motives to the act; grant that, unfore-
warned, I would slay myself outright at the time appointed: yet, foretold
of it, and resolved to test the decree to the uttermost, under such circumstances, I say, would it be possible for me not to kill myself? If possible,
then predestination is not a thing absolute; and Heaven is wise to keep
secret from us those decrees, whose virtue consists in secrecy. But if not
possible, then that suicide would not be mine, but Oro's. And, by consequence, not only that act, but all my acts, are Oro's. In sum, my lord, he who
believes that in times past, prophets have prophesied, and their prophecies
have been fulfilled; when put to it, inevitably must allow that every man
now living is an irresponsible being."

"In sooth, a very fine argument very finely argued," said Media. "You
have done marvels, Babbalanja. But hark ye, were I so disposed, I could
deny you all over, premises and conclusions alike. And furthermore, my
cogent philosopher, had you published that anarchical dogma among my
subjects in Odo, I had silenced you by my spear-headed scepter, instead of
my uplifted finger."

"Then, all thanks and all honor to your generosity, my lord, in granting
us the immunities you did at the outset of this voyage. But, my lord, permit
me one word more. Is not Oro omnipresent—absolutely every where?"

"So you mortals teach, Babbalanja."

"But so do they *mean*, my lord? Often do we Mardians stick to terms
for ages, yet truly apply not their meanings."

"Well, Oro is every where. What now?"

"Then, if that be absolutely so, Oro is not merely a universal on-looker,
but occupies and fills all space; and no vacancy is left for any being, or any
thing but Oro. Hence, Oro is *in* all things, and himself *is* all things—the
time-old creed. But since evil abounds, and Oro is all things, then he can
not be perfectly good; wherefore, Oro's omnipresence and moral perfection
seem incompatible. Furthermore, my lord those orthodox systems which
ascribe to Oro almighty and universal attributes every way, those systems,
I say, destroy all intellectual individualities but Oro, and resolve the universe

into him. But this is a heresy; wherefore, orthodoxy and heresy are one. And thus is it, my lord, that upon these matters we Mardians all agree and disagree together, and kill each other with weapons that burst in our hands. Ah, my lord, with what mind must blessed Oro look down upon this scene! Think you he discriminates between the deist and atheist? Nay; for the Searcher of the cores of all hearts well knoweth that atheists there are none. For in things abstract, men but differ in the sounds that come from their mouths, and not in the wordless thoughts lying at the bottom of their beings. The universe is all of one mind. Though my twin-brother sware to me, by the blazing sun in heaven at noon-day, that Oro is not; yet would he belie the thing he intended to express. And who lives that blasphemes? What jargon of human sounds so puissant as to insult the unutterable majesty divine? Is Oro's honor in the keeping of Mardi?—Oro's conscience in man's hands? Where our warrant, with Oro's sign-manual, to justify the killing, burning, and destroying, or far worse, the social persecutions we institute in his behalf? Ah! how shall these self-assumed attorneys and vice-gerents be astounded, when they shall see all heaven peopled with heretics and heathens, and all hell nodding over with miters! Ah! let us Mardians quit this insanity. Let us be content with the theology in the grass and the flower, in seed-time and harvest. Be it enough for us to know that Oro indubitably is. My lord! my lord! sick with the spectacle of the madness of men, and broken with spontaneous doubts, I sometimes see but two things in all Mardi to believe:—that I myself exist, and that I can most happily, or least miserably exist, by the practice of righteousness. All else is in the clouds; and naught else may I learn, till the firmament be split from horizon to horizon. Yet, alas! too often do I swing from these moorings."

"Alas! his fit is coming upon him again," whispered Yoomy.

"Why, Babbalanja," said Media, "I almost pity you. You are too warm, too warm. Why fever your soul with these things? To no use you mortals wax earnest. No thanks, but curses, will you get for your earnestness. You yourself you harm most. Why not take creeds as they come? It is not so hard to be persuaded; never mind about believing."

"True, my lord; not very hard; no act is required; only passiveness. Stand still and receive. Faith is to the thoughtless, doubts to the thinker."

"Then, why think at all? Is it not better for you mortals to clutch error as in a vice, than have your fingers meet in your hand? And to what end your eternal inquisitions? You have nothing to substitute. You say all is a lie; then out with the truth. Philosopher, your devil is but a foolish one, after all. I, a demi-god, never say nay to these things."

"Yea, my lord, it would hardly answer for Oro himself, were he to come down to Mardi, to deny men's theories concerning him. Did they not strike at the rash deity in Alma?"

"Then, why deny those theories yourself? Babbalanja, you almost affect my immortal serenity. Must you forever be a sieve for good grain to run through, while you retain but the chaff? Your tongue is forked. You speak two languages: flat folly for yourself, and wisdom for others. Babbalanja, if you have any belief of your own, keep it; but, in Oro's name, keep it secret."

"Ay, my lord, in these things wise men are spectators, not actors; wise men look on, and say 'ay.'"

"Why not say so yourself, then?"

"My lord, because I have often told you, that I am a fool, and not wise."

"Your Highness," said Mohi, "this whole discourse seems to have grown out of the subject of Necessity and Free Will. Now, when a boy, I recollect hearing a sage say, that these things were reconcilable."

"Ay?" said Media, "what say you to that, now, Babbalanja?"

"It may be even so, my lord. Shall I tell you a story?"

"Azzageddi's stirring now," muttered Mohi.

"Proceed," said Media.

"King Normo had a fool, called Willi, whom he loved to humor. Now, though Willi ever obeyed his lord, by the very instinct of his servitude, he flattered himself that he was free; and this conceit it was, that made the fool so entertaining to the king. One day, said Normo to his fool,— 'Go, Willi, to yonder tree, and wait there till I come.' 'Your Majesty, I will,' said Willi, bowing beneath his jingling bells; 'but I presume your Majesty has no objections to my walking on my hands:—I am free, I hope.' 'Perfectly,' said Normo, 'hands or feet, it's all the same to me; only do my bidding.' 'I thought as much,' said Willi; so, swinging his limber legs into the air, Willi, thumb after thumb, essayed progression. But soon, his bottled blood so rushed downward through his neck, that he was fain to turn a somerset and regain his feet. Said he, 'Though I am free to do it, it's not so easy turning digits into toes; I'll walk, by gad! which is my other option.' So he went straight forward, and did King Normo's bidding in the natural way."

"A curious story that," said Media; "whence came it?"

"My lord, where every thing, but one, is to be had:—within."

"You are charged to the muzzle, then," said Braid-Beard.

"Yes, Mohi; and my talk is my overflowing, not my fullness."

"And what may you be so full of?"

"Of myself."

"So it seems," said Mohi, whisking away a fly with his beard.

"Babbalanja," said Media, "you did right in selecting this ebon night for discussing the theme you did; and truly, you mortals are but too apt to talk in the dark."

"Ay, my lord, and we mortals may prate still more in the dark, when we are dead; for methinks, that if we then prate at all, 'twill be in our sleep. Ah! my lord, think not that in aught I've said this night, I would assert any wisdom of my own. I but fight against the armed and crested Lies of Mardi, that like a host, assail me. I am stuck full of darts; but, tearing them from out me, gasping, I discharge them whence they come."

So saying, Babbalanja slowly drooped, and fell reclining; then lay motionless as the marble Gladiator, that for centuries has been dying.

Chapter 136

My Lord Media summons Mohi to the Stand

WHILE SLOWLY THE NIGHT WORE ON, and the now scudding clouds flown past, revealed again the hosts in heaven, few words were uttered save by Media; who, when all others were most sad and silent, seemed but little moved, or not stirred a jot.

But that night, he filled his flagon fuller than his wont, and drank, and drank, and pledged the stars.

"Here's to thee, old Arcturus! To thee, old Aldebaran! who ever poise your wine-red, fiery spheres on high. A health to *thee*, my regal friend, Alphacca, in the constellation of the Crown: Lo! crown to crown, I pledge thee! I drink to *ye*, too, Alphard! Markab! Denebola! Capella!— to *ye*, too, sailing Cygnus! Aquila soaring!—All round, a health to all your diadems! May they never fade! nor mine!"

At last, in the shadowy east, the Dawn, like a gray, distant sail before the wind, was descried; drawing nearer and nearer, till her gilded prow was perceived.

And as in tropic gales, the winds blow fierce, and more fierce, with the advent of the sun; so with King Media; whose mirth now breezed up afresh. But, as at sunrise, the sea-storm only blows harder, to settle down at last into a steady wind; even so, in good time, my lord Media came to be more decorous of mood. And Babbalanja abated his reveries.

For who might withstand such a morn!

431

As on the night-banks of the far-rolling Ganges, the royal bridegroom sets forth for his bride, preceded by nymphs, now this side, now that, lighting up all the flowery flambeaux held on high as they pass; so came the Sun, to his nuptials with Mardi:—the Hours going on before, touching all the peaks, till they glowed rosy-red.

By reflex, the lagoon, here and there, seemed on fire; each curling wave-crest a flame.

Noon came as we sailed.

And now, citrons and bananas, cups and calabashes, calumets and to-bacco, were passed round; and we were all very merry and mellow indeed. Smacking our lips, chatting, smoking, and sipping. Now a mouthful of citron to season a repartee; now a swallow of wine to wash down a precept; now a fragrant whiff to puff away care. Many things did beguile. From side to side, we turned and grazed, like Juno's white oxen in clover meads.

Soon, we drew nigh to a charming cliff, overrun with woodbines, on high suspended from flowering Tamarisk and Tamarind-trees. The blossoms of the Tamarisks, in spikes of small, red bells; the Tamarinds, wide-spreading their golden petals, red-streaked as with streaks of the dawn. Down sweeping to the water, the vines trailed over to the crisp, curling waves,—little pages, all eager to hold up their trains.

Within, was a bower; going behind it, like standing inside the sheet of the falls of the Genesee.

In this arbor we anchored. And with their shaded prows thrust in among the flowers, our three canoes seemed baiting by the way, like wearied steeds in a hawthorn lane.

High midsummer noon is more silent than night. Most sweet a siesta then. And noon dreams are day-dreams indeed; born under the meridian sun. Pale Cynthia begets pale specter shapes; and her frigid rays best illuminate white nuns, marble monuments, icy glaciers, and cold tombs.

The sun rolled on. And starting to his feet, arms clasped, and wildly staring, Yoomy exclaimed—"Nay, nay, thou shalt not depart, thou maid! —here, here I fold thee for aye!—Flown?—A dream! Then siestas henceforth while I live. And at noon, every day will I meet thee, sweet maid! And, oh Sun! set not; and poppies bend over us, when next we embrace!"

"What ails that somnambulist?" cried Media, rising. "Yoomy, I say! what ails thee?"

"He must have indulged over freely in those citrons," said Mohi, sympathetically rubbing his fruitery. "Ho, Yoomy! a swallow of brine will help thee."

"Alas," cried Babbalanja, "do the fairies then wait on repletion? Do our dreams come from below, and not from the skies? Are we angels, or dogs? Oh, Man, Man, Man! thou art harder to solve, than the Integral Calculus —yet plain as a primer; harder to find than the philosopher's-stone—yet ever at hand; a more cunning compound, than an alchemist's—yet a hundred weight of flesh, to a penny weight of spirit; soul and body glued together, firm as atom to atom, seamless as the vestment without joint, warp or woof—yet divided as by a river, spirit from flesh; growing both ways, like a tree, and dropping thy topmost branches to earth, like thy beard or a banian!—I give thee up, oh Man! thou art twain—yet indivisible; all things—yet a poor unit at best."

"Philosopher you seem puzzled to account for the riddles of your race," cried Media, sideways reclining at his ease. "Now, do thou, old Mohi, stand up before a demi-god, and answer for all.—Draw nigh, so I can eye thee. What art thou, mortal?"

"My worshipful lord, a man."

"And what are men?"

"My lord, before thee is a specimen."

"I fear me, my lord will get nothing out of that witness," said Babbalanja. "Pray you, King Media, let another inquisitor cross-question."

"Proceed; take the divan."

"A pace or two farther off, there, Mohi; so I can garner thee all in at a glance.—Attention! Rememberest thou, fellow-being, when thou wast born?"

"Not I. Old Braid-Beard had no memory then."

"When, then, wast thou first conscious of being?"

"What time I was teething: my first sensation was an ache."

"What dost thou, fellow-being, here in Mardi?"

"What doth Mardi here, fellow-being, under me?"

"Philosopher, thou gainest but little by thy questions," cried Yoomy advancing. "Let a poet endeavor."

"I abdicate in your favor, then, gentle Yoomy; let me smooth the divan for you;—there: be seated."

"Now, Mohi, who art thou?" said Yoomy, nodding his bird-of-paradise plume.

"The sole witness, it seems, in this case."

"Try again minstrel," cried Babbalanja.

"Then, what art thou, Mohi?"

"Even what thou art, Yoomy."

"He is too sharp or too blunt for us all," cried King Media. "His devil is even more subtle than yours, Babbalanja. Let him go."

"Shall I adjourn the court then, my lord?" said Babbalanja.

"Ay."

"Oyez! Oyez! Oyez! All mortals having business at this court, know ye, that it is adjourned till sundown of the day, which hath no to-morrow."

Chapter 137

Wherein Babbalanja and Yoomy embrace

H OW THE ISLES GROW and multiply around us!" cried Babbalanja, as turning the bold promontory of an uninhabited shore, many distant lands bluely loomed into view. "Surely, our brief voyage, may not embrace all Mardi like its reef?"

"No," said Media, "much must be left unseen. Nor every where can Yillah be sought, noble Taji."

Said Yoomy, "We are as birds, with pinions clipped, that in unfathomable and endless woods, but flit from twig to twig of one poor tree."

"More isles! more isles!" cried Babbalanja, erect, and gazing abroad. "And lo! round all is heaving that infinite ocean. Ah! gods! what regions lie beyond?"

"But whither now?" he cried, as in obedience to Media, the paddlers suddenly altered our course.

"To the bold shores of Diranda," said Media.

"Ay; the land of clubs and javelins, where the lord seigniors Hello and Piko celebrate their famous games," cried Mohi.

"Your clubs and javelins," said Media, "remind me of the great battle-chant of Narvi—Yoomy!"—turning to the minstrel, gazing abstractedly into the water;—"awake, Yoomy, and give us the lines."

"My lord Media, 'tis but a rude, clanging thing; dissonant as if the north

435

wind blew through it. Methinks the company will not fancy lines so in-
harmonious. Better sing you, perhaps, one of my sonnets."

"Better sit and sob in our ears, silly Yoomy that thou art!—no! no!
none of your sentiment now; my soul is martially inclined; I want clarion
peals, not lute warblings. So throw out your chest, Yoomy: lift high your
voice; and blow me the old battle-blast.—Begin, sir minstrel."

And warning all, that he himself had not composed the odious chant,
Yoomy thus:—

Our clubs! our clubs!
The thousand clubs of Narvi!
Of the living trunk of the Palm-tree made;
Skull breakers! Brain spatterers!
Wielded right, and wielded left;
Life quenchers! Death dealers!
Causing live bodies to run headless!

Our bows! our bows!
The thousand bows of Narvi!
Ribs of Tara, god of War!
Fashioned from the light Tola their arrows;
Swift messengers! Heart piercers!
Barbed with sharp pearl shells;
Winged with white tail-plumes;
To wild death-chants, strung with the hair of wild maidens!

Our spears! our spears!
The thousand spears of Narvi!
Of the thunder-riven Moo-tree made:
Tall tree, couched on the long mountain Lana!
No staves for gray-beards! no rods for fishermen!
Tempered by fierce sea-winds,
Splintered into lances by lightnings,
Long arrows! Heart seekers!
Toughened by fire their sharp black points!

Our slings! our slings!
The thousand slings of Narvi!
All tasseled, and braided, and gayly bedecked.
In peace, our girdles; in war, our war-nets;
Wherewith catch we heads as fish from the deep!

The pebbles they hurl, have been hurled before,—
Hurled up on the beach by the stormy sea!
Pebbles, buried erewhile in the head of the shark:
To be buried erelong in the heads of our foes!
Home of hard blows, our pouches!
Nest of death-eggs! How quickly they hatch!

Uplift, and couch we our spears, men!
Ring hollow on the rocks our war clubs!
Bend we our bows, feel the points of our arrows:
Aloft, whirl in eddies our sling-nets;
To the fight, men of Narvi!
Sons of battle! Hunters of men!
Raise high your war-wood!
Shout Narvi! her groves in the storm!

"By Oro!" cried Media, "but Yoomy has well nigh stirred up all
Babbalanja's devils in me. Were I a mortal, I could fight now on a pretense.
And did any man say me nay, I would charge upon him like a spear-point.
Ah, Yoomy, thou and thy tribe have much to answer for; ye stir up all
Mardi with your lays. Your war chants make men fight; your drinking
songs, drunkards; your love ditties, fools. Yet there thou sittest, Yoomy,
gentle as a dove.—What art thou, minstrel, that thy soft, singing soul should
so master all mortals? Yoomy, like me, you sway a scepter."

"Thou honorest my calling overmuch," said Yoomy, "we minstrels
but sing our lays carelessly, my lord Media."

"Ay: and the more mischief they make."

"But sometimes we poets are didactic."

"Didactic and dull; many of ye are but too apt to be prosy unless mis-
chievous."

"Yet in our verses, my lord Media, but few of us purpose harm."

"But when all harmless to yourselves, ye may be otherwise to Mardi."

"And are not foul streams often traced to pure fountains, my lord?"
said Babbalanja. "The essence of all good and all evil is in us, not out of us.
Neither poison nor honey lodgeth in the flowers on which, side by side,
bees and wasps oft alight. My lord, nature is an immaculate virgin, forever
standing unrobed before us. True poets but paint the charms which all eyes
behold. The vicious would be vicious without them."

"My lord Media," impetuously resumed Yoomy, "I am sensible of a thousand sweet, merry fancies, limpid with innocence; yet my enemies account them all lewd conceits."

"There be those in Mardi," said Babbalanja, "who would never ascribe evil to others, did they not find it in their own hearts; believing none can be different from themselves."

"My lord, my lord!" cried Yoomy. "The air that breaths my music from me is a mountain air! Purer than others am I; for though not a woman, I feel in me a woman's soul."

"Ah, have done, silly Yoomy," said Media. "Thou art becoming flighty, even as Babbalanja, when Azzageddi is uppermost."

"Thus ever: ever thus!" sighed Yoomy. "They comprehend us not."

"Nor me," said Babbalanja. "Yoomy: poets both, we differ but in seeming; thy airiest conceits are as the shadows of my deepest ponderings; though Yoomy soars, and Babbalanja dives, both meet at last. Not a song you sing, but I have thought its thought; and where dull Mardi sees but your rose, I unfold its petals, and disclose a pearl. Poets are we, Yoomy, in that we dwell without us; we live in grottoes, palms, and brooks; we ride the sea, we ride the sky; poets are omnipresent."

Chapter 138

Of the Isle of Diranda

IN GOOD TIME the shores of Diranda were in sight. And, introductory to landing, Braid-Beard proceeded to give us some little
account of the island, and its rulers.

As previously hinted, those very magnificent and illustrious lord seigniors, the lord seigniors Hello and Piko, who between them divided Diranda,
delighted in all manner of public games, especially warlike ones; which
last were celebrated so frequently, and were so fatal in their results, that,
notwithstanding the multiplicity of nuptials taking place in the isle, its
population remained in equilibrio. But, strange to relate, this was the very
object which the lord seigniors had in view; the very object they sought to
compass, by instituting their games. Though, for the most part, they wisely
kept the secret locked up.

But to tell how the lord seigniors Hello and Piko came to join hands
in this matter.

Diranda had been amicably divided between them ever since the day
they were crowned; one reigning king in the East, the other in the West.
But King Piko had been long harassed with the thought, that the un-
obstructed and indefinite increase of his browsing subjects might eventually
denude of herbage his portion of the island. Posterity, thought he, is marshaling her generations in squadrons, brigades, and battalions, and ere long

439

will be down upon my devoted empire. Lo! her locust cavalry darken the skies; her light-troop pismires cover the earth. Alas! my son and successor, thou wilt inhale choke-damp for air, and have not a private corner to say thy prayers.

By a sort of arithmetical progression, the probability, nay, the certainty of these results, if not in some way averted, was proved to King Piko; and he was furthermore admonished, that war—war to the haft with King Hello—was the only cure for so menacing an evil.

But so it was, that King Piko, at peace with King Hello, and well content with the tranquillity of the times, little relished the idea of picking a quarrel with his neighbor, and running its risks, in order to phlebotomize his redundant population.

"Patience, most illustrious seignior," said another of his sagacious Ahithophels, "and haply a pestilence may decimate the people."

But no pestilence came. And in every direction the young men and maidens were recklessly rushing into wedlock; and so salubrious the climate, that the old men stuck to the outside of the turf, and refused to go under.

At last some Machiavel of a philosopher suggested, that peradventure the object of war might be answered without going to war; that peradventure King Hello might be brought to acquiesce in an arrangement, whereby the men of Diranda might be induced to kill off one another voluntarily, in a peaceable manner, without troubling their rulers. And to this end, the games before mentioned were proposed.

"Egad! my wise ones, you have hit it," cried Piko; "but will Hello say ay?"

"Try him, most illustrious seignior," said Machiavel.

So to Hello went embassadors ordinary and extraordinary, and ministers plenipotentiary and peculiar; and anxiously King Piko awaited their return.

The mission was crowned with success.

Said King Hello to the ministers, in confidence:—"The very thing, Dons, the very thing I have wanted. My people are increasing too fast. They keep up the succession too well. Tell your illustrious master it's a bargain. The games! the games! by all means."

So, throughout the island, by proclamation, they were forthwith established; succeeding to a charm.

And the lord seigniors, Hello and Piko, finding their interests the same, came together like bride and bridegroom; lived in the same palace; dined off the same cloth; cut from the same bread-fruit; drank from the same calabash; wore each other's crowns; and often locking arms with a charming frankness, paced up and down in their dominions, discussing the prospect of the next harvest of heads.

In his old-fashioned way, having related all this, with many other particulars, Mohi was interrupted by Babbalanja, who inquired how the people of Diranda relished the games, and how they fancied being coolly thinned out in that manner.

To which in substance the chronicler replied, that of the true object of the games, they had not the faintest conception; but hammered away at each other, and fought and died together, like jolly good fellows.

"Right again, immortal old Bardianna!" cried Babbalanja.

"And what has the sage to the point this time?" asked Media.

"Why, my lord, in his chapter on 'Cracked Crowns,' Bardianna, after many profound ponderings, thus concludes: 'In this cracked sphere we live in, then, cracked skulls would seem the inevitable allotments of many. Nor will the splintering thereof cease, till this pugnacious animal we treat of be deprived of his natural maces: videlicet, his arms. And right well doth man love to bruise and batter all occiputs in his vicinity.'"

"Seems to me, our old friend must have been on his stilts that time," interrupted Mohi.

"No, Braid-Beard. But by way of apologizing for the unusual rigidity of his style in that chapter, he says in a note, that it was written upon a straight-backed settle, when he was ill of a lumbago, and a crick in the neck."

"That incorrigible Azzageddi again," said Media. "Proceed with your quotation, Babbalanja."

"Where was I, Braid-Beard?"

"Battering occiputs at the last accounts," said Mohi.

"Ah, yes.—'And right well doth man love to bruise and batter all occiputs in his vicinity; he but follows his instincts; he is but one member of a fighting world. Spiders, vixens, and tigers all war with a relish; and on every side is heard the howls of hyenas, the throttlings of mastiffs, the din of belligerant beetles, the buzzing warfare of the insect battalions: and the shrill cries of lady Tartars rending their lords. And all this existeth of necessity. To war it is, and other depopulators, that we are beholden for elbow-room in Mardi, and for all our parks and gardens, wherein we are wont to expatiate. Come on, then, plague, war, famine and viragos! Come on, I say, for who shall stay ye? Come on, and healthfulize the census! And more especially, oh War! do thou march forth with thy bludgeon! Cracked are our crowns by nature, and henceforth forever, cracked shall they be by hard raps.'"

"And hopelessly cracked the skull, that hatched such a tirade of nonsense," said Mohi.

"And think you not, old Bardianna knew that?" asked Babbalanja. "He wrote an excellent chapter on that very subject."

"What, on the cracks in his own pate?"

"Precisely. And expressly asserts, that to those identical cracks, was he indebted for what little light he had in his brain."

"I yield, Babbalanja; your old Ponderer is older than I."

"Ay, ay, Braid-Beard; his crest was a tortoise; and this was the motto:— 'I bite, but am not to be bitten.'"

Chapter 139

They visit the Lords Piko and Hello

IN GOOD TIME, we landed at Diranda. And that landing was like landing at Greenwich among the Waterloo pensioners. The people were docked right and left; some without arms; some without legs; not one with a tail; but to a man, all had heads, though rather the worse for wear; covered with lumps and contusions.

Now, those very magnificent and illustrious lord seigniors, the lord seigniors Hello and Piko, lived in a palace, round which was a fence of the cane called Malacca, each picket helmed with a skull, of which there were fifty, one to each cane. Over the door was the blended arms of the high and mighty houses of Hello and Piko: a Clavicle crossed over an Ulna.

Escorted to the sign of the Skull-and-Cross-Bones, we received the very best entertainment which that royal inn could afford. We found our hosts Hello and Piko seated together on a dais or throne, and now and then drinking some claret-red wine from an ivory bowl, too large to have been wrought from an elephant's tusk. They were in glorious good spirits, shaking ivory coins in a skull.

"What says your majesty?" said Piko. "Heads or tails?"

"Oh, heads, your majesty," said Hello.

"And heads say I," said Piko.

And heads it was. But it was heads on both sides, so both were sure to win.

443

And thus they were used to play merrily all day long; beheading the gourds of claret by one slicing blow with their sickle-shaped scepters. Wide round them lay empty calabashes, all feathered, red dyed, and betasseled, trickling red wine from their necks, like the decapitated pullets in the old baronial barn yard at Kenilworth, the night before Queen Bess dined with my lord Leicester.

The first compliments over; and Media and Taji having met with a reception suitable to their rank, the kings inquired, whether there were any good javelin-flingers among us: for if that were the case, they could furnish them plenty of sport. Informed, however, that none of the party were professional warriors, their majesties looked rather glum, and by way of chasing away the blues, called for some good old stuff that was red.

It seems, this soliciting guests, to keep their spears from decaying, by cut and thrust play with their subjects, was a very common thing with their illustrious majesties.

But if their visitors could not be prevailed upon to spear a subject or so, our hospitable hosts resolved to have a few speared, and otherwise served up for our special entertainment. In a word, our arrival furnished a fine pretext for renewing their games; though, we learned, that only ten days previous, upward of fifty combatants had been slain at one of these festivals.

Be that as it might, their joint majesties determined upon another one; and also upon our tarrying to behold it.

We objected, saying we must depart.

But we were kindly assured, that our canoes had been dragged out of the water, and buried in a wood; there to remain till the games were over.

The day fixed upon, was the third subsequent to our arrival; the interval being devoted to preparations; summoning from their villages and valleys the warriors of the land; and publishing the royal proclamations, whereby the unbounded hospitality of the kings' household was freely offered to all heroes whatsoever, who for the love of arms, and the honor of broken heads, desired to cross battle-clubs, hurl spears, or die game in the royal valley of Deddo.

Meantime, the whole island was in a state of uproarious commotion, and strangers were daily arriving.

The spot set apart for the festival, was a spacious down, mantled with white asters; which, waving in windrows, lay upon the land, like the cream-surf surging the milk of young heifers. But that whiteness, here and there, was spotted with strawberries; tracking the plain, as if wounded creatures had been dragging themselves bleeding from some deadly encounter. All round the down, waved scarlet thickets of sumach, moaning in the wind, like the gory ghosts environing Pharsalia the night after the battle; scaring away the peasants, who with bushel-baskets came to the jewel-harvest of the rings of Pompey's knights.

Beneath the heaped turf of this down, lay thousands of glorious corpses of anonymous heroes, who here had died glorious deaths.

Whence, in the florid language of Diranda, they called this field "The Field of Glory."

Chapter 140

They attend the Games

AT LAST the third day dawned; and facing us upon entering the plain, was a throne of red log-wood, canopied by the foliage of a red-dyed Pandannus. Upon this throne, purple-robed, reclined those very magnificent and illustrious lords seigniors, the lord seigniors Hello and Piko. Before them, were many gourds of wine; and crosswise, staked in the sod, their own royal spears.

In the middle of the down, as if by a furrow, a long, oval space was margined off, about which, a crowd of spectators were seated. Opposite the throne, was reserved a clear passage to the arena, defined by air-lines, indefinitely produced from the leveled points of two spears, so poised by a brace of warriors.

Drawing near, our party was courteously received, and assigned a commodious lounge.

The first encounter was a club-fight between two warriors. Nor casque of steel, nor skull of Congo could have resisted their blows, had they fallen upon the mark; for they seemed bent upon driving each other, as stakes, into the earth. Presently, one of them faltered; but his adversary rushing in to cleave him down, slipped against a guava-rind; when the falterer, with one lucky blow, high into the air sent the stumbler's club, which descended upon the crown of a spectator, who was borne from the plain.

446

"All one," muttered Piko.

"As good dead as another," muttered Hello.

The second encounter was a hugging-match; wherein two warriors, masked in Grisly-bear skins, hugged each other to death.

The third encounter was a bumping-match between a fat warrior and a dwarf. Standing erect, his paunch like a bass-drum before a drummer, the fat man was run at, head-a-tilt by the dwarf, and sent spinning round on his axis.

The fourth encounter was a tussle between two-score warriors, who all in a mass, writhed like the limbs in Sebastiano's painting of Hades. After obscuring themselves in a cloud of dust, these combatants, uninjured, but hugely blowing, drew off; and separately going among the spectators, rehearsed their experience of the fray.

"Braggarts!" mumbled Piko.

"Poltroons!" growled Hello.

While the crowd were applauding, a sober-sided observer, trying to rub the dust out of his eyes, inquired of an enthusiastic neighbor, "Pray, what was all that about?"

"Fool! saw you not the dust?"

"That I did," said Sober-Sides, again rubbing his eyes. "But I can raise a dust myself."

The fifth encounter was a fight of single sticks between one hundred warriors, fifty on a side.

In a line, the first fifty emerged from the sumachs, their weapons interlocked in a sort of wicker-work. In advance marched a priest, bearing an idol with a cracked cocoanut for a head,—Krako, the god of Trepans. Preceded by damsels flinging flowers, now came on the second fifty, gayly appareled, weapons poised, and their feet nimbly moving in a martial measure.

Midway meeting, both parties touched poles, then retreated. Very courteous, this; but tantamount to bowing each other out of Mardi; for upon Piko's tossing a javelin, they rushed in, and each striking his man, all fell to the ground.

"Well done!" cried Piko.

"Brave fellows!" cried Hello.

"But up and at it again, my heroes!" joined both. "Lo! we kings look on, and there stand the bards!"

These bards were a row of lean, sallow, old men, in thread-bare robes, and chaplets of dead leaves.

"Strike up!" cried Piko.

"A stave!" cried Hello.

Whereupon, the old croakers, each with a quinsy, sang thus in cracked strains:—

Quack! Quack! Quack!
With a toorooloo whack;
Hack away, merry men, hack away.
Who would not die brave,
His ear smote by a stave?
Thwack away, merry men, thwack away!
'Tis glory that calls,
To each hero that falls,
Hack away, merry men, hack away!
Quack! Quack! Quack!
Quack! Quack!
Quack!

Thus it tapered away.

"Ha, ha!" cried Piko, "how they prick their ears at that!"

"Hark ye, my invincibles!" cried Hello. "That pean is for the slain. So all ye who have lives left, spring to it! Die and be glorified! Now's the time!—Strike up again, my ducklings!"

Thus incited, the survivors staggered to their feet; and hammering away at each other's sconces, till they rung like a chime of bells going off with a triple-bob-major, they finally succeeded in immortalizing themselves by quenching their mortalities all round; the bards still singing.

"Never mind your music now," cried Piko.

"It's all over," said Hello.

"What valiant fellows we have for subjects," cried Piko.

"Ho! grave-diggers, clear the field," cried Hello.

"Who else is for glory?" cried Piko.

"There stand the bards!" cried Hello.

But now there rushed among the crowd a haggard figure, trickling with blood, and wearing a robe, whose edges were burned and blacked by fire. Wielding a club, it ran to and fro, with loud yells menacing all.

A noted warrior this; who, distracted at the death of five sons slain in recent games, wandered from valley to valley, wrestling and fighting.

With wild cries of "The Despairer! The Despairer!" the appalled multitude fled; leaving the two kings frozen on their throne, quaking and quailing, their teeth rattling like dice.

The Despairer strode toward them; when, recovering their senses, they ran; for a time pursued through the woods by the phantom.

Chapter 141

Taji still hunted, and beckoned

PREVIOUS TO THE KINGS' FLIGHT, we had plunged into the
neighboring woods; and from thence emerging, entered brakes of
cane, sprouting from morasses. Soon we heard a whirring, as if
three startled partridges had taken wing; it proved three feathered arrows,
from three unseen hands.

Grazing us, two buried in the ground, but from Taji's arm, the third
drew blood.

On all sides round we turned; but none were seen.

"Still the avengers follow," said Babbalanja.

"Lo! the damsels three!" cried Yoomy. "Look where they come!"

We joined them by the sumach-wood's red skirts; and there, they waved
their cherry stalks, and heavy bloated cactus leaves, their crimson blossoms
armed with nettles; and before us flung shining, yellow, tiger-flowers
spotted red.

"Blood!" cried Yoomy, starting, "and leopards on your track!"

And now the syrens blew through long reeds, tasseled with their pan-
nicles, and waving verdant scarfs of vines, came dancing toward us, proffer-
ing clustering grapes.

"For all now yours, Taji; and all that yet may come," cried Yoomy,
"fly to me! I will dance away your gloom, and drown it in inebriation."

"Away! woe is its own wine. What may be mine, that will I endure, in its own essence to the quick. Let me feel the poniard if it stabs."

They vanished in the wood; and hurrying on, we soon gained sun-light, and the open glade.

Chapter 142

They embark from Diranda

RRIVED at the Sign of the Skulls, we found the illustrious lord
seigniors at rest from their flight, and once more quaffing their claret,
all thoughts of the specter departed. Instead of rattling their own
ivory in the heads on their shoulders, they were rattling their dice in the
skulls in their hands. And still "Heads," was the cry, and "Heads," was the
throw.

That evening they made known to my lord Media that an interval of
two days must elapse ere the games were renewed, in order to reward the
victors, bury their dead, and provide for the execution of an Islander, who
under the provocation of a blow, had killed a stranger.

As this suspension of the festivities had been wholly unforeseen, our
hosts were induced to withdraw the embargo laid upon our canoes. Nevertheless, they pressed us to remain; saying, that what was to come would far
exceed in interest, what had already taken place. The games in prospect
being of a naval description, embracing certain hand-to-hand contests in the
water between shoals of web-footed warriors.

However, we decided to embark on the morrow.

It was in the cool of the early morning, at that hour when a man's face
can be known, that we set sail from Diranda; and in the ghostly twilight,
our thoughts reverted to the phantom that so suddenly had cleared the
plain. With interest we hearkened to the recitals of Mohi; who discoursing

452

of the sad end of many brave chieftains in Mardi, made allusion to the youthful Adondo, one of the most famous of the chiefs of the chronicles. In a canoe-fight, after performing prodigies of valor, he was wounded in the head, and sunk to the bottom of the lagoon.

"There is a noble monody upon the death of Adondo," said Yoomy. "Shall I sing it, my lord? It is very beautiful; nor could I ever repeat it without a tear."

"We will dispense with your tears, minstrel," said Media, "but sing it, if you will."

And Yoomy sang:—

> Departed the pride, and the glory of Mardi:
> The vaunt of her isles sleeps deep in the sea,
>   That rolls o'er his corse with a hush.
>   His warriors bend over their spears,
>   His sisters gaze upward and mourn.
>   Weep, weep, for Adondo is dead!
>   The sun has gone down in a shower;
>   Buried in clouds the face of the moon;
> Tears stand in the eyes of the starry skies,
>   And stand in the eyes of the flowers;
> And streams of tears are the trickling brooks,
>   Coursing adown the mountains.—
> Departed the pride, and the glory of Mardi:
> The vaunt of her isles sleeps deep in the sea.
> Fast falls the small rain on its bosom that sobs,—
> Not showers of rain, but the tears of Oro.

"A dismal time it must have been," yawned Media, "not a dry brook then in Mardi, not a lake that was not moist. Lachrymose rivulets, and inconsolable lagoons! Call you this poetry, minstrel?"

"Mohi has something like a tear in his eye," said Yoomy.

"False!" cried Mohi, brushing it aside.

"Who composed that monody?" said Babbalanja. "I have often heard it before."

"None know, Babbalanja; but the poet must be still singing to himself; his songs bursting through the turf, in the flowers over his grave."

"But gentle Yoomy, Adondo is a legendary hero, indefinitely dating back. May not his monody, then, be a spontaneous melody, that has been with us since Mardi began? What bard composed the soft verses that our palm boughs sing at even? Nay, Yoomy, that monody was not written by man."

"Ah! Would that I had been the poet, Babbalanja; for then had I been famous indeed; those lines are chanted through all the isles, by prince and peasant. Yes, Adondo's monody will pervade the ages, like the low undertone you hear, when many singers do sing."

"My lord, my lord," cried Babbalanja, "but this were to be truly immortal;—to be perpetuated in our works, and not in our names. Let me, oh Oro! be anonymously known!"

Chapter 143

Wherein Babbalanja discourses of himself

A N INTERVAL OF SILENCE was at last broken by Babbalanja. Pointing to the sun, just gaining the horizon, he exclaimed, "As old Bardianna says—shut your eyes, and believe."

"And what may Bardianna have to do with yonder orb?" said Media.

"This much, my lord; the astronomers maintain that Mardi moves round the sun; which I, who never formally investigated the matter for myself, can by no means credit; unless, plainly seeing one thing, I blindly believe another. Yet even thus blindly does all Mardi subscribe to an astronomical system, which not one in fifty thousand can astronomically prove. And not many centuries back, my lord, all Mardi did equally subscribe to an astronomical system, precisely the reverse of that which they now believe. But the mass of Mardians have not as much reason to believe the first system, as the exploded one; for all who have eyes must assuredly see, that the sun seems to move, and that Mardi seems a fixture, eternally *here*. But doubtless there are theories which may be true, though the face of things belie them. Hence, in such cases, to the ignorant, disbelief would seem more natural than faith; though they too often reject the testimony of their own senses, for what to them, is a mere hypothesis. And thus, my lord, is it, that the mass of Mardians do not believe because they know, but because they know *not*. And they are as ready to receive one thing as another, if it comes from a canonical source. My lord, Mardi is as an ostrich, which will swallow aught you offer, even a bar of iron, if placed endwise. And though the iron be indigestible, yet it serves to fill: in feeding, the end proposed. For Mardi must have something to exercise its digestion, though that something be forever indigestible. And as fishermen for sport, throw two lumps of bait, united by a cord, to albatrosses floating on the sea; which are greedily attempted to be swallowed, one lump by this fowl, the other by that; but forever are kept reciprocally going up and down in them, by means of the cord; even so, my lord, do I sometimes fancy, that our theorists divert themselves with the greediness of Mardians to believe."

"Ha, ha," cried Media, "methinks this must be Azzageddi who speaks."

"No, my lord; not long since, Azzageddi received a furlough to go home and warm himself for a while. But this leaves me not alone."

"How?"

"My lord,—for the present putting Azzageddi entirely aside,—though I have now been upon terms of close companionship with myself for nigh five hundred moons, I have not yet been able to decide who or what I am. To you, perhaps, I seem Babbalanja; but to myself, I seem not myself. All I am sure of, is a sort of prickly sensation all over me, which they call life; and, occasionally, a headache or a queer conceit admonishes me, that there is something astir in my attic. But how know I, that these sensations are identical with myself? For aught I know, I may be somebody else. At any rate, I keep an eye on myself, as I would on a stranger. There is something going on in me, that is independent of me. Many a time, have I willed to do one thing, and another has been done. I will not say by myself, for I was not consulted about it; it was done instinctively. My most virtuous thoughts are not born of my musings, but spring up in me, like bright fancies to the poet; unsought, spontaneous. Whence they come I know not. I am a blind man pushed from behind; in vain, I turn about to see what propels me. As vanity, I regard the praises of my friends; for what they commend pertains not to me, Babbalanja; but to this unknown something that forces me to it. But why am I, a middle aged Mardian, less prone to excesses than when a youth? The same inducements and allurements are around me. But no; my more ardent passions are burned out; those which are strongest when we are least able to resist them. Thus, then, my lord, it is not so much outer temptations that prevail over us mortals; but inward instincts."

"A very curious speculation," said Media.—"But Babbalanja, have you mortals no moral sense, as they call it?"

"We have. But the thing you speak of is but an after-birth; we eat and drink many months before we are conscious of thoughts. And though some adults would seem to refer all their actions to this moral sense, yet, in reality, it is not so; for, dominant in them, their moral sense bridles their instinctive passions; wherefore, they do not govern themselves, but are governed by their very natures. Thus, some men in youth are constitutionally as staid as I am now. But shall we pronounce them pious and worthy youths for this? Does he abstain, who is not incited? And on the other hand, if the instinctive passions through life naturally have the supremacy over the moral sense, as in extreme cases we see it developed in irreclaimable male-factors,—shall we pronounce such, criminal and detestable wretches? My lord, it is easier for some men to be saints, than for others not to be sinners."

"That will do, Babbalanja; you are on the verge, take not the leap! Go back whence you set out, and tell us of that other, and still more myste-rious Azzageddi; him whom you hinted to have palmed himself off on you for you yourself."

"Well, then, my lord,—Azzageddi still set aside,—upon that self-same inscrutable stranger, I charge all those past actions of mine, which in the retrospect appear to me such eminent folly, that I am confident, it was not I, Babbalanja, now speaking, that committed them. Nevertheless, my lord, this very day I may do some act, which at a future period may seem equally senseless; for in one life-time we live a hundred lives. By the incompre-hensible stranger in me, I say, this body of mine has been rented out scores of times, though always one dark chamber in me is retained by the old mystery."

"Will you never come to the mark, Babbalanja? Tell me something direct of the stranger. Who, what is he? Introduce him."

"My lord, I can not. He is locked up in me. In a mask, he dodges me. He prowls about in me, hither and thither; he peers, and I stare. This is he who talks in my sleep, revealing my secrets; and takes me to unheard of realms, beyond the skies of Mardi. So present is he always, that I seem not so much to live of myself, as to be a mere apprehension of the unaccountable being that is in me. Yet all the time, this being is I, myself."

"Babbalanja," said Media, "you have fairly turned yourself inside out."

"Yes, my lord," said Mohi, "and he has so unsettled me, that I begin to think all Mardi a square circle."

"How is that, Babbalanja," said Media, "is a circle square?"

"No, my lord, but ever since Mardi began, we Mardians have been essaying our best to square it."

"Cleverly retorted. Now, Babbalanja, do you not imagine, that you may do harm by disseminating these sophisms of yours; which like your devil theory, would seem to relieve all Mardi from moral accountability?"

"My lord, at bottom, men wear no bonds that other men can strike off; and have no immunities, of which other men can deprive them. Tell a good man that he is free to commit murder,—will he murder? Tell a murderer that at the peril of his soul he indulges in murderous thoughts,—will that make him a saint?"

"Again on the verge, Babbalanja? Take not the leap, I say."

"I can leap no more, my lord. Already I am down, down, down."

"Philosopher," said Media, "what with Azzageddi, and the mysterious indweller you darkly hint of, I marvel not that you are puzzled to decide upon your identity. But when do you seem most yourself?"

"When I sleep, and dream not, my lord."

"Indeed?"

"Why then, a fool's cap might be put on you, and you would not know it."

"The very turban he ought to wear," muttered Mohi.

"Yet, my lord, I live while consciousness is not mine, while to all appearances I am a clod. And may not this same state of being, though but alternate with me, be continually that of many dumb, passive objects we so carelessly regard? Trust me, there are more things alive than those that crawl, or fly, or swim. Think you, my lord, there is no sensation in being a tree? feeling the sap in one's boughs, the breeze in one's foliage? think you it is nothing to be a world? one of a herd, bison-like, wending its way across boundless meadows of ether? In the sight of a fowl, that sees not our souls, what are our own tokens of animation? That we move, make a noise, have organs, pulses, and are compounded of fluids and solids. And all these are in this Mardi as a unit. Daily the slow, majestic throbbings of its heart are perceptible on the surface in the tides of the lagoon. Its rivers are its veins; when agonized, earthquakes are its throes; it shouts in the thunder, and weeps in the shower; and as the body of a bison is covered with hair, so Mardi is covered with grasses and vegetation, among which, we parasitical things do but crawl, vexing and tormenting the patient creature to which we cling. Nor yet, hath it recovered from the pain of the first foundation that was laid. Mardi is alive to its axis. When you pour water, does it not gurgle? When you strike a pearl shell, does it not ring? Think you there is no sensation in being a rock?—To exist, is to be; to be, is to be something: to be something, is—"

"Go on," said Media.

"And what is it, to be something?" said Yoomy artlessly.

"Bethink yourself of what went before," said Media.

"Lose not the thread," said Mohi.

"It has snapped," said Babbalanja.

"I breathe again," said Mohi.

"But what a stepping-off place you came to then, philosopher," said Media. "By the way, is it not old Bardianna who says, that no Mardian should undertake to walk, without keeping one foot foremost?"

"To return to the vagueness of the notion I have of myself," said Babbalanja.

"An appropriate theme," said Media, "proceed."

"My lord," murmured Mohi, "Is not this philosopher like a centipede? Cut off his head, and still he crawls."

"There are times when I fancy myself a lunatic," resumed Babbalanja.

"Ah, now he's beginning to talk sense," whispered Mohi.

"Surely you forget, Babbalanja," said Media. "How many more theories have you? First, you are possessed by a devil; then rent yourself out to the indweller; and now turn yourself into a mad-house. You are inconsistent."

"And for that very reason, my lord, *not* inconsistent; for the sum of my inconsistencies makes up my consistency. And to be consistent to one's self, is often to be inconsistent to Mardi. Common consistency implies unchangeableness; but much of the wisdom here below lives in a state of transition."

"Ah!" murmured Mohi, "my head goes round again."

"Azzageddi aside, then, my lord, and also, for the nonce, the mysterious indweller, I come now to treat of myself as a lunatic. But this last conceit is not so much based upon the madness of particular actions, as upon the whole drift of my ordinary and hourly ones; those, in which I most resemble all other Mardians. It seems like going through with some nonsensical whim-whams, destitute of fixed purpose. For though many of my actions seem to have objects, and all of them somehow run into each other; yet, where is the grand result? To what final purpose, do I walk about, eat, think, dream? To what great end, does Mohi there, now stroke his beard?"

"But I was doing it unconsciously," said Mohi, dropping his hand, and lifting his head.

"Just what I would be at, old man. 'What we do, we do blindly,' says old Bardianna. Many things we do, we do without knowing,—as with you and your beard, Mohi. And many others we know not, in their true bearing at least, till they are past. Are not half our lives spent in reproaches for foregone actions, of the true nature and consequences of which, we were wholly ignorant at the time? Says old Bardianna, 'Did I not so often feel an appetite for my yams, I should think every thing a dream;'— so puzzling to him, seemed the things of this Mardi. But Alla-Malolla goes further. Says he, 'Let us club together, fellow-riddles:—Kings, clowns, and inter-mediates. We are bundles of comical sensations; we bejuggle ourselves into strange phantasies: we are air, wind, breath, bubbles; our being is told in a tick.'"

"Now, then, Babbalanja," said Media, "what have you come to in all this rhapsody? You everlastingly travel in a circle."

"And so does the sun in heaven, my lord; like me, it goes round, and gives light as it goes. Old Bardianna, too, revolved. He says so himself. In his roundabout chapter on Cycles and Epicycles, with Notes on the Ecliptic, he thus discourseth:—'All things revolve upon some center, to them, fixed; for the centripetal is ever too much for the centrifugal. Where-fore, it is a perpetual cycling with us, without progression; and we fly round, whether we will or no. To stop, were to sink into space. So, over and over we go, and round and round; double-shuffle, on our axis, and round the sun.' In another place, he says:—'There is neither apogee nor perigee, north nor south, right nor left; what to-night is our zenith, to-morrow is our nadir; stand as we will, we stand on our heads; essay to spring into the air, and down we come; here we stick; our very bones make glue.'"

"Enough, enough, Babbalanja," cried Media. "You are a very wise Mardian; but the wisest Mardians make the most consummate fools."

"So they do, my lord; but I was interrupted. I was about to say, that there is no place but the universe; no limit but the limitless; no bottom but the bottomless."

Chapter 144

Of the Sorcerers in the Isle of Minda

"TIFFIN! tiffin!" cried Media; "time for tiffin! Up, comrades! and while the mat is being spread, walk we to the bow, and inhale the breeze for an appetite. Hark ye, Vee-Vee! forget not that calabash with the sea-blue seal, and a round ring for a brand. Rare old stuff, that, Mohi; older than you: the circumnavigator, I call it. My sire had a canoe launched for the express purpose of carrying it thrice round Mardi for a flavor. It was many moons on the voyage; the mariners never sailed faster than three knots. Ten would spoil the best wine ever floated."

Tiffin over, and the blue-sealed calabash all but hid in the great cloud raised by our pipes, Media proposed to board it in the smoke. So, goblet in hand, we all gallantly charged, and came off victorious from the fray.

Then seated again, and serenely puffing in a circle, the circumnavigator meanwhile pleasantly going the rounds, Media called upon Mohi for something entertaining.

Now, of all the old gossips in Mardi, surely our delightful old Diodorus was furnished with the greatest possible variety of histories, chronicles, anecdotes, memoirs, legends, traditions, and biographies. There was no end to the library he carried. In himself, he was the whole history of Mardi, amplified, not abridged, in one volume.

461

In obedience, then, to King Media's command, Mohi regaled the company with a narrative, in substance as follows:—

In a certain quarter of the Archipelago was an island called Minda; and in Minda were many sorcerers, employed in the social differences and animosities of the people of that unfortunate land. If a Mindarian deemed himself aggrieved or insulted by a countryman, he forthwith repaired to one of these sorcerers; who, for an adequate consideration, set to work with his spells, keeping himself in the dark, and directing them against the obnoxious individual. And full soon, by certain peculiar sensations, this individual, discovering what was going on, would straightway hie to his own professor of the sable art, who, being well feed, in due time brought about certain counter-charms, so that in the end it sometimes fell out that neither party was gainer or loser, save by the sum of his fees.

But the worst of it was, that in some cases all knowledge of these spells was at the outset hidden from the victim; who, hearing too late of the mischief brewing, almost always fell a prey to his foe; which calamity was held the height of the art. But as the great body of sorcerers were about matched in point of skill, it followed that the parties employing them were so likewise. Hence arose those interminable contests, in which many moons were spent, both parties toiling after their common destruction.

Indeed, to say nothing of the obstinacy evinced by their employers, it was marvelous, the pertinacity of the sorcerers themselves. To the very last tooth in their employer's pouches, they would stick to their spells; never giving over till he was financially or physically defunct.

But much as they were vilified, no people in Minda were half so disinterested as they. Certain indispensable conditions secured, some of them were as ready to undertake the perdition of one man as another; good, bad, or indifferent, it made little matter.

What wonder, then, that such abominable mercenaries should cause a mighty deal of mischief in Minda; privately going about, inciting peaceable folks to enmities with their neighbors; and with marvelous alacrity, proposing themselves as the very sorcerers to rid them of the annoyances suggested as existing.

Indeed, it even happened that a sorcerer would be secretly retained to work spells upon a victim, who, from his bodily sensations, suspecting something wrong, but knowing not what, would repair to that self-same sorcerer, engaging him to counteract any mischief that might be brewing. And this worthy would at once undertake the business; when, having both parties in his hands, he kept them forever in suspense; meanwhile seeing to it well, that they failed not in handsomely remunerating him for his pains.

At one time, there was a prodigious excitement about these sorcerers, growing out of some alarming revelations concerning their practices. In several villages of Minda, they were sought to be put down. But fruitless the attempt; it was soon discovered that already their spells were so spread abroad, and they themselves so mixed up with the every-day affairs of the isle, that it was better to let their vocation alone, than, by endeavoring to suppress it, breed additional troubles. Ah! they were a knowing and a cunning set, those sorcerers; very hard to overcome, cajole, or circumvent.

But in the name of the Magi, what were these spells of theirs, so potent and occult? On all hands it was agreed, that they derived their greatest virtue from the fumes of certain compounds, whose ingredients—horrible to tell—were mostly obtained from the human heart; and that by variously mixing these ingredients, they adapted their multifarious enchantments.

They were a vain and arrogant race. Upon the strength of their dealing in the dark, they affected even more mystery than belonged to them; when interrogated concerning their science, would confound the inquirer by answers couched in an extraordinary jargon, employing words almost as long as anacondas. But all this greatly prevailed with the common people.

Nor was it one of the least remarkable things, that oftentimes two sorcerers, contrarily employed upon a Mindarian,—one to attack, the other to defend,—would nevertheless be upon the most friendly terms with each other; which curious circumstance never begat the slightest suspicions in the mind of the victim.

Another phenomenon: If from any cause, two sorcerers fell out, they seldom exercised their spells upon each other; ascribable to this, perhaps,—that both being versed in the art, neither could hope to get the advantage.

But for all the opprobrium cast upon these sorcerers, part of which they deserved, the evils imputed to them were mainly, though indirectly, ascribable to the very persons who abused them; nay, to the very persons who employed them; the latter being by far the loudest in their vilifyings; for which, indeed, they had excellent reason.

Nor was it to be denied, that in certain respects, the sorcerers were productive of considerable good. The nature of their pursuits leading them deep into the arcana of mind, they often lighted upon important discoveries; along with much that was cumbersome, accumulated valuable examples concerning the inner working of the hearts of the Mindarians; and often waxed eloquent in elucidating the mysteries of iniquity.

Yet was all this their lore graven upon so uncouth, outlandish, and antiquated tablets, that it was all but lost to the mass of their countrymen; and some old sachem of a wise man is quoted as having said, that their treasures were locked up after such a fashion, that for old iron, the key was worth more than the chest and its contents.

Chapter 145

Chiefly of King Bello

"NOW TAJI," said Media, "with old Bello of the Hump whose island of Dominora is before us, I am at variance."

"Ah! How so?"

"A dull recital, but you shall have it."

And forthwith his Highness began.

This princely quarrel originated, it seems, in a slight jostling concerning the proprietorship of a barren islet in a very remote quarter of the lagoon. At the outset the matter might have been easily adjusted, had the parties but exchanged a few amicable words. But each disdaining to visit the other, to discuss so trivial an affair, the business of negotiating an understanding was committed to certain plenipos, men with lengthy tongues, who scorned to utter a word short of a polysyllable.

Now, the more these worthies penetrated into the difficulty, the wider became the breach; till what was at first a mere gap, became a yawning gulf.

But that which had perhaps tended more than any thing else to deepen the variance of the kings, was hump-backed Bello's dispatching to Odo, as his thirtieth plenipo, a diminutive little negotiator, who all by himself, in a solitary canoe, sailed over to have audience of Media; into whose presence he was immediately ushered.

Darting one glance at him, the king turned to his chieftains, and said:—
"By much straining of your eyes, my lords, can you perceive this insignificant manikin? What! are there no tall men in Dominora, that King Bello
must needs send this dwarf hither?"

And charging his attendants to feed the embassador extraordinary with
the soft pap of the cocoanut, and provide nurses during his stay, the monarch
retired from the arbor of audience.

"As I am a man," shouted the despised plenipo, raising himself on his
toes, "my royal master will resent this affront!—A dwarf, forsooth!—
Thank Oro, I am no long-drawn giant! There is as much stuff in me, as
in others; what is spread out in their clumsy carcasses, in me is condensed.
I am much in little! And that much, thou shalt know full soon, disdainful
King of Odo!"

"Speak not against our lord the king," cried the attendants.

"And speak not ye to me, ye headless spear poles!"

And so saying, under sufferance of being small, the plenipo was permitted to depart unmolested; for all his bravadoes, fobbing his credentials
and affronts.

Apprized of his servant's ignoble reception, the choleric Bello burst
forth in a storm of passion; issuing orders for one thousand conch shells
to be blown, and his warriors to assemble by land and by sea.

But bethinking him of the hostilities that might ensue, the sagacious
Media hit upon an honorable expedient to ward off an event for which
he was then unprepared. With all haste he dispatched to the hump-backed
king a little dwarf of his own; who voyaging over to Dominora in a
canoe, sorry and solitary as that of Bello's plenipo, in like manner, received
the same insults. The effect whereof, was, to strike a balance of affronts;
upon the principle, that a blow given, heals one received.

Nevertheless, these proceedings but amounted to a postponement of
hostilities; for soon after, nothing prevented the two kings from plunging into war, but the following judicious considerations. First: Media was
almost afraid of being beaten. Second: Bello was almost afraid to conquer.
Media, because he was inferior in men and arms; Bello, because his ag-
grandizement was already a subject of warlike comment among the neighboring kings.

Indeed, did the old chronicler Braid-Beard speak truth, there were
some tribes in Mardi, that accounted this king of Dominora a testy, quarrelsome, rapacious old monarch; the indefatigable breeder of contentions and
wars; the elder brother of this household of nations, perpetually essaying

to lord it over the juveniles; and though his patrimonial dominions were situated to the north of the lagoon, not the slightest misunderstanding took place between the rulers of the most distant islands, than this doughty old cavalier on a throne, forthwith thrust his insolent spear into the matter, though it in no wise concerned him, and fell to irritating all parties by his gratuitous interference.

Especially was he officious in the concerns of Porpheero, a neighboring island, very large and famous, whose numerous broad valleys were divided among many rival kings:—the king of Franko, a small-framed, poodle-haired, fine, fiery gallant; finical in his tatooing; much given to the dance and glory;—the king of Ibeereea, a tall and stately cavalier, proud, generous, punctilious, temperate in wine; one hand forever on his javelin, the other, in superstitious homage, lifted to his gods; his limbs all over marks of stakes and crosses;—the king of Luzianna; a slender, dark-browed chief; at times wrapped in a moody robe, beneath which he fumbled something, as if it were a dagger; but otherwise a sprightly troubadour, given to serenades and moonlight;—the many chiefs of sunny Latianna; minstrel monarchs, full of song and sentiment; fiercer in love than war; glorious bards of freedom: but rendering tribute while they sang;—the priest-king of Vatikanna; his chest marked over with antique tatooings; his crown, a cowl; his rusted scepter swaying over falling towers, and crumbling mounds; full of the superstitious past; askance, eyeing the suspicious time to come;—the king of Hapzaboro; portly, pleasant; a lover of wild boar's meat; a frequent quaffer from the can; in his better moods, much fancying solid comfort;—the eight-and-thirty banded kings, chieftains, seigniors, and oligarchies of the broad hill and dale of Tutoni; clubbing together their domains, that none might wrest his neighbor's; an earnest race; deep thinkers, deeper drinkers; long pipes, long heads; their wise ones given to mystic cogitations, and consultations with the devil;—the twin kings of Zandinavia; hardy, frugal mountaineers; upright of spine and heart; clad in skins of bears;—the king of Jutlanda; much like their Highnesses of Zandinavia; a seal-skin cap his crown; a fearless sailor of his frigid seas;—the king of Muzkovi; a shaggy, icicled White-bear of a despot in the north; said to reign over millions of acres of glaciers; had vast provinces of snow-drifts, and many flourishing colonies among the floating ice-bergs. Absolute in his rule as Predestination in metaphysics, did he command all his people to give up the ghost, it would be held treason to die last. Very precise and foppish in his imperial tastes was this monarch. Disgusted with the want of uniformity in the stature of his subjects, he was said to nourish thoughts of killing off all those below his prescribed standard—six feet, long measure. Immortal souls were of no account in his fatal wars; since, in some of his serf-breeding estates, they were daily manufactured to order.

Now, to all the above-mentioned monarchs, old Bello would frequently dispatch heralds; announcing, for example, his unalterable resolution, to espouse the cause of this king, against that; at the very time, perhaps, that their Serene Superfluities, instead of crossing spears, were touching flagons. And upon these occasions, the kings would often send back word to old Bello, that instead of troubling himself with their concerns, he might far better attend to his own; which, they hinted, were in a sad way, and much needed reform.

The royal old warrior's pretext for these and all similar proceedings, was the proper adjustment in Porpheero, of what he facetiously styled the "Equipoise of Calabashes;" which he stoutly swore was essential to the security of the various tribes in that country.

"But who put the balance into thy hands, King Bello?" cried the indignant nations.

"Oro!" shouted the hump-backed king, shaking his javelin.

Superadded to the paternal interest which Bello betrayed in the concerns of the kings of Porpheero, according to our chronicler, he also manifested no less interest in those of the remotest islands. Indeed, where he found a rich country, inhabited by a people, deemed by him barbarous and incapable of wise legislation, he sometimes relieved them from their political anxieties, by assuming the dictatorship over them. And if incensed at his conduct, they flew to their spears, they were accounted rebels, and treated accordingly. But as old Mohi very truly observed,—herein, Bello was not alone; for throughout Mardi, all strong nations, as well as all strong men, loved to govern the weak. And those who most taunted King Bello for his political rapacity, were open to the very same charge. So with Vivenza, a distant island, at times very loud in denunciations of Bello, as a great national brigand. Not yet wholly extinct in Vivenza, were its aboriginal people, a race of wild Nimrods and hunters, who year by year were driven further and further into remoteness, till as one of their sad warriors said, after continual removes along the log, his race was on the point of being remorselessly pushed off the end.

Now, Bello was a great geographer, and land surveyor, and gauger of the seas. Terraqueous Mardi, he was continually exploring in quest of strange empires. Much he loved to take the altitude of lofty mountains, the depth of deep rivers, the breadth of broad isles. Upon the highest pinnacles of commanding capes and promontories, he loved to hoist his flag. He circled Mardi with his watch-towers: and the distant voyager passing wild rocks in the remotest waters, was startled by hearing the tattoo, or the reveille, beating from hump-backed Bello's omnipresent drum. Among Antartic glaciers, his shrill bugle calls mingled with the scream of the gulls; and so impressed seemed universal nature with the sense of his dominion, that the very clouds in heaven never sailed over Dominora without rendering the tribute of a shower; whence the air of Dominora was more moist than that of any other clime.

In all his grand undertakings, King Bello was marvelously assisted by his numerous fleets of war-canoes; his navy being the largest in Mardi. Hence his logicians swore that the entire Lagoon was his; and that all prowling whales, prowling keels, and prowling sharks were invaders. And with this fine conceit to inspire them, his poets-laureat composed some glorious old salt-water odes, enough to make your very soul sing to hear them.

But though the rest of Mardi much delighted to list to such noble minstrelsy, they agreed not with Bello's poets in deeming the lagoon their old monarch's hereditary domain.

Once upon a time, the paddlers of the hump-backed king, meeting upon the broad lagoon certain canoes belonging to the before-mentioned island of Vivenza; these paddlers seized upon several of their occupants; and feeling their pulses, declared them born men of Dominora; and therefore, not free to go whithersoever they would; for, unless they could somehow get themselves born over again, they must forever remain subject to Bello. Shed your hair; nay, your skin, if you will, but shed your allegiance you can not; while you have bones, they are Bello's. So, spite of all expostulations and attempts to prove alibis, these luckless paddlers were dragged into the canoes of Dominora, and commanded to paddle home their captors.

Whereof hearing, the men of Vivenza were thrown into a great ferment; and after a mighty pow-wow over their council fire, fitting out several double-keeled canoes, they sallied out to sea, in quest of those, whom they styled the wholesale corsairs of Dominora.

But lucky perhaps it was, that at this juncture, in all parts of Mardi, the fleets of the hump-backed king, were fighting, gunwale and gunwale, alongside of numerous foes; else there had borne down upon the canoes of the men of Vivenza so tremendous an armada, that the very swell under its thousand prows might have flooded their scattered proas forever out of sight.

As it was, Bello dispatched a few of his smaller craft to seek out, and incidentally run down the enemy; and without returning home, straightway proceed upon more important enterprises.

But it so chanced, that Bello's crafts, one by one meeting the foe, in most cases found the canoes of Vivenza much larger than their own; and manned by more men, with hearts bold as theirs; whence, in the ship-duels that ensued, they were worsted; and the canoes of Vivenza, locking their yard-arms into those of the vanquished, very courteously gallanted them into their coral harbors.

Solely imputing these victories to their superior intrepidity and skill, the people of Vivenza were exceedingly boisterous in their triumph; raising such obstreperous peans, that they gave themselves hoarse throats; insomuch, that according to Mohi, some of the present generation are fain to speak through their noses.

Chapter 146

Dominora and Vivenza

THE THREE CANOES still gliding on, some further particulars were narrated concerning Dominora; and incidentally, of other isles.

It seems that his love of wide dominion sometimes led the otherwise sagacious Bello into the most extravagant actions. If the chance accumulation of soil and drift-wood about any detached shelf of coral in the lagoon held forth the remotest possibility of the eventual existence of an islet there, with all haste he dispatched canoes to the spot, to take prospective possession of the as yet nearly sub-marine territory; and if possible, eject the zoophytes.

During an unusually low tide, here and there baring the outer reef of the Archipelago, Bello caused his royal spear to be planted upon every place thus exposed, in token of his supreme claim thereto.

Another anecdote was this: that to Dominora there came a rumor, that in a distant island dwelt a man with an uncommonly large nose; of most portentous dimensions, indeed; by the soothsayers supposed to foreshadow some dreadful calamity. But disregarding these superstitious conceits, Bello forthwith dispatched an agent, to discover whether this huge promontory of a nose was geographically available; if so, to secure the same, by bringing the proprietor back.

Now, by sapient old Mohi, it was esteemed a very happy thing for Mardi at large, that the subjects whom Bello sent to populate his foreign

471

acquisitions, were but too apt to throw off their vassalage, so soon as they deemed themselves able to cope with him.

Indeed, a fine country in the western part of Mardi, in this very manner, became a sovereign—nay, a republican state. It was the nation to which Mohi had previously alluded—Vivenza. But in the flush and pride of having recently attained their national majority, the men of Vivenza were perhaps too much inclined to carry a vauntful crest. And because intrenched in their fastnesses, after much protracted fighting, they had eventually succeeded in repelling the warriors dispatched by Bello to crush their insurrection, they were unanimous in the opinion, that the hump-backed king had never before been so signally chastised. Whereas, they had not so much vanquished Bello, as defended their shores; even as a young lion will protect its den against legions of unicorns, though, away from home, he might be torn to pieces. In truth, Braid-Beard declared, that at the time of this war, Dominora couched ten long spears for every short javelin Vivenza could dart; though the javelins were stoutly hurled as the spears.

But, superior in men and arms, why, at last, gave over King Bello the hope of reducing those truculent men of Vivenza? One reason was, as Mohi said, that many of his fighting men were abundantly occupied in other quarters of Mardi; nor was he long in discovering, that fight he never so valiantly, Vivenza—not yet its inhabitants—was wholly unconquerable. Thought Bello, Mountains are sturdy foes; fate hard to dam.

Yet, the men of Vivenza were no dastards; not to lie, coming from lion-like loins, they were a lion-loined race. Did not their bards pronounce them a fresh start in the Mardian species; requiring a new world for their full development? For be it known, that the great land of Kolumbo, no inconsiderable part of which was embraced by Vivenza, was the last island discovered in the Archipelago.

In good round truth, and as if an impartialist from Arcturus spoke it, Vivenza was a noble land. Like a young tropic tree she stood, laden down with greenness, myriad blossoms, and the ripened fruit thick-hanging from one bough. She was promising as the morning.

Or Vivenza might be likened to St. John, feeding on locusts and wild honey, and with prophetic voice, crying to the nations from the wilderness. Or, child-like, standing among the old robed kings and emperors of the Archipelago, Vivenza seemed a young Messiah, to whose discourse the bearded Rabbis bowed.

So seemed Vivenza in its better aspect. Nevertheless, Vivenza was a braggadocio in Mardi; the only brave one ever known. As an army of spurred and crested roosters, her people chanticleered at the resplendent rising of their sun. For shame, Vivenza! Whence thy undoubted valor? Did ye not bring it with ye from the bold old shores of Dominora, where there is a fullness of it left? What isle but Dominora could have supplied thee with that stiff spine of thine?—That heart of boldest beat? Oh, Vivenza! know that true grandeur is too big for a boast; and nations, as well as men, may be too clever to be great.

But what more of King Bello? Notwithstanding his territorial acquisitiveness, and aversion to relinquishing stolen nations, he was yet a glorious old king; rather choleric—a word and a blow—but of a right royal heart. Rail at him as they might, at bottom, all the isles were proud of him. And almost in spite of his rapacity, upon the whole, perhaps, they were the better for his deeds. For if sometimes he did evil with no very virtuous intentions, he had fifty ways of accomplishing good with the best; and a thousand ways of doing good without meaning it. According to an ancient oracle, the hump-backed monarch was but one of the most conspicuous pieces on a board, where the gods played for their own entertainment.

But here it must not be omitted, that of late, King Bello had somewhat abated his efforts to extend his dominions. Various causes were assigned. Some thought it arose from the fact that already he found his territories too extensive for one scepter to rule; that his more remote colonies largely contributed to his tribulations, without correspondingly contributing to his revenues. Others affirmed that his hump was getting too mighty for him to carry; others still, that the nations were waxing too strong for him. With prophetic solemnity, head-shaking sages averred that he was growing older and older; had passed his grand climacteric; and though it was a hale old age with him, yet it was not his lusty youth; that though he was daily getting rounder, and rounder in girth, and more florid of face, that these, howbeit, were rather the symptoms of a morbid obesity, than of a healthful robustness. These wise ones predicted that very soon poor Bello would go off in an apoplexy.

But in Vivenza there were certain blusterers, who often thus prated: "The Hump-back's hour is come; at last the old teamster will be gored by the nations he's yoked; his game is done,—let him show his hand and throw up his scepter; he cumbers Mardi,—let him be cut down and burned; he stands in the way of his betters,—let him sheer to one side; he has shut up many eyes, and now himself grows blind; he hath committed horrible atrocities during his long career, the old sinner!—now, let him quickly say his prayers and be beheaded."

Howbeit, Bello lived on; enjoying his dinners, and taking his jorums as of yore. Ah, I have yet a jolly long lease of life, thought he over his wine; and like unto some obstinate old uncle, he persisted in flourishing, in spite of the prognostications of the nephew nations, which at his demise, perhaps hoped to fall heir to odd parts of his possessions: Three streaks of fat valleys to one of lean mountains!

Chapter 147

They land at Dominora

A S EREWHILE RECOUNTED, not being on the best terms in
Mardi with the King of Dominora, Media saw fit to draw nigh
unto his dominions in haughty state; he (Media) being upon excellent terms with himself. Our sails were set, our paddles paddling, streamers streaming, and Vee-Vee in the shark's mouth, clamorous with his
conch. The din was soon heard; and sweeping into a fine broad bay we
beheld its margin seemingly pebbled in the distance with heads; so populous
the land.

Winding through a noble valley, we presently came to Bello's palace,
couchant and bristling in a grove. The upright canes composing its front
projected above the eaves in a long row of spear-heads fluttering with
scarlet pennons; while below, from the intervals of the canes, were slant-
ingly thrust three tiers of decorated lances. A warlike aspect! The entire
structure looking like the broadside of the Macedonian phalanx, advancing
to the charge, helmeted with a roof.

"Ah, Bello," said Media, "thou dwellest among thy quills like the
porcupine."

"I feel a prickly heat coming over me," cried Mohi, "my lord Media,
let us enter."

"Ay," said Babbalanja, "safer the center of peril, than the circumference."

Passing under an arch, formed by two pikes crossed, we found ourselves targets in prospective, for certain flingers of javelins, with poised weapons, occupying the angles of the palace.

Fronting us, stood a portly old warrior, spear in hand, hump on back, and fire in eye.

"Is it war?" he cried, pointing his pike, "or peace?" reversing it.

"Peace," said Media.

Whereupon advancing, King Bello courteously welcomed us.

He was an arsenal to behold: Upon his head the hereditary crown of Dominora,—a helmet of the sea-porcupine's hide, bristling all over with spikes, in front displaying a river-horse's horn, leveled to the charge; thrust through his ears were barbed arrows; and from his dyed shark-skin girdle, depended a kilt of strung javelins.

The broad chest of Bello was the chart of Mardi. Tattooed in sea-blue were all the groups and clusters of the Archipelago; and every time he breathed, rose and fell the isles, as by a tide: Dominora full upon his heart.

His sturdy thighs were his triumphal arch; whereon in numerous medallions, crests, and shields, were blazoned all his victories by sea and land.

His strong right arm was Dominora's scroll of Fame, where all her heroes saw their names recorded.—An endless roll!

Our chronicler avouched, that on the sole of Bello's dexter foot was stamped the crest of Franko's king, his hereditary foe. "Thus, thus," cried Bello, stamping, "thus I hourly crush him."

In stature, Bello was a mountaineer; but, as over some tall tower impends the hill-side cliff, so Bello's Athos hump hung over him. Could it be, as many of his nobles held, that the old monarch's hump was his sensorium and source of strength; full of nerves, muscles, ganglions and tendons? Yet, year by year it grew, ringed like the bole of his palms. The toils of war increased it. But another skirmish with the isles, said the wise-acres of Porpheero, and Bello's mount will crush him.

Against which calamity to guard, his medicos and Sangredos sought the hump's reduction. But down it would not come. Then by divers mystic rites, his magi tried. Making a deep pit, many teeth they dropped therein. But they could not fill it. Hence, they called it the Sinking Pit, for bottom it had none. Nevertheless, the magi said, when this pit is filled, Bello's hump you'll see no more. "Then, hurrah for the hump!" cried the nobles, "for he will never hurl it off. Long life to the hump! By the hump we will rally and die! Cheer up, King Bello! Stand up, old king!"

But these were they, who when their sovereign went abroad, with that

Athos on his back, followed idly in its shade; while Bello leaned heavily upon his people, staggering as they went.

Ay, sorely did Bello's goodly stature lean; but though many swore he soon must fall; nevertheless, like Pisa's Leaning Tower, he may long lean over, yet never nod.

Visiting Dominora in a friendly way, in good time, we found King Bello very affable; in hospitality, almost exceeding portly Borabolla: October-plenty reigned throughout his palace borders.

Our first reception over, a sumptuous repast was served, at which much lively talk was had.

Of Taji, Bello sought to know, whether his solar Majesty had yet made a province of the moon; whether the Astral hosts were of much account as territories, or mere Motoos, as the little tufts of verdure are denominated, here and there clinging to Mardi's circle reef; whether the people in the sun vilified him (Bello) as they did in Mardi; and what they thought of an event, so ominous to the liberties of the universe, as the addition to his navy of three large canoes.

Ere long, so fused in social love we grew, that Bello, filling high his can, and clasping Media's palm, drank everlasting amity with Odo.

So over their red cups, the two kings forgot their differences, and concerning the disputed islet nothing more was ever heard; especially, as it so turned out, that while they were most hot about it, it had suddenly gone out of sight, being of volcanic origin.

Chapter 148

Through Dominora, they wander after Yillah

A T LAST, withdrawing from the presence of King Bello, we went
forth, still intent on our search.

Many brave sights we saw. Fair fields; the whole island a garden;
green hedges all round; neat lodges, thick as white mice in the landscape;
old oak woods, hale and hearty as ever; old temples buried in ivy; old
shrines of old heroes, deep buried in broad groves of bay trees; old rivers
laden down with heavy-freighted canoes; humped hills, like droves of
camels, piled up with harvests; every sign and token of a glorious abundance, every sign and token of generations of renown. Rare sight! fine
sight! none rarer, none finer in Mardi.

But roving on through this ravishing region, we passed through a corn-
field in full beard, where a haggard old reaper laid down his hook, be-
seeching charity for the sake of the gods.—"Bread, bread! or I die mid
these sheaves!"

"Thrash out your grain, and want not."

"Alas, masters, this grain is not mine; I plough, I sow, I reap, I bind,
I stack,—Lord Primo garners."

Rambling on, we came to a hamlet, hidden in a hollow; and beneath
weeping willows saw many mournful maidens seated on a bank; beside
each, a wheel that was broken. "Lo, we starve," they cried, "our distaffs
are snapped; no more may we weave and spin!"

478

Then forth issued from vaults clamorous crowds of men, hands tied to their backs.—"Bread! Bread!" they cried. "The magician hath turned us out from our glen, where we labored of yore in the days of the merry Green Queen. He has pinioned us hip and arm that we starve. Like sheep we die off with the rot.—Curse on the magician. A curse on his spell."

Bending our steps toward the glen, roaring down the rocks we descried a stream from the mountains. But ere those waters gained the sea, vassal tribute they rendered. Conducted through culverts and moats, they turned great wheels, giving life to ten thousand fangs and fingers, whose gripe no power could withstand, yet whose touch was soft as the velvet paw of a kitten. With brute force, they heaved down great weights, then daintily wove and spun; like the trunk of the elephant, which lays lifeless a river-horse, and counts the pulses of a moth. On all sides, the place seemed alive with its spindles. Round and round, round and round; throwing off wondrous births at every revolving; ceaseless as the cycles that circle in heaven. Loud hummed the loom, flew the shuttle like lightning, red roared the grim forge, rung anvil and sledge; yet no mortal was seen.

"What ho, magician! Come forth from thy cave!"

But all deaf were the spindles, as the mutes, that mutely wait on the Sultan.

"Since we are born, we will live!" so we read on a crimson banner, flouting the crimson clouds, in the van of a riotous red-bonneted mob, racing by us as we came from the glen. Many more followed: black, or blood-stained:—

"Mardi is man's!"

"Down with landholders!"

"Our turn now!"

"Up rights! Down wrongs!"

"Bread! Bread!"

"Take the tide, ere it turns!"

Waving their banners, and flourishing aloft clubs, hammers, and sickles, with fierce yells the crowd ran on toward the palace of Bello. Foremost, and inciting the rest by mad outcries and gestures, were six masks; "This way! This way!" they cried,—"by the wood; by the dark wood!" Whereupon all darted into the groves; when of a sudden, the masks leaped forward, clearing a long covered trench, into which fell many of those they led. But on raced the masks; and gaining Bello's palace, and raising the alarm, there sallied from thence a woodland of spears, which charged upon the disordered ranks in the grove. A crash as of icicles against icebergs round Zembla, and down went the hammers and sickles. The host fled, hotly pursued. Meanwhile brave heralds from Bello advanced, and with chaplets crowned the six masks.—"Welcome, heroes! worthy and valiant!" they cried. "Thus our lord Bello rewards all those, who to do him a service, for hire betray their kith and their kin."

Still pursuing our quest, wide we wandered through all the sun and shade of Dominora; but nowhere was Yillah found.

Chapter 149

They behold King Bello's State Canoe

AT LAST, bidding adieu to King Bello; and in the midst of the lowing of oxen, breaking away from his many hospitalities, we departed for the beach. But ere embarking, we paused to gaze at an object, which long fixed our attention.

Now, as all bold cavaliers have ever delighted in special chargers, gayly caparisoned, whereon upon grand occasions to sally forth upon the plains: even so have maritime potentates ever prided themselves upon some holiday galley, splendidly equipped, wherein to sail over the sea.

When of old, glory-seeking Jason, attended by his promising young lieutenants, Castor and Pollux, embarked on that hardy adventure to Colchis, the brave planks of the good ship Argos he trod, its model a swan to behold.

And when Trojan Æneas wandered West, and discovered the pleasant land of Latium, it was in the fine craft Bis Taurus that he sailed: its stern gloriously emblazoned, its prow a leveled spear.

And to the sound of sackbut and psaltery, gliding down the Nile, in the pleasant shade of its pyramids to welcome mad Mark, Cleopatra was throned on the cedar quarter-deck of a glorious gondola, silk and satin hung; its silver plated oars, musical as flutes. So, too, Queen Bess was wont to disport on old Thames.

481

And tough Torf-Egill, the Danish Sea-king, reckoned in his stud, a slender yacht; its masts young Zetland firs; its prow a seal, dog-like holding a sword-fish blade. He called it the Grayhound, so swift was its keel; the Sea-hawk, so blood-stained its beak.

And groping down his palace stairs, the blind old Doge Dandolo, oft embarked in his gilded barge, like the lord-mayor setting forth in civic state from Guildhall in his chariot. But from another sort of prow leaped Dandolo, when at Constantinople, he foremost sprang ashore, and with a right arm ninety years old, planted the standard of St. Mark full among the long chin-pennons of the long-bearded Turks.

And Kumbo Sama, Emperor of Japan, had a dragon-beaked junk, a floating Juggernaut, wherein he burnt incense to the sea-gods.

And Kannakoko, King of New Zealand; and the first Tahitian Pomaree; and the Pelew potentate, each possessed long state canoes; sea-snakes, all; carved over like Chinese card-cases, and manned with such scores of warriors, that dipping their paddles in the sea, they made a commotion like shoals of herring.

What wonder then, that Bello of the Hump, the old sea-king of Mardi, should sport a brave ocean-chariot?

In a broad arbor by the water-side, it was housed like Alp Arslan's war-horse, or the charger Caligula deified; upon its stern a wilderness of sculpture:—shell-work, medallions, masques, griffins, gulls, ogres, finned-lions, winged walruses; all manner of sea-cavalry, crusading centaurs, crocodiles, and sharks; and mermen, and mermaids, and Neptune only knows all.

And in this craft, Doge-like, yearly did King Bello stand up and wed with the Lagoon. But the custom originated not in the manner of the Doge's, which was as follows; so, at least, saith Ghibelli, who tells all about it:—

When, in a stout sea-fight, Ziani defeated Barbarossa's son Otho, sending his feluccas all flying, like frightened water-fowl from a lake, then did his Holiness, the Pope, present unto him a ring; saying, "Take this, oh Ziani, and with it, the sea for thy bride; and every year wed her again."

So the Doge's tradition; thus Bello's:—

Ages ago, Dominora was circled by a reef, which expanding in proportion to the extension of the isle's naval dominion, in due time embraced the entire lagoon; and this marriage ring zoned all the world.

But if the sea was King Bello's bride, an Adriatic Tartar he wedded; who, in her mad gales of passions, often boxed about his canoes, and led his navies a very boisterous life indeed.

And hostile prognosticators opined, that ere long she would desert her old lord, and marry again. Already, they held, she had made advances in the direction of Vivenza.

But truly, should she abandon old Bello, he would straightway after her with all his fleets; and never rest till his queen was regained.

Now, old sea-king! look well to thy barge of state: for, peradventure, the dry-rot may be eating into its keel; and the wood-worms exploring into its spars.

Without heedful tending, any craft will decay; yet, forever may its first, fine model be preserved, though its prow be renewed every spring, like the horns of the deer, if, in repairing, plank be put for plank, rib for rib, in exactest similitude. Even so, then, oh Bello! do thou with thy barge.

Chapter 150

Wherein Babbalanja bows thrice

T HE NEXT MORNING'S TWILIGHT found us once more
afloat; and yielding to that almost sullen feeling, but too apt to
prevail with some mortals at that hour, all but Media long remained silent.

But now, a bright mustering is seen among the myriad white Tartar
tents in the Orient; like lines of spears defiling upon some upland plain,
the sunbeams thwart the sky. And see! amid the blaze of banners, and the
pawings of ten thousand thousand golden hoofs, day's mounted Sultan,
Xerxes-like, moves on: the Dawn his standard, East and West his cymbals.

"Oh, morning life!" cried Yoomy, with a Persian air; "would that all
time were a sunrise, and all life a youth."

"Ah! but these striplings whimper of youth," said Mohi, caressing his
braids, "as if they wore this beard."

"But natural, old man," said Babbalanja. "We Mardians never seem
young to ourselves; childhood is to youth what manhood is to age:—
something to be looked back upon, with sorrow that it is past. But childhood
recks of no future, and knows no past; hence, its present passes in a vapor."

"Mohi, how's your appetite this morning?" said Media.

"Thus, thus, ye gods," sighed Yoomy, "is feeling ever scouted. Yet,
what might seem feeling in me, I can not express."

"A good commentary on old Bardianna, Yoomy," said Babbalanja, "who somewhere says, that no Mardian can out with his heart, for his unyielding ribs are in the way. And indeed, pride, or something akin thereto, often holds check on sentiment. My lord, there are those who like not to be detected in the possession of a heart."

"Very true, Babbalanja; and I suppose that pride was at the bottom of your old Ponderer's heartless, unsentimental, bald-pated style."

"Craving pardon, my lord is deceived. Bardianna was not at all proud; though he had a queer way of showing the absence of pride. In his essay, entitled,—'On the Tendency to curl in Upper Lips,' he thus discourses. 'We hear much of pride and its sinfulness in this Mardi wherein we dwell: whereas, I glory in being brimmed with it;—my sort of pride. In the presence of kings, lords, palm-trees, and all those who deem themselves taller than myself, I stand stiff as a pike, and will abate not one vertebra of my stature. But accounting no Mardian my superior, I account none my inferior; hence, with the social, I am ever ready to be sociable.'"

"An agrarian!" said Media; "no doubt he would have made the headsman the minister of equality."

"At bottom we are already equal, my honored lord," said Babbalanja, profoundly bowing—"One way we all come into Mardi, and one way we withdraw. Wanting his yams a king will starve, quick as a clown; and smote on the hip, saith old Bardianna, he will roar as loud as the next one."

"Roughly worded, that, Babbalanja.—Vee-Vee! my crown!—So; now, Babbalanja, try if you can not polish Bardianna's style in that last saying you father upon him."

"I will, my ever honorable lord," said Babbalanja, salaming. "Thus we'll word it, then: In their merely Mardian nature, the sublimest demi-gods are subject to infirmities; for struck by some keen shaft, even a king ofttimes dons his crown, fearful of future darts."

"Ha, ha!—well done, Babbalanja; but I bade you polish, not sharpen the arrow."

"All one, my thrice honored lord;—to polish is not to blunt."

Chapter 151

Babbalanja philosophizes, and my Lord Media passes round the Calabashes

AN INTERVAL OF SILENCE PASSED; when Media cried, "Out upon thee, Yoomy! curtail that long face of thine."

"How can he, my lord," said Mohi, "when he is thinking of furlongs?"

"Fathoms you mean, Mohi; see you not he is musing over the gunwale? And now, minstrel, a banana for thy thoughts. Come, tell me how you poets spend so many hours in meditation."

"My lord, it is because, that when we think, we think so little of ourselves."

"I thought as much," said Mohi, "for no sooner do I undertake to be sociable with myself, than I am straightway forced to beat a retreat."

"Ay, old man," said Babbalanja, "many of us Mardians are but sorry hosts to ourselves. Some hearts are hermits."

"If not of yourself, then, Yoomy, of whom else do you think?" asked Media.

"My lord, I seldom think," said Yoomy; "I but give ear to the voices in my calm."

"Did Babbalanja speak?" said Media. "But no more of your reveries;" and so saying Media gradually sunk into a reverie himself.

The rest did likewise; and soon, with eyes enchanted, all reclined: gazing at each other, witless of what we did.

486

It was Media who broke the spell; calling for Vee-Vee our page, his calabashes and cups, and nectarines for all.

Eyeing his goblet, Media at length threw himself back, and said: "Babbalanja, not ten minutes since, we were all absent-minded; now, how would you like to step out of your body, in reality; and, as a spirit, haunt some shadowy grove?"

"But our lungs are not wholly superfluous, my lord," said Babbalanja, speaking loud.

"No, nor our lips," said Mohi, smacking his over his wine.

"But could you really be disembodied here in Mardi, Babbalanja, how would you fancy it?" said Media.

"My lord," said Babbalanja, speaking through half of a nectarine, "defer putting that question, I beseech, till after my appetite is satisfied; for, trust me, no hungry mortal would forfeit his palate, to be resolved into the impalpable."

"Yet pure spirits we must all become at last, Babbalanja," said Yoomy, "even the most ignoble."

"Yes, so they say, Yoomy; but if all boors be the immortal sires of endless dynasties of immortals, how little do our pious patricians bear in mind their magnificent destiny, when hourly they scorn their companionship. And if here in Mardi they can not abide an equality with plebeians, even at the altar; how shall they endure them, side by side, throughout eternity? But since the prophet Alma asserts, that Paradise is almost entirely made up of the poor and despised, no wonder that many aristocrats of our isles pursue a career, which, according to some theologies, must forever preserve the social distinctions so sedulously maintained in Mardi. And though some say, that at death every thing earthy is removed from the spirit, so that clowns and lords both stand on a footing; yet, according to the popular legends, it has ever been observed of the ghosts of boors when revisiting Mardi, that invariably they rise in their smocks. And regarding our intellectual equality hereafter, how unjust, my lord, that after whole years of days and nights consecrated to the hard gaining of wisdom, the wisest Mardian of us all should in the end find the whole sum of his attainments, at one leap outstripped by the veriest dunce, suddenly inspired by light divine. And though some hold, that all Mardian lore is vain, and that at death all mysteries will be revealed; yet, none the less, do they toil and ponder now. Thus, their tongues have one mind, and their understanding another."

"My lord," said Mohi, "we have come to the lees; your pardon, Babbalanja."

"Then, Vee-Vee, another calabash! Fill up, Mohi; wash down wine with wine. Your cup, Babbalanja; any lees?"

"Plenty, my lord; we philosophers come to the lees very soon."

"Flood them over, then; but cease not discoursing; thanks be to the gods, your mortal palates and tongues can both wag together; fill up, I say, Babbalanja; you are no philosopher, if you stop at the tenth cup; endurance is the test of philosophy all Mardi over; drink, I say, and make us wise by precept and example.—Proceed, Yoomy, you look as if you had something to say."

"Thanks, my lord. Just now, Babbalanja, you flew from the subject;— you spoke of boors; but has not the lowliest peasant an eye that can take in the vast horizon at a sweep: mountains, vales, plains, and oceans? Is such a being nothing?"

"But can that eye see itself, Yoomy?" said Babbalanja, winking. "Taken out of its socket, will it see at all? Its connection with the body imparts to it its virtue."

"He questions every thing," cried Mohi. "Philosopher, have you a head?"

"I have," said Babbalanja, feeling for it; "I am finished off at the helm very much as other Mardians, Mohi."

"My lord, the first yea that ever came from him."

"Ah, Mohi," said Media, "the discourse waxes heavy. I fear me we have again come to the lees. Ho, Vee-Vee, a fresh calabash; and with it we will change the subject. Now, Babbalanja, I have this cup to drink, and then a question to propound. Ah, Mohi, rare old wine this; it smacks of the cork. But attention, Philosopher. Supposing you had a wife—which, by the way, you have not—would you deem it sensible in her to imagine you no more, because you happened to stroll out of her sight?"

"However that might be," murmured Yoomy, "young Nina bewailed herself a widow, whenever Arhinoo, her lord, was absent from her side."

"My lord Media," said Babbalanja, "during my absence, my wife would have more reason to conclude that I was not living, than that I was. To the former supposition, every thing tangible around her would tend; to the latter, nothing but her own fond fancies. It is this imagination of ours, my lord, that is at the bottom of these things. When I am in one place, there exists no other. Yet am I but too apt to fancy the reverse. Nevertheless, when I am in Odo, talk not to me of Ohonoo. To me it is not, except when I am there. If it be, prove it. To prove it, you carry me thither; but you only prove, that to its substantive existence, as cognizant to me, my presence is indispensable. I say that, to me, all Mardi exists by virtue of my sovereign pleasure; and when I die, the universe will perish with me."

"Come you of a long-lived race," said Mohi, "one free from apoplexies? I have many little things to accomplish yet, and would not be left in the lurch."

"Heed him not, Babbalanja," said Media. "Dip your beak again, my eagle, and soar."

"Let us be eagles, then, indeed, my lord: eagle-like, let us look at this red wine without blinking; let us grow solemn, not boisterous, with good cheer."

Then, lifting his cup, "My lord, serenely do I pity all such who are stirred one jot from their centers by ever so much drinking of this fluid. Ply him hard as you will, through the live-long polar night, a wise man can not be made drunk. Though, toward sunrise, his body may reel, it will reel round its center; and though he make many tacks in going home, he reaches it at last; while scores of over-plied fools are foundering by the way. My lord, when wild with much thought, 'tis to wine I fly, to sober me; its magic fumes breathe over me like the Indian summer, which steeps all nature in repose. To me, wine is no vulgar fire, no fosterer of base passions; my heart, ever open, is opened still wider; and glorious visions are born in my brain; it is then that I have all Mardi under my feet, and the constellations of the firmament in my soul."

"Superb!" cried Yoomy.

"Pooh, pooh!" said Mohi, "who does not see stars at such times? I see the Great Bear now, and the little one, its cub; and Andromeda, and Perseus' chain-armor, and Cassiopea in her golden chair, and the bright, scaly Dragon, and the glittering Lyre, and all the jewels in Orion's sword-hilt."

"Ay," cried Media, "the study of astronomy is wonderfully facilitated by wine. Fill up, old Ptolemy, and tell us should you discover a new planet. Methinks this fluid needs stirring. Ho, Vee-Vee, my scepter! be we sociable. But come, Babbalanja, my gold-headed aquila, return to your theme;— the imagination, if you please."

"Well, then, my lord, I was about to say, that the imagination is the Voli-Donzini; or, to speak plainer, the unical, rudimental, and all-comprehending abstracted essence of the infinite remoteness of things. Without it, we were grass-hoppers."

"And with it, you mortals are little else; do you not chirp all over, Mohi? By my demi-god soul, were I not what I am, this wine would almost get the better of me."

"Without it—" continued Babbalanja.

"Without what?" demanded Media, starting to his feet. "This wine? Traitor, I'll stand by this to the last gasp; you are inebriated, Babbalanja."

"Perhaps so, my lord; but I was treating of the imagination, may it please you."

"My lord," added Mohi, "of the unical, and rudimental fundament of things, you remember."

"Ah! there's none of them sober; proceed, proceed, Azzageddi!"

"My lord waves his hand like a banner," murmured Yoomy.

"Without imagination, I say, an armless man, born blind, could not be made to believe, that he had a head of hair, since he could neither see it, nor feel it, nor has hair any feeling of itself."

"Methinks though," said Mohi, "if the cripple had a Tartar for a wife, he would not remain skeptical long."

"You all fly off at tangents," cried Media, "but no wonder: your mortal brains can not endure much quaffing. Return to your subject, Babbalanja. Assume now, Babbalanja,—assume, my dear prince—assume it, assume it, I say!—Why don't you?"

"I am willing to assume any thing you please, my lord: what is it?"

"Ah! yes!—Assume that—that upon returning home, you should find your wife had newly wedded, under the—the—the metaphysical presumption, that being no longer visible, you—*you* Azzageddi, had departed this life; in other words, out of sight, out of mind; what then, my dear prince?"

"Why then, my lord, I would demolish my rival in a trice."

"Would you?—then—then so much for your metaphysics, Bab— Babbalanja."

Babbalanja rose to his feet, muttering to himself—"Is this assumed, or real?—Can a demi-god be mastered by wine? Yet, the old mythologies make bacchanals of the gods. But he was wondrous keen! He felled me, ere he fell himself."

"Yoomy, my lord Media is in a very merry mood to-day," whispered Mohi, "but his counterfeit was not well done. No, no, a bacchanal is not used to be so logical in his cups."

Chapter 152

They sail round an Island without landing; and talk round a Subject without getting at it

PURPOSING A VISIT to Kaleedoni, a country integrally united to Dominora, our course now lay northward along the western white cliffs of the isle. But finding the wind ahead, and the current too strong for our paddlers, we were fain to forego our destination; Babbalanja observing, that since in Dominora we had not found Yillah, then in Kaleedoni the maiden could not be lurking.

And now, some conversation ensued concerning the country we were prevented from visiting. Our chronicler narrated many fine things of its people; extolling their bravery in war, their amiability in peace, their devotion in religion, their penetration in philosophy, their simplicity and sweetness in song, their loving-kindness and frugality in all things domestic:—running over a long catalogue of heroes, metaphysicians, bards, and good men.

But as all virtues are convertible into vices, so in some cases did the best traits of these people degenerate. Their frugality too often became parsimony; their devotion grim bigotry; and all this in a greater degree perhaps than could be predicated of the more immediate subjects of King Bello.

In Kaleedoni was much to awaken the fervor of its bards. Upland and lowland were full of the picturesque; and many unsung lyrics yet lurked

491

in her glens. Among her blue, heathy hills, lingered many tribes, who in their wild and tattooed attire, still preserved the garb of the mightiest nation of old times. They bared the knee, in token that it was honorable as the face, since it had never been bent.

While Braid-Beard was recounting these things, the currents were sweeping us over a strait, toward a deep green island, bewitching to behold.

Not greener that midmost terrace of the Andes, which under a torrid meridian steeps fair Quito in the dews of a perpetual spring;—not greener the nine thousand feet of Pirohitee's tall peak, which, rising from out the warm bosom of Tahiti, carries all summer with it into the clouds;—nay, not greener the famed gardens of Cyrus,—than the vernal lawn, the knoll, the dale of beautiful Verdanna.

"Alas, sweet isle! Thy desolation is overrun with vines," sighed Yoomy, gazing.

"Land of caitiff curs!" cried Media.

"Isle, whose future is in its past. Hearth-stone, from which its children run," said Babbalanja.

"I can not read thy chronicles for blood, Verdanna," murmured Mohi.

Gliding near, we would have landed, but the rolling surf forbade. Then thrice we circumnavigated the isle for a smooth, clear beach; but it was not found.

Meanwhile all still conversed.

"My lord," said Yoomy, "while we tarried with King Bello, I heard much of the feud between Dominora and this unhappy shore. Yet is not Verdanna as a child of King Bello's?"

"Yes, minstrel, a step-child," said Mohi.

"By way of enlarging his family circle," said Babbalanja, "an old lion once introduced a deserted young stag to his den; but the stag never became domesticated, and would still charge upon his foster-brothers.—Verdanna is not of the flesh and blood of Dominora, whence, in good part, these dissensions."

"But Babbalanja, is there no way of reconciling these foes?"

"But one way, Yoomy:—By filling up this strait with dry land; for, divided by water, we Mardians must ever remain more or less divided at heart. Though Kaleedoni was united to Dominora long previous to the union of Verdanna, yet Kaleedoni occasions Bello no disquiet; for, geographically one, the two populations insensibly blend at the point of junction. No hostile strait flows between the arms, that to embrace must touch."

"But, Babbalanja," said Yoomy, "what asks Verdanna of Dominora, that Verdanna so clamors at the denial?"

"They are arrant cannibals, Yoomy," said Media, "and desire the privilege of eating each other up."

"King Bello's idea," said Babbalanja; "but, in these things, my lord, you demi-gods are ever unanimous. But, whatever be Verdanna's demands, Bello persists in rejecting them."

"Why not grant every thing she asks, even to renouncing all claim upon the isle," said Mohi; "for thus, Bello would rid himself of many perplexities."

"And think you, old man," said Media, "that, bane or blessing, Bello will yield his birthright? Will a tri-crowned king resign his triple diadem? And even did Bello what you propose, he would only breed still greater perplexities. For if granted, full soon would Verdanna be glad to surrender many things she demands. And all she now asks, she has had in times past; but without turning it to advantage:—and is she wiser now?"

"Does she not demand her harvests, my lord?" said Yoomy, "and has not the reaper a right to his sheaf?"

"Cant! cant! Yoomy. If you reap for me, the sheaf is mine."

"But if the reaper reaps on his own harvest-field, whose then the sheaf, my lord?" said Babbalanja.

"His for whom he reaps—his lord's!"

"Then let the reaper go with sickle and with sword," said Yoomy, "with one hand, cut down the bearded grain; and with the other, smite his bearded lords."

"Thou growest fierce, in thy lyric moods, my warlike dove," said Media, blandly. "But for thee, philosopher, know thou, that Verdanna's men are of blood and brain inferior to Bello's native race; and the better Mardian must ever rule."

"Verdanna inferior to Dominora, my lord!—Has she produced no bards, no orators, no wits, no patriots? Mohi, unroll thy chronicles! Tell me, if Verdanna may not claim full many a star along King Bello's tattooed arm of Fame?"

"Even so," said Mohi. "Many chapters bear you out."

"But my lord," said Babbalanja, "as truth, omnipresent, lurks in all things, even in lies: so, does some germ of it lurk in the calumnies heaped on the people of this land. For though they justly boast of many lustrous names, these jewels gem no splendid robe. And though like a bower of grapes, Verdanna is full of gushing juices, spouting out in bright sallies of wit, yet not all her grapes make wine; and here and there, hang goodly clusters mildewed; or half devoured by worms, bred in their own tendrils."

"Drop, drop your grapes and metaphors!" cried Media. "Bring forth your thoughts like men; let them come naked into Mardi.—What do you mean, Babbalanja?"

"This, my lord, Verdanna's worst evils are her own, not of another's giving. Her own hand is her own undoer. She stabs herself with bigotry, superstition, divided councils, domestic feuds, ignorance, temerity; she wills, but does not; her East is one black storm-cloud, that never bursts; her utmost fight is a defiance; she showers reproaches, where she should rain down blows. She stands a mastiff baying at the moon."

"Tropes on tropes!" said Media. "Let me tell the tale,—straight-forward like a line. Verdanna is a lunatic—"

"A trope! my lord," cried Babbalanja.

"My tropes are not tropes," said Media, "but yours are.—Verdanna is a lunatic, that after vainly striving to cut another's throat, grimaces before a standing pool and threatens to cut his own. And is such a madman to be intrusted with himself? No; let another govern him, who is ungovernable to himself. Ay, and tight hold the rein; and curb, and rasp the bit. Do I exaggerate?—Mohi, tell me, if, save one lucid interval, Verdanna, while independent of Dominora, ever discreetly conducted her affairs? Was she not always full of fights and factions? And what first brought her under the sway of Bello's scepter? Did not her own Chief Dermoddi fly to Bello's ancestor for protection against his own seditious subjects? And thereby did not her own king unking himself? What wonder, then, and where the wrong, if Henro, Bello's conquering sire, seized the diadem?"

"What my lord cites is true," said Mohi, "but cite no more, I pray; lest, you harm your cause."

"Yet for all this, Babbalanja," said Media, "Bello but holds lunatic Verdanna's lands in trust."

"And may the guardian of an estate also hold custody of the ward, my lord?"

"Ay, if he can. What *can* be done, may be: that's the creed of demi-gods."

"Alas, alas!" cried Yoomy, "why war with words over this poor, suffering land. See! for all her bloom, her people starve; perish her yams, ere taken from the soil; the blight of heaven seems upon them."

"Not so," said Media. "Heaven sends no blights. Verdanna will not learn. And if from one season's rottenness, rottenness they sow again, rottenness must they reap. But Yoomy, you seem earnest in this matter;—come: on all hands it is granted that evils exist in Verdanna; now sweet sympathizer, what must the royal Bello do to mend them?"

"I am no sage," said Yoomy, "what would my lord Media do?"

"What would *you* do, Babbalanja?" said Media.

"Mohi, what you?" asked the philosopher.

"And what would the company do?" added Mohi.

"Now, though these evils pose us all," said Babbalanja, "there lately died in Verdanna, one, who set about curing them in a humane and peaceable way, waving war and bloodshed. That man was Konno. Under a huge caldron, he kept a roaring fire."

"Well, Azzageddi, how could that answer his purpose?" asked Media.

"Nothing better, my lord. His fire boiled his bread-fruit; and so convinced were his countrymen, that he was well employed, that they almost stripped their scanty orchards to fill his caldron."

"Konno was a knave," said Mohi.

"Your pardon, old man, but that is only known to his ghost, not to us. At any rate he was a great man; for even assuming he cajoled his country, no common man could have done it."

"Babbalanja," said Mohi, "my lord has been pleased to pronounce Verdanna crazy; now, may not her craziness arise from the irritating, tantalizing practices of Dominora?"

"Doubtless, Braid-Beard, many of the extravagances of Verdanna, are in good part to be ascribed to the cause you mention; but, to be impartial, none the less does Verdanna essay to taunt and provoke Dominora; yet not with the like result. Perceive you, Braid-Beard, that the trade-wind blows dead across this strait from Dominora, and not from Verdanna? Hence, when King Bello's men fling gibes and insults, every missile hits; but those of Verdanna are blown back in its teeth: her enemies jeering her again and again."

"King Bello's men are dastards for that," cried Yoomy.

"It shows neither sense, nor spirit, nor humanity," said Babbalanja.

"All wide of the mark," cried Media. "What is to be done for Verdanna?"

"What will she do for herself?" said Babbalanja.

"Philosopher, you are an extraordinary sage; and since sages should be seers, reveal Verdanna's future."

"My lord, you will ever find true prophets, prudent; nor will any prophet risk his reputation upon predicting aught concerning this land.

The isles are Oro's. Nevertheless, he who doctors Verdanna aright, will first medicine King Bello; who in some things is himself a patient, though he would fain be a physician. However, my lord, there is a demon of a doctor in Mardi, who at last deals with these desperate cases. He employs only pills, picked off the Couroupita Guianensis tree."

"And what sort of a vegetable is that?" asked Mohi.

"Consult the botanists," said Babbalanja.

Chapter 153

*They draw nigh to Porpheero; where they behold
a terrific Eruption*

G LIDING AWAY from Verdanna at the turn of the tide, we cleared
the strait, and gaining the more open lagoon, pointed our prows
for Porpheero, from whose magnificent monarchs my lord Media
promised himself a glorious reception.

"They are one and all demi-gods," he cried, "and have the old demi-
god feeling. We have seen no great valleys like theirs:—their scepters are
long as our spears; to their sumptuous palaces, Donjalolo's are but inns:—
their banquetting halls are as vistas; no generations run parallel to theirs:—
their pedigrees reach back into chaos.

"Babbalanja! here you will find food for philosophy:—the whole land
checkered with nations, side by side contrasting in costume, manners, and
mind. Here you will find science and sages; manuscripts in miles; bards
singing in choirs.

"Mohi! here you will flag over your page; in Porpheero the ages have
hived all their treasures: like a pyramid, the past shadows over the land.

"Yoomy! here you will find stuff for your songs:—blue rivers flowing
through forest arches, and vineyards; velvet meads, soft as ottomans:
bright maidens braiding the golden locks of the harvest; and a background
of mountains, that seem the end of the world. Or if nature will not content
you, then turn to the landscapes of art. See! mosaic walls, tattooed like our
faces; paintings, vast as horizons; and into which, you feel you could rush:

497

See! statues to which you could off turban; cities of columns standing thick as mankind; and firmament domes forever shedding their sunsets of gilding: See! spire behind spire, as if the land were the ocean, and all Bello's great navy were riding at anchor.

"Noble Taji! you seek for your Yillah;—give over despair! Porpheero's such a scene of enchantment, that there, the lost maiden must lurk."

"A glorious picture!" cried Babbalanja, "but turn the medal, my lord; —what says the reverse?"

"Cynic! have done.—But bravo! we'll ere long be in Franko, the good-liest vale of them all; how I long to take her old king by the hand!"

The sun was now setting behind us, lighting up the white cliffs of Domi-nora, and the green capes of Verdanna; while in deep shade lay before us the long winding shores of Porpheero.

It was a sunset serene.

"How the winds lowly warble in the dying day's ear," murmured Yoomy.

"A mild, bright night, we'll have," said Media.

"See you not those clouds over Franko, my lord," said Mohi, shaking his head.

"Ah, aged and weather-wise as ever, sir chronicler;—I predict a fair night, and many to follow."

"Patience needs no prophet," said Babbalanja. "The night is at hand."

Hitherto the lagoon had been smooth: but anon, it grew black, and stirred; and out of the thick darkness came clamorous sounds. Soon, there shot into the air a vivid meteor, which bursting at the zenith, radiated down the firmament in fiery showers, leaving treble darkness behind.

Then, as all held their breath, from Franko there spouted an eruption, which seemed to plant all Mardi in the foreground.

As when Vesuvius lights her torch, and in the blaze, the storm-swept surges in Naples' bay rear and plunge toward it; so now, showed Franko's multitudes, as they stormed the summit where their monarch's palace blazed, fast by the burning mountain.

"By my eternal throne!" cried Media, starting, "the old volcano has burst forth again!"

"But a new vent, my lord," said Babbalanja.

"More fierce this, than the eruption which happened in my youth," said Mohi—"methinks that Franko's end has come."

"You look pale, my lord," said Babbalanja, "while all other faces glow; —Yoomy, doff that halo in the presence of a king."

Over the waters came a rumbling sound, mixed with the din of warfare, and thwarted by showers of embers that fell not, for the whirling blasts.

"Off shore! off shore!" cried Media; and with all haste we gained a place of safety.

Down the valley now poured Rhines and Rhones of lava, a fire-freshet, flooding the forests from their fastnesses, and leaping with them into the seething sea.

The shore was lined with multitudes pushing off wildly in canoes.

Meantime, the fiery storm from Franko, kindled new flames in the distant valleys of Porpheero; while driven over from Verdanna came frantic shouts, and direful jubilees. Upon Dominora a baleful glare was resting.

"Thrice cursed flames!" cried Media. "Is Mardi to be one conflagration? How it crackles, forks, and roars!—Is this our funeral pyre?"

"Recline, recline, my lord," said Babbalanja. "Fierce flames are ever brief—a song, sweet Yoomy! Your pipe, old Mohi! Greater fires than this have ere now blazed in Mardi. Let us be calm;—the isles were made to burn;—Braid-Beard! hereafter, in some quiet cell, of this whole scene you will but make one chapter;—come, digest it now."

"My face is scorched," cried Media.

"The last, last day!" cried Mohi.

"Not so, old man," said Babbalanja, "when that day dawns, 'twill dawn serene. Be calm, be calm, my potent lord."

"Talk not of calm brows in storm-time!" cried Media fiercely. "See! how the flames blow over upon Dominora!"

"Yet the fires they kindle there are soon extinguished," said Babbalanja. "No, no; Dominora ne'er can burn with Franko's fires; only those of her own kindling may consume her."

"Away! Away!" cried Media. "We may not touch Porpheero now.— Up sails! and westward be our course."

So dead before the blast, we scudded.

Morning broke, showing no sign of land.

"Hard must it go with Franko's king," said Media, "when his people rise against him with the red volcanoes. Oh, for a foot to crush them! Hard, too, with all who rule in broad Porpheero. And may she we seek, survive this conflagration!"

"My lord," said Babbalanja, "where'er she hide, ne'er yet did Yillah lurk in this Porpheero; nor have we missed the maiden, noble Taji! in not touching at its shores."

"This fire must make a desert of the land," said Mohi; "burn up and bury all her tilth."

"Yet, Mohi, vineyards flourish over buried villages," murmured Yoomy.

"True, minstrel," said Babbalanja, "and prairies are purified by fire. Ashes breed loam. Nor can any skill make the same surface forever fruitful. In all times past, things have been overlaid; and though the first fruits of the marl are wild and poisonous, the palms at last spring forth; and once again the tribes repose in shade. My lord, if calms breed storms, so storms calms; and all this dire commotion must eventuate in peace. It may be, that Porpheero's future has been cheaply won."

Chapter 154

Wherein King Media celebrates the Glories of Autumn;
the Minstrel, the Promise of Spring

"HO, NOW!" cried Media, "across the wide waters, for that New Mardi, Vivenza! Let us indeed see, whether she who eludes us elsewhere, be at last found in Vivenza's vales."

"There or nowhere, noble Taji," said Yoomy.

"Be not too sanguine, gentle Yoomy," said Babbalanja.

"Does Yillah choose rather to bower in the wild wilderness of Vivenza, than in the old vineyards of Porpheero?" said Braid-Beard.

Sang Yoomy:—

> Her bower is not of the vine,
> But the wild, wild eglantine!
> Not climbing a moldering arch,
> But upheld by the fir-green larch.
>   Old ruins she flies:
>   To new valleys she hies;—
>   Not the hoar, moss-wood,
>   Ivied trees each a rood—
>   Not in Maramma she dwells,
>   Hollow with hermit cells.
>
>   'Tis a new, new isle!

501

An infant's its smile,
  Soft-rocked by the sea.
Its bloom all in bud;
No tide at its flood,
  In that fresh-born sea!

Spring! Spring! where she dwells,
In her sycamore dells,
Where Mardi is young and new:
Its verdure all eyes with dew.
There, there! in the bright, balmy morns,
The young deer sprout their horns,
Deep-tangled in new-branching groves,
Where the Red-Rover Robin roves,—

  Stooping his crest,
  To his molting breast—
  Rekindling the flambeau there!
Spring! Spring! where she dwells,
In her sycamore dells:—
Where, fulfilling their fates,
All creatures seek mates—
  The thrush, the doe, and the hare!

"Thou art most musical, sweet Yoomy," said Media, "concerning this spring-land Vivenza. But are not the old autumnal valleys of Porpheero more glorious than those of vernal Vivenza? Vivenza shows no trophies of the summer time, but Dominora's full-blown rose hangs blushing on her garden walls; her autumn groves are glory-dyed."

"My lord, autumn soon merges in winter, but the spring has all the seasons before. The full-blown rose is nearer withering than the bud. The faint morn is a blossom: the crimson sunset the flower."

Chapter 155

*In which Azzageddi seems to use Babbalanja
for a Mouth-piece*

ORPHEERO FAR ASTERN, the spirits of the company rose.
Once again, old Mohi serenely unbraided, and rebraided his beard;
and sitting Turk-wise on his mat, my lord Media smoking his gonfalon, diverted himself with the wild songs of Yoomy, the wild chronicles
of Mohi, or the still wilder speculations of Babbalanja; now and then, as
from pitcher to pitcher, pouring royal old wine down his soul.

Among other things, Media, who at times turned over Babbalanja for
an encyclopædia, however unreliable, demanded information upon the
subject of neap tides and their alleged slavish vassalage to the moon.

When true to his cyclopædiatic nature, Babbalanja quoted from a still
older and better authority than himself; in brief, from no other than eternal
Bardianna. It seems that that worthy essayist had discussed the whole matter
in a chapter thus headed: "On Seeing into Mysteries through Mill-Stones;"
and throughout his disquisitions he evinced such a profundity of research,
though delivered in a style somewhat equivocal, that the company were
much struck by the erudition displayed.

"Babbalanja, that Bardianna of yours must have been a wonderful
student," said Media after a pause; "no doubt he consumed whole thickets
of rush-lights."

"Not so, my lord.—'Patience, patience, philosophers,' said Bardianna;

503

'blow out your tapers, bolt not your dinners, take time, wisdom will be plenty soon.'"

"A notable hint! Why not follow it, Babbalanja?"

"Because, my lord, I have overtaken it, and passed on."

"True to your nature, Babbalanja; you stay nowhere."

"Ay, keep moving is my motto; but speaking of hard students, did my lord ever hear of Midni the ontologist and entomologist?"

"No."

"Then, my lord, you shall hear of him now. Midni was of opinion that day-light was vulgar; good enough for taro-planting and traveling; but wholly unadapted to the sublime ends of study. He toiled by night; from sunset to sunrise poring over the works of the old logicians. Like most philosophers, Midni was an amiable man; but one thing invariably put him out. He read in the woods by glow-worm light; insect in hand, tracing over his pages, line by line. But glow-worms burn not long: and in the midst of some calm intricate thought, at some imminent comma, the insect often expired, and Midni groped for a meaning. Upon such an occasion, 'Ho, Ho,' he cried; 'but for one instant of sun-light to see my way to a period!' But sun-light there was none; so Midni sprang to his feet, and parchment under arm, raced about among the sloughs and bogs for another glow-worm. Often, making a rapid descent with his turban, he thought he had caged a prize; but nay. Again he tried; yet with no better success. Nevertheless, at last he secured one; but hardly had he read three lines by its light, when out it went. Again and again this occurred. And thus he forever went halting and stumbling through his studies, and plunging through his quagmires after a glim."

At this ridiculous tale, one of our silliest paddlers burst into uncontrollable mirth. Offended at which breach of decorum, Media sharply rebuked him.

But he protested he could not help laughing.

Again Media was about to reprimand him, when Babbalanja begged leave to interfere.

"My lord, he is not to blame. Mark how earnestly he struggles to suppress his mirth; but he can not. It has often been the same with myself. And many a time have I not only vainly sought to check my laughter, but at some recitals I have both laughed and cried. But can opposite emotions be simultaneous in one being? No. I wanted to weep; but my body wanted to smile; and between us we almost choked. My lord Media, this man's body laughs; not the man himself."

"But his body is his own, Babbalanja; and he should have it under better control."

"The common error, my lord. Our souls belong to our bodies, not our bodies to our souls. For which has the care of the other? which keeps house? which looks after the replenishing of the aorta and auricles, and stores away the secretions? Which toils and ticks while the other sleeps? Which is ever giving timely hints, and elderly warnings? Which is the most authoritative? —Our bodies, surely. At a hint, you must move; at a notice to quit, you depart. Simpletons show us, that a body can get along almost without a soul; but of a soul getting along without a body, we have no tangible and indisputable proof. My lord, the wisest of us breathe involuntarily. And how many millions there are who live from day to day by the incessant operation of subtle processes in them, of which they know nothing, and care less? Little ween they, of vessels lacteal and lymphatic, of arteries femoral and temporal; of pericranium or pericardium; lymph, chyle, fibrin, albumen, iron in the blood, and pudding in the head; they live by the charity of their bodies, to which they are but butlers. I say, my lord, our bodies are our betters. A soul so simple, that it prefers evil to good, is lodged in a frame, whose minutest action is full of unsearchable wisdom. Knowing this superiority of theirs, our bodies are inclined to be willful: our beards grow in spite of us; and as every one knows, they sometimes grow on dead men."

"You mortals are alive, then, when you are dead, Babbalanja."

"No, my lord; but our beards survive us."

"An ingenious distinction; go on, philosopher."

"Without bodies, my lord, we Mardians would be minus our strongest motive-passions, those which, in some way or other, root under our every action. Hence, without bodies, we must be something else than we essentially are. Wherefore, that saying imputed to Alma, and which, by his very followers, is deemed the most hard to believe of all his instructions, and the most at variance with all preconceived notions of immortality, I Babbalanja, account the most reasonable of his doctrinal teachings. It is this;— that at the last day, every man shall rise in the flesh."

"Pray, Babbalanja, talk not of resurrections to a demi-god."

"Then let me rehearse a story, my lord. You will find it in the 'Very Merry Marvelings' of the Improvisator Quiddi; and a quaint book it is. Fugle-fi is its finis:—fugle-fi, fugle-fo, fugle-fogle-orum!"

"That wild look in his eye again," murmured Yoomy.

"Proceed, Azzageddi," said Media.

"The philosopher Grando had a sovereign contempt for his carcass.

Often he picked a quarrel with it; and always was flying out in its disparagement. 'Out upon you, you beggarly body! you clog, drug, drag! You keep me from flying; I could get along better without you. Out upon you, I say, you vile pantry, cellar, sink, sewer; abominable body! what vile thing are you not? And think you, beggar! to have the upper hand of me? Make a leg to that man if you dare, without my permission. This smell is intolerable; but turn from it, if you can, unless I give the word. Bolt this yam!—it is done. Carry me across yon field!—off we go. Stop!—it's a dead halt. There, I've trained you enough for to-day; now, sirrah, crouch down in the shade, and be quiet.—I'm rested. So, here's for a stroll, and a reverie homeward:—Up, carcass, and march.' So the carcass demurely rose and paced, and the philosopher meditated. He was intent upon squaring the circle; but bump he came against a bough. 'How now, clodhopping bumpkin! you would take advantage of my reveries, would you? But I'll be even with you;' and seizing a cudgel, he laid across his shoulders with right good will. But one of his backhanded thwacks injured his spinal cord; the philosopher dropped; but presently came to. 'Adzooks! I'll bend or break you! Up, up, and I'll run you home for this.' But wonderful to tell, his legs refused to budge; all sensation had left them. But a huge wasp happening to sting his foot, not him, for he felt it not, the leg incontinently sprang into the air, and of itself, cut all manner of capers. 'Be still! Down with you!' But the leg refused. 'My arms are still loyal,' thought Grando; and with them he at last managed to confine his refractory member. But all commands, volitions, and persuasions, were as naught to induce his limbs to carry him home. It was a solitary place; and five days after, Grando the philosopher was found dead under a tree."

"Ha, ha!" laughed Media, "Azzageddi is full as merry as ever."

"But, my lord," continued Babbalanja, "some creatures have still more perverse bodies than Grando's. In the fables of Ridendiabola, this is to be found. 'A fresh-water Polyp, despising its marine existence, longed to live upon air. But all it could do, its tentacles or arms still continued to cram its stomach. By a sudden preternatural impulse, however, the Polyp at last turned itself inside out; supposing that after such a proceeding it would have no gastronomic interior. But its body proved ventricle outside as well as in. Again its arms went to work; food was tossed in, and digestion continued.'"

"Is the literal part of that a fact?" asked Mohi.

"True as truth," said Babbalanja; "the Polyp will live turned inside out."

"Somewhat curious, certainly," said Media.—"But methinks, Babbalanja, that somewhere I have heard something about organic functions, so called; which may account for the phenomena you mention; and I have heard too, methinks, of what are called reflex actions of the nerves, which, duly considered, might deprive of its strangeness that story of yours concerning Grando and his body."

"Mere substitutions of sounds for inexplicable meanings, my lord. In some things science cajoles us. Now, what is undeniable of the Polyp some physiologists analogically maintain with regard to us Mardians; that forasmuch, as the lining of our interiors is nothing more than a continuation of the epidermis, or scarf-skin, therefore, that in a remote age, we too must have been turned wrong side out: an hypothesis, which, indirectly might account for our moral perversities: and also, for that otherwise nonsensical term—'the coat of the stomach;' for originally it must have been a surtout, instead of an inner garment."

"Pray, Azzageddi," said Media, "are you not a fool?"

"One of a jolly company, my lord; but some creatures besides wearing their surtouts within, sport their skeletons without: witness the lobster and turtle, who alive, study their own anatomies."

"Azzageddi, you are a zany."

"Pardon, my lord," said Mohi, "I think him more of a lobster; it's hard telling his jaws from his claws."

"Yes, Braid-Beard, I am a lobster, a mackerel, any thing you please; but my ancestors were kangaroos, not monkeys, as old Boddo erroneously opined. My idea is more susceptible of demonstration than his. Among the deepest discovered land fossils, the relics of kangaroos are discernible, but no relics of men. Hence, there were no giants in those days; but on the contrary, kangaroos; and those kangaroos formed the first edition of mankind, since revised and corrected."

"What has become of our finises, or tails, then?" asked Mohi, wriggling in his seat.

"The old question, Mohi. But where are the tails of the tadpoles, after their gradual metamorphosis into frogs? Have frogs any tails, old man? Our tails, Mohi, were worn off by the process of civilization; especially at the period when our fathers began to adopt the sitting posture: the fundamental evidence of all civilization, for neither apes, nor savages, can be said to sit; invariably, they squat on their hams. Among barbarous tribes benches and settles are unknown. But, my lord Media, as your liege and loving subject I can not sufficiently deplore the deprivation of your royal tail.

That stiff and vertebrated member, as we find it in those rustic kinsmen we have disowned, would have been useful as a supplement to your royal legs; and whereas my good lord is now fain to totter on two stanchions, were he only a kangaroo, like the monarchs of old, the majesty of Odo would be dignified, by standing firm on a tripod."

"A very witty conceit! But have a care, Azzageddi; your theory applies not to me."

"Babbalanja," said Mohi, "you must be the last of the kangaroos."

"I am, Mohi."

"But the old fashioned pouch or purse of your grandams?" hinted Media.

"My lord, I take it, that must have been transferred; nowadays our sex carries the purse."

"Ha, ha!"

"My lord, why this mirth? Let us be serious. Although man is no longer a kangaroo, he may be said to be an inferior species of plant. Plants proper are perhaps insensible of the circulation of their sap: we mortals are physically unconscious of the circulation of the blood; and for many ages were not even aware of the fact. Plants know nothing of their interiors:—three score years and ten we trundle about ours, and never get a peep at them; plants stand on their stalks:—we stalk on our legs; no plant flourishes over its dead root:—dead in the grave, man lives no longer above ground; plants die without food:—so we. And now for the difference. Plants elegantly inhale nourishment, without looking it up: like lords, they stand still and are served; and though green, never suffer from the colic:—whereas, we mortals must forage all round for our food: we cram our insides; and are loaded down with odious sacks and intestines. Plants make love and multiply; but excel us in all amorous enticements, wooing and winning by soft pollens and essences. Plants abide in one place, and live: we must travel or die. Plants flourish without us: we must perish without them."

"Enough Azzageddi!" cried Media. "Open not thy lips till to-morrow."

Chapter 156

The charming Yoomy sings

THE MORROW CAME; and three abreast, with snorting prows, we raced along; our mat-sails panting to the breeze. All present partook of the life of the air; and unanimously Yoomy was called upon for a song. The canoes were passing a long, white reef, sparkling with shells, like a jeweler's case: and thus Yoomy sang in the same old strain as of yore; beginning aloud, where he had left off in his soul:—

> Her sweet, sweet mouth!
>   The peach-pearl shell:—
> Red edged its lips,
>   That softly swell,
> Just oped to speak,
> With blushing cheek,
>   That fishermen
> With lonely spear
>   On the reef ken,
> And lift to ear
> Its voice to hear,—
>   Soft sighing South!
> Like this, like this,—
> The rosy kiss!—

That maiden's mouth.
A shell! a shell!
A vocal shell!
Song-dreaming,
In its inmost dell!

Her bosom! Two buds half blown, they tell;
A little valley between perfuming;
That roves away,
Deserting the day,—
The day of her eyes illuming;—
That roves away, o'er slope and fell,
Till a soft, soft meadow becomes the dell.

Thus far, old Mohi had been wriggling about in his seat, twitching his beard, and at every couplet looking up expectantly, as if he desired the company to think, that he was counting upon that line as the last. But now, starting to his feet, he exclaimed, "Hold, minstrel! thy muse's drapery is becoming disordered: no more!"

"Then no more it shall be," said Yoomy. "But you have lost a glorious sequel."

Chapter 157

They draw nigh unto Land

I N GOOD TIME, after many days' sailing, we snuffed the land from
afar, and came to a great country, full of inland mountains, north and
south stretching far out of sight. "All hail, Kolumbo!" cried Yoomy.

Coasting by a portion of it, which Mohi called Kanneeda, a province
of King Bello's, we perceived the groves rocking in the wind; their flexible
boughs bending like bows; and the leaves flying forth, and darkening the
landscape, like flocks of pigeons.

"Those groves must soon fall," said Mohi.

"Not so," said Babbalanja. "My lord, as these violent gusts are formed
by the hostile meeting of two currents, one from over the lagoon, the other
from land; they may be taken as significant of the occasional variances
between Kanneeda and Dominora."

"Ay," said Media, "and as Mohi hints, the breeze from Dominora must
soon overthrow the groves of Kanneeda."

"Not if the land-breeze holds, my lord;—one breeze oft blows another
home.—Stand up, and gaze! From cape to cape, this whole main we see,
is young and froward. And far southward, past this Kanneeda and Vivenza,
are haughty, overbearing streams, which at their mouths dam back the
ocean, and long refuse to mix their freshness with the foreign brine:—so
bold, so strong, so bent on hurling off aggression is this brave main, Kolumbo;—last sought, last found, Mardi's estate, so long kept back;—pray Oro,

it be not squandered foolishly. Here lie plantations, held in fee by stout hearts and arms; and boundless fields, that may be had for seeing. Here, your foes are forests, struck down with bloodless maces.—Ho! Mardi's Poor, and Mardi's Strong! ye, who starve or beg; seventh-sons who slave for earth's first-born—here is your home; predestinated yours; Come over, Empire-founders! fathers of the wedded tribes to come!—abject now, illustrious evermore:—Ho: Sinew, Brawn, and Thigh!"

"A very fine invocation," said Media, "now Babbalanja, be seated; and tell us whether Dominora and the kings of Porpheero do not own some small portion of this great continent, which just now you poetically pronounced as the spoil of any vagabonds who may choose to settle therein? Is not Kanneeda, Dominora's?"

"And was not Vivenza once Dominora's also? And what Vivenza now is, Kanneeda soon must be. I speak not, my lord, as wishful of what I say, but simply as fore-knowing it. The thing must come. Vain for Dominora to claim allegiance from all the progeny she spawns. As well might the old patriarch of the flood reappear, and claim the right of rule over all mankind, as descended from the loins of his three roving sons.

" 'Tis the old law:—the East peoples the West, the West the East; flux and reflux. And time may come, after the rise and fall of nations yet unborn, that, risen from its future ashes, Porpheero shall be the promised land, and from her surplus hordes Kolumbo people it."

Still coasting on, next day, we came to Vivenza; and as Media desired to land first at a point midway between its extremities, in order to behold the convocation of chiefs supposed to be assembled at this season, we held on our way, till we gained a lofty ridge, jutting out into the lagoon, a bastion to the neighboring land. It terminated in a lofty natural arch of solid trap. Billows beat against its base. But above, waved an inviting copse, wherein was revealed an open temple of canes, containing one only image, that of a helmeted female, the tutelar deity of Vivenza.

The canoes drew near.

"Lo! what inscription is that?" cried Media, "there, chiseled over the arch?"

Studying those immense hieroglyphics awhile, antiquarian Mohi still eyeing them, said slowly:—

"In-this-re-publi-can-land-all-men-are-born-free-and-equal."

"False!" said Media.

"And how long stay they so?" said Babbalanja.

"But look lower, old man," cried Media, "methinks there's a small hieroglyphic or two hidden away in yonder angle.—Interpret them, old man."

After much screwing of his eyes, for those characters were very minute, Champollion Mohi thus spoke—"Except-the-tribe-of-Hamo."

"That nullifies the other," cried Media. "Ah, ye republicans!"

"It seems to have been added for a postscript," rejoined Braid-Beard, screwing his eyes again.

"Perhaps so," said Babbalanja, "but some wag must have done it."

Shooting through the arch, we rapidly gained the beach.

Chapter 158

They visit the great central Temple of Vivenza

THE THRONG THAT GREETED US upon landing were exceedingly boisterous.

"Whence came ye?" they cried. "Whither bound? Saw ye ever such a land as this? Is it not a great and extensive republic? Pray, observe how tall we are; just feel of our thighs; are we not a glorious people? Here, feel of our beards. Look round; look round; be not afraid; behold those palms; swear now, that this land surpasses all others. Old Bello's mountains are mole-hills to ours; his rivers, rills; his empires, villages; his palm-trees, shrubs."

"True," said Babbalanja. "But great Oro must have had some hand in making your mountains and streams.—Would ye have been as great in a desert?"

"Where is your king?" asked Media, drawing himself up in his robe, and cocking his crown.

"Ha, ha, my fine fellow! We are all kings here; royalty breathes in the common air. But come on, come on. Let us show you our great Temple of Freedom."

And so saying, irreverently grasping his sacred arm, they conducted us toward a lofty structure, planted upon a bold hill, and supported by thirty pillars of palm; four quite green; as if recently added; and beyond these, an almost interminable vacancy, as if all the palms in Mardi, were at some future time, to aid in upholding that fabric.

Upon the summit of the temple was a staff; and as we drew nigh, a man with a collar round his neck, and the red marks of stripes upon his back, was just in the act of hoisting a tappa standard—correspondingly striped. Other collared menials were going in and out of the temple.

Near the porch, stood an image like that on the top of the arch we had seen. Upon its pedestal, were pasted certain hieroglyphical notices; according to Mohi, offering rewards for missing men, so many hands high.

Entering the temple, we beheld an amphitheatrical space, in the middle of which, a great fire was burning. Around it, were many chiefs, robed in long togas, and presenting strange contrasts in their style of tattooing.

Some were sociably laughing, and chatting; others diligently making excavations between their teeth with slivers of bamboo; or turning their heads into mills, were grinding up leaves and ejecting their juices. Some were busily inserting the down of a thistle into their ears. Several stood erect, intent upon maintaining striking attitudes; their javelins tragically crossed upon their chests. They would have looked very imposing, were it not, that in rear their vesture was sadly disordered. Others, with swelling fronts, seemed chiefly indebted to their dinners for their dignity. Many were nodding and napping. And, here and there, were sundry indefatigable worthies, making a great show of imperious and indispensable business; sedulously folding banana leaves into scrolls, and recklessly placing them into the hands of little boys, in gay turbans and trim little girdles, who thereupon fled as if with salvation for the dying.

It was a crowded scene; the dusky chiefs, here and there, grouped together, and their fantastic tattooings showing like the carved work on quaint old chimney-stacks, seen from afar. But one of their number overtopped all the rest. As when, drawing nigh unto old Rome, amid the crowd of sculptured columns and gables, St. Peter's grand dome soars far aloft, serene in the upper air; so, showed one calm grand forehead among those of this mob of chieftains. That head was Saturnina's. Gall and Spurzheim! saw you ever such a brow?—poised like an avalanche, under the shadow of a forest! woe betide the devoted valleys below! Lavater! behold those lips,—like mystic scrolls! Those eyes,—like panthers' caves at the base of Popocatepetl!

"By my right hand, Saturnina," cried Babbalanja, "but thou wert made in the image of thy Maker! Yet, have I beheld men, to the eye as commanding as thou; and surmounted by heads globe-like as thine, who never had thy caliber. We must measure brains, not heads, my lord; else, the sperm-whale, with his tun of an occiput, would transcend us all."

Near by, were arched ways, leading to subterranean places, whence issued a savory steam, and an extraordinary clattering of calabashes, and smacking of lips, as if something were being eaten down there by the fattest of fat fellows, with the heartiest of appetites, and the most irresistible of relishes. It was a quaffing, guzzling, gobbling noise. Peeping down, we beheld a company, breasted up against a board, groaning under numerous viands. In the middle of all, was a mighty great gourd, yellow as gold, and jolly round like a pumpkin in October, and so big it must have grown in the sun. Thence flowed a tide of red wine. And before it, stood plenty of paunches being filled therewith like portly stone jars at a fountain. Melancholy to tell, before that fine flood of old wine, and among those portly old topers, was a lean man; who occasionally ducked in his bill. He looked like an ibis standing in the Nile at flood tide, among a tongue-lapping herd of hippopotami.

They were jolly as the jolliest; and laughed so uproariously, that their hemispheres all quivered and shook, like vast provinces in an earthquake. Ha! ha! ha! how they laughed, and they roared. A deaf man might have heard them; and no milk could have soured within a forty-two-pounder ball shot of that place.

Now, the smell of good things is no very bad thing in itself. It is the savor of good things beyond; proof positive of a glorious good meal. So snuffing up those zephyrs from Araby the blest, those boisterous gales, blowing from out the mouths of baked boars, stuffed with bread-fruit, bananas, and sage, we would fain have gone down and partaken.

But this could not be; for we were told that those worthies below, were a club in secret conclave; very busy in settling certain weighty state affairs upon a solid basis. They were all chiefs of immense capacity:—how many gallons, there was no finding out.

Be sure, now, a most riotous noise came up from those catacombs, which seemed full of the ghosts of fat Lamberts; and this uproar it was, that heightened the din above-ground.

But heedless of all, in the midst of the amphitheater, stood a tall, gaunt warrior, ferociously tattooed, with a beak like a buzzard; long dusty locks; and his hands full of headless arrows. He was laboring under violent paroxysms; three benevolent individuals essaying to hold him. But repeatedly breaking loose, he burst anew into his delirium; while with an absence of sympathy, distressing to behold, the rest of the assembly seemed wholly engrossed with themselves; nor did they appear to care how soon the unfortunate lunatic might demolish himself by his frantic proceedings.

Toward one side of the amphitheatrical space, perched high upon an elevated dais, sat a white-headed old man with a tomahawk in his hand: earnestly engaged in overseeing the tumult; though not a word did he say. Occasionally, however, he was regarded by those present with a mysterious sort of deference; and when they chanced to pass between him and the crazy man, they invariably did so in a stooping position; probably to elude the atmospheric grape and cannister, continually flying from the mouth of the lunatic.

"What mob is this?" cried Media.

"'Tis the grand council of Vivenza," cried a bystander. "Hear ye not Alanno?" and he pointed to the lunatic.

Now coming close to Alanno, we found, that with incredible volubility, he was addressing the assembly upon some all-absorbing subject connected with King Bello, and his presumed encroachments toward the northwest of Vivenza.

One hand smiting his hip, and the other his head, the lunatic thus proceeded; roaring like a wild beast, and beating the air like a windmill:—

"I have said it! the thunder is flashing, the lightning is crashing! already there's an earthquake in Dominora! Full soon will old Bello discover that his diabolical machinations against this ineffable land must soon come to naught. Who dare not declare, that we are not invincible? I repeat it, we are. Ha! ha! Audacious Bello must bite the dust! Hair by hair, we will trail his gory gray beard at the end of our spears! Ha, ha! I grow hoarse; but would mine were a voice like the wild bulls of Bullorom, that I might be heard from one end of this great and gorgeous land to its farthest zenith; ay, to the uttermost diameter of its circumference. Awake! oh Vivenza. The signs of the times are portentous; nay, extraordinary; I hesitate not to add, peculiar! Up! up! Let us not descend to the bathos, when we should soar to the climax! Does not all Mardi wink and look on? Is the great sun itself a frigid spectator? Then let us double up our mandibles to the deadly encounter. Methinks I see it now. Old Bello is crafty, and his oath is recorded to obliterate us! Across this wide lagoon he casts his serpent eyes; whets his insatiate bill; mumbles his barbarous tusks; licks his forked tongues; and who knows when we shall have the shark in our midst? Yet be not deceived; for though as yet, Bello has forborne molesting us openly, his emissaries are at work; his infernal sappers, and miners, and wet-nurses, and midwives, and grave-diggers are busy! His canoe-yards are all in commotion! In navies his forests are being launched upon the wave; and ere long typhoons, zephyrs, white-squalls, balmy breezes, hurricanes, and besoms will be raging round us!"

His philippic concluded, Alanno was conducted from the place; and being now quite exhausted, cold cobble-stones were applied to his temples, and he was treated to a bath in a stream.

This chieftain, it seems, was from a distant western valley, called Hio-Hio, one of the largest and most fertile in Vivenza, though but recently settled. Its inhabitants, and those of the vales adjoining,—a right sturdy set of fellows,—were accounted the most dogmatically democratic and ultra of all the tribes in Vivenza; ever seeking to push on their brethren to the uttermost; and especially were they bitter against Bello. But they were a fine young tribe, nevertheless. Like strong new wine they worked violently in becoming clear. Time, perhaps, would make them all right.

An interval of greater uproar than ever now ensued; during which, with his tomahawk, the white-headed old man repeatedly thumped and pounded the seat where he sat, apparently to augment the din, though he looked anxious to suppress it.

At last, tiring of his posture, he whispered in the ear of a chief, his friend; who, approaching a portly warrior present, prevailed upon him to rise and address the assembly. And no sooner did this one do so, than the whole convocation dispersed, as if to their yams; and with a grin, the little old man leaped from his seat, and stretched his legs on a mat.

The fire was now extinguished, and the temple deserted.

Chapter 159

Wherein Babbalanja comments upon the Speech of Alanno

A S WE LINGERED in the precincts of the temple after all others had departed, sundry comments were made upon what we had seen; and having remarked the hostility of the lunatic orator toward Dominora, Babbalanja thus addressed Media:—

"My lord, I am constrained to believe, that all Vivenza can not be of the same mind with the grandiloquent chief from Hio-Hio. Nevertheless, I imagine, that between Dominora and this land, there exists at bottom a feeling akin to animosity, which is not yet wholly extinguished; though but the smoldering embers of a once raging fire. My lord, you may call it poetry if you will, but there are nations in Mardi, that to others stand in the relation of sons to sires. Thus with Dominora and Vivenza. And though, its majority attained, Vivenza is now its own master, yet should it not fail in a reverential respect for its parent. In man or nation, old age is honorable; and a boy, however tall, should never take his sire by the beard. And though Dominora did indeed ill merit Vivenza's esteem, yet by abstaining from criminations, Vivenza should ever merit its own. And if in time to come, which Oro forbid, Vivenza must needs go to battle with King Bello, let Vivenza first cross the old veteran's spear with all possible courtesy. On the other hand, my lord, King Bello should never forget, that whatever be glorious in Vivenza, redounds to himself. And as some gallant old lord

proudly measures the brawn and stature of his son; and joys to view in his
noble young lineaments the likeness of his own; bethinking him, that
when at last laid in his tomb, he will yet survive in the long, strong life of
his child, the worthy inheritor of his valor and renown; even so, should
King Bello regard the generous promise of this young Vivenza of his own
lusty begetting. My lord, behold these two states! Of all nations in the
Archipelago, they alone are one in blood. Dominora is the last and greatest
Anak of Old Times; Vivenza, the foremost and goodliest stripling of the
Present. One is full of the past; the other brims with the future. Ah! did
this sire's old heart but beat to free thoughts, and back his bold son, all
Mardi would go down before them. And high Oro may have ordained for
them a career, little divined by the mass. Methinks, that as Vivenza will
never cause old Bello to weep for his son; so, Vivenza will not, this many a
long year, be called to weep over the grave of its sire. And though King
Bello may yet lay aside his old-fashioned cocked hat of a crown, and comply
with the plain costume of the times; yet will his frame remain sturdy as of
yore, and equally grace any habiliments he may don. And those who say,
Dominora is old and worn out, may very possibly err. For if, as a nation,
Dominora be old—her present generation is full as young as the youths in
any land under the sun. Then, Ho! worthy twain! Each worthy the other,
join hands on the instant, and weld them together. Lo! the past is a prophet.
Be the future, its prophecy fulfilled."

Chapter 160

A Scene in the Land of Warwicks, or King-makers

WENDING OUR WAY from the temple, we were accompanied by a fluent, obstreperous wight, one Znobbi, a runaway native of Porpheero, but now an enthusiastic inhabitant of Vivenza.

"Here comes our great chief!" he cried. "Behold him! It was *I* that had a hand in making him what he is!"

And so saying, he pointed out a personage, no way distinguished, except by the tattooing on his forehead—stars, thirty in number; and an uncommonly long spear in his hand. Freely he mingled with the crowd.

"Behold, how familiar I am with him!" cried Znobbi, approaching, and pitcher-wise taking him by the handle of his face.

"Friend," said the dignitary, "thy salute is peculiar, but welcome. I reverence the enlightened people of this land."

"Mean-spirited hound!" muttered Media, "were I him, I had impaled that audacious plebeian."

"There's a Head-Chief for you, now, my fine fellow!" cried Znobbi. "Hurrah! Three cheers! Ay, ay! All kings here—all equal. Every thing's in common."

Here, a bystander, feeling something grazing his side, looked down; and perceived Znobbi's hand in clandestine vicinity to the pouch at his girdle-end.

Whereupon the crowd shouted, "A thief! a thief!" And with a loud voice the starred chief cried—"Seize him, people, and tie him to yonder tree."

And they seized, and tied him on the spot.

"Ah," said Media, "this chief has something to say, after all; he pinions a king at a word, though a plebeian takes him by the nose. Beshrew me, I doubt not, that spear of his, though without a tassel, is longer and sharper than mine."

"There's not so much freedom here as these freemen think," said Babbalanja, turning; "I laugh and admire."

Chapter 161

They hearken unto a Voice from the Gods

NEXT DAY we retraced our voyage northward, to visit that section of Vivenza.

In due time we landed.

To look round was refreshing. Of all the lands we had seen, none looked more promising. The groves stood tall and green; the fields spread flush and broad; the dew of the first morning seemed hardly vanished from the grass. On all sides was heard the fall of waters, the swarming of bees, and the rejoicing hum of a thriving population.

"Ha, ha!" laughed Yoomy, "Labor laughs in this land; and claps his hands in the jubilee groves! methinks that Yillah will yet be found."

Generously entertained, we tarried in this land; till at length, from over the Lagoon, came full tidings of the eruption we had witnessed in Franko, with many details. The conflagration had spread through Porpheero; and the kings were to and fro hunted, like malefactors by blood-hounds; all that part of Mardi was heaving with throes.

With the utmost delight, these tidings were welcomed by many; yet others heard them with boding concern.

Those, too, there were, who rejoiced that the kings were cast down; but mourned that the people themselves stood not firmer. A victory, turned to no wise and enduring account, said they, is no victory at all. Some victories revert to the vanquished.

But day by day great crowds ran down to the beach, in wait for canoes periodically bringing further intelligence. Every hour new cries startled the air. "Hurrah! another kingdom is burnt down to the earth's edge; another demi-god is unhelmed; another republic is dawning. Shake hands, freemen, shake hands! Soon will we hear of Dominora down in the dust; of hapless Verdanna free as ourselves; all Porpheero's volcanoes are bursting! Who may withstand the people? The times tell terrible tales to tyrants! Ere we die, freemen, all Mardi will be free."

Overhearing these shouts, Babbalanja thus addressed Media:—"My lord, I can not but believe, that these men, are far more excited than those with whom they so ardently sympathize. But no wonder. The single discharges which are heard in Porpheero; here come condensed in one tremendous report. Every arrival is a firing off of events by platoons."

Now, during this tumultuous interval, King Media very prudently kept himself exceedingly quiet. He doffed his regalia; and in all things carried himself with a dignified discretion. And many hours he absented himself; none knowing whither he went, or what his employment.

So also with Babbalanja. But still pursuing our search, at last we all journeyed into a great valley, whose inhabitants were more than commonly inflated with the ardor of the times.

Rambling on, we espied a clamorous crowd gathered about a conspicuous palm, against which, a scroll was fixed.

The people were violently agitated; storming out maledictions against the insolent knave, who, over night must have fixed there, that scandalous document. But whoever he may have been, certain it was, he had contrived to hood himself effectually.

After much vehement discussion, during which sundry inflammatory harangues were made from the stumps of trees near by, it was proposed, that the scroll should be read aloud, so that all might give ear.

Seizing it, a fiery youth mounted upon the bowed shoulders of an old man, his sire; and with a shrill voice, ever and anon interrupted by outcries, read as follows:—

"Sovereign-kings of Vivenza! it is fit you should hearken to wisdom. But well aware, that you give ear to little wisdom except of your own; and that as freemen, you are free to hunt down him who dissents from your majesties; I deem it proper to address you anonymously.

"And if it please you, you may ascribe this voice to the gods: for never will you trace it to man.

"It is not unknown, sovereign-kings! that in these boisterous days, the lessons of history are almost discarded, as superseded by present experiences. And that while all Mardi's Present has grown out of its Past, it is becoming obsolete to refer to what has been. Yet, peradventure, the Past is an apostle.

"The grand error of this age, sovereign-kings! is the general supposition, that the very special Diabolus is abroad; whereas, the very special Diabolus has been abroad ever since Mardi began.

"And the grand error of your nation, sovereign-kings! seems this:— The conceit that Mardi is now in the last scene of the last act of her drama; and that all preceding events were ordained, to bring about the catastrophe you believe to be at hand,—a universal and permanent Republic.

"May it please you, those who hold to these things are fools, and not wise.

"Time is made up of various ages; and each thinks its own a novelty. But imbedded in the walls of the pyramids, which outrun all chronologies, sculptured stones are found, belonging to yet older fabrics. And as in the mound-building period of yore, so every age thinks its erections will forever endure. But as your forests grow apace, sovereign-kings! overrunning the tumuli in your western vales; so, while deriving their substance from the past, succeeding generations overgrow it; but in time, themselves decay.

"Oro decrees these vicissitudes.

"In chronicles of old, you read, sovereign kings! that an eagle from the clouds presaged royalty to the fugitive Taquinoo; and a king, Taquinoo reigned; no end to my dynasty, thought he.

"But another omen descended, foreshadowing the fall of Zooperbi, his son; and Zooperbi returning from his camp, found his country a fortress against him. No more kings would she have. And for five hundred twelve-moons the Regifugium or King's-flight, was annually celebrated like your own jubilee day. And rampant young orators stormed out detestation of kings; and augurs swore that their birds presaged immortality to freedom.

"Then, Romara's free eagles flew over all Mardi, and perched on the topmost diadems of the east.

"Ever thus must it be.

"For, mostly, monarchs are as gemmed bridles upon the world, checking the plungings of a steed from the Pampas. And republics are as vast reservoirs, draining down all streams to one level; and so, breeding a fullness which can not remain full, without overflowing. And thus, Romara flooded all Mardi, till scarce an Ararat was left of the lofty kingdoms which had been.

"Thus, also, did Franko, fifty twelve-moons ago. Thus may she do again. And though not yet, have you, sovereign-kings! in any large degree done likewise, it is because you overflow your redundancies within your own mighty borders; having a wild western waste, which many shepherds with their flocks could not overrun in a day. Yet overrun at last it will be; and then, the recoil must come.

"And, may it please you, that thus far your chronicles had narrated a very different story, had your population been pressed and packed, like that of your old sire-land Dominora. Then, your great experiment might have proved an explosion; like the chemist's who, stirring his mixture, was blown by it into the air.

"For though crossed, and recrossed by many brave quarterings, and boasting the great Bull in your pedigree; yet, sovereign-kings! you are not meditative philosophers like the people of a small republic of old; nor enduring stoics, like their neighbors. Pent up, like them, may it please you, your thirteen original tribes had proved more turbulent, than so many mutinous legions. Free horses need wide prairies; and fortunate for you, sovereign-kings! that you have room enough, wherein to be free.

"And, may it please you, you are free, partly, because you are young. Your nation is like a fine, florid youth, full of fiery impulses, and hard to restrain; his strong hand nobly championing his heart. On all sides, freely he gives, and still seeks to acquire. The breath of his nostrils is like smoke in spring air; every tendon is electric with generous resolves. The oppressor he defies to his beard; the high walls of old opinions he scales with a bound. In the future he sees all the domes of the East.

"But years elapse, and this bold boy is transformed. His eyes open not as of yore; his heart is shut up as a vice. He yields not a groat; and seeking no more acquisitions, is only bent on preserving his hoard. The maxims once trampled under foot, are now printed on his front; and he who hated oppressors, is become an oppressor himself.

"Thus, often, with men; thus, often, with nations. Then marvel not, sovereign-kings! that old states are different from yours; and think not, your own must forever remain liberal as now.

"Each age thinks its own is eternal. But though for five hundred twelve-moons, all Romara, by courtesy of history, was republican; yet, at last, her terrible king-tigers came, and spotted themselves with gore.

"And time was, when Dominora was republican, down to her sturdy back-bone. The son of an absolute monarch became the man Karolus; and his crown and head, both rolled in the dust. And Dominora had her patriots by thousands; and lusty Defenses, and glorious Areopagiticas were written, not since surpassed; and no turban was doffed save in homage of Oro.

"Yet, may it please you, to the sound of pipe and tabor, the second King Karolus returned in good time; and was hailed gracious majesty by high and low.

"Throughout all eternity, the parts of the past are but parts of the future reversed. In the old foot-prints, up and down, you mortals go, eternally traveling your Sierras. And not more infallible the ponderings of the Calculating Machine than the deductions from the decimals of history.

"In nations, sovereign-kings! there is a transmigration of souls; in you, is a marvelous destiny. The eagle of Romara revives in your own mountain bird, and once more is plumed for her flight. Her screams are answered by the vauntful cries of a hawk; his red comb yet reeking with slaughter. And one East, one West, those bold birds may fly, till they lock pinions in the midmost beyond.

"But, soaring in the sky over the nations that shall gather their broods under their wings, that bloody hawk may hereafter be taken for the eagle.

"And though crimson republics may rise in constellations, like fiery Aldebarans, speeding to their culminations; yet, down must they sink at last, and leave the old sultan-sun in the sky; in time, again to be deposed.

"For little longer, may it please you, can republics subsist now, than in days gone by. For, assuming that Mardi is wiser than of old; nevertheless, though all men approached sages in intelligence, some would yet be more wise than others; and so, the old degrees be preserved. And no exemption would an equality of knowledge furnish, from the inbred servility of mortal to mortal; from all the organic causes, which inevitably divide mankind into brigades and battalions, with captains at their head.

"Civilization has not ever been the brother of equality. Freedom was born among the wild eyries in the mountains; and barbarous tribes have sheltered under her wings, when the enlightened people of the plain have nestled under different pinions.

"Though, thus far, for you, sovereign-kings! your republic has been fruitful of blessings; yet, in themselves, monarchies are not utterly evil. For many nations, they are better than republics; for many, they will ever so remain. And better, on all hands, that peace should rule with a scepter, than that the tribunes of the people should brandish their broadswords. Better be the subject of a king, upright and just; than a freeman in Franko, with the executioner's ax at every corner.

"It is not the prime end, and chief blessing, to be politically free. And freedom is only good as a means; is no end in itself. Nor, did man fight it out against his masters to the haft, not then, would he uncollar his neck from the yoke. A born thrall to the last, yelping out his liberty, he still remains a slave unto Oro; and well is it for the universe, that Oro's scepter is absolute.

"World-old the saying, that it is easier to govern others, than oneself. And that all men should govern themselves as nations, needs that all men be better, and wiser, than the wisest of one-man rulers. But in no stable democracy do all men govern themselves. Though an army be all volunteers, martial law must prevail. Delegate your power, you leagued mortals must. The hazard you must stand. And though unlike King Bello of Dominora, your great chieftain, sovereign-kings! may not declare war of himself; nevertheless, has he done a still more imperial thing:—gone to war without declaring intentions. You yourselves were precipitated upon a neighboring nation, ere you knew your spears were in your hands.

"But, as in stars you have written it on the welkin, sovereign-kings! you are a great and glorious people. And verily, yours is the best and happiest land under the sun. But not wholly, because you, in your wisdom, decreed it: your origin and geography necessitated it. Nor, in their germ, are all your blessings to be ascribed to the noble sires, who of yore fought in your behalf, sovereign-kings! Your nation enjoyed no little independence before your Declaration declared it. Your ancient pilgrims fathered your liberty; and your wild woods harbored the nursling. For the state that to-day is made up of slaves, can not to-morrow transmute her bond into free; though lawlessness may transform them into brutes. Freedom is the name for a thing that is *not* freedom; this, a lesson never learned in an hour or an age. By some tribes it will never be learned.

"Yet, if it please you, there may be such a thing as being free under Cæsar. Ages ago, there were as many vital freemen, as breathe vital air to-day.

"Names make not distinctions; some despots rule without swaying scepters. Though King Bello's palace was not put together by yoked men; your federal temple of freedom, sovereign-kings! was the handiwork of slaves.

"It is not gildings, and gold maces, and crown-jewels alone, that make a people servile. There is much bowing and cringing among you yourselves, sovereign-kings! Poverty is abased before riches, all Mardi over; any where, it is hard to be a debtor; any where, the wise will lord it over fools; every where, suffering is found.

"Thus, freedom is more social than political. And its real felicity is not to be shared. *That* is of a man's own individual getting and holding. It is not, who rules the state, but who rules me. Better be secure under one king, than exposed to violence from twenty millions of monarchs, though oneself be of the number.

"But superstitious notions you harbor, sovereign kings! Did you visit Dominora, you would not be marched straight into a dungeon. And though you would behold sundry sights displeasing, you would start to inhale such liberal breezes; and hear crowds boasting of their privileges; as you, of yours. Nor has the wine of Dominora, a monarchical flavor.

"Now, though far and wide, to keep equal pace with the times, great reforms, of a verity, be needed; nowhere are bloody revolutions required. Though it be the most certain of remedies, no prudent invalid opens his veins, to let out his disease with his life. And though all evils may be assuaged; all evils can not be done away. For evil is the chronic malady of the universe; and checked in one place, breaks forth in another.

"Of late, on this head, some wild dreams have departed.

"There are many, who erewhile believed that the age of pikes and javelins was passed; that after a heady and blustering youth, old Mardi was at last settling down into a serene old age; and that the Indian summer, first discovered in your land, sovereign kings! was the hazy vapor emitted from its tranquil pipe. But it has not so proved. Mardi's peaces are but truces. Long absent, at last the red comets have returned. And return they must, though their periods be ages. And should Mardi endure till mountain melt into mountain, and all the isles form one table-land; yet, would it but expand the old battle-plain.

"Students of history are horror-struck at the massacres of old; but in the shambles, men are being murdered to-day. Could time be reversed, and the future change places with the past, the past would cry out against us, and our future, full as loudly, as we against the ages foregone. All the Ages are his children, calling each other names.

"Hark ye, sovereign-kings! cheer not on the yelping pack too furiously. Hunters have been torn by their hounds. Be advised; wash your hands. Hold aloof. Oro has poured out an ocean for an everlasting barrier between you and the worst folly which other republics have perpetrated. That barrier hold sacred. And swear never to cross over to Porpheero, by manifesto or army, unless you traverse dry land.

"And be not too grasping, nearer home. It is not freedom to filch. Expand not your area too widely, now. Seek you proselytes? Neighboring nations may be free, without coming under your banner. And if you can not lay your ambition, know this: that it is best served, by waiting events.

"Time, but Time only, may enable you to cross the equator; and give you the Arctic Circles for your boundaries."

So read the anonymous scroll; which straightway, was torn into shreds.

"Old tory, and monarchist!" they shouted, "Preaching over his benighted sermons in these enlightened times! Fool! does he not know that all the Past and its graves are being dug over?"

They were furious; so wildly rolling their eyes after victims, that well was it for King Media, he wore not his crown; and in silence, we moved unnoted from out the crowd.

"My lord, I am amazed at the indiscretion of a demi-god," said Babbalanja, as we passed on our way; "I recognized your sultanic style the very first sentence. This, then, is the result of your hours of seclusion."

"Philosopher! I am astounded at your effrontery. I detected your philosophy the very first maxim. Who posted that parchment for you?"

So, each charged the other with its authorship: and there was no finding out, whether, indeed, either knew aught of its origin.

Now, could it have been Babbalanja? Hardly. For, philosophic as the document was, it seemed too dogmatic and conservative for him. King Media? But though imperially absolute in his political sentiments, Media delivered not himself so boldly, when actually beholding the eruption in Franko.

Indeed, the settlement of this question must be left to the commentators on Mardi, some four or five hundred centuries hence.

Chapter 162

They visit the extreme South of Vivenza

WE PENETRATED FURTHER and further into the valleys around; but, though, as elsewhere, at times we heard whisperings that promised an end to our wanderings;—we still wandered on; and once again, even Yoomy abated his sanguine hopes.

And now, we prepared to embark for the extreme south of the land.

But we were warned by the people, that in that portion of Vivenza, whither we were going, much would be seen repulsive to strangers. Such things, however, indulgent visitors overlooked. For themselves, they were well aware of those evils. Northern Vivenza had done all it could to assuage them; but in vain; the inhabitants of those southern valleys were a fiery, and intractable race; heeding neither expostulations, nor entreaties. They were wedded to their ways. Nay, they swore, that if the northern tribes persisted in intermeddlings, they would dissolve the common alliance, and establish a distinct confederacy among themselves.

Our coasting voyage at an end, our keels grated the beach among many prostrate palms, decaying, and washed by the billows. Though part and parcel of the shore we had left, this region seemed another land. Fewer thriving things were seen; fewer cheerful sounds were heard.

"Here labor has lost his laugh!" cried Yoomy.

It was a great plain where we landed; and there, under a burning sun, hundreds of collared men were toiling in trenches, filled with the taro plant; a root most flourishing in that soil. Standing grimly over these, were men unlike them; armed with long thongs, which descended upon the toilers, and made wounds. Blood and sweat mixed; and in great drops, fell.

"Who eat these plants thus nourished?" cried Yoomy.

"Are these men?" asked Babbalanja.

"Which mean you?" said Mohi.

Heeding him not, Babbalanja advanced toward the foremost of those with the thongs,—one Nulli: a cadaverous, ghost-like man; with a low ridge of forehead; hair, steel-gray; and wondrous eyes;—bright, nimble, as the twin Corposant balls, playing about the ends of ships' royal-yards in gales.

The sun passed under a cloud; and Nulli, darting at Babbalanja those wondrous eyes, there fell upon him a baleful glare.

"Have they souls?" he asked, pointing to the serfs.

"No," said Nulli, "their ancestors may have had; but their souls have been bred out of their descendants; as the instinct of scent is killed in pointers."

Approaching one of the serfs, Media took him by the hand, and felt of it long; and looked into his eyes; and placed his ear to his side; and exclaimed, "Surely this being has flesh that is warm; he has Oro in his eye; and a heart in him that beats. I swear he is a man."

"Is this our lord the king?" cried Mohi, starting.

"What art thou," said Babbalanja to the serf. "Dost ever feel in thee a sense of right and wrong? Art ever glad or sad?— They tell us thou art not a man:—speak, then, for thyself; say, whether thou beliest thy Maker."

"Speak not of my Maker to me. Under the lash, I believe my masters, and account myself a brute; but in my dreams, bethink myself an angel. But I am bond; and my little ones;—their mother's milk is gall."

"Just Oro!" cried Yoomy, "do no thunders roll,—no lightnings flash in this accursed land!"

"Asylum for all Mardi's thralls!" cried Media.

"Incendiaries!" cried he with the wondrous eyes, "come ye, firebrands, to light the flame of revolt? Know ye not, that here are many serfs, who, incited to obtain their liberty, might wreak some dreadful vengeance? Avaunt, thou king! thou horrified at this? Go back to Odo, and right her wrongs! These serfs are happier than thine; though thine, no collars wear;

more happy as they are, than if free. Are they not fed, clothed, and cared for? Thy serfs pine for food: never yet did these; who have no thoughts, no cares."

"Thoughts and cares are life, and liberty, and immortality!" cried Babbalanja; "and are their souls, then, blown out as candles?"

"Ranter! they are content," cried Nulli. "They shed no tears."

"Frost never weeps," said Babbalanja; "and tears are frozen in those frigid eyes."

"Oh fettered sons of fettered mothers, conceived and born in manacles," cried Yoomy; "dragging them through life; and falling with them, clank-ing in the grave:—oh, beings as ourselves, how my stiff arm shivers to avenge you! 'Twere absolution for the matricide, to strike one rivet from your chains. My heart outswells its home!"

"Oro! Art thou?" cried Babbalanja; "and doth this thing exist? It shakes my little faith." Then, turning upon Nulli, "How can ye abide to sway this curs'd dominion?"

"Peace, fanatic! Who else may till unwholesome fields, but these? And as these beings are, so shall they remain; 'tis right and righteous! Maramma champions it!—I swear it! The first blow struck for them, dissolves the union of Vivenza's vales. The northern tribes well know it; and know me."

Said Media, "Yet if—"

"No more! another word, and, king as thou art, thou shalt be dun-geoned:—here, there is such a law; thou art not among the northern tribes."

"And this is freedom!" murmured Media; "when heaven's own voice is throttled. And were these serfs to rise, and fight for it; like dogs, they would be hunted down by her pretended sons!"

"Pray, heaven!" cried Yoomy, "they may yet find a way to loose their bonds without one drop of blood. But hear me, Oro! were there no other way, and should their masters not relent, all honest hearts must cheer this tribe of Hamo on; though they cut their chains with blades thrice edged, and gory to the haft! 'Tis right to fight for freedom, whoever be the thrall."

"These South savannahs may yet prove battle-fields," said Mohi, gloomily, as we retraced our steps.

"Be it," said Yoomy. "Oro will van the right."

"Not always has it proved so," said Babbalanja. "Ofttimes, the right fights single-handed against the world; and Oro champions none. In all things, man's own battles, man himself must fight. Yoomy: so far as feeling goes, your sympathies are not more hot than mine; but for these serfs you would cross spears; yet, I would not. Better present woes for some, than future woes for all."

"No need to fight," cried Yoomy, "to liberate that tribe of Hamo instantly; a way may be found, and no irretrievable evil ensue."

"Point it out, and be blessed, Yoomy."

"That is for Vivenza; but the head is dull, where the heart is cold."

"My lord," said Babbalanja, "you have startled us by your kingly sympathy for suffering; say thou, then, in what wise manner it shall be relieved."

"That is for Vivenza," said Media.

"Mohi, you are old: speak thou."

"Let Vivenza speak," said Mohi.

"Thus, then, we all agree; and weeping, all but echo hard-hearted Nulli. Tears are not swords; and wrongs seem almost natural as rights. For the righteous to suppress an evil, is sometimes harder than for others to uphold it. Humanity cries out against this vast enormity:—not one man knows a prudent remedy. Blame not, then, the North; and wisely judge the South. Ere, as a nation, they became responsible, this thing was planted in their midst. Such roots strike deep. Place to-day those serfs in Dominora; and with them, all Vivenza's Past;—and serfs, for many years, in Dominora, they would be. Easy is it to stand afar and rail. All men are censors who have lungs. We can say, the stars are wrongly marshaled. Blind men say the sun is blind. A thousand muscles wag our tongues; though our tongues were housed, that they might have a home. Whoso is free from crime, let him cross himself—but hold his cross upon his lips. That he is not bad, is not of him. Potters' clay and wax are all, molded by hands invisible. The soil decides the man. And, ere birth, man wills not to be born here or there. These southern tribes have grown up with this thing; bond-women were their nurses, and bondmen serve them still. Nor are all their serfs such wretches as those we saw. Some seem happy: yet not as men. Unmanned, they know not what they are. And though, of all the south, Nulli must stand almost alone in his insensate creed; yet, to all wrong-doers, custom backs the sense of wrong. And if to every Mardian, conscience be the awarder of its own doom; then, of these tribes, many shall be found exempted from the least penalty of this sin. But sin it is, no less;—a blot, foul as the crater-pool of hell; it puts out the sun at noon; it parches all fertility; and, conscience or no conscience—ere he die—let every master who wrenches bond-babe from mother, that the nipple tear; unwreathes the arms of sisters; or cuts the holy unity in twain; till apart fall man and wife, like one bleeding body cleft:—let that master thrice shrive his soul; take every sacrament; on his bended knees give up the ghost;—yet shall he die despairing; and live again, to die forever damned. The future is all hieroglyphics. Who may read? But, methinks the great laggard Time must now march up apace, and somehow befriend these thralls. It can not be, that misery is perpetually entailed; though, in a land proscribing primogeniture, the first-born and last of Hamo's tribe must still succeed to all their sires' wrongs. Yes: Time—all-healing Time—Time, great Philanthropist!—Time must befriend these thralls!"

"Oro grant it!" cried Yoomy, "and let Mardi say, amen!"

"Amen! amen! amen!" cried echoes echoing echoes.

We traversed many of these southern vales; but as in Dominora,—so, throughout Vivenza, North and South,—Yillah harbored not.

Chapter 163

They converse of the Mollusca, Kings, Toad-stools and other Matters

ONCE MORE EMBARKING, we gained Vivenza's southwestern side; and there, beheld vast swarms of laborers discharging from canoes, great loads of earth; which they tossed upon the beach.

"It is true, then," said Media, "that these freemen are engaged in digging down other lands, and adding them to their own, piece-meal. And this, they call extending their dominions agriculturally, and peaceably."

"My lord, they pay a price for every canoe-load," said Mohi.

"Ay, old man, holding the spear in one hand, and striking the bargain with the other."

"Yet charge it not upon all Vivenza," said Babbalanja. "Some of her tribes are hostile to these things: and when their countrymen fight for land, are only warlike in opposing war."

"And therein, Babbalanja, is involved one of those anomalies in the condition of Vivenza," said Media, "which I can hardly comprehend. How comes it, that with so many things to divide them, the valley-tribes still keep their mystic league intact?"

"All plain, it is because the model, whence they derive their union, is one of nature's planning. My lord, have you ever observed the mysterious federation subsisting among the mollusca of the Tunicata order,—in other words, a species of cuttle-fish, abounding at the bottom of the lagoon?"

"Yes: in clear weather about the reefs, I have beheld them time and again: but never with an eye to their political condition."

"Ah! my lord king, we should not cut off the nervous communication between our eyes, and our cerebellums."

"What were you about to say concerning the Tunicata order of mollusca, sir philosopher?"

"My very honorable lord, I hurry to conclude. They live in a compound structure; but though connected by membranous canals, freely communicating throughout the league—each member has a heart and stomach of its own; provides and digests its own dinners; and grins and bears its own gripes, without imparting the same to its neighbors. But if a prowling shark touches one member, it ruffles all. Precisely thus now with Vivenza. In that confederacy, there are as many consciences as tribes; hence, if one member on its own behalf, assumes aught afterwards repudiated, the sin rests on itself alone; is not participated."

"A very subtle explanation, Babbalanja. You must allude, then, to those recreant tribes; which, while in their own eyes presenting a sublime moral spectacle to Mardi,—in King Bello's, do but present a hopeless example of bad debts. And these, the tribes that boast of boundless wealth."

"Most true, my lord. But Bello errs, when for this thing, he stigmatizes all Vivenza, as a unity."

"Babbalanja, you yourself are made up of members:—then, if you be sick of a lumbago,—'tis not *you* that are unwell; but your spine."

"As you will, my lord. I have said. But to speak no more on that head—what sort of a sensation, think you, life is to such creatures as those mollusca?"

"Answer your own question, Babbalanja."

"I will; but first tell me what sort of a sensation life is to you, yourself, my lord."

"Pray answer that along with the other, Azzageddi."

"Directly; but tell me, if you will, my lord, what sort of a sensation life is to a toad-stool."

"Pray, Babbalanja put all three questions together; and then, do what you have often done before,—pronounce yourself a lunatic."

"My lord, I beseech you, remind me not of that fact so often. It is true, but annoying. Nor will any wise man call another a fool."

"Do you take me for a mere man, then, Babbalanja, that you talk to me thus?"

"My demi-divine lord and master, I was deeply concerned at your indisposition last night:—may a loving subject inquire, whether his prince is completely recovered from the effect of those guavas?"

"Have a care, Azzageddi; you are far too courteous, to be civil. But proceed."

"I obey. In kings, mollusca, and toad-stools, life is one thing and the same. The Philosopher Dumdi pronounces it a certain febrile vibration of organic parts, operating upon the vis inertia of unorganized matter. But Bardianna says nay. Hear him. 'Who put together this marvelous mechanism of mine; and wound it up, to go for three score years and ten; when it runs out, and strikes Time's hours no more? And what is it, that daily and hourly renews, and by a miracle, creates in me my flesh and my blood? What keeps up the perpetual telegraphic communication between my outpost toes and digits, and that domed grandee up aloft, my brain?—It is not I; nor you; nor he; nor it. No; when I place my hand to that king muscle my heart, I am appalled. I feel the great God himself at work in me. Oro is life.'"

"And what is death?" demanded Media.

"Death, my lord!—it is the deadest of all things."

Chapter 164

Wherein, that gallant Gentleman and Demi-god, King Media, Scepter in Hand, throws himself into the Breach

SAILING SOUTH from Vivenza, not far from its coast, we passed a cluster of islets, green as new fledged grass; and like the mouths of floating cornucopias, their margins brimmed over upon the brine with flowers. On some, grew stately roses; on others stood twin-pillars; across others, tri-hued rainbows rested.

Cried Babbalanja, pointing to the last, "Franko's pledge of peace! with that, she loudly vaunts she'll span the reef!—Strike out all hues but red,—and the token's nearer truth."

All these isles were prolific gardens; where King Bello, and the Princes of Porpheero grew their most delicious fruits,—nectarines and grapes.

But, though hard by, Vivenza owned no garden here; yet longed and lusted; and her hottest tribes oft roundly swore, to root up all roses the half-reef over; pull down all pillars; and dissolve all rainbows. "Mardi's half is ours;" said they. "Stand back invaders!" Full of vanity; and mirroring themselves in the future; they deemed all reflected there, their own.

'Twas now high noon.

"Methinks the sun grows hot," said Media, retreating deeper under the canopy. "Ho! Vee-Vee; have you no cooling beverage? none of that golden wine distilled from torrid grapes, and then sent northward to be cellared in an iceberg? That wine was placed among our stores. Search,

539

search the crypt, little Vee-Vee! Ha, I see it!—that yellow gourd!—Come: drag it forth, my boy. Let's have the amber cups: so: pass them round;—fill all! Taji! my demi-god, up heart! Old Mohi, my babe, may you live ten thousand centuries! Ah! this way you mortals have of dying out at three score years and ten, is but a craven habit. So, Babbalanja! may you never die. Yoomy! my sweet poet, may you live to sing to me in Paradise. Ha, ha! would that we floated in this glorious stuff, instead of this pestilent brine.—Hark ye! were I to make a Mardi now, I'd have every continent a huge haunch of venison; every ocean a wine-vat! I'd stock every cavern with choice old spirits, and make three surplus suns to ripen the grapes all the year round. Let's drink to that!—Brimmers! So: may the next Mardi that's made, be one entire grape; and mine the squeezing!"

"Look, look! my lord," cried Yoomy, "what a glorious shore we pass."

Sallying out into the high golden noon, with golden-beaming goblets suspended, we gazed.

"This must be Kolumbo of the south," said Mohi.

It was a long, hazy reach of land; piled up in terraces, traced here and there with rushing streams, that worked up gold dust alluvian, and seemed to flash over pebbled diamonds. Heliotropes, sun-flowers, marigolds gemmed, or starred the violet meads, and vassal-like, still sunward bowed their heads. The rocks were pierced with grottoes, blazing with crystals, many-tinted.

It was a land of mints and mines; its east a ruby; west a topaz. Inland, the woodlands stretched an ocean, bottomless with foliage; its green surges bursting through cable-vines; like Xerxes' brittle chains which vainly sought to bind the Hellespont. Hence flowed a tide of forest sounds; of parrots, paroquets, macaws; blent with the howl of jaguars, hissing of anacondas, chattering of apes, and herons screaming.

Out from those depths up rose a steam.

The land lay basking in the world's round torrid brisket, hot with solar fire.

"No need here to land," cried Yoomy, "Yillah lurks not here."

"Heat breeds life, and sloth, and rage," said Babbalanja. "Here live bastard tribes and mongrel nations; wrangling and murdering to prove their freedom.—Refill, my lord."

"Methinks, Babbalanja, you savor of the mysterious parchment, in Vivenza read:—Ha? Yes, philosopher, these are the men, who toppled castles to make way for hovels; these, they who fought for freedom, but find it despotism to rule themselves. These, Babbalanja, are of the race, to whom a tyrant would prove a blessing." So saying he drained his cup.

"My lord, that last sentiment decides the authorship of the scroll. But, with deference, tyrants seldom can prove blessings; inasmuch as evil seldom eventuates in good. Yet will these people soon have a tyrant over them, if long they cleave to war. Of many javelins, one must prove a scepter; of many helmets, one a crown. It is but in the wearing.—Refill, my lord."

"Fools, fools!" cried Media, "these tribes hate us kings; yet know not, that Peace is War against all kings. We seldom are undone by spears, which are our ministers.—This wine is strong."

"Ha, now's the time! In his cups learn king-craft from a king. Ay, ay, my lord, your royal order will endure, so long as men will fight. Break the spears, and free the nations. Kings reap the harvests that wave on battle-fields. And oft you kings do snatch the aloe-flower, whose slow blossoming mankind watches for a hundred years.—Say on, my lord."

"All this I know; and, therefore, rest content. My children's children will be kings; though, haply, called by other titles. Mardi grows fastidious in names: we royalties will humor it. The steers would burst their yokes, but have not hands. The whole herd rears and plunges, but soon will bow again: the old, old way!"

"Yet, in Porpheero, strong scepters have been wrested from anointed hands. Mankind seems in arms."

"Let them arm on. They hate us:—good;—they always have; yet still we've reigned, son after sire. Sometimes they slay us, Babbalanja; pour out our marrow, as I this wine; but they spill no kinless blood. 'Twas justly held of old, that but to touch a monarch, was to strike at Oro.—Truth. The palest vengeance is a royal ghost; and regicides but father slaves. Thrones, not scepters, have been broken. Mohi, what of the past? Has it not ever proved so?"

"Pardon, my lord; the times seem changed. 'Tis held, that demi-gods no more rule by right divine. In Vivenza's land, they swear the last kings now reign in Mardi."

"Is the last day at hand, old man? Mohi, your beard is gray; but, Yoomy, listen. When you die, look around; mark then if any mighty change be seen. Old kingdoms may be on the wane; but new dynasties advance. Though revolutions rise to high spring-tide, monarchs will still drown hard; —monarchs survived the flood!"

"Are all our dreams, then, vain?" sighed Yoomy. "Is this no dawn of day that streaks the crimson East! Naught but the false and flickering lights which sometimes mock Aurora in the north! Ah, man, my brother! have all martyrs for thee bled in vain; in vain we poets sang, and prophets spoken? Nay, nay; great Mardi, helmed and mailed, strikes at Oppression's shield, and challenges to battle! Oro will defend the right, and royal crests must roll."

"Thus, Yoomy, ages since, you mortal poets sang; but the world may not be moved from out the orbit in which first it rolled. On the map that charts the spheres, Mardi is marked 'the world of kings.' Round centuries on centuries have wheeled by:—has all this been its nonage? Now, when the rocks grow gray, does man first sprout his beard? Or, is your golden time, your equinoctial year, at hand, that your race fast presses toward perfection; and every hand grasps at a scepter, that kings may be no more?"

"But free Vivenza! Is she not the star, that must, ere long, lead up the constellations, though now unrisen? No kings are in Vivenza; yet, spite her thralls, in that land seems more of good than elsewhere. Our hopes are not wild dreams: Vivenza cheers our hearts. She is a rainbow to the isles!"

"Ay, truth it is, that in Vivenza they have prospered. But thence it comes not, that all men may be as they. Are all men of one heart and brain; one bone and sinew? Are all nations sprung of Dominora's loins? Or, has Vivenza yet proved her creed? Yoomy! the years that prove a man, prove not a nation. But two kings'-reigns have passed since Vivenza was a monarch's. Her climacteric is not come; hers is not yet a nation's manhood even; though now in childhood, she anticipates her youth, and lusts for empire like any czar. Yoomy! judge not yet. Time hath tales to tell. Many books, and many long, long chapters, are wanting to Vivenza's history; and what history but is full of blood?"

"There stop, my lord," said Babbalanja, "nor aught predict. Fate laughs at prophets; and of all birds, the raven is a liar!"

Chapter 165

They round the stormy Cape of Capes

LONG LEAGUES, for weary days, we voyaged along that coast, till we came to regions where we multiplied our mantles.

The sky grew overcast. Each a night, black storm-clouds swept the wintry sea; and like Sahara caravans, which leave their sandy wakes—so, thick and fleet, slanted the scud behind. Through all this rack and mist, ten thousand foam-flaked dromedary-humps uprose.

Deep among those panting, moaning fugitives, the three canoes raced on.

And now, the air grew nipping cold. The clouds shed off their fleeces; a snow-hillock, each canoe; our beards, white-frosted.

And so, as seated in our shrouds, we sailed in among great mountain passes of ice-isles; from icy ledges scaring shivering seals, and white bears, musical with icicles, jingling from their shaggy ermine.

Far and near, in towering ridges, stretched the glassy Andes; with their own frost, shuddering through all their domes and pinnacles. Ice-splinters rattled down the cliffs, and seethed into the sea.

Broad away, in amphitheaters undermined by currents, whole cities of ice-towers, in crashes, toward one center, fell.—In their earthquakes, Lisbon and Lima never saw the like. Churned and broken in the boiling tide, they swept off amain;—over and over rolling; like porpoises to vessels tranced in calms, bringing down the gale.

At last, rounding an antlered headland, that seemed a moose at bay—ere long, we launched upon blue lake-like waters, serene as Windermere, or Horicon. Thus, from the boisterous storms of youth, we glide upon senility.

But as we northward voyaged, another aspect wore the sea.

In far-off, endless vistas, colonnades of water-spouts were seen: all heaven's dome upholding on their shafts: and bright forms gliding up and down within. So at Luz, in his strange vision, Jacob saw the angels.

A boundless cave of stalactites, it seemed; the cloud-born vapors downward spiraling, till they met the whirlpool-column from the sea; then, uniting, over the waters stalked, like ghosts of gods. Or midway sundered—down, sullen, sunk the watery half; and far up into heaven, was drawn the vapory. As, at death, we mortals part in twain; our earthy half still here abiding; but our spirits flying whence they came.

In good time, we gained the thither side of great Kolumbo of the South; and sailing on, long waited for the day; and wondered at the darkness.

"What steadfast clouds!" cried Yoomy, "yonder! far aloft: that ridge, with many points; it fades below, but shows a faint white crest."

"Not clouds, but mountains," said Babbalanja, "the vast spine, that traverses Kolumbo; spurring off in ribs, that nestle loamy valleys, veined with silver streams, and silver ores."

It was a long, embattled line of pinnacles. And high posted in the East, those thousand bucklered peaks stood forth, and breasted back the Dawn. Before their purple bastions bold, Aurora long arrayed her spears, and clashed her golden shells. The summons dies away. But now, her lancers charge the steep, and gain its crest a-glow;—their glittering spears and blazoned shields triumphant in the morn.

But ere that sight, we glided on for hours in twilight; when, on those mountains' farther side, the hunters must have been abroad, morning-glories all astir.

Chapter 166

They encounter Gold-hunters

NOW, NORTHWARD COASTING along Kolumbo's Western
shore, whence came the same wild forest-sounds, as from the
Eastern; and where we landed not, to seek among those wrangling tribes;—after many, many days, we spied prow after prow, before the
wind all northward bound: sails wide-spread, and paddles plying: scaring
the fish from before them.

Their inmates answered not our earnest hail.

But as they sped, with frantic glee, in one long chorus thus they sang:—

> We rovers bold,
> To the land of Gold,
> Over bowling billows are gliding:
> Eager to toil,
> For the golden spoil,
> And every hardship biding.
> See! See!
> Before our prows' resistless dashes,
> The gold-fish fly in golden flashes!
> 'Neath a sun of gold,
> We rovers bold,
> On the golden land are gaining;

And every night,
We steer aright,
By golden stars unwaning!
All fires burn a golden glare:
No locks so bright as golden hair!
All orange groves have golden gushings:
All mornings dawn with golden flushings!
In a shower of gold, say fables old,
A maiden was won by the god of gold!
In golden goblets wine is beaming:
On golden couches kings are dreaming!
The Golden Rule dries many tears!
The Golden Number rules the spheres!
Gold, gold it is, that sways the nations:
Gold! gold! the center of all rotations!
On golden axles worlds are turning:
With phosphorescence seas are burning!
All fire-flies flame with golden gleamings:
Gold-hunters' hearts with golden dreamings!
With golden arrows kings are slain:
With gold we'll buy a freeman's name!
In toilsome trades, for scanty earnings,
At home we've slaved, with stifled yearnings:
No light! no hope! Oh, heavy woe!
When nights fled fast, and days dragged slow.
But joyful now, with eager eye,
Fast to the Promised Land we fly:
Where in deep mines,
The treasure shines;
Or down in beds of golden streams,
The gold-flakes glance in golden gleams!
How we long to sift,
That yellow drift!
Rivers! Rivers! cease your going!
Sand-bars! rise, and stay the tide!
'Til we've gained the golden flowing;
And in the golden haven ride!

"Quick, quick, my lord," cried Yoomy, "let us follow them; and from the golden waters where she lies, our Yillah may emerge."

"No, no," said Babbalanja,—"no Yillah there!—from yonder promised-land, fewer seekers will return, than go. Under a gilded guise, happiness is still their instinctive aim. But vain, Yoomy, to snatch at Happiness.
Of that we may not pluck and eat. It is the fruit of our own toilsome planting; slow it grows, nourished by many tears, and all our earnest tendings.
Yet ere it ripen, frosts may nip;—and then, we plant again; and yet again.
Deep, Yoomy, deep, true treasure lies; deeper than all Mardi's gold, rooted
to Mardi's axis. But unlike gold, it lurks in every soil,—all Mardi over.
With golden pills and potions is sickness warded off?—the shrunken veins
of age, dilated with new wine of youth? Will gold the heart-ache cure? turn
toward us hearts estranged? will gold, on solid centers empires fix? 'Tis
toil world-wasted to toil in mines. Were all the isles gold globes, set in a
quicksilver sea, all Mardi were then a desert. Gold is the only poverty; of
all glittering ills the direst. And that man might not impoverish himself
thereby, Oro hath hidden it, with all other banes,—saltpeter and explosives,
deep in mountain bowels, and river-beds. But man still will mine for it;
and mining, dig his doom.—Yoomy, Yoomy!—she we seek, lurks not in
the Golden Hills!"

"Lo, a vision!" cried Yoomy, his hands wildly passed across his eyes. "A
vast and silent bay, belted by silent villages:—gaunt dogs howling over
grassy thresholds at stark corpses of old age and infancy; gray hairs mingling
with sweet flaxen curls; fields, with turned furrows, choked with briers;
arbor-floors strown over with hatchet-helves, rotting in the iron; a
thousand paths, marked with foot-prints, all inland leading, none villageward; and strown with traces, as of a flying host. On: over forest—hill, and
dale—and lo! the golden region! After the glittering spoil, by strange rivermargins, and beneath impending cliffs, thousands delve in quicksands; and,
sudden, sink in graves of their own making: with gold dust mingling their
own ashes. Still deeper, in more solid ground, other thousands slave; and
pile their earth so high, they gasp for air, and die; their comrades mounting on them, and delving still, and dying—grave piled on grave! Here, one
haggard hunter murders another in his pit; and murdering, himself is
murdered by a third. Shrieks and groans! cries and curses! It seems a golden
Hell! With many camels, a sleek stranger comes—pauses before the shining
heaps, and shows *his* treasures: yams and bread-fruit. 'Give, give,' the
famished hunters cry—'a thousand shekels for a yam!—a prince's ransom
for a meal!—Oh, stranger! on our knees we worship thee:—take, take our
gold; but let us live!' Yams are thrown them; and they fight. Then he who
toiled not, dug not, slaved not, straight loads his caravans with gold;

regains the beach, and swift embarks for home. 'Home! home!' the hunters cry, with bursting eyes. 'With this bright gold, could we but join our waiting wives, who wring their hands on distant shores, all then were well. But we can not fly; our prows lie rotting on the beach. Ah! home! thou only happiness!—better thy silver earnings than all these golden findings. Oh, bitter end to all our hopes—we die in golden graves.'"

Chapter 167

They seek through the Isles of Palms; and pass the Isles of Myrrh

NOW, OUR PROWS WE TURNED due west, across the blue lagoon.

Soon, no land appeared. Far as the eye could sweep, one azure plain; all over flaked with foamy fleeces:—a boundless flock upon a boundless mead!

Again, all changed. Like stars in multitude, bright islets multiplied around. Emerald-green, they dotted shapes fantastic: circles, arcs, and crescents;—atolls all, or coral carcanets, begemmed and flashing in the sun.

By these we glided, group after group; and through the foliage, spied sweet forms of maidens, like Eves in Edens ere the Fall, or Proserpines in Ennas. Artless airs came from the shore; and from the censer-swinging roses, a bloom, as if from Hebe's cheek.

"Here, at last, we find sweet Yillah!" murmured Yoomy. "Here must she lurk in innocence! Quick! Let us land and search."

"If here," said Babbalanja, "Yillah will not stay our coming, but fly before us through the groves. Wherever a canoe is beached, see you not the palm-trees pine? Not so, where never keel yet smote the strand. In mercy, let us fly from hence. I know not why, but our breath here, must prove a blight."

These regions passed, we came to savage islands, where the glittering

549

coral seemed bones imbedded, bleaching in the sun. Savage men stood naked on the strand, and brandished uncouth clubs, and gnashed their teeth like boars.

The full red moon was rising; and, in long review there passed before it, phantom shapes of victims, led bound to altars through the groves. Death-rattles filled the air. But a cloud descended, and all was gloom.

Again blank water spread before us; and after many days, there came a gentle breeze, fraught with all spicy breathings; cinnamon aromas; and in the rose-flushed evening air, like glow worms, glowed the islets, where this incense burned.

"Sweet isles of myrrh! oh crimson groves," cried Yoomy. "Woe, woe's your fate! your brightness and your bloom, like musky fire-flies, double-lure to death! On ye, the nations prey like bears that gorge themselves with honey."

Swan-like, our prows sailed in among these isles; and oft we landed; but in vain; and leaving them, we still pursued the setting sun.

Chapter 168

Concentric, inward, with Mardi's Reef, they leave their
Wake around the World

WEST, WEST! West, West! Whitherward point Hope and prophet-fingers; whitherward, at sun-set, kneel all worshipers of fire; whitherward in mid-ocean, the great whales turn to die; whitherward face all the Moslem dead in Persia; whitherward lie Heaven and Hell!—West, West! Whitherward mankind and empires—flocks, caravans, armies, navies; worlds, suns, and stars all wend!—West, West!—Oh boundless boundary! Eternal goal! Whitherward rush, in thousand worlds, ten thousand thousand keels! Beacon, by which the universe is steered!—Like the north-star, attracting all needles! Unattainable forever; but forever leading to great things this side thyself!—Hive of all sunsets!—Gabriel's pinions may not overtake thee!

Over balmy waves, still westward sailing! From dawn till eve, the bright, bright days sped on, chased by the gloomy nights; and, in glory dying, lent their luster to the starry skies. So, long the radiant dolphins fly before the sable sharks; but seized, and torn in flames—die, burning:—their last splendor left, in sparkling scales that float along the sea.

Cymbals, drums and psalteries! the air beats like a pulse with music!—High land! high land! and moving lights, and painted lanterns!—What grand shore is this?

"Reverence we render thee, Old Orienda!" cried Media, with bared brow. "Original of all empires and emperors!—a crowned king salutes thee!"

"Mardi's father-land!" cried Mohi, "grandsire of the nations,—hail!"

"All hail!" cried Yoomy. "Kings and sages hither coming, should come like palmers,—scrip and staff! Oh Orienda! thou wert our East, where first dawned song and science, with Mardi's primal mornings! But now, how changed! the dawn of light become a darkness, which we kindle with the gleam of spears! On the world's ancestral hearth, we spill our brothers' blood!"

"Herein," said Babbalanja, "have many distant tribes proved parricidal. In times gone by, Luzianna hither sent her proas; Franko, her scores of captains; and the Dykemen, their peddler hosts, with yard-stick spears! But thou, oh Bello! lord of the empire lineage! Noah of the moderns. Sire of the long line of nations yet in germ!—thou, Bello, and thy locust armies, are the present curse of Orienda. Down ancient streams, from holy plains, in rafts thy murdered float! The pestilence that thins thy armies here, is bred of corpses, made by thee. Maramma's priests, thy pious heralds, loud proclaim that of all pagans, Orienda's most resist the truth!—ay! vain all pious voices, that speak from clouds of war! The march of conquest through wild provinces, may be the march of Mind; but not the march of Love."

"Thou, Bello!" cried Yoomy, "would'st wrest the crook from Alma's hand, and place in it a spear. But vain to make a conqueror of him, who put off the purple when he came to Mardi; and declining gilded miters, entered the nations meekly on an ass."

"Oh curse of commerce!" cried Babbalanja, "that it barters souls for gold. Bello! with opium, thou wouldst drug this land, and murder it in sleep!—And what boot thy conquests here? Seed sown by spears but seldom springs; and harvests reaped thereby, are poisoned by the sickle's edge."

Yet on, and on we coasted; counting not the days.

"Oh, folds and flocks of nations! dusky tribes innumerable!" cried Yoomy, "camped on plains and steppes; on thousand mountains, worshiping the stars; in thousand valleys, offering up first-fruits, till all the forests seem in flames;—where, in fire, the widow's spirit mounts to meet her lord! —Oh, Orienda, in thee 'tis vain to seek our Yillah!"

"How dark as death the night!" said Mohi, shaking the dew from his braids, "the Heavens blaze not here with stars, as over Dominora's land, and broad Vivenza."

One only constellation was beheld; but every star was brilliant as the one, that promises the morning. That constellation was the Crux-Australis, —the badge, and type of Alma.

And now, southwest we steered, till another island vast, was reached;— Hamora! far trending toward the Antarctic Pole.

Coasting on by barbarous beaches, where painted men, with spears, charged on all attempts to land, at length we rounded a mighty bluff,—lit by a beacon; and heard a bugle call:—Bello's! hurrying to their quarters, the World-End's garrison.

Here, the sea rolled high, in mountain surges: mid which, we toiled and strained, as if ascending cliffs of Caucasus.

But not long thus. As when from howling Rhætian heights, the traveler spies green Lombardy below, and downward rushes toward that pleasant plain; so, sloping from long rolling swells, at last we launched upon the calm lagoon.

But as we northward sailed, once more the storm-trump blew, and charger-like, the seas ran mustering to the call; and in battalions crouched before a towering rock, far distant from the main. No moon, eclipsed in Egypt's skies, looked half so lone. But from out that darkness, on the loftiest peak, Bello's standard waved.

"Oh rifled tomb!" cried Babbalanja. "Wherein lay the Mars and Moloch of our times, whose constellated crown, was gemmed with diadems. Thou god of war! who didst seem the devouring Beast of the Apocalypse; casting so vast a shadow over Mardi, that yet it lingers in old Franko's vale; where still they start at thy tremendous ghost; and, late, have hailed a phantom, King! Almighty hero-spell! that after the lapse of half a century, can so bewitch all hearts! But one drop of hero-blood will deify a fool.

"Franko! thou wouldst be free; yet thy free homage is to the buried ashes of a King; thy first choice, the exaltation of his race. In furious fires, thou burn'st Ludwig's throne; and over thy new-made chieftain's portal, in golden letters print'st—'The Palace of our Lord!' In thy New Dispensation, thou cleavest to the exploded Law. And on Freedom's altar—ah, I fear—still, may slay thy hecatombs. But Freedom turns away; she is sick with burnt blood of offerings. Other rituals she loves; and like Oro, unseen herself, would be worshiped only by invisibles. Of long drawn cavalcades, pompous processions, frenzied banners, mystic music, marching nations, she will none. Oh, may thy peaceful Future, Franko, sanctify thy bloody Past. Let not history say: 'To her old gods, she turned again.'"

This rocky islet passed, the sea went down; once more we neared

Hamora's western shore. In the deep darkness, here and there, its margin was lit up by foam-white, breaking billows rolled over from Vivenza's strand, and down from northward Dominora; marking places where light was breaking in, upon the interior's jungle-gloom.

In heavy sighs, the night-winds from shore came over us.

"Ah, vain to seek sweet Yillah here," cried Yoomy.—"Poor land! curst of man, not Oro! how thou faintest for thy children, torn from thy soil, to till a stranger's. Vivenza! did these winds not spend their plaints, ere reaching thee, thy every vale would echo them. Oh, tribe of Hamo! thy cup of woe so brims, that soon it must overflow upon the land which holds ye thralls. No misery born of crime, but spreads and poisons wide. Suffering hunteth sin, as the gaunt hound the hare, and tears it in the greenest brakes."

Still on we sailed: and after many tranquil days and nights, a storm came down, and burst its thousand bombs. The lightnings forked and flashed; the waters boiled; our three prows lifted themselves in supplication; but the billows smote them as they reared.

Said Babbalanja, bowing to the blast: "Thus, oh Vivenza! retribution works! Though long delayed, it comes at last—Judgment, with all her bolts."

Now, a current seized us, and like three darts, our keels sped eastward, through a narrow strait, far in, upon a smooth expanse, an inland ocean, without a throb.

On our left, Porpheero's southwest point, a mighty rock, long tiers of galleries within, deck on deck; and flag-staffs, like an admiral's masts: a line-of-battle-ship, all purple stone, and anchored in the sea. Here Bello's lion crouched; and, through a thousand port-holes, eyed the world.

On our right, Hamora's northern shore gleamed thick with crescents; numerous as the crosses along the opposing strand.

"How vain to say, that progress is the test of truth, my lord," said Babbalanja, "when, after many centuries, those crescents yet unwaning shine, and count a devotee for every worshiper of yonder crosses. Truth and Merit have other symbols than success; and in this mortal race, all competitors may enter; and the field is clear for all. Side by side, Lies run with Truths, and fools with wise; but, like geometric lines, though they pierce infinity, never may they join."

Over that tideless sea we sailed; and landed right, and landed left; but the maiden never found; till, at last, we gained the water's limit; and inland saw great pointed masses, crowned with halos.

"Granite continents," cried Babbalanja, "that seem created like the planets, not built with human hands. Lo, Landmarks! upon whose flanks Time leaves its traces, like old tide-rips of diluvian seas."

As, after wandering round and round some purple dell, deep in a boundless prairie's heart, the baffled hunter plunges in; then, despairing, turns once more to gain the open plain; even so we seekers now curved round our keels; and from that inland sea emerged. The universe again before us; our quest, as wide.

Chapter 169

Sailing on

MORNING DAWNED upon the same mild, blue Lagoon as erst; and all the lands that we had passed, since leaving Piko's shore of spears, were faded from the sight.

Part and parcel of the Mardian isles, they formed a cluster by themselves; like the Pleiades, that shine in Taurus, and are eclipsed by the red splendor of his fiery eye, and the thick clusterings of the constellations round.

And as in Orion, to some old king-astronomer,—say, King of Rigel, or Betelgeuse,—this Earth's four quarters show but four points afar; so, seem they to terrestrial eyes, that broadly sweep the spheres.

And, as the sun, by influence divine, wheels through the Ecliptic; threading Cancer, Leo, Pisces, and Aquarius; so, by some mystic impulse am I moved, to this fleet progress, through the groups in white-reefed Mardi's zone.

Oh, reader, list! I've chartless voyaged. With compass and the lead, we had not found these Mardian Isles. Those who boldly launch, cast off all cables; and turning from the common breeze, that's fair for all, with their own breath, fill their own sails. Hug the shore, naught new is seen; and "Land ho!" at last was sung, when a new world was sought.

That voyager steered his bark through seas, untracked before; ploughed his own path mid jeers; though with a heart that oft was heavy with the

thought, that he might only be too bold, and grope where land was none.
So I.

And though essaying but a sportive sail, I was driven from my course, by a blast resistless; and ill-provided, young, and bowed to the brunt of things before my prime, still fly before the gale;—hard have I striven to keep stout heart.

And if it harder be, than e'er before, to find new climes, when now our seas have oft been circled by ten thousand prows,—much more the glory!

But this new world here sought, is stranger far than his, who stretched his vans from Palos. It is the world of mind; wherein the wanderer may gaze round, with more of wonder than Balboa's band roving through the golden Aztec glades.

But fiery yearnings their own phantom-future make, and deem it present. So, if after all these fearful, fainting trances, the verdict be, the golden haven was not gained;—yet, in bold quest thereof, better to sink in boundless deeps, than float on vulgar shoals; and give me, ye gods, an utter wreck, if wreck I do.

Chapter 170

A flight of Nightingales from Yoomy's Mouth

B Y NOON, down came a calm.
"Oh Neeva! good Neeva! kind Neeva! thy sweet breath, dear Neeva!"

So from his shark's-mouth prayed little Vee-Vee to the god of Fair Breezes. And along they swept; till the three prows neighed to the blast; and pranced on their path, like steeds of Crusaders.

Now, that this fine wind had sprung up; the sun riding joyously in the heavens; and the Lagoon all tossed with white, flying manes; Media called upon Yoomy to ransack his whole assortment of songs:—warlike, amorous, and sentimental,—and regale us with something inspiring; for too long the company had been gloomy.

"Thy best," he cried.

"Then will I e'en sing you a song, my lord, which is a song-full of songs. I composed it long, long since, when Yillah yet bowered in Odo. Ere now, some fragments have been heard. Ah, Taji! in this my lay, live over again your happy hours. Some joys have thousand lives; can never die; for when they droop, sweet memories bind them up.—My lord, I deem these verses good; they came bubbling out of me, like live waters from a spring in a silver mine. And by your good leave, my lord, I have much faith in inspiration. Whoso sings is a seer."

"Tingling is the test," said Babbalanja. "Yoomy, did you tingle, when that song was composing?"

"All over, Babbalanja."

"From sole to crown?"

"From finger to finger."

"My life for it! true poetry, then, my lord! For this self-same tingling, I say, is the test."

"And infused into a song," cried Yoomy, "it evermore causes it so to sparkle, vivify, and irradiate, that no son of man can repeat it without tingling himself. This very song of mine may prove what I say."

"Modest youth!" sighed Media.

"Not more so, than sincere," said Babbalanja. "He who is frank, will often appear vain, my lord. Having no guile, he speaks as freely of himself, as of another; and is just as ready to honor his own merits, even if imaginary, as to lament over undeniable deficiencies. Besides, such men are prone to moods, which to shallow-minded, unsympathizing mortals, make their occasional distrust of themselves, appear but as a phase of self-conceit. Whereas, the man who, in the presence of his very friends, parades a barred and bolted front,—that man so highly prizes his sweet self, that he cares not to profane the shrine he worships, by throwing open its portals. He is locked up; and Ego is the key. Reserve alone is vanity. But all mankind are egotists. The world revolves upon an I; and we upon ourselves; for we are our own worlds:—all other men as strangers, from outlandish, distant climes, going clad in furs. Then, whate'er they be, let us show our worlds; and not seek to hide from men, what Oro knows."

"Truth, my lord," said Yoomy, "but all this applies to men in mass; not specially, to my poor craft. Of all mortals, we poets are most subject to contrary moods. Now, heaven over heaven in the skies; now layer under layer in the dust. This, the penalty we pay for being what we are. But Mardi only sees, or thinks it sees, the tokens of our self-complacency: whereas, all our agonies operate unseen. Poets are only seen when they soar."

"The song! the song!" cried Media. "Never mind the metaphysics of genius."

And Yoomy, thus clamorously invoked, hemmed thrice, tuning his voice for the air.

But here, be it said, that the minstrel was miraculously gifted with

three voices; and, upon occasions, like a mocking-bird, was a concert of
sweet sounds in himself. Had kind friends died, and bequeathed him their
voices? But hark! in a low, mild tenor, he begins:—

Half-vailed above the hills, yet rosy bright,
 Stands fresh, and fair, the meek and blushing morn!
So Yillah looks! her pensive eyes the stars,
 That mildly beam from out her cheek's young dawn!

  But the still meek Dawn,
  Is not aye the form
  Of Yillah nor Morn!
   Soon rises the sun,
   Day's race to run:
  His rays abroad,
  Flash each a sword,—
   And merrily forth they flare!
   Sun-music in the air!
  So Yillah now rises and flashes!
  Rays shooting from out her long lashes,—
   Sun-music in the air!

   Her laugh! How it bounds!
   Bright cascade of sounds!
  Peal after peal, and ringing afar,—
  Ringing of waters, that silvery jar,
   From basin to basin fast falling!
   Fast falling, and shining, and streaming:—
  Yillah's bosom, the soft, heaving lake,
  Where her laughs at last dimple, and flake!

Oh, beautiful Yillah! Thy step so free!—
 Fast fly the sea-ripples,
Revealing their dimples,
 When forth, thou hie'st to the frolicsome sea!

  All the stars laugh,
   When upward she looks:
  All the trees chat
   In their woody nooks:

All the brooks sing;
All the caves ring;
All the buds blossom;
  All the boughs bound;
All the birds carol;
  And leaves turn round,
  Where Yillah looks!

Light wells from her soul's deep sun
Causing many toward her to run!
Vines to climb, and flowers to spring;
And youths their love by hundreds bring!

"Proceed, gentle Yoomy," said Babbalanja.

"The meaning," said Mohi.

"The sequel," said Media.

"My lord, I have ceased in the middle; the end is not yet."

"Mysticism!" cried Babbalanja. "What, minstrel; must nothing ultimate come of all that melody? no final and inexhaustible meaning? nothing that strikes down into the soul's depths; till, intent upon itself, it pierces in upon its own essence, and is resolved into its pervading original; becoming a thing constituent of the all embracing deific; whereby we mortals become part and parcel of the gods; our souls to them as thoughts; and we privy to all things occult, ineffable, and sublime? Then, Yoomy, is thy song nothing worth. Alla Malolla saith, 'That is no true, vital breath, which leaves no moisture behind.' I mistrust thee, minstrel! that thou hast not yet been impregnated by the arcane mysteries; that thou dost not sufficiently ponder on the Adyta, the Monads, and the Hyparxes; the Dianoias, the Unical Hypostases, the Gnostic powers of the Psychical Essence, and the Supermundane and Pleromatic Triads; to say nothing of the Abstract Noumenons."

"Oro forbid!" cried Yoomy; "the very sound of thy words affrights me." Then, whispering to Mohi—"Is he daft again?"

"My brain is battered," said Media. "Azzageddi! you must diet, and be bled."

"Ah!" sighed Babbalanja, turning; "how little they ween of the Rudimental Quincunxes, and the Hecatic Spherula!"

Chapter 171

They visit one Doxodox

NEXT MORNING, we came to a deep, green wood, slowly nodding over the waves; its margin frothy-white with foam. A charming sight!

While delighted, all our paddlers gazed, Media, observing Babbalanja plunged in reveries, called upon him to awake; asking what might so absorb him.

"Ah, my lord! what seraphic sounds have ye driven from me!"

"Sounds! Sure, there's naught heard but yonder murmuring surf; what other sound heard you?"

"The thrilling of my soul's monochord, my lord. But prick not your ears to hear it; that divine harmony is overheard by the rapt spirit alone; it comes not by the auditory nerves."

"No more, Azzageddi! No more of that. Look yonder!"

"A most lovely wood, in truth. And methinks it is here the sage Doxodox, surnamed the Wise One, dwells."

"Hark, I hear the hootings of his owls," said Mohi.

"My lord, you must have read of him. He is said to have penetrated from the zoned, to the unzoned principles. Shall we seek him out, that we may hearken to his wisdom? Doubtless he knows many things, after which we pant."

The lagoon was calm, as we landed; not a breath stirred the plumes of the trees; and as we entered the voiceless shades, lifting his hand, Babbalanja whispered:—"This silence is a fit introduction to the portals of Telestic lore. Somewhere, beneath this moss, lurks the mystic stone Mnizuris; whereby Doxodox hath attained unto a knowledge of the ungenerated essences. Nightly, he bathes his soul in archangelical circumlucencies. Oh, Doxodox! whip me the Strophalunian top! Tell o'er thy Jynges!"

"Down, Azzageddi! down!" cried Media. "Behold: there sits the Wise One; now, for true wisdom!"

From the voices of the party, the sage must have been aware of our approach: but seated on a green bank, beneath the shade of a red mulberry, upon the boughs of which, many an owl was perched, he seemed intent upon describing divers figures in the air, with a jet-black wand.

Advancing with much deference and humility, Babbalanja saluted him.

"Oh wise Doxodox! Drawn hither by thy illustrious name, we seek admittance to thy innermost wisdom. Of all Mardians, thou alone comprehendest those arcane combinations, whereby to drag to day the most deftly hidden things, present and to come. Thou knowest what we are, and what we shall be. We beseech thee, evoke thy Tselmns!"

"Tetrads; Pentads; Hexads; Heptads; Ogdoads:— meanest thou those?"

"New terms all!"

"Foiled at thy own weapons," said Media.

"Then, if thou comprehendest not my nomenclature:—how my science? But let me test thee in the portico.—Why is it, that as some things extend more remotely than others; so, Quadammodotatives are larger than Qualitatives; forasmuch, as Quadammodotatives extend to those things, which include the Quadammodotatives themselves."

"Azzageddi has found his match," said Media.

"Still posed, Babbalanja?" asked Mohi.

"At a loss, most truly! But I beseech thee, wise Doxodox! instruct me in thy dialectics, that I may embrace thy more recondite lore."

"To begin then, my child:—all Dicibles reside in the mind."

"But what are Dicibles?" said Media.

"Meanest thou, Perfect or Imperfect Dicibles?"

"Any kind you please;—but what are they?"

"Perfect Dicibles are of various sorts: Interrogative; Percontative; Adjurative; Optative; Imprecative; Execrative; Substitutive; Compellative; Hypothetical; and lastly, Dubious."

"Dubious enough! Azzageddi! forever, hereafter, hold thy peace."

"Ah, my children! I must go back to my Axioms."

"And what are they?" said old Mohi.

"Of various sorts; which, again, are diverse. Thus: my contrary axioms are Disjunctive, and Subdisjunctive; and so, with the rest. So, too, in degree, with my Syllogisms."

"And what of them?"

"Did I not just hint what they were, my child? I repeat, they are of various sorts: Connex, and Conjunct, for example."

"And what of them?" persisted Mohi; while Babbalanja, arms folded, stood serious and mute; a sneer on his lip.

"As with other branches of my dialectics: so, too, in their way, with my Syllogisms. Thus: when I say,—If it be warm, it is not cold:—that's a simple Sumption. If I add, But it *is* warm:—that's an *As*sumption."

"So called from the syllogist himself, doubtless;" said Mohi, stroking his beard.

"Poor ignorant babe! no. Listen:—if finally, I say,—Therefore it is not cold:—that's the final inference."

"And a most triumphant one it is!" cried Babbalanja. "Thrice profound, and sapient Doxodox! Light of Mardi! and Beacon of the Universe! didst ever hear of the Shark-Syllogism?"

"Though thy epithets be true, my child, I distrust thy sincerity. I have not yet heard of the syllogism to which thou referrest."

"It was thus. A shark seized a swimmer by the leg; addressing him: 'Friend, I will liberate you, if you truly answer whether you think I purpose harm.' Well knowing that sharks seldom were magnanimous, he replied: —'Kind sir, you mean me harm; now go your ways.' 'No, no; my conscience forbids. Nor will I falsify the words of so veracious a mortal. You were to answer truly; but you say I mean you harm:—so harm it is:— here goes your leg.'"

"Profane jester! Would'st thou insult me with thy tomfoolery? Begone—all of ye! tramp! pack! I say: away with ye!" and into the woods Doxodox himself disappeared.

"Bravely done, Babbalanja!" cried Media. "You turned the corner to admiration."

"I have hopes of our Philosopher yet," said Mohi.

"Outrageous impostor! fool, dotard, oaf! Did he think to bejuggle me with his preposterous gibberish? And is this shallow phraseman the renowned Doxodox whom I have been taught so highly to reverence? Alas, alas—Odonphi there is none!"

"His fit again," sighed Yoomy.

Chapter 172

King Media dreams

THAT AFTERNOON was melting down to eve; all but Media broad awake; yet all motionless, as the slumberer upon the purple mat. Sailing on, with open eyes, we slept the wakeful sleep of those, who to the body only give repose, while the spirit still toils on, threading her mountain passes.

King Media's slumbers were like the helmed sentry's in the saddle. From them, he started like an antlered deer, bursting from out a copse. Some said he never slept; that deep within himself he but intensified the hour; or, leaving his crowned brow in marble quiet, unseen, departed to far-off councils of the gods. Howbeit, his lids never closed; in the noonday sun, those crystal eyes, like diamonds, sparkled with a fixed light.

As motionless we thus reclined, Media turned and muttered:—"Brother gods, and demi-gods, it is not well. These mortals should have less or more. Among my subjects is a man, whose genius scorns the common theories of things; but whose still mortal mind can not fathom the ocean at his feet. His soul's a hollow, wherein he raves."

"List, list," whispered Yoomy—"our lord is dreaming; and what a royal dream."

"A very royal and imperial dream," said Babbalanja—"he is arraigning me before high heaven;—ay, ay; in dreams, at least, he deems himself a demi-god."

"Hist," said Mohi—"he speaks again."

"Gods and demi-gods! With one gesture all abysses we may disclose; and before this Mardi's eyes, evoke the shrouded time to come. Were this well? Like lost children groping in the woods, they falter through their tangled paths; and at a thousand angles, baffled, start upon each other. And even when they make an onward move, 'tis but an endless vestibule, that leads to naught. In my own isle of Odo—Odo! Odo! How rules my viceroy there?—Down, down, ye madding mobs! Ho, spearmen, charge! By the firmament, but my halberdiers fly!"

"His dream has changed," said Babbalanja. "He is in Odo, whither his anxieties impel him."

"Hist, hist," said Yoomy.

"I leap upon the soil! Render thy account, Almanni! Where's my throne? Mohi, am I not a king? Do not thy chronicles record me? Yoomy, am I not the soul of some one glorious song? Babbalanja, speak.—Mohi! Yoomy!"

"What is it, my lord? thou dost but dream."

Staring wildly; then calmly gazing round, Media smiled.

"Ha! how we royalties ramble in our dreams! I've told no secrets?"

"While he seemed to sleep, my lord spoke much," said Mohi.

"I knew it not, old man; nor would now; but that ye tell me."

"We dream not ourselves," said Babbalanja, "but the thing within us."

"Ay?—good-morrow Azzageddi!—But come; no more dreams:—Vee-Vee! wine."

And straight through that livelong night, immortal Media plied the can.

Chapter 173

After a long Interval, by Night they are becalmed

NOW SUNS ROSE, and set; moons grew, and waned; till, at last, the star that erewhile heralded the dawn, presaged the eve; to us, sad token!—while deep within the deepest heart of Mardi's circle, we sailed from sea to sea; and isle to isle; and group to group;— vast empires explored, and inland valleys, to their utmost heads; and for every ray in heaven, beheld a king.

Needless to recount all that then befell; what tribes and caravans we saw; what vast horizons; boundless plains; and sierras, in their every intervale, a nation nestling.

Enough that still we roamed.

It was evening; and as the red sun, magnified, launched into the wave, once more, from a wild strand, we launched our three canoes.

Soon, from her clouds, hooded Night, like a nun from a convent, drew nigh. Rustled her train, yet no spangles were there. But high on her brow, still shone her pale crescent; haloed by bandelets—violet, red, and yellow. So looked the lone watcher through her rainbow-iris; so sad, the night without stars.

The winds were laid; the lagoon, still, as a prairie of an August noon.

"Let us dream out the calm," said Media. "One of ye paddlers, watch: Ho companions! who's for Cathay?"

Sleep reigned throughout the canoes, sleeping upon the waters. But nearer and nearer, low-creeping along, came mists and vapors, a thousand; spotted with twinklings of Will-o-Wisps from neighboring shores. Dusky leopards, stealing on by crouches, those vapors seemed.

Hours silently passed. When startled by a cry, Taji sprang to his feet; against which something rattled; then, a quick splash! and a dark form bounded into the lagoon.

The dozing watcher had called aloud; and, about to stab, the assassin, dropping his stiletto, plunged.

Peering hard through those treacherous mists, two figures in a shallop, were espied; dragging another, dripping, from the brine.

"Foiled again, and foiled forever. No foe's corpse was I."

As we gazed, in the gloom quickly vanished the shallop; ere ours could be reversed to pursue.

Then, from the opposite mists, glided a second canoe; and beneath the Iris round the moon, shone now another:—Hautia's flowery flag!

Vain to wave the sirens off; so still they came.

One waved a plant of sickly silver-green.

"The Midnight Tremella!" cried Yoomy; "the falling-star of flowers! —Still I come, when least foreseen; then, flee."

The second waved a hemlock top, the spike just tapering to its final point. The third, a convolvulus, half closed.

"The end draws nigh, and all thy hopes are waning."

Then they proffered grapes.

But once more waved off, silently they vanished.

Again the buried barb tore at my soul; again Yillah was invoked, but Hautia made reply.

Slowly wore out the night. But when uprose the sun, fled clouds, and fled sadness.

Chapter 174

They land at Hooloomooloo

K EEP ALL THREE PROWS, for yonder rock," cried Media.
"No sadness on this merry morn! And now for the Isle of Cripples,
—even Hooloomooloo."

"The Isle of Cripples?"

"Ay; why not? Mohi, tell how they came to club."

In substance, this was the narration.

Averse to the barbarous custom of destroying at birth all infants not
symmetrically formed; but equally desirous of removing from their sight
those unfortunate beings; the islanders of a neighboring group had long
ago established an asylum for cripples; where they lived, subject to their
own regulations; ruled by a king of their own election; in short, forming
a distinct class of beings by themselves.

One only restriction was placed upon them: on no account must they
quit the isle assigned them. And to the surrounding islanders, so unpleasant
the sight of a distorted mortal, that a stranger landing at Hooloomooloo,
was deemed a prodigy. Wherefore, respecting any knowledge of aught
beyond them, the cripples were well nigh as isolated, as if Hooloomooloo
was the only terra-firma extant.

Dwelling in a community of their own, these unfortunates, who otherwise had remained few in number, increased and multiplied greatly. Nor did successive generations improve in symmetry upon those preceding them.

Soon, we drew nigh to the isle.

Heaped up, and jagged with rocks; and, here and there, covered with dwarfed, twisted thickets, it seemed a fit place for its denizens.

Landing, we were surrounded by a heterogeneous mob; and thus escorted, took our way inland, toward the abode of their lord, King Yoky.

What a scene!

Here, helping himself along with two crotched roots, hobbled a dwarf without legs; another stalked before, one arm fixed in the air, like a lightning rod; a third, more active than any, seal-like, flirted a pair of flippers, and went skipping along; a fourth hopped on a solitary pin, at every bound, spinning round like a top, to gaze; while still another, furnished with feelers or fins, rolled himself up in a ball, bowling over the ground in advance.

With curious instinct, the blind stuck close to our side; with their chattering fingers, the deaf and the dumb described angles, obtuse and acute in the air; and like stones rolling down rocky ravines, scores of stammerers stuttered. Discord wedded deformity. All asses' brays were now harmonious memories; all Calibans, as angels.

Yet for every stare we gave them, three stares they gave us.

At last, we halted before a tenement of rude stones; crooked Banian boughs its rafters, thatched with fantastic leaves. So rambling and irregular its plan, it seemed thrown up by the eruption, according to sage Mohi, the origin of the isle itself.

Entering, we saw King Yoky.

Ah! sadly lacking was he, in all the requisites of an efficient ruler. Deaf and dumb he was; and save arms, minus every thing but an indispensable trunk and head. So huge his all-comprehensive mouth, it seemed to swallow up itself.

But shapeless, helpless as was Yoky,—as king of Hooloomooloo, he was competent; the state being a limited monarchy, of which his Highness was but the passive and ornamental head.

As his visitors advanced, he fell to gossiping with his fingers: a servitor interpreting. Very curious to note the rapidity with which motion was translated into sound; and the simultaneousness with which meaning made its way through four successive channels to the mind—hand, sight, voice, and tympanum.

Much amazement His Highness now expressed; horrified his glances.

"Why club such frights as ye? Herd ye, to keep in countenance; or are afraid of your own hideousness, that ye dread to go alone? Monsters! speak."

"Great Oro!" cried Mohi, "are we then taken for cripples, by the very King of the Cripples? My lord, are not our legs and arms all right?"

"Comelier ones were never turned by turners, Mohi. But royal Yoky! in sooth we feel abashed before thee."

Some further stares were then exchanged; when His Highness sought to know, whether there were any Comparative Anatomists among his visitors.

"Comparative Anatomists! not one."

"And why may King Yoky ask that question?" inquired Babbalanja.

Then was made the following statement.

During the latter part of his reign, when he seemed fallen into his dotage, the venerable predecessor of King Yoky had been much attached to an old gray-headed Chimpanzee, one day found meditating in the woods. Rozoko was his name. He was very grave, and reverend of aspect; much of a philosopher. To him, all gnarled and knotty subjects were familiar; in his day he had cracked many a crabbed nut. And so in love with his Timonean solitude was Rozoko, that it needed many bribes and bland persuasions, to induce him to desert his mossy, hillside, misanthropic cave, for the distracting tumult of a court.

But ere long, promoted to high offices, and made the royal favorite, the woodland sage forgot his forests; and, love for love, returned the aged king's caresses. Ardent friends they straight became; dined and drank together; with quivering lips, quaffed long-drawn, sober bumpers; comparing all their past experiences; and canvassing those hidden themes, on which octogenarians dilate.

For when the fires and broils of youth are passed, and Mardi wears its truer aspect—then we love to think, not act; the present seems more unsubstantial than the past; then, we seek out gray-beards like ourselves; and hold discourse of palsies, hearses, shrouds, and tombs; appoint our undertakers; our mantles gather round us, like to winding-sheets; and every night lie down to die. Then, the world's great bubble bursts; then, Life's clouds seem sweeping by, revealing heaven to our straining eyes; then, we tell our beads, and murmur pater-nosters; and in trembling accents cry—"Oro! be merciful."

So, the monarch and Rozoko.

But not always were they thus. Of bright, cheerful mornings, they took slow, tottering rambles in the woods; nodding over grotesque walking-sticks, of the Chimpanzee's handiwork. For sedate Rozoko was a dilletante-arborist: an amateur in canes. Indeed, canes at last became his hobby. For half daft with age, sometimes he straddled his good staff and gently rode abroad, to take the salubrious evening air; deeming it more befitting exercise, at times, than walking. Into this menage, he soon initiated his friend, the king; and side by side they often pranced; or, wearying of the saddle, dismounted; and paused to ponder over prostrate palms, decaying across the path. Their mystic rings they counted; and for every ring, a year in their own calendars.

Now, so closely did the monarch cleave to the Chimpanzee, that, in good time, summoning his subjects, earnestly he charged it on them, that at death, he and his faithful friend should be buried in one tomb.

It came to pass, the monarch died; and Poor Rozoko, now reduced to second childhood, wailed most dismally:—no one slept that night in Hoo-loomooloo. Never did he leave the body; and at last, slowly going round it thrice, he laid him down; close nestled; and noiselessly expired.

The king's injunctions were remembered; and one vault received them both.

Moon followed moon; and wrought upon by jeers and taunts, the people of the isle became greatly scandalized, that a base-born baboon should share the shroud of their departed lord; though they themselves had tucked in the aged Æneas fast by the side of his Achates.

They straight resolved, to build another vault; and over it, a lofty cairn; and thither carry the remains they reverenced.

But at the disinterring, a sad perplexity arose. For lo! surpassing Saul and Jonathan, not even in decay were these fast friends divided. So mingled every relic,—ilium and ulna, carpus and metacarpus;—and so similar the corresponding parts, that like the literary remains of Beaumont and of Fletcher, which was which, no spectacles could tell. Therefore, they desisted; lest the towering monument they had reared, might commemorate an ape, and not a king.

Such the narration; hearing which, my lord Media kept stately silence. But in courtly phrase, as beseemed him, Babbalanja, turban in hand, thus spoke:—

"My concern is extreme, King Yoky, at the embarrassment into which your island is thrown. Nor less my grief, that I myself am not the man, to put an end to it. I could weep that Comparative Anatomists are not so numerous now, as hereafter they assuredly must become; when their services shall be in greater request; when, at the last, last day of all, millions of noble and ignoble spirits will loudly clamor for lost skeletons; when contending claimants shall start up for one poor, carious spine; and, dog-like, we shall quarrel over our own bones."

Then entered dwarf-stewards, and major-domos; aloft bearing twisted antlers; all hollowed out in goblets, grouped; announcing dinner.

Loving not, however, to dine with misshapen Mardians, King Media was loth to move. But Babbalanja, quoting the old proverb—"Strike me in the face, but refuse not my yams," induced him to sacrifice his fastidiousness.

So, under a flourish of ram-horn bugles, court and company proceeded to the banquet.

Central was a long, dislocated trunk of a wild Banian; like a huge centipede crawling on its hundred branches, sawn of even lengths for legs. This table was set out with wry-necked gourds; deformities of calabashes; and shapeless trenchers, dug out of knotty woods.

The first course was shrimp-soup, served in great clam-shells; the second, lobsters, cuttle-fish, crabs, cockles, cray-fish; the third, hunchbacked roots of the Taro-plant—plantains, perversely curling at the end, like the inveterate tails of pertinacious pigs; and for dessert, ill-shaped melons, huge as idiots' heads, plainly suffering from water in the brain.

Now these viands were commended to the favorable notice of all guests; not only for their delicacy of flavor, but for their symmetry.

And in the intervals of the courses, we were bored with hints to admire numerous objects of vertu: bow-legged stools of mangrove wood; zig-zag rapiers of bone; armlets of grampus-vertebræ; outlandish tureens of the callipees of terrapin; and cannakins of the skulls of baboons.

The banquet over, with many congees, we withdrew.

Returning to the water-side, we passed a field, where dwarfs were laboring in beds of yams, heaping the soil around the roots, by scratching it backward; as a dog.

All things in readiness, Yoky's valet, a tri-armed dwarf, treated us to a glorious start, by giving each canoe a vigorous triple-push, crying, "Away with ye, monsters!"

Nor must it be omitted that just previous to embarking, Vee-Vee, spying a curious looking stone, turned it over, and found a snake.

Chapter 175

A Book from the "Ponderings of old Bardianna"

NOW," SAID BABBALANJA, lighting his trombone as we sailed from the isle, "who are the monsters, we or the cripples?"

"You yourself are a monster, for asking the question," said Mohi.

"And so, to the cripples I am; though not, old man, for the reason you mention. But I am, as I am; whether hideous, or handsome, depends upon who is made judge. There is no supreme standard yet revealed, whereby to judge of ourselves; 'Our very instincts are prejudices,' saith Alla Malolla; 'Our very axioms, and postulates are far from infallible.' 'In respect of the universe, mankind is but a sect,' saith Diloro: 'and first principles but dogmas.' What ethics prevail in the Pleiades? What things have the synods in Sagittarius decreed?"

"Never mind your old authors," said Media. "Stick to the cripples; enlarge upon them."

"But I have done with them now, my lord; the sermon is not the text. Give ear to old Bardianna. I know him by heart. Thus saith the sage in Book X. of the Ponderings, 'Zermalmende,' the title: 'Je pense,' the motto: —'My supremacy over creation, boasteth man, is declared in my natural attitude:—I stand erect! But so do the palm-trees; and the giraffes that graze off their tops. And the fowls of the air fly high over our heads; and from the place where we fancy our heaven to be, defile the tops of our temples. Belike, the eagles, from their eyries look down upon us Mardians, in our hives, even as upon the beavers in their dams, marveling at our in-comprehensible ways. And cunning though we be, some things, hidden from us, may not be mysteries to them. Having five keys, hold we all that open to knowledge? Deaf, blind, and deprived of the power of scent, the bat will steer its way unerringly:—could we? Yet man is lord of the bat and the brute; lord over the crows; with whom, he must needs share the grain he garners. We sweat for the fowls, as well as ourselves. The curse of labor rests only on us. Like slaves, we toil: at their good leisure they glean.

"'Mardi is not wholly ours. We are the least populous part of creation. To say nothing of other tribes, a census of the herring would find us far in the minority. And what life is to us,—sour or sweet,—so is it to them. Like us, they die, fighting death to the last; like us, they spawn and depart. We inhabit but a crust, rough surfaces, odds and ends of the isles; the abounding lagoon being its two-thirds, its grand feature from afar; and forever un-fathomable.

"'What shaft has yet been sunk to the antipodes? What underlieth the gold mines?

"'But even here, above-ground, we grope with the sun at meridian. Vainly, we seek our Northwest Passages,—old alleys, and thoroughfares of the whales.

"'Oh men! fellow men! we are only what we are; not what we would be; nor every thing we hope for. We are but a step in a scale, that reaches further above us than below. We breathe but oxygen. Who in Arcturus hath heard of us? They know us not in the Milky Way. We prate of facul-ties divine: and know not how sprouteth a spear of grass; we go about shrugging our shoulders: when the firmament-arch is over us; we rant of etherealities: and long tarry over our banquets; we demand Eternity for a lifetime: when our mortal half-hours too often prove tedious. We know not of what we talk. The Bird of Paradise outflies our flutterings. What it is to be immortal, has not yet entered into our thoughts. At will, we build our futurities; tier above tier, all galleries full of laureates: resounding with everlasting oratorios! Pater-nosters forever, or eternal Misereres! forgetting that in Mardi, our breviaries oft fall from our hands. But divans there are, some say, whereon we shall recline, basking in effulgent suns, knowing neither Orient nor Occident. Is it so? Fellow men! our mortal lives have an end; but that end is no goal: no place of repose. Whatever it may be, it will prove but as the beginning of another race. We will hope, joy, weep, as before; though our tears may be such as the spice-trees shed. Supine we can only be, annihilated.

" 'The thick film is breaking; the ages have long been circling. Fellow-men! if we live hereafter, it will not be in lyrics; nor shall we yawn, and our shadows lengthen, while the eternal cycles are revolving. To live at all, is a high vocation; to live forever, and run parallel with Oro, may truly appall us. Toil we not here? and shall we be forever slothful elsewhere? Other worlds differ not much from this, but in degree. Doubtless, a pebble is a fair specimen of the universe.

" 'We point at random. Peradventure at this instant, there are beings gazing up to this very world as their future heaven. But the universe is all over a heaven: nothing but stars on stars, throughout infinities of expansion. All we see are but a cluster. Could we get to Boötes, we would be no nearer Oro, than now; he hath no place; but is here. Already, in its un-imaginable roamings, our system may have dragged us through and through the spaces, where we plant cities of beryl and jasper. Even now, we may be inhaling the ether, which we fancy seraphic wings are fanning. But look round. There is much to be seen here, and now. Do the archangels survey aught more glorious than the constellations we nightly behold? Continually we slight the wonders, we deem in reserve. We await the present. With marvels we are glutted, till we hold them no marvels at all. But had these eyes first opened upon all the prodigies in the Revelation of the Dreamer, long familiarity would have made them appear, even as these things we see. Now, *now*, the page is outspread: to the simple, easy as a primer; to the wise, more puzzling than hieroglyphics. The eternity to come, is but a prolongation of time present: and the beginning may be more wonderful than the end.

" 'Then let us be wise. But much of the knowledge we seek, already we have in our cores. Yet so simple it is, we despise it; so bold, we fear it.

" 'In solitude, let us exhume our ingots. Let us hear our own thoughts. The soul needs no mentor, but Oro; and Oro, without proxy. Wanting Him, it is both the teacher and the taught. Undeniably, reason was the first revelation; and so far as it tests all others, it has precedence over them. It comes direct to us, without suppression or interpolation; and with Oro's indisputable imprimatur. But inspiration though it be, it is not so arrogant as some think. Nay, far too humble, at times it submits to the grossest in-dignities. Though in its best estate, not infallible; so far as it goes, for us, it is reliable. When at fault, it stands still. We speak not of visionaries. But if this our first revelation stops short of the uttermost, so with all others. If, often, it only perplexes: much more the rest. They leave much unexpound-ed; and disclosing new mysteries, add to the enigma. Fellow-men; the ocean we would sound is unfathomable; and however much we add to our line, when it is out, we feel not the bottom. Let us be truly lowly, then; not lifted up with a Pharisaic humility. We crawl not like worms; nor wear we the liveries of angels.

" 'The firmament-arch has no key-stone; least of all, is man its prop. He stands alone. We are every thing to ourselves, but how little to others. What are others to us? Assure life everlasting to this generation, and their immediate forefathers;—and what tears would flow, were there no resurrection for the countless generations from the first man to five cycles since? And soon we ourselves shall have fallen in with the rank and file of our sires. At a blow, annihilate some distant tribe, now alive and jocund—and what would we reck? Curiosity apart, do we really care whether the people in Bellatrix are immortal or no?

" 'Though they smite us, let us not turn away from these things, if they be really thus.

" 'There was a time, when near Cassiopeia, a star of the first magnitude, most lustrous in the North, grew lurid as a fire, then dim as ashes, and went out. Now, its place is a blank. A vast world, with all its continents, say the astronomers, blazing over the heads of our fathers; while in Mardi were merry-makings, and maidens given in marriage. Who now thinks of that burning sphere? How few are aware that ever it was?

" 'These things are so.

" 'Fellow-men! we must go, and obtain a glimpse of what we are from the Belts of Jupiter and the Moons of Saturn, ere we see ourselves aright. The universe can wax old without us; though by Oro's grace we may live to behold a wrinkle in the sky. Eternity is not ours by right; and, alone, unrequited sufferings here, form no title thereto, unless resurrections are reserved for maltreated brutes. Suffering is suffering; be the sufferer man, brute, or thing.

" 'How small;—how nothing, our deserts! Let us stifle all vain speculations; we need not to be told what righteousness is; we were born with the whole Law in our hearts. Let us do: let us act: let us down on our knees. And if, after all, we should be no more forever;—far better to perish meriting immortality, than to enjoy it unmeritorious. While we fight over creeds, ten thousand fingers point to where vital good may be done. All round us, Want crawls to her lairs; and, shivering, dies unrelieved. Here, *here*, fellow-men, we can better minister as angels, than in heaven, where want and misery come not.

" 'We Mardians talk as though the future was all in all; but act as though the present was every thing. Yet so far as, in our theories, we dwarf our Mardi; we go not beyond an archangel's apprehension of it, who takes in all suns and systems at a glance. Like pebbles, were the isles to sink in space, Sirius, the Dog-star, would still flame in the sky. But as the atom to the animalculae, so Mardi to us. And lived aright, these mortal lives are long; looked into, these souls, fathomless as the nethermost depths.

"'Fellow-men; we split upon hairs; but stripped, mere words and phrases cast aside, the great bulk of us are orthodox. None who think, dissent from the grand belief. The first man's thoughts were as ours. The paramount revelation prevails with us; and all that clashes therewith, we do not so much believe, as believe that we can not disbelieve. Common sense is a sturdy despot; that, for the most part, has its own way. It inspects and ratifies much independent of it. But those who think they do wholly reject it, are but held in a sly sort of bondage; under a semblance of something else, wearing the old yoke.'"

"Cease, cease, Babbalanja," said Media, "and permit me to insinuate a word in your ear. You have long been in the habit, philosopher, of regaling us with chapters from your old Bardianna; and with infinite gusto, you have just recited the longest of all. But I do not observe, oh, Sage! that for all these things, you yourself are practically the better or wiser. You live not up to Bardianna's main thought. Where he stands, he stands immovable; but you are a Dog-vane. How is this?"

"Gogle-goggle, fugle-fi, fugle-fogle-orum!"

"Mad, mad again," cried Yoomy.

Chapter 176

Babbalanja starts to his Feet

FOR TWENTY-FOUR HOURS, seated stiff, and motionless, Babbalanja spoke not a word; then, almost without moving a muscle, muttered thus:—"At banquets surfeit not, but fill; partake, and retire; and eat not again till you crave. Thereby you give nature time to work her magic transformings; turning all solids to meat, and wine into blood. After a banquet you incline to repose:—do so: digestion commands. All this follow those, who feast at the tables of Wisdom; and all such are they, who partake of the fare of old Bardianna."

"Art resuscitated, then, Babbalanja?" said Media.

"Ay, my lord, I am just risen from the dead."

"And did Azzageddi conduct you to their realms?"

"Fangs off! fangs off! depart, thou fiend!—unhand me! or by Oro, I will die and spite thee!"

"Quick, quick, Mohi! let us change places," cried Yoomy.

"How now, Babbalanja?" said Media.

"Oh my lord man—not *you* my lord Media!—high and mighty Puissance! great King of Creation!—thou art but the biggest of braggarts! In every age, thou boastest of thy valorous advances:—flat fools, old dotards, and numskulls, our sires! All the Past, wasted time! the Present knows all! right lucky, fellow-beings, we live now! every man an author!

579

books plenty as men! strike a light in a minute! teeth sold by the pound! all the elements fetching and carrying! lightning running on errands! rivers made to order! the ocean a puddle!—But ages back they boasted like us; and ages to come, forever and ever, they'll boast. Ages back they black-balled the past, thought the last day was come; so wise they were grown. Mardi could not stand long; have to annex one of the planets; invade the great sun; colonize the moon;—conquerors sighed for new Mardis; and sages for heaven—having by heart all the primers here below. Like us, ages back they groaned under their books; made bonfires of libraries, leaving ashes behind, mid which we reverentially grope for charred pages, forgetting we are so much wiser than they.—But amazing times! astounding revelations; preternatural divulgings!—How now?—more wonderful than all our discoveries is this: that they never were discovered before. So simple, no doubt our ancestors overlooked them; intent on deeper things—the deep things of the soul. All we discover has been with us since the sun began to roll; and much we discover, is not worth the discovering. We are children, climbing trees after birds' nests, and making a great shout, whether we find eggs in them or no. But where are our wings, which our fore-fathers surely had not? Tell us, ye sages! something worth an archangel's learning; discover, ye discoverers, something new. Fools, fools! Mardi's not changed: the sun yet rises in its old place in the East; all things go on in the same old way; we cut our eye-teeth just as late as they did, three thousand years ago."

"Your pardon," said Mohi, "for beshrew me, they are not yet all cut. At threescore and ten, here have I a new tooth coming now."

"Old man! it but clears the way for another. The teeth sown by the alphabet-founder were eye-teeth, not yet all sprung from the soil. Like spring-wheat, blade by blade, they break ground late; like spring-wheat, many seeds have perished in the hard winter glebe. Oh, my lord! though we galvanize corpses into St. Vitus' dances, we raise not the dead from their graves! Though we have discovered the circulation of the blood, men die as of yore; oxen graze, sheep bleat, babies bawl, asses bray—loud and lusty as the day before the flood. Men fight and make up; repent and go at it; feast and starve; laugh and weep; pray and curse; cheat, chaffer, trick, truckle, cozen, defraud, fib, lie, beg, borrow, steal, hang, drown—as in the laughing and weeping, tricking and truckling, hanging and drowning times that have been. Nothing changes, though much be new-fashioned: new fashions but revivals of things previous. In the books of the past we learn naught but of the present; in those of the present, the past. All Mardi's

history—beginning, middle, and finis—was written out in capitals in the
first page penned. The whole story is told in a title-page. An exclamation
point is entire Mardi's autobiography."

"Who speaks now?" said Media, "Bardianna, Azzageddi, or Babbalanja?"

"All three: is it not a pleasant concert?"

"Very fine: very fine.—Go on; and tell us something of the future."

"I have never departed this life yet, my lord."

"But just now you said you were risen from the dead."

"From the buried dead within me; not from myself, my lord."

"If you, then, know nothing of the future—did Bardianna?"

"If he did, naught did he reveal. I have ever observed, my lord, that
even in their deepest lucubrations, the profoundest, frankest, ponderers
always reserve a vast deal of precious thought for their own private behoof.
They think, perhaps, that 'tis too good, or too bad; too wise, or too foolish,
for the multitude. And this unpleasant vibration is ever consequent upon
striking a new vein of ideas in the soul. As with buried treasures, the ground
over them sounds strange and hollow. At any rate, the profoundest ponderer seldom tells us all he thinks; seldom reveals to us the ultimate, and the
innermost; seldom makes us open our eyes under water; seldom throws
open the totus-in-toto; and never carries us with him, to the unconsub-
sistent, the idea-immanens, the super-essential, and the One."

"Confusion! Remember the Quadammodatatives!"

"Ah!" said Braid-Beard, "that's the crack in his calabash, which all the
Dicibles of Doxodox will not mend."

"And from that crazy calabash he gives us to drink, old Mohi."

"But never heed his leaky gourd nor its contents, my lord. Let these
philosophers muddle themselves as they will, we wise ones refuse to partake."

"And fools like me drink till they reel," said Babbalanja. "But in these
matters one's calabash must needs go round to keep afloat. Fogle-orum!"

Chapter 177

*At last, the last Mention is made of old Bardianna;
and His last Will and Testament is recited at Length*

THE DAY WAS WANING. And, as after many a tale of ghosts, around their forest fire, Hungarian gipsies silent sit; watching the ruddy glow kindling each other's faces;—so, now we solemn sat; the crimson West our fire; all our faces flushed.

"Testators!" then cried Media, "when your last wills are all round settled, speak, and make it known!"

"Mine, my lord, has long been fixed," said Babbalanja.

"And how runs it?"

"Fugle-fogle—"

"Hark ye, intruding Azzageddi! rejoin thy merry mates below;—go there, and wag thy saucy tail; or I will nail it to our bow, till ye roar for liberation. Begone, I say."

"Down, devil! deeper down!" rumbled Babbalanja. "My lord, I think he's gone. And now, by your good leave, I'll repeat old Bardianna's Will. It's worth all Mardi's hearing; and I have so studied it, by rote I know it."

"Proceed then; but I mistrust that Azzageddi is not yet many thousand fathoms down."

"Attend my lord:—'Anno Mardis 50,000,000, o.s. I, Bardianna, of the island of Vamba, and village of the same name, having just risen from my yams, in high health, high spirits, and sound mind, do hereby cheerfully make and ordain this my last will and testament.

" 'Imprimis:

" 'All my kith and kin being well to do in Mardi, I wholly leave them out of this my will.

" 'Item. Since, in divers ways, verbally and otherwise, my good friend Pondo has evinced a strong love for me, Bardianna, as the owner and proprietor of all that capital messuage with the appurtenances, in Vamba aforesaid, called 'The Lair,' wherein I now dwell; also for all my Bread-fruit orchards, Palm-groves, Banana-plantations, Taro-patches, gardens, lawns, lanes, and hereditaments whatsoever, adjoining the aforesaid mes-suage;—I do hereby give and bequeath the same to Bomblum of the island of Adda; the aforesaid Bomblum having never expressed any regard for me, as a holder of real estate.

" 'Item. My esteemed neighbor Lakreemo having since the last lunar eclipse called daily to inquire after the state of my health: and having nightly made tearful inquiries of my herb-doctor, concerning the state of my viscera;—I do hereby give and bequeath to the aforesaid Lakreemo all and sundry those vegetable pills, potions, powders, aperients, purgatives, expellatives, evacuatives, tonics, emetics, cathartics, clysters, injections, scarifiers, cataplasms, lenitives, lotions, decoctions, washes, gargles, and phlegmagogues; together with all the jars, calabashes, gourds, and galipots, thereunto pertaining; situate, lying, and being, in the west-by-north corner of my east-southeast crypt, in my aforesaid tenement known as 'The Lair.'

" 'Item. The woman Pesti; a native of Vamba, having oftentimes hinted that I, Bardianna, sorely needed a spouse, and having also intimated that she bore me a conjugal affection; I do hereby give and bequeath to the aforesaid Pesti:—my blessing; forasmuch, as by the time of the opening of this my last will and testament, I shall have been forever delivered from the afore-said Pesti's persecutions.

" 'Item. Having a high opinion of the probity of my worthy and excel-lent friend Bidiri, I do hereby entirely, and wholly, give, will, grant, be-stow, devise, and utterly hand over unto the said Bidiri, all that tenement where my servant Oram now dwelleth; with all the lawns, meadows, up-lands and lowlands, fields, groves, and gardens, thereunto belonging:—IN TRUST NEVERTHELESS to have and to hold the same for the sole use and benefit of Lanbranka Hohinna, spinster, now resident of the aforesaid island of Vamba.

" 'Item. I give and bequeath my large carved drinking gourd to my good comrade Topo.

" 'Item. My fast friend Doldrum having at sundry times, and in sundry places, uttered the prophecy, that upon my decease his sorrow would be great; I do hereby give and bequeath to the aforesaid Doldrum, ten yards of my best soft tappa, to be divided into handkerchiefs for his sole benefit and behoof.

" 'Item. My sensible friend Solo having informed me, that he intended to remain a bachelor for life; I give and devise to the aforesaid Solo, the mat for one person, whereon I nightly repose.

" 'Item. Concerning my private Arbor and Palm-groves, adjoining, lying, and being in the isle of Vamba, I give and devise the same, with all appurtenances whatsoever, to my friend Minta the Cynic, to have and to hold, in trust for the first through-and-through honest man, issue of my neighbor Mondi; and in default of such issue, for the first through-and-through honest man, issue of my neighbor Pendidda; and in default of such issue, for the first through-and-through honest man, issue of my neighbor Wynodo: and in default of such issue, to any through-and-through honest man, issue of any body, to be found through the length and breadth of Mardi.

" 'Item. My friend Minta the Cynic to be sole judge of all claims to the above-mentioned devise; and to hold the said premises for his own use, until the aforesaid person be found.

" 'Item. Knowing my devoted scribe Marko to be very sensitive touching the receipt of a favor; I willingly spare him that pain; and hereby bequeath unto the aforesaid scribe, three milk-teeth, not as a pecuniary legacy, but as a very slight token of my profound regard.

" 'Item. I give to the poor of Vamba the total contents of my red-labeled bags of bicuspids and canines (which I account three-fourths of my whole estate); to my body servant Fidi, my staff, all my robes and togas, and three hundred molars in cash; to that discerning and sagacious philosopher my disciple Krako, one complete set of denticles, to buy him a vertebral bone ring; and to that pious and promising youth Vangi, two fathoms of my best kaiar rope, with the privilege of any bough in my groves.

" 'All the rest of my goods, chattels and household stuff whatsoever; and all my loose denticles, remaining after my debts and legacies are paid, and my body is out of sight, I hereby direct to be distributed among the poor of Vamba.

" 'Ultimo. I give and bequeath to all Mardi this my last advice and counsel:—videlicet: live as long as you can; close your own eyes when you die.

"'I have no previous wills to revoke; and publish this to be my first and last.

"'In witness whereof, I have hereunto set my right hand; and hereunto have caused a true copy of the tattooing on my right temple to be affixed, during the year first above written.

"'By me, BARDIANNA.'"

"Babbalanja, that's an extraordinary document," said Media.

"Bardianna was an extraordinary man, my lord."

"Were there no codicils?"

"The will is all codicils; all after-thoughts; Ten thoughts for one act, was Bardianna's motto."

"Left he nothing whatever to his kindred?"

"Not a stump."

"From his will, he seems to have lived single."

"Yes: Bardianna never sought to improve upon nature; a bachelor he was born, and a bachelor he died."

"According to the best accounts, how did he depart, Babbalanja?" asked Mohi.

"With a firm lip, and his hand on his heart, old man."

"His last words?"

"'Calmer, and better!'"

"Where think you, he is now?"

"In his Ponderings. And those, my lord, we all inherit; for like the great chief of Romara, who made a whole empire his legatee; so, great authors have all Mardi for an heir."

Chapter 178

A Death-cloud sweeps by them, as they sail

NEXT DAY, a fearful sight!
As in Sooloo's seas, one vast water-spout will, sudden, form: and
whirling, chase the flying Malay keels; so, before a swift-winged
cloud, a thousand prows sped by, leaving braided, foaming wakes; their
crowded inmates' arms, in frenzied supplications wreathed; like tangled
forest-boughs.

"See, see," cried Yoomy, "how the Death-cloud flies! Let us dive down
in the sea."

"Nay," said Babbalanja. "All things come of Oro; if we must drown,
let Oro drown us."

"Down sails: drop paddles," said Media: "here we float."

Like a rushing bison, sweeping by, the Death-cloud grazed us with its
foam; and whirling in upon the thousand prows beyond, sudden burst in
deluges; and scooping out a maelström, dragged down every plank and
soul.

Long we rocked upon the circling billows, which expanding from that
center, dashed every isle, till, moons afterward, faint, they laved all Mardi's
reef.

"Thanks unto Oro," murmured Mohi, "this heart still beats."

That sun-flushed eve, we sailed by many tranquil harbors, whence fled those thousand prows. Serene, the waves ran up their strands; and chimed around the unharmed stakes of palm, to which the thousand prows that morning had been fastened.

"Flying death, they ran to meet it," said Babbalanja. "But 'tis not that they fled, they died; for maelströms, of these harbors, the Death-cloud might have made. But they died, because they might not longer live. Could we gain one glimpse of the great calendar of eternity, all our names would there be found, glued against their dates of death. We die by land, and die by sea; we die by earthquakes, famines, plagues, and wars; by fevers, agues; woe, or mirth excessive. This mortal air is one wide pestilence, that kills us all at last. Whom the Death-cloud spares, sleeping, dies in silent watches of the night. He whom the spears of many battles could not slay, dies of a grape-stone, beneath the vine-clad bower he built, to shade declining years. We die, because we live. But none the less does Babbalanja quake. And if he flies not, 'tis because he stands the center of a circle; its every point a leveled dart; and every bow, bent back:—a twang, and Babbalanja dies."

Chapter 179

They visit the palmy King Abrazza

NIGHT AND MORN DEPARTED; and in the afternoon, we drew nigh to an island, overcast with shadows; a shower was falling; and pining, plaintive notes forth issued from the groves: half-suppressed, and sobbing whisperings of leaves. The shore sloped to the water; thither our prows were pointed.

"Sheer off! no landing here," cried Media, "let us gain the sunny side; and like the care-free bachelor Abrazza, who here is king, turn our back on the isle's shadowy side, and revel in its morning-meads."

"And lord Abrazza:—who is he?" asked Yoomy.

"The one hundred and twentieth in lineal descent from Phipora," said Mohi; "and connected on the maternal side to the lord seigniors of Klivonia. His uttermost uncle was nephew to the niece of Queen Zmiglandi; who flourished so long since, she wedded at the first Transit of Venus. His pedigree is endless."

"But who is lord Abrazza?"

"Has he not said?" answered Babbalanja. "Why so dull?—Uttermost nephew to him, who was nephew to the niece of the peerless Queen Zmiglandi; and the one hundred and twentieth in descent from the illustrious Phipora."

"Will none tell, who Abrazza is?"

"Can not a man then, be described by running off the catalogue of his

588

ancestors?" said Babbalanja. "Or must we e'en descend to himself? Then, listen, dull Yoomy! and know that lord Abrazza is six feet two: plump thighs; blue eyes; and brown hair; likes his bread-fruit baked, not roasted; sometimes carries filberts in his crown: and has a way of winking when he speaks. His teeth are good."

"Are you publishing some decamped burglar," said Media, "that you speak thus of my royal friend, the lord Abrazza? Go on, sir! and say he reigns sole king of Bonovona!"

"My lord, I had not ended. Abrazza, Yoomy, is a fine and florid king: high-fed, and affluent of heart; of speech, mellifluent. And for a royalty extremely amiable. He is a sceptered gentleman, who does much good. Kind king! in person he gives orders for relieving those, who daily dive for pearls, to grace his royal robe; and gasping hard, with blood-shot eyes, come up from shark-infested depths, and fainting, lay their treasure at his feet. Sweet lord Abrazza! how he pities those, who in his furthest wood-lands day-long toil to do his bidding. Yet king-philosopher, he never weeps; but pities with a placid smile; and that but seldom."

"There seems much iron in your blood," said Media. "But say your say."

"Say I not truth, my lord? Abrazza, I admire. Save his royal pity all else is jocund round him. He loves to live for life's own sake. He vows he'll have no cares; and often says, in pleasant reveries,—'Sure, my lord Abrazza, if any one should be care-free, 'tis thou; who strike down none, but pity all the fallen!' Yet none he lifteth up."

At length we gained the sunny side, and shoreward tended. Vee-Vee's horn was sonorous; and issuing from his golden groves, my lord Abrazza, like a host that greets you on the threshold, met us, as we keeled the beach.

"Welcome! fellow demi-god, and king! Media, my pleasant guest!"

His servitors salamed; his chieftains bowed; his yeoman-guard, in meadow-green, presented palm-stalks,—royal tokens; and hand in hand, the nodding, jovial, regal friends, went up a lane of salutations; dragging behind, a train of envyings.

Much we marked Abrazza's jeweled crown; that shot no honest blaze of ruddy rubies; nor looked stern-white like Media's pearls; but cast a green and yellow glare; rays from emeralds, crossing rays from many a topaz. In those beams, so sinister, all present looked cadaverous: Abrazza's cheek alone beamed bright, but hectic.

Upon its fragrant mats a spacious hall received the kings; and gathering courtiers blandly bowed; and gushing with soft flatteries, breathed idol-incense round them.

The hall was terraced thrice; its elevated end was curtained; and thence, at every chime of words, there burst a girl, gay scarfed, with naked bosom, and poured forth wild and hollow laughter, as she raced down all the terraces, and passed their merry kingships.

Wide round the hall, in avenues, waved almond-woods; their whiteness frosted into bloom. But every vine-clad trunk was hollow-hearted; hollow sounds came from the grottos: hollow broke the billows on the shore: and hollow pauses filled the air, following the hollow laughter.

Guards, with spears, paced the groves, and in the inner shadows, oft were seen to lift their weapons, and backward press some ugly phantom, saying, "Subjects! haunt him not; Abrazza would be merry; Abrazza feasts his guests."

So, banished from our sight seemed all things uncongenial; and pleasant times were ours, in these dominions. Not a face passed by, but smiled; mocking-birds perched on the boughs; and singing, made us vow the woods were warbling forth thanksgiving, with a thousand throats! The stalwart yeomen grinned beneath their trenchers, heaped with citrons, pomegranates, grapes; the pages tittered, pouring out the wine; and all the lords loud laughed, smote their gilded spears, and swore the isle was glad.

Such the isle, in which we tarried; but in our rambles, found no Yillah.

Chapter 180

Some pleasant, shady Talk in the Groves, between my Lords Abrazza and Media, Babbalanja, Mohi, and Yoomy

ABRAZZA HAD A COOL RETREAT—a grove of dates; where we were used to lounge of noons, and mix our converse with the babble of the rills; and mix our punches in goblets chased with grapes. And as ever, King Abrazza was the prince of hosts.

"Your crown," he said to Media; and with his own, he hung it on a bough.

"Be not ceremonious:" and stretched his royal legs upon the turf.

"Wine!" and his pages poured it out.

So on the grass we lounged; and King Abrazza, who loved his antique ancestors; and loved old times; and would not talk of moderns;—bade Yoomy sing old songs; bade Mohi rehearse old histories; bade Babbalanja tell of old ontologies; and commanded all, meanwhile, to drink his old, old wine.

So, all round we quaffed and quoted.

At last, we talked of old Homeric bards:—those who, ages back, harped, and begged, and groped their blinded way through all this charitable Mardi; receiving coppers then, and immortal glory now.

ABRAZZA.—How came it, that they all were blind?

BABBALANJA.—It was endemical, your Highness. Few grand poets have good eyes; for they needs blind must be, who ever gaze upon the sun. Vavona himself was blind; when, in the silence of his secret bower, he said

—"I will build another world. Therein, let there be kings and slaves, philosophers and wits; whose checkered actions—strange, grotesque, and merry-sad, will entertain my idle moods." So, my lord, Vavona played at kings and crowns, and men and manners; and loved that lonely game to play.

ABRAZZA.—Vavona seemed a solitary Mardian; who seldom went abroad; had few friends; and shunning others, was shunned by them.

BABBALANJA.—But shunned not himself, my lord; like gods, great poets dwell alone; while round them, roll the worlds they build.

MEDIA.—You seem to know all authors:—you must have heard of Lombardo, Babbalanja; he who flourished many ages since.

BABBALANJA.—I have; and his grand Koztanza know by heart.

MEDIA (to Abrazza.)—A very curious work, that, my lord.

ABRAZZA.—Yes, my dearest king. But, Babbalanja, if Lombardo had aught to tell to Mardi—why choose a vehicle so crazy?

BABBALANJA.—It was his nature, I suppose.

ABRAZZA.—But so it would not have been, to me.

BABBALANJA.—Nor would it have been natural, for my noble lord Abrazza, to have worn Lombardo's head:—every man has his own, thank Oro!

ABRAZZA.—A curious work: a very curious work. Babbalanja, are you acquainted with the history of Lombardo?

BABBALANJA.—None better. All his biographies have I read.

ABRAZZA.—Then, tell us how he came to write that work. For one, I can not imagine how those poor devils contrive to roll such thunders through all Mardi.

MEDIA.—Their thunder and lightning seem spontaneous combustibles, my lord.

ABRAZZA.—With which, they but consume themselves, my prince beloved.

BABBALANJA.—In a measure, true, your Highness. But pray you, listen; and I will try to tell the way in which Lombardo produced his great Koztanza.

MEDIA.—But hark you, philosopher! this time no incoherencies; gag that devil, Azzageddi. And now, what was it that originally impelled Lombardo to the undertaking?

BABBALANJA.—Primus and forever, a full heart:—brimful, bubbling, sparkling; and running over like the flagon in your hand, my lord. Secundo, the necessity of bestirring himself to procure his yams.

ABRAZZA.—Wanting the second motive, would the first have sufficed, philosopher?

BABBALANJA.—Doubtful. More conduits than one to drain off the soul's overflowings. Besides, the greatest fullnesses overflow not spontaneously; and, even when decanted, like rich syrups, slowly ooze; whereas, poor fluids glibly flow, wide-spreading. Hence, when great fullness weds great indolence;—that man, to others, too often proves a cipher; though, to himself, his thoughts form an Infinite Series, indefinite, from its vastness; and incommunicable;—not for lack of power, but for lack of an omnipotent volition, to move his strength. His own world is full before him; the fulcrum set; but lever there is none. To such a man, the giving of any boor's resoluteness, with tendons braided, would be as hanging a claymore to Valor's side, before unarmed. Our minds are cunning, compound mechanisms; and one spring, or wheel, or axle wanting, the movement lags, or halts. Cerebrum must not overbalance cerebellum; our brains should be round as globes; and planted on capacious chests, inhaling mighty morning-inspirations. We have had vast developments of parts of men; but none of manly wholes. Before a full-developed man, Mardi would fall down and worship. We are idiot, younger-sons of gods, begotten in dotages divine; and our mothers all miscarry. Giants are in our germs; but we are dwarfs, staggering under heads overgrown. Heaped, our measures burst. We die of too much life.

MEDIA (to Abrazza).—Be not impatient, my lord; he'll recover presently. You were talking of Lombardo, Babbalanja.

BABBALANJA.—I was, your Highness. Of all Mardians, by nature, he was the most inert. Hast ever seen a yellow lion, all day basking in the yellow sun:—in reveries, rending droves of elephants; but his vast loins supine, and eyelids winking? Such, Lombardo; but fierce Want, the hunter, came and roused his roar. In hairy billows, his great mane tossed like the sea; his eyeballs flamed two hells; his paw had stopped a rolling world.

ABRAZZA.—In other words, yams were indispensable, and, poor devil, he roared to get them.

BABBALANJA (bowing).—Partly so, my literal lord. And as with your own golden scepter, at times upon your royal teeth, indolent tattoos you beat; then, potent, sway it o'er your isle; so, Lombardo. And ere Necessity plunged spur and rowel into him, he knew not his own paces. That churned him into consciousness; and brought ambition, ere then dormant, seething to the top, till he trembled at himself. No mailed hand lifted up against a traveler in woods, can so appall, as we ourselves. We are full of ghosts and spirits; we are as grave-yards full of buried dead, that start to life before us. And all our dead sires, verily, are in us; *that* is their immortality. From sire to son, we go on multiplying corpses in ourselves; for all of which, are resurrections. Every thought's a soul of some past poet, hero, sage. We are fuller than a city. Woe it is, that reveals these things. He knows himself, and all that's in him, who knows adversity. To scale great heights, we must come out of lowermost depths. The way to heaven is through hell. We need fiery baptisms in the fiercest flames of our own bosoms. We must feel our hearts hot—hissing in us. And ere their fire is revealed, it must burn its way out of us; though it consume us and itself. Oh, sleek-cheeked Plenty! smiling at thine own dimples;—vain for thee to reach out after greatness. Turn! turn! from all your tiers of cushions of eider-down—turn! and be broken on the wheels of many woes. At white-heat, brand thyself; and count the scars, like old war-worn veterans, over camp-fires. Soft poet! brushing tears from lilies—this way! and howl in sackcloth and in ashes! Know, thou, that the lines that live are turned out of a furrowed brow. Oh! there is a fierce, a cannibal delight, in the grief that shrieks to multiply itself. That grief is miserly of its own; it pities all the happy. Some damned spirits would not be otherwise, could they.

ABRAZZA (*to Media*).—Pray, my lord, is this good gentleman a devil?

MEDIA.—No, my lord; but he's possessed by one. His name is Azzaged-di. You may hear more of him. But come, Babbalanja, hast forgotten all about Lombardo? How set he about that great undertaking, his Koztanza?

ABRAZZA (*to Media*).—Oh, for all the ravings of your Babbalanja, Lombardo took no special pains; hence, deserves small commendation. For, genius must be somewhat like us kings,—calm, content, in consciousness of power. And to Lombardo, the scheme of his Koztanza must have come full-fledged, like an eagle from the sun.

BABBALANJA.—No, your Highness; but like eagles, his thoughts were first callow; yet, born plumeless, they came to soar.

ABRAZZA.—Very fine. I presume, Babbalanja, the first thing he did, was to fast, and invoke the muses.

BABBALANJA.—Pardon, my lord; on the contrary he first procured a ream of vellum, and some sturdy quills: indispensable preliminaries, my worshipful lords, to the writing of the sublimest epics.

ABRAZZA.—Ah! then the muses were afterward invoked.

BABBALANJA.—Pardon again. Lombardo next sat down to a fine plantain pudding.

YOOMY.—When the song-spell steals over me, I live upon olives.

BABBALANJA.—Yoomy, Lombardo eschewed olives. Said he, "What fasting soldier can fight? and the fight of all fights is to write." In ten days Lombardo had written—

ABRAZZA.—Dashed off, you mean.

BABBALANJA.—He never dashed off aught.

ABRAZZA.—As you will.

BABBALANJA.—In ten days, Lombardo had written full fifty folios; he loved huge acres of vellum whereon to expatiate.

MEDIA.—What then?

BABBALANJA.—He read them over attentively; made a neat package of the whole: and put it into the fire.

ALL.—How?

MEDIA.—What! these great geniuses writing trash?

ABRAZZA.—I thought as much.

BABBALANJA.—My lords, they abound in it! more than any other men in Mardi. Genius is full of trash. But genius essays its best to keep it to itself; and giving away its ore, retains the earth; whence, the too frequent wisdom of its works, and folly of its life.

ABRAZZA.—Then genius is not inspired, after all. How they must slave in their mines! I weep to think of it.

BABBALANJA.—My lord, all men are inspired; fools are inspired; your highness is inspired; for the essence of all ideas is infused. Of ourselves, and in ourselves, we originate nothing. When Lombardo set about his work, he knew not what it would become. He did not build himself in with plans; he wrote right on; and so doing, got deeper and deeper into himself; and like a resolute traveler, plunging through baffling woods, at last was rewarded for his toils. "In good time," saith he, in his autobiography, "I came out into a serene, sunny, ravishing region; full of sweet scents, singing birds, wild plaints, roguish laughs, prophetic voices. Here we are at last, then," he cried; "I have created the creative." And now the whole boundless landscape stretched away. Lombardo panted; the sweat was on his brow; he off mantle; braced himself; sat within view of the ocean; his face to a cool rushing breeze; placed flowers before him; and gave himself plenty of room. On one side was his ream of vellum—

ABRAZZA.—And on the other, a brimmed beaker.

BABBALANJA.—No, your Highness; though he loved it, no wine for Lombardo while actually at work.

MOHI.—Indeed? Why, I ever thought that it was to the superior quality of Lombardo's punches, that Mardi was indebted for that abounding humor of his.

BABBALANJA.—Not so; he had another way of keeping himself well braced.

YOOMY.—Quick! tell us the secret.

BABBALANJA.—He never wrote by rush-light. His lamp swung in heaven.—He rose from his East, with the sun; he wrote when all nature was alive.

MOHI.—Doubtless, then, he always wrote with a grin; and none laughed louder at his quips, than Lombardo himself.

BABBALANJA.—Hear you laughter at the birth of a man child, old man? The babe may have many dimples; not so, the parent. Lombardo was a hermit to behold.

MEDIA.—What! did Lombardo laugh with a long face?

BABBALANJA.—His merriment was not always merriment to him, your Highness. For the most part, his meaning kept him serious. Then he was so intensely riveted to his work, he could not pause to laugh.

MOHI.—My word for it; but he had a sly one, now and then.

BABBALANJA.—For the nonce, he was not his own master: a mere amanuensis writing by dictation.

YOOMY.—Inspiration, that!

BABBALANJA.—Call it as you will, Yoomy, it was a sort of sleep-walking of the mind. Lombardo never threw down his pen: it dropped from him; and then, he sat disenchanted: rubbing his eyes; staring; and feeling faint—sometimes, almost unto death.

MEDIA.—But pray, Babbalanja, tell us how he made acquaintance with some of those rare worthies, he introduces us to, in his Koztanza.

BABBALANJA.—He first met them in his reveries; they were walking about in him, sour and moody: and for a long time, were shy of his advances; but still importuned, they at last grew ashamed of their reserve; stepped forward; and gave him their hands. After that, they were frank and friendly. Lombardo set places for them at his board; when he died, he left them something in his will.

MEDIA.—What! those imaginary beings?

ABRAZZA.—Wondrous witty! infernal fine!

MEDIA.—But, Babbalanja; after all, the Koztanza found no favor in the eyes of some Mardians.

ABRAZZA.—Ay: the arch-critics Verbi and Batho denounced it.

BABBALANJA.—Yes: on good authority, Verbi is said to have detected a superfluous comma; and Batho declared that, with the materials he could have constructed a far better world than Lombardo's. But, didst ever hear of his laying his axis?

ABRAZZA.—But the unities; Babbalanja, the unities! they are wholly wanting in the Koztanza.

BABBALANJA.—Your Highness; upon that point, Lombardo was frank. Saith he, in his autobiography: "For some time, I endeavored to keep in the good graces of those nymphs; but I found them so captious, and exacting; they threw me into such a violent passion with their fault-findings; that, at last, I renounced them."

ABRAZZA.—Very rash!

BABBALANJA.—No, your Highness; for though Lombardo abandoned all monitors from without; he retained one autocrat within—his crowned and sceptered instinct. And what, if he pulled down one gross world, and ransacked the etherial spheres, to build up something of his own—a composite:—what then? matter and mind, though matching not, are mates; and sundered oft, in his Koztanza they unite:—the airy waist, embraced by stalwart arms.

MEDIA.—Incoherent again! I thought we were to have no more of this!

BABBALANJA.—My lord Media, there are things infinite in the finite; and dualities in unities. Our eyes are pleased with the redness of the rose, but another sense lives upon its fragrance. Its redness you must approach, to view: its invisible fragrance pervades the field. So, with the Koztanza. Its mere beauty is restricted to its form: its expanding soul, past Mardi does embalm. Modak is Modako; but fogle-foggle is not fugle-fi.

MEDIA (to Abrazza).—My lord, you start again; but 'tis only another phase of Azzageddi; sometimes he's quite mad. But all this you must needs overlook.

ABRAZZA.—I will, my dear prince; what one can not see through, one must needs look over, as you say.

YOOMY.—But trust me, your Highness, some of those strange things fall far too melodiously upon the ear, to be wholly deficient in meaning.

ABRAZZA.—Your gentle minstrel, this must be, my lord. But Babbalanja, the Koztanza lacks cohesion; it is wild, unconnected, all episode.

BABBALANJA.—And so is Mardi itself:—nothing but episodes; valleys and hills; rivers, digressing from plains; vines, roving all over; boulders and diamonds; flowers and thistles; forests and thickets; and, here and there, fens and moors. And so, the world in the Koztanza.

ABRAZZA.—Ay, plenty of dead-desert chapters there; horrible sands to wade through.

MEDIA.—Now, Babbalanja, away with your tropes; and tell us of the work, directly it was done. What did Lombardo then? Did he show it to any one for an opinion?

BABBALANJA.—Yes, to Zenzori; who asked him where he picked up so much trash; to Hauto, who bade him not be cast down, it was pretty good; to Lucree, who desired to know how much he was going to get for it; to Roddi, who offered a suggestion.

MEDIA.—And what was that?

BABBALANJA.—That he had best make a faggot of the whole; and try again.

ABRAZZA.—Very encouraging.

MEDIA.—Any one else?

BABBALANJA.—To Pollo; who, conscious his opinion was sought, was thereby puffed up; and marking the faltering of Lombardo's voice, when the manuscript was handed him, straightway concluded, that the man who stood thus trembling at the bar, must needs be inferior to the judge. But his verdict was mild. After sitting up all night over the work; and diligently taking notes:—"Lombardo, my friend! here, take your sheets. I have run through them loosely. You might have done better; but then you might have done worse. Take them, my friend; I have put in some good things for you."

MEDIA.—And who was Pollo?

BABBALANJA.—Probably some one who lived in Lombardo's time, and went by that name. He is incidentally mentioned, and cursorily immortalized in one of the posthumous notes to the Koztanza.

MEDIA.—What is said of him there?

BABBALANJA.—Not much. In a very old transcript of the work—that of Aldina—the note alludes to a brave line in the text, and runs thus:— "Diverting to tell, it was this passage that an old prosodist, one Pollo, claimed for his own. He maintained he made a free-will offering of it to Lombardo. Several things are yet extant of this Pollo, who died some weeks ago. He seems to have been one of those, who would do great things if they could; but are content to compass the small. He imagined, that the precedence of authors he had established in his library, was their Mardi order of merit. He condemned the sublime poems of Vavona to his lowermost shelf. 'Ah,' thought he, 'how we library princes, lord it over these beggarly authors!' Well read in the history of their woes, Pollo pitied them all, particularly the famous; and wrote little essays of his own, which he read to himself."

MEDIA.—Well: and what said Lombardo to those good friends of his, —Zenzori, Hauto, and Roddi?

BABBALANJA.—Nothing. Taking home his manuscript, he glanced it over; making three corrections.

ABRAZZA.—And what then?

BABBALANJA.—Then, your Highness, he thought to try a conclave of professional critics; saying to himself, "Let them privately point out to me, now, all my blemishes; so that, what time they come to review me in public, all will be well." But curious to relate, those professional critics, for the most part, held their peace, concerning a work yet unpublished. And, with some generous exceptions, in their vague, learned way, betrayed such base, beggarly notions of authorship, that Lombardo could have wept, had tears been his. But in his very grief, he ground his teeth. Muttered he, "They are fools. In their eyes, bindings not brains make books. They criticise my tattered cloak, not my soul, caparisoned like a charger. He is the great author, think they, who drives the best bargain with his wares: and no bargainer am I. Because he is old, they worship some mediocrity of an ancient, and mock at the living prophet with the live coal on his lips. They are men who would not be men, had they no books. Their sires begat them not; but the authors they have read. Feelings they have none: and their very opinions they borrow. They can not say yea, nor nay, without first consulting all Mardi as an Encyclopedia. And all the learning in them, is as a dead corpse in a coffin. Were they worthy the dignity of being damned, I would damn them; but they are not. Critics?—Asses! rather mules!—so emasculated, from vanity, they can not father a true thought. Like mules, too, from dunghills, they trample down gardens of roses: and deem that crushed fragrance their own.—Oh! that all round the domains of genius should lie thus unhedged, for such cattle to uproot! Oh! that an eagle should be stabbed by a goose-quill! But at best, the greatest reviewers but prey on my leavings. For I am critic and creator; and as critic, in cruelty surpass all critics merely, as a tiger, jackals. For ere Mardi sees aught of mine, I scrutinize it myself, remorseless as a surgeon. I cut right and left; I probe, tear, and wrench; kill, burn, and destroy; and what's left after that, the jackals are welcome to. It is *I* that stab false thoughts, ere hatched; *I* that pull down wall and tower, rejecting materials which would make palaces for others. Oh! could Mardi but see how we work, it would marvel more at our primal chaos, than at the round world thence emerging. It would marvel at our scaffoldings, scaling heaven; marvel at the hills of earth, banked all round our fabrics ere completed.—How plain the pyramid! In this grand silence, so intense, pierced by that pointed mass,—could ten thousand slaves have ever toiled? ten thousand hammers rung?—There it stands,—part of Mardi: claiming kin with mountains;—was this thing piecemeal built?—It was. Piecemeal?—atom by atom it was laid. The world is made of mites."

YOOMY (*musing.*)—It is even so.

ABRAZZA.—Lombardo was severe upon the critics; and they as much so upon him;—of that, be sure.

BABBALANJA.—Your Highness, Lombardo never presumed to criticise true critics; who are more rare than true poets. A great critic is a sultan among satraps; but pretenders are thick as ants, striving to scale a palm, after its aerial sweetness. And they fight among themselves. Essaying to pluck eagles, they themselves are geese, stuck full of quills, of which they rob each other.

ABRAZZA (*to Media.*)—Oro help the victim that falls in Babbalanja's hands!

MEDIA.—Ay, my lord; at times, his every finger is a dagger: every thought a falling tower that whelms! But resume, philosopher—what of Lombardo now?

BABBALANJA.—"For this thing," said he, "I have agonized over it enough.—I can wait no more. It has faults—all mine;—its merits all its own;—but I can toil no longer. The beings knit to me implore; my heart is full; my brain is sick. Let it go—let it go—and Oro with it. Somewhere Mardi has a mighty heart—*that* struck, all the isles shall resound!"

ABRAZZA.—Poor devil! he took the world too hard.

MEDIA.—As most of these mortals do, my lord. That's the load, self-imposed, under which Babbalanja reels. But now, philosopher, ere Mardi saw it, what thought Lombardo of his work, looking at it objectively, as a thing out of him, I mean.

ABRAZZA.—No doubt, he hugged it.

BABBALANJA.—Hard to answer. Sometimes, when by himself, he thought hugely of it, as my lord Abrazza says; but when abroad, among men, he almost despised it; but when he bethought him of those parts, written with full eyes, half blinded; temples throbbing; and pain at the heart—

ABRAZZA.—Pooh! pooh!

BABBALANJA.—He would say to himself, "Sure, it can not be in vain!"

Yet again, when he bethought him of the hurry and bustle of Mardi, dejection stole over him. "Who will heed it," thought he; "what care these fops and brawlers for me? But am I not myself an egregious coxcomb? Who will read me? Say one thousand pages—twenty-five lines each—every line ten words—every word ten letters. That's two million five hundred thousand *a*'s, and *i*'s, and *o*'s to read! How many are superfluous? Am I not mad to saddle Mardi with such a task? Of all men, am I the wisest, to stand upon a pedestal, and teach the mob? Ah, my own Koztanza! child of many prayers!—in whose earnest eyes, so fathomless, I see my own; and recall all past delights and silent agonies—thou may'st prove, as the child of some fond dotard:—beauteous to me; hideous to Mardi! And methinks, that while so much slaving merits that thou should'st not die; it has not been intense, prolonged enough, for the high meed of immortality. Yet, things immortal have been written; and by men as me;—men, who slept and waked; and ate; and talked with tongues like mine. Ah, Oro! how may we know or not, we are what we would be? Hath genius any stamp and imprint, obvious to possessors? Has it eyes to see itself; or is it blind? Or do we delude ourselves with being gods, and end in grubs? Genius, genius?—a thousand years hence, to be a household-word?—I?—Lombardo? but yesterday cut in the market-place by a spangled fool!—Lombardo immortal?—Ha, ha, Lombardo! but thou art an ass, with vast ears brushing the tops of palms! Ha, ha, ha! Methinks I see thee immortal! 'Thus great Lombardo saith; and thus; and thus; and thus:—thus saith he—illustrious Lombardo!—Lombardo, our great countryman! Lombardo, prince of poets—Lombardo! great Lombardo!'—Ha, ha, ha!—go, go! dig thy grave, and bury thyself!"

ABRAZZA.—He was very funny, then, at times.

BABBALANJA.—Very funny, your Highness:—amazing jolly! And from my nethermost soul, would to Oro, thou could'st but feel one touch of that jolly woe! It would appall thee, my Right Worshipful lord Abrazza!

ABRAZZA (*to Media*).—My dear lord, his teeth are marvelously white and sharp: some she-shark must have been his dam:—does he often grin thus? It was infernal!

MEDIA.—Ah! that's Azzageddi. But, prithee, Babbalanja, proceed.

BABBALANJA.—Your Highness, even in his calmer critic moods, Lombardo was far from fancying his work. He confesses, that it ever seemed to him but a poor scrawled copy of something within, which, do what he would, he could not completely transfer. "My canvas was small," said he; "crowded out were hosts of things that came last. But Fate is in it." And

Fate it was, too, your Highness, which forced Lombardo, ere his work was well done, to take it off his easel, and send it to be multiplied. "Oh, that I was not thus spurred!" cried he; "but like many another, in its very child-hood, this poor child of mine must go out into Mardi, and get bread for its sire."

ABRAZZA (*with a sigh*).—Alas, the poor devil! But methinks 'twas won-drous arrogant in him to talk to all Mardi at that lofty rate.—Did he think himself a god?

BABBALANJA.—He himself best knew what he thought; but, like all others, he was created by Oro to some special end; doubtless, partly answered in his Koztanza.

MEDIA.—And now that Lombardo is long dead and gone—and his work, hooted during life, lives after him—what think the present company of it? Speak, my lord Abrazza! Babbalanja! Mohi! Yoomy!

ABRAZZA (*tapping his sandal with his scepter*).—I never read it.

BABBALANJA (*looking upward*).—It was written with a divine intent.

MOHI (*stroking his beard*).—I never hugged it in a corner, and ignored it before Mardi.

YOOMY (*musing*).—It has bettered my heart.

MEDIA (*rising*).—And I have read it through nine times.

BABBALANJA (*starting up*).—Ah, Lombardo! this must make thy ghost glad!

Chapter 181

They sup

THERE SEEMED something sinister, hollow, heartless, about Abrazza, and that green-and-yellow, evil-starred crown that he wore.

But why think of that? Though we like not something in the curve of one's brow, or distrust the tone of his voice; yet, let us away with suspicions if we may, and make a jolly comrade of him, in the name of the gods. Miserable! thrice miserable he, who is forever turning over and over one's character in his mind, and weighing by nice avoirdupois, the pros and the cons of his goodness and badness. For we are all good and bad. Give me the heart that's huge as all Asia; and unless a man be a villain outright, account him one of the best tempered blades in the world.

That night, in his right regal hall, King Abrazza received us. And in merry good time a fine supper was spread.

Now, in thus nocturnally regaling us, our host was warranted by many ancient and illustrious examples.

For old Jove gave suppers; the god Woden gave suppers; the Hindoo deity Brahma gave suppers; the Red Man's Great Spirit gave suppers:—chiefly venison and game.

And many distinguished mortals besides.

Ahasuerus gave suppers; Xerxes gave suppers; Montezuma gave suppers; Powhattan gave suppers; the Jews' Passovers were suppers; the Pharaohs gave suppers; Julius Cæsar gave suppers:—and rare ones they

603

were; Great Pompey gave suppers; Nabob Crassus gave suppers; and Heliogabalus, surnamed the Gobbler, gave suppers.

It was a common saying of old, that King Pluto gave suppers; some say he is giving them still. If so, he is keeping tip-top company, old Pluto:— Emperors and Czars; Great Moguls and Great Khans; Grand Lamas and Grand Dukes; Prince Regents and Queen Dowagers:—Tamerlane hob-a-nobbing with Bonaparte; Antiochus with Solyman the Magnificent; Pisistratus pledging Pilate; Semiramis eating bon-bons with Bloody Mary, and her namesake of Medicis; the Thirty Tyrants quaffing three to one with the Council of Ten; and Sultans, Satraps, Viziers, Hetmans, Soldans, Landgraves, Bashaws, Doges, Dauphins, Infantas, Incas, and Caçiques looking on.

Again: at Arbela, the conqueror of conquerors, conquering son of Olympia by Jupiter himself, sent out cards to his captains,—Hephestion, Antigonus, Antipater, and the rest—to join him at ten, P.M., in the Temple of Belus; there, to sit down to a victorious supper, off the gold plate of the Assyrian High Priests. How majestically he poured out his old Madeira that night!—feeling grand and lofty as the Himmalehs; yea, all Babylon nodded her towers in his soul!

Spread, heaped up, stacked with good things; and redolent of citrons and grapes, hilling round tall vases of wine; and here and there, waving with fresh orange-boughs, among whose leaves, myriads of small tapers gleamed like fire-flies in groves,—Abrazza's glorious board showed like some banquet in Paradise: Ceres and Pomona presiding; and jolly Bacchus, like a recruit with a mettlesome rifle, staggering back as he fires off the bottles of vivacious champagne.

In ranges, roundabout stood living candelabras:—lackeys, gayly bedecked, with tall torches in their hands; and at one end, stood trumpeters, bugles at their lips.

"This way, my dear Media!—this seat at my left.—Noble Taji!—my right. Babbalanja!—Mohi—where you are. But where's pretty Yoomy?— Gone to meditate in the moonlight? ah!—Very good. Let the banquet begin. A blast there!"

And charge all did.

The venison, wild boar's meat, and buffalo-humps, were extraordinary; the wine, of rare vintages, like bottled lightning; and the first course, a brilliant affair, went off like a rocket.

But as yet, Babbalanja joined not in the revels. His mood was on him; and apart he sat; silently eyeing the banquet; and ever and anon muttering, —"Fogle-foggle, fugle-fi—"

The first fury of the feast over, said King Media, pouring out from a heavy flagon into his goblet, "Abrazza, these suppers are wondrous fine things."

"Ay, my dear lord, much better than dinners."

"So they are, so they are. The dinner-hour is the summer of the day: full of sunshine, I grant; but not like the mellow autumn of supper. A dinner, you know, may go off rather stiffly; but invariably suppers are jovial. At dinners, 'tis not till you take in sail, furl the cloth, bow the lady-passengers out, and make all snug; 'tis not till then, that one begins to ride out the gale with complacency. But at these suppers—Good Oro! your cup is empty, my dear demi-god!—But at these suppers, I say, all is snug and ship-shape before you begin; and when you begin, you waive the beginning, and begin in the middle. And as for the cloth,—but tell us, Braid-Beard, what that old king of Franko, Ludwig the Fat, said of that matter. The cloth for suppers, you know. It's down in your chronicles."

"My lord,"—wiping his beard,—"Old Ludwig was of opinion, that at suppers the cloth was superfluous, unless on the back of some jolly good friar. Said he, 'For one, I prefer sitting right down to the unrobed table.'"

"High and royal authority, that of Ludwig the Fat," said Babbalanja, "far higher than the authority of Ludwig the Great:—the one, only great by courtesy; the other, fat beyond a peradventure. But they are equally famous; and in their graves, both on a par. For after devouring many a fair province, and grinding the poor of his realm, Ludwig the Great has long since, himself, been devoured by very small worms, and ground into very fine dust. And after stripping many a venison rib, Ludwig the Fat has had his own polished and bleached in the Valley of Death; yea, and his cranium chased with corrodings, like the carved flagon once held to its jaws."

"My lord! my lord!"—cried Abrazza to Media—"this ghastly devil of yours grins worse than a skull. I feel the worms crawling over me!—By Oro we must eject him!"

"No, no, my lord. Let him sit there, as of old the Death's-head graced the feasts of the Pharaohs—let him sit—let him sit—for Death but imparts a flavor to Life—Go on: wag your tongue without fear, Azzageddi!—But come, Braid-Beard! let's hear more of the Ludwigs."

"Well, then, your Highness, of all the eighteen royal Ludwigs of Franko—"

"Who like so many ten-pins, all in a row," interposed Babbalanja—"have been bowled off the course by grim Death."

"Heed him not," said Media—"go on."

"The Debonnaire, the Pious, the Stammerer, the Do-Nothing, the Juvenile, the Quarreler:—of all these, I say, Ludwig the Fat was the best table-man of them all. Such a full orbed paunch was his, that no way could he devise of getting to his suppers, but by getting right into them. Like the Zodiac his table was circular, and full in the middle he sat, like a sun;—all his jolly stews and ragouts revolving around him."

"Yea," said Babbalanja, "a very round sun was Ludwig the Fat. No wonder he's down in the chronicles; several ells about the waist, and King of cups and Tokay. Truly, a famous king: three hundred-weight of lard, with a diadem on top: lean brains and a fat doublet—a demi-john of a demi-god!"

"Is this to be longer borne?" cried Abrazza, starting up. "Quaff that sneer down, devil! on the instant! down with it, to the dregs! This comes, my lord Media, of having a slow drinker at one's board. Like an iceberg, such a fellow frosts the whole atmosphere of a banquet, and is felt a league off. We must thrust him out. Guards!"

"Back! touch him not, hounds!"—cried Media. "Your pardon, my lord, but we'll keep him to it; and melt him down in this good wine. Drink! I command it, drink, Babbalanja!"

"And am I not drinking, my lord? Surely you would not that I should imbibe more than I can hold. The measure being full, all poured in after that is but wasted. I am for being temperate in these things, my good lord. And my one cup outlasts three of yours. Better to sip a pint, than pour down a quart. All things in moderation are good; whence, wine in moderation is good. But all things in excess are bad: whence wine in excess is bad."

"Away with your logic and conic sections! Drink!—But no, no: I am too severe. For of all meals a supper should be the most social and free. And going thereto we kings, my lord, should lay aside our scepters.—Do as you please, Babbalanja."

"You are right, you are right, after all, my dear demi-god," said Abrazza. "And to say truth, I seldom worry myself with the ways of these mortals; for no thanks do we demi-gods get. We kings should be ever indifferent. Nothing like a cold heart; warm ones are ever chafing, and getting into trouble. I let my mortals here in this isle take heed to themselves; only barring them out when they would thrust in their petitions. This very instant, my lord, my yeoman-guard is on duty without, to drive off intruders. —Hark!—what noise is that?—Ho, who comes?"

At that instant, there burst into the hall, a crowd of spearmen, driven before a pale, ragged rout, that loudly invoked King Abrazza.

"Pardon, my lord king, for thus forcing an entrance! But long in vain have we knocked at thy gates! Our grievances are more than we can bear! Give ear to our spokesman, we beseech!"

And from their tumultuous midst, they pushed forward a tall, grim, pine-tree of a fellow, who loomed up out of the throng, like the Peak of Teneriffe among the Canaries in a storm.

"Drive the knaves out! Ho, cowards, guards, turn about! charge upon them! Away with your grievances! Drive them out, I say, drive them out! —High times, truly, my lord Media, when demi-gods are thus annoyed at their wine. Oh, who would reign over mortals!"

So at last, with much difficulty, the ragged rout were ejected; the Peak of Teneriffe going last, a pent storm on his brow; and muttering about some black time that was coming.

While the hoarse murmurs without still echoed through the hall, King Abrazza refilling his cup thus spoke:—"You were saying, my dear lord, that of all meals a supper is the most social and free. Very true. And of all suppers those given by us bachelor demi-gods are the best. Are they not?"

"They are. For Benedict mortals must be home betimes: bachelor demi-gods are never away."

"Ay, your Highnesses, bachelors are all the year round at home;" said Mohi: "sitting out life in the chimney corner, cozy and warm as the dog, whilome turning the old-fashioned roasting-jack."

"And to us bachelor demi-gods," cried Media, "our to-morrows are as long rows of fine punches, ranged on a board, and waiting the hand."

"But my good lords," said Babbalanja, now brightening with wine; "if, of all suppers those given by bachelors be the best:—of all bachelors, are not your priests and monks the jolliest? I mean, behind the scenes? Their prayers all said, and their futurities securely invested,—who so care-free and cozy as they? Yea, a supper for two in a friar's cell in Maramma, is merrier far, than a dinner for five-and-twenty, in the broad right wing of Donjalolo's great Palace of the Morn."

"Bravo, Babbalanja!" cried Media, "your iceberg is thawing. More of that, more of that. Did I not say, we would melt him down at last, my lord?"

"Ay," continued Babbalanja, "bachelors are a noble fraternity: I'm a bachelor myself. One of ye, in that matter, my lord demi-gods. And if un-like the patriarchs of the world, we father not our brigades and battalions;

and send not out into the battles of our country whole regiments of our own individual raising;—yet do we oftentimes leave behind us goodly houses and lands; rare old brandies and mountain Malagas; and more especially, warm doublets and togas, and spatterdashes, wherewithal to keep comfortable those who survive us;—casing the legs and arms, which others beget. Then compare not invidiously Benedicts with bachelors, since thus we make an equal division of the duties, which both owe to posterity."

"Suppers forever!" cried Media. "See, my lord, what yours has done for Babbalanja. He came to it a skeleton; but will go away, every bone padded!"

"Ay, my lord demi-gods," said Babbalanja, drop by drop refilling his goblet. "These suppers are all very fine, very pleasant, and merry. But we pay for them roundly. Every thing, my good lords, has its price, from a marble to a world. And easier of digestion, and better for both body and soul, are a half-haunch of venison and a gallon of mead, taken under the sun at meridian, than the soft bridal breast of a partridge, with some gentle negus, at the noon of night!"

"No lie that!" said Mohi. "Beshrew me, in no well-appointed mansion doth the pantry lie adjoining the sleeping-chamber. A good thought: I'll fill up, and ponder on it."

"Let not Azzageddi get uppermost again, Babbalanja," cried Media. "Your goblet is only half-full."

"Permit it to remain so, my lord. For whoso takes much wine to bed with him, has a bedfellow, more restless than a somnambulist. And though Wine be a jolly blade at the board, a sulky knave is he under a blanket. I know him of old. Yet, your Highness, for all this, to many a Mardian, suppers are still better than dinners, at whatever cost purchased. Forasmuch, as many have more leisure to sup, than dine. And though you demi-gods, may dine at your ease; and dine it out into night: and sit and chirp over your Burgundy, till the morning larks join your crickets, and wed matins to vespers;—far otherwise, with us plebeian mortals. From our dinners, we must hie to our anvils: and the last jolly jorum evaporates in a cark and a care."

"Methinks he relapses," said Abrazza.

"It waxes late," said Mohi; "your Highnesses, is it not time to break up?"

"No, no!" cried Abrazza; "let the day break when it will: but no breakings for us. It's only midnight. This way with the wine; pass it along, my dear Media. We are young yet, my sweet lord; light hearts and heavy purses; short prayers and long rent-rolls. Pass round the Tokay! We demi-gods have all our old age for a dormitory. Come!—Round and round with the flagons! Let them disappear like mile-stones on a race-course!"

"Ah!" murmured Babbalanja, holding his full goblet at arm's length on the board, "not thus with the hapless wight, born with a hamper on his back, and blisters in his palms.—Toil and sleep—sleep and toil, are his days and his nights; he goes to bed with a lumbago, and wakes with the rheu-matics;—I know what it is;—he snatches lunches, not dinners, and makes of all life a cold snack! Yet praise be to Oro, though to such men dinners are scarce worth the eating; nevertheless, praise Oro again, a good supper is something. Off jack-boots; nay, off shirt, if you will, and go at it. Hurrah! the fagged day is done: the last blow is an echo. Twelve long hours to sun-rise! And would it were an Antarctic night, and six months to to-morrow! But, hurrah! the very bees have their hive, and after a day's weary wander-ing, hie home to their honey. So they stretch out their stiff legs, rub their lame elbows, and putting their tired right arms in a sling, set the others to fetching and carrying from dishes to dentals, from foaming flagon to the demijohn which never pours out at the end you pour in. Ah! after all, the poorest devil in Mardi lives not in vain. There's a soft side to the hardest oak-plank in the world!"

"Methinks I have heard some such sentimental gabble as this before from my slaves, my lord," said Abrazza to Media. "It has the old gibberish flavor."

"Gibberish, your Highness? Gibberish? I'm full of it—I'm a gibbering ghost, my right worshipful lord! Here, pass your hand through me—here, *here*, and scorch it where I most burn. By Oro! King! but I will gibe and gibber at thee, till thy crown feels like another skull clapped on thy own. Gibberish? ay, in hell we'll gibber in concert, king! we'll howl, and roast, and hiss together!"

"Devil that thou art, begone! Ho, guards! seize him!"

"Back, curs!" cried Media. "Harm not a hair of his head. I crave pardon, King Abrazza, but no violence must be done Babbalanja."

"Trumpets there!" said Abrazza; "so: the banquet is done—lights for King Media! Good-night, my lord!"

Now, thus, for the nonce, with good cheer, we close. And after many fine dinners and banquets—through light and through shade; through mirth, sorrow, and all—drawing nigh to the evening end of these wander-ings wild—meet is it that all should be regaled with a supper.

Chapter 182

They embark

NEXT MORNING, King Abrazza sent frigid word to Media that the day was very fine for yachting; but he much regretted that indisposition would prevent his making one of the party, who that morning doubtless would depart his isle.

"My compliments to your king," said Media to the chamberlains, "and say the royal notice to quit was duly received."

"Take Azzageddi's also," said Babbalanja; "and say, I hope his Highness will not fail in his appointment with me:—the first midnight after he dies; at the grave-yard corner;—there I'll be, and grin again!"

Sailing on, the next land we saw was thickly wooded: hedged round about by mangrove trees; which growing in the water, yet lifted high their boughs. Here and there were shady nooks, half verdure and half water. Fishes rippled, and canaries sung.

"Let us break through, my lord," said Yoomy, "and seek the shore. Its solitudes must prove reviving."

"Solitudes they are," cried Mohi.

"Peopled but not enlivened," said Babbalanja. "Hard landing here, minstrel! see you not the isle is hedged?"

"Why break through, then," said Media. "Yillah is not here."

"I mistrusted it," sighed Yoomy; "an imprisoned island! full of uncomplaining woes: like many others we must have glided by, unheedingly.

Yet of them have I heard. This isle many pass, marking its outward brightness, but dreaming not of the sad secrets here embowered. Haunt of the
hopeless! In those inland woods brood Mardians who have tasted Mardi,
and found it bitter—the draught so sweet to others!—maidens whose un-
imparted bloom has cankered in the bud; and children, with eyes averted
from life's dawn—like those new-oped morning blossoms which, foreseeing storms, turn and close."

"Yoomy's rendering of the truth," said Mohi.

"Why land, then?" said Media. "No merry man of sense—no demi-
god like me, will do it. Let's away; let's see all that's pleasant, or that seems
so, in our circuit, and, if possible, shun the sad."

"Then we have circled not the round reef wholly," said Babbalanja,
"but made of it a segment. For this is far from being the first sad land, my
lord, that we have slighted at your instance."

"No more. I will have no gloom. A chorus! there, ye paddlers! spread
all your sails; ply paddles; breeze up, merry winds!"

And so, in the saffron sunset, we neared another shore.

A gloomy-looking land! black, beetling crags, rent by volcanic clefts;
ploughed up with water-courses, and dusky with charred woods. The
beach was strewn with scoria and cinders; in dolorous soughs, a chill wind
blew; wails issued from the caves; and yellow, spooming surges, lashed
the moaning strand.

"Shall we land?" said Babbalanja.

"Not here," cried Yoomy; "no Yillah here."

"No," said Media. "This is another of those lands far better to avoid."

"Know ye not," said Mohi, "that here are the mines of King Klanko,
whose scourged slaves, toiling in their pits, so nigh approach the volcano's
bowels, they hear its rumblings? 'Yet they must work on,' cries Klanko,
'the mines still yield!' And daily his slaves' bones are brought above
ground, mixed with the metal masses."

"Set all sail there, men! away!"

"My lord," said Babbalanja; "still must we shun the unmitigated evil;
and only view the good; or evil so mixed therewith, the mixture's both?"

Half vailed in misty clouds, the harvest-moon now rose; and in that
pale and haggard light, all sat silent; each man in his own secret mood:
best knowing his own thoughts.

Chapter 183

Babbalanja at the Full of the Moon

HO, MORTALS! Go we to a funeral, that our paddles seem thus muffled? Up heart, Taji! or does that witch Hautia haunt thee? Be a demi-god once more, and laugh. Her flowers are not barbs; and the avengers' arrows are too blunt to slay. Babbalanja! Mohi! Yoomy! up heart! up heart!—By Oro! I will debark the whole company on the next land we meet. No tears for me. Ha, ha! let us laugh. Ho, Vee-Vee! awake; quick, boy,—some wine! and let us make glad, beneath the glad moon. Look! it is stealing forth from its clouds. Perdition to Hautia! Long lives, and merry ones to ourselves! Taji, my charming fellow, here's to you:—May your heart be a stone! Ha, ha!—will nobody join me? My laugh is lonely as his who laughed in his tomb. Come, laugh; will no one quaff wine, I say? See! the round moon is abroad."

"Say you so, my lord? then for one, I am with you;" cried Babbalanja. "Fill me a brimmer. Ah! but this wine leaps through me like a panther. Ay, let us laugh: let us roar: let us yell! What, if I was sad but just now? Life is an April day, that both laughs and weeps in a breath. But whoso is wise, laughs when he can. Men fly from a groan, but run to a laugh. Vee-Vee! your gourd. My lord, let me help you. Ah, how it sparkles! Cups, cups, Vee-Vee, more cups! Here, Taji, take that: Mohi, take that: Yoomy, take that. And now let us drown away grief. Ha! ha! the house of mourning, is deserted, though of old good cheer kept the funeral guests; and so keep I mine; here I sit by my dead, and replenish your wine cups. Old Mohi, your cup: Yoomy, yours: ha! ha! let us laugh, let us scream! Weeds are put off at a fair; no heart bursts but in secret; it is good to laugh, though the laugh be hollow; and wise to make merry, now and for aye. Laugh, and make friends: weep, and they go. Women sob, and are rid of their grief: men laugh, and retain it. There is laughter in heaven, and laughter in hell. And a deep thought whose language is laughter. Though wisdom be wedded to woe, though the way thereto is by tears, yet all ends in a shout. But wisdom wears no weeds; woe is more merry than mirth; 'tis a shallow grief that is sad. Ha! ha! how demoniacs shout; how all skeletons grin; we all die with a rattle. Laugh! laugh! Are the cherubim grave? Humor, thy laugh is divine; whence, mirth-making idiots have been revered; and therefore may I. Ho! let us be gay, if it be only for an hour, and Death hand us the goblet. Vee-Vee! bring on your gourds! Let us pledge each other in bumpers!— let us laugh, laugh, laugh it out to the last. All sages have laughed,—let us; Bardianna laughed,—let us; Demorkriti laughed,—let us; Amoree laughed, —let us; Rabeelee roared,—let us; the hyenas grin, the jackals yell,—let us. —But you don't laugh, my lord? laugh away!"

"No, thank you, Azzageddi, not after that infernal fashion; better weep."

"He makes me crawl all over, as if I were an ant-hill," said Mohi.

"He's mad, mad, mad!" cried Yoomy.

"Ay, mad, mad, mad!—mad as the mad fiend that rides me!—But come, sweet minstrel, wilt list to a song?—We madmen are all poets, you know:—Ha! ha!—

> Stars laugh in the sky:
> Oh fugle-fi!
> The waves dimple below:
> Oh fugle-fo!

The wind strikes her dulcimers; the groves give a shout; the hurricane is only an hysterical laugh; and the lightning that blasts, blasts only in play. We must laugh or we die; to laugh is to live. Not to laugh is to have the tetanus. Will you weep? then laugh while you weep. For mirth and sorrow are kin; are published by identical nerves. Go, Yoomy: go study anatomy: there is much to be learned from the dead, more than you may learn from the living, and I am dead though I live; and as soon dissect myself as another; I curiously look into my secrets: and grope under my ribs. I have found that the heart is not whole, but divided; that it seeks a soft cushion whereon to repose; that it vitalizes the blood; which else were weaker than water: I have found that we can not live without hearts; though the heartless live longest. Yet hug your hearts, ye handful that have them; 'tis a blessed inheritance! Thus, thus, my lord, I run on; from one pole to the other; from this thing to that. But so the great world goes round, and in one somerset, shows the sun twenty-five thousand miles of a landscape!"

At that instant, down went the fiery full-moon, and the Dog-Star; and far down into Media, a Tivoli of wine.

Chapter 184

Morning

LIFE OR DEATH, weal or woe, the sun stays not his course. On: over battle-field and bower; over tower, and town, he speeds;—peers in at births, and death-beds; lights up cathedral, mosque, and pagan shrine;—laughing over all;—a very Democritus in the sky; and in one brief day sees more than any pilgrim in a century's round.

So, the sun; nearer heaven than we:—with what mind, then, may blessed Oro downward look.

It was a purple, red, and yellow East;—streaked, and crossed. And down from breezy mountains, robust and ruddy Morning came,—a plaided Highlander, waving his plumed bonnet to the isles.

Over the neighboring groves the larks soared high; and soaring, sang in jubilees; while across our bows, between two isles, a mighty moose swam stately as a seventy-four; and backward tossed his antlered wilderness in air.

Just bounding from fresh morning groves, with the brine he mixed the dew of leaves,—his antlers dripping on the swell, that rippled before his brown and bow-like chest.

"Five hundred thousand centuries since," said Babbalanja, "this same sight was seen. With Oro, the sun is co-eternal; and the same life that moves that moose, animates alike the sun and Oro. All are parts of One. In me, in *me*, flit thoughts participated by the beings peopling all the stars.

Saturn, and Mercury, and Mardi, are brothers, one and all; and across their orbits, to each other talk, like souls. Of these things what chapters might be writ! Oh! that flesh can not keep pace with spirit. Oh! that these myriad germ-dramas in me, should so perish hourly, for lack of power mechanic. —Worlds pass worlds in space, as men, men,—in thoroughfares; and after periods of thousand years, cry:—"Well met, my friend, again!"—To me, to *me*, they talk in mystic music; I hear them think through all their zones. —Hail, furthest worlds! and all the beauteous beings in ye! Fan me, sweet Zenora! with thy twilight wings!—Ho! let's voyage to Aldebaran.—Ha! indeed, a ruddy world! What a buoyant air! Not like to Mardi, this. Ruby columns: minarets of amethyst: diamond domes! Who is this?—a god? What a lake-like brow! transparent as the morning air. I see his thoughts like worlds revolving—and in his eyes—like unto heavens—soft falling stars are shooting.—How these thousand passing wings winnow away my breath:—I faint:—back, back to some small asteroid.—Sweet being! if, by Mardian word I may address thee—speak!—'I bear a soul in germ within me; I feel the first, faint trembling, like to a harp-string, vibrate in my inmost being. Kill me, and generations die.'—So, of old, the unbegotten lived within the virgin; who then loved her God, as new-made mothers their babes ere born. Oh, Alma, Alma, Alma!—Fangs off, fiend!—will that name ever lash thee into foam?—Smite not my face so, forked flames!"

"Babbalanja! Babbalanja! rouse, man! rouse! Art in hell and damned, that thy sinews so snake-like coil and twist all over thee? Thy brow is black as Ops! Turn, turn! see yonder moose!"

"Hail! mighty brute!—thou feelest not these things: never canst *thou* be damned. Moose! would thy soul were mine; for if that scorched thing, mine, be immortal—so thine; and thy life hath not the consciousness of death. I read profound placidity—deep—million—violet fathoms down, in that soft, pathetic, woman eye! What is man's shrunk form to thine, thou woodland majesty?—Moose, moose!—my soul is shot again—Oh, Oro! Oro!"

"He falls!" cried Media.

"Mark the agony in his waning eye," said Yoomy;—"alas, poor Babbalanja! Is this thing of madness conscious to thyself? If ever thou art sane again, wilt thou have reminiscences? Take my robe:—here, I strip me to cover thee and all thy woes. Oro! by this, thy being's side, I kneel:—grant death or happiness to Babbalanja!"

Chapter 185

L'Ultima sera

THUS FAR, through myriad islands, had we searched: of all, no one pen may write: least, mine;—and still no trace of Yillah.

But though my hopes revived not from their ashes; yet, so much of Mardi had we searched, it seemed as if the long pursuit must, ere many moons, be ended; whether for weal or woe, my frenzy sometimes recked not.

After its first fair morning flushings, all that day was overcast. We sailed upon an angry sea, beneath an angry sky. Deep scowled on deep; and in dun vapors, the blinded sun went down, unseen; though full toward the West our three prows were pointed; steadfast as three printed points upon the compass-card.

"When we set sail from Odo, 'twas a glorious morn in spring," said Yoomy; "toward the rising sun we steered. But now, beneath autumnal night-clouds, we hasten to its setting."

"How now?" cried Media; "why is the minstrel mournful?—He whose place it is to chase away despondency: not be its minister."

"Ah, my lord, so *thou* thinkest. But better can my verses soothe the sad, than make them light of heart. Nor are we minstrels so gay of soul as Mardi deems us. The brook that sings the sweetest, murmurs through the loneliest woods:

617

The isles hold thee not, thou departed!
From thy bower, now issues no lay:—
In vain we recall perished warblings:
Spring birds, to far climes, wing their way!"

As Yoomy thus sang; unmindful of the lay, with paddle plying, in low, pleasant tones, thus hummed to himself our bowsman, a gamesome wight:—

Ho! merrily ho! we paddlers sail!
Ho! over sea-dingle, and dale!—
Our pulses fly,
Our hearts beat high,
Ho! merrily, merrily, ho!

But a sudden splash, and a shrill, gurgling sound, like that of a fountain subsiding, now broke upon the air. Then all was still, save the rush of the waves by our keels.

"Save him! Put back!"

From his elevated seat, the merry bowsman, too gleefully reaching forward, had fallen into the lagoon.

With all haste, our speeding canoes were reversed; but not till we had darted in upon another darkness than that in which the bowsman fell.

As, blindly, we groped back, deep Night dived deeper down in the sea.

"Drop paddles all, and list."

Holding their breath, over the six gunwales all now leaned; but the only moans were the wind's.

Long time we lay thus; then slowly crossed and recrossed our track, almost hopeless; but yet loth to leave him who, with a song in his mouth, died and was buried in a breath.

"Let us away," said Media—"why seek more? He is gone."

"Ay, gone," said Babbalanja, "and whither? But a moment since, he was among us: now, the fixed stars are not more remote than he. So far off, can he live? Oh, Oro! this death thou ordainest, unmans the manliest. Say not nay, my lord. Let us not speak behind Death's back. Hard and horrible is it to die: blindfold to leap from life's verge! But thus, in clouds of dust, and with a trampling as of hoofs, the generations disappear; death driving them all into his treacherous fold, as wild Indians the bison herds. Nay, nay, Death is Life's last despair. Hard and horrible is it to die. Oro himself, in Alma, died not without a groan. Yet why, why live? Life is wearisome to all: the same dull round. Day and night, summer and winter, round about us revolving for aye. One moment lived, is a life. No new stars appear in the sky; no new lights in the soul. Yet, of changes there are many. For though, with rapt sight, in childhood, we behold many strange things beneath the moon, and all Mardi looks a tented fair—how soon every thing fades. All of us, in our very bodies, outlive our own selves. I think of green youth as of a merry playmate departed; and to shake hands, and be pleasant with my old age, seems in prospect even harder, than to draw a cold stranger to my bosom. But old age is not for me. I am not of the stuff that grows old. This Mardi is not our home. Up and down we wander, like exiles transported to a planet afar:—'tis not the world *we* were born in; not the world once so lightsome and gay; not the world where we once merrily danced, dined, and supped; and wooed, and wedded our long-buried wives. Then let us depart. But whither? We push ourselves forward —then, start back in affright. Essay it again, and flee. Hard to live; hard to die; intolerable suspense! But the grim despot at last interposes; and with a viper in our winding-sheets, we are dropped in the sea."

"To me," said Mohi, his gray locks damp with night-dews, "death's dark defile at times seems at hand, with no voice to cheer. That all have died, makes it not easier for me to depart. And that many have been quenched in infancy seems a mercy to the slow perishing of my old age, limb by limb and sense by sense. I have long been the tomb of my youth. And more has died out of me, already, than remains for the last death to finish. Babbalanja says truth. In childhood, death stirred me not; in middle age, it pursued me like a prowling bandit on the road; now, grown an old man, it boldly leads the way; and ushers me on; and turns round upon me its skeleton gaze: poisoning the last solaces of life. Maramma but adds to my gloom."

"Death! death!" cried Yoomy, "must I be not, and millions be? Must I go, and the flowers still bloom? Oh, I have marked what it is to be dead;— how shouting boys, of holidays, hide-and-seek among the tombs, which must hide all seekers at last."

"Clouds on clouds!" cried Media, "but away with them all! Why not leap your graves, while ye may? Time to die, when death comes, without dying by inches. 'Tis no death, to die; the only death is the fear of it. I, a demi-god, fear death not."

"But when the jackals howl round you?" said Babbalanja.

"Drive them off! Die the demi-god's death! On his last couch of crossed spears, my brave old sire cried, 'Wine, wine; strike up, conch and cymbal; let the king die to martial melodies!'"

"More valiant dying, than dead," said Babbalanja. "Our end of the winding procession resounds with music, and flaunts with banners with brave devices:—'Cheer up!' 'Fear not!' 'Millions have died before!'—but in the endless van, not a pennon streams; all there, is silent and solemn. The last wisdom is dumb."

Silence ensued; during which, each dip of the paddles in the now calm water, fell full and long upon the ear.

Anon, lifting his head, Babbalanja thus:—"Yillah still eludes us. And in all this tour of Mardi, how little have we found to fill the heart with peace: how much to slaughter all our yearnings."

"Croak no more, raven!" cried Media. "Mardi is full of spring-time sights, and jubilee sounds. I never was sad in my life."

"But for thy one laugh, my lord, how many groans! Were all happy, or all miserable,—more tolerable then, than as it is. But happiness and misery are so broadly marked, that this Mardi may be the retributive future of some forgotten past.—Yet vain our surmises. Still vainer to say, that all Mardi is but a means to an end; that this life is a state of probation: that evil is but permitted for a term; that for specified ages a rebel angel is viceroy.— Nay, nay. Oro delegates his scepter to none; in his everlasting reign there are no interregnums; and Time is Eternity; and we live in Eternity now. Yet, some tell of a hereafter, where all the mysteries of life will be over; and the sufferings of the virtuous recompensed. Oro is just, they say.— Then always,—now, and evermore. But to make restitution implies a wrong; and Oro can do no wrong. Yet what seems evil to us, may be good to him. If he fears not, nor hopes,—he has no other passion; no ends, no purposes. He lives content; all ends are compassed in Him; He has no past, no future; He is the everlasting now; which is an everlasting calm; and things that are,—have been,—will be. This gloom's enough. But hoot! hoot! the night-owl ranges through the woodlands of Maramma; its dismal notes pervade our lives; and when we would fain depart in peace, that bird flies on before:—cloud-like, eclipsing our setting suns, and filling the air with dolor."

"Too true!" cried Yoomy. "Our calms must come by storms. Like helmless vessels, tempest-tossed, our only anchorage is when we founder."

"Our beginnings," murmured Mohi, "are lost in clouds; we live in darkness all our days, and perish without an end."

"Croak on, cowards!" cried Media, "and fly before the hideous phantoms that pursue ye."

"No coward he, who hunted, turns and finds no foe to fight," said Babbalanja. "Like the stag, whose brow is beat with wings of hawks, perched in his heavenward antlers; so I, blinded, goaded, headlong, rush! this way and that; nor knowing whither; one forest wide around!"

Chapter 186

They sail from Night to Day

ERE LONG the three canoes lurched heavily in a violent swell. Like palls, the clouds swept to and fro, hooding the gibbering winds. At every head-beat wave, our arching prows reared up, and shuddered; the night ran out in rain.

Whither to turn we knew not; nor what haven to gain; so dense the darkness.

But at last, the storm was over. Our shattered prows seemed gilded. Day dawned; and from his golden vases poured red wine upon the waters.

That flushed tide rippled toward us; floating from the east, a lone canoe; in which, there sat a mild old man; a palm-bough in his hand: a bird's beak, holding amaranth and myrtles, his slender prow.

"Alma's blessing upon ye, voyagers! ye look storm-worn."

"The storm we have survived, old man; and many more, we yet must ride," said Babbalanja.

"The sun is risen; and all is well again. We but need to repair our prows," said Media.

"Then, turn aside to Serenia, a pleasant isle, where all are welcome; where many storm-worn rovers land at last to dwell."

"Serenia?" said Babbalanja; "methinks Serenia is that land of enthusiasts, of which we hear, my lord; where Mardians pretend to the unnatural conjunction of reason with things revealed; where Alma, they say, is restored to his divine original; where, deriving their principles from the same sources whence flow the persecutions of Maramma,—men strive to live together in gentle bonds of peace and charity;—folly! folly!"

"Ay," said Media, "much is said of those people of Serenia; but their social fabric must soon fall to pieces; it is based upon the idlest of theories. Thanks for thy courtesy, old man, but we care not to visit thy isle. Our voyage has an object, which, something tells me, will not be gained by touching at thy shores. Elsewhere we may refit. Farewell! 'Tis breezing; set the sails! Farewell, old man."

"Nay, nay! think again; the distance is but small; the wind fair,—but 'tis ever so, thither;—come: we, people of Serenia, are most anxious to be seen of Mardi; so that if our manner of life seem good, all Mardi may live as we. In blessed Alma's name, I pray ye, come!"

"Shall we then, my lord?"

"Lead on, old man! We will e'en see this wondrous isle."

So, guided by the venerable stranger, by noon we descried an island blooming with bright savannas, and pensive with peaceful groves.

Wafted from this shore, came balm of flowers, and melody of birds: a thousand summer sounds and odors. The dimpled tide sang round our splintered prows; the sun was high in heaven, and the waters were deep below.

"The land of Love!" the old man murmured, as we neared the beach, where innumerable shells were gently rolling in the playful surf, and murmuring from their tuneful valves. Behind, another, and a verdant surf played against lofty banks of leaves; where the breeze, likewise, found its shore.

And now, emerging from beneath the trees, there came a goodly multitude in flowing robes; palm-branches in their hands; and as they came, they sang:—

> Hail! voyagers, hail!
> Whence e'er ye come, where'er ye rove,
> No calmer strand,
> No sweeter land,
> Will e'er ye view, than the Land of Love!
>
> Hail! voyagers, hail!
> To these, our shores, soft gales invite:
> The palm plumes wave,
> The billows lave,
> And hither point fix'd stars of light!

Hail! voyagers, hail!
Think not our groves wide brood with gloom;
In this, our isle,
Bright flowers smile:
Full urns, rose-heaped, these valleys bloom.

Hail! voyagers, hail!
Be not deceived; renounce vain things;
Ye may not find
A tranquil mind,
Though hence ye sail with swiftest wings.

Hail! voyagers, hail!
Time flies full fast; life soon is o'er;
And ye may mourn,
That hither borne,
Ye left behind our pleasant shore.

Chapter 187

They land

THE SONG was ended; and as we gained the strand, the crowd embraced us; and called us brothers; ourselves and our humblest attendants.

"Call ye us brothers, whom ere now ye never saw?"

"Even so," said the old man, "is not Oro the father of all? Then, are we not brothers? Thus Alma, the master, hath commanded."

"This was not our reception in Maramma," said Media, "the appointed place of Alma; where his precepts are preserved."

"No, no," said Babbalanja; "old man! your lesson of brotherhood was learned elsewhere than from Alma; for in Maramma and in all its tributary isles true brotherhood there is none. Even in the Holy Island many are oppressed; for heresies, many murdered; and thousands perish beneath the altars, groaning with offerings that might relieve them."

"Alas! too true. But I beseech ye, judge not Alma by all those who profess his faith. Hast thou thyself his records searched?"

"Fully, I have not. So long, even from my infancy, have I witnessed the wrongs committed in his name; the sins and inconsistencies of his followers; that thinking all evil must flow from a congenial fountain, I have scorned to study the whole record of your Master's life. By parts I only know it."

"Ah! baneful error! But thus is it, brothers! that the wisest are set against the Truth, because of those who wrest it from itself."

"Do ye then claim to live what your Master hath spoken? Are your precepts practices?"

"Nothing do we claim: we but earnestly endeavor."

"Tell me not of your endeavors, but of your life. What hope for the fatherless among ye?"

"Adopted as a son."

"Of one poor, and naked?"

"Clothed, and he wants for naught."

"If ungrateful, he smite you?"

"Still we feed and clothe him."

"If yet an ingrate?"

"Long, he can not be; for Love is a fervent fire."

"But what, if widely he dissent from your belief in Alma;—then, surely, ye must cast him forth?"

"No, no; we will remember, that if he dissent from us, we then equally dissent from him; and men's faculties are Oro-given. Nor will we say that he is wrong, and we are right; for this we know not, absolutely. But we care not for men's words; we look for creeds in actions; which are the truthful symbols of the things within. He who hourly prays to Alma, but lives not up to world-wide love and charity—that man is more an unbeliever than he who verbally rejects the Master, but does his bidding. Our lives are our Amens."

"But some say that what your Alma teaches is wholly new—a revelation of things before unimagined, even by the poets. To do his bidding, then, some new faculty must be vouchsafed, whereby to apprehend aright."

"So have I always thought," said Mohi.

"If Alma teaches love, I want no gift to learn," said Yoomy.

"All that is vital in the Master's faith, lived here in Mardi, and in humble dells was practiced, long previous to the Master's coming. But never before was virtue so lifted up among us, that all might see; never before did rays from heaven descend to glorify it. But are Truth, Justice, and Love, the revelations of Alma alone? Were they never heard of till he came? Oh! Alma but opens unto us our own hearts. Were his precepts strange we would recoil—not one feeling would respond; whereas, once hearkened to, our souls embrace them as with the instinctive tendrils of a vine."

"But," said Babbalanja, "since Alma, they say, was solely intent upon the things of the Mardi to come—which to all, must seem uncertain—of what benefit his precepts for the daily lives led here?"

"Would! would that Alma might once more descend! Brother! were the turf our everlasting pillow, still would the Master's faith answer a blessed end;—making us more truly happy *here. That* is the first and chief result; for holy here, we must be holy elsewhere. 'Tis Mardi, to which loved Alma gives his laws; not Paradise."

"Full soon will I be testing all these things," murmured Mohi.

"Old man," said Media, "thy years and Mohi's lead ye both to dwell upon the unknown future. But speak to me of other themes. Tell me of this island and its people. From all I have heard, and now behold, I gather that here, there dwells no king; that ye are left to yourselves; and that this mystic Love, ye speak of, is your ruler. Is it so? Then, are ye full as visionary, as Mardi rumors. And though for a time, ye may have prospered,—long, ye can not be, without some sharp lesson to convince ye, that your faith in Mardian virtue is entirely vain."

"Truth. We have no king; for Alma's precepts rebuke the arrogance of place and power. He is the tribune of mankind; nor will his true faith be universal Mardi's, till our whole race is kingless. But think not we believe in man's perfection. Yet, against all good, he is not absolutely set. In his heart, there is a germ. *That* we seek to foster. To *that* we cling; else, all were hopeless!"

"Your social state?"

"It is imperfect; and long must so remain. But we make not the miserable many support the happy few. Nor by annulling reason's laws, seek to breed equality, by breeding anarchy. In all things, equality is not for all. Each has his own. Some have wider groves of palms than others; fare better; dwell in more tasteful arbors; oftener renew their fragrant thatch. Such differences must be. But none starve outright, while others feast. By the abounding, the needy are supplied. Yet not by statute, but from dictates, born half dormant in us, and warmed into life by Alma. Those dictates we but follow in all we do; we are not dragged to righteousness; but go running. Nor do we live in common. For vice and virtue blindly mingled, form a union where vice too often proves the alkali. The vicious we make dwell apart, until reclaimed. And reclaimed they soon must be, since every thing invites. The sin of others rests not upon our heads: none we drive to crime. Our laws are not of vengeance bred, but Love and Alma."

"Fine poetry all this," said Babbalanja, "but not so new. Oft do they warble thus in bland Maramma!"

"It sounds famously, old man!" said Media, "but men are men. Some must starve; some be scourged.—Your doctrines are impracticable."

"And are not these things enjoined by Alma? And would Alma inculcate the impossible? of what merit, his precepts, unless they may be practiced? But, I beseech ye, speak no more of Maramma. Alas! did Alma revisit Mardi, think you, it would be among those Morais he would lay his head?"

"No, no," said Babbalanja, "as an intruder he came; and an intruder would he be this day. On all sides, would he jar our social systems."

"Not here, not here! Rather would we welcome Alma hungry and athirst, than though he came floating hither on the wings of seraphs; the blazing zodiac his diadem! In all his aspects we adore him; needing no pomp and power to kindle worship. Though he came from Oro; though he did miracles; though through him is life;—not for these things alone, do we thus love him. We love him from an instinct in us;—a fond, filial, reverential feeling. And this would yet stir in our souls, were death our end; and Alma incapable of befriending us. We love him because we do."

"Is this man divine?" murmured Babbalanja. "But thou speakest most earnestly of adoring Alma:—I see no temples in your groves."

"Because this isle is all one temple to his praise; every leaf is consecrated his. We fix not Alma here and there; and say,—'those groves for Him, and these broad fields for us.' It is all his own; and we ourselves; our every hour of life; and all we are, and have."

"Then, ye forever fast and pray; and stand and sing; as at long intervals the censer-bearers in Maramma supplicate their gods."

"Alma forbid! We never fast; our aspirations are our prayers; our lives are worship. And when we laugh, with human joy at human things,— *then* do we most sound great Oro's praise, and prove the merit of sweet Alma's love! Our love in Alma makes us glad, not sad. Ye speak of temples; —behold! 'tis by not building *them*, that we widen charity among us. The treasures which, in the islands round about, are lavished on a thousand fanes;—with these we every day relieve the Master's suffering disciples. In Mardi, Alma preached in open fields,—and must his worshipers have palaces?"

"No temples, then no priests;" said Babbalanja, "for few priests will enter where lordly arches form not the portal."

"We have no priests, but one; and he is Alma's self. We have his precepts: we seek no comments but our hearts."

"But without priests and temples, how long will flourish this your faith?" said Media.

"For many ages has not this faith lived, in spite of priests and temples? and shall it not survive them? What we believe, we hold divine; and things divine endure forever."

"But how enlarge your bounds? how convert the vicious, without persuasion of some special seers? Must your religion go hand in hand with all things secular?"

"We hold not, that one man's words should be a gospel to the rest; but that Alma's words should be a gospel to us all. And not by precepts would we have some few endeavor to persuade; but all, by practice, fix convictions, that the life we lead is the life for all. We are apostles, every one. Where'er we go, our faith we carry in our hands, and hearts. It is our chiefest joy. We do not put it wide away six days out of seven; and then, assume it. In it we all exult, and joy; as that which makes us happy here; as that, without which, we could be happy nowhere; as something meant for this time present, and henceforth for aye. It is our vital mode of being; not an incident. And when we die, this faith shall be our pillow; and when we rise, our staff; and at the end, our crown. For we are all immortal. Here, Alma joins with our own hearts, confirming nature's promptings."

"How eloquent he is!" murmured Babbalanja. "Some black cloud seems floating from me. I begin to see. I come out in light. The sharp fang tears me less. The forked flames wane. My soul sets back like ocean streams, that sudden change their flow. Have I been sane? Quickened in me is a hope. But pray you, old man—say on—methinks, that in your faith must be much that jars with reason."

"No, brother! Right-reason, and Alma, are the same; else Alma, not reason, would we reject. The Master's great command is Love; and here do all things wise, and all things good, unite. Love is all in all. The more we love, the more we know; and so reversed. Oro we love; this isle; and our wide arms embrace all Mardi like its reef. How can we err, thus feeling? We hear loved Alma's pleading, prompting voice, in every breeze, in every leaf; we see his earnest eye in every star and flower."

"Poetry!" cried Yoomy, "and poetry is truth! He stirs me."

"When Alma dwelt in Mardi, 'twas with the poor and friendless. He fed the famishing; he healed the sick; he bound up wounds. For every precept that he spoke, he did ten thousand mercies. And Alma is our loved example."

"Sure, all this is in the histories!" said Mohi, starting.

"But not alone to poor and friendless, did Alma wend his charitable way. From lowly places, he looked up; and long invoked great chieftains in their state; and told them all their pride was vanity; and bade them ask their souls. 'In *me*,' he cried, 'is that heart of mild content, which in vain ye seek in rank and title. I am Love: love ye then me.'"

"Cease, cease, old man!" cried Media; "thou movest me beyond my seeming. What thoughts are these? Have done! Wouldst thou unking me?"

"Alma is for all; for high and low. Like heaven's own breeze, he lifts the lily from its lowly stem, and sweeps, reviving, through the palmy groves. High thoughts he gives the sage, and humble trust the simple. Be the measure what it may, his grace doth fill it to the brim. He lays the lashings of the soul's wild aspirations after things unseen; oil he poureth on the waters; and stars come out of night's black concave at his great command. In him is hope for all; for all, unbounded joys. Fast locked in his loved clasp, no doubts dismay. He opes the eye of faith, and shuts the eye of fear. He is all we pray for, and beyond; all, that in the wildest hour of ecstasy, rapt fancy paints in bright Auroras upon the soul's wide, boundless Orient!"

"Oh, Alma, Alma! prince divine!" cried Babbalanja, sinking on his knees—"in *thee*, at last, I find repose. Hope perches in my heart a dove;—a thousand rays illume;—all Heaven's a sun. Gone, gone! are all distracting doubts. Love and Alma now prevail. I see with other eyes:—Are these my hands? What wild, wild dreams were mine;—I have been mad. Some things there are, we must not think of. Beyond one obvious mark, all human lore is vain. Where have I lived till now? Had dark Maramma's zealot tribe but murmured to me as this old man, long since had I been wise! Reason no longer domineers; but still doth speak. All I have said ere this, that wars with Alma's precepts, I here recant. Here I kneel, and own great Oro and his sovereign son."

"And here another kneels and prays," cried Yoomy. "In Alma all my dreams are found, my inner longings for the Love supreme, that prompts my every verse. Summer is in my soul."

"Nor now, too late for these gray hairs," cried Mohi, with devotion. "Alma, thy breath is on my soul. I see bright light."

"No more a demigod," cried Media, "but a subject to our common chief. No more shall dismal cries be heard from Odo's groves. Alma, I am thine."

With swimming eyes the old man kneeled; and round him grouped king, sage, gray hairs, and youth.

There, as they kneeled, and as the old man blessed them, the setting sun burst forth from mists, gilded the island round about, shed rays upon their heads, and went down in a glory—all the East radiant with red burnings, like an altar-fire.

Chapter 188

Babbalanja relates to them a Vision

LEAVING BABBALANJA in the old man's bower, deep in meditation; thoughtfully we strolled along the beach, inspiring the
musky, midnight air; the tropical stars glistening in heaven, like
drops of dew among violets.

The waves were phosphorescent, and laved the beach with a fire that
cooled it.

Returning, we espied Babbalanja advancing in his snow-white mantle.
The fiery tide was ebbing; and in the soft, moist sand, at every step, he left
a lustrous foot-print.

"Sweet friends! this isle is full of mysteries," he said. "I have dreamed
of wondrous things. After I had laid me down, thought pressed hard upon
me. By my eyes passed pageant visions. I started at a low, strange melody,
deep in my inmost soul. At last, methought my eyes were fixed on heaven;
and there, I saw a shining spot, unlike a star. Thwarting the sky, it grew,
and grew, descending; till bright wings were visible: between them, a
pensive face angelic, downward beaming; and, for one golden moment,
gauze-vailed in spangled Berenice's Locks.

"Then, as white flame from yellow, out from that starry cluster it
emerged; and brushed the astral Crosses, Crowns, and Cups. And as in
violet, tropic seas, ships leave a radiant-white, and fire-fly wake; so, in

632

long extension tapering, behind the vision, gleamed another Milky-Way.

"Strange throbbings seized me; my soul tossed on its own tides. But soon the inward harmony bounded in exulting choral strains. I heard a feathery rush; and straight beheld a form, traced all over with veins of vivid light. The vision undulated round me.

"'Oh! Spirit! angel! god! whate'er thou art,'—I cried, 'leave me; I am but man.'

"Then, I heard a low, sad sound,—no voice. It said, or breathed upon me,—'Thou hast proved the grace of Alma: tell me what thou'st learned.'

"Silent replied my soul, for voice was gone,—'This have I learned, oh! spirit!—In things mysterious, to seek no more; but rest content, with knowing naught but Love.'

"'Blessed art thou for that: thrice blessed,' then I heard, 'and since humility is thine, thou art one apt to learn. That which thy own wisdom could not find, thy ignorance confessed shall gain. Come, and see new things.'

"Once more it undulated round me; its lightning wings grew dim; nearer, nearer; till I felt a shock electric,—and nested 'neath its wing.

"We clove the air; passed systems, suns, and moons: what seem from Mardi's isles, the glow-worm stars.

"By distant fleets of worlds we sped, as voyagers pass far sails at sea, and hail them not. Foam played before them as they darted on; wild music was their wake; and many tracks of sound we crossed, where worlds had sailed before.

"Soon, we gained a point, where a new heaven was seen; whence all our firmament seemed one nebula. Its glories burned like thousand steadfast-flaming lights.

"Here hived the worlds in swarms: and gave forth sweets ineffable.

"We lighted on a ring, circling a space, where mornings seemed forever dawning over worlds unlike.

"'Here,' I heard, 'thou viewest thy Mardi's Heaven. Herein each world is portioned.'

"As he who climbs to mountain tops pants hard for breath; so panted I for Mardi's grosser air. But that which caused my flesh to faint, was new vitality to my soul. My eyes swept over all before me. The spheres were plain as villages that dot a landscape. I saw most beauteous forms, yet like our own. Strange sounds I heard of gladness that seemed mixed with sadness:—a low, sweet harmony of both. Else, I know not how to phrase what never man but me e'er heard.

" 'In these blest souls are blent,' my guide discoursed, 'far higher thoughts, and sweeter plaints than thine. Rude joy were discord here. And as a sudden shout in thy hushed mountain-passes brings down the awful avalanche; so one note of laughter here, might start some white and silent world.'

"Then low I murmured:—'Is theirs, oh guide! no happiness supreme? their state still mixed? Sigh these yet to know? Can these sin?'

"Then I heard:—'No mind but Oro's can know all; no mind that knows not all can be content; content alone approximates to happiness. Holiness comes by wisdom; and it is because great Oro is supremely wise, that He's supremely holy. But as perfect wisdom can be only Oro's; so, perfect holiness is his alone. And whoso is otherwise than perfect in his holiness, is liable to sin.

" 'And though death gave these beings knowledge, it also opened other mysteries, which they pant to know, and yet may learn. And still they fear the thing of evil; though for them, 'tis hard to fall. Thus hoping and thus fearing, then, theirs is no state complete. And since Oro is past finding out, and mysteries ever open into mysteries beyond; so, though these beings will for aye progress in wisdom and in good; yet, will they never gain a fixed beatitude. Know, then, oh mortal Mardian! that when translated hither, thou wilt but put off lowly temporal pinings, for angel and eternal aspirations. Start not: thy human joy hath here no place: no name.'

"Still, I mournful mused; then said:—'Many Mardians live, who have no aptitude for Mardian lives of thought: how then endure more earnest, everlasting, meditations?'

" 'Such have their place,' I heard.

"Then low I moaned, 'And what, oh! guide! of those who, living thoughtless lives of sin, die unregenerate; no service done to Oro or to Mardian?'

" 'They, too, have their place,' I heard; 'but 'tis not here. And Mardian! know, that as your Mardian lives are long preserved through strict obedience to the organic law, so are your spiritual lives prolonged by fast keeping of the law of mind. Sin is death.'

" 'Ah, then,' yet lower moan made I; 'and why create the germs that sin and suffer, but to perish?'

" 'That,' breathed my guide; 'is the last mystery which underlieth all the rest. Archangel may not fathom it; that makes of Oro the everlasting mystery he is; that to divulge, were to make equal to himself in knowledge all the souls that are; that mystery Oro guards; and none but him may know.'

"Alas! were it recalled, no words have I to tell of all that now my guide discoursed, concerning things unsearchable to us. My sixth sense which he opened, sleeps again, with all the wisdom that it gained.

"Time passed; it seemed a moment, might have been an age; when from high in the golden haze that canopied this heaven, another angel came; its vans like East and West; a sunrise one, sunset the other. As silver-fish in vases, so, in his azure eyes swam tears unshed.

"Quick my guide close nested me; through its veins the waning light throbbed hard.

"'Oh, spirit! archangel! god! whate'er thou art,' it breathed; 'leave me: I am but blessed, not glorified.'

"So saying, as down from doves, from its wings dropped sounds. Still nesting me, it crouched its plumes.

"Then, in a snow of softest syllables, thus breathed the greater and more beautiful:—'From far away, in fields beyond thy ken, I heard thy fond discourse with this lone Mardian. It pleased me well; for thy humility was manifest; no arrogance of knowing. Come *thou* and learn new things.'

"And straight it overarched us with its plumes; which, then, downsweeping, bore us up to regions where my first guide had sunk, but for the power that buoyed us, trembling, both.

"My eyes did wane, like moons eclipsed in overwhelming dawns: such radiance was around; such vermeil light, born of no sun, but pervading all the scene. Transparent, fleckless, calm, all glowed one flame.

"Then said the greater guide:—'This is the night of all ye here behold— its day ye could not bide. Your utmost heaven is far below.'

"Abashed, smote down, I, quaking, upward gazed; where, to and fro, the spirits sailed, like broad-winged crimson-dyed flamingos, spiraling in sunset-clouds. But a sadness glorified, deep-fringed their mystic temples, crowned with weeping halos, bird-like, floating o'er them, wheresoe'er they roamed.

"Sights and odors blended. As when new-morning winds, in summer's prime, blow down from hanging gardens, wafting sweets that never pall; so, from those flowery pinions, at every motion, came a flood of fragrance.

"And now the spirits twain discoursed of things, whose very terms, to me, were dark. But my first guide grew wise. For me, I could but blankly list; yet comprehended naught; and, like the fish that's mocked with wings, and vainly seeks to fly;—again I sought my lower element.

"As poised, we hung in this rapt ether, a sudden trembling seized the four wings now folding me. And afar off, in zones still upward reaching, suns' orbits off, I, tranced, beheld an awful glory. Sphere in sphere, it burned:—the one Shekinah! The air was flaked with fire;—deep in which, fell showers of silvery globes, tears magnified—braiding the flame with rainbows. I heard a sound; but not for me, nor my first guide, was that unutterable utterance. Then, my second guide was swept aloft, as rises a cloud of red-dyed leaves in autumn whirlwinds.

"Fast clasping me, the other drooped, and, instant, sank, as in a vacuum; myriad suns' diameters in a breath;—my five senses merged in one, of falling; till we gained the nether sky, descending still.

"Then strange things—soft, sad, and faint, I saw or heard; as, when, in sunny, summer seas, down, down, you dive, starting at pensive phantoms, that you can not fix.

"'These,' breathed my guide, 'are spirits in their essences; sad, even in undevelopment. With these, all space is peopled;—all the air is vital with intelligence, which seeks embodiment. This it is, that unbeknown to Mardians, causes them to strangely start in solitudes of night, and in the fixed flood of their enchanted noons. From hence, are formed your mortal souls; and all those sad and shadowy dreams, and boundless thoughts man hath, are vague remembrances of the time when the soul's sad germ, wide wandered through these realms. And hence it is, that when ye Mardians feel most sad, then ye feel most immortal.'

"Like a spark new-struck from flint, soon Mardi showed afar. It glowed within a sphere, which seemed, in space, a bubble, rising from vast depths to the sea's surface. Piercing it, my Mardian strength returned; but the angel's veins once more grew dim.

"Nearing the isles, thus breathed my guide:—'Loved one, love on! But know, that heaven hath no roof. To know all is to be all. Beatitude there is none. And your only Mardian happiness is but exemption from great woes—no more. Great Love is sad; and heaven is Love. Sadness makes the silence throughout the realms of space; sadness is universal and eternal; but sadness is tranquillity; tranquillity the uttermost that souls may hope for.'

"Then, with its wings it fanned adieu; and disappeared where the sun flames highest."

We heard the dream and, silent, sought repose, to dream away our wonder.

Chapter 189

They depart from Serenia

AT SUNRISE, we stood upon the beach.

Babbalanja thus:—"My voyage is ended. Not because what we sought is found; but that I now possess all which may be had of what I sought in Mardi. Here, I tarry to grow wiser still:—then I am Alma's and the world's. Taji! for Yillah thou wilt hunt in vain; she is a phantom that but mocks thee; and while for her thou madly huntest, the sin thou didst cries out, and its avengers still will follow. But here they may not come: nor those, who, tempting, track thy path. Wise counsel take. Within our hearts is all we seek: though in that search many need a prompter. Him I have found in blessed Alma. Then rove no more. Gain now, in flush of youth, that last wise thought, too often purchased, by a life of woe. Be wise: be wise.

"Media! thy station calls thee home. Yet from this isle, thou carriest that, wherewith to bless thy own. These flowers, that round us spring, may be transplanted: and Odo made to bloom with amaranths and myrtles, like this Serenia. Before thy people act the things, thou here hast heard. Let no man weep, that thou may'st laugh; no man toil too hard, that thou may'st idle be. Abdicate thy throne: but still retain the scepter. None need a king; but many need a ruler.

"Mohi! Yoomy! do we part? then bury in forgetfulness much that

637

hitherto I've spoken. But let not one syllable of this old man's words be lost.

"Mohi! Age leads thee by the hand. Live out thy life; and die, calm-browed.

"But Yoomy! many days are thine. And in one life's span, great circles may be traversed, eternal good be done. Take all Mardi for thy home. Nations are but names; and continents but shifting sands.

"Once more: Taji! be sure thy Yillah never will be found; or found, will not avail thee. Yet search, if so thou wilt; more isles, thou say'st, are still unvisited; and when all is seen, return, and find thy Yillah here.

"Companions all! adieu."

And from the beach, he wended through the woods.

Our shallops now refitted, we silently embarked; and as we sailed away, the old man blessed us.

For a time, each prow's ripplings were distinctly heard: ripple after ripple.

With silent, steadfast eyes, Media still preserved his noble mien; Mohi his reverend repose; Yoomy his musing mood.

But as a summer hurricane leaves all nature still, and smiling to the eye; yet, in deep woods, there lie concealed some anguished roots torn up:—so, with these.

Much they longed, to point our prows for Odo's isle; saying our search was over.

But I was fixed as fate.

On we sailed, as when we first embarked; the air was bracing as before. More isles we visited:—thrice encountered the avengers: but unharmed; thrice Hautia's heralds: but turned not aside;—saw many checkered scenes—wandered through groves, and open fields—traversed many vales —climbed hill-tops whence broad views were gained—tarried in towns— broke into solitudes—sought far, sought near:—Still Yillah there was none.

Then again they all would fain dissuade me.

"Closed is the deep blue eye," said Yoomy.

"Fate's last leaves are turning, let me home and die," said Mohi.

"So nigh the circuit's done," said Media, "our morrow's sun must rise o'er Odo; Taji! renounce the hunt."

"I am the hunter, that never rests! the hunter without a home! She I seek, still flies before; and I will follow, though she lead me beyond the reef; through sunless seas; and into night and death. Her, will I seek, through all the isles and stars; and find her, whate'er betide!"

Again they yielded; and again we glided on;—our storm-worn prows, now pointed here, now there;—beckoned, repulsed;—their half-rent sails, still courting every breeze.

But that same night, once more, they wrestled with me. Now, at last, the hopeless search must be renounced: Yillah there was none: back must I hie to blue Serenia.

Then sweet Yillah called me from the sea;—still must I on! but gazing whence that music seemed to come, I thought I saw the green corse drifting by: and striking 'gainst our prow, as if to hinder. Then, then! my heart grew hard, like flint; and black, like night; and sounded hollow to the hand I clenched. Hyenas filled me with their laughs; death-damps chilled my brow; I prayed not, but blasphemed.

Chapter 190

They meet the Phantoms

T HAT STARLESS MIDNIGHT, there stole from out the darkness, the Iris flag of Hautia.

Again the sirens came. They bore a large and stately urn-like flower, white as alabaster, and glowing, as if lit up within. From its calyx, flame-like, trembled forked and crimson stamens, burning with intensest odors.

The phantoms nearer came; their flower, as an urn of burning niter. Then it changed, and glowed like Persian dawns; or passive, was shot over by palest lightnings;—so variable its tints.

"The night-blowing Cereus!" said Yoomy, shuddering, "that never blows in sun-light; that blows but once; and blows but for an hour.— 'For the last time I come; now, in your midnight of despair, and promise you this glory. Take heed! short time hast thou to pause; through me, perhaps, thy Yillah may be found.'"

"Away! away! tempt me not by that, enchantress! Hautia! I know thee not; I fear thee not; but instinct makes me hate thee. Away! my eyes are frozen shut; I will not be tempted more."

"How glorious it burns!" cried Media. "I reel with incense:—can such sweets be evil?"

"Look! look!" cried Yoomy, "its petals wane, and creep; one moment

640

more, and the night-flower shuts up forever the last, last hope of Yillah!"

"Yillah! Yillah! Yillah!" bayed three vengeful voices far behind.

"Yillah! Yillah!—dash the urn! I follow, Hautia! though thy lure be death."

The Cereus closed; and in a mist the siren prow went on before; we, following.

When day dawned, three radiant pilot-fish swam in advance: three ravenous sharks astern.

And, full before us, rose the isle of Hautia.

Chapter 191

They draw nigh to Flozella

AS IF Mardi were a poem, and every island a canto, the shore now in sight was called Flozella-a-Nina, or The-Last-Verse-of-the-Song.

According to Mohi, the origin of this term was traceable to the remotest antiquity.

In the beginning, there were other beings in Mardi besides Mardians; winged beings, of purer minds, and cast in gentler molds, who would fain have dwelt forever with mankind. But the hearts of the Mardians were bitter against them, because of their superior goodness. Yet those beings returned love for malice, and long entreated to virtue and charity. But in the end, all Mardi rose up against them, and hunted them from isle to isle; till, at last, they rose from the woodlands like a flight of birds, and disappeared in the skies. Thereafter, abandoned of such sweet influences, the Mardians fell into all manner of sins and sufferings, becoming the erring things their descendants were now. Yet they knew not, that their calamities were of their own bringing down. For deemed a victory, the expulsion of the winged beings was celebrated in choruses, throughout Mardi. And among other jubilations, so ran the legend, a pean was composed, corresponding in the number of its stanzas, to the number of islands. And a band of youths, gayly appareled, voyaged in gala canoes all round the lagoon, singing upon each isle, one verse of their song. And Flozella being the last

642

isle in their circuit, its queen commemorated the circumstance, by new naming her realm.

That queen had first incited Mardi to wage war against the beings with wings. She it was, who had been foremost in every assault. And that queen was ancestor of Hautia, now ruling the isle.

Approaching the dominions of one who so long had haunted me, conflicting emotions tore up my soul in tornadoes. Yet Hautia had held out some prospect of crowning my yearnings. But how connected were Hautia and Yillah? Something I hoped; yet more I feared. Dire presentiments, like poisoned arrows, shot through me. Had they pierced me before, straight to Flozella would I have voyaged; not waiting for Hautia to woo me by that last and victorious temptation. But unchanged remained my feelings of hatred for Hautia; yet vague those feelings, as the language of her flowers. Nevertheless, in some mysterious way seemed Hautia and Yillah connected. But Yillah was all beauty, and innocence; my crown of felicity; my heaven below;—and Hautia, my whole heart abhorred. Yillah I sought; Hautia sought me. One, openly beckoned me here; the other dimly allured me there. Yet now was I wildly dreaming to find them together. But so distracted my soul, I knew not what it was, that I thought.

Slowly we neared the land. Flozella-a-Nina!—An omen? Was this isle, then, to prove the last place of my search, even as it was the Last-Verse-of-the-Song?

Chapter 192

They land

A JEWELED TIARA, nodding in spray, looks flowery Flozella, approached from the sea. For, lo you! the glittering foam all round its white marge; where, forcing themselves underneath the coral ledge, and up through its crevices, in fountains, the blue billows gush. While, within, zone above zone, thrice zoned in belts of bloom, all the isle, as a hanging-garden soars; its tapering cone blending aloft, with heaven's own blue.

"What flies through the spray! what incense is this?" cried Media.

"Ha! you wild breeze! you have been plundering the gardens of Hautia," cried Yoomy.

"No sweets can be sweeter," said Braid-Beard, "but no Upas more deadly."

Anon we came nearer; sails idly flapping, and paddles suspended; sleek currents our coursers. And round about the isle, like winged rainbows, shoals of dolphins were leaping over floating fragments of wrecks:—dark-green, long-haired ribs, and keels of canoes. For many shallops, inveigled by the eddies, were oft dashed to pieces against that flowery strand. But what cared the dolphins? Mardian wrecks were their homes. Over and over they sprang: from east to west: rising and setting: many suns in a moment; while all the sea, like a harvest plain, was stacked with their glittering sheaves of spray.

And far down, fathoms on fathoms, flitted rainbow hues:—as seines-full of mermaids; half-screening the bones of the drowned.

Swifter and swifter the currents now ran; till with a shock, our prows were beached.

There, beneath an arch of spray, three dark-eyed maidens stood; garlanded with columbines, their nectaries nodding like jesters' bells; and robed in vestments blue.

"The pilot-fish transformed!" cried Yoomy.

"The night-eyed heralds three!" said Mohi.

Following the maidens, we now took our way along a winding vale; where, by sweet-scented hedges, flowed blue-braided brooks; their tributaries, rivulets of violets, meandering through the meads.

On one hand, forever glowed the rosy mountains with a tropic dawn; and on the other, lay an Arctic eve;—the white daisies drifted in long banks of snow, and snowed the blossoms from the orange boughs. There, summer breathed her bridal bloom; her hill-top temples crowned with bridal wreaths.

We wandered on, through orchards arched in long arcades, that seemed baronial halls, hung o'er with trophies:—so spread the boughs in antlers. This orchard was the frontlet of the isle.

The fruit hung high in air, that only beaks, not hands, might pluck.

Here, the peach tree showed her thousand cheeks of down, kissed often by the wooing winds; here, in swarms, the yellow apples hived, like golden bees upon the boughs; here, from the kneeling, fainting trees, thick fell the cherries, in great drops of blood; and here, the pomegranate, with cold rind and sere, deep pierced by bills of birds revealed the mellow of its ruddy core. So, oft the heart, that cold and withered seems, within yet hides its juices.

This orchard passed, the vale became a lengthening plain, that seemed the Straits of Ormus bared; so thick it lay with flowery gems:—torquoise-hyacinths, ruby-roses, lily-pearls. Here roved the vagrant vines; their flaxen ringlets curling over arbors, which laughed and shook their golden locks. From bower to bower, flew the wee bird, that ever hovering, seldom lights; and flights of gay canaries passed, like jonquils, winged.

But now, from out half-hidden bowers of clematis, there issued swarms of wasps, which flying wide, settled on all the buds.

And, fifty nymphs preceding, who now follows from those bowers, with gliding, artful steps:—the very snares of love!—Hautia. A gorgeous amaryllis in her hand; Circe-flowers in her ears; her girdle tied with vervain.

She came by privet hedges, drooping; downcast honey-suckles; she trod on pinks and pansies, blue-bells, heath, and lilies. She glided on: her crescent brow calm as the moon, when most it works its evil influences.

Her eye was fathomless.

But the same mysterious, evil-boding gaze was there, which long before had haunted me in Odo, ere Yillah fled.—Queen Hautia the incognito! Then two wild currents met, and dashed me into foam.

"Yillah! Yillah!—tell me, queen!" But she stood motionless; radiant, and scentless: a dahlia on its stalk.

"Where? Where?"

"Is not thy voyage now ended?—Take flowers! Damsels, give him wine to drink. After his weary hunt, be the wanderer happy."

I dashed aside their cups, and flowers; still rang the vale with Yillah!

"Taji! did I know her fate, naught would I now disclose; my heralds pledged their queen to naught. Thou but comest here to supplant thy mourner's night-shade, with marriage roses. Damsels! give him wreaths; crowd round him; press him with your cups!"

Once more I spilled their wine, and tore their garlands.

"Is not that, the evil eye that long ago did haunt me? and thou, the Hautia who hast followed me, and wooed, and mocked, and tempted me, through all this long, long voyage? I swear! thou knowest all."

"I am Hautia. Thou hast come at last. Crown him with your flowers! Drown him in your wine! To all questions, Taji! I am mute.—Away!—damsels dance; reel round him; round and round!"

Then, their feet made music on the rippling grass, like thousand leaves of lilies on a lake. And, gliding nearer, Hautia welcomed Media; and said, "Your comrade here is sad:—be ye gay. Ho, wine!—I pledge ye, guests!"

Then, marking all, I thought to seem what I was not, that I might learn at last the thing I sought.

So, three cups in hand I held; drank wine, and laughed; and half-way met Queen Hautia's blandishments.

Chapter 193

They enter the Bower of Hautia

CONDUCTED TO THE ARBOR, from which the queen had emerged, we came to a sweet-brier bower within; and reclined upon odorous mats.

Then, in citron cups, sherbet of tamarinds was offered to Media, Mohi, Yoomy; to me, a nautilus shell, brimmed with a light-like fluid, that welled, and welled like a fount.

"Quaff, Taji, quaff! every drop drowns a thought!"

Like a blood-freshet, it ran through my veins.

A philter?—How Hautia burned before me! Glorious queen! with all the radiance, lighting up the equatorial night.

"Thou art most magical, oh queen! about thee a thousand constellations cluster."

"They blaze to burn," whispered Mohi.

"I see ten million Hautias!—all space reflects her, as a mirror."

Then, in reels, the damsels once more mazed, the blossoms shaking from their brows; till Hautia, glided near; arms lustrous as rainbows: chanting some wild invocation.

My soul ebbed out; Yillah there was none! but as I turned round open-armed, Hautia vanished.

"She is deeper than the sea," said Media.

647

"Her bow is bent," said Yoomy.

"I could tell wonders of Hautia and her damsels," said Mohi.

"What wonders?"

"Listen; and in his own words will I recount the adventure of the youth Ozonna. It will show thee, Taji, that the maidens of Hautia are all Yillahs, held captive, unknown to themselves; and that Hautia, their enchantress, is the most treacherous of queens.

"'Camel-like, laden with woe,' said Ozonna, 'after many wild rovings in quest of a maiden long lost—beautiful Ady! and after being repelled in Maramma; and in vain hailed to land at Serenia, represented as naught but another Maramma;—with vague promises of discovering Ady, three sirens, who long had pursued, at last inveigled me to Flozella; where Hautia made me her thrall. But ere long, in Rea, one of her maidens, I thought I discovered my Ady transformed. My arms opened wide to embrace; but the damsel knew not Ozonna. And even, when after hard wooing, I won her again, she seemed not lost Ady, but Rea. Yet all the while, from deep in her strange, black orbs, Ady's blue eyes seemed pensively looking:—blue eye within black: sad, silent soul within merry. Long I strove, by fixed ardent gazing, to break the spell, and restore in Rea my lost one's Past. But in vain. It was only Rea, not Ady, who at stolen intervals looked on me now. One morning Hautia started as she greeted me; her quick eye rested on my bosom; and glancing there, affrighted, I beheld a distinct, fresh mark, the impress of Rea's necklace drop. Fleeing, I revealed what had passed to the maiden, who broke from my side; as I, from Hautia's. The queen summoned her damsels, but for many hours the call was unheeded; and when at last they came, upon each bosom lay a necklace-drop like Rea's. On the morrow, lo! my arbor was strown over with bruised Linden-leaves, exuding a vernal juice. Full of forebodings, again I sought Rea: who, casting down her eyes, beheld her feet stained green. Again she fled; and again Hautia summoned her damsels: malicious triumph in her eye; but dismay succeeded: each maid had spotted feet. That night Rea was torn from my side by three masks; who, stifling her cries, rapidly bore her away; and as I pursued, disappeared in a cave. Next morning, Hautia was surrounded by her nymphs, but Rea was absent. Then, gliding near, she snatched from my hair, a jet-black tress, loose-hanging. 'Ozonna is the murderer! See! Rea's torn hair entangled with his!' Aghast, I swore that I knew not her fate. 'Then let the witch Larfee be called!' The maidens darted from the bower; and soon after, there rolled into it a green cocoa-nut, followed by the witch, and all the damsels, flinging anemones upon it. Bowling this way and that, the nut at last rolled to my feet.—'It is he!' cried all.—Then they bound me with osiers; and at midnight, unseen and irresistible hands placed me in a shallop; which sped far out into the lagoon, where they tossed me to the waves; but so violent the shock, the osiers burst; and as the shallop fled one way, swimming another, ere long I gained land.

"'Thus in Flozella, I found but the phantom of Ady, and slew the last hope of Ady the true.'"

This recital sank deep into my soul. In some wild way, Hautia had made a captive of Yillah; in some one of her black-eyed maids, the blue-eyed One was transformed. From side to side, in frenzy, I turned; but in all those cold, mystical eyes, saw not the warm ray that I sought.

"Hast taken root within this treacherous soil?" cried Media.—"Away! thy Yillah is behind thee, not before. Deep she dwells in blue Serenia's groves; which thou would'st not search. Hautia mocks thee; away! The reef is rounded; but a strait flows between this isle and Odo, and thither its ruler must return. Every hour I tarry here, some wretched serf is dying there, for whom, from blest Serenia, I carry life and joy. Away!"

"Art still bent on finding evil for thy good?" cried Mohi.—"How can Yillah harbor here?—Beware!—Let not Hautia so enthrall thee."

"Come away, come away," cried Yoomy. "Far hence is Yillah! and he who tarries among these flowers, must needs burn juniper."

"Look on me, Media, Mohi, Yoomy. Here I stand, my own monument, till Hautia breaks the spell."

In grief they left me.

Vee-Vee's conch I heard no more.

Chapter 194

Taji with Hautia

AS THEIR LAST ECHOES died away down the valley, Hautia glided near;—zone unbound, the amaryllis in her hand. Her bosom ebbed and flowed; the motes danced in the beams that darted from her eyes.

"Come! let us sin, and be merry. Ho! wine, wine, wine! and lapfuls of flowers! let all the cane-brakes pipe their flutes. Damsels! dance; reel, swim, around me:—I, the vortex that draws all in. Taji! Taji!—as a berry, that name is juicy in my mouth!—Taji, Taji!" and in choruses, she warbled forth the sound, till it seemed issuing from her syren eyes.

My heart flew forth from out its bars, and soared in air; but as my hand touched Hautia's, down dropped a dead bird from the clouds.

"Ha! how he sinks!—but did'st ever dive in deep waters, Taji? Did'st ever see where pearls grow?—To the cave!—damsels, lead on!"

Then wending through constellations of flowers, we entered deep groves. And thus, thrice from sun-light to shade, it seemed three brief nights and days, ere we paused before the mouth of the cavern.

A bow-shot from the sea, it pierced the hill-side like a vaulted way; and glancing in, we saw far gleams of water; crossed, here and there, by long-flung distant shadows of domes and columns. All Venice seemed within.

From a stack of golden palm-stalks, the damsels now made torches; then stood grouped; a sheaf of sirens in a sheaf of flame.

Illuminated, the cavern shone like a Queen of Kandy's casket: full of dawns and sunsets.

From rocky roof to bubbling floor, it was columned with stalactites; and galleried all round, in spiral tiers, with sparkling, coral ledges.

And now, their torches held aloft, into the water the maidens softly glided; and each a lotus floated; while, from far above, into the air Hautia flung her flambeau; then bounding after,—in the lake, two meteors were quenched.

Where she dived, the flambeaux clustered; and up among them, Hautia rose; hands, full of pearls.

"Lo! Taji; all these may be had for the diving; and Beauty, Health, Wealth, Long Life, and the Last Lost Hope of man. But through me alone, may these be had. Dive thou, and bring up one pearl if thou canst."

Down, down! down, down, in the clear, sparkling water, till I seemed crystalized in the flashing heart of a diamond; but from those bottomless depths, I uprose empty handed.

"Pearls, pearls! thy pearls! thou art fresh from the mines. Ah, Taji! for thee, bootless deep diving. Yet to Hautia, one shallow plunge reveals many Golcondas. But come; dive with me:—join hands—let me show thee strange things."

"Show me that which I seek, and I will dive with thee, straight through the world, till we come up in oceans unknown."

"Nay, nay; but join hands, and I will take thee, where thy Past shall be forgotten; where thou wilt soon learn to love the living, not the dead."

"Better to me, oh Hautia! all the bitterness of my buried dead, than all the sweets of the life thou canst bestow; even, were it eternal."

Chapter 195

Mardi behind: an Ocean before

RETURNED FROM THE CAVE, Hautia reclined in her clematis bower, invisible hands flinging fennel around her. And nearer, and nearer, stole dulcet sounds dissolving my woes, as warm beams, snow. Strange languors made me droop; once more within my inmost vault, side by side, the Past and Yillah lay:—two bodies tranced;—while like a rounding sun, before me Hautia magnified magnificence; and through her fixed eyes, slowly drank up my soul.

Thus we stood:—snake and victim: life ebbing out from me, to her.

But from that spell, I burst again, as all the Past smote all the Present in me.

"Oh Hautia! thou knowest the mystery I die to fathom. I see it crouching in thine eye:—Reveal!"

"Weal or woe?"

"Life or death!"

"See, see!" and Yillah's rose-pearl danced before me.

I snatched it from her hand:—"Yillah! Yillah!"

"Rave on: she lies too deep to answer; stranger voices than thine she hears:—bubbles are bursting round her."

"Drowned! drowned then, even as she dreamed:—I come, I come!— Ha, what form is this?—hast mosses? sea-thyme? pearls?—Help, help! I

652

sink!—Back, shining monster!—What, Hautia,—is it thou?—Oh vipress, I could slay thee!"

"Go, go,—and slay thyself: I may not make thee mine;—go,—dead to dead!—There is another cavern in the hill."

Swift I fled along the valley-side; passed Hautia's cave of pearls; and gained a twilight arch; within, a lake transparent shone. Conflicting currents met, and wrestled; and one dark arch led to channels, seaward tending.

Round and round, a gleaming form slow circled in the deepest eddies: —white, and vaguely Yillah.

Straight I plunged; but the currents were as fierce headwinds off capes, that beat back ships.

Then, as I frenzied gazed; gaining the one dark arch, the revolving shade darted out of sight, and the eddies whirled as before.

"Stay, stay! let me go with thee, though thou glidest to gulfs of blackness;—naught can exceed the hell of this despair!—Why beat longer in this corpse oh, my heart!"

As somnambulists fast-frozen in some horrid dream, ghost-like glide abroad, and fright the wakeful world; so that night, with death-glazed eyes, to and fro I flitted on the damp and weedy beach.

"Is this specter, Taji?"—and Mohi and the minstrel stood before me.

"Taji lives no more. So dead, he has no ghost. I am his spirit's phantom's phantom."

"Nay, then, phantom! the time has come to flee."

They dragged me to the water's brink, where a prow was beached. Soon—Mohi at the helm—we shot beneath the far-flung shadow of a cliff; when, as in a dream, I hearkened to a voice.

Arrived at Odo, Media had been met with yells. Sedition was in arms, and to his beard defied him. Vain all concessions then. Foremost stood the three pale sons of him, whom I had slain, to gain the maiden lost. Avengers, from the first hour we had parted on the sea, they had drifted on my track; survived starvation; and lived to hunt me round all Mardi's reef; and now at Odo, that last threshold, waited to destroy; or there, missing the revenge they sought, still swore to hunt me round Eternity.

Behind the avengers, raged a stormy mob, invoking Media to renounce his rule. But one hand waving like a pennant above the smoke of some sea-fight, straight through that tumult Media sailed serene: the rioters parting from before him, as wild waves before a prow inflexible.

A haven gained, he turned to Mohi and the minstrel:—"Oh, friends! after our long companionship, hard to part! But henceforth, for many moons, Odo will prove no home for old age, or youth. In Serenia only, will ye find the peace ye seek; and thither ye must carry Taji, who else must soon be slain, or lost. Go: release him from the thrall of Hautia. Outfly the avengers, and gain Serenia. Reck not of me. The state is tossed in storms; and where I stand, the combing billows must break over. But among all noble souls, in tempest-time, the headmost man last flies the wreck. So, here in Odo will I abide, though every plank breaks up beneath me. And then, —great Oro! let the king die clinging to the keel! Farewell!"

Such Mohi's tale.

In trumpet-blasts, the hoarse night-winds now blew; the Lagoon, black with the still shadows of the mountains, and the driving shadows of the clouds. Of all the stars, only red Arcturus shone. But through the gloom, and on the circumvallating reef, the breakers dashed ghost-white.

An outlet in that outer barrier was nigh.

"Ah! Yillah! Yillah!—the currents sweep thee oceanward; nor will I tarry behind.—Mardi, farewell!—Give me the helm, old man!"

"Nay, madman! Serenia is our haven. Through yonder strait, for thee, perdition lies. And from the deep beyond, no voyager e'er puts back."

"And why put back? is a life of dying worth living o'er again?—Let *me*, then, be the unreturning wanderer. The helm! By Oro, I will steer my own fate, old man.—Mardi, farewell!"

"Nay, Taji: commit not the last, last crime!" cried Yoomy.

"He's seized the helm! eternity is in his eye! Yoomy: for our lives we must now swim."

And plunging, they struck out for land: Yoomy buoying Mohi up, and the salt waves dashing the tears from his pallid face, as through the scud, he turned it on me mournfully.

"Now, I am my own soul's emperor; and my first act is abdication! Hail! realm of shades!"—and turning my prow into the racing tide, which seized me like a hand omnipotent, I darted through.

Churned in foam, that outer ocean lashed the clouds; and straight in my white wake, headlong dashed a shallop, three fixed specters leaning o'er its prow: three arrows poising.

And thus, pursuers and pursued flew on, over an endless sea.

THE END

Editorial Appendix

HISTORICAL NOTE
By Elizabeth S. Foster

TEXTUAL RECORD
By the Editors

RELATED DOCUMENTS

THE FIRST *of the three parts of this* EDITORIAL APPENDIX *is a note on the composition, publication, reception, and later critical history of* Mardi, *contributed by Elizabeth S. Foster. The second, which records textual information, has been prepared by the editors, Harrison Hayford, Hershel Parker, and G. Thomas Tanselle. It consists of a note on the textual history of* Mardi *and on the editorial principles of this edition, followed by discussions of certain problematical readings, a list of emendations made in this edition, a report of line-end hyphenation, and a full list of substantive variants between the first American and English editions. The third part presents a reproduction and transcript of the two surviving manuscript fragments. In verifying the information in this* APPENDIX, *the editors have been aided by the bibliographical associate, Richard Colles Johnson, and the editorial assistants, Watson G. Branch and Amy Puett. To insure uniform policy, the same three editors bear full responsibility for establishing the texts in all volumes of the Edition, except when other editors are specifically named (as in the case of certain writings edited from manuscript). Although most of the historical notes have been written by other contributing scholars, the task of writing textual commentary and of preparing the textual lists has been the joint responsibility of the three editors. Hershel Parker is the editor who coordinated the preparation of this volume.*

At appropriate points in the APPENDIX *acknowledgment is made for generous assistance received from scholars not directly connected with the Edition. The editors also wish to recognize the indispensable services of these members of their staff: Virginia Heiserman, Michael Klee, Joel Myerson, Eugene Perchak, Eileen Peterson, Karleen Redle, R. E. Steinhauer, Sister Mary Dominic Stevens, and the chief proofreader, Justine Smith.*

Historical Note

HERMAN MELVILLE'S THIRD BOOK, *Mardi: and A Voyage Thither*, was begun as a sequel to *Omoo*, which concludes as the narrator abandons his picaresque beachcombing in the Pacific and ships on a whaler with a hurrah "for the coast of Japan!" and for the sport of chasing whales. *Mardi* was completed, some year and a half or two years later, as a continuum of adventure in an open boat and a derelict ship, wild allegorical romance, and fantastic travelogue-satire. Melville's book changed as he wrote it, but not so much or so momentously as the writing of the book changed Melville. It freed his imagination and his intellect to roam the universe from the silliest custom of man to Dantean heavens, to hobnob with the great writers and thinkers of the ages, to match wits with them and learn to speak their language. It stirred up demonic powers within him and gave him more than an inkling of his own genius. That is to say, it made possible *Moby-Dick*.

Melville was to write Hawthorne later that he dated his life from the year, 1844–45, when he returned from three and a half years of whaling and wandering in the Pacific and, at the age of twenty-five, began to write. "Three weeks have scarcely passed, at any time between then and now," he explained, "that I have not unfolded within myself."[1] The unfolding within

1. Documentation of this NOTE is explained at the end, in the section on "Sources."

himself which took place between January, 1847, when he finished work on the proof sheets of *Omoo*, and January, 1849, when he finished the proof sheets of *Mardi*, was the most astonishing and the most accelerated in any two-year period of his life.

Whatever the causes of this extraordinary "unfolding," it was nourished and stimulated by the new kind of life Melville was enjoying while working on *Mardi*. He courted Elizabeth Shaw, daughter of Chief Justice Lemuel Shaw of Massachusetts, and married her on August 4, 1847, three days after his twenty-eighth birthday. He moved from Lansingburgh, near Albany, to New York City, and he and his bride set up housekeeping at 103 Fourth Avenue, along with his brother Allan, a lawyer who took a hand in politics; Allan's bride; and Herman's and Allan's mother and four sisters. He spent convivial evenings at the hospitable home of Evert A. Duyckinck in talk with literary and other notable men, and he borrowed freely from Duyckinck's large library and from the New York Society Library. He was steadily buying books of his own. At Boston he met Richard Henry Dana, Jr., and other men interested in literature and politics. He attended the opening of the Art Union Hall and occasionally the opera, but he tried to avoid late evening parties and hoarded his time and energy for *Mardi*. In the latter months of these two years of spiritual plenty, he knew he was the father of a child; a son was born to him and Elizabeth in Boston on February 16, 1849, just half a month after he ended his final proofreading labors on *Mardi*.

Melville had begun thinking about the book that was to become *Mardi* even before *Omoo* was published. "If 'Omoo' succeeds I shall follow it up by something else, immediately," he wrote on March 31, 1847, to John Murray, who had just brought out that book in London. But Melville could work only intermittently at best on *Mardi* during the first nine months of 1847. Early in February he tried for a job in the Treasury Department at Washington, probably because he felt that entire dependence on his pen would be risky for a householder and married man; no government job was available. He wrote a double review of J. Ross Browne's *Etchings of a Whaling Cruise* and Captain Ringbolt's *Sailors' Life and Sailors' Yarns* for the new weekly, the *Literary World* (March 6), of which his friend Evert A. Duyckinck was editor. In April and May he may have been writing the early chapters of his new book; he was buying books of voyages and exploration, the kind of books he had found helpful to his imagination and memory as he wrote *Typee* and *Omoo*. By June 19 he had made some plans, at the very least, for his new book; in a letter of that date to the English

publisher Richard Bentley, Melville spoke of it as "a new work of South
Sea adventure . . . occupying entirely fresh ground." Bentley had made
"overtures" toward publishing Melville's next book in London, but Melville explained that he could not "at present" meet them because he had
mentioned the book to Murray. He was also busy, before his wedding in
August, with his mother's garden at Lansingburgh and other family obli-
gations; with professional business in New York and the writing of a series
of "Authentic Anecdotes of 'Old Zack,' " humorous articles on General
Zachary Taylor which appeared in the comic weekly *Yankee Doodle* between July 24 and September 11; and with visits to Boston and preparations
for his wedding.

After the wedding, the wedding trip, and a visit to Lansingburgh,
Herman and Elizabeth, or Lizzie, settled down in New York in September,
and by October he could begin to work steadily on his new book. It was still
a tale of South Sea adventure, perhaps the whaling story that the conclusion
of *Omoo* points toward. On October 29 he wrote Murray that his new
"book of South Sea Adventure" was "continued from, tho' wholly independent of, 'Omoo,' " and that it would "enter into scenes altogether new"
and more interesting than those of *Omoo*. Duyckinck had written his
brother, George, in September that Melville's new book would "exhaust
the South Sea marvels." But Melville's fictional ideas were already expanding: he told Murray that his "own peculiar province" was "wide & fresh"
and that "indeed, I only but begin, as it were, to feel my hand." He thought
his book would be ready for the press probably late the next spring, certainly by the fall of 1848.

The book, however, which began as what Melville called "a bona-vide
narrative of my adventures in the Pacific, continued from 'Omoo,' "
underwent a radical change in plan sometime before the end of 1847. For on
January 1, 1848, Melville wrote Murray that his plan "clothes the whole
subject in new attractions & combines in one cluster all that is romantic,
whimsical & poetic in Polynusia."[2] This makes it likely that he had let his
hero pose as a demigod by this time—a "romantic" episode yet one not un-
precedented in the history of Pacific exploration. Though he had dropped
autobiography, he could still think of his book as the factual narrative that
Murray required. Melville had confidence in his "rather bold aim" and
believed that Murray might double the advance of 100 guineas that he had

2. Quotations from Melville's letters follow the Davis and Gilman transcription
(1960) *literatim*, retaining Melville's erratic spellings, such as "bona-vide" and "Polynusia".

tentatively offered, after he saw the new book. Since Murray steadfastly refused to publish fiction and continued to be disturbed because reviewers
were insisting that *Typee* and *Omoo* must be romances rather than narratives
of fact, Melville assured him that the new book was "authentic." But then
he crossed out that statement and merely promised that it would have "the
right stuff" in it to redeem any faults. Perhaps the really sizable amount of
Pacific and Polynesian fact in his new book, and also the exhilaration of
writing in the new vein, had made him forget until the moment of con-
fronting Murray by letter how far he had strayed from Murray's idea of
authenticity. Melville's "It is yet a continuous narrative" betrays his own
sense of the awkward difference in genre between the open boat and the
"whimsical & poetic" chapters.

In the early months of 1848, then, the new book was in its second phase,
and by March 25 Melville recognized that it had become "in downright
earnest" a romance. On that date he wrote Murray a long letter to explain
how and why the promised bona fide narrative of his adventures in the
Pacific had turned into a romance and to say he hoped that nevertheless
Murray would publish it the following summer: "The truth is, Sir, that the
reiterated imputation of being a romancer in disguise has at last pricked me
into a resolution to show . . . that a *real* romance of mine is no Typee or
Omoo, & is made of different stuff altogether." Melville had been "pricked"
not only when reviewers lightly linked him with Gulliver and Munchausen
but when Murray himself wished that "some means could be taken to convince the English Public" that Melville's books were not fictitious imitations
of *Robinson Crusoe* and twice asked him to send "documentary evidence" of
his having been in the South Seas. In retrospect at least, Melville thought
that all this incredulity had been "the main inducement" in altering his
plans. But other inducements, he explained, were his wish to exploit the
"rich poetical material" of Polynesia, "which to bring out suitably, required only that play of freedom & invention accorded only to the
Romancer & poet"; a feeling of being "irked, cramped & fettered" by a
narrative of facts; and "a longing to plume my pinions for a flight." His
romance, he assured Murray, "is no dish water nor its model borrowed
from the Circulating Library. . . . It opens like a true narrative—like Omoo
for example, on ship board—& the romance & poetry of the thing thence
grow continually, till it becomes a story wild enough I assure you & with a
meaning too." He would forward the proofs to Murray and let him judge
the book's merits for himself. He proposed an advance of £150, instead of
Murray's suggested 100 guineas, and half profits "of all future editions . . .

when *all* expences of outlay on your part shall have been defraid by the book itself."

Despite Murray's "Antarctic" reply to this letter, on June 19 Melville was still resolved to submit *Mardi* to him with the hope that Murray would "for once relent" in his abhorrence of romances. And, since the papers had recently come into his possession, Melville promised to send along soon "one or two original documents, evidencing the incredible fact, that I have actually been a common sailor before the mast, in the Pacific."

"He has borrowed Sir Thomas Brown[e] of me," Evert A. Duyckinck wrote his brother on March 18, 1848, "and says finely of the speculations of the Religio Medici that Browne is a kind of 'crack'd Archangel!' Was ever any thing of this sort said before by a sailor?" In the first months of 1848 the sailor had borrowed from Duyckinck not only the four volumes of Sir Thomas Browne but also the second, third, and fourth volumes of a four-volume Rabelais and *Frithiof's Saga*, by Esaias Tegnér, as well as *A Narrative of the Sufferings and Adventures of Capt. Charles H. Barnard*. From the New York Society Library he had borrowed David Hartley's *Observations on Man* as well as Louis de Bougainville's *A Voyage Round the World*. In January he had bought a volume of Shakespeare, probably the poems, and Montaigne; in February, DeFoe's *The Fortunate Mistress*, a complete edition of Burton's *Anatomy of Melancholy* (he had bought selections a year earlier), and Coleridge's *Biographia Literaria*; and sometime in early 1848 James Macpherson's *Fingal* and *Seneca's Morals by Way of Abstract*. He was still mining books of Pacific travel and exploration and using some of the ore, especially from William Ellis' *Polynesian Researches* and Frederick Debell Bennett's *Narrative of a Whaling Voyage*. But three things were going on concurrently and more or less interdependently: the shift of direction in *Mardi*; its author's avid reading of great and near-great writers—a remarkably varied but by no means random cluster of them; and his rapid intellectual development.

As *Mardi* deepened, in the travelogue chapters, into an intermittent symposium on religion, philosophy, science, politics, and the poet's art, on faith and knowledge, on necessity and free will, on time and death and eternity, Melville's reading and also his writing were rushing him into such an intellectual expansion and exhilaration that his very being was ringing with the voices of the great dead. At the same time, like his Lombardo in *Mardi*, as he wrote he "got deeper and deeper into himself" (595.26).[3] And there the release of dormant powers and thoughts also released what he

3. Parenthetical references are to page and line of the present edition.

later called "a certain something unmanageable." As Melville confessed, "And though essaying but a sportive sail, I was driven from my course, by a blast resistless" (557.3–4).

Lombardo writing his Koztanza is frequently taken to be a parallel of Melville writing *Mardi*. Babbalanja says of Lombardo: "And ere Necessity plunged spur and rowel into him, he knew not his own paces. *That* churned him into consciousness; and brought ambition, ere then dormant, seething to the top, till he trembled at himself" (593.35–38). Necessity was indeed holding the spur to Melville's side, for returns from *Typee* and *Omoo*, though steady and supplemented by a loan or gift from his father-in-law, barely supported him and his wife even in their economical household; and Necessity was hurrying him to finish *Mardi* even though he knew—if Lombardo doubles for him here—that all his "slaving" had not been "intense, prolonged enough, for the high meed of immortality" (601.12–13).

"The book is done now, . . . and the copy for the press is in progress," Lizzie wrote to her stepmother on May 5, 1848, and on June 6 she expected to complete the copying "this week." So Melville had finished according to the loose schedule he had set himself as early as October 29, 1847, and according to the more exact schedule revealed in his letter to Murray of March 25. When he wrote that letter, he expected to get his manuscript to an American publisher in time to have the American proof sheets in Murray's hands by the middle of July.

But even while Melville was making his final revisions and his wife and at least one of his sisters were copying the completed work, the "blast resistless" kept on blowing. *Mardi* went into its third phase. During the summer and fall of 1848 the sequence describing the voyage around the real, contemporary geographical world was written and inserted, that is to say, all or most of the twenty-five chapters from 145 through 169, and also perhaps Chapter 180, about Lombardo, which can be read as Melville's apology for his own artistic waywardness in *Mardi*. Merrell R. Davis, in *Melville's MARDI: A Chartless Voyage*, showed that Chapters 145–149, on the visit to Dominora (England), could not have been written before May 1, the day the news of the "Great Chartist Meeting" and fiasco of April 10 reached New York; and that, although the news of the Revolution of 1848 in France began to arrive in New York on March 18, Chapter 153, on Franko (France), was probably written after the chapters on Dominora. As evidence, Davis pointed out the allusions in the Franko chapter to remarks or incidents in the preceding Dominora section; he also found in *Mardi* a certain skepticism about Franko's "eruption" which is more consonant with the disillusion spreading in New York by the early summer than with the sympathy and congratulations that had at first greeted the news of the Revolution.

Vivenza (the United States), the next stop on the Mardian cruise (Chapters 157–163), found its way into the book in the summer or autumn or both. As Davis showed, political events of the spring and summer of 1848 are alluded to in these chapters: for example, the admission of the thirtieth state, Wisconsin, to the union on May 29; John Van Buren's "political capital" movement; the Buffalo Free-Soil Convention of August 9–10, or perhaps, alternatively, the Barnburner Convention at Utica on June 22. In the middle of September, New York and other eastern newspapers began printing the more exciting stories of the California gold rush and some of the subsequent tragedies, the subject of Chapter 166. It was not until November 15, 1848, that Melville signed an agreement with Harper & Brothers, New York, for the publication of *Mardi*. On January 27, 1849, Melville's sister Augusta wrote to Lizzie in Boston: "The last proof sheets are through. 'Mardi's' a book. . . . 'Ah my own Koztanza! child of many prayers.' Oro's blessing on thee."

On January 28 Melville wrote Murray that he was sending the proof sheets "herewith" and proposed new terms: "I can hardly consent to dispose of the book for less than 200 guineas, in advance, on the day of publication, & half the profits of any editions which may be sold after the book shall have paid for itself—of course, including the outlay of the 200 guineas." He reminded him of Murray's own earlier suggestion that the new book not be published in the "cheap" Home and Colonial Library form adopted for *Typee* and *Omoo* but rather "in handsome style, & independently of any series," and added: "Unless you should deem it *very* desirable do not put me down on the title page as 'the author of Typee & Omoo.' I wish to separate '*Mardi*' as much as possible from those books."

The proof sheets were actually sent to Murray by Allan Melville on the steamer leaving February 7, after Herman had gone to Boston to be with Lizzie for the birth of their child. In spite of Melville's hopes, Murray refused *Mardi*. John Romeyn Brodhead, Secretary of the American Legation in London, who was acting as go-between for Melville with British publishers, wrote of *Mardi* in his diary on February 24: "I am now to offer [it] to Bentley as Melville's agent. It is a fiction & Mr Murray says it don't suit him."

Bentley responded quickly. On March 1 he agreed to publish *Mardi*, and on March 3 he contracted to advance Melville 200 guineas toward "his

moiety of the profits that may accrue"—just the terms Melville had asked
of Murray, and the largest advance payment that he ever received from an
English publisher for any of his books. The reputation of his first two tales
of adventure in the South Seas had made him a "guinea author" and doubtless influenced Bentley to bring the new book out handsomely as a "three-
decker" novel at 31s. 6d. for the set. Acting with dispatch, Bentley was able
to publish *Mardi: and A Voyage Thither* on March 16, 1849, in a text faithful
in all essentials to the American edition.

Melville's contract with Harper & Brothers provided that he receive an
advance of $500, due December 1, 1848, and half profits, with settlement
on February 1 and August 1 of each year; that Melville own the copyright
and that Harper & Brothers be the only American publishers; and that the
Harpers wait four months before bringing out the book. Such a delay of
publication in America was customary because British publishers at the
time believed that by being the first to publish a work by a foreigner they
in effect secured a British copyright on it. The American copyright for
Mardi: and A Voyage Thither was registered on February 5, 1849, and a copy
of the book was deposited with the Clerk of the Southern District of New
York on April 14. On that day *Mardi* was published in New York, in two
duodecimo volumes, to sell for $1.75 in muslin, and $1.50 in paper.

II

In Britain *Mardi* was reviewed promptly and on the whole not un-
favorably. No critic admired the book without reservation, but of the
fifteen British reviews in 1849 which have been studied, nine commended,
sometimes with high praise, more than one quality or part of *Mardi*, and
four were very harshly adverse; two are negligible as being little more than
mosaics of bits from other reviews.

What most of the reviews gave their highest praise to were the superb
adventures in the first part of the book, the brilliant pictorial power shown
in the scenes from nature, and the portraits of people like Jarl and Samoa—
in other words, the parts and qualities of *Mardi* that were most like *Typee*
and *Omoo*. Melville's descriptions of the Devil Fish, the swordfish, and the
sharks were enthusiastically acclaimed in many reviews and extracted,
usually at length, in five of them. "No one paints a shark better than Mr.
Melville," said the *Examiner* (March 31). Even the hostile critic of the
Athenæum (March 24) liked the sharks and quoted a long extract about them
and another long one about the boarding and exploring of the *Parki*,
another favorite passage with reviewers.

The worst that was said about *Mardi* appeared in four very severe reviews. The *Athenæum* said: "If this book be meant as a pleasantry, the mirth has been oddly left out—if as an allegory, the key of the casket is 'buried in ocean deep'—if as a romance, it fails from tediousness—if as a prose-poem, it is chargeable with puerility." The *Spectator* (April 21) was caustic and contumelious: "He has neither the mind nor the mental training requisite for fiction." The adventures among the islands "defy description to depict their absurdity or their total lack of interest." *Sharpe's London Journal* (May 15) demolished *Mardi* in one short paragraph as a book that "aims at many things and achieves none satisfactorily" and preaches "certain transcendental nonsense which is meant for *bona fide* transcendental philosophy." Perhaps most grievous was the blow from the influential *Blackwood's Edinburgh Magazine* (August), for *Blackwood's* had been delighted with *Omoo* but was disgusted with *Mardi*—"a rubbishing rhapsody," "trash," "mingled, too, with attempts at a Rabelaisian vein, and with strainings at smartness—the style of the whole being affected, pedantic, and wearisome exceedingly."

Several of the more or less friendly reviewers were also disturbed by opacity of meaning, uncertainty of aim, and rhapsodical language. The *Literary Gazette* (March 24) put the question of the meaning most kindly in wondering "how aught so luminous can be so dark," and went on to say, "We never saw a book so like a kaleidoscope." The allegory puzzled and seems to have annoyed most of the reviewers who mention it. But *John Bull* (April 21) gave an admirable insight into it: Yillah represents "the poetry of the soul's high romance, and its ideal happiness, before it has become effaced by contact with a base world." The satire on human foibles and the often satirical political allusions and comments were too vague or obscure for some reviewers, but others relished the "sly hits at many mortal absurdities" and at America's shortcomings.

Melville's high-hearted excursion into "the world of mind" elicited a few disapproving cries of Transcendentalism! German metaphysics! But the *Atlas* (March 24) remarked: "The great questions of natural religion, necessity, free-will, and so on" are "treated with much ingenuity, and frequently with a richness of imagination which disguises the triteness of the leading ideas." On the ground of religion the *New Monthly Magazine* (April) found Babbalanja's speculations on the immortality of whales "objectionable." And *John Bull* felt "profound regret that a pen so talented" should irreverently introduce the Saviour "under a fabulous name" and talk down "the verities of the Christian faith by sophistry."

Many literary kinships were noticed by the reviewers. Most frequently mentioned were *Gulliver's Travels* and *Robinson Crusoe*—"a transcendental *Gulliver*, or *Robinson Crusoe* run mad," the *Examiner* said. Others were "The Ancient Mariner," *The Arabian Nights*, Ossian, Rabelais, Munchausen, Spenser's *Faerie Queene*, Southey's *Thalaba*, More's *Utopia*, Harrington's *Oceana*, Cook's *Voyages*, Purchas, Mandeville, Charles Lamb, Macaulay's style, Disraeli's "sarcasm," Carlyle, Emerson, Sterne, Sir Thomas Browne, and Robert Burton. American reviewers also mentioned many of these and added *Rasselas*, Scott, and Irving.

By May, 1849, while it was still being reviewed, *Mardi* had become widely enough known to justify an amusing burlesque and parody in *The Man in the Moon*, a humorous London monthly. During the next few years *Mardi* was remembered occasionally in the British press, with less amusement, and was confirmed in the place it was to hold into the twentieth century as the first of the series of books (with *Moby-Dick*, *Pierre*, and *The Confidence-Man*) fatal to Melville's popularity, in which, as his contemporaries thought, he obstinately turned away from his true direction and lost himself in the fogs of dark philosophy and obscure meanings and, except in *The Confidence-Man*, extravagant, half-insane writing. The reviewer in the *Dublin University Magazine* (January, 1856) wrote as glowingly as anyone has ever written before or since of Melville's "unrivalled powers of diction," "his wealth of fancy," "his exuberance of imagination," and "his pathos, vigour, and exquisite graces of style" in *Mardi*. Nevertheless he thought that *Mardi* was "one of the saddest, most melancholy, most deplorable, and humiliating perversions of genius of a high order in the English language."

In the United States, the *Literary World*, of which Melville's friends the Duyckinck brothers, Evert and George, were now owners as well as editors, gave its front page to *Mardi* on April 7, 1849, a week ahead of the publication in New York, and heralded the book as "an onward development, with new traits, of all the fine literary qualities" of Melville's previous works. For a sample it printed Chapter 84, "Taji Sits Down to Dinner with Five-and-Twenty Kings. . . ." In the next two issues, April 14 and April 21, the *Literary World* gave a lengthy summary of *Mardi* with numerous long extracts and a running criticism which praised the many beauties of the earlier parts of *Mardi* and the richness of this well-filled book and then laid its emphasis on Melville's serious and thoughtful exploration of "the condition, the duties, the destiny of men," and his "poetical, thoughtful, ingenious moral writing . . . which Emerson would not disclaim." America has reached true manhood, said Duyckinck, speaking as the pleased champion of Young America throughout this essay, when a young writer boldly tells his country the truth about itself. His only reservation was that the "high discourse" occasionally got "into the clouds, attempting to handle the problem of the universe." The *Literary World*, in one way or another, generously kept *Mardi* before the public through the summer of 1849.

In America twice as many reviews of *Mardi* appeared during 1849 as in Britain. Of the thirty-odd that have been discovered, more than a third were very brief notices that praised the author of *Typee* and *Omoo* and spoke well or hopefully of a *Mardi* which, it is clear, most of these reviewers had not read and the rest had only glanced at. Of the nineteen more or less informed, though often very brief, reviews, eleven found a great deal to praise in *Mardi*, three found a little, and five thought the book a failure. Most of the American reviews were more general, less precise, particularly in their praise, than the British; they used the word "genius" freely. No American journal was as harsh as Britain's contemptuous *Spectator*.

It is clear that the American reviewers who liked *Mardi* tended more than the British did to like the whole book rather than only or mainly the first part. Others besides Duyckinck enjoyed the rich variety. They chose for their longer extracts from the first part of *Mardi* mostly the same passages that were popular in Britain—Samoa, scenes on the *Parki*, the fish chapters, for instance. But, significantly, fully half of their longer extracts came from the later parts of the book—the suffering of the poor and the heretical in Odo, the scenes of banqueting and drinking, Nora-Bamma, King Bello. And the *United States Magazine and Democratic Review* (July) printed the whole rhapsodical chapter on "Dreams." Six journals besides the *Literary World* maintained that *Mardi* showed an "onward development" of Melville's powers. *Graham's Magazine* (June) thought that it was "altogether the most striking work which Mr. Melville has produced"; *Mardi*'s very defects indicated "that the author has not yet reached the limits of his capacity."

The most profoundly perceptive of all the criticism of *Mardi*, probably written by William Alfred Jones, appeared in the *Democratic Review*. *Typee* and *Omoo*, "books that made the multitude crazy with delight," were to *Mardi*, this critic said, "as a seven-by-nine sketch of a sylvan lake, with a lone hunter, or a boy fishing, compared with the cartoons of Raphael." Blaming *Mardi*'s readers for its relative unsuccess, he said that some of "those who rejoiced in the flute-like music of Melville's Typee and Omoo . . . had not the slightest conception of the meaning of his magnificent orchestra in Mardi." "The man who expects and asks for loaf sugar will not be satisfied with marble, though it be built into a palace."

Three of the numerous critics who preferred flute warblings to orchestrated meanings wrote what were probably the most injurious reviews because they were fairly long and explicit in condemnation—those in the Boston *Post* (April 18), the New York *Daily Tribune* (May 10), and *Saroni's Musical Times* (September 29). All three had hoped for something amusing and delightful and like *Typee*, and had instead been wearied to exhaustion by a tedious, floundering work of uncertain meaning or no meaning at all. A hodgepodge, added the *Post*, Rabelais without coarseness but also without wit or humor. A story without movement, or proportions, or end, said the *Tribune*, or point—unless it is perhaps a huge, unwieldy allegory. "An undigested mass of rambling metaphysics," *Saroni's* reviewer complained, a "fathomless sea of Allegory, from which we have just emerged, gasping for breath." Still, the *Tribune* thought the first part of *Mardi* was excellent, and *Saroni's* praised *Mardi*'s poetic style: "Style is its sole redeeming feature." The *Southern Literary Messenger* (May) and the *American Whig Review* (September) also dismissed *Mardi* as a failure.

There was no outcry in Melville's own country, as there was in Britain, against *Mardi*'s "Transcendentalism." Indeed, besides Duyckinck and the reviewer in *Saroni's*, only a few Americans even mentioned the philosophical side of *Mardi*, and then only in a distant and general way. Some reviewers deplored the "affectations of style," and some praised the style as "graceful, pure and glowing" and lauded its poetic quality—"majestic poetry, which reminds us of the Hebrew," said the *Democratic Review*. The satire was beyond the reach of *Holden's Dollar Magazine* (June) and the Boston *Post*, but the *Albion* (April 21), the *Democratic Review*, and *Graham's* enjoyed what *Graham's* called the "capital audacities of satire, which are inimitable." As in Britain, there was a large amount of puzzlement over the meaning, a bewildered feeling of having been in a dream. In the United States, there was also some resentment at the call to mental exertion. Only the *Democratic Review* made much out of the allegory. "Mardi is an allegory that mirrors the world." A "far-seeking and high-aspiring youth, afloat on the ocean of life, which as yet is . . . bright with the rainbow of hope and beauty . . . finds his heart's first love, his Yillah." She is "as dreamy, and beautiful, and unsubstantial as the lady love of a boy-poet usually is. At length he comes into this actual world of ours, where he loses his Yillah" yet not his love of his ideal; "and everywhere he seeks that the shine of his Yillah may fall again on his soul."

No other critic spoke so gravely of the satiric and moral aims of *Mardi* as this reviewer did. "But whoso wishes to see the spirit of philosophy and humanity, love and wisdom, showing man to himself as he is, that he may know his evil and folly, and be saved from them, will be reverently thankful for this book." The center of Melville's greatness is "this mighty love [for humanity] that wells up always in his heart." "There is an immortality in love . . . and the author, whose heart burns within him like a live coal from God's own altar, need take no care for his fame. Such an one is Herman Melville."

This writer was the only American reviewer who raised any religious objection to *Mardi*, and he raised the deepest. Only he sensed that the "great Heart" was open to a radical pessimism—"the doctrine that this world can be a failure."

It is not surprising that the man who found such depths of life and meaning in *Mardi* should see as flame upon the lips what some others were calling insane rhapsody. "We have small respect for authors who are wilful, and cannot be advised," he says; "but we reverence a man when God's *must* is upon him, and he does his work in his own and other's spite. Portions of Mardi are written with this divine impulse, and they thrill through every fibre of the reader with an electric force."

From Paris came a review of *Mardi* that was equally exceptional but in a different way. "Voyages réels et fantastiques d'Hermann Melville," in the *Revue des Deux Mondes* for May 15, was an article on Melville's first three books by Philarète Chasles, a French critic of some standing, and it not only was the unique review of *Mardi* in continental Europe but also was very long—thirty pages, eleven of them on *Mardi*. No wonder the Duyckincks hailed it and translated it and printed it in the *Literary World* (August 4 and 11); they were pleased with it for giving a young American author "so cordial, appreciative a reception" and for clearing the way for him to be read "at Paris, St. Petersburgh, and Madrid, as well as London and Edinburgh."

The cordiality of Chasles's article appears chiefly in its length and consequent implication of Melville's importance. Chasles, who was interested in what happens to people and to literature in a new nation created from old nations, found *Mardi*, to quote the *Literary World*'s translation, "worthy of a Rabelais without gaiety, a Cervantes without grace, a Voltaire without taste," but said we should nevertheless look for what is "new and remarkable" in this product of a young nation. The first part of *Mardi* is "charming and full of life," but after "fairy land and somnambulism commence," the meaning is obscure, the ideas trite, the style strained and incorrect. The most "piquant" part of the book, he says, is the allegory of the modern political world.

Now comes the most piquant part of Chasles's criticism. He bestowed the highest praise of his review upon what purported to be a three-paragraph excerpt from *Mardi* in French translation, beginning: "Salut, mon Amérique libre, terre du printemps!" "There are few lyric chants more beautiful than this," he exclaimed. But alas for the author of *Mardi*. The author of the beautiful lyric chant is M. Philarète Chasles, though he does incorporate a few images from Yoomy's song about Yillah in Chapter 154 and a phrase from Babbalanja in Chapter 159. If the translation in the *Literary World* had not omitted all Chasles's excerpts from *Mardi*, or rather pseudo-excerpts, someone would have noticed, and would probably have pointed out long ago, that it was his own amendments of and substitutions for Melville that Chasles found most worthy of wonder and praise. He concluded his essay with his own fervent advice to revolution-prone France, but again he pretended that the passage came from *Mardi*. "The words which he [Melville] addresses to France," he gravely said, "deserve to be pondered."

Melville was more disappointed and hurt by the reception of his "child of many prayers" than the full tenor of the reviews perhaps justifies. "I see that Mardi has been cut into by the London Atheneum, and also burnt by the common hangman in the Boston Post," he wrote to his father-in-law on April 23. He encouraged both himself and Shaw by adding that some other papers had "done differently. These attacks are matters of course, and are essential to the building up of any permanent reputation—if such should ever prove to be mine." But the knife of the critic tormented him. He would never again, he wrote Duyckinck from London on December 14, say anything " ' critical' about another man's book. . . . Hereafter I shall no more stab at a book (in print, I mean) than I would stab at a man." And when, on February 2, 1850, he was making Duyckinck a present of the London edition of *Mardi*, he wrote of his book as a plant that "may possibly —by some miracle, that is—flower like the aloe, a hundred years hence— or not flower at all, which is more likely by far, for some aloes never flower"; and he said that Duyckinck's library would be affording refuge to a work "which almost everywhere else has been driven forth like a wild, mystic Mormon into shelterless exile."

As American reviewers discussed later works of Melville, their occasional and brief critical remarks on *Mardi* merely reiterated earlier judgments, except that the Duyckincks, in their *Cyclopædia of American Literature* (1855), spoke briefly and coolly of the book they had so cordially befriended at its debut. The only later criticism of any length in the American press was by Fitz-James O'Brien, who wrote for *Putnam's Monthly Magazine* an article on Melville alone (February, 1853) and one on Melville and Curtis (April, 1857). Although both first and last O'Brien confessed that he did not know what *Mardi* meant, in 1853 he declared that he did not want to know, that he accepted it as a rhapsody and delighted in its "vague, dreamy, poetic charm," its "splendor of imagery," its "gorgeous and fantastic" descriptive painting. But in 1857, with Melville's ten books before him, O'Brien was not content to dream in Mardi, "that enchanted, mysterious place"; he was urgent in his attempt to persuade Melville "to give up metaphysics and take to nature and the study of mankind."

In the forty-two years between its publication and Melville's death in 1891, *Mardi* sold a few more than 2,900 copies in the United States—not many, but a great many more than the English edition sold. The Harper edition of *Mardi* in April, 1849, numbered 3,048 two-volume sets. Of these, 2,054 were sold before the first audit (on September 10), 1,971 in muslin and 83 in paper; thereafter the sale in Melville's lifetime averaged about twenty copies a year, more in the earlier years, fewer in the later. On December 10, 1853, a fire destroyed the buildings and stock, except the stereotype plates, of Harper & Brothers. All but ten sets of *Mardi* were lost. The Harpers printed 260 additional copies in 1855, bound a few in half-calf and the rest in muslin, and discontinued the paper-bound line. In 1864 they printed another 250 copies. By March, 1887, Melville and his American publisher had each made a total profit of $740.87 on *Mardi*. In London, Bentley had difficulty disposing of the 1,000 copies he had printed, and in 1851 he reissued the remaining sheets with new title pages. In all he lost £68 7s. 6d.; he took in £141 12s. 6d. above the expenses of production, but he had paid Melville £210—or $970.65, two hundred dollars more than Melville earned from the greater Harper sales over a forty-year period.

Since Melville's death and before the present edition, *Mardi* has been set in type at least six times, four times from the American edition and twice from the British edition.

III

In the revival of critical interest in Melville, which began about 1919, scholars have not been slow in searching out the sources of *Mardi*. Not all their discoveries can be reported here, but enough to give an idea of what is known.

The first page or so of *Mardi*, it has been found, is in essence a continuation of Melville's own story from where it left off in *Omoo*. The ship which picked him up in the Society Islands and carried him as a "boat steerer" for a six-month cruise to the Hawaiian Islands, where he landed at Lahaina, Maui, about May 3, 1843, was the Nantucket whaler *Charles and Henry*; Melville called this ship the *Leviathan* at the end of *Omoo*, and the *Arcturion* in *Mardi*. Its captain, John B. Coleman, was apparently the model for the captain of the *Leviathan*, "a Vineyarder, . . . a sailor, and no tyrant," and also for the sociable and kindly skipper of the *Arcturion*, who was "a trump."

Melville's residence in the Hawaiian Islands for three and a half months in the summer of 1843 undoubtedly helped to inform him about the numerous places, people, and events in Hawaiian geography and history that appear in Mardian transmutation: for example, Ohonoo, "midway cloven down to the sea" (272.3–4), is like Oahu; the battle in which warriors were forced over a precipice (278.25–27) is like the battle of Nuuanu, 1795; the precipice of Mondo is like the Nuuanu Pali cliff. Donjalolo (Chapter 74) in some ways resembles Kamehameha III, who was king of Hawaii when Melville was there.

Of the strange Mardian customs, legends, myths, anecdotes, names, and bits of history and geography that make Mardi seem sometimes a real place and sometimes a *Mandeville's Travels* world, a great many have been traced back to books of travel and exploration. Some of the Polynesian background, of course, like the surfboarding which he describes at Ohonoo (Oahu) and which he read about in William Ellis, *Polynesian Researches*, Melville had probably seen for himself. For *Mardi* he drew heavily on Ellis, as he had done in *Omoo*. In Ellis he found, for example, a description of the operation of trepanning in which a piece of coconut shell was substituted for a piece of the patient's skull and pig's brains were sometimes used to replace an injured part of the human brain; the belief that sharks, "a sort of demigods of the sea," congratulate a new king and play harmlessly with him; an idol-maker's statement that his carved wooden logs become gods when placed in a temple; the material on sorcerers and witchcraft that Melville, prompted by Rabelais on the Furred Law-Cats, heightened into satire on lawyers; the model for Aleema's headdress and double canoe; the appearance of royalty in public on men's shoulders; the uncovering of a subject's body to the waist to show homage to a king; the prostration of natives with noses touching the ground when a king appeared; the Hawaiian custom of expressing grief for the dead by knocking out some of the front teeth; and the four classes of gods in South Sea mythology, including the gods of thieves, of ghosts, and of house-thatchers mentioned by Mohi. From Ellis or other writers or during his own Polynesian rambles Melville learned that a foremost god of the South Sea Islands was named Oro.

Frederick Debell Bennett, in *Narrative of a Whaling Voyage Round the Globe*, also furnished much useful information. For example, Melville found material in Bennett for his descriptions of flying fish, sharks, and pilot fish, for his remarks on the swordfish and on marine phosphorescence, for most of what he says about albinos, and for his description of the Great Morai and its environs.

Mohi's story (212.3–8) of the god Upi, who shot an arrow through a promontory on a neighboring island and made an arch through it, is like the myth of the god Pae, who shot an arrow at the island of Eimeo from Tahiti, pierced the rock, and left an orifice; the myth is related in Daniel Tyerman and George Bennet, *Journal of Voyages and Travels*, which Melville had cited in *Omoo*. This journal of travels in the South Seas also records a custom that Melville modified amusingly in his first chapter on Hivohitee (334.2–5): natives avoid having names that even slightly resemble those of the sovereign or members of the privileged order and therefore from time to time must change their own names and names of plants and animals.

In Charles Wilkes, *Narrative of the United States Exploring Expedition*, are long discussions of the Samoan Islands, the customs of the Kingsmill Islanders, and the currents near those islands. Since his escaping sailors were headed for the Kingsmill Islands, Melville may well have gathered much of his material from Wilkes, including details for his portrait and biography of the Upoluan Samoa. He had bought Wilkes in April, 1847, and used it in writing *Omoo*.

Books of travel and exploration in Egypt and the Levant may also have contributed details to some passages in *Mardi*. The descent into Oh-Oh's vault (Chapter 123), for example, may be derived from Belzoni's entry into a tomb at Kurnah, related in Giovanni Belzoni's *Narrative*.

Melville's wide-ranging reading before and during the composition of *Mardi* obviously took him among the philosophers, from Plato, a major influence on Melville, through Spinoza and the moderns, probably not always read at first hand. Babbalanja's gibberish (Chapter 170) about the

"Adyta, the Monads, and the Hyparxes; the Dianoias, the Unical Hypo-stases," etc., and also Doxodox's esoteric jargon (Chapter 171) are straight out of Proclus, in Thomas Taylor's translation of *The Six Books of Proclus on the Theology of Plato* (London, 1816), and form the first of several satirical attacks in Melville's works on the "transcendentalisms" and "oracular gibberish" of some philosophers. "A Happy Life," the old manuscript that Babbalanja read with such pleasure (Chapter 124), derives from Sir Roger L'Estrange's *Seneca's Morals by Way of Abstract* (London, 1746), another of Melville's purchases in 1848. Among the modern philosophers whose ideas garnish Babbalanja's and Mohi's discourse are David Hartley, on fate, free will, and necessity (Chapter 135); Coleridge, on reason (Chapters 135, 175); and Malthus, on population (Chapter 138).

Another stream that fed into Melville's "billow from afar" was science. The imagery of stars and galaxies which gives *Mardi* much of its distinctive poetic character, and the talk in the book of planets being formed and of a comet which had actually just been discovered (577.16–18), suggest that the series of lectures in New York by distinguished astronomers in the winter of 1847–48 had excited Melville's imagination. Without doubt Melville's insatiable interest in all that might unriddle the universe led him about this time to read attentively works on geology and paleontology. Babbalanja's "celebrated sandwich System" (Chapter 132) is, in humorous form, a brief compendium of paleontology which shows an extraordinarily accurate knowledge of the latest scientific findings in a science which was unsettling many religious minds.

An oddly mixed literary ancestry has been discovered for the Yillah-Taji-Hautia story—sentimental German romance, books about the language of the flowers, Spenser's *Faerie Queene*, probably works of various Romantic poets, and perhaps works of Arabian and Persian literature. La Motte-Fouqué's *Undine*, a translation of which Melville very likely read with Elizabeth when he was visiting her in Boston before their marriage, is a tale of a water spirit, Undine, who appears to her mortal lover as a beautiful fair-haired girl, marries him and lives with him on an island, returns to her underwater home and is seen by him in a dream as she sits weeping at the bottom of the sea, and in the end, in the form of a little stream, lovingly encircles the grave of her unfaithful, dead lover. *Undine's* companion piece in the same volume, *Sintram and His Companions*, probably influenced the pursuit of Taji by the avengers of Aleema. For the flower messages from Hautia, Melville drew on the currently popular books on the language of flowers; he used Mrs. Frances S. Osgood's *The Poetry of*

Flowers or other similar flower books, at least one of which Elizabeth Melville owned.

The Faerie Queene looms behind *Mardi*, most conspicuously in the symbolic contrast between Yillah and Hautia. Hautia has been likened to the false Florimel, to Duessa, and frequently to the seductive Acrasia. It has been shown that Taji's approach to Hautia's island and some of his discoveries and experiences there are closely similar to Sir Guyon's when he visits Acrasia's bower of sensual bliss.

Hautia also belongs to the tradition of the witch-women of the Romantic poets—Coleridge's Geraldine and Keats's Lamia, for example. Like lamias in general and as described in Burton's *Anatomy of Melancholy*, and like the enchantresses of Southey's *Thalaba, the Destroyer* and Wieland's *Oberon*, Hautia loses her power over the hero and is seen by him to be a "shining monster" at the instant when he remembers and calls upon Yillah. There are other parallels with *Thalaba*.

Taji's pursuit of the ideal is vividly reminiscent of *Alastor*, even in some details, and of *Endymion*, though Melville is not known to have read Shelley or Keats when he wrote *Mardi*. Indeed, almost all the elements of the Mardian romance are common in Romantic literature. Besides the enchantress and the final defiant voyage into the fearful unknown, there are, in one scholar's words, "the voyaging boat, the search for the lost maiden, the island symbol, and the aspiring youth whose character is completed by his mysterious sin, volcanic emotions, and withdrawal from mankind." There are a few echoes of Byron, especially from *The Island*, and perhaps echoes of *Adonais* in Yoomy's song about Adondo; Yoomy as a poet resembles Shelley himself and Shelley's poet in *A Defence of Poetry*.

Mardi reminded some British reviewers of *The Arabian Nights*, and Melville may well have known that famous work; Duyckinck, whose father had published an English translation in 1815, was much interested in it. One modern scholar not only hears "Arabian overtones" throughout *Mardi*, particularly in such names as Taji, Yillah, Yoomy, Babbalanja, Mohi, Alla-Malolla, and Donjalolo, and in Donjalolo's large harem, but also sees Arabian parallels to the Taji-Yillah story: in the tale of Taj-el-Mulook the hero assumes a supernatural character and goes on a quest for the beloved; "Mejnoun and Leila" corresponds in some details to the Taji-Yillah story and also was interpreted as "the human soul groping for divine love." This scholar also finds the influence of the Persian poets, particularly in Yoomy, and parallels in popular oriental romances of the nineteenth century, such as James Morier's tale of Ayesha and (also noticed by others) Byron's *The Giaour* and Moore's *Lalla Rookh*.

When he read Rabelais in the winter and spring of 1848, Melville's humor-loving and free, nonconforming spirit found an instant affinity in him. Beginning with the first reviews of *Mardi*, Rabelais's influence on Melville's panoramic travelogue-satire has been noted and renoted by critics. The Mardian voyage is "sometimes an exact" parallel of Pantagruel's in search of the Holy Bottle. Satire on "bigotry, dogmatism, and pedantry" and the praise of eating and drinking are "Rabelaisian in intention"; Maramma brings to mind the superstitions of Papimany; Oh-Oh's curios and books with comic titles are a Rabelaisian catalogue and burlesque of absurd antiquarianism; Bardiana's will burlesques in Rabelaisian form and wording the will of John Jacob Astor, which had been published in the New York press in April, 1848.

IV

Interpretation and criticism of *Mardi* have burgeoned in the twentieth century along with studies of its sources, and we may glance at some of the main branches here. Melville's early interpreters, beginning with Raymond Weaver, tended to read his books as in large part autobiographical and to see *Mardi* in the light of the Melville family relationships they thought they had discovered in his other books, particularly *Pierre*. Weaver's *Herman Melville: Mariner and Mystic* (1921) held that "*Mardi* is a quest after some total and undivined possession of that holy and mysterious joy that touched Melville during the period of his courtship: a joy he had felt in the crucifixion of his love for his mother; a joy that had dazzled him in his love for Elizabeth Shaw. When he wrote *Mardi* he was married, and his wife was with child. And *Mardi* is a pilgrimage for a lost glamour." Yillah is "the symbol of this faded ecstasy." Weaver's words were quoted or paraphrased by several subsequent critics, and his idea tinges foreign criticism—for example, Jean-Jacques Mayoux, *Melville par lui-même* (Paris, 1958).

Autobiographical reading of *Mardi* has continued. Newton Arvin, for example, in his more or less Freudian interpretation, *Herman Melville* (1950), found *Mardi* "extremely revealing" in the "personal and biographical sense." The Taji-Yillah-Hautia story he took to be a reflection of conjectured experiences in Melville's life which drove him to intense remorse and, "in *Mardi*, to an act of symbolic suicide." William Braswell, in *Melville's Religious Thought* (1943), believed that in *Mardi* Melville was writing an allegory of his inner life; his will (Taji) refuses to be guided by his understanding (Babbalanja), and so he pursues introspective reasoning (Yillah) even to destruction. Merrell Davis countered the identification of Melville with the minds of his characters by insisting that "Melville was writing as an author with his imaginary characters clearly in focus."

One group of modern critics has found the center of gravity in many-sided *Mardi* to be Melville's concern with questions of politics, culture, and civilization. *Mardi* "recapitulates Melville's search among individuals and societies for the rationale of the evil which one man or group of men inflicts upon others," said R. E. Watters in 1940; he called *Mardi* Melville's sociology of evil, as *Moby-Dick* is his metaphysics of evil and *Pierre* his psychology of evil. What Melville wished to do in *Mardi*, according to Pierre Frédérix, *Herman Melville* (1950), was: "Composer une saga de son temps; refaire Pantagruel." Richard Chase, in his *Herman Melville* (1949), looked at *Mardi* from the point of view of his thesis that Melville was "a profound and prophetic critic of liberal-progressivism," which Chase hoped would be supplanted, with Melville's help, by the "new liberalism," a movement which was, by contrast, free of dogma and absolutism, "open-minded, skeptical, and humanist." *Mardi* is important, in this reading, because here for the first time in Melville's works emerges the figure of the "false Prometheus," the titanic figure who "betrays his humanity through some monstrous pride" or abdication from the ambiguities or social loyalties of life.

Without considering it the center of *Mardi*, several critics, for example Willard Thorp and Leon Howard, have found Melville's survey of the modern political world the best part, or among the best and most mature parts, of *Mardi*.

Most critics have seen Melville's quest for truth as the main impulsion in *Mardi*. Whether Taji's search for Yillah represents man's yearning for the harmonious union of spiritual and sensuous delight, for "the eternal lure," for absolute or ultimate truth, "for a lost innocence, for a transcendent ideal, for the transfigured past, for absolute perfection, for total happiness, for a good unalloyed with evil—all unattainable in this world," or for all these together, *Mardi* was the book, they say, in which Herman Melville himself, with eternity in his eye, "was off on his long quest for the ultimate truth." This quest is related to a fundamental concern or theme of Melville, the balanced development of the mind and the heart in man, a theme which he first fully explored in *Mardi*, as Nathalia Wright explained in 1951.

William Ellery Sedgwick took the quest for truth to be both Melville's and his hero's in *Mardi*, *Moby-Dick*, and *Pierre*, and he studied that quest as "the tragedy of mind," the subtitle of his *Herman Melville* (1944). "In Melville's view of life," he said, "a great man [the potential tragic hero] combines a great heart with a great mind." The human heart "fulfills itself in the loving acceptance of men and women as they are within the limits of our common human nature." The mind "spurns these commonplaces. It insists on striving for the ultimate truth, which is to say that it proposes a noble, impossible ideal for the nature in which it shares," and so in the end "brings ruin. At the centre of the destruction which it wreaks is the death of the heart." Yet, though *Mardi* has force, "it fails of the force . . . of tragedy." Before he could command full tragic force, Melville "would have to command pity."

Ronald Mason, in *The Spirit Above the Dust* (1951), also treated *Mardi* as a quest for truth and as tragedy *manqué*; though Melville never really faces tragedy in *Mardi*, he said, the conclusion of the book produces both pity and terror, "those two authentic companions of great tragedy. Innocence has been overwhelmed by the evil implicit in Experience." Milton R. Stern's very full analysis and criticism of *Mardi*, in *The Fine Hammered Steel of Herman Melville* (1957), called the object of Taji's search not truth but "ideality" and showed how the quest for the impossible ideal dehumanizes the quester, "kills his heart, . . . and changes his quest from heavenly aspiration to the diabolism of pride."

Charles Feidelson, Jr., in *Symbolism and American Literature* (1953), discussed *Mardi* as "a study of what it entails to regard thinking as a metaphysical journey" and as a dramatization of that journey by the symbolistic imagination.

Approaching the subject from a fresh direction, H. Bruce Franklin, in *The Wake of the Gods: Melville's Mythology* (1963), argued that Melville used his knowledge of mythology in his quest for truth: Melville drew "upon the mythologies of the Hindus, the Polynesians, the Incas, the Hebrews, the Greeks, the Christians, the Romans, and the Norse," compared them, and quested through them "for a truth behind and beyond them." *Mardi* is "a textbook of comparative mythology"; it dramatizes Sir William Jones's "four principal sources of all mythology": the distortions of historical and natural truth, illustrated in the chronicles of Mohi and in the product of this distortion—the demigodhood of Media and other kings; "a wild admiration of the heavenly bodies," which produces such cosmic demigods as Taji; poetic invention, exemplified by Yoomy; and metaphysical invention, seen in Babbalanja's hypotheses and in

Azzageddi, "the metaphysical devil." In the end "Melville rejects the mythological basis of religion. In a world in which history, poetry, and philosophy offer mere myths, the only safe basis for religion seems to be intuitive psychological and moral truth."

A good many critics maintain that Melville is not altogether a spontaneous warbler of native wood-notes wild but an artist who thought long and hard about the craft of literature and worked at that craft, and the place of *Mardi* in his development as an artist has been variously studied. For example, not only did Melville, who was "among the American literary discoverers of the principle of organic form," set Babbalanja and Yoomy to discussing and endorsing that principle, but *Mardi* illustrates it, as Nathalia Wright showed in 1952. Melville's increased power of characterization and his luxuriant use of "allusiveness" in *Mardi* were brought out by Leon Howard in 1940. Melville's own version of the metaphysical style, later achieved in *Moby-Dick*, grew in *Mardi* under the tutelage of Sir Thomas Browne and through the "ventriloquism" of *Mardi*, his first intense response to Browne; this is demonstrated in F. O. Matthiessen, *American Renaissance* (1941). That in *Mardi* Melville was "feeling his way forward . . . to a genuinely mythopoeic form" has been explained by Newton Arvin and noticed by others. How Melville's power of comedy grew from the "jocular-hedonic" of *Typee* and *Omoo* through an increasing depth and ambiguity in *Mardi* until in that book he came very close to his mature comic style, was traced by Edward H. Rosenberry in *Melville and the Comic Spirit* (1955). James Baird wrote in *Ishmael* (1956): "Melville, the artist, is a supreme example of the artistic creator engaged in the act of making new symbols to replace the 'lost' symbols of Protestant Christianity." *Mardi* "is the most important of all American experimental literary works documenting the development of the symbolistic imagination."

So the aloe flowered at last. It is probably fair to say that most modern critics forgive the gaucheries of *Mardi* for the sake of its riches of the spirit and of language, and it is obvious that modern critics study *Mardi* as the first bold stroke of Melville's greatest work.

SOURCES

FOR THE FACTS about Melville's life and the composition and publication of *Mardi*, I have relied upon Merrell R. Davis, *Melville's MARDI: A Chartless Voyage* (New Haven: Yale University Press, 1952), the vade

mecum of students of *Mardi*; Leon Howard, *Herman Melville: A Biography*
(Berkeley and Los Angeles: University of California Press, 1951); Harrison
Hayford and Merrell Davis, "Herman Melville as Office-Seeker," *Modern
Language Quarterly*, X (June, 1949), 168–83; *The Letters of Herman Melville*,
ed. Merrell R. Davis and William H. Gilman (New Haven: Yale University
Press, 1960); and Jay Leyda, *The Melville Log* (New York: Harcourt,
Brace, 1951). Documents quoted may show slight differences in detail as
transcribed in these and other sources. The editors of the present edition
have supplied me with information about nineteenth-century English and
American printings, sales, and profits, from Melville's accounts with
Harper & Brothers and Richard Bentley, and about the publication date
of *Mardi* in London—March 16, according to the Bentley papers in the
British Museum and the published *List of the Principal Publications* of Bentley
(London: Richard Bentley, 1897); they have also supplied information
about later editions from copies collected at The Newberry Library. My
list of periodicals and books that criticized *Mardi* in the nineteenth century
was drawn from Hugh W. Hetherington, *Melville's Reviewers: British and
American, 1846–1891* (Chapel Hill: University of North Carolina Press,
1961), and supplemented by two recent discoveries: John T. Flanagan,
"*The Spirit of the Times* Reviews Melville," *Journal of English and Germanic
Philology*, LXIV (January, 1965), 57–64; and Theodore R. Ellis III,
"Another Broadside into *Mardi*," which is about the burlesque in *The
Man in the Moon, American Literature*, XLI (November, 1969), 419–22. The
reviews themselves are the source of what I have to say about the reception
of *Mardi* in Melville's time; I am indebted to Mr. Hetherington's kind-
ness for transcripts of four of the more inaccessible of the reviews. The
studies of Melville's sources for the Polynesian elements in *Mardi* upon
which I have drawn are Charles Roberts Anderson, *Melville in the South
Seas* (New York, 1939); David Jaffé, "Some Sources of Melville's *Mardi*,"
American Literature, IX (March, 1937), 56–69; A. Grove Day, "Hawaiian
Echoes in Melville's *Mardi*," *Modern Language Quarterly*, XVIII (March,
1957), 3–8; and Davis. On Melville's reading in philosophy I report work of
Merton M. Sealts, Jr., in his "Melville's 'Neoplatonical Originals,'"
Modern Language Notes, LXVII (February, 1952), 80–96; William Braswell,
in "Melville's Use of Seneca," *American Literature*, XII (March, 1940), 98–
104; and Davis. For Melville and science, Davis again and my article,
"Melville and Geology," *American Literature*, XVII (March, 1945), 50–65,
are my sources. All the attributions of literary influence and discoveries or
reports of literary analogues come from Davis except as here noted:

Nathalia Wright has worked out the similarities between Hautia's isle and Acrasia's bower in "A Note on Melville's Use of Spenser: Hautia and the Bower of Bliss," *American Literature*, XXIV (March, 1952), 83–85; Dorothee Metlitsky Finkelstein, *Melville's Orienda* (New Haven and London: Yale University Press, 1961), found the Arabian and Persian parallels and possible influences that are mentioned; Edward H. Rosenberry, *Melville and the Comic Spirit* (Cambridge: Harvard University Press, 1955), Newton Arvin, *Herman Melville* (New York: William Sloan Associates, 1950), and Davis are my sources for all the references to Rabelais. Works referred to in Section IV by author only are Willard Thorp, "Herman Melville," *Literary History of the United States* (New York: Macmillan, 1948); and Leon Howard, *Herman Melville*. Articles referred to in Section IV by author and date only are: R. E. Watters, "Melville's Metaphysics of Evil," *University of Toronto Quarterly*, IX (January, 1940), 170–82; Nathalia Wright, "The Head and the Heart in Melville's *Mardi*," *Publications of the Modern Language Association of America*, LXVI (June, 1951), 351–62, and "Form as Function in Melville," *ibid.*, LXVII (June, 1952), 330–40; and Leon Howard, "Melville's Struggle with the Angel," *Modern Language Quarterly*, I (June, 1940), 195–206. The quotation about what Taji's search means (beginning with "for a lost innocence") comes from James E. Miller, Jr., "The Many Masks of *Mardi*," *Journal of English and Germanic Philology*, LVIII (July, 1959), 400–413. The quotation "was off on his long quest for the ultimate truth" comes from Thorp.

Note on the Text

THIS EDITION of *Mardi* presents an unmodernized critical text, reconstructed according to the theory of copy-text formulated by Sir Walter Greg.[1] Central to that theory is the distinction between substantive variants (those which affect meaning, such as verbal changes) and accidental variants (those which affect form, such as changes in punctuation and spelling).[2] When an author makes substantive revisions in printed forms of his work, he is not always equally concerned with accidentals. The fact that he does not alter certain accidentals which were not his own but were changes made by the copyist, publisher, or compositor does not amount to an endorsement of those accidentals. Since the aim of a critical edition is to establish a text which represents as nearly as possible the author's intentions, it follows that the formal texture of his work will be most

1. "The Rationale of Copy-Text," *Studies in Bibliography*, III (1950–51), 19–36. For an application of this method to the period of Melville, see Fredson Bowers, "Some Principles for Scholarly Editions of Nineteenth-Century American Authors," *Studies in Bibliography*, XVII (1964), 223–28; and his "A Preface to the Text," in the Centenary Edition of Hawthorne's *The Scarlet Letter* (Columbus: Ohio State University Press, 1962), pp. xxix–xlvii (reprinted in the later volumes of the Centenary Edition).

2. The line between the two is not rigid, for some changes of punctuation and spelling do affect meaning and accordingly would be classed as substantives.

accurately reproduced by adopting as copy-text[3] either the fair-copy manuscript or the first printing based on it. The printed form is chosen if the manuscript does not exist or if the author worked in such a way that corrected proof became in effect the final form of the manuscript. This basic text may then be emended with any later authorial alterations (whether substantive or accidental) and with other obvious corrections. Following this procedure maximizes the probability of having authorial readings in cases which are inconclusive as to the source of an alteration in a later authorized edition. The resulting text is *critical* in that it does not correspond exactly to any authorized edition, but it is closer to the author's intentions—insofar as they are recoverable—than any single authorized edition.

As the preceding HISTORICAL NOTE has shown, the first English edition of *Mardi*, though published earlier than the first American, was set from the American proof sheets. The American edition was the one set directly from the manuscript Melville supplied, and, in the absence of that manuscript, the first impression of the American edition becomes the copy-text for the present edition.[4] Any impressions or editions published during Melville's lifetime are a potential source for emendations in this copy-text, since theoretically it would have been possible for Melville to make corrections or changes in them. The two authorized editions—those of Harper & Brothers in the United States and Richard Bentley in England—were the only ones published before Melville's death in 1891,[5] and they have been fully collated in the following pattern:

1. American against English Edition

    a. Two complete sight collations[6] of the first American impression (1849) against the English impression (as issued in 1849 and 1851)

3. "Copy-text" is the text accepted as the basis for an edition.

4. The particular copy of the first American impression which served (in the form of a marked Xerox reproduction) as printer's copy is M67–722–115 (see footnote 7).

5. Although several extracts from *Mardi* appeared in Evert A. Duyckinck's *Literary World* on April 7, 14, 21, 1849 (IV, 309–10, 333–36, 351–52), Melville was probably not in a position to have made revisions in the copy furnished to Duyckinck, and a complete collation of the passages as published in the *Literary World* and as they appeared in the Harper edition reveals that the few minor differences between the two texts are clearly not authorial but editorial or compositorial changes. (Copies used for collation: M67–1296 *vs.* M67–722–108. See footnote 7.) Likewise, the extract (Chapter 50) in N. P. Willis's *Home Journal* on April 21, 1849, taken "from the proof-sheets," has among its half-dozen minor substantive variants from the published Harper text none that can be considered authorial.

6. Collations between two *editions*, which (because they are printed from different

    b. Four substantive sight collations of the first American impression (1849) against the English impression (as issued in 1849 and 1851)

2. Impressions of the American Edition
    Two machine collations of the first impression of this edition (1849) against the last (1864)

3. Issues of the English Edition
    Two machine collations of the first issue of this edition (1849) against the last (1851)[7]

The text was thus collated for record 10 times.[8] In addition, routine procedures in the process of compiling, checking, and preparing the in-

settings of type) cannot be performed on the Hinman Collator, are "sight collations." Those between *impressions* of the same edition are "machine collations"—so called because that machine, by superimposing page images, enables the human collator's eye to see differences, including minute changes not otherwise easily detected, such as resettings and type damage. A "complete sight collation" is one in which both substantive and accidental variants are recorded; a "substantive collation" is one in which only substantive variants are recorded. The terms *edition, impression (printing), issue,* and *state,* as used here, follow the definitions of Fredson Bowers in *Principles of Bibliographical Description* (Princeton: Princeton University Press, 1949), pp. 379–426.

    7. The English edition of *Mardi* is in three volumes, the American edition in two. Since each volume of any multivolume work is a separate entity, no bibliographical significance attaches to any particular combination of volumes. In these collations, therefore, no attempt was made to treat presently constituted sets as units, particularly since the scarcity of copies (sometimes on limited loan from libraries and private collectors) made it convenient to separate sets for collation. The copies used for these collations are here recorded by identification number (for books in the Melville Collection, now at The Newberry Library), or by library name and call number (for books not in the Melville Collection): (1a) M67–722–2 *vs.* M67–103–7a; M67–722–5 (through I, 321) and M66–2471–37 *vs.* M67–722–12 (I) [1851] and M67–103–7a (II, III); (1b) M67–722–109 *vs.* Yale Ix.M497.849; M66–2471–38 *vs.* M67–722–12 (I) and Lake Forest College PS2384M3 (II, III) [1851]; M67–722–153 (I) and M67–722–15 (II) *vs.* Lake Forest College PS2384M3 (I) [1851] and M67–722–12 (III), with M67–722–23 *vs.* M67–722–12 (II); M66–2718–3 *vs.* William S. Akin copy (I, III), with Northwestern 813.3M531Ma 1855 (I) and M67–103–8 (II) *vs.* Akin copy (II); (2) M67–722–23 *vs.* Portland (Maine) Public Library #2338; Gift M67–12 (W. M. Gibson copy) *vs.* M67–1306–1; (3) M67–722–12 *vs.* University of Michigan PS2384M2 1851; M67–103–7a (I, II) and M67–722–12 (III) *vs.* Lake Forest College PS2384M3.

    8. The number of collations which must be performed in order to detect all significant variations in a given text can never be prescribed with certainty, since chance determines, at least to some extent, the particular copies available to any group of editors. Whether or

formation for publication have resulted in a larger total number of collations.[9]

Analysis of the variants (in both substantives and accidentals) disclosed by these collations has resulted in the adoption of 134 emendations in the copy-text; and 90 other emendations, not taken from English variants, have been made by the present editors. In order to make clear the evidence and rationale on which these decisions rest, an account of the textual history of the work is given below, followed by a discussion of the treatment in this text of substantives and accidentals, and an explanation of the editorial apparatus through which the evidence is presented.

THE TEXTS

NO MANUSCRIPT of *Mardi* survives (except for two draft fragments, reproduced on pp. 727, 728). The text published first is not the one closest to Melville's final manuscript (i.e., to the printer's copy, which was copied from his own final draft by his wife and one or more of his sisters, then punctuated and revised by himself). Although the English edition was published on March 16, 1849, about a month earlier than the American, it was set from proofs of the American edition which were shipped to England in the first week of February. What is technically the second edition of the book (2 vols.; New York: Harper & Brothers, 1849) is the one set directly from the manuscript the author supplied. Copies of this American edition dated 1849 on the title page exist in at least two states,

---

not variant states of a first impression are detected, for example, depends largely upon whether or not at least one copy of an earlier state is present in the collection of copies assembled for collation; regardless of the size of this collection, there is always the chance that an unknown earlier state is missing. To reduce the element of chance somewhat, the present editors have checked many points in every copy of *Mardi* in the Melville Collection at The Newberry Library and have examined numerous copies in other collections. For making copies of *Mardi* available, the editors are indebted to William S. Akin, William M. Gibson, M. Douglas Sackman, and Howard P. Vincent, and to the London Library, the Portland (Maine) Public Library, and the libraries of Lake Forest College, the University of Michigan, Northwestern University, and Yale University.

9. Proofreading provided the chief opportunity for making these additional collations. Copies of the first American and the first English editions were simultaneously compared with two sets of the Northwestern–Newberry page proofs; besides this group proofreading, five individual proofreadings were made of the page proofs against copies of the first American edition.

distinguishable by the presence or absence of plate damage in the inner forme of sheet F in Volume II. The damage consists of a broken last letter in "follow" at A2.122.35[10] and the absence of the period following the word. Since this damage persists throughout later printings, the undamaged state is clearly the earlier one, but it does not follow that copies with the later sheet F in Volume II necessarily have later states of the other sheets as well. The only other variations among copies with the 1849 title page (such as variations of inking in the heading for the thirteenth chapter in Volume I) are not of a kind which can indicate priority or differentiate states or impressions. The copy-text for the present edition may therefore be defined simply as the Harper printing with 1849 on the title page and with a period after the word "follow" at A2.122.35.[11]

The Harper edition was printed twice more from these plates, in 1855 and 1864; since all of the slight variations resulted from plate damage (and, in one instance, an attempt to correct plate damage), none has any textual authority.[12]

10. Reference numbers with prefixed letters refer to volume, page, and line of the American edition (A) or the English edition (E); when these letters do not appear, reference is to page and line of the Northwestern–Newberry Edition.

11. Historical facts about the dates, sizes, and background of the various printings and editions are given in the HISTORICAL NOTE; precise physical descriptions will appear in the full-scale bibliography to be published in conjunction with the Northwestern–Newberry Edition. The present discussion is not concerned with bibliographical details discovered in the process of collation unless they bear on textual questions. Type or plate damage, for example, which may distinguish the states within an impression or the impressions within a given year, is not reported here if it does not create a textual variant (as defined in the following footnote) and if the states or impressions involved are not otherwise of textual significance.

12. In the 1855 printing seven commas were lost (after "also", 64.22; "woman", 66.35; "reality", 89.3; "difference", 152.18; "heads", 302.2; "strange", 303.10; and "here", 627.12), and plate damage caused three semicolons to be unrecognizable (after "been", 228.18; "downs", 365.7; and "blind", 591.24). In the 1864 impression four additional commas disappeared (after "name", 59.19; "friends", 128.21; "disposed", 234.3; and "Moreover", 246.32), as well as three hyphens (after "whale", 87.4; "many", 344.34; and "for", 483.9), one semicolon (after "up", 76.3), and one period (after "bystander", 517.12); another semicolon appeared to be a colon (after "itself", 356.4), two others appeared as commas (after "ripple", 54.24; and "smile", 504.37), and one colon looked like a period (after "Yes", 535.9). In addition, in 1864 an "e" and hyphen were supplied to create "de-" (344.33), probably in error for "dis-", and the "t" in "at" (350.1), which had been absent from the earlier impressions, printed properly. In this NOTE, when changes are listed within

The English edition, unlike the American, was printed only once but was issued at two different times, two years apart. The first issue (3 vols.; London: Richard Bentley, 1849) exists in various states, distinguishable by the presence or absence of certain type-impressions in at least eleven places. In one of these instances the priority of readings is certain: on the first page of sheet D in Volume III, the signature line in the earlier state reads "VOL. I.", and in the later state it is corrected to "VOL. III." However, copies with the earlier state of sheet D cannot be assumed necessarily to have the earliest states of all sheets, and the variations present in other sheets are of a kind which offer no sure indication of priority. Since the book was printed from type rather than plates, the shifting (or failure to print) of individual pieces of type does not furnish evidence of an irreversible progression. For example, the absence in some copies of the word "a" following "pointed to" (381.9) and of the first three letters of "sausages" (382.15)—or the absence of punctuation after "busy" (517.39), "exhausted" (518.5), and "mantle" (595.33)—probably represents a later state, but not necessarily. The other variations, mainly shifting or missing letters (such as the absence in some copies of the first letter of "inquired" at 447.17), do not occur at points where they create substantive differences. In 1851 Bentley issued the remaining sheets of his edition with a new title page (dated 1851); some of the variations present in copies with the 1849 title page (such as "gloriously", with and without the "g", at 481.17) also occur in the same states in copies with the 1851 title page. In addition, a few other variations not so far discovered in any 1849 copies have been noted—such as the absence in some 1851 copies of "Yet" at 14.37. None of these differences between copies of the English edition—except the one alteration of a signature line—gives any evidence of intervention during the course of printing.

The text of the English edition differs substantively from the American edition at 142 points (there are hundreds of changes in spelling and punctuation). Most of these English substantive variants are simply the result of careless typesetting and proofreading or routine substitutions of English idioms,[13] but nine of them correct obvious substantive errors in the

---

either the American or the English edition, the many instances of battered type or plates and missing letters are not included when it is clear what letter is intended, nor is missing end-punctuation listed when the absent mark is a period; and missing hyphens at the ends of lines are not reported when the divided word is not a possible compound. Missing commas, however, which might pass unnoticed, are listed. In other words, type or plate wear is noted only when it could pass unnoticed or be mistaken for intentional revision.

13. Among the outright errors in the English edition are "an" for "and" (203.23);

American edition.[14] The only difference involving more than a short phrase
is the evidently inadvertent omission of one complete eight-word sentence
in Chapter 89 (270.18). In no instance do both the American and the
English variants appear to be unmistakably authorial, and in no instance
does an English variant appear to be an unmistakable authorial correction
or revision of a nonauthorial American reading.[15]

Since Melville's death in 1891, *Mardi* has been set in type at least six
times,[16] and some of these editions have been reprinted or issued by more
than one publisher. For example, the edition published in 1923 by the

---

"a of" for "of a" (379.9); "inhabitants" for "habiliments" (405.12); the transposition of
letters that changed "startled . . . fainted" to "started . . . faintled" (406.30) and "Great . . .
Grand" to "Gread . . . Grant" (604.5–6)—each of these instances resulting in one substantive error (a different word) and one mere misspelling; the repetition of "at" (396.19)
and "by" (487.34); and the omission of "in" (127.3), "of" (298.12), and "a" (359.26).
Among the other variants (including some less obvious errors, such as casual anglicizations
and routine compositorial substitutions) are about two dozen differences in nouns or verbs
(the American "existing" at 35.10, for example, is changed to "existance", and "ensue" at
81.23 to "follow"); nearly two dozen changes in the forms of nouns and verbs; three and a
half dozen more in the forms of other parts of speech, mainly adjectives; nearly two dozen
rearrangements of words or substitutions of idioms, ranging from reversal of word order
(76.2; 101.17–18; 125.18; 307.34; and 328.1) to slight shifts of syntax (192.26; 430.5); and
about three dozen omissions or insertions of single words or short phrases (such as the
insertion of "said" at 369.13 and the omission of "the Conqueror" at 91.22). Since certain
variants can be classified in more than one way, precise figures are not given here.

14. The English edition corrected "of" to "off" (xi.23); "an" to "on" (55.4); "of" to
"as" (87.38); "month" to "mouth" (233.6); "Braid-Bead" to "Braid-Beard" (348.10–11);
"an another" to "another" (460.21); "were" to "was" (462.15); "than" to "that" (527.36);
and "countryman" to "countrymen" (536.14).

15. Comment on certain individual readings will be found in the following section and
in the DISCUSSIONS OF ADOPTED READINGS.

16. The number cannot be stated with assurance, since further editions—which have
not been discovered in an extensive search of catalogues, libraries, and bookstores—
occasionally still turn up. Details of all these editions will be included in the forthcoming
descriptive bibliography. The Melville Collection being formed at The Newberry Library
during preparation of the Northwestern–Newberry Edition contains many of these later
editions (and ideally will contain all of them in time). Charles R. Anderson, in *Melville in
the South Seas* (New York: Columbia University Press, 1939), states that 11 "editions" of
Mardi had been published by 1938 (p. 439); but he is not using "edition" in the sense
employed here, as a technical bibliographical term which encompasses all the impressions
from a given setting of type.

St. Botolph Society in the United States and Jonathan Cape in England has also appeared under the imprints of L. C. Page and D. D. Nickerson and was issued in 1964 as a Capricorn paperback. This edition followed the American (Harper) text, as did the Pickwick (1928) and Signet (1964) editions; the English (Bentley) text, on the other hand, served as copy-text for the Abbey Classics edition (1923)—published in England by Chapman & Dodd and in the United States by Small, Maynard & Company—and for the Albert & Charles Boni edition (1925). The Constable edition of *Mardi* (1922)—in the collected *Works*—is significant because it was the first edition of the book after Melville's death and because it is part of the only complete set of his work that has been available in the past (and is therefore often cited as standard). Its text is based on the Harper rather than the Bentley edition but often departs from it, especially in spelling and punctuation.[17] None of these editions offers an explanation of its editorial policy or an account of the textual history of the work.

TREATMENT OF SUBSTANTIVES

THE TEXT of *Mardi* presents no complications, since the English edition follows the wording of the American except in a scattering of inconsequential variants (relatively few for so long a book) and since Melville made no later revisions. An editor, after adopting some obvious corrections from the English variants, has only two problems. The first is to determine whether any of the remaining English variants are authorial, and if so whether to adopt them as later or to reject them as earlier than the corresponding American (copy-text) readings. The second is to find and correct any readings that are corrupt in both editions—readings, that is, where the English text follows the American in printing words that cannot be the ones Melville intended. Neither problem is particularly difficult in *Mardi*.

Nine of the English variants are corrections obviously called for (see p. 689, footnote 14). Whether compositors' errors or slips of the author's pen, the American readings can hardly have been intended by Melville, and whether the correction was made by Melville or by someone at Bentley's is immaterial.

17. This generalization is based on a collation of a copy of the 1849 American edition (M66-2471-37) with a copy of the Constable *Mardi* in the Russell & Russell reissue (New York, 1963; M67-722-123). For some background relating to the Constable texts, see Philip Durham, "Prelude to the Constable Edition of Melville," *Huntington Library Quarterly*, XXI (1957-58), 285-89.

In determining whether to adopt as authorial any of the remaining English variants, an editor must consider the question of the priority of American and English readings. In general, the English text is later, since the Bentley edition was set from Harper proof sheets. Most or all of the English readings are obviously not authorial alterations but changes introduced in the course of resetting the book in England; and even authorial English variants, if any exist, are not necessarily later than the corresponding American readings, since changes (authorial or otherwise) could theoretically have been made in the Harper proofs after Melville sent a set of proof sheets to England—in which cases the English text would of course preserve the earlier readings.[18] However, in the few scattered and minor instances where the English variant readings appear to be possibly authorial (because arguably better than the American), they are of a kind that someone at Bentley's or even an alert compositor would have been able to make. In no instance does the priority of readings pose a real editorial problem.

In sum, the present editors have seen no sufficient reason to adopt any of the English variants except those few which correct obvious errors. The only other substantive emendations they have made are of corrupt readings, where the English edition follows the American in scribal or compositorial misreadings of Melville's manuscript (or in errors of the manuscript itself). In these instances, the emendations restore what Melville must originally have written or at least intended to write.[19] No substantive emendations have been made under any other circumstances. If, for example, an English reading fits the sense of a passage as well as the copy-text reading (or is in some respects even better) but cannot be convincingly defended as Mel-

---

18. This possibility is quite remote, for Melville was in Boston between the time the proofs were sent to London and the week the Harper edition was printed. From Boston on April 5, 1849, he wrote Evert A. Duyckinck about *Mardi*: "it seems so long now since I wrote it, & my mood has so changed, that I dread to look into it, & have purposely abstained from so doing since I thanked God it was off my hands."

19. Such changes are of course made only when the copy-text reading is unsatisfactory. The emendation must be a word that Melville would have used in the context (judging from his literary practice); it must be a word that improves the sense and fits the tone of the context; and it must be a word that in Melville's hand could have been misread as the word in the copy-text (or that Melville himself could mistakenly have written). Under these three criteria, "as" is emended to "of" (88.1); "from" to "of" (262.20); "saucers" to "sauces" (417.34); "Oro" to "Odo" (427.23); "others' " to "other's" (448.23); "fisherman" to "fishermen" (509.15); "stream" to "steam" (540.29); and "pile" to "piled" (547.31).

ville's, then the copy-text reading is retained (see, for instance, the discussion of the reading at 6.5). In other words, substantive emendations have not been made on the basis of the subjective stylistic judgments of the editors. Since the copy-text is likely to retain more manuscript readings than a later text, there is no choice but to follow it in those few cases which are otherwise indeterminable.

TREATMENT OF ACCIDENTALS

IN THE ABSENCE of a final manuscript, the degree to which the author was responsible for the accidentals—the punctuation and spelling—of a printed text is a matter impossible to settle conclusively. Greg's theory of copy-text provides a method for playing the odds to advantage: adhering to the printed text closest to the manuscript will allow a maximum number of characteristic authorial usages to be retained, since each successive impression or edition offers further opportunities for corruption, in the form of publishers' changes, compositors' errors, or plate damage. Even though changes in the spelling and punctuation of *Mardi* were undoubtedly made at Harper & Brothers, the American edition was nevertheless set directly from Melville's manuscript and inevitably preserves more of its accidentals than the English edition, another step removed, could possibly do. Even if some of the variants in accidentals in the English edition are changes Melville made on the proofs he sent to Bentley, it is impossible to determine just which ones; to accept the English variants which appear to be improvements would be to risk adopting many instances of nonauthorial spelling and punctuation on the chance of acquiring a few authorial alterations— and to defeat the purpose of selecting a copy-text on Greg's principles.

Accordingly, the accidentals of the first American impression of *Mardi* have been retained in the present edition except in a few unusual instances, even when the spelling and punctuation may appear incorrect or inconsistent by mid-twentieth-century standards. Some of the inconsistencies in the spelling and punctuation may have been in the manuscript, and although Melville presumably did not intend them, they constitute a suggestive part of his total expression, since patterns of accidentals do affect the texture of a literary work. On the other hand, some of the inconsistencies in accidentals may have resulted either from an imperfectly realized attempt to make the manuscript conform to a house style or from compositorial alterations. To regularize the punctuation and spelling would be to risk choosing nonauthorial forms.[20] Therefore no attempt has been made to impose general consistency on either spelling or punctuation,[21] and any changes have been made sparingly, according to the following guidelines:

SPELLING. The general rule adopted here is to correct spellings which were unacceptable by the standards of 1849, but to retain any acceptable variants. One available guide for decisions about spelling is the 1847 revision of Webster's *American Dictionary of the English Language* (Springfield, Mass., 1848). Webster's was the dictionary used (in one or more editions) by Harper & Brothers at the time, for Melville remarked, in his letter to Murray on January 28, 1849: "my printers here 'go for' Webster." The Harper accounts show that Melville ordered at least three copies of Webster's (on April 10 and November 15, 1847, and on November 16, 1848), the third of which could have been the new 1847 revision published in 1848. In any case, Webster's in various editions of the 1840's can be taken as a generally accepted standard for 1847 and 1848, when Melville was writing *Mardi*. Recourse to Webster's and to other contemporary dictionaries such as Joseph E. Worcester's (and to editions of American novels and works of travel published in the 1840's by Harpers and other American publishers) has resulted in retention of a good many anomalous-appearing copy-text forms, such as "aigulette," "alluvian," "Antartic," "barbacue," "belligerant," "bucanier," "cimeter," "Cnaster," "dilletante," "guanos" (for "iguanas"), "hypogriffs," "inuendoes," "lea," "mollymeux," "numskulls," "pean," "rarified," "salam," "taught" (for "taut"), "torquoise," "vallies," "verdent," "vertu," and "waving" (for "waiving"). Some other forms, not found in reliable parallels in such contemporary sources, have been corrected,[22] such as "Abysinnians," "Carribean," "chisseled," "Conroupta Quiancensis" (to "Couroupita Guianensis"), "Crocket," "friccasied," "Gaudentia" (to "Gaudentio"), "Kamschatska," "minis-

20. Melville's habits in the extant manuscripts and letters are not definite enough to offer grounds to emend for consistency (and in any case the letters, not intended for publication, do not provide a parallel situation). Neither is the Harper house styling consistent enough to be helpful in determining precisely what elements of the punctuation of *Mardi* resulted from it.

21. For example, no emendations are made to secure consistency in the use (or non-use) of capital letters; of apostrophes in contractions; of italics or of quotation marks (or both at once) for such items as foreign words, the first occurrence of special terms (nautical terminology, slang, and the like), names of ships, and titles of books.

22. Several such words have been corrected to standard forms found elsewhere in *Mardi*, but the aim is correctness, not consistency.

trelsy," "myrh," "obstreporous," "phillipic," "Piaggi" (to "Piaggio"), "reminiscenses," "Rhœtian" (to "Rhætian"), and "Tremmella"; and random misspellings of names invented by Melville have been regularized, such as "Alla Mallolla" (to "Alla Malolla"), "Babballanja" (to "Babbalanja"), "Braid-Bead" (to "Braid-Beard"), and "Doxdox" (to "Doxodox"). Any changes to bring spellings into conformity with an 1840's standard have been made cautiously so as to preserve the wide latitude allowed in contemporary usage (especially for proper names) and to preserve the deliberately archaic or literary flavor of many passages in *Mardi*.

PUNCTUATION. Emendations in punctuation have been made in two kinds of instances. First are the simple corrections of obvious typographical errors, such as the commas after "attendants" (196.21) and "vale" (251.5), which should be periods, and various obvious errors involving the misuse or omission of quotation marks.[23] Second are the corrections at places where a mark of punctuation (or the absence of one) creates an ambiguity serious enough to interfere with the meaning of a sentence. Such emendations are, in effect, substantive, since they impose a particular meaning on a passage that is ambiguous in its Harper punctuation.[24]

EDITORIAL APPARATUS

THE BASIC EVIDENCE for textual decisions in the present edition is given in the preceding parts of this NOTE and in the four sections which follow it and complete the TEXTUAL RECORD :[25]

23. In some cases there are beginning or ending quotation marks where none are required (for example, see the entries in the LIST OF EMENDATIONS for 185.4; 292.3; 369.13; 373.39; and 376.34) or the reverse situation where necessary ones are omitted at the beginning or end of a passage (271.1; 274.9; 275.18–20; 323.21; 338.12; 354.37; 419.9; 420.19; 423.1; 425.19; 433.31; 511.14; 539.17; 602.2; and 606.18); in other cases single quotation marks are misplaced (356.27) or misused for the regular double ones (383.19). In several instances (listed in the next footnote) emendation requires a decision affecting the meaning, since the misuse or omission of quotation marks calls into question either who is speaking or what is said. In at least five instances (after "foe", 150.5; "Plujii", 264.10; "rate", 264.17; "puff", 377.10; and "speeds", 615.4) marks of punctuation printed so faintly in the American edition that they could easily be overlooked or misconstrued and in some copies did not print at all. These marks, which appear in the present edition, could at first seem to be emendations but of course are not.

24. See the LIST OF EMENDATIONS at 274.9; 275.18–20; 292.3; 356.27–28; 369.13; 455.7; 539.17; 610.21; and 640.14–16.

25. On file in the Melville Collection at The Newberry Library is a complete list of

DISCUSSIONS OF ADOPTED READINGS. These discussions take up any reading (whether a copy-text reading or an emendation) adopted in the Northwestern–Newberry text which seems to require discussion or explanation beyond the general guidelines already stated. Certain instances of decisions not to emend, as well as some actual emendations, are commented upon.

LIST OF EMENDATIONS. This list records every change made in the copy-text for the present edition, accidentals as well as substantives. The left column gives the Northwestern–Newberry readings, the right column the rejected copy-text readings. Each emendation is followed by a symbol to indicate whether the source is the English edition (E) or the present editors (NN).[26] Items marked with an asterisk are commented on in the DISCUSSIONS OF ADOPTED READINGS.

It will be seen that 202 emendations have been made in accidentals, 22 in substantives. Of the accidentals, 125 are corrections made in the English edition, and the other 77 have been made by the present editors; of the substantives, 9 come from the English edition and 13 from the present editors. No emendations of any sort have been made silently; using the LIST OF EMENDATIONS and the REPORT OF LINE-END HYPHENATION, one can reconstruct the copy-text in every detail.[27]

REPORT OF LINE-END HYPHENATION. Since some possible compound words are hyphenated at the ends of lines in the copy-text, the intended

---

variants between the American and the English editions, including both substantives (which are reported in the LIST OF SUBSTANTIVE VARIANTS) and accidentals (which are reported, in the LIST OF EMENDATIONS, only when they are adopted). Also on file is the evidence for the decisions in the first list of the REPORT OF LINE-END HYPHENATION.

26. The presence of an NN symbol signifies only that the reading does not occur in the two authorized texts; it does not imply that no one has ever thought of it before.

27. That is, every *textual* detail: features of the styling or design of the copy-text print—such as the length of lines; the form and content of the title page and running titles; the typography and punctuation of chapter numbers, chapter titles, and poems and lists within the text; and the display capitalization of chapter openings and half-titles—are of course not recoverable from these lists. (However, in this volume, capitalization of words in the chapter titles, both in the Table of Contents and at the heads of the chapters, follows the capitalization in the Table of Contents of the copy-text.) Opening quotation marks are omitted before the display capitals at the beginning of the following chapters: 88 (p. 267); 95 (p. 290); 104 (p. 316); 121 (p. 371); 122 (p. 378); 133 (p. 419); 137 (p. 435); 144 (p. 461); 145 (p. 465); 154 (p. 501); 174 (p. 569); 175 (p. 574); and 183 (p. 612). Chapters which constitute the second volume of the copy-text (numbered 1–91) have been renumbered as Chapters 105–195, and the two separate "Contents" tables have been joined.

forms of these words become a matter for editorial decision. When such a word appears elsewhere in the copy-text in only one form, that form is followed; when its treatment is not consistent (and the inconsistency is an acceptable one, to be retained in the present text), the form which occurs more times in analogous situations is followed. If the word does not occur elsewhere in the copy-text, the form is determined by a survey of similar words, by the usage in the 1848 Webster's, and by any relevant evidence in a Melville manuscript. The first list in the REPORT OF LINE-END HYPHEN-ATION records these decisions by listing the adopted Northwestern–Newberry forms of possible compounds which are hyphenated at the ends of lines in the copy-text. The second list records the copy-text forms of possible compounds which are hyphenated at the ends of lines in the Northwestern–Newberry Edition. No editorial decisions are involved in this second list,[28] but the information recorded is essential for reconstructing the copy-text and making exact quotations from the present edition.

LIST OF SUBSTANTIVE VARIANTS. This list is a historical record of all variant substantive readings in the two editions authorized by Melville.[29] The left column gives the readings of the first American impression (and also the Northwestern–Newberry readings when they differ from those of the copy-text). The right column lists the English substantive readings which are at variance with the copy-text. Editions are designated by three symbols: A (American), E (English), and NN (Northwestern–Newberry).

In these four lists the reader has before him all the copy-text readings and all the substantive variations from them in authorized editions. With the lists he can examine and reconsider for himself the textual decisions for the present edition and in the process see more clearly the relationships between the texts of *Mardi* available during Melville's lifetime and the one which is offered here as a more faithful representation of the author's intentions.

(Chapters in the English edition were also numbered in separate series, with separate "Contents" tables for each of the three volumes: 1–70, 1–66, 1–59, in Roman numerals.)

28. Except in the cases of words hyphenated at the ends of lines in the copy-text as well. These words, which appear in both lists and are marked with daggers, are given in the forms which the present editors adopted but which are obscured by hyphenation at the ends of lines in this edition.

29. Such variants as "ambassadors/embassadors," "ay/aye," "hereabout/hereabouts," "strewing/strowing," and "vailing/veiling" are considered accidentals whenever the 1848 Webster's or other contemporary dictionaries classify them as interchangeable forms of the same word.

Discussions of Adopted Readings

I N THESE COMMENTS on emendations and on decisions not to emend, the following symbols are employed:

A American Edition (1849–1864)
E English Edition (1849–1851)
NN Northwestern–Newberry Edition

xi.23   *off*]   The A reading "of" was corrected in E to "off"; the change from "off" to "*off*" is made in conformity with the styling of NN.

xii.3   *Donjalolo*]   The comma after "Donjalolo" in A was removed in E; the change from "Donjalolo" to "*Donjalolo*" is made in conformity with the styling of NN.

xv.8   *They*]   The lower-case letter at the beginning of the title of Chapter 171 in A is corrected in E; the change from "They" to "*They*" is made in conformity with the styling of NN.

6.5   Hartz]   The A reading "Hartz forest" is retained by NN, though geographically impossible. The E reading "Black Forest", which corrects the geographical error that placed Hartz Forest logs in the Rhine, is not necessarily an authorial correction, and indeed may more likely have been made by someone at Bentley's.

7.7   farthest]   NN retains the A and E reading as part of Melville's emphatic description, although "nearest" would be more logical in the context.

13.10   Jesus]   The omission in E of the word "Jesus" is perhaps the one example in *Mardi* suggesting the kind of deliberate publishing house excision to spare religious sensibilities that characterized Wiley's treatment of *Typee*, to some extent Murray's of *Omoo*, and on a wholesale scale Bentley's of *The Whale*. Even this omission, however, may be a compositorial oversight rather than a deliberate excision, since the sense remains unimpaired.

17.33   old hints]   The adjective "old" occurs in both A and E, but its meaning is not altogether clear and it may be a corrupt reading.

30.34   Geoffry]   The spelling "Geoffry Hudson" is retained in preference to the more frequent "Jeffrey Hudson"; it occurs as "Geoffrey Hudson" in Scott's *Peveril of the Peak* (1823) which gave currency to the erroneous idea, followed here by Melville, that Hudson died in prison.

73.3   while]   E alters the awkward echo "while all the while" to "while all the time", a stylistic improvement not adopted by NN since a Bentley editor or the compositor could have made it.

88.1   of]   The A reading "as", though followed by E, is emended in NN. Presumably some accident caused two words in the American edition to become transposed before plating. In the first volume, A107.23 begins with "of" and A107.25 with "as" (an indented paragraph opening intervenes). The first word is obviously wrong, since it creates the phrase "of it turned out", and it was altered to "as" in the English edition (followed by NN at 87.38); but the "as" in "Jarl's discovery as the occupant", two lines later, at least makes sense and was retained in the English edition. Undoubtedly, however, the "of" and "as" were transposed in the American edition and the second reading should be "of the occupant" (88.1). This change, called for by the context, is thus supported by physical evidence.

88.3   was]   The E correction of "was" to "were" is not adopted by NN since there is no reason to suppose it was authorial. In this instance, as in others (e.g., 441.32, 443.11) where E corrected agreement in number of subject and verb, NN retains the copy-text form, which seems colloquially acceptable and is probably Melville's usage, rather than a blunder requiring correction.

95.33   sometime]   Although the A reading was changed by E to "some times", the meaning "now and then; occasionally" is listed under the first definition of "sometime" by the *Oxford English Dictionary*, with many citations, the latest in 1809, and similarly (as rare) by Worcester's *Dictionary* (1860). It is possible, however, that Melville wrote "sometimes" and that his final "s", often indistinctly formed, was overlooked by the copyist or compositor.

228.6 Gaudentio] See note on 228.7.

228.7 -sixty-] NN emends the A and E reading "three-hundred-and-seventy-five" to "three-hundred-and-sixty-five". Nathalia Wright called the editors' attention to this reading, pointing out that in Simon Berington's fictional *Memoirs of Sigr. Gaudentio di Lucca* (1737) the number of pillars in the "Temple of the Year," which is alluded to here, is appropriately 365. It is unlikely that in making the allusion Melville was not aware of the obvious point that the number of pillars corresponds to the number of days in the year and so wrote out the pointless number 375. Probably he saw the point and wrote out the proper number but in a way that induced a misreading by a copyist or compositor unaware of the point. Also corrected by NN is the A and E misspelling "Gaudentia" (228.6) for "Gaudentio", likewise on grounds of a probable misreading of Melville's manuscript.

248.2 *Donjalolo*] The comma after "DONJALOLO" in A was removed in E; the change from "DONJALOLO" to "*Donjalolo*" is made in conformity with the styling of NN.

275.18–20 "The . . . hopes."] This paragraph was not enclosed in quotation marks in A and E, but NN supplies the quotation marks since the comments are clearly the conclusion of Braid-Beard's speech.

281.34 above] Both the A reading, retained by NN, and the E reading "about" make good sense in the context. As he "began over again" Yoomy either (as E has it) repeated the phrase "about ten hundred thousand moons" or (as A has it), having been challenged by Mohi the historian, he defiantly increased the time to "above ten hundred thousand moons". No ground exists for rejecting the copy-text reading.

298.5 them] E repeats "stay-at-homes" in place of "them"; the change seems deliberately made to avoid the possible faulty reference of "them" to "travelers" rather than to "stay-at-homes". The change is not adopted by NN, however, since someone at Bentley's or even the compositor could have made it.

327.19 desire] The E reading "require" somewhat strengthens Media's question, since in fact the old man does require, not merely desire, recompense. The change may be deliberate, not merely a compositorial misreading. Since, however, it cannot be taken as necessarily an authorial change, it is not adopted by NN.

368.1–2 enter many nations] NN retains the A and E reading, assuming that the sense is merely that the speaker casually enters many nations, even as Mungo Park rested (or visited) in many African cots, and that no exact equivalence is intended between the number of nations and the number of cots (in which case "as" would be required after "enter").

380.14   shark's]   NN retains the A reading with the apostrophe before the "s" even though the E reading "sharks' " would be more accurate since more than one shark is involved. Repeated parallel instances in Melville's writings establish the usage with the singular possessive form.

430.5   the . . . did]   The E change from the A reading "the theme you did" to "this theme of yours" is so colloquial in its direction, and otherwise so apparently unmotivated, as to suggest Melville's hand rather than an editorial or compositorial change. The suggestion is not strong enough, however, to justify adoption of the E form.

443.19   "Heads]   The quotation marks, missing in A, are adopted from E, but the capital "H" (which E changed to lower-case) is retained from A.

447.10   Sebastiano's]   The name in A, "Sebastioni" ("Sebastiani" in E), has been emended because no painter of that name has been located (the form is unlikely in Italian) and presumably Melville meant to allude to a well-known figure. The most likely such painter with a closely similar name is Sebastiano del Piombo, whose name either Melville or the compositor could well have rendered as "Sebastioni." From Melville's description it seems possible that the picture he had in mind may not in fact have been a painting by Sebastiano but some such commonly known work as Signorelli's *Punishments of the Damned*. Among other Italian names in *Mardi*, a few (such as "Piaggi" for "Piaggio" and "Gaudentia" for "Gaudentio") are anomalous forms of actual names and are readily ascribable to authorial or compositorial error, of the kind evidently involved in this instance. Others (such as "Ghibelli" at 482.27), though they may involve such error, probably belong among Melville's literary inventions, since they do not resemble any appropriate actual names so closely as do those in the first group.

452.21   be]   The E insertion of "just" after "be" makes the sense much clearer: the hour of morning when a man's face becomes "just" recognizable. The improvement, which seems probably deliberate, was not, however, necessarily authorial, and so is not adopted by NN.

455.14   first]   Since "first" may mean first-mentioned rather than first in time, the A and E reading is retained, although it may be an authorial slip for "second".

495.10   waving]   The A and E reading is retained as an acceptable variant of "waiving".

585.21   " 'Calmer, and better!' "]   NN emends the A and E reading which has only double quotation marks, by supplying single quotation marks, assuming that Babbalanja is quoting the last words of Bardianna in response to Mohi's question. To be correct, the A and E reading would have to mean merely that

Bardianna's last words were calmer and better than some previous words—a sense hard to justify by the context.

598.7, 599.4   Hauto]   The A and E reading "Hanto" is emended by NN, following the suggestion of Nathalia Wright that since the names of the other three critics are thinly concealed versions of salient qualities displayed in their criticisms (Zenzori/Censor; Lucree/Lucre; Roddi/Rod) so probably is that of this fourth critic. "Hanto", however, suggests no such quality, while "Hauto" suggests the "haughty" advice he gives. The emendation assumes that "Hanto" is a copyist's or compositor's misreading of Melville's "u" as "n".

638.27   heralds:]   In all examined copies of A the punctuation mark after "heralds" registered only as a single dot which could be taken as the top member of either a colon or a semicolon. The parallel punctuation marks in the series indicate that a colon (as in E) is required.

List of Emendations

I N THIS LIST of changes made in the copy-text by the present editors, the following abbreviations are used to designate the sources of readings:

> A American Edition (1849–1864)
> E English Edition (1849–1851)
> NN Northwestern–Newberry Edition

For further comment on this list, see p. 695 above; for discussions of the emendations marked with an asterisk (*), see the DISCUSSIONS OF ADOPTED READINGS, pp. 697–701. The wavy dash (∼) stands for the word cited in the left column and signals that only a punctuation mark is emended. The caret (∧) indicates the absence of a punctuation mark. Empty brackets ([ ]) indicate space where a letter or letters failed to print. The slash (/) stands for a line end.

	NN READING	COPY-TEXT READING
*xi.23	*off* E	of
*xii.3	*Donjalolo*∧ E	∼,
*xv.8	*They* E	they

	NN Reading	Copy-text Reading
4.32	symptoms E	symptons
6.1	Kamschatka NN	Kamschatska
15.4	reminiscences E	reminiscenses
22.17	the crew E	thc crew
40.6	Caribbean NN	Carribean
43.4	jackknife NN	jacknife
55.4	on E	an
62.10	brakes NN	breaks
66.28	Annatoo!" E	~!ᴧ
87.38	as E	of
*88.1	of NN	as
104.35	lunge NN	lounge
105.30	Crockett's NN	Crocket's
119.8	pump-brakes NN	pump-breaks
123.11	phosphorescence E	phosphoresence
147.9	philippic NN	phillipic
150.9	fish, we E	Fish, we
175.13	Archipelago. E	~ᴧ
175.25	transmissible NN	transmissable
185.4	twelve.ᴧ E	~."
192.12	windrows NN	winrows
196.21	attendants. E	~,
203.26	itself. E	~,
210.12	us, E	~.
211.10	shall NN	Shall
212.13	Braid-Beard NN	Braid-beard
220.8	to the E	to tho
*228.6	Gaudentio NN	Gaudentia
*228.7	-sixty- NN	-seventy-
233.6	mouth E	month
246.21	nut. NN	~,
247.5	'Ah E	"~
247.5	fancy,' E	~,"

	NN Reading	Copy-text Reading
*248.2	*Donjalolo*ᴧ E	DONJALOLO,
249.32	face? E	~.
251.5	vale. E	~,
257.30	everlasting. E	~ᴧ
259.27	absorbed E	aborbed
262.20	of NN	from
266.5	Nora-Bamma E	~ᴧ~
271.1	Time!" E	~!ᴧ
274.8	Babbalanja, E	~ᴧ
274.9	ᴧBut E	"~
275.6	more, E	~ᴧ
275.7	cried; E	~ᴧ
275.16	'When E	"~
275.17	Mardi.' NN	~."
*275.18	"The NN	ᴧ~
*275.20	hopes." NN	~.ᴧ
277.6	Monlova. E	~ᴧ
278.33	precipice, E	~.
281.15	Babbalanja E	Babballanja
284.4	Mohi. E	~,
289.20	Gibraltar E	Gibralter
291.22	Media, E	~ᴧ
291.33	you, E	~ᴧ
291.37	Borabolla, NN	~ᴧ
292.3	ᴧThen NN	"~
298.8	Abyssinians E	Abysinnians
314.12	haunts, E	~ᴧ
323.21	back." NN	~.ᴧ
327.17	Media, E	~ᴧ
328.5	And NN	and
338.12	"These E	ᴧ~
344.33	new-disposed E	new-d[ ]/posed
348.10–11	Braid-Beard E	Braid-Bead

	NN Reading	Copy-text Reading
348.15	elapsed E	elasped
350.1	at E	a[ ]
354.37	"Stick E	∧~
356.27	∧all NN	'~
356.28	'there NN	∧~
358.13	Casuarinas NN	Casaurinas
364.21	revenge. E	~∧
369.13	will,∧ NN	~,"
369.13	∧but NN	"~
372.34	leg E	[ ]eg
372.35	pipe-bowl E	pipe-/[ ]owl
373.39	trunks.∧ NN	~."
375.11	Media. E	~∧
376.34	∧So NN	"~
376.36	Puff! Puff! E	~!~:
377.15	Media. NN	~,
380.37	Chiropodist NN	Chiropedist
382.9	lord, E	~∧
383.19	"The E	'~
385.32	antiquary. E	~,
392.19	day. E	~∧
393.20	∧Full NN	"~
393.21	harms!∧ NN	~!"
394.9	bound, NN	~.
396.19	'Oh NN	∧~
396.20	brow!' " NN	~!∧"
396.31	'but E	∧~
397.19	" 'Bear NN	"∧~
397.19	gods!' NN	~!∧
397.20	'that NN	∧~
397.22	unbeheld.' " NN	~·∧"
401.7	unexplored." E	~·∧
403.20	roots." NN	~·∧

	NN Reading	Copy-text Reading
410.5	robustious NN	robustuous
411.3	courteous E	courteus
412.3	pipe. E	~ ∧
415.10	Piaggio NN	Piaggi
416.29	chiseled NN	chisseled
417.34	sauces NN	saucers
418.13	fricasseed NN	friccasied
419.9	"Hark E	∧ ~
420.19	"My E	∧ ~
422.22	Yoomy. E	~ ∧
423.1	these?" NN	~ ? ∧
423.22	cure. E	~ ,
425.19	Necessity." E	~ . ∧
425.34	lord," E	~ , ∧
426.16	things? E	~ .
427.23	Odo NN	Oro
427.29	lord? NN	~ .
429.25	come. E	~ ,
432.7	flame. E	~ ∧
433.31	"Let NN	∧ ~
435.9	∧Said E	" ~
437.15	Oro!" E	~ ! ∧
441.13	'Cracked E	" ~
441.13	Crowns,' E	~ ,"
441.25	Media. E	~ ,
442.2	raps.'" E	~ . ∧ "
*443.19	"Heads NN	∧ ~
*447.10	Sebastiano's NN	Sebastioni's
447.20	eyes. E	~ ;
448.23	other's NN	others'
455.7	lord; NN	~ ,
460.21	another E	an another
462.15	was E	were

	NN Reading	Copy-text Reading
466.5	attendants E	attendents
469.17	minstrelsy E	ministrelsy
485.10	'On NN	"∼
485.10	Lips,' NN	∼,"
485.11	'We E	"∼
485.16	sociable.' " NN	∼·∧"
486.19	Yoomy; NN	∼,
488.31	during NN	During
490.10	born∧ E	∼,
495.5	Babbalanja? E	∼,
496.2	is∧ E	∼,
496.5	Couroupita Guianensis NN	Conroupta Quiancensis
498.2	firmament E	firmanent
499.37	where'er E	where'ere
500.4	Yoomy. E	∼∧
502.22	Media,∧ E	∼·"
502.22	"concerning E	∧∼
503.21	pause; NN	∼,
504.12	logicians E	logicans
504.22	success E	succcess
505.35	Improvisator E	Improvisitor
509.15	fishermen NN	fisherman
510.15	last. E	∼;
510.18	Yoomy. E	∼,
511.3	days' E	∼∧
511.14	Dominora." NN	∼·∧
514.7	are we E	Are we
514.8	behold NN	Behold
515.34	Lavater E	Lavatar
516.29	basis. E	∼,
517.37	forborne E	forborn
521.4	obstreperous E	obstreporous
521.18	"Hurrah E	∧∼

	NN Reading	Copy-text Reading
524.3	another‿ E	~,
527.36	that E	than
531.20	heard. E	~‿
535.11	Yoomy, E	~‿
536.7	Media, E	~‿
536.14	countrymen E	countryman
538.6	febrile NN	febral
539.17	"Stand NN	‿~
539.17	invaders!" NN	~!‿
540.29	steam NN	stream
546.36	'Til NN	'Till
547.31	piled NN	pile
550.11	myrrh E	myrh
552.1	brow. E	~,
553.11	Rhætian NN	Rhœtian
553.38	say: E	~;
556.10	Betelgeuse NN	Betelguese
559.2	Babbalanja. NN	~,
560.31	hie'st NN	hi'st
561.23	Malolla NN	Mollolla
568.19	Tremella NN	Tremmella
569.3	rock, E	~.
569.3	Media. NN	~;
573.17	clam-shells NN	clamp-shells
573.33	Away E	away
574.9	Malolla NN	Mallolla
580.23	ago.‿" NN	~.' "
581.1	beginning, E	~‿
581.25	Doxodox E	Doxdox
*585.21	" 'Calmer NN	"‿~
*585.21	better!' " NN	~!‿"
589.1	himself? E	~.
590.17	citrons, E	~‿

	NN Reading	Copy-text Reading
590.18	pomegranates E	pomegrantes
593.30	world. E	~,
595.30	‸Here E	"~
*598.7	Hauto NN	Hanto
*599.4	Hauto NN	Hanto
602.2	"Oh E	‸~
606.18	hounds!" NN	~!‸
606.31	please, E	~‸
607.25	Media, E	~‸
608.28	purchased. NN	~‸
610.21	Why‸ NN	~,
613.17	us; Amoree E	~ : ~
613.37	living, E	~.
616.6	me, E	~‸
634.6	theirs E	their's
634.17	theirs E	their's
634.23	name.' E	~.‸
634.28	"‸Then E	" '~
636.23	immortal.' E	~.‸
*638.27	heralds: E	~.
640.14	'For NN	‸~
640.16	found.' " NN	~.‸"
640.20	"I E	‸~
648.28	forebodings E	forbodings

Report of Line-End Hyphenation

THE FIRST LIST below records the forms adopted in the present
edition (NN) for possible compound words which were hyphenated at line-ends in the copy-text (A) and which the editors had to
decide whether to print as single-word compounds without hyphens or as
hyphenated compounds. The second list records the A reading of possible
compounds which happen to be hyphenated at the ends of lines in the
present edition; any possible compound hyphenated at the end of a line in
NN occurs as one unhyphenated word in A unless it appears in this list.
Those words coincidentally hyphenated between the same elements at line
ends in both A and NN are listed in the forms which would have been
adopted if they had fallen within a line in NN and are marked with daggers
(†). A slash (/) indicates the line-end break in A in a word with two or more
hyphens.

To make the record of editorial decisions complete, a few words
hyphenated at the ends of lines in A are included in the first list even
though (1) they always appear as one unhyphenated word when they occur
within the line in the copy-text (e.g., "whirlpool"), or (2) they always
appear either as a hyphenated compound or as two separate words when
they occur within the line in the copy-text (e.g., "palm-trees" or "palm
trees"). Both lists exclude two classes of line-end hyphenation: (1) those

which unquestionably mark only compositorial syllabication of non-compound words (or non-compound parts of compound words—for example, the "loneli-" of "heart-loneliness"), and (2) those which separate two or more elements that could not possibly be run together as one word without a hyphen (e.g., "Do-Nothing" and "Froth-of-the-Sea"). For further comment on these lists, see pp. 695–96 above.

I. NN *forms of possible compounds which were hyphenated at copy-text line-ends*

4.36	half-score	86.8	overturning
5.23	†sea-moss	87.4	whale-boat
11.11	Kingsmill	87.6	half-breeds
13.12	circumnavigated	90.12	shipmates
16.11	fore-/mast-head	93.10	state-room
21.8	straight-forwardness	94.9	dead-wall
22.12	boats-/crew-watches	94.30	noteworthy
23.36	sea-dog	102.6	ground-tier
27.5	lurking-places	103.8	steel-blue
41.19	cross-roads	104.26	anchor-stocks
42.8	clipper-built	105.14	alongside
44.20	boat-kegs	107.16	everpresent
44.24	dog-like	111.9	headway
44.38	Daddy-/long-legs	112.2	rain-water
48.22	mid-day	114.13	horror-struck
49.25	pilot-boat	115.22	scandalmongers
53.10	link-boys	119.8	pump-brakes
53.10	ray-fish	126.3	tail-feathers
54.7	Shovel-nosed	126.5	low-sailing
58.4	main-chains	126.32	long-drawn
61.3	forecastle	135.4	death-deed
62.12	mainmast	136.18	gauze-like
66.2	supernatural	140.20	demi-god
70.10	bow-sprit	141.18	mat-sail
70.33	outlet	151.3	outskirts
71.26	half-breeds	156.30	milk-white
71.35	sea-hawks	159.14	whirlpool
73.5	sideways	160.7	midmost
74.17	overhaul	160.13	†erewhile
75.5	bulkhead	172.8	lock-jaw
76.7	foremast	176.7	rent-roll
79.8	steel-gloved	177.12	high-priests

178.19	jet-black	333.28	forty-seven
179.5	scroll-prowed	335.6	water-course
185.13	bulkheads	336.26	forest-tree
189.25	whirlpool	344.11	to-day
191.38	demi-god	344.28	anaconda-like
197.34	high-spirited	344.34	many-limbed
200.23	paddle-blades	352.10	stopping-places
200.26	shark's-mouth	366.16	vineyards
201.5	arrow-flights	367.24	land-locked
203.15	To-day	367.31	sea-side
212.13	Braid-Beard	372.8	cocoa-nut
217.27	sea-cavern	372.16	red-barked
225.3	†overarched	372.16	†net-work
226.29	†sweet-scented	372.20	†mouth-piece
231.15	overlooking	372.35	pipe-bowl
232.2	overlapping	373.10	pipe-bowls
237.37	balsam-dropping	374.15	black-letter
240.2	torch-light	374.23	coffin-lid
240.5	sea-girt	376.4	berry-brown
240.8	golden-rinded	376.25	skull-bowl
243.13	woe-begone	379.35	†foot-prints
243.28	burial-place	380.13	†swordfish
246.11	under-breeding	385.14	midmost
246.12	Arva-root	385.33	worm-eaten
253.17	milk-white	387.13	undertaker
256.38	lordly-looking	396.2	market-place
268.1	moss-roses	406.33	semi-transparent
271.10	overstepped	416.21	foot-prints
282.37	star-fish	418.21	cocoa-nuts
282.39	swordfish	423.20	rose-balm
283.16	moonbeams	426.39	†foreordained
285.14	close-grappling	446.5	purple-robed
286.8	overstrained	446.20	guava-rind
287.19	merry-making	456.39	after-birth
288.28	nursery-talk	463.23	oftentimes
289.1	tiger-sharks	467.34	snow-drifts
290.23	circumnavigated	467.35	ice-bergs
295.23	cocoa-nut	479.12	†river-horse
297.20	Commonwealth's	482.6	lord-mayor
330.9	palm-nuts	482.11	dragon-beaked
330.19	†halberd-shaped	482.18	sea-king
332.22	demi-gods	489.27	sword-hilt

489.36	grass-hoppers	575.29	outflies
498.28	foreground	576.22	outspread
512.15	fore-knowing	577.37	fellow-men
516.33	above-ground	580.18	†fore-fathers
517.5	overseeing	581.22	idea-immanens
524.4	demi-god	583.8	Taro-patches
525.16	mound-building	601.19	household-word
525.17	sovereign-kings	601.20	market-place
526.2	sovereign-kings	606.32	demi-god
530.11	demi-god	607.25	to-morrows
532.9	foremost	607.30	care-free
533.36	Ofttimes	608.19	well-appointed
540.14	golden-beaming	608.20	sleeping-chamber
540.25	cable-vines	613.13	mirth-making
543.5	storm-clouds	619.19	night-dews
544.10	whirlpool-column	622.14	storm-worn
547.26	†river-margins	632.9	snow-white
559.31	self-complacency	644.8	hanging-garden
562.13	overheard	644.18	long-haired
564.29	tomfoolery	645.11	blue-braided
565.12	far-off	646.1	honey-suckles
571.33	winding-sheets	648.27	Linden-leaves
573.17	clam-shells	652.22	sea-thyme
573.18	cray-fish	653.10	headwinds
574.20	palm-trees	653.17	ghost-like

II. *Copy-text forms of possible compounds which are hyphenated at line-ends in* NN

5.23	†sea-moss	64.2	ill-starred
5.34	sun-strokes	65.6	main-chains
15.1	Fidus-Achates-ship	70.18	fore-top-gallant-
26.20	quarter-deck		yard
33.6	whale-boat's	77.21	breast-high
39.13	sea-serpent	78.38	knight-errants
40.5	sea-monsters	84.1	over-keenly
54.17	sucking-fish	86.10	fore-top
60.4	bell-buttons	86.26	sailor-like
63.13	phantom-like	103.18	knight-errants
63.27	fore-rigging	109.19	night-watches
63.32	futtock-shrouds	125.10	wooden-walled

128.1	shark-tails	344.10	new-marshal
130.8	deep-graven	344.11	to-morrow
146.5	one-armed	344.23	arrow-slits
147.6	old-fashioned	346.6	pearl-shells
153.20	re-echoed	351.9	mile-stones
160.13	†ere-while	358.15	Morning-glory
171.13	palmetto-thatched	359.21	mule-track
176.13	all-permeating	372.16	†net-work
183.17	law-giving	372.20	†mouth-piece
183.32	suspicious-looking	373.18	terra-firma
184.2	sour-looking	374.10	gold-fishes'
186.12	tower-shadowed	376.20	demi-gods
187.30	witch-hazels	379.35	†foot-prints
203.20	open-handed	380.13	†sword-fish
216.12	gable-pointed	381.5	ant-hill
225.3	†over-arched	382.12	tomb-like
226.29	†sweet-scented	382.18	weeping-willows
226.33	moss-rose	382.19	sea-noddy
228.9	cross-cut	383.32	Swiftly-Going
229.3	All-Plastic	385.13	lung-cells
231.22	seed-cocoanuts	405.13	frame-work
239.10	passage-way	417.37	sea-beeves
239.19	sky-lights	418.17	cock-billed
240.4	universe-rounded	426.39	†fore-ordained
240.5	mountain-locked	432.6	wave-crest
246.5	frost-white	432.17	wide-spreading
248.10	story-tellers	435.19	battle-chant
250.1	reef-bar	441.35	elbow-room
251.20	king-belted	444.37	cream-surf
254.24	demi-divine	454.6	under-tone
276.7	demi-gods	460.22	to-morrow
282.9	red-plumaged	467.9	poodle-haired
282.35	sea-nettles	478.13	corn-field
289.2	orang-outang	479.12	†river-horse
296.8	port-hole	482.20	war-horse
306.1	blood-red	485.27	demi-gods
309.6	wax-myrtle	494.33	demi-gods
317.2	steering-paddle	497.8	demi-god
319.4	orang-outang	514.10	palm-trees
330.16	thick-ranked	517.38	wet-nurses
330.19	†halberd-shaped	525.27	twelve-moons
333.8	plantain-pudding	526.34	twelve-moons

528.29	to-day		593.16	morning-
535.7	first-born			inspirations
539.15	half-reef		600.28	self-imposed
544.30	morning-glories		605.8	lady-passengers
547.26	†river-margins		609.2	demi-gods
550.12	double-lure		611.9	demi-god
572.1	walking-sticks		619.14	long-buried
572.2	dilletante-arborist		635.20	down-sweeping
573.3	dog-like		638.3	calm-browed
576.1	Fellow-men		644.17	dark-green
580.4	black-balled		645.1	seines-full
580.18	†fore-fathers		645.30	torquoise-hyacinths
583.7	Bread-fruit		647.20	open-armed
589.38	idol-incense		653.35	sea-fight

List of Substantive Variants

I N THIS LIST, which is a historical record of the substantive variants in the authorized editions during Melville's lifetime, the following abbreviations are used to designate the sources of readings:

A American Edition (1849–1864)
E English Edition (1849–1851)
NN Northwestern–Newberry Edition

Copy-text readings are listed in the left column and readings differing from them in the right. (In the instances of emendations made by the present editors, the NN reading also appears in the left column to provide a reference to the text.) If a reading does not remain constant throughout all the impressions of a given edition, a date or inclusive dates are appended to the symbol to show the period during which new impressions carried the reading in question. Features of the styling or design of the American edition are not necessarily followed in the present edition, and such deviations are not recorded here (see the NOTE ON THE TEXT, p. 695, footnote 27). Empty brackets ([ ]) indicate space where a letter or letters failed to print. The slash (/) stands for a line end.

xi.23   *off* NN   ———
               of A
                                           off E

717

xvii.1–9	PREFACE ... 1849 A	[*omitted*] E
6.5	Hartz A	Black E
6.14	aboard A	on board E
13.10	Jesus A	[*omitted*] E
13.35	be A	may be E
20.1	way A	away E
27.34	the body A	of the body E
35.10	existing A	existance E
35.11	people's A	peoples' E
39.16	ever ever A	ever E
44.12	dry A	as dry E
44.17	was A	was as E
45.11	of A	[*omitted*] E
46.18	one of A	one E
51.7	currents A	current E
55.4	on NN	
	an A	on E
60.13	and the A	and E
61.1	that A	the E
62.20	this A	the E
63.32	in A	in the E
69.31	thither A	other E
71.29	Now on A	On E
73.3	while A	time E
76.2	anew break out A	break out anew E
78.39	prison A	imprison E
81.23	ensue A	follow E
87.38	as NN	
	of A	as E
88.3	was A	were E
91.22	the Conqueror A	[*omitted*] E
91.31	with A	[*omitted*] E
94.6	unbeknown A	unknown E
95.33	sometime A	some times E

101.17–18	blue boundless A	boundless blue E
105.10	spiteful A	[*omitted*] E
106.18	could A	[*omitted*] E
106.18	see A	saw E
108.6	then A	[*omitted*] E
123.3	to A	by E
123.39	upon A	on E
125.16	And at A	At E
125.18	sedulously kept A	kept sedulously E
127.3	in A	[*omitted*] E
136.14	cheek A	cheeks E
144.12	as A	a E
150.32	the A	a E
153.14	was A	must have been E
157.14	would A	should E
176.37	one A	[*omitted*] E
192.26	over A	our E
202.22	loyal A	royal E
203.23	and A	an E
211.16	for A	that, for E
211.17	but A	[*omitted*] E
211.17	a A	a mere E
228.7	that A	the E
233.6	mouth NN month A	mouth E
239.4	of the A	of E
246.13	then A	just then E
265.4	pass A	passed E
270.18	And . . . Mohi. A	[*omitted*] E
280.11	he A	the E
281.34	above A	about E
285.9	Kings A	King's E
289.4	a A	an E
297.9	swab A	to swab E

297.16	Charles the Fifth A	Charles V E
298.5	them A	stay-at-homes E
298.12	infernalest of A	infernalest E
307.34	know only A	only know E
317.17	a A	[omitted] E
317.29	sage A	savage E
318.12	said A	cried E
327.19	desire A	require E
328.1	over all A	all over E
344.33	new-disposed NN	
	new-d[ ]/posed A 1849– 1855	new-disposed E new-de-/posed A1864
345.14	our thoughts A	our own thoughts E
348.10–11	Braid-Beard NN	
	Braid-Bead A	Braid-Beard E
350.1	at NN	
	a[ ] A	at E
359.11	with A	by E
359.26	a A	[omitted] E
360.17	through the A	through an E
360.26	itself A	himself E
366.15	forests A	forest E
367.10	cables A	cable E
367.10	hamper A	hampers E
369.13	Babbalanja A	said Babbalanja E
372.18	Versailles A	Versailles' E
379.9	of a A	a of E
380.14	shark's A	sharks' E
381.9	a A	[omitted] E
383.20	And A	A E
386.1	he A	[omitted] E
389.1	thing A	things E
389.6	better A	had better E
396.19	at A	at at E

396.31	saith A	said E
396.37	unintermitting A	unremitting E
405.12	habiliments A	inhabitants E
406.17	Thinking A	Think- E
406.30	startled A	started E
408.17	their A	heir E
411.12	those A	these E
413.16	I A	[omitted] E
429.27	objections A	objection E
430.5	the A	this E
430.5	you did A	of yours E
430.12	them A	them from E
441.32	is A	are E
443.11	was A	were E
444.30	kings' A	king's E
446.6	lord A	lords E
447.32	tossing A	throwing E
452.21	be A	be just E
460.21	another NN	
	an another A	another E
462.11	feed A	fed E
462.15	was NN	
	were A	was E
466.2	much A	such E
466.20	in A	into E
472.15	for A	fro E
477.5	yet A	but E
487.34	by the A	by by the E
507.30	our A	their E
511.3	days' NN	
	days A	days' E
527.35–36	than that NN	
	than than A	than that E
536.14	countrymen NN	
	countryman A	countrymen E

545.9	hail A	hailing E
561.11	hundreds A	hundred's E
572.2	the A	[omitted] E
580.11	much A	much the E
593.18	manly A	many E
598.27	to the A	to E
604.6	Grand A	Grant E
611.19	woods A	wood E
616.27	hath A	has E
627.30	by A	from E
633.7	man A	a man E
636.23	then A	[omitted] E
637.20	the A	thy E
640.19	I A	and I E
648.4	adventure A	adventures E
653.8	slow A	slowly E

Manuscript Fragments

ONLY TWO FRAGMENTS of *Mardi* manuscript survive. Each consists of one paragraph in Melville's hand, on a single leaf. The first is now owned by Mr. Parkman Howe, by whose generous permission it is reproduced and transcribed here. (The other side of the same leaf was used earlier by Melville for a preliminary draft of the Round-Robin in *Omoo* and is reproduced in the Northwestern–Newberry Edition, page 379.) The second fragment, on the verso of a part-leaf clipping attached to the foot of page 25 of the manuscript of Melville's essay on "Hawthorne and His Mosses," is preserved in the Duyckinck Collection, Manuscript Division, New York Public Library, and is also reproduced and transcribed here by permission.

The first manuscript fragment is an early version of the opening paragraph of Chapter 2, "A Calm." This version may well be Melville's earliest draft of the paragraph, since it has the many false starts and revisions characteristic of his process of composition, as seen in his surviving first-draft manuscripts. More likely, however, it is an intermediate draft, copied from an earlier one, since it is written in ink rather than pencil, and since in copying as well as in composing Melville often made such false starts and revisions. It is not at all likely that in inscribing this paragraph he intended it as final fair copy, since he wrote it with no care for spelling or legibility,

723

on the verso of a salvaged sheet used earlier for drafting the *Omoo* Round-Robin, the ink of which shows through so heavily that he would have seen at once he could not write on most of the page. A possible inference from Melville's making use of such a portion of a discarded leaf for a single paragraph, and from his placing at the head the word "Chapter" without a chapter number, is that he may have composed the paragraph after he had already written the passage on the calm, which it introduces, in order to provide an opening paragraph when he decided to make a chapter division at this point. In any case, the paragraph as printed in the American edition shows that Melville had revised this version thoroughly by the time printer's copy for it was prepared. (See 9.1–7 and the right column of Parallel Texts, p. 726.)

The second surviving manuscript fragment is an early version of the fifth paragraph (and the last five words of the fourth) of Chapter 38, "The Sea on Fire." Like the first fragment, most of whose inscriptional characteristics it shares, it is possibly the earliest draft of the passage but is more likely an intermediate one. Certainly it was not printer's copy, for the writing, though more flowing and less impeded by revisions than that of the first fragment, shows no concern for legibility; furthermore, the wording of the passage as printed in the American edition was arrived at by Melville through subsequent revisions, transpositions, and a certain amount of expansion, all to good effect. (See 122.2–8 and the right column of Parallel Texts, p. 729.)

The form in which the manuscript fragments are given below in genetic transcription is designed to show the order in which Melville put down the words. It distinguishes, that is, among: (1) the words Melville first wrote down, (2) words he canceled at once and replaced by others on the same line, and (3) words he canceled at some later time and replaced by others inserted above the line or added. Words are transcribed here in standard spelling, except for words clearly misspelled, even though Melville frequently did not form all the letters distinctly. Usually the word he intended can be made out, sometimes only by aid of the context; but an occasional word may offer equally plausible alternative choices (e.g., "discerning" or "discovering" in line 10 of the second fragment). Other words, which Melville dashed off in rough approximations of the shape and number of letters, would be quite uncertain without reference to the printed text.

Following each genetic transcription, the final text of the passage as it stood in the manuscript and the corresponding text of the first American impression are presented in parallel columns. In the left column is the text of the manuscript fragment, incorporating the latest revisions; it does not include canceled readings and does not alter spelling or punctuation. In the right column is the 1849 Harper text, which is identical with the North-western–Newberry text.

SYMBOLS USED

→ ••• →	revision enclosed between arrows was made at time leaf was first being inscribed
[...]	revision enclosed in brackets was made later than initial inscription of leaf
>	the word(s) following were inserted above, with caret
⤴	the word(s) following were inserted above, without caret
<	the word(s) following were canceled (by lining out)
add	the word(s) following were added, on same line
/	end of line in manuscript
‖...‖	letter or word enclosed is conjectured by the editors (uncertain because unclear)
...	word(s) lost by mutilation of manuscript
	all words in roman are Melville's; all words in italics are the editors'

GENETIC TRANSCRIPTION

[*First fragment*]

Chapter

[*device*]

A clam which came on about this time / addded not a little to my impatience
of the ship, and / eventually brought → <eventually brought→ it → <it→
seemed to revive → <seemed to ✃ by certain nameles associations *alter* revive
to revived→ in me my first → <first→ previous → <previous *add* first→ /
strange → <strange→ impressions of this → <of this→ upon first witnessing
this / phenomenon of the sea. But who can descirbe the [<the >ones]
emotions of → <of→ / upon such an occasion. Let us undertake it / however.
→ <But . . . however.→ It may be worth while to venture a description. /

PARALLEL TEXTS

[*First fragment*]
Chapter

A clam which came on about
this time addded not a little to my
impatience of the ship, and
by certain nameles
associations revived in me my first
impressions upon first witnessing

this phenomenon of the sea.
It may be worth while to venture
a description.

[*American edition*]
CHAPTER II.
A CALM.

Next day there was a calm,
which added not a little to my
impatience of the ship. And,
furthermore, by certain nameless
associations revived in me my old
impressions upon first witnessing
as a landsman
this phenomenon of the sea.
Those impressions may merit
a page.

Chapter

A calm which came on about this time
added not a little to my impatience of the ship. And
~~certainly~~ by certain novelty attracted ~~it seemed to~~ remind me my first impressions first
step impression of this upon first returning this
phenomenon of the sea. ~~But who can describe the~~ emotion of
upon ~~such~~ an occasion. ~~Let me understand it~~
~~herein~~. It may be well while to venture a description.

spouting canal of the whale. ———

We here in fact been that lest
the monsters might with any near
intention might occasion destroy as by
coming in rude contact with the boat.
But we observed that the leviathans
would chose madness while they
with spray about the craft seemed to
deter them from approaching — Several of them, apparently descry us f
sudden, plunged heavily down into the water

GENETIC TRANSCRIPTION

[*Second fragment*]
spouting canal of the whale. ———— /
     We were in great fear that [< that *add* lest] / the monsters might →
< might→ without any vicious / intention might occasion → < occasion→
destroy us by / coming in rude contact with the boat. / But we observed that
the peculiarly / vivid appea → < appea→ irradiation which clung → < clung→
shot / forth from about the craft seemed to / deter them from approaching——
for / several of them, apparently ‖discerning *or* discovering‖ us of a / sudden,
plunged headlong down into the water / [*leaf cut across through the next line of
writing, leaving perhaps three words mutilated and six intact*] . . . ⊁the water . . .
the white → < the white→ still more / [*entire passage canceled by two heavy ink
lines, evidently the lower segments of two corner-to-corner diagonal lines that canceled
the original whole leaf*]

PARALLEL TEXTS

[*Second fragment*]	[*American edition*]
spouting canal of the whale. ————	spouting canal of the whales.
We were in great fear lest the	We were in great fear, lest
monsters without any vicious intention	without any vicious intention the
might destroy us by	Leviathans might destroy us, by
coming in rude contact with the boat.	coming into close contact with our
	boat.
	We would have shunned them; but
	they were all round and round us.
But we observed that	Nevertheless we were safe; for as we
	parted the pallid brine,
the peculiarly vivid irradiation which	the peculiar irradiation which
shot forth from about the craft seemed	shot from about our keel seemed
to deter them from approaching ——	to deter them.
for several of them, apparently	Apparently
discerning [discovering ?] us of a sudden,	discovering us of a sudden, many
plunged headlong down	of them plunged headlong down
into the water. . . .	into the water . . .

COLOPHON

THE TEXT *of the Northwestern–Newberry Edition of* THE WRITINGS OF HERMAN MELVILLE *is set in eleven-point Monophoto Bembo, two points leaded. This exceptionally handsome type face is a modern rendering of designs made by Francesco Griffo for the office of Aldus Manutius in Venice and first used for the printing, in 1495, of the tract* De Aetna *by Cardinal Pietro Bembo. The display face is Bruce Rogers's Centaur, a twentieth-century design based on and reflective of the late-fifteenth-century Venetian models of Nicolas Jenson.*

This volume was composed by William Clowes & Sons, Ltd., of Beccles, Suffolk, England. It was printed and bound by the Colonial Press, Inc., of Clinton, Massachusetts. The paper for the clothbound edition, Melville Text, was made expressly for this edition by the S. D. Warren Company, of Boston, and has a specially designed watermark embodying a representation of the signature of Herman Melville. It is an acid-free paper that has withstood tests simulating 300 years' wear with no signs of serious deterioration. The cloth-bound copies are covered with a library buckram manufactured by Arkwright-Interlaken, Inc., of Fiskeville, Rhode Island. The typography and binding design of the edition are by Paul Randall Mize.